14 Stones

A River of Rocks

First Book of the Stones Series

Paul Telegdi

Paul Telegdi

Dedicated to my wife, Melanie Telegdi, my strength and support.

Written: July 1997

Copyright © 2014, Paul Telegdi

All rights reserved, including the right to reproduce this book or portions thereof in any form whatsoever

Edited by Melanie Telegdi

Published by Paul Telegdi at Amazon

To enjoy other books by Paul Telegdi please visit
www.seeWordFactory.com

Dreamcast I, II, III, IV and V (paranormal series)

The Call at 3:18 am (paranormal)

14-, 15-, 16-, 17- and 18 Stones (prehistoric series)

Seize the Day (Roman)

Strike the Red Hammer (Norman)

The Locksmith's Dilemma (medieval)

Where Arrows Fly (medieval)

Dark Fires (medieval)

Learning Berserk (Viking)

Unlearning Berserk (Viking)

Chance Encounter (a life in progress)

On the Razor's Edge (prison novel)

Remembering PT-927 (WWII)

The Lady Bug (WWII)

At the Point of the Quarrel (next)

Contents

Foreword	5
Chapter 1	6
Chapter 2	17
Chapter 3	26
Chapter 4	37
Chapter 5	54
Chapter 6	63
Chapter 7	83
Chapter 8	94
Chapter 9	104
Chapter 10	115
Chapter 11	128
Chapter 12	141
Chapter 13	158
Chapter 14	177
Chapter 15	190
Chapter 16	206
Chapter 17	214
Chapter 18	230
Chapter 19	241
Chapter 20	250
Chapter 21	261
Chapter 22	270
Chapter 23	282
Chapter 24	294
Chapter 25	305
Chapter 26	315
Chapter 27	325
Chapter 28	336
Chapter 29	349
Chapter 30	356
Chapter 31	368
Chapter 32	378
Chapter 33	388
Chapter 34	400
Chapter 35	412
Chapter 36	423
Chapter 37	434
Chapter 38	446
Chapter 39	457
Epilogue	468
A Parting Word from the Author	469

Foreword

This isn't the first book I've started, but the first that I completed—around summer of 1997. Back then I wasn't so sure of my writer's voice, yet four more books grew into the Stones Series. I was still learning the craft of storytelling. I wrote fifteen more books and published them before I felt confident to revisit my firsts and do the necessary polish and edits.

Fourteen Stones is Young Adult fiction that taught me to write, to persevere through dry spells, to weave a story line into something I could be proud of. Chaiko, the main character, has always remained close to my heart, and in one way or other influenced all my other characters who followed.

Young or old, I'm confident you will like this story. I set it in prehistoric times, thinking it would be simpler not having to deal with the ponderous weight of civilization. To my surprise it was harder, because I was unable to reference thoughts and institutions (like church, government and taxation) everyone is familiar with.

Yet because of where the story takes place, I always had to keep track of the surroundings, the weather and the time of year in careful detail. You will see…

So, welcome to the prehistoric. I wish you good reading.

Chapter 1

Some inner sense roused him from a light sleep. Chaiko surfaced into awareness of the night around him and though he had no prescience of danger, from longstanding habit he remained motionless, listening intently, testing the night air. A light wind played among the trees a little further down the slope but was not loud enough to mask a possible threat. He was reassured by the small habitual sounds: the hum of insects, now and then the strident call of crickets, wing beats of a bat hunting and an occasional frog calling under a quarter moon. From behind him came the sounds of the cave sleeping, comfortingly expected: a cough, a snore, the creaking of a hide, all softened by the depth of the cave.

With deliberate slowness he scanned his immediate surroundings. Dull embers glowed in the guard fire in front and only a wisp of smoke curled upward along the towering cliff face which loomed above in the pale light, with the cave it sheltered lost in the shadows. The wan glow of the moon barely illuminated the landscape; it hid more than it revealed. The broad ledge faced outward, seemingly empty. The access slope was barely visible, and the bush and trees beyond merely hinted at. Everything else farther down was lost in the darkness and the ambiguity of shadows, some threat hidden within. Chaiko shook his head to clear the suggestions his mind painted.

He drew a deep breath through his nostrils tasting the air, but smelled nothing disturbing. His lids closed against the distraction of his eyes; he willed himself to thought-walk into the darkness. He focused his mind and "walked" the area with his senses in a deliberate, slow sweep in front of the cave and then beyond; past the gathering place by Standing-Rock, which gave the clan its name; along the water run and onto Tall-Frog Tree. His senses vibrated, ears attuned, nostrils sniffing the air. He concentrated, projecting himself into the memory of the land, and swept on, resisting an impulse to hurry through the ritual. He followed the path worn into the grass, passing by the solitary rose-hip bush that grew there. There was an odd itching sensation at the back of his head; his ears twitched. Had he heard something? He was aware suddenly of the quiet all around. He nearly lost the mental vision of thought-walking but he forced himself to go on. There was a group of rocks, then a bare, sandy spot next to a clump of dried grass ... but wait ... did he just hear the dry grass crackling as if something brushed by? The hairs on his back rose. Trembling with concentration, his senses straining sharply, he listened. There was something there! With his whole being he reached out into that spot of darkness and felt awareness meet awareness, a feeling like cold water on the naked skin, shockingly unexpected even though he had been probing for just such a thing. He felt a creature as clearly as if he were touching it. The darkness growled; it too had felt the contact, palpably real. The menace grew in the low rumble and Chaiko knew there was a cougar on the prowl - a fearsome hunter of the night, sinewy, quick, agile and merciless.

"The fire will protect me..." Chaiko reasoned, but the presence approached brazenly, paused at the edge of the circle of firelight, crouched and made ready to jump at the puny creature in its sight.

"Animals are not supposed to do this ..." his mind protested. "Only man does not fear fire ..." The rumble grew again, ending in a half cough that echoed deep within its chest. The animal shifted its weight and gathered itself, ready to spring. There was something odd about that movement. "It's hurt," flashed through Chaiko's mind, every detail sharp in his heightened state of awareness, but his heart missed a beat and a warning scream froze in his throat.

Chaiko felt the beast's intent to spring; he felt its wish to slash into soft flesh with sharpened claws; he felt its need to escape the throbbing pain in an explosion of violence, blood and bleeding flesh. Let someone else carry its pain. No! Chaiko resisted that vicious purpose, resisted the weakness of his own mind succumbing to the terror in front of him. He roused himself to fight, dropped to the ground as his hand grabbed a burning limb from the fire and threw it at the face of the crouching animal. The cat sprang back in one fluid motion easily avoiding the wood, but the shower of sparks confused it. Its body low to the ground, it surged forward again, snarling, flecks of foam spitting through its bared teeth. Yellow fire blazed in those eyes, half crazed with pain far beyond any restraint of caution. Still between growls, it whimpered, licked its paw then shook its head in denial. Then the lips curled in renewed rage as a fresh paroxysm of pain exploded throughout its body. Every sinew taut, every nerve aflame, claws unfurled and dug deep into the soil, it made ready to spring.

Hate burned in that gaze, but the human returned it look for look. The eyes locked. Measure for measure, the son of the Standing-Rock Clan stood up against the beast. The cougar trembled with murderous intent, but that thin thread of resolve shining in the human eyes held him at bay. "You will not jump! You will not pounce!" Chaiko aimed the thought at the cougar, coiled and ready. The eyes bored into each other, and each saw the nature of the other, the manchild's and the beast's, and it was the beast that flinched and looked away.

The cougar reared and roared again, its claws ripping the soil, but they both knew the struggle between them was already decided, and it was the cougar that backed away. Favoring its injured paw, it wheeled, screaming its frustration into the night. In reply, Chaiko howled in victory like the wolf his people revered. The cougar slunk away and the darkness covered its retreat.

People came boiling out of the cave. "What is it?" Baer, the leader, demanded. "Cougar," Chaiko could reply almost calmly, though his heart thundered in his chest. Then he hurried to add by way of explanation, "It was crazed with hurt. Nearly ignored the fire."

A stocky man strode to the fore, spear in hand, clutching some skins around himself. He bent over the signs on the ground and confirmed, "Wounded." He looked into the darkness, then at the smallness of Chaiko. He wondered what could have stopped the crazed cougar; its intentions were clear in the sand. There was nothing in its way that he could see. Puzzled, he shook his head. Certainly not a cripple.

Baer called out loudly, "Only a cougar that passed by," and he herded the people back into the cave. "Go to sleep," he told his mate, reassuringly calm, and pulled the covers over himself. All around people settled down, but sleep did not come so easily, for there were few things in life as bone-chilling as a cougar's full scream of rage when frustrated.

Chaiko was again alone in the flickering circle of the fire. Slowly his heart settled to a steady rhythm, and his breath came more easily. The wonderful clarity of his mind faded as his perception dulled. The cave behind him stirred a few more times, but eventually settled into a troubled sleep.

This had been a very unusual night, Chaiko concluded. No animal had ever challenged the cave so, with the guard fire protecting its approach. But Chaiko knew that this time it was not the fire that had turned back the animal, but human spirit that had dared to stare danger down. He had not flinched, he realized in triumph, warmed with the victory. But then came the chilling realization of what could have happened, the rampage of a crazed beast among the sleepers and the terror they had so narrowly escaped.

Chaiko stirred the fire, coaxing the embers with dry tinder and twigs, and soon the dancing flames lit up the mouth of the cave, a circle of light that stood against the darkness and the dangers outside. He placed a few larger pieces of wood among the leaping flames, big enough to provide a steady glow till daybreak without wasting wood that had to be brought from the valley below. This was his task, to tend the fire, to keep the prowling night animals and hostile spirits away. This night he had proven the worth of his service.

He looked to the east and saw a softening in the darkness there. The morning was near, and already the stars were fading as the depth of sky gradually dissolved in the rising light. This was always a time of danger, as predators hunted the unwary caught between night and the coming day. The night belonged to the giant hunting cats, to the rarer pack of dogs, to the hyena and the wolves. But daybreak was also the time when spirits were said to be most restless. Feeling the weight of the approaching light of day, they too would search out the shadows. The fire gave shelter against them, but the dance of shadows also hid them. Out of the corner of his eyes, Chaiko could feel a spirit slide away behind him. By the fire, in the comforting circle of heat, light and smoke, he felt safe.

Yesterday, Chaiko had seen the first red-necked thrush of the season, and recalled (as his mother often used to) how he was born on the day the thrush had arrived at the summer feeding grounds, now fourteen years ago. In a pouch around his neck were thirteen small stones marking each year since his birth. He unlaced the pouch and spilled its contents onto the soft leather spanning his lap. With the practice of many years he ordered them, the feel of each stone familiar even in the uncertain firelight. The first five stones for the Growing Years had been selected for him by his father. He clicked through the stones in order.

> "The year of birth.................you were born crying.
> The year of walking.............you learned by trying.
> The year of words...............you measured out meaning.
> The year of listening...........to teach your ear hearing.
> The year of thought.............to find your way to reason.
> It takes five years................to make you a person."

He dropped each stone into the pouch as he counted through the singsong cadence of the mnemonic. He hurried through five more for the Learning Years, then slowed as he encountered the more recent three years of impatient waiting for the fourteenth year: Becoming, a much anticipated event when a boy was asked to sit among the men in formal recognition of maturity. Yet to Chaiko it would be a bitter event, for as a cripple he was destined to remain a child forever. Four years had gone by since a rock slide had severed his left leg a handbreadth beneath the knee in a melee of rolling stones. Each day since he had had to fight the bitterness, for inside there was a body that still remembered being whole.

Veering away from that excruciating memory, Chaiko returned to the comfort of the stones. They clicked through his fingers, thirteen stones for thirteen years. He had found four likely pieces for his Year of Becoming, but could not focus on that bitter task of choosing one over another. Becoming? He had already been stamped a cripple, robbed of becoming. Just what would lie ahead? The fifteenth year was the Year of Search, of seeking a mate, but for him, just another empty quest. It was all too painful to contemplate.

There followed five years of power, the peak of a person's strength and abilities, then five years of hope, when a person would see the children grow and hope for them in the future. After that, though people collected the year-stones still, the count was not worth remembering. A man was considered lucky who lived long enough to see his children reach Becoming, for most faced an unkind future of decline and ill health and the dependence of old age. There were few as old as Samar who, having accumulated wisdom from a long life, was now serving the clan. Could he, Chaiko, live as long as Samar and be as wise? To a cripple each day was long, he sighed, there was little wisdom in anguish, just suffering.

With great effort Chaiko focused on the four candidate stones. The year still had to be commemorated. Tradition dictated that the stone had to have some affinity for the purpose; after all the stone too had a history and maybe its own destiny. Perhaps most important, could the stone enhance his luck? Chaiko needed luck. He, more than others, had to be careful, to neglect nothing of significance. A rock slide had made him a cripple, and the cripple inside had made him cautious, always whispering, "Do not try too hard, for the harder you try, the harder it will be to accept giving in."

Which one then? His fingers read the stones, one by one, to divine its suitability by feel. He chose one, a crystal embedded in basalt. Sharp points protruded from its core, giving it a painful bite. Yes, Chaiko was inclined to settle on it, but in the end put it aside, thinking best to consult Samar.

His thoughts turned even sadder, arriving to a place which he knew all too well. He had no past; both his parents were dead and his childhood was obliterated by an accident. Likewise he had no present; he was a burden to himself and to the clan. He had no future for he was destined to remain a child forever. Or was there yet a way to escape his fate? Dejectedly he shook his head. He had only his brother.

The thought of his brother warmed him and allowed him to escape the obsession with his hurt and to look at the clan more dispassionately. Baer stood out in their ranks, radiating a commanding presence, for he had won the clan's respect by proving his courage and intelligence many times. He was a skilled hunter, with few to match him even though Tusk, his right hand and lead hunter, was stronger and Cosh, his left hand, age-mate and chief scout, was faster and keener in his senses. Still, Baer's strength was combined with reason and unfailing fairness. Baer was usually serious, and only his young daughter Lana could make him laugh freely and lighten the burden of his cares for the clan. Chaiko was filled with admiration and love for his brother because Baer always had time for him, made him feel more than just a burden.

The two brothers looked very different. Twice Chaiko's age, Baer was tall and barrel-chested, with great strength in his arms anchored in his sloping shoulders, and big hands that could easily cinch the waist of his mate, Tanya, before Lana was born. He used to hold the baby protectively in his arms cradled against his hairy chest, surprisingly gentle for such a powerful man.

Next to his brother, Chaiko looked slight, built along tough lean lines of long muscles. His greatest assets had been speed, agility and dexterity ... the very things his injury robbed him of. Then, for about two years after his accident his body had stopped growing. Now, at age fourteen, he was noticeably smaller than his age-mate Crow.

Yet, in spite of all dissimilarities, people were often struck by the likeness the two brothers shared. It was most noticeable in the dark brown color and the set of their eyes, as they looked about, alert, inquisitive, full of intelligence, always watchful and aware. They had the habit of squinting a bit as if looking beyond things, searching for causes that shaped events and moved people, seeing more than did most and considering matters carefully. There was an openness about them, an acceptance of others which made both very approachable; that is, until Chaiko's accident. Thus, while Baer had the wealth of experience that gave him confidence to channel his thoughts into decisions for the benefit of the whole clan, Chaiko had been robbed of the promise of a future. For Chaiko, one thought increasingly fed another, and he became more and more a thinker, an observer, destined to experience life second-hand.

It was generally considered by the clan that Baer made up for Chaiko's lack. If Chaiko was unlucky, Baer was considered lucky. To many of the clan, it was bad luck that Chaiko survived; most felt that it would have been kinder for him to have died, because there was no role for a cripple. Chaiko felt the weight of the consequence of his survival, and was driven by it. He sought ways of making himself useful: his severed leg made him useless as a hunter, but he could fish, and when the hunters returned empty-handed, the fish he caught were welcomed. He could get around awkwardly with the help of stout crutches. In the presence of others, he tried not to move much. He hid his deformity from himself and his clan, and they conspired with him to overlook it.

Above all, Chaiko felt that he must repay his brother for his protection, by somehow contributing to the care and well-being of the clan and thereby easing the load his brother carried. So when others relaxed around the fire, given over to the enjoyment of peaceful moments of inactivity, Chaiko was still thinking of ways to be of service. He kept watch, tending the guard fire throughout long nights, allowing others to rest. He worked wood into spears and digging sticks: each smooth, well-balanced and fire-hardened. Though his skill at spear-making was recognized, people were leery of his work, thinking it tainted by his

14 Stones

bad luck. It stood to reason a hunter needed luck, so a less well made implement by Kray was often preferred over his.

It seemed that all thoughts eventually led back to himself again. Tonight he had stood face to face with the cougar, had looked into the fury in its eyes and had recognized that its agony had eaten away the reason of the beast, and in time had turned it into hate of everything around him. "Be careful," Chaiko warned himself, "lest your own bitterness make such a cougar out of you." He shifted his seat, and the year-stones clicked in the pouch. Thirteen stones for thirteen years behind him, and four others awaiting his choice. He wondered what lay ahead. The year coming was called the Year of Search, when a young person searched for a mate, and if the fates were kind he would find one. Men were mated at fourteen, fifteen; girls even earlier - some as young as twelve. Given the short span of their lives, it was best to live it early. Could he, Chaiko, expect the future to reward him with a mate? Not likely.

Chaiko put a few more sticks on the fire, and bathed his face in the rising smoke, a habit to keep insects away especially in spring. By now, the grayness reached across the whole sky. A few morning birds uttered greeting calls announcing the imminent arrival of the sun. Then everything seemed to pause as the first ray of sun raced over the land and light unfolded over the horizon. Birds responded with raucous noises, frogs from a nearby pond joining in. With each heartbeat, the sun rose higher, and the land was filled with light and emerging color. Chaiko as always felt a sense of relief, released from the responsibility of guarding the cave. The spirit world retreated back into the darkest of the shadows and underground, into rocks and trees.

The sun broke free of the earth. A sparse cloud cover high up shone in gold, reflecting the light back down onto the ground. A thick mist hid the valley below and the lake beyond. A gentle wind swept up the slope and swirled at the rock facade of the cliff sheltering the cave. The curved cliff face, facing to the south and east, directed the early light into the cave with a welcoming warmth.

Uma as always was the first to get up. She coughed to clear her weak lungs, and wheezing she moved off to relieve herself. Ela's new baby cried wanting to be fed; Ela obliged. Then slowly, one by one, the rest awoke and began their morning routines.

The women came to the guard fire and each took a burning twig back to start her own. This morning they lingered, casting sideways looks at Chaiko, whispering among themselves about the unseen terror of the night before, the blood chilling screams still fresh on their minds. These had to be talked about and shared with one another.

"I nearly fainted when I heard the cougar scream," confided Nebu, clutching her five-year-old son Ork, until he complained of the pressure of her grip and wrenched himself free to run off.

"I nearly wet myself in fright," confessed Yaya shamefaced, but now that she was safe, she enjoyed the delicious shudder of terror that swept up and down her back at the memory of last night.

"That's nothing. I nearly died. I could not catch my breath," contributed Calla self-importantly.

"Tael said to me, 'Woman, come lie down! It's only a cat.' That is what he said," Ela complained about her mate. "Imagine that! He called it just a cat. Have you seen those claw marks in the sand?" Secretly she was proud of him, for she had seen fat Simm cowering under the covers, as if the cougar were after him alone.

"It's good that the guard fire was bright and kept the beast out," said Tanya with studied complacency, as if a passing cougar was an every night event. Befitting the mate of a leader, she wanted to calm their fears.

Only slowly did the women disperse. Soon swirling smoke from several fires filled the air. The cheerful noise of youngsters rose above the normal muted sounds of the morning. Eight-year-old Ruba bragged to his mother how he would have disposed of the intruder, and how she would have been cleaning its pelt for him this morning, but alas, Chaiko had chased the cougar off before brave Ruba could do all this. The mother smiled at him in indulgent pride; he would be a great hunter someday.

All about, people called out to each other, "Are you well?" This morning they added, "Did you hear the commotion last night?" as if anybody could sleep through those bloodcurdling screams. Makar, as usual, mimed the crane fresh from sleep, rising ungainly from its nest only to fall down, floundering and thrashing to overcome its stiffness and sleepiness, stumbling over its own long legs. This had been part of the morning ritual for years, yet people still laughed at it. This time Makar added the mountain lion that burned its paws and retreated, swinging its tail as it slunk away. Even Chaiko had to smile at that performance.

One by one, the hunters came to examine the prints left in the soil. They looked at Chaiko and at the prints. It was hard to believe that the animal had dared to come this close! Most shook their heads, inclined to dismiss the incident; the guard fire had done its job well.

Baer looked at the prints more closely, tracing the outline of the paw with his finger, judging its size and strength, reading the intention of the animal. He saw the sharp imprint of the claws fully extended; the cat had been ready to slash and shred. He could feel the tenseness of the coiled muscles ready to spring on its victim. What had stopped it? He looked at his brother and smiled. Surely not he?

Cosh, the lead scout who had backtracked the animal's approach and followed its retreat a good way, confirmed that the cougar had been hurt; the right front paw barely touched the ground. It had limped down the slope onto the plain and finally holed up in dense bush near the stream soaking its burning wound in the cool water, lapping to quench its fever-induced thirst. Cosh did not follow him in there. He reported back to Baer and everyone was warned to avoid the area.

Emma, her kindly face crinkled up in concern, said timorously, "But that's where we found old Sokar not too many years ago, stretched out on the grass, quite dead. Do you suppose his spirit entered the cougar???" She shuddered at her thoughts; it was easy to see where her son Crow got his superstitious bent.

"Sokar's spirit would not hurt us," Tanya said, dismissing the thought quickly before it could take root in the imaginations of the women. When she came back to the fire again, she grumbled in an undertone of light scorn, "Such a superstitious lot."

Chaiko, his night duty done, moved back to Baer's and Tanya's hearth. The few who saw him looked away, though this morning the looks lingered. Chaiko was used to their reactions, and planned his days to at least minimize movement that would call attention to his crippleness. On his sleeping place, he gathered his furs around him, then settled down to await the day's events. The usual sense of relief at being released from his self-appointed duty was overlaid by a sense of triumph. He relished the feeling for it was a long time since he had felt this good. Lana scampered over to him, and affectionately hugged him. In her eyes, he was the brave lion-slayer that saved them all last night.

"Would you give me its tail?" she asked him eagerly.

"What tail? The tail that's still attached to the cougar?"

"The tail that you could have cut off if you'd really wanted to," she replied with the self-assurance of a child though she was past eleven, just three years younger than he. But at that age of impatience, three years was a lifetime. She hugged him again, grateful that he was safe, grateful that he had kept out the terror of the night. He smiled broadly at her; with her large open eyes and expression of delight, she was irresistible. Tanya gave Chaiko a piece of smoke-hardened meat for his morning meal and a handful of nuts and cava-seeds to chew into a nourishing pulp. He munched on the mix without much appetite. They needed fresh meat soon. They all dreamed of mouth-wateringly tender chunks of roast, sizzling over the fire, juices dripping hissing into the flames, the fat shrinking and curling in the heat, singed ... served on a bed of fresh onions and white roots. They had not seen the like since bagging a rare elk in a midwinter hunt.

Crow, Chaiko's age-mate and closest friend hurried over. He too had no doubts that Chaiko had saved them. Still he asked, "And you looked the cougar right in the eye?" worried that the animal might have stolen a bit of his friend's spirit. But Chaiko looked the same, with that characteristic, slightly sardonic smile he always had when confronting Crow's superstitious views of the world. But then Chaiko relented, for this time he, Chaiko, had taken something from the animal, its confidence perhaps, certainly its purpose. This time, he had won.

Chapter 2

Baer went to Lookout, a small ledge higher up, which gave a good view to the south, down the slope to the shores of a broad lake that extended out of view into the distance. To the north the cave backed onto the cliff that hid the broad plain that was their chief hunting domain. To the east was a line of hills crowding that edge of the lake and to the west was a distant mountain range that bordered the plain. Baer noted nothing unusual this morning and ambled back to a fire set aside from the rest to give the leaders space to discuss issues without the whole clan being privy to them. Tusk and Cosh came to join him and more slowly, joints aching, the old one, Samar. In unhurried tones they conferred, watched discreetly by the rest of the cave. This morning their gestures seemed more deliberate than usual. A stir of expectation swept through everyone; a hunt was due. Not just a small hunting party going out for some chance game, this would be an organized effort involving all of the men, women and children. "Except me," Chaiko thought with bitterness. Even his brother's standing could not give him access to the circle of hunters. People usually felt uneasy around him anyway, and especially at times of import, like a big hunt, they shunned him, afraid that his bad luck could infect them somehow.

"We're going to hunt, I tell you," declared Tael, quite certain. Like the rest he was hungry for fresh meat, but he was even hungrier for the excitement a hunt promised. Besides, he craved recognition and was looking forward to a hunt to advance himself.

"If so, I'll be the one who will cast the first spear and kill the first animal," gloated Kray, rubbing in that he had been on the midwinter hunting party that brought in the last elk. It galled Tael to have his friend come ahead of him in anything.

Stow, a young hunter, sharpening the tip of his spear, overheard their talk from across the boundary stones of the hearths. He wanted to ingratiate himself with the older hunters. "With Cosh scouting, Baer leading one hunting party, Tusk the other, we should all have a chance at a kill," he said expressing his confidence in the hierarchy of the clan into whose ranks he hoped to climb one day. The older hunters exchanged looks, but ignored him. It was indeed a long way to the top of even such a small heap.

Samar rose from his seat, scanned the landscape, searching for some portents in the view. All knew this was in part an act, since Samar's eyes were weak and watery, and the view of the real hunting ground, the great plain, lay to the north blocked by the cliff. Yet he was seeing with the spiritual eye, the one he remembered with and the one that looked into the future needing no light.

In spite of their skepticism, people wanted to believe that he could call forth hunting magic, that he could evoke good luck, and do all that a shaman should to ensure success. No one dared to risk the consequences of doubting him and thereby somehow jinx the hunt. Their need added to their hopes, their hopes added to the stature of Samar and the ritual he acted out for them. The old man leaned down, picked up a handful of sand; straightening, he let the sand trickle through his fingers, his favorite way of signaling the end of most rituals. His body posture showed he was satisfied, and with his free hand he made the good hunting sign. Everyone let out their breath, releasing the impatient anticipation that had been building. Everyone then looked at Baer, for after the spirit world he was their authority; he simply nodded and gave a wave and the whole cave erupted into activity.

Crow hurried over to Chaiko, his face aglow with excitement; he would be going along on this hunt in recognition of his fourteen years, as a hunter-to-be. He carried two spears that Chaiko had made for him, smooth and fire-hardened. Bubbling with anticipation, he was oblivious of Chaiko's envy and hurt. Chaiko hid his disappointment in front of his friend, for he was truly happy for him. "Watch Cosh and do what he does," he advised unnecessarily, fussing over Crow who was growing more impatient with each seeming delay.

"Bison, bison...," Crow was muttering his wish list, "or at least an elk." He ached to fulfill the pent-up desires of years and to start on his first true hunt. It seemed to Chaiko that Crow wanted to hurry his destiny, to break out of camp and find something to cast his spear at, but he would not look beyond it. In contrast, Chaiko saw the hunt as a whole, a communal effort, a smooth progression of interlocking events that foresaw the end result, the hunters returning with the game. It always amazed Chaiko that his friend seemed to live in the here and now, as if the future did not exist. For Crow, like most of the others, the day itself was all the future he craved. In like manner, yesterday was the memory of all the past that mattered. But for Chaiko the past was the larger part of future; the present had a foot in each. He sought meaning behind meaning, as the lizard searches out the shade beneath the shade on a hot day.

The pace of preparation going on all around Chaiko stirred up all of his emotions. The aching to go along was overpowering. He remembered his childhood wish to become the hunter that he was meant to be. He silently cursed his fate; as a cripple he would always be left behind, would always eat someone else's kill at someone else's fire. He felt sorry for himself and wanted to cry. It was not the past he resented, nor the pain and rejection, but the future he had lost. Swallowing his tears, he forced the crying into anger. This cascade of emotions was much too overpowering so he turned away from it, trying not to think and not to feel at all.

A tight group of hunters had gathered about Tusk besieging him with questions, eager to begin. Kneeling in front of them was Cosh who drew lines in the soil, sketching out their route. Baer still conferred with Samar, after which he exchanged a few words with Tanya to include the women. She nodded her head to him, then collected a group of women around her. Tanya made sure they all had something, a carrying skin or a basket with which to bring the meat back. Kor shuffled about the group, parsimoniously handing out sharp flint blades he had recently made, to cut up and butcher the meat.

An excited group of boys chased about noisily waving their spears. As they all wanted to be hunters, they forced the youngest, five year old Sosa, to be a bison. He ran with the rest close on his heels. "There he goes... Head off the beast!" Everyone was infected with the excitement and enthusiastically cheered on the chase.

In the hunt, the clan's effort would be to make a major sweep of the great plain for bigger game, the first large kill of the season. This meant a trek there, stalk and chase, and a trek back loaded down with meat. Chaiko was unable to range very far from the cave; nonetheless, he too made plans. He would look for large calo-leaves used to wrap meat for roasting, both to flavor and to protect it from charring. There should be lots on the south slope by the bend of the creek, not really big enough yet, but this early in the season they would have to do. A few charo roots would be welcome as seasoning too.

Next to Chaiko, Crow was bursting with impatience. When someone uttered the deep-chested call of a bison, he eagerly joined in, the call taken up and passed along. He then started a new round of calls, tentative at first, then growing bolder as more people joined in, letting it be known, if anybody could still be unaware, that he would be a hunter on this hunt. In recognition of this special event even the more experienced hunters joined in. It was polite as well as politic to give recognition, confer status, and build self-confidence, a hunter's keenest weapon. When the bellows finally died out, people smiled at each other and exchanged knowing looks.

"It will be a good thing for the clan to have a new hunter," said Rea, a seasoned veteran, summing up the prevailing view. It remained unspoken that with each new hunter initiated into their midst, the rank and status of every other hunter increased, for there was one more beneath on the ladder of status and importance.

"A new hunter makes an old hunter older," dismissed Gill, who delighted in disagreeing with Rea in all things. He also wanted to remind Rea that he was ahead of him in rank.

Chaiko felt the excitement and honor for his friend Crow, while simultaneously feeling the emptiness that this recognition would be denied to him. "Why is happiness such a brief visitor, and why is bitterness such a constant, jealous companion?" he thought, swallowing the sudden sour taste in his mouth.

The whole clan was gathered around Samar and Baer ready for action. The old one had a burning twist of grass in his hand; he went from hunter to hunter blowing the smoke at them, purifying each.

He chanted: "... Good luck ... have the patience of stone ... the strength of a bear ... the eye of an eagle ... the swiftness of an antelope ..." exhorting the hunters, then casting a net to ensnare the hunted: "You'll call and the antelope will hear you... you will go and the elk will come to you... you will run and the bison will stop for you ... and will lie down in his bright blood ... and give its life to you that you may thank the beast for feeding you, your family and all of the clan..." Everyone made the good hunting sign, the thumb curled under the rest of the fingers, a full fist instead of an empty turned-up hand.

Chaiko reviewed the clan quickly. Everyone was dressed lightly, ready to move at speed. Each hunter carried two spears and some, a heavy-headed club as well. Two experienced hunters carried live embers in a clay-lined leather pouch. The women and girls held digging sticks, and were loaded down with wicker baskets or leather carryalls. Boys carried their spears and throwing sticks. Some of the spears were made by him, Chaiko noted with some pride; they would not fail. A small mark like a falcon's claw was etched into the shaft for good luck and accuracy. Of all the hunting birds, the falcon was Chaiko's favorite, the embodiment of much admired qualities, precision of flight, swiftness and lethal accuracy. Most of the digging sticks that the women carried had been made by him, too.

Then the whole clan broke into a final howl of anticipation, stomping their feet, jumping up and down, shaking spears and digging sticks. The high pitched tones of the women overrode the lower resonance of the men. Makar, unable to contain himself, ran around the entire group, whooping and hollering. Then the exuberance burst, and everyone settled into an easy stride: speed, endurance, and quiet purpose.

At a sign from Baer, Cosh in the lead with Tael and Stow broke away from the rest and swiftly disappeared from view, ranging ahead scouting for game. Baer and the rest of the hunters followed. His face aglow with pride and anticipation, Crow waved to Chaiko and held both his spears high. "I will bring a bison back for you," he called back to his friend. Chaiko gave him the good hunting sign.

The women and children shouldering carry-wraps made up the rear. The procession soon disappeared from sight down the slope and into the hidden cut that gave access to the valley and the plain behind the cliffs. For a while sounds drifted back: a voice calling out direction, a dislodged stone, then that too faded away. A little while later only a rising flock of birds marked their progress.

Chaiko was left with only Samar, Uma and Kor, all too old or infirm to go along. They gathered into a cluster instinctively, held together by the regret of not being able to take part in the hunt. Choking down the bitterness at being left behind, Chaiko set out on his crutches to find calo-leaf and charo-root as he intended. Though he depended on the convenience of the movement these crutches gave him, he hated them, seeing in them a symbol of all his shortcomings and an accusation of failed promise, that he would never measure up to what he was born to be.

Chaiko worked down the slope to where open grass replaced the scrub brush and stands of birch. He passed a young ash sapling standing by itself, just thick enough to make a spear. He sat down and with a chopper stone, nibbled at the wood. It was tedious work, and he soon broke into a sweat, but finally he had a straight piece of wood, green yet, but promising. He resumed his way. He found the calo-leaf where he expected, in the hollow of the creek bank open to the sun, and collected a large bundle. The load was not heavy but awkward and tended to overbalance him, making the trip back to the cave more awkward.

It was afternoon by the time he returned, the sun hot on his skin. Without speaking, Uma took the bundle from him and draped each leaf over the warm rocks to let the taste improve. Resignation was etched in her face; she too, being so old, sickly and without children, shared Chaiko's lack of status. Their efforts went unrecognized, unthanked.

Chaiko rested in the shade, expectantly scanning for any sign of the hunters but could find none. It was still too early, but that knowledge did not stop the anxious anticipation. Questions filled the waiting. Had they found something? Did Crow get his first kill? Was everyone all right? Wait, he told himself, he must wait. A cripple had better learn to wait well.

By the fire, Kor was working stones, making choppers with sharp edges, or blades, as there would be need for more of them to cut up the meat. The stone obeyed his gnarled hand, and with rhythmic clicking, chip by chip, a tool emerged from the shapeless rock. Chaiko watched him secretly. One day he too would work the stone. In the clan no one had Kor's expertise. Young Tael worked at it but did not have the patience nor the eye for it. He did not see the stone, the promise of it, what it could be; he forced his will on it, rather than the nature of the stone being coaxed. Stone had a good memory since every shard remembered every other, unlike water that flowed carelessly without memory. Chaiko felt unworthy to ask Kor to teach him and was afraid of rejection. So he surreptitiously watched and learned the old craftsman's technique. Thus whenever Tael made his frequent mistakes, invoking the correction of the old craftsman, Chaiko rejoiced not out of malice, but because of the opportunity to learn something of value. He reflected that perhaps it was unfair for Tael to be born with a driving wish but not the talent. A cripple often struggled with what was fair and what was not.

Chaiko busied himself cleaning a young green sapling with a shard of flint. He had already stripped off all the bark and was scraping some bumps off the main core of wood. The stick was slender and flexible; it was to be a spear for eight-year-old Ruba. Halfway down though, it had a slight bend in it which Chaiko repeatedly tried to straighten. But every time the wood sprang back, it was still crooked. Chaiko knew from experience that few pieces of wood were ever really straight; most started to warp as they dried and needed some work to right them. He carefully examined the shaft, but could not see any irregularities in the grain. Finally he stood up, then hopped to one side of the cave where there were a few crevices filled with rain water, which people used for washing and cleaning up. He submerged the shaft in a long fissure, weighed down with stones, and left it to soak.

"Chaiko," Kor called, waving for him to come. "We must clean out the storage cairns and make them ready for the meat."

So, with Kor and Uma, Chaiko went to the back of the cave, where it was cool and dry and examined the pits dug into the hard-packed dirt of the cave floor. Food, be it meat, roots, grain, or fruit was stored here for winter use. In spring the pits were cleaned, relined with mud then hardened by a slow fire. The fires were now out. Chaiko and the two others scooped out the ashes with their hands. There were fifteen pits, each easily able to hold a seated man. Hope we will fill a few after this hunt, Chaiko wished to himself, knowing their winter well-being was dependent on it. By winter, ten had to be filled to avoid hunger, but twelve would be better. They worked in silence, and were soon covered in fine ash etched by sweat.

Uma had to rest repeatedly and fight her growing shortness of breath. Kor watched her in sympathy. His problem was that his joints ached and did not want to bend anymore. In a way, he felt more of a cripple than Chaiko, but he could at least work flint and be useful, and retain ranking in the clan.

"When I was young," said Kor conversationally without the usual regret for one so old, "we took the first hunt of the season most seriously. We danced for days beforehand, to limber up our muscles and increase endurance. Nowadays, we're always in such hurry."

Uma asked, "Did you see Simm? He was jiggling as he went off to hunt; the winter melted the fat off him, and his skin was a loose bag hanging on his bones." She cackled in amusement; it was rare for her to dare to slight anyone, but Simm's indulgence in food made him a target even for her.

Finished with the pits, Chaiko returned to the fissure and checked on the shaft now thoroughly soaked. He took it back to the fire and held the bend just beyond the reach of the flames. In no time a thin thread of vapor rose from the drying wood. Again and again he flexed the shaft trying to straighten it. When the wood had dried completely, he repeated the whole process into early evening. There were still no signs of the hunting party.

Samar was in the back of the cave, chanting a hunting song, asking the spirits for assistance, as he fussed over a single paw of a Grey Wolf, the only relic of the wolves his clan revered. Samar, more than anyone, recognized that he was not a true shaman since he had been merely appointed to the title, and perhaps that was why he insisted upon rigid adherence to the form of any ritual, so vital for their survival. It was a deep-seated worry to the clan that even Samar was growing old, his memory fading, and his interest in life ebbing. There was no one suitable to replace him.

Samar looked down at Chaiko, his eyes watery and red. He folded his wasted limbs under him and joined Chaiko by the fire. "The hunt will succeed." It behooved him as shaman to hold that thought. "I have called on the Spirit of Grey Wolf and on the spirits of our fathers for help." More he could not do. Still he worried, because a shaman was often blamed for a hunt that failed.

"Baer will succeed," Chaiko uttered on faith. The old man smiled at him thinly; his watery eyes recognized him for an instant, then turned inward to continue to deal with the spirit world. Chaiko watched the eyes intently and wondered what and where the spirit world was. He had asked the shaman, of course, but was not enlightened by the reply. "The spirit world is behind the world you see. Just because you do not see the wind, would you deny it, even when you feel it on your face?

You do not see the rays of the sun, but see all illuminated by it. So it is with the spirit world. You look onto it, and as if looking at a pond, the depth of it is hidden by the reflection of its surface. Do not be dazzled by mere reflections."

With the sky darkening, Chaiko settled in his usual night spot and tended the guard fire. It felt strange to be guarding a nearly empty cave. To fill the time, he returned to work on the staff. He wetted the wood, applied counter-pressure to the bend, dried it over the fire. He filled a ragged piece of skin with sand and rubbed along the shaft to smooth it, but the work would take time to finish. But time he had. So he was still at it as the moon rose and moved across the face of night.

Chapter 3

It was midmorning when the first group returned from the hunt, a party of women and children with Stow in lead. As soon as he was in sight he signaled, with broad gestures, both success and that no one was hurt. All were burdened with loads of meat, already cut into chunks and fire-seared. The smell of their burden followed them, an invitation to any carnivore, so even this close to the cave they were watchful on all sides with spears and digging sticks held ready.

"We got an auroch and a small herd of bison against a cliff and killed three there and two others trying to cross a stream. You should have seen the water turn red with their blood," Stow exulted, none of his enthusiasm dampened by the long way back.

"That fills about two cairns," calculated Kor from Stow's account. Calla, his mate, came wearily up to him, dropped her burden of carrying skin and straightened stiffly, the small bones of her back crackling audibly. Because of her age, her load had been light. "This bison meat is tough," she pronounced derisively, kicking the bag with her foot, but was too tired to say much more. Kor looked her over. Tougher than you? he asked himself silently. He would never say that aloud, for he did not want to direct her sharp tongue toward himself more than it was already wont to do. He was concerned about the grey pallor of her face and hurried off to get her some water to drink.

Stow walked to Standing-Rock and in the customary ritual, dipped his hand in blood from a bag and pressed it upon the rock face to mark the success of six kills. Later when the work was done, and the celebrations were over, maybe Malek would paint one of the animals in the gallery of pictures in the back of the cave to capture the spirit of the animals, bind them to the cave, and to ensure many successful hunts.

As after any hunt, the first priority was to secure the meat: kill, butcher, protect, prepare and store in that order. Not until the meat was safely stashed in the pits could people relax and enjoy the fruits of the hunt.

They had worked all night, butchering the kill, cutting the meat into chunks wrapped in fronds and readied for transport. The smell of blood and gore from the butchering brought the hyenas, and even a curious lion that came to investigate, but were kept off by a circle of fires. The lion roared its displeasure and tore up large chunks of the turf with front paws, but left, disliking the odor of humans. The hunters had had to drive off the bolder dogs and hyenas who had less respect for man. With daylight the carrion birds arrived, circling high in the air, landing heavily among the rest, starting a fresh squabble for the best spot. With all the attention the kill was attracting it was best not to tarry, and as soon as the first batch of meat was prepared, a group was sent home, the honor to lead given to Stow, who had done well on the hunt.

Once back at the cave, there was still a lot of work to be done. The meat was cut into even smaller strips and put to dry on rocks or strung onto strings, with many fires smoking thickly from aromatic grass to flavor the meat. Chaiko tended a number of fires, carefully keeping the smoke even. He chewed on a fresh piece of meat, almost nauseated by its full flavor after lean winter fare.

Throughout the morning small groups continued to arrive burdened with meat wrapped in hides, and in baskets covered with leaves to keep insects off. The air rang with happy shouts and laughter in greetings, for the moment their tiredness forgotten. By the afternoon everyone was back and working. A group was busy cutting up a bison quarter. "How can you carry a whole bison on your small back?" Tael asked Sosa, who did not yet know the answer. "A strip at a time!" chorused everyone else at the oft-told saying. The flint blades cut through muscle and sinew and little by little the carcass disappeared.

Crow was among the hunters, rejoicing that he had thrust his spear into a young bison and caused it grievous injuries, and it was already known that the others who also shared in the kill would renounce their rights to allow him to claim it to earn the rank of hunter. He walked around, pride in every gesture, making sure everybody could see the tail of the bison he took as a token of his accomplishment. It was common courtesy for all to listen and to allow the passions to subside in the retelling. A new hunter was a big event. None smiled more broadly or laughed more loudly than Emma, swelled up with pride for her son.

After the meat, the hides needed attention. They had to be scraped, cleaned of any flesh that might invite bugs or rot to spoil them. This was a woman's job, and small groups of them surrounded a hide, stretched it out on the ground, inner side up, and attacked it with bone scrapers. An older, experienced woman would go around the edges patiently trimming it clean with a small flint knife. And so it went: spit, rub, scrape, pull the hide taut. Spit, rub, scrape and pull in an easy rhythm, humming a simple melody.

Ela straightened from her work and asked loudly, "Did you see that fool of my man on the hunt? Tael got his spear stuck into the side of a great big bison, then would not let go of the spear, the fool, but suffered the lumbering animal to drag him quite a way before it crashed to the ground, nearly on top of him. Now I ask you, is that any way for a grown man to act, risking life and limb?" Pride in him, however, shone clearly in her voice. "Why, we are most likely working the very hide. Look, here is the hole in its side."

Yaya looked at her askance. Everybody knew of the competition between their men, and everybody knew that Tael would do anything to win over Kray. One could always count on Ela to trumpet each victory. Yaya's mouth pulled into a tight line of disapproval.

The ground in the open places was covered with hides, stretched and pegged, curing in the air. The auroch hide was particularly tough and would be used for footwear. The bison hides were prized for wraps and blankets. One would be given to Crow.

Toward evening the pace slowed. The many hands had made short work of all tasks that needed to be done. The fires smoked as people finally rested. There was no more pleasant odor than meat curing over smoking fires, Chaiko thought, awash in feelings of well-being. Now at last there was time to relive the excitement of the last two days. There were animated discussions all over the cave. Painfully conscious that he had nothing to tell, Chaiko listened to as many stories as he could.

Nearby Baer was talking with Cosh and Tusk. "We moved too soon on the herd. We should have waited for them to cross the creek bed before we gave chase. We lost over half that herd," he said critically more to himself than to anyone specific.

Cosh, picking on a piece of smoked bone, agreed, "We chose the wrong animal to turn; we should have gone after the older bull, not the younger one."

Baer did his own calculation. "We have enough meat to fill about one and a half storage pits. Had we had gotten all, we would have over three. As it is, we need to hunt again to fill the second pit so we can seal it."

"We could try a sweep by the marshes. It's easy to corner some beasts between the ridge and the marsh," Tusk contributed. After all he was the lead hunter.

Baer considered awhile. "We must consult Samar," which he said often when he did not want to be rushed into a decision. Then he frowned. Samar was sleeping by his fire. It was obvious that the old one could not be depended on much longer. Someone would have to take his place. But who? Baer worried.

At another fire with Chaiko near, Crow loudly told the story of his first kill. As he spoke, he felt once again the pounding of hooves as a herd of bison had come thundering at them, but they had been instructed to close rank to block their way and turn them into the waiting trap. The older bison with half the herd swept by them on the open side to safety, while the less experienced bull, carried away by his rage, led the rest into the blind washout, and was forced to turn toward the closing hunters. Tusk, Tael and Crow all went for the young bull; without him the rest would be easier to kill. Approaching from three sides, Tael, the quickest, feinted a rush, distracting the bull, and as the young animal turned to face him, Tusk moved in and thrust his spear into the bull's side, just between the second and third ribs. The bull, roaring with rage, whipped around to face the pain, whereupon Tael and Crow lunged to make their thrust into the exposed side. The bull's breath sprayed out a bloody mist, and choked off any further bellows. He fell to his knees, half struggled up again, rolled onto his side, lifted his head one last time, then died with a long whimper of escaping breath. Crow, thrilled in the bloodlust of the kill, saw the vapor rise from the gushing blood. He was now a hunter, the shed blood proclaimed it. Chaiko smiled at the exuberance of his friend and was grateful that the spear he had made for Crow had not failed.

"When the bison charged at me, I forgot everything I ever learned and froze," Crow later admitted to his friend in private. "It was heading straight for me. I saw its eyes aimed at me. I could feel the beat of his hooves already dancing on my chest, and I could even smell its breath of sour grass. And still I could not move. If it had not been for the others distracting the beast, it would have trampled me into the dirt." He paused, his moment of indecision agonizingly painful. "But when it presented its side to me, I rushed in and stabbed it with my spear. I felt the shaft go through the hairs, through the hide and muscle into its innards in a horrible squish of sound." He shuddered as he tried to exorcise the memory by retelling, again and again. "I twisted and drove the spear even deeper. Blood sprayed on my face and before the animal was dead the taste of his blood was in my mouth. A very strange feeling." He paused trying to sort out his reactions. "Then it fell and died. Its legs still moving, still wanting to get away." It was not the first time he had killed, but who worries over the death of a rabbit or a fox? The passing from life of an imposing bison, however, had to be remembered.

"You are a hunter now," said Chaiko, reminding him of this most important consequence of the hunt, and watched pride brighten his friend's face. For Chaiko it was a bitter sweet moment; sweet feeling of affirmation for his friend but mixed with a bitter taste of his own hopelessness.

A little later, when the rush of excitement had receded, Crow felt nauseated having seen death so close up, seeing great strength ebbing away with so much blood flowing, the final clouding of the eyes and the deep death rattle of the last breath. Death, the final consequence of a life lived. A life that started with a breath and ended with one. But as they rolled the carcass of the young bull to one side for easier butchering, trapped air escaped noisily. Crow had jumped back, frightened that the spirit of the bull had returned to reclaim the body ... and was looking for him in order to exact revenge for the pain of its death.

Taking a life had its consequences. The bloodshed was on the hunter's hands and he was guilty of it. He must therefore treat the animal with respect - lest the hunter become callous and inured to the pain he caused and thus lose the spiritual link that tied him to the animal he hunted. According to clan wisdom, such a one had forgotten how the animal felt, and could not lure its like to face his spear again. The carcass was therefore to be respected for its spirit's sake and the hunter purified by regret for his own sake.

Crow was thus torn between his desire to brag about his exploits and his fear of arousing the bison's spirit against him. Chaiko hastened to reassure him. "It is the waste of an animal that shows disrespect. Pride in the kill confers recognition of worth and does not dishonor the animal." Crow still looked dubious.

At the next fire, Ile, Cosh's mate, was telling how tough the auroch hide had been and how it took five of them half the morning to skin it. It would make strong footwear that could stand up to a lot of use. Only a moose hide was prized more for its tightness against water. Ile and Tanya were trying to guess how many pairs could be made from one hide.

"Not just for footwear," Ile remarked rather tartly. "It is high time that Tay is fully covered. I don't know what her mother is thinking, letting the girl run around naked."

Tanya looked with surprise at her friend. "Yaya is a good mother and Tay is only three," she hurried to add. Ile sometimes acted as if she had never raised a child of her own. Their daughters were best of friends, Lana turned eleven, Ido just past ten.

Tanya was smiling with contentment at the success of the hunt. Though her mate led the clan, the cave and all women's work was her responsibility, and storing food her special joy. Kind and gracious, she was a perfect fit for Baer, who was strong and fair. She had a natural courtesy to which others responded by gladly doing as she asked or suggested. She needed not use her authority because people loved and admired her for her beauty combined with her warmth. When she smiled, eyes twinkling and face aglow, they found themselves smiling back.

Even after two childbirths, the first had died, she had retained a youthful figure, but she was most proud of her long hair which she wore tied up out of the way of work. When she was yet unattached, she had worn her hair down all of the time. In the sunlight, the unusual tawny color sparkled with copper highlights as her hair cascaded about her shoulders down her back.

Nowadays, when she felt romantic, she let her hair down to catch her mate's attention - and he'd better or else - but he never failed to respond. She thought it was a private signal to him alone, not realizing that everybody in the cave knew but pretended to overlook it out of respect for her. But then, they were all happy for her.

Awash in the smoke of his fire, Kor was recalling a more successful hunt years ago when he was young and a better hunter than all here. Calla, his mate, smiled a toothless grin. "You were better at many things back then," she said. That effectively silenced Kor.

Just a little further off Rea and Gill, near in age, shared a claim to one of the bison pelts and were working out who would get possession of this one. "You well remember that last season the moose hide went to you," Rea claimed. "But you gave it to some visiting girl in hope of her favors. Remember?"

"Yes, that was White Dove, a beauty indeed," Gill recalled. "But it went for nothing in the end. She smiled sweetly and thanked me most nicely, but of her favors I saw none." There was genuine regret in his voice. But that was then and this was now. "Look, Rea, you already have a nice new robe to keep you warm and mine is so worn, nearly lost all its hair. Soon it will be entirely bald, like Kor. I have no woman to keep me warm." Obviously Gill placed a high value on being warm.

"Neither have I," countered Rea, not about to be moved by need alone. "I warn you, women will be the death of you. You should find a girl and settle down." As if there were that many to choose from.

"It is a poor bee that settles on one flower in a field of blooms. Surely, it will go hungry on the same old fare and crave to taste some other," Gill muttered, conjuring up even more girls to fill their lives. After some further bickering they finally agreed that Gill could have the new robe but now owed Rea a new spear and his prized bear claw.

All around stories were told, exploits exaggerated, rival disputes of shares negotiated and claims settled. This was a normal preoccupation that followed any hunt.

Makar, hoping next year to be a hunter himself, pretended to be one now, running from a herd of bison after him. His knees were pumping higher and higher, his mouth agape in exaggerated terror. "No! Not me!" he shrieked, then fell, rolled and got to his feet again, just avoiding being trampled by the imaginary herd. Afterwards he dusted himself off – a big grin on his face. He earned appreciative laughter from all around.

"What would we do without him?" Chaiko smiled to himself. Makar acted out all their terror but robbed it of its bite by his humor. "Laughter is the recognition of all our frailties," Chaiko thought, shaking his head admiringly. "No one else could get away with the things that sprang from Makar's fertile imagination and zest for life. Can you hold onto water? It always seeps through your fingers."

While Chaiko listened, his hands had been busy with the shaft he was working on. In spite of all his effort the shaft was still noticeably crooked. If anything, the bend seemed to be increasing. As the tree grew and the limbs extended, it had fought its own weight, the tug of the wind and the press of snow caught in its branches. The strength and weakness was thus built into its grain, stronger on one side, more yielding on the other. It was a wonder then that any wood was straight! Chaiko frowned at the shaft in hand, thought of discarding it, demoting it into a digging stick, but the wood had the proper denseness for a spear. The point would hold its fire-hardened sharpness for a long time, so Chaiko decided to keep working on it. He took a handful of sand and rubbed it along the shaft. It was already smooth, and Chaiko was now using finer sand. The wood was taking on a burnished look. Only the bend needed to be worked out. He hobbled to the back wall of the cave, out of the way. He jammed the shaft into a niche, with the bend facing up. He wrapped a thong around a rock, and affixed it to the spear so the full weight would work against the bend. The shaft straightened to accommodate the weight, but Chaiko judged not enough, so he attached a heavier stone and was more satisfied. He hobbled back to the hearth, as always conscious of those who would watch, though they hid it. Only Baer smiled at him with open acceptance.

The cave had quieted, the work mostly done. Some were still checking pieces of meat and packing them into the storage pits. The first pit was full, covered with bitter herbs to repel bugs and insects, a clean hide, a layer of ash and rocks to press it all down, and finally sealed with fire-dried dirt tamped firmly into place.

After two days of fetching, carrying and generally helping wherever they could with small tasks, the younger children were tired, but still too excited to rest. They grew impatient listening to the adults' retelling of technical details and wanted a diversion of their own. They collected around Samar and pestered him for a story. The general excitement had warmed his spirits as well, so as long as it did not involve any physical exertion Samar was happy to oblige. Besides, this was also his responsibility. To teach by telling stories, to pass along values and traditions. An eye might see to imitate, an ear might hear to remember. Chaiko quietly joined the group, glad of a chance to rest.

Samar settled himself comfortably on a pile of hides, and scowled as he considered the many possibilities. "There once lived an eagle, just a nestling who had little to do but eat, sleep and grow. All of which she did with great enthusiasm, but undertook nothing else. Doing nothing soon became a habit. When the time came, she refused to learn to fly, for she did not want to leave the nest. The parents had to feed her extra. The more she ate, the more she grew and the more food she demanded. Her voice could be heard a long way complaining shrilly, 'Give me more.' They tried to throw her out of the nest but she was heavy and resisted piteously. Finally, it was the parents who left, one late summer day, and did not return. Vainly she called and called, they did not appear with food, and a strange feeling she had not known before grew more insistent in her belly. When she no longer could tolerate the hunger, she spread her wings as she saw her parents do, stepped off and fell out of the nest. But without the parents to teach and encourage, she fluttered awkwardly to the ground. Again she tried but could not fly, shamed that a bird had to walk like a fox, or a rat. All the animals came to see a bird that walked, and made fun of her. Finally a kind-hearted owl tried to teach her. 'When one flies, it is well to remember to think light thoughts of soaring and gather as much air under your wings as you can and not let it escape. When you can so hold the air and not spill it, you will be flying,' the old wise owl said. For one has to be wise to grow old, as one has to be old to be wise..." Samar's story was interrupted by a fit of coughing. Makar was already imitating the bird that walked, earning some laughter. Chaiko was puzzled by the story, for it was not one he had heard before.

14 Stones

The spasm finally ceased, and Samar was able to continue. "Now an owl is a good-natured bird and he told the eagle that she was born with wings and feathers because she was meant to fly and also pointed out that the eagle's feet were short and stubby, not meant for walking, sure to get caught in grass and bushes. Encouraged by the kind words, the eagle tried to fly, spreading her wings wide to hold the air, but to no avail. 'I can't, I can't,' the eagle cried, flapping her wings, fanning the air ineffectually. The owl considered awhile then said, 'To fly, my young friend, you must want to fly. Fear sits heavy in your heart like a lode stone. Give up the stone and your spirit will be light and ready to soar.' The eagle screamed, 'You stupid bird, there is no stone! There is nothing ... but a biting emptiness.' Now an owl will brook no disrespect. Without a further word he gathered himself, jumped into the air and with a few powerful strokes of his wide wings he was away."

Samar paused again. Most of the kids were disappointed that the eagle had not learned to fly, for they well understood her feelings, since they themselves were constantly trying things too hard for them, but so easy for an adult. Chaiko was puzzled; the eagle had closed her mind it seemed, and Chaiko knew many who did likewise, wishing for something but then telling themselves why they could not have it.

"The eagle hopped to the river where she found a catfish sunning itself near the surface asleep, unaware of the danger so near. The eagle would have had a feast, had she not been afraid of getting wet. But instead of pouncing, she called to the catfish to come closer. The catfish was quite surprised to hear what the eagle wanted, so it let itself into a conversation and soon found out what the problem was. 'You can't fly? Well, let me teach you.' 'How?' asked the eagle, astonished to hear a fish speak so. 'Next to birds fishes know more about flying than any other creature. You fly in the air, fishes fly in the water. It is really almost the same. There are currents in the water and there are currents in the air and we slip among them. And does not water flow, just as air?' The eagle had to admit that the fish made some sense, and was ready to listen.

"The catfish continued smoothly, 'Yes, we have much in common, you and I.' The eagle was taken aback by this assertion. 'How?' she wanted to know, for she saw little in the fish that she could find familiar. 'Why, look at my scales and then look at your feathers. Surely you see some similarities? Are not my fins like your wings to fly in water? And we are both shaped to fit our worlds, I, to slip smoothly through water, and you, to glide effortlessly in air. When I rest, I face the current like the eagle that faces into the wind. Or do you like the wind to get under your feathers, ruffling and bending them backward?' the fish continued its reasoning. 'No, no. That's most uncomfortable,' the eagle hastened to reply.

"Then the fish mentioned what most mattered to the eagle. 'How will you eat? You are an eagle. You soar, you hunt from the air. Surely you will not **run** after an animal in a vain attempt to catch it? How will you then fill your stomach? Maybe you had better learn to eat grass like a moose. Maybe you had better eat dirt like a pig.' 'No, no,' protested the eagle as those things did not stir her appetite. 'I don't want to walk anymore. Teach me to fly,' begged the eagle of the fish.

"After some consideration, the fish had this to say, 'To learn to fly you must first learn to swim. It is that simple.' The eagle was too stunned to speak; she could only open and close her beak. 'It stands to reason,' the fish maintained impatiently, 'to fly you must sense the wind and air currents swirling about you. Swimming will teach you to feel the water flowing by your feathers. And don't forget, you can never fall out of water, whereas you can fall out of the sky and get hurt, perhaps even die.' Well even a young eagle could see the wisdom in that argument; if there was one thing an eagle was afraid of, it was of falling out of the sky. 'Well come on, the water is soft and cozy, and there is no place like it on earth or in air ... So jump in,' the catfish said smiling, whiskers quivering with delight, droplets of water sparkling on his wide smile. The eagle thought the catfish was a lot wiser than the owl and so decided to learn from it; after all, she could still eat it later. So the eagle did as the fish suggested and jumped in." Samar clapped his hands to show how the eagle hit the water with a splash. He broke off a long-stemmed grass and chewed on it.

The children stirred expectantly, looking at each other and at Samar, waiting. They murmured among themselves but Samar remained quiet, unconcerned. Finally, Makar asked, "Well, did the eagle learn to fly?"

"The eagle?" Samar mused, his eyes twinkling, "No the eagle did not learn to fly. The eagle drowned. Everybody knows eagles can't swim." He waved his hand deprecatingly, to the chorus of groans as the logic, or lack of it, sank in. But long after the group melted away, Chaiko was still intrigued by the riddle. "What if the fish was right about water and air? The owl certainly was about flying," he muttered to himself. He resolved to learn how to keep his thoughts light to let his spirit soar.

Chapter 4

The morning found the clan awake earlier than usual. There was an air of expectation for everybody knew that the feast would be called, but still one could not act as if it had been decreed already; that would be a presumption of leadership. Any rite, especially one as important as the feast of First-Fires, had to be done correctly. It could easily be ruined by over-eagerness.

Outside the cave the fires were still smoldering, bathing the bison meat drying in the flow of smoke. At Makar's direction the boys Ruba, Sosa and Ork were given the task of tending the fires, while Lana and Ido were checking the strips of meat.

Calla came over to greet Tanya and gave her a bundle of bay leaves and a bag of sage, herbs for the upcoming feast. Tanya thanked her sincerely, aware of the generosity of the gift after a long winter. She knew, of course, that almost everybody considered Calla to be a pretentious busybody, but she knew the woman to be compassionate, more than some of the others who prided themselves on being so.

"It is best to wait for the meat to be at least half done, then season it thoroughly," Calla instructed. "That way the seasoning won't lose its potency through overcooking, but will still have plenty of time to flavor the entire roast." It was presumptuous of Calla to lecture Tanya on the use of such well known herbs, but Tanya listened to the directions with her customary courtesy. After all, the woman meant well and was being generous.

Ile joined them, giving Calla a telling sideways look. The two nodded to each other coolly, each feeling that she had a better claim on Tanya's attention than the other, but Tanya remained scrupulously neutral between them. The smaller the clan the more intense were its loyalties.

The three of them standing together acted like a magnet, and soon all the women were standing about expectantly. Tanya found herself talking in hushed tones, as everyone was waiting for the words to be spoken that would release all the activity related to the festivities.

Not too long ago, this had been known as the feast of the First-Kill, but the well-loved shaman, Bogan, had shown people that though their physical needs were fed by the hunt, the inner self was nourished by higher things. Bogan was often quoted, "If you are hungry, and share it, your neighbor will be hungry too. If you are full and share it, then all will be full together. The hunt decides whether you are full or hungry, but the sharing makes you people." The fire was a symbol of this communal spirit, for it stood for the whole cave. Hence the First-Fires rites celebrated the first successful hunt but also became a symbol of a new beginning, giving honor to all, recognizing the contribution of everyone, not just the hunters and their deeds.

Bogan was revered, by all the clans and caves far away, and though some of his reasoning was lost with his death, it added to the mysticism that grew like moss around his reputation and made it all the more prized. People were afraid of losing the thread. Bogan had been very good at making them feel bigger than themselves: he had found them a place in the nature of things. Besides, if things were understood by everybody, there would be no need for a shaman to balance the known and the unknown. Bogan's name still had great value, and in most situations it was sufficient to say, "Bogan said...," to close an argument. You could only counter a bogan with a bogan, "Yes, but Bogan also said..." Everything else fell short.

Samar was not trained. Age gave him wisdom, but it was the need of the cave that made him an acting shaman. He did not have the imagination to command the respect Bogan had earned but he was fair-minded and thoughtful, listened first, and was slow to come to a decision. Lately he saw more with his memories than with his eyes, and often it seemed he was merely going through the motions. It was up to Baer to look into the future with the eyes of his people. Though everybody knew that Samar had little time left, it was Baer who worried about who would replace him; he worried about it like a dog chewing on a piece of bone, the bone would not let him go. There was no likely successor. Baer frowned deeply every time he thought of this problem.

This morning many eyes followed Baer to the council fire. They did not miss the exaggeration of his posture, just a little statelier for the benefit of the occasion; he knew what was expected of him. Of course, no one showed any impatience. Baer was their leader, and he rightly gave expression to all their undertakings. Chaiko could appreciate more than any other the weight of leadership his brother bore. He noted that in the close confines of the cave, where it was impossible to escape or to hide, manners and polite conventions were so important. It was not good to mix in other people's affairs too closely, but if so, then with the authority of the whole community. And when needed, Baer was that authority, but it was a wise consensual exercise of the will of the whole.

Baer and Cosh were conferring, and the old shaman joined them. The three, conscious of their role, played out the scene as rehearsed through many shared tasks, mindful that like a fire the suspense had to be fed. Appetite should precede hunger.

"Whom do you need to assist you?" Baer asked of the shaman. "Makar is much too impetuous to come into question, but there are Tael and Stow; either could fit the role."

Samar paused to consider the suggestion in the slow deliberate manner that old people were wont to show, as if they were living at a different rate of time, as if they had all the time in the world, when in fact, they had the least.

"In my view, Tael is much too pushy for any honors," Cosh interjected into the pause. "Take Stow, he is steady and reliable."

"Wanting is the mother of all deeds," the old man muttered. "Tael will do, but I have use of both."

"That's it then," Baer agreed, and Cosh went to inform the young men of their honor in being selected.

Samar's near-blind eyes scanned the whole cave, feeling the people there rather than seeing them individually. He scooped up a handful of sand and let it trickle through his fingers forming a design on the ground. He took small pieces of stone and sticks and arranged them within the design, muttering to himself. Baer and Cosh exchanged curious glances; the old one was making a special effort. Could he sense that this might be his last First-Fire?

Baer waited patiently, for the physical must always wait upon the spiritual, until finally, Samar gave his approval with emphatic nods of his head. Baer then gave the formal command, raised his hand to show the closed fist, the symbol of authority, then opened the fingers in a sign of consent. Released from the waiting, the clan erupted into activity. Women and children started dragging skins and furs out of the cave, spreading them on the bare rocks and open grass in the full sun. The men collected every implement, every stick, carried them outside and sorted them into neat piles. The women doused the fires with water, then scooped the soggy ashes into worn skins, dragged and dumped them down the slope, where years of litter had already stained the face of the incline. Every stone around the fires had to be turned and cleaned, every pit swept and newly laid. Throughout the whole cave any loose dirt was swept up, and carted away to be dumped. Fresh dirt, sand, and clay were brought in and scattered, tramped down, the place made anew. The watch fire too was put out - ashes dug up then rebuilt with kindling and seasoned wood. But the fire was not lit yet. The sleeping places were remade with winter-dried moss and last year's grass with a bit of aromatic dried flowers mixed in. The sleeping furs were shaken and aired out.

Clearing out the bottom layer of furs, Sosa found a piece of rancid rabbit skin that was discolored with mold. "Ugh!" He smelled the sudden odor of death clinging to the fur and shuddering with disgust, flung the thing as far as he could.

It was an unfortunate Simm who walked right into the path of this flying piece, and it wrapped itself, like some living thing, around his neck. Startled out of his wits, Simm uttered a shrill screech of displeasure. He then flung the offending item farther, disgusted with the smell still clinging to him. He went off sniffing the air warily.

This time the loathsome piece landed upon the bedding of Malek and Nebu where it remained unnoticed for a while, and it was not until Nebu was taking the furs to be shaken and aired did she become aware of a vile odor. In fright, she examined the fur but could not account for the smell. Ashamed to own up to it, she went aside from the rest and shook and shook the fur wondering why the smell still clung so stubbornly to it. She soaked the area with water, scrubbed it assiduously with a scouring stone, but no use, the smell still permeated the piece. She rubbed it with aromatic grass, with only modest results. "Will nothing rid me of this pestilent smell?" she despaired. To her horror, the next covering needed similar extreme measures to purge it. She was on a verge of panic, when she discovered that the next piece was likewise affected, reeking of this indescribable odor of dead fish.

"What in all ....? What was wrong?" She began to sniff at herself. It did not seem to come from her, but how could she be sure? In alarm she retreated when a friend came near.

A short time later, young Ork came running up complaining to his mother, and brandishing a piece of rabbit fur for her inspection. Here at last was the accursed source! Horrified, Nebu took the piece and hurried into the bush where she dug a sizeable hole to cover the guilty evidence. Then she grabbed Ork, and the two of them spent nearly an hour standing in cold water, rubbing and scrubbing every body part.

Her antics, however, went unnoticed, since the whole cave was busy taking every item out, cleaning its place and bringing things back in. The men wiped and oiled their spears and throwing sticks. The women beat the furs with sticks, or washed items with water. This was also the time to throw away things that were worn, rather a rare event as things were used over and over again till they fell apart completely.

Well outside the cave, fresh meats were being roasted over cooking fires. The children collected around, sniffing at the delicious aroma. But there was no nibbling, not at First-Fire; the hunger that grew throughout the day was to remind people of winter, the roasting meat the promise of the season ahead.

The last of the nuts and dried berries, and all the roots and grains still left, were mixed together with water, allowed to soak and soften, then cooked slowly over a small fire into a thick porridge. It was allowed to cool and made into palm-sized flat pieces set to harden in the sun. A youngster would come and snatch one, then run and was given a gleeful chase by the more nimble, while the older people cheered on the contest. The people were chasing away a scavenging hyena, therefore showing vigilance, an important lesson at all times. The chase always ended with the hyena caught, for it was deemed proper not to allow a hyena to get away with its booty, though the cakes were almost always eaten by then. Chaiko yelled with the rest, "Oy, Oy, Oy ..." and rejoiced when the hyena was brought down and the chasers all piled on.

"Get off me," Sosa was yelling from under a pile of squirming bodies. When they did not respond quickly enough, he flailed back with elbows which was not received passively by the others. Soon the pile was in the throes of a free-for-all. Kray had to wade into the fray and separate them. Held by the scruff of the neck, Sosa was still trying to get at Ork, who was straining to get at him. Kray admonished him sternly to hold his peace. But to most of the men, a fight was a good sign that the mood had built to a fever pitch and had found an outlet. To the women, wiping a bloody nose or pressing a cold skin onto a bruise, the men's logic was unfathomable.

Chaiko had been sitting quietly at the periphery of all the activity. He had cleaned his possessions, ordered them, but there was no communal task assigned to him. Not to a cripple. Not on as an important day as this. He did not want to be underfoot with everybody busy preparing for the feast. He retrieved the shaft he had been working on, releasing the weight of stone. The shaft sprang back - unhappily still showing the bend. Exasperated he again considered giving up on the spear, but once again was mollified by the rich look and smooth feel of the wood. It felt right, a perfect balance of weight, length, and grip. He took it outside to the small pile of his possessions, mostly pieces of wood in various stages of workmanship ... his current life spread out in front of him.

A little later Chaiko kept Lana occupied by tying twisted cords of dried grass into a deer shape with branches for antlers. He was astonishingly good at this art and the girl applauded in delight, clamoring for the item like the young child she sometimes pretended to be for his and her own amusement. With a few deft adjustments Chaiko had captured the characteristic stance of the animal. But he was like that in most things he undertook, he had to do it better than anyone, the cripple driving him. He knew that he was secretly admired for his skills and had he been whole, he would have shared in many praises, but because he was a cripple, it prevented people outside his family expressing their appreciation, for then they would also have to acknowledge his crippleness. It was considered more polite to ignore both his handicap and his skill. Besides, skill was still no substitute for luck.

Chaiko looked at Lana with the proprietary pleasure that only kin could have with other kin. She had a shock of brown hair from her father, that tended to turn into an unruly mop of haphazard curls, but it was tinted with tawny highlights from her mother, although it came far short of Tanya's in both length and silky texture. The eyes were like his, lively dark brown, darting about, questioning. For a girl her mouth was a bit too generous but wonderfully expressive and the rest of her features well proportioned. Thankfully, she had inherited her mother's light, smooth complexion rather than Baer's swarthier, tougher skin.

Her body was still narrow, but was slowly adapting, preparing for womanhood, with a few interesting changes just becoming noticeable. The young males had started to pay more attention to her. This was a potential problem, as there were two males for every female in the clan. With Lana's ripening, the unattached males started to hope for her companionship, although Gill and Rae were past their prime and Tusk was unwilling by disposition. Of the rest, Simm was obsessed with food to the exclusion of everything else. Left were Stow, Chaiko, Crow and Makar, who was a year younger, to vie for the affections of but two budding girls, Lana, eleven, and Ido, only ten. Yet the time was not far off as girls were mated at thirteen or even twelve.

Lana sensed the changes in her body and in the expectations of people around her, but tried to keep these transformations from intruding into her awareness. She had an innocent, naive way about her that allowed her to shut out things she did not want to see. She never "saw" Chaiko's missing leg, but loved him all the more for it. Such selective blindness often called for some adroit balancing. But with her, Chaiko never felt his bitterness.

Lana was secure in her parents' love but they were strong, charismatic people, emanating a power she herself did not yet feel, and was therefore still shy and somewhat timid. She tended to be quiet and thoughtful but loved jokes and laughter. She ran around with Ido most of the time; the two were best of friends.

From Chaiko she ran to Ido to show her the straw deer he had made for her. "Ido, look what Chaiko made for me. Isn't it good? See, it even has antlers."

"It's ... good," Ido allowed, with a tone of hesitation in her voice she used whenever she talked about Chaiko.

"What is it with you?" Lana asked her, displeased at the lack of enthusiasm her friend was showing.

"Nothing," said Ido. "But he scares me."

"Chaiko?" Lana was incredulous. "He's the sweetest of persons."

"I know he's your father's brother, but he frightens me."

"Are we talking about Chaiko?" Lana could not believe her ears.

"Well, he sits there all day and watches," she said defensively. "I can feel his eyes on me, but when I look, he looks away, but then I feel him looking again."

"He likes to watch people," admitted Lana, "but that's because he can't mingle freely with them."

"He's like some black bird, sitting on a tree, watching and waiting." Ido tried to put words to her apprehension; dare she say it? "Like a vulture."

"Ido!" Lana remonstrated in protest.

"Well he does. And ... and I can never look at his leg ... the missing one. I mean his stump," she stammered out her confusion.

"Ido, I will hear no more of this, or I will never speak to you again!" Both were shocked by these revelations. Lana stormed away, leaving Ido to wonder why she had said all those things, because she knew how much Lana liked Chaiko.

With the cleaning done, people began to wander off to wash in final preparations for the feast. Some went to the stream and splashed the frigid waters over themselves. A few, more fastidious than the rest, stood in the cold waters, shivering, washing away a whole winter's accumulation of dirt, then rubbed and rubbed their hair with slippery root working out the tangles..

By late afternoon most tasks were done, and people hungrily gathered in front of the cave waiting to be invited in as First-Fire prescribed. Under Samar's direction Tael wove a path through the cave waving a smoldering cord of sweet grass, chanting:

> "Old, old, old ... hold and fold ... throw out ... what's too old
> Be new ... like the dew ... fresh each day ... made anew
> Fire old ... is fire dead ... ash is ash ... sad is sad
> Fire lit ... fire stay ... First Fire ... bright as day."

The onlookers soon joined in clapping and chanting. The pressure of the insistent rhythm built and Chaiko, his chest bursting, found himself howling and soon the whole cave joined in like a pack of wolves under a full moon.

Then, as was required by the ceremony, even the few remaining cooking fires outside were extinguished, in preparation for making the First-Fire of the new year. "Out, out ..." people yelled as the flames were doused and the still steaming ashes dug up and carted off. Samar then called for Kray and gave him a bundle containing the fire drill and wood. Kray, conscious of the honor, settled down on his haunches, his feet on a piece of dry seasoned wood, and began to spin the stick between his palms. The stick drilled into the wood, the friction building up the heat. Samar intoned and the rest joined in chorus:

> "The people learned to live in caves from the Bear ... from the bear learned to hunt bison and deer, from wolves ... from the wolves but fire was a gift of the sky ... the sky, blue sky"

The stick was spinning back and forth, the hands working down its length, pausing but an instant to reposition to the top, to spin down again. Kray was concentrating, willing the wood to light. He was sweating and soon grunting from the effort. His face became a straining mask, the wood drilling deeper into the hole. A wisp of smoke finally appeared and Yaya, his mate, dropped on all fours and gently blew on the awakening glow. The whole clan called out anxious encouragement as this was their fire that would burn the rest of the year, the parent to all other fires in the cave. A small tongue of flame burst forth and quickly enveloped the dried tinder. Yaya fed it carefully. Nervously, the two conveyed the burning bundle to the guard fire and nested it there, carefully nursing the flame. The burn flared and spread and First-Fire came alive to the cheers of relief (for it was considered unlucky if the transfer did not succeed the first time as befitting the ritual). The fire took hold, the flames spreading through the well-seasoned wood, aromatic herbs and pine cones, and in the failing light, the flames began their dance.

The food was passed around, ample portions wrapped in broad leaves, holding a juicy chunk of meat, a small porridge cake and a steaming piece of root.

"What was hunted and what has been found, we now share and pass around," intoned Samar in dedication. "We thank the animals that provided this sustenance. May they find peace in the spirit world. Health to you all."

For a little while, all conversations ceased as people got down to the serious task of eating a meal of such abundance. As the harshness of their lives dictated, there was a certain rhythm to their existence: prolonged hunger followed by an occasional binge of eating. "Whether you are full or empty, sharing makes you people. We all sit around the fire, sharing its warmth, and the fire is generous, warms all, and shines even on the undeserving," Bogan had said.

Simm could not be happier. There was plenty of food of all kinds, enough even for his appetite. One bite after the other he stuffed into his mouth. He took great gulps of fresh water to refresh his palate so he could taste again the full flavor of the food. He munched on some bitter herbs to further heighten the sensitivity of his flavor buds. His initial hunger satisfied, he was now settling into slow and measured eating. His grease-covered face beamed with delight. Such portions they should eat everyday! Ah, there was no tastier morsel than freshly roasted bison hump, unless it were wild boar baked in a pit, or perhaps sautéed antelope ribs served on watercress with carrots, or maybe steamed goose wrapped in callo-leaf with a side serving of a nest of eggs with onions ... There was really no end to this list of delicacies he reviewed so fondly.

He stuffed boiled white-root into his mouth, only momentarily slowed by the heat of the piece. He was visibly filling out and could feel his skin tightening the more he ate. Soon he would be back to normal, he thought with great contentment, except for a bothersome strange smell that found its way to his nose from time to time. Damn that piece of fur!

On the other side of the fire, Malek and Nebu were feasting on their portions with Ork half asleep at their feet. Their five year old son and pride of their existence, Ruba, came to sit with them, noisily sucking marrow from a bone. He was full to bursting, but after being hungry for so long, eating was hard to stop. Unexpectedly, he stuck his grease covered face into his mother's furs and wiped his face on them. "Ruba!" she cried out scandalized. Belatedly, she swung at him, but he easily avoided her blow. He sniffed derisively in her direction a few times, then ran off. Agitated, Nebu sniffed at herself, frowned, then ran toward the creek, to wash herself yet again. Where did that skin come from? she puzzled angrily to herself.

Chaiko sat beside Crow, and watched him stuff himself, his friend's face full of grease and smiles for all around. Chaiko himself was still too full of excitement to eat much, but he relished the stringy sinewy root. People nodded knowingly at Crow; he was soon to be initiated as a hunter. Excitement, however, did not dull his appetite. He ate his seed cakes, then Chaiko's too. Aside from Lana, he was the only one who did not "respect" Chaiko's crippleness; a blind insensitivity that had its advantages as well as its drawbacks.

"Today, I'll be made a hunter and will sit among the men." Crow was trying to fit himself into the role. "I will no longer keep the company of children ... and the women." Did that include Lana?— not likely.

"You have grown in the measure of the world. Soon you will not deign even to talk to me," said Chaiko, his voice infused with regret.

"Oh, no, I won't! You are my friend for life," Crow hastened in denial at this shocking utterance, but then saw the mischief in Chaiko's grin. He smote his friend lightly on the shoulder, just hard enough to let him know his saying was not overly appreciated. Chaiko laughed, almost as freely as he used to when they were children with the whole of their future still ahead of them. Now, the future was opening up for Crow, as it had already closed for Chaiko. A hunter was a hunter, as long as he carried a spear and sat among hunters. A cripple remained forever a cripple.

Crow had a positive buoyancy of mood and people joked that he could not sink because of it. His favorite expression was a half-smile playing about his face, laugh-lines curling an already round countenance. He would not have known sorrow had it not been for Chaiko's loss, but this burden he was careful to hide.

He was long of limbs set on a lanky frame. His muscles were always aching for some task to test their strength. Indeed, he liked pushing against something immovable, pretending dismay when it did not budge. He had made his first real kill, a good-sized bison, and for the moment it was enough.

Emma came over to Crow with her basket. She sat down next to her son and combed her son's hair with her fingers, gently separating the strands. Crow grimaced as she pulled at a knot then growled under his breath when she persisted. "Hold still!" she admonished him with a light slap, probably for the last time. After this he would be a hunter and beyond the reach of her discipline, she thought with pride. She rubbed some fat into his hair until it glistened, and then onto his face and chest. Finally she braided his hair into a long rope and tied it with a soft deer skin thong to the side. Still she fussed over him, joy shining in her eyes, intent that he be fully presentable to the whole clan.

Baer and the hunters sat together, quietly discussing Crow's elevation to their rank. They were all glad of an extra spear, because Simm was getting slower and slower as his stomach grew larger and larger. However, he was well liked for his humor, which saved him from an excess of ridicule.

Samar sat sunk into himself, with Tael by his side waiting for instruction. Could Tael take Samar's place? Baer asked himself. Tael was not of a reflective nature and was too impulsive to be used for anything but lesser roles. Tael always pushed himself forward, hungry for recognition. A shaman must serve his people, not bask in their regard as Tael was wont to do. No, Tael would not do. No, in the whole cave there was none suitable. Should he ask for help from another cave? This was a problem that needed to be solved. But not today!

Baer felt good about the feast of First-Fires proceeding so smoothly. Each year the ceremonies seemed easier and engaged his attention less and less. He made a few gestures, said a few words, and then the formalities seemed to run on their own. He was aware that Tanya did more actual work than he, in organizing and directing with gentle suggestions, even cajoling if need be. Nowadays he could sit back and enjoy the feast.

"The food tasted good," he said inconsequentially to Tusk and Cosh near him. "Especially the bison."

Tusk merely grunted, the food heavy in his stomach and his mind in the grip of an after meal lassitude. Cosh was not given to small talk and could not understand why people wasted their breath with such mundane conversations. Even Baer could not get a rise out of him until the talk got serious.

"What think you of young Crow?" Baer asked.

Cosh considered briefly. "He froze at first, but when opportunity presented itself, he made good use of it. He was second spear." Second spear meant he had second claim on the bison they killed. Not surprisingly Tusk was first spear and Tael third. It was not practical to extend beyond three. In any case, Tusk had renounced his claim and so had Tael, so that the kill could be presented to the clan on Crow's behalf for such an important ceremony. Thus the hide belonged to Crow though the meat remained communal property.

"Yes, he will do," Baer nodded approvingly. Of course, they had had this conversation many times before as they periodically reassessed the capabilities of each person, to see how well each fitted into the whole. A leader works with his head, thought Baer to himself, seeing his mate busily arranging the next phase of the festivities.

Chaiko felt the shift in the mood throughout the cave. The people had eaten and exchanged the required pleasantries. Baer signaled to Tael to wake the old shaman. Wrenched from heavy reverie, Samar looked older than ever; it took him a full moment to orient himself and even longer to realize what was wanted of him. He wobbled to the centre, trying to work the stiffness out of his limbs. A girl brought him a bowl of water and he drank greedily, water spilling down his narrow chest. He motioned for people to gather around the open space in the centre of the cave. Tael then started to bang two heavy sticks together and Samar attempted to shuffle to the slow beat. On alternating beats he shook a rattle, the bone-dry sound surprisingly loud in the heightened expectation. A circle of fires illuminated the central area, but the highlights and shadows reflected off his narrow limbs, emphasized their thinness and length; Samar looked more like a spider caught in a jerky dance in his own web. Still he danced. Others now joined in, clapping and banging sticks and rocks to build a wave of sound, and gradually a pulsing beat filled the cave. The excitement was building. Even Samar looked more convincing, as the rhythms energized his frail body. The sound grew in volume, filling every vestige of awareness, adding to every heartbeat, expanding every chest. The rhythm then ran away with itself, faster and faster, till it imploded into confusion. People collapsed panting, some laughing if they had breath to spare. Samar grinned wickedly, his face alive, his eyes glowing, the music making him forget his age.

Baer exchanged looks with Tanya, agreeing. The cave was ready. He nodded and she gave a sign to Ile.

A group of women, girls, boys and children pushed Crow to the centre. "Go, you do not belong with us anymore. You have hunted and you have killed. You have brought back much meat. You have fed the people. You do not sit with the children anymore. You do not sit with the women. Go. Go." As tradition required, Crow resisted their shoves. Not too much, just enough to honor the women and children. They gleefully thrust him in front of the hunters sitting in a group. Baer turned toward the commotion and demanded with mock severity, "Women, what brings you forth for our consideration?"

"We bring you one who would be a hunter," his mate replied with the required modesty.

"Call the shaman to test his spirit. Let him ask if that is so," Baer said resolutely.

Samar came forward. He walked around Crow, poking at his body, testing the strength of his muscles, tracing designs in the grease paint covering his chest. He took a burning twig from the fire, shook it till the flame went out, then with the glowing ember drew intricate patterns around Crow as if outlining a new person. Indeed, already Crow looked different; he was nearly unrecognizable under the grease paint and he stayed very quiet, his heart thumping, unsure of how much was wanted of him. Samar scattered a handful of kuma-seeds over him, which appeared to envelop him in a shower of sparks; a few that landed in the fire burst into flames and the air was filled with their heavy oily odor.

Samar then pushed Crow in front of the hunters again and Baer took note of him. "Shaman, he who-wants-to-be-a-hunter, is he fit?"

Samar nodded energetically. "His legs are like roots of oak, stout and strong. His arms are like branches holding up the sky. His eyes are clear as rainwater. And his thoughts are straight."

"Do you smell fear in him?"

"I smell fear in everyone. Even the rocks fear falling and shattering. Only water has no fear because water has no memory. It flows but knows not where it has been. A man who would be a hunter had better know fear from the inside, master it and earn respect."

"Does he need a spirit guide?"

"I have looked behind his eyes. There is a cave there, where he hides his thoughts and dreams, but there is light in that cave, not filled with brooding darkness. When he is ready the spirits will heed him." Chaiko knew what the shaman was talking about. Crow's eyes were always open and clear, the light freely reflected back. "The boy is sound, ready to be a man," was the final pronouncement.

"Does anyone here speak for him?" Baer asked as custom demanded.

It was Tusk, the lead hunter of the clan, who stood up, giving much honor to Crow. "I have known him since he was a boy and watched him grow. It is now many years since his father died in crossing the Swift-Waters and we, the hunters became like a father to him. We showed him the path a hunter must follow. Now he has grown tall and strong, and has learned the skills needed. He's proud to serve the clan, and the People-of-Standing-Rock are proud to have him. We know it and so say we." He spoke with exaggerated solemnity and sat down to a chorus of approval from the other hunters. The tension in Crow's chest tightened and he had to swallow hard to keep tears from his eyes. His stomach was pounding like a drum. Those who remembered the father now gave back to him, as they recognized Crow as one of them. One by one the hunters came and touched him, showing their acceptance of him. Proud of his friend, his chest swelling with happiness, Chaiko forgot for a moment that he was a cripple.

A crowd collected around Crow, patting him, wishing him well. There were smiles all around. It was going to be good to have an extra hunter. There would be no more hunger now for sure. Watch out, women, he will keep you busy cooking all the meat he will bring back from the hunt and curing hides all the time. Watch out, women, for the hunter will surely want more.

Baer stood once more, "Does anyone speak against him?" he asked as was required, momentarily putting a hole in the festivities. When no one answered, the whole crowd broke into a rising howl of approval.

When the noise died down somewhat, Samar laid his hand on Crow. His shrunken fist hit the young man's chest twice then he called out in a surprisingly strong voice, "From hence, you will not be called Crow the child ... you will answer only to Crow the Hunter, and may luck be your shadow..." Samar intended to continue, but the whole cave was in no mood to listen any longer. A few burst into a chant and soon the whole crowd was clapping, beating out a rhythm with everyone, from youngest to oldest, joining in a dance around the fires. Tael, beating on a hollow log with a pleasing, deep resonance, finally established dominance as others fell in behind. Everyone was aglow with the energy of the moment, inflamed by the pulse of sound. The dancing continued as the fires burned and as the moon advanced across the sky.

The clan was warmed by the frenzy of motion inspired by the pulsing beat, reinforced by the echoes of the cave. When Samar judged the excitement at its peak, he signaled and Stow, covered with a bison hide, moved to the centre of the crowd. A dark, shaggy beast with short curved horns spun about, pawing the ground, snorting. The beat changed to a sound of thundering hoofs, the staccato rhythm of a herd on the move. Then with head down the bison charged into the crowd that gave way amidst screams of alarm tinged with real fear. The fire and its shadows stirred their imagination and made the make-believe possible. The pelt became a real bison, powerful and dangerous. Yet, as the bison turned away, the crowd surged back in its wake, daring the danger. Then, starting with Baer and the hunters, each stalked the bison and laid a hand on its hump, claiming a piece of his spirit. It was strange to see all the vaunted hunters engaged in this seeming child play, but the solemn ritual affirmed their status rather than diminished it. The horns of the beast flashed right, then up in a vicious uppercut, and the bison charged into the crowd, scattering them. Crow the youngest hunter came last, his dance the longest and certainly the most felt, in a re-enactment of the hunt. When the bison bellowing in rage and pain fell before the spear thrusts, the rest of the crowd, children, women and old people rushed in to make their claim. "Spirit of bison, be free! Harbor no resentment, we hunt only because we must, to survive. You have lived and died honorably. We thank you for your generosity." Tael was beating the hollow log as fast as he could and the sound rolled about in the cave in a fitting climax to the ceremony. They all howled the call of the wolf who had taught them to hunt. Ahhhuww!!

Tay cried, for it was a lesson that for everything that lived, something had to die. Death was a basic fact of life that needed respect and ritual to tame it. How else was a hunter to prove his dominance over the beast he hunted, often stronger, faster than he and even better armed and protected?

With the death of the bison the ceremony was over and people collapsed for a rest. But the youngsters, with a fresh desire to feel the pulse of the dance, badgered Tael to start up the beat again. Soon the cave was again filled with stomping feet and swaying bodies in the firelight. The call to dance commanded by the beat was irresistible and the whole cave joined in, even Samar and Uma. For a time the sounds of celebration radiated out into the darkness of night proclaiming that a new year had begun.

The older people were the first to drop out, collecting near the walls, talking quietly, watching the merriment. The youngest, trying desperately to stay awake, fell asleep where they came to rest and had to be carried to the safety of the walls. Then one by one, the grownups drifted back to their sleeping places. Each time the singing got thinner and more ragged. When only the young were left, only the refrains were sung, with gaps, as they had not yet memorized the whole.

A group of young people collected around Crow, the newest hunter. With him they still felt a kinship of the past companionship and were not yet shy of his new stature. The boys examined admiringly his new spear, which Chaiko had given him in honor of Becoming. Their hands luxuriated at the smooth feel of the wood shaft, and at the snug way it filled the hand; and they marveled at its fine balance, as well as at the deadly spearhead and the sharpness of the serrated edge of the flint, worked so carefully by Kor. It was obvious the boys were interested by the trappings of status, the outward signs of a hunter. They could hardly wait for their Becoming, and wanted a finely worked spear from Chaiko, just like Crow's. To them Chaiko's luck was a lesser consideration than his obvious skill. It took experience of repeated failure to teach one the meaning of luck. The boys looked at Crow with new eyes: the spear, the new pendant around his neck: an odd shaped stone, a tell-mark carried by every hunter to remind each to be patient, a great virtue for a hunter.

The girls were more interested in Crow himself, and noted a new shine in his eyes, the straightness of his back as he walked conscious of the fact that he was now a hunter, a new assurance in his voice that had not been there this morning. He was slower to speak, aware that people were already taking him at his word. "It's amazing," Chaiko observed to himself, "how quick the transformation was. Yesterday he was but a boy, today he's a hunter, and he knows it." This night Crow was saying good-by to his childhood, not realizing fully what that meant but suspecting, anticipating his new role. The fires shrank, and the voices muted to a murmur as this group also melted away.

Chaiko was left alone at his post, tending the guard fire, watching the sparks fly into the dark sky. The feast of First-Fire was over, a new hunter had been invested, and a new year awaited them.

Paul Telegdi

Chapter 5

The quarter moon, moving in and out of high clouds, was visible to the west following its arch across the sky. Here and there a cluster of stars shone brightly into a colder than usual night, but there was no wind to put a real bite to the cold. The fire had collapsed into a few embers glowing weakly among the white ashes. Chaiko sat huddled over it, wrapped tightly in a bundle of furs, only his face and hands free. He was working on the ash sapling, rubbing it with a handful of coarse sand held in a piece of skin. He would drift off, his mind wandering, and his hands would fall asleep. Then suddenly he would jerk awake, peer into the night, thought-walk into the darkness, then reassured he would check the fire and get back to polishing the wood. He put a branch with last year's leaves still clinging to it into the fire. The flames leaped joyously through the dry leaves, then just as suddenly retreated, leaving the night darker than before.

Chaiko looked around, but there was not much to see. The lake to the south was a dull mirror of the sky that faded when the moon disappeared behind a bank of clouds. The slope to the cave was hidden also and there was a quiet that nagged at Chaiko. Were the insects so paralyzed with the cold? Or was his head still so full of the sounds of celebration that the ears listened for meaning in the strange stillness now? His breath smoked as he exhaled a lungful of air which he had been holding to listen. No insect sounds, no birds, and no wind permeated this silence. Even the cave seemed quieter than usual; people had sung and danced themselves into a deep, deep sleep. The occasional sound therefore was made louder by contrast. A child whimpered and somewhere to the left, water trickled quietly in the undergrowth.

Chaiko still felt stuffed. The meal had been too much and too rich, which after the privation of winter did not sit well with him. Yet for the moment, winter's long hunger was sated. Though he had not danced, he had helped the rhythm with sticks and swayed back and forth, the movement helping to settle the lump in his stomach. But now a tension was building again in his gut and it bothered him. A worry was nibbling away in his mind at the very edge of awareness. It made him very uneasy that he could not account for it. He listened again, but heard nothing. He looked, but could see nothing. He thought-walked into the darkness, sensing nothing. Yet he felt much too conscious of nothing to dismiss it; in an odd way the silence was confirming its own significance. He then brooded over this, like a raccoon that worried over a piece of bone, looking at it, washing it and nibbling at it; even when the bone was bare and gnawed clean, the creature still could not let go of it.

Were the spirits who had been banished by the general cleansing of the First-Fires still hovering about, reluctant to depart? Could he be feeling their presence? He squinted apprehensively into the shadows of darkness and noted its many tones. What did he expect to find? Could he see a hole within the hole, the larger subsuming the lesser? Wisdom held that it was not possible to see spirits directly, but that you could feel their effects. Was that it? He wondered. He did not like to trust something that he could not see, yet his world was full of things he could not understand but had to accept because they were. His strength as well as his weakness was that he had to have explanations for things.

Spirits talked to the living in dreams, did they not? Did not Samar say the like? "If you dream of a river," he had said, "it's not the river itself but the spirit of the river that flows through your mind. If you look at the river, it's there and you see the water flowing between its banks. But the eyes see only the surface whereas the mind knows its depth, the fish that swim in it, the water plants that cling to its bottom and even the sand and mud that are carried along by it. The eye is content with what it sees but the mind is more impressed with what it doesn't see, but knows is there." Were then thoughts mere reflections of reality? What were thoughts? An inner voice that sounded in one's head? Just a voice, or was there something more substantial? A voice alone could not explain memory, but then what could?

Could it all just be spirit effects? he asked again. He knew his friend Crow believed strongly in a spirit world; he could not explain it, but used it to explain everything else. Such blindness did not suffice for Chaiko. He looked for meaning behind meaning, though he often came short of it. He shook his head, thoroughly frustrated. Why was he so different from the rest? Why could he not be satisfied with the simple answers that everyone else settled for? Did all his questions lead back to a river of rocks, rolling, rolling, taking everything with it, including his leg, and with his leg his life? He shook his head again to get rid of the thoughts, but they remained like obstinate leeches. There needed to be a compromise somewhere, otherwise he would end up like the cougar—obsessed with its injury, hating everything else.

Warding off the uncomfortable thoughts, he focused on the stick in his hand. The shaft was smooth, but still showed the undesirable bend about halfway along its length. A spear had to be straight to be true in flight. Often as wood dried and aged, it developed a twist, however he had worked this piece before to straighten it. The surprise was its tenacity; yet that very quality argued for the wood, not against it, and Chaiko resolved yet again to keep working it some more. He applied steady pressure against the bend, testing the flexibility of the wood. As it cured it was stiffening, but possessed considerable springiness still. To one end he tied a length of string made of tough river grass, then bending the wood he tied it to the other end. The shaft bowed, the string holding the curve in the wood, straining against the bend. Testing the tension, his fingers plucked the string and he was surprised by the pleasing sound produced as the string vibrated along its length. It hummed, sounding like the wingbeat of a hummingbird hovering over a flower, excited by the promise of nectar. A rich sound, taking pleasure in itself, fading slowly, reluctantly, aching for more. Delighted, Chaiko struck again and again, enjoying each tone as it sprang into being, hovered briefly then evaporated into silence, leaving the night poorer than before. He hurried to fill the void with new tones; each with its own accent, its own moods and surprising range of emotions. In succession he felt joy rising, shadowed by sadness, followed by a new longing. How could the sounds do all that? Was it a new language? To be felt, but not to be spoken of or explained? Fascinated, he experimented.

He soon found that the more he bent the wood, the more the wood resisted and put greater tension on the string, and the higher the tones sounded. The string unraveled and snapped several times but he retied it stronger than before and noted how the sound changed.

The tones he made were not very loud, certainly not loud enough to wake anyone sleeping. He quickly noticed that some sounds sounded clean, while others sounded muddy and displeasing. He also found it was easier to make unpleasant sounds, but the few good ones were worth all the rest. He kept at it. He tried to think of ways of using it. Perhaps while chanting, but the sounds were so unpredictable. It would be hard to fit into a chant unless the sounds could be made to obey. But how?

Suddenly he froze, amazed that he was enjoying himself. He was driven by pleasure rather than by a grim need to be useful. Earlier, when Crow was elevated to the rank of a hunter, he had also been happy. But that was for his friend whereas now, he was enjoying himself on his own account. This had not happened since ... since the rock slid out from under him four years ago. He sensed himself approaching the barrier he had erected around that memory, but this time he did not veer off. He cringed in expectation of the surge of pain that had always stopped him before when his thoughts came this close to the rock slide. Even now he dared not face it directly. Instead he started from afar, recalling the time when he was just a child, healthy and whole.

He had held such promise then. He had been quick, agile both of limb and of mind, full of intelligence much like his brother, and showed every indication of growing up just like him to serve the clan. But there were differences that had set them apart; he was always pestering adults with unusual questions that they could not answer. Even Samar often had to send the boy away because his many queries, and the detail and clarity of the answers he expected, often brought on a headache from confusion. Samar was fond of saying, "Confusion of thought is the mother of all ignorance, and I can hear my mother calling." He would then retreat from any further onslaught. So while his brother Baer achieved stature and reputation through his dedication of service to the clan, Chaiko gradually acquired a reputation of being peculiar. But the more people retreated from him the more insistent he became and his questions became interrogations.

As Chaiko grew, he learned to ask fewer questions that nobody could answer anyway. His father, sensing his need, taught him all the lore and wisdom of the clan, but could not satisfy the hunger of his son. His mother worried about him and Baer tried to mentor him, to shield him with his own prestige. With the years Chaiko suppressed his inquisitiveness, kept it from view, and tried behaving normally to win back some of the acceptance he had lost. He had made good progress, when four years ago his life abruptly changed.

When he was ten, he had been with a group returning from a hunt loaded down with meat. They had come to a slope obstructed by a spillway of stones cutting across the entire width of the hill. There was no way around it but straight across the precariously balanced river of rocks. Chaiko with the exuberance of youth had raced ahead to be the first, lightly bounding from rock to rock like a mountain goat, unconcerned and unafraid. Crow had followed to the warning shout of others. "Be careful," his mother had yelled. Baer had lifted his arms in caution.

It had been a beautiful day; the sun was shining brightly with no build-up of heat yet and it was too early in the year for pestering bugs. They had eaten, but had walked off the fullness and Chaiko had felt strong and light and invincible. It had been a good hunt. His brother had gotten a bison and promised the hide to him. He knew that he too would be a great hunter, just like his brother, he knew, on that day with the sun shining on a river of rocks.

Crow slightly behind him had made a dash to be across first, when a light scattering of rocks rolled down the slope. Chaiko was not going to be beaten, not by Crow, for he knew himself to be the faster. Laughing, he leapt from rock to rock, oft tottering, sometimes feeling them shift and give way under his weight, but he kept on. He was almost across, then looked back one more time to taunt Crow still struggling to make up the distance. He jumped a wide gap to a large protruding rock, landed on it, felt the rock jerk as it absorbed the impact of his weight then steadied, but he was still off balance wobbling. He righted himself and called out in triumph - he was going to win. Crow should have known he could never best him! There were shouts of encouragement from the group behind; they too were caught up in the race. Which goat would be first?

Then it happened. Slowly and without warning the rock began to shift, to roll, but nimbly Chaiko managed to stay on top of it, his feet dancing. But the more he danced the more the rock rolled, and it was now slipping down the hill taking smaller rocks along with it. Still Chaiko was not alarmed; the rocks around were small, most mere pebbles, tinkling ticking their way down. But the speed of the slide increased, and Chaiko gathered himself for a long jump to safety. He snapped his legs straight and pushed off, but found nothing to push against. The whole ground was now sliding, the trickle had turned into a rumble, then to the sound of thunder as the whole slope gave way. He lost his footing completely, and became a mere helpless piece of flesh carried by the avalanche. He had one final glimpse of the group of people strung out on the far side, their faces frozen in shock. Then his world turned to dust, to thunder, as he kept rolling, tumbling with the rock. But it was not he. This was not happening to him. It must be someone else caught in that melee. A bright searing pain filled his mind and body, then time stood still and the pain was everlasting, ageless. It laughed at his puny efforts to escape and save himself—much too late. And though time stopped to look at itself, the rock kept on moving, rolling down, down. The red film in front of his eyes turned black and he no longer cared.

Later those who had been on the slope told him he was lucky that being so light, he was deflected out of the path of the full weight of the rocks coming to a crashing halt on the bottom. He was lucky, they said, for the rocks severed his leg cleanly, no jagged bone or chips, a clean break, and the blood flow was stopped by crushed arteries. He was lucky they assured him, but they really meant it would have been luckier had he died.

He had not been this close to the memory since. For four years his mind had turned away each and every time even from a hint of recollection. It had simply refused to revisit the trauma. With a shock he now realized there were holes in what he could recall, huge gaps. He did not remember the pain much, though he knew that it had been there, as close as his shadow, constant and personal. He did not remember the even worse anguish when he must have first realized that his fate was forever sealed; but he knew it had been there, a desperate, hopeless moment in time, his entire future taken away. He had become and would forever be a cripple. And all the future he would have was his brother. As long as Baer was strong, Chaiko would not go hungry. As long as Baer was healthy, a cripple would not lack a place to stay. And as long as Baer would smile at him, he could go on living. Baer was his only status.

It was not that the clan lacked compassion; it took good care of the sick and nursed the old with patience and understanding. But it was facing a world that had become harsher over the last generations. Climatic changes had disrupted the migrating patterns of animals they depended on. Floods, fire, and drought had obstructed the herds, which were delayed or reduced or did not show up at all. Life for the People became harder and less predictable. The changes forced the larger groups to disperse into smaller clans to scavenge for food over a wider area. The clans became smaller, leaner, hardened by winter hunger and accompanying sickness and death. Far fewer children were born, as if they did not want to arrive into such a harsh world. And far fewer survived their first years.

In turn, the clan looked at the world with narrower, hardened eyes. They responded to hurt with sympathy, to sickness with care and to death with sorrow, but also with an acceptance of how things were and were meant to be. So their behavior toward Chaiko was not driven by callousness; it was just that they could not afford an easy sentimentality. There was simply no role foreseen for him; a cripple would remain a child forever, a dependant.

Thinking now of the past, Chaiko was overwhelmed by the intensity of sadness that welled up in him—but this time he did not turn away. Tears sprang to his eyes, and he cried for the first time—for himself. He dared to think what he could have been. Today he would have been a hunter like Crow, and the clan would have looked at him also with pride and great expectations. Instead they had looked away, around, or through him. He became a shadow that did not go away. That hurt the most, the loss of identity that was still buried under rocks somewhere along with his childhood. Panic-stricken he backed off the thought and tried to press all the emotions back where they came from. That place must be in his stomach, for it was pounding and shortening his breath. In time he calmed down, though his feelings remained in disarray. He soothed himself with reason; once one disturbs the lay of sand, one can never get it as smooth and faceless as before - the tracks might be hidden, but a trace would always remain.

His life had started all over again; born of pain in a river of rocks, nourished by sorrow, sustained by bitterness. It was as if the former Chaiko had never lived, the child that could run, that could laugh. Yet Chaiko still remembered the joy of running, the carefree laughter, but was cut off from the child he had been. The loss had been great, the anguish continued to torment him, and the child in him that still craved recognition kicked him in the stomach again. This time, however, he was better prepared for it.

He was a cripple. He had to face that. As a cripple he could never be a hunter. But who was he then? What about the longing that had been building the past years as he took more interest in the girls and women around him? He dared not dream of a mate. Without hunting he had no status. Without status a man could not mate, he could not have children. And without children he had neither respect, nor a future. The best that he could expect was to share in the warmth of his brother's hearth, but from the rest, to be overlooked - a shadow that did not go away.

In spite of his pain, Chaiko could see that self-pity would lead him into despair, with bitterness as its fruit, until he would eventually succumb and become far less than what he still could be. "I must spit out the bitterness. Must let go of the anger that is gnawing at me from the inside. But how to do that?" Perhaps by looking at himself with other eyes, with Baer's or Crow's, the two he trusted most.

Crow's attitude had never changed toward him; he remained a friend, though no longer a playmate, since playing had disappeared from both their lives. For with Chaiko's injury and slow recovery, Crow too had quieted down. It was as if he also had lost something in that rock slide, no longer constantly challenging Chaiko as before. But he always had time for him. He refused to let the loss come between them; he overlooked Chaiko's moodiness, letting him brood, but refusing to brood with him. Still, they no longer talked of a future as they used to, with the anticipation of youth; they both knew that a cripple had no future.

"I have two persons I can depend on," Chaiko concluded, his heart warmed by the thought. "But can they depend on me?" He thought that over awhile, watching the odd spark from the fire jump into the night and wink out in the frigid air.

He had tried to help. He had tried to be useful and serve in any way he could, but was that enough? There was an angry hurt driving him, for he had to prove that he still had value. But the more he drove himself, the more he hurt, from an inner sense of uselessness and from the subtle and not so subtle rejection from others. He would have to let go of the hurt; he would have to stop proving himself; he would keep helping, but he would do so because help was needed and because he could. Freely, without recompense. And he would learn to smile again, he promised himself. He thought of Lana, and smiled. Perhaps someday he would dare even to laugh.

When the sun came up, a bright orange circle on the horizon, Chaiko was calm. He had a new sense of purpose instead of the well-intentioned stumbling about driven by desperation. He would help where he could with what he could. If one could not have the legs to hunt, then one could be the eyes of the cave, watchful at all times, always looking ahead, guarding their future as well as the present. A deep sigh escaped him, so be it! He had drawn a line between the present and the past, at peace with himself at last.

Without realizing it, he had finally buried his leg in that River of Rocks.

Chapter 6

The morning was crisp. The rising sun, however, soon warmed the air and the chill retreated into the shadows until the rising temperature penetrated even there.

The cave stirred and people eased themselves into the new day. Chaiko went from the guard fire to his brother's hearth, sat and chewed absently on the remains of last night's feast, still too preoccupied to enjoy the taste. Lana sought to engage him in a morning play of teasing but had to make a disappointed face when he did not respond. Finally she went off to search for Ido, and the two of them spent a great deal of time avoiding eight-year-old Ruba, who was making a nuisance of himself, dismayed as he was by the interest the older boys were showing in the girls, thereby devaluing his attentions.

Chaiko felt so disoriented by an unusual sense of peace that he quickly backtracked to his rededication of the night before. The inner turmoil was absent, as every heartbeat no longer reminded him that he was a cripple. There was a quiet inside, a quiet that needed to be filled. Chaiko looked about at all the activity with fresh eyes, taking nothing for granted. The next hearth was occupied by Cosh, Ile and Ido but they were already up and about. Beyond them was the fire of Kor and Calla, a much older couple. Calla kept her place tidy; nothing was left lying about. She even made Kor take his stone work elsewhere as she did not want any stone chips about her fire. He preferred to be away from her sharp tongue that could cut him more than the flint shards he worked. Their only son had left years ago to take the skill he learned from his father to a clan that needed it. Because Kor was such a valued craftsman, they always had plenty to eat when there was food to be had, and piles of soft furs to cover them. Calla tended to give herself airs about their importance and pretended to have a status near that of Baer's and Tanya's. The rest of the cave took no issue with her view.

The hearth on the other side was occupied by Kray and Yaya. She was five years older than he, but he counted himself happy that he had a mate at all, as women were scarce. Kray worked wood and hunted, was reasonably accomplished in both endeavors, but was not an inspired craftsman like Kor. Still he was lucky, attested to by a mate, a five-year-old boy Sosa, and a three-year-old girl Tay.

Beyond them were Tael, Ela and the baby. Corpulent Simm shared their fire, benefiting from Ela's excellent cooking. He certainly had the girth to prove it.

There was no question that Tael was the focus at that hearth. Still aglow from the importance of being the shaman's assistant in yesterday's festivities, he lolled about the fire, luxuriating in feelings of accomplishment. Soon this feeling would fade and he would be driven by his ambition to prove himself all over again, or until someone of worth finally took notice.

Ela was an attractive young woman with thick, brown hair. She was petite in size, her body soft and rounded. She had big, expressive eyes that she would turn on Tael shining with admiration. She liked attention fully as much as he, but was content to bask in any glory that reflected off her mate. She did not mind that he was jealously possessive of any luster, as long as he paid her some attention. Which he did, for a perfect man deserving of credit must have a perfect mate. So even when he faulted her, he did so gently so as not to devalue her.

This morning, Tael was in no hurry to get up, and stretched on his furs while Ela hand-fed him some seed cakes. Playfully he snapped after her hands and she squealed in mock alarm. In between, she would steal a few seconds to attend to the baby, to play and pat him. Not yet a year old, already having learned that he was not the centre of their little world, he was quiet and undemanding.

"Who's the best tracker of the lot?" Tael asked, self-satisfied as he was, and in a mood to preen.

"Why, you are, of course," Ela chimed in on cue.

"By Thunder, right you are! It was I who first picked up the bison tracks on the hard-packed ground. Cosh nearly missed them." The last he said in lowered tones to her alone. "Who's the best hunter of them all?" he asked, watching her closely.

"But you surely are," she said without hesitation.

"Right again. I should have got first spear on the kill of the young bull and you would now have a nice new robe. But we had to be unselfish and give Crow a claim to become a hunter. Am I not generous?"

"Indeed you are," she affirmed without missing a beat. He beamed at her approvingly.

"Who has the nicest, most obedient mate in the whole cave?"

"Why, you have ..." only belatedly realizing the meaning of his question. She blushed first in confusion, then in pleasure. He beamed at her even more brightly.

Simm watched this little private show with good-natured tolerance. He appreciated Ela's cooking so much that he could find no fault with her. He confided to Malek that he thought that Tael was looking for a herd of his own to lead, like any young bull. "He, who would lead, must first learn to follow," responded Malek, parroting a clan saying, but well out of Tael's hearing.

In any case, Simm was very fond of Ela, and would not hurt her in any way. He praised her often, and she rewarded him by cooking more for him than for Tael, who was not as zealous for the taste of food. To him it mattered more that a meal looked right.

Late into last winter when food was scarce, the hunger was long, and Simm felt he was melting away; he had had to find the farthest recess of the cave to hide his growing irritation at Tael and his constant self-aggrandizement. But once food was at hand, he reverted back to the easygoing, good-natured Simm again.

Chaiko looked, and Chaiko saw, his eyes missing little of the interplay. But when his eyes were intercepted, he quickly averted them. One's presence should end at the border stones that outlined the extent of each hearth. Ears and eyes should not stray beyond, or so good manners required. But it was hard to pretend not to have heard or not to have seen the myriad little things that made up their lives.

Chaiko's sense of foreboding that had nagged him throughout the night returned. In the full light he concluded that it could not be spirit effects, for spirits hid throughout the day. There was something wrong, but he could not see it or hear it; he could only feel it, an upsurge of unease just behind his thoughts, a tension that was building across his chest, the roots clamped on his stomach, and an ache that was throbbing behind his eyes. When he had listened at dawn, some birds sounded too quiet and some too loud. Their flight was short, as if interrupted or hesitant. Chaiko searched his memory to check out every detail of what he had seen and heard over the past few days, but found nothing concrete except the vague feeling of doom weighing on him. After finishing his breakfast, he decided to do something about it. He made his way to where Baer was seated with Cosh, as was their habit in the mornings. Tusk would join them soon, and the coming day would be discussed. Baer immediately noticed his brother's purposeful approach, and was surprised enough to interrupt a comment he was making to Cosh. Startled, Cosh also turned. Chaiko stopped at a respectful distance and waited until his brother beckoned him closer. Chaiko moved onto the ledge, reserved for the leaders, and sat down.

"Did you sleep well?" Baer asked, his voice encouraging, using the courteous form, knowing full well that Chaiko had not, tending the guard-fire all night. It was unusual, though not unheard of, for anyone to disturb the morning ritual, and Baer was assessing its possible import. Cosh hid his thoughts behind an impassive face. He knew of Baer's regard for the boy, and was concerned that Baer's judgment would be overly affected by his feelings. It was not that Cosh approved or disapproved of Chaiko, it was that he had no expectations of him, whereas he knew Baer had: "Watch his eyes," Baer had said more than once, "and you'll see that he is very deep. Swift water rushing is shallow, all the motion on the surface, like Crow ... every mood and every thought transparent for all to see. But with Chaiko the very calmness of his eyes hides all thoughts. Yet I can feel those eyes measuring me and measuring everything around. You, too, he has measured." Cosh did not care; he needed to think about the clan, and as far as he could tell, Chaiko had little to offer.

"It looks to be a good day," Baer said, half statement, half question, inviting Chaiko to voice his concern.

"But the night was long, and dark," Chaiko said, then paused for if time allowed, it was better to come at things sideways rather than head on; there was less chance to offend. Baer and Cosh exchanged quick looks. What was it about the night? Cosh fervently hoped this was not going to be some trivial small talk, the bane of his existence. He wanted every instant to be of significance, and if not, then silence was a better companion than chatter without aim or content.

"Yes, there were clouds, and little moonlight," Baer responded, keeping his voice flat, not too interested as the form required, though he arched his eyebrows in encouragement.

"The night was empty," Chaiko returned in the same flat tone.

Once again Baer and Cosh exchanged looks. Obviously there was meaning behind these words but where? Everybody knows that the night was not empty. They leaned forward expectantly.

"The night was full of emptiness," Chaiko said again for emphasis, knowing that he had their attention, though he noted the tightening around Cosh's eyes. He did not really know how to explain something that he could only feel. How do you explain sight to a blind man, when you are blind yourself? he wondered to himself, but tried, "The bats were not hunting last night."

"They weren't??" both asked, taken aback. Not knowing much about the habits of bats, they did not know what to do with this information.

"The owl didn't hoot," Chaiko volunteered in enlightenment.

"It didn't?" Cosh's irritation was rising, but Baer looked more and more thoughtful. What was his brother trying to say?

"The crickets did not chirp and the frogs did not croak."

This statement was greeted by silence, for neither Baer nor Cosh knew what to say. Bats? Owl? Crickets and frogs? Where could this be leading?

"When you throw a stone in the water, what do you expect to hear?" Chaiko asked.

The two were totally thrown off any scent they could have followed. They looked at each other in puzzlement, but it was Baer who finally ventured, "A splash?"

"What if you threw the stone, the stone hit the water, but there was NO splash. What would you think then?"

"If you threw the stone, and the stone hit the water, there would be a splash," Cosh said with an edge of irritation in his voice.

"Yes, there should have been." Chaiko agreed with him, noting Cosh's reaction. "But last night, there was no splash. Last night, the bats did not hunt; every night before they did. Last night the owl did not hoot; every other night it did. Last night the frogs did not croak and they should have for it is their season to mate."

The three sat there on the ledge. Chaiko wondered how he could put it better; the other two were trying to digest this information.

"So what does it mean? We aren't really talking about bats, owls and frogs, are we?" Baer asked directly, breaking the form, for he was beginning to suspect that this was beyond mere curiosity.

"I don't know," Chaiko answered simply, "But if a wolf started running backward, I would want to know why." With that they could all agree. A wolf was a smart animal. The People had learned to hunt from the wolf. "I can't see it, but there's some danger out there. I can almost feel it, touch it, just out of reach. Even taste it at times but I can find no words for it... Some great danger." They sat in silence, each busy with his own thoughts. Danger was a key word for Baer; it always got his attention. It was now obvious that this had to be dealt with. But how? How does one deal with something not seen and not heard? How does danger hide itself in silence and emptiness? Baer the Hunter knew that quiet often forebode danger. When things got very quiet, then someone, something was hunting—better be careful. The hunter hid in silence, the hunted feared it. Baer also trusted instincts that sensed even when the mind could find no reason for it. Bogan had said, "Do not always trust only what you can see, for sometimes your eyes lead you astray, but your feelings sometimes have sharper vision. Walk in darkness, and your feet will find the path that your eyes have not seen."

After several moments stretched into silence, Baer roused himself and sent Cosh for Samar. It seemed good to get the shaman's view on this oddity. By now the unusual conference had drawn everybody's attention, and Tusk came over to join them. Samar came much more slowly, and sat down wearily among them. He screwed his face up in concentration and listened to each. Tusk's questions also had to be answered. Samar nodded encouragingly as he listened, but Tusk was quick to shake his head in denial. He was not interested in Chaiko's twisted reasoning. Can you hunt a bat? A frog? Who would want to?

Then there was silence, and expectant eyes looked at the shaman, waiting. He waited too, looking somewhere in his head, occasionally muttering to himself. Finally he shook himself and said in a shaman's voice: "When we hunt, do we not look for a flight of birds to see if something has disturbed them? We do. Are we not warned by the call of a bird giving alarm that danger is near? We do. Last night, in the silence there was a warning. Take heed, Baer, there's some danger surely afoot."

"But there was no noise... there was nothing..." Both Tusk and Cosh stumbled over each other in protest.

"Sometimes silence is louder than shouting," Samar said, shaking his fingers at them. "Take heed. For what you can't see or can't hear, can still kill you!" His tone was almost spitefully vehement. He rose and shuffled off toward his fire, adding cryptically, "You have been warned! Make what you will of it."

"Could it be spirits...?" Tusk called after him faltering, expressing what they were all considering, hoping to account so easily for the unexplained.

"Spirits, spirits..." the old man muttered, shrugging his shoulders, not pausing in his slow shuffle. So later, half who believed in spirits took it to mean yes, and the others who did not, took it to mean no. Chaiko smiled thinly to himself at this ready acceptance, but then saw his brother watching him understandingly. The two grinned at each other so broadly that Chaiko had to look away from the sudden rush of pain that filled him from the opening their smiles created. When their eyes met again, both were tempered with understanding.

Baer, Tusk, and Cosh now settled down to work out what to do about this situation. It was clear that Baer accepted the warning at full value. Tusk was inclined to ignore it. "Let's go out; we must hunt, we are hunters," he suggested, hunting being his answer to everything. Baer wanted to be more cautious and quickly added, "But not alone ... and not too far." So they began to discuss who would go where and with whom. Chaiko, having now finished his mission, started to withdraw, but Baer reached out a long arm and gently pushed him back down. The gesture was not lost on the others. Cosh was sympathetic to Baer's wishes, but Tusk was plainly vexed. He did not want to share counsel with a crippled brother. It was insult added to injury; after all, he should have been the leader of the Standing-Rock Clan, not Baer.

The whole cave was reacting to these new developments. "Chaiko saw a spirit last night," someone suggested, having overheard something. And then, when some of the news started to filter through the cave from hearth to hearth, this was quickly expanded to "Chaiko saw an owl eat a bat last night." "No, not a bat, the owl ate a frog." "No, he saw nothing." "How could he see nothing?" At the farthest hearth, it was Chaiko who ate a bat. "Yuucch! How could he?" Young Sosa was shaking with revulsion.

A fresh flurry of speculation had arisen when Samar was summoned to the impromptu council. "Chaiko must have swallowed a spirit, why else would a shaman be required?" somebody suggested. "More like a spirit swallowed him," someone else immediately countered. That unleashed a new round of speculation but it soon quieted as they all heard the shaman's dire warning to take heed. A general shiver of dread swept through the cave. What did it all mean? Take heed of what?

It was decided to send out a cautious scouting party to hunt and look around, not too far, just to see what they could flush out of the thicket along the river's edge. To see how the animals reacted— if they too, could feel something. All were cautioned not to lose sight of each other. A group of women looking for early herbs also had to venture forth under hunter escort. Everyone was warned again to be vigilant. The morning meeting then dissolved and people dispersed to whatever task they were assigned. Most stayed close to the cave, apprehensive of the nothing everyone was talking about.

"Nothing is made of nothing. Where's the harm in that?" Rea demanded of Gill.

"Chaiko set us a puzzle with that, and that's for sure. It's hard to see how nothing could hurt us." Gill was chewing on the problem, but had trouble swallowing it. "If he had said something will hurt us, I could believe that. Something has weight, shape and size, and you need those qualities for impact, like a spear or a casting-stone. But nothing? How can you get hold of nothing?"

"Yes, it's hard to see how I could hit you over the head with nothing and still hurt you." Rea was not done wrestling with the problem and seemed willing to experiment.

Meanwhile, ignoring the prevailing mood of unease, the younger children played together in a group, chasing each other. Now that Lana and Ido were interested in the young men, Ruba had to spend more time with the pair of five-year-old boys, Sosa and Ork. The three years gave him a huge advantage and he lorded over them. They had to do his games according to his rules. Conspiratorially, the two delighted in frustrating him in little ways, always pretending innocent misunderstanding of his instructions.

"No! No! No!" Ruba was yelling at them now, complaining of their lackluster efforts in a game of tug. Though he was stronger than the two of them together, the pull had been too easy and he suspected they were not playing in earnest. Sosa and Ork sported ill-concealed smirks but protested their innocence all the same. He was too strong for them, they were too weak for him, the ground was too slippery to get a good foothold, and so on.

"Look! There goes Lana," Sosa called in feigned surprise.

"Where?" Ruba wanted to know, his head turning in all directions.

"And there goes Ido," contributed Ork gleefully, pointing in the other direction. "Probably to watch the young men practicing throwing their spears." The pair of five-year-olds looked at each other conspiratorially. They had an alliance and a shared mission, and for the rest of their lives would strive to outwit and frustrate Ruba.

Stow, Crow and Makar were indeed practicing throwing spears, a ceaseless occupation for hunters. The spears flew through the air in graceful arcs, vying for distance. Their shouts of encouragement to each other filled the air. Boys were always so loud. Did they not know the meaning of quiet or good manners? Nearby a group of women was weaving grass mats from long broad leaves for fresh bedding. They were singing or trying to, but Ido kept pulling them off the melody, and their songs would dissolve into fits of laughter. Nonetheless, it occurred to no one to ask Ido to refrain from singing. The poor girl could not be blamed for having no voice or ear to keep her on pitch. But why, they wondered, do people so afflicted strive to make up for said deficiencies by singing even louder? In contrast, Lana's pure light voice stood out from the rest. She had no difficulty with any melody, and could sing in harmony, enriching any song.

The singing reminded Chaiko of the stick that hummed. He got the piece out, the ends tied together by a thong, and sat down in his favorite place along the cliff, out of everyone's way. He strummed the thong and was struck anew with delight at the quiet pleasing hum it produced. He untied the thong and let the stick spring straight, well, not quite straight; there was still a bend, less now, but still a bend. He decided that the method was working, and with care he would have it trained straight. Without much thinking he took a handful of sand and rubbed it along the shaft, smoothing an already smooth piece of wood.

While his hands kept busy, he was thinking. He knew that this morning he had gained something. In front of the whole cave, Baer had acknowledged him and heard him out. In spite of the ridiculous sound of the dilemma he presented, they took him seriously enough, especially Samar. It was now clear that the whole cave was thinking of the warning, looking at him with wondering eyes. Chaiko felt taller for the status that the attention had given him. Now he must earn it, he told himself. He lowered the work in his hands and looked around the countryside, trying to spot something unusual. But under such an intense scrutiny, everything looked unusual. The flight of birds seemed erratic. The familiar view looked eerily strange. The clouds building above the far-off mountains looked menacing. Last night, you saw nothing. Last night you heard nothing. Use your feelings then, for last night you felt the nothing. But last night the nothing felt very real. He closed his eyes and tried to see with his mind. The noise of the children playing intruded and he could not find anything to grasp upon. The tightness in his chest and stomach was still there, a compact knot, and the headache still throbbed behind his eyes. He felt a threat hanging in the air. In sudden anxiety he opened his eyes but saw everything as he had left it. He shook his head, hoping to clear out the foreboding, and tried to concentrate on the piece of wood in his hand.

Crow, who had gone off to collect firewood with a group, returned and came to sit beside Chaiko. His smile was broad and grew broader as Chaiko returned it. Crow picked up the bent spear, his hands luxuriating in the smooth feel of the wood, and the nice dense weight of it. He marveled at Chaiko's skill, as few things in his life showed the same workmanship or functional beauty. However, Chaiko belittled his own effort, "It's just patience." Crow discovered the slight bend and frowned at it. It was not like Chaiko to leave such obvious imperfection in his handiwork. Instead of answering, Chaiko bent the wood, tied both ends, and strummed the tight string. Crow was delighted with the sound. Chaiko adjusted the tension till it gave a more pleasing sound. "What is it?" Crow wanted to know, but Chaiko only shrugged; he had no word for it. "Singing-Stick," he finally said. Crow looked at him appraisingly. It was he, Crow the Hunter, who had gained recognition and standing in the clan, yet why did he feel so much smaller than Chaiko? Was it because Chaiko could hear and see the nothing? Or because of things like this Singing-Stick? Chaiko was always full of surprises. And today he had smiled.

By early afternoon all the foragers had returned. The hunters had seen no game, no game at all, and the women also had seen nothing. All the animals seemed to have disappeared. People sat in uneasy groupings, debating whether the scarcity of game confirmed or disputed Chaiko's warning. Questions were being asked, not challenging Baer's authority, but questioning Chaiko's reliability. "How would he know? He's no shaman. He's only a boy." And not a few would add to themselves "and a cripple," as a silent afterthought.

Following an early meal of seasoned meat and some fresh roots, Chaiko sat by Baer's fire, staring at the coals, lost in thought. He had been aware of the quizzical looks around him, but he had chosen not to acknowledge them. In truth, after the elation of presenting himself in full view of the clan, he felt the resultant letdown and an emotional flatness. He started to wonder if he had been foolish after all, warning of something that was not there. Yet, he could still feel it, as a weight on his chest, and in the headache that continued to torment him. The feeling of apprehension was the strongest when he was not directly searching for it, for when he focused on it, it would elude him.

With dusk approaching, the people collected in the usual groupings. Men with men, women with women, and the children playfully flowing between them. Baer, Samar, Tusk and Cosh sat in their usual place, discussing the situation. They were concerned about the scarcity of game. Last year was not a bad hunting year, but the year previous to that had been and the winter was especially long on empty stomachs. This ever-present worry supplanted Chaiko's unseen danger, and after all, only Baer really took that to heart. But once he had accepted it, the rest had to follow his lead.

Tusk was pressing, "Tomorrow we should hunt along the swamp. There it is always easy to trap some beast in the soft mud."

After a moment of consideration, Baer cautioned, "That's too far from the cave. Until we know what's threatening us, we had better stay together. It's hard to be on guard when you do not know what you are looking out for."

"Perhaps, Chaiko's nightmares..." said Tusk derisively. "There's something wrong with that boy. Have you seen bats hunt?" he challenged, daring Baer to respond.

There was no ready answer to that. Though bats lived in caves, they did not share it well with humans. The noise and the smoke drove them out. They all knew what bats were, of course, but of their habits and ways they knew little. There was some superstition that being night creatures they were somehow spirits trapped in small, misshapen bodies. It was not a popular view, for it ultimately implied the possibility that any one of them could end up as a bat, hanging about upside down from the roof of a cave, defecating.

Baer beckoned Chaiko over, but Chaiko could not elaborate on his earlier warning, though he repeated it with somewhat more conviction than he felt. This time, too, Baer did not dismiss him, but motioned for him to sit there while he thought. An uneasy silence ensued. Tusk was fidgeting. He could see no reason why Chaiko was being tolerated in their presence. It was as if Chaiko diminished his stature. He was frowning, casting brooding sideways looks at Baer, who was still busy with his thoughts, "If I were the leader..." Cosh was aware of the trouble brewing. Though both by age and temperament he allied himself with Baer, he was very much aware of Tusk's sensibilities. He looked appraisingly at Chaiko. What had Baer seen there that he had not? Perhaps just a brother's love. He shrugged, Baer asked so little for himself.

Samar was in a world of his own. He was not concerned by the prescience of danger, for in his long life he had often been in situations fraught with such threats which all too often evaporated. Fear, he reasoned, often distorted reality so.

Baer was concerned about any danger, especially one so undefined. He had the frozen reaction of an animal which sensed trouble though it had not yet seen it, but was trying to make up its mind whether to stay motionless or to run for cover. If his brother was wrong and there was no danger out there, then they would have been careful for naught, losing only time. But if he was right and there was a danger, then hopefully being watchful, they could yet avoid it. He looked at his brother and nodded. It was good to see him with his eyes alive. He sensed Tusk's disapproval, and shifted his gaze to him. Years ago, when the parent clan had grown too large and needed to be split to find new hunting grounds, he had been chosen to lead the people now known as the Standing-Rock Clan. Tusk had been his only rival for leadership then, and Tusk had never forgiven him for having been chosen over him. "If the clan would accept you, you could have it," Baer thought without resentment. Together with Cosh, the three formed the leadership with Samar called into consultation as needed. Samar was his other most pressing concern. The old one was getting too old. Often he became confused about events, and mixed the present with the past. But when lucid, he gave good, practical advice. Soon after, the group dispersed to their hearths and readied themselves for the night. Chaiko crabbed his way to the guard-fire and settled in.

The sun had set already. The western sky was still alight with a glowing blue, but the land was quickly being swallowed up by the spreading dusk. Behind it, darkness was rapidly extending its wings from the east toward the west. In its shadow, the earth faded. Above, the moon grew brighter, sharper in focus, and the stars emerged. The sky became full of lights, twinkling, distant and unreachable. A shooting star traced a glowing line across to the far horizon and Chaiko craned his neck to follow its path. With darkness completely encompassing the earth, the sky deepened even more and the stars built a luminous cloud of their own. The lights had to be from fires, Chaiko reasoned, burning of the stars, blazing, but they appeared without any warmth. Chaiko wondered how distant a star had to be to turn fire into the coldness of an ice crystal.

Chaiko was leaning over the fire arranging the wood when he felt a sudden flash of pain course through his body. It was not intense, but so unexpected that he cried out in surprise. He took a quick look around but everything seemed normal. Well, not everything. In the shallow lake waters near the shore, a large flight of birds erupted into the air, their white feathers flashing in the moonlight. What had disturbed them? Normally they would have settled down for the night, relatively safe upon the water.

The pain was gone as quickly as it had come, but Chaiko could not relax. There was still a throbbing of his temples, not painful but disturbingly conspicuous. The feeling in his chest seemed tighter, and he had to consciously try to breathe against its pressure. Then he heard something, not a noise, merely an awareness, as if something passed by his ears. At the same time, there was a sudden brief commotion from the bushes, as some startled birds half took to flight, then dropped to the ground looking for a hiding place. "They heard it too!" the thought flashed through his mind. Instantly he became totally alert, his senses sharp, his body coiled to react. A prescience of danger welled up within, a peril grown more ominous. He peered into the cave, but there was no indication that anyone else had noticed. From farther away, he heard a faltering howl of a wolf trailing off unnaturally into a questioning silence. And then the silence was deep and profound. There was a flash of pain again, followed by a murmur of noise, spreading like a ripple across the face of silence, then silence again.

Chaiko's sense of alarm that something was terribly wrong took command of him. He closed his eyes still trying to make sense of it, swallowed his unease, willed his mind to quiet. He tried to listen with his intuition. There was a feeling of ponderous weight, a push and pull that made him nauseated, then a sudden clear impression of imminent danger, that had something to do with the cave. He roused himself, and on all fours scampered as fast as he could to Baer's sleeping place.

"Wake up! Wake up!" he shouted at Baer, roughly shaking him. His brother looked at him with wide-eyed shock. "The cliff is going to come down," is all Chaiko could say. "The cliff... the cliff!!"

Roused from sleep, Baer did not understand, but he heard the tone and recognized the panic underneath and the magnitude of danger being conveyed. He knew that there was not even time for questions. He threw off his cover, one hand reaching toward his mate, the other toward his daughter, helping them up. He was yelling at the top of his voice for everyone to get up and get out of the cave. He jammed Lana into Tanya's arm and shoved them toward the open. "GO! Everyone up. NOW! OUT! GET OUT!" He grabbed a confused woman with a clinging child and threw them toward the opening. "OUT! EVERYONE OUT OF THE CAVE! NOW!" his voice rang over the confused hubbub as people fell over each other in the darkness. But by and large most were leaving, whipped into action by his commanding tone. Baer strode to the back of the cave, picked up Samar forcefully, and carried him into the open air.

The whole cave was assembled on the broad knoll opposite the cave entrance about two stone-throws from the cliff. From there they had a dim view of the lake peacefully reflecting a starlit sky. They were shivering with cold and shock. Some had covers, while others were naked, hugging themselves protectively. The children were stunned into silence, but the baby was crying. There was a babble of questions as people tried to figure out what had happened. "Is everybody here?" Baer's voice cut through the noise. People looked around and accounted for themselves. They were looking at each other confused, standing in darkness. But yes, everyone had gotten out.

In front of the cave the guard fire burned invitingly, while the other fires gave off weak glows. "What are we doing out here?" people were asking, a murmur of discontent rising in their midst.

"The cliff is going to come down," Baer stated, then realized how lame it sounded out here in the open. He looked questioningly toward Chaiko, but his brother, feeling all the inquiring eyes on him, lost all his self-assurance. "Chaiko warned me that the cliff was going to collapse," restated Baer, his voice calm and measured once more - forestalling a flood of questions.

Chaiko swallowed, then tried to explain, "First I felt pain. Then the birds flew into the air. Then a wolf howled, then stopped. Then I heard ..." Heard what? How was he going to explain that? He took a deep breath to steady himself and tried again. "I felt something I had never felt before. But not I alone. The animals felt it too. The birds flew into the air, whole flocks of them all at once and the wolves howled a question. Maybe some of you heard it too?" He looked around hopefully, but most merely looked more bewildered.

The shock of being suddenly ripped out of sleep and warm covers was wearing off, and here and there voices of indignation were heard and found echo in anger. The mood was quickly turning ugly. People were scared, trying to get over their fright. By now, the settling dampness was chilling them and many were shivering. The murmuring rose.

"I believe there is danger," Baer declared in reasonable but forceful tones. "Chaiko has felt the danger. So have the animals. We will stay here in the open and consider what to do. Mothers, get your children together, have them share whatever covers they have. Men, share your furs and skins with your mates." His clear voice gave reassurance and they started to respond. "Tusk, Cosh, Samar, Chaiko." He motioned them to follow him to the side.

"We cannot stay here unprotected," he stated without preamble.

"Chaiko is driving us crazy with his nightmares. There's no reason for us to be out here. We should go back to our sleeping places," Tusk retorted with choked anger. He was not going to be appeased this time with some smooth talk. If need be he was ready to take on Baer.

Baer looked him straight in the eye and reiterated, "I believe there is danger. We will stay here till we decide what we need to do." He thrust his face into Tusk's. He also was ready, if need be, making it clear that in this case he would not tolerate opposition even though in his statement he had stressed the we. The tension rose between them ready to explode. Cosh edged himself between the two. "We have work to do," he said quietly, afraid that any harsh word would set them off.

Tusk wanted to berate Chaiko, but contained his anger. The fire went out of his eyes, but his nostrils still flared. He let his breath out explosively. He had not experienced Baer so unyielding before.

Baer looked at Chaiko, "Are we safe here?"

Chaiko said yes, feeling fairly sure, though uncertain as to why or how he would know. The hillock they were on was far enough away from the crushing weight of the cliff face: this was all he could formulate into coherent thought. With his feelings he sensed a pent-up power quivering to be let loose. But what power? And when?

"Cosh," Baer ordered, "get some of the quicker, younger men to fetch furs and covers from the cave. Then get some of the piled-up firewood and bring it out here. Only one at a time. Do not linger, stay out from under the overhang as much as you can."

Samar came out of his silence. "The spirit bag..." his voice trembled remembering the Gray-Wolf relics. "Someone must get the spirit bag." His voice shook with worry; his whole authority was tied up in that bag.

"In time, all in good time," Baer reassured him. They stood there peering into the cave, straining to watch the young men carry out their tasks. There was not much to see, only shadows moving in the darkness. Somebody picked up a burning branch from the guard-fire, and the glowing end traced his way as he returned.

A short time later people were covered with their furs and had arranged themselves around three new fires brightly burning under a dark sky. The children were quick to drop off to sleep but the rest were still too stirred up. Baer organized a further expedition to retrieve vital weapons and some food stores. That was accomplished uneventfully, but with some sense of comfort returning, the level of indignation was again rising against Chaiko.

"Chaiko's crazy," was the general opinion. "Were it not for his leg, today he would be a hunter like his friend Crow," the more charitable among them countered. "That would drive me crazy too." Though they were used to sleeping under the open skies during hunting trips, no one liked to be yanked out of warm furs with the night falling, and told to go make camp. Tusk was the most upset of all, not so much at Chaiko, for Chaiko was barely above recognition, but at Baer. Today's confrontation was the first real spark of the underlying animosity between them that showed through the usual cool and distant collaboration. In spite of these differences, they had worked well together. Tusk was a good hunter. Because of his great strength and endurance he was widely respected. He had few weaknesses. He had an instinctive knack of leadership, and rarely did he allow his impulsiveness or his temper to show. But he was driven by some inner conviction that he was right without ever feeling the need to question it. This was his strength but also his greatest weakness. It gave him confidence on the one hand that he communicated to his followers, but on the other he was unable to appreciate another person's view. Baer, by contrast, always listened to others when coming to a decision. He was also quick to give credit where due. Though both men were respected, Baer was also well liked. Tusk resented Baer's popularity and thought that Baer's "pandering to others' whims" weakened the leadership that rightly belonged to him. Baer was aware of Tusk's feelings toward him, and though he regretted the brief sparks that escaped, he thought it good for a wolf to show a few fangs occasionally.

In spite of the excitement, the clan finally settled down. Chaiko sat by one of the fires, the guard-fire for the night. Near him Lana lay folded in her mother's arms with Baer protectively on the outside. Cosh and his family, and Kor and Calla also shared the fire. Chaiko was thinking about the rush of events. Things were moving all too fast, and he was the centre of attention. He did not like it. It was preferable to be ignored. Though the sense of danger was still strong, doubt was eating away at his conviction. What if he was wrong? People would ridicule him for the rest of his life, he knew. But if he was right, then here in the open air the clan was safe. That far outweighed all risk of derision.

In the open, with less protection from the cold, the night air flowed unhindered about them. Chaiko shivered, piled more wood on the fire and watched the flames awaken and do their dance, illuminating the surrounding darkness. In the light, he could see Lana's face, in sleep so composed, not like the animated girl throughout the day. Chaiko examined Tanya's face in the warm glow. He was struck by her beauty in the peacefulness of sleep; no worry lines disturbing her face now. Being the mate of the leader had its privileges but also its responsibilities that weighed heavier than they should have on her easily aroused maternal instincts and conscience. Chaiko studied her face carefully. That was something he dared not do too obviously in daylight. It was not good to show undue interest in another person's mate, not even a brother's. Baer was lucky, for Tanya was beautiful as well as tender, and always sought to please. He felt a pang of loneliness as he realized anew that the warmth and comfort of a mate were denied to him. He would have cried, but he abhorred the weakness of tears.

He lost himself in the fire, the glowing embers drawing him in, a blue light flickering amid the glow. He was half-asleep. The flames danced their dance, changing from blue to yellow and then to orange. Suddenly the flames brightened, a shower of sparks leaping toward the sky to escape. At the same time Chaiko felt something let go deep in his mind and instantly he was fully alert. He heard a loud groan and realized that the ground was shaking, slowly and gently at first, then more and more violently. Alarmed shouts erupted all around, cries and screams. The ground heaved. Everyone was tossed about, into each other, their utterances incoherent. Some tried to stand up, but that was impossible with all the shaking and the tossing. Most were on all fours, hugging the earth. Ile had her furs about her head trying to shut out the world. Cosh was digging his fingers into the soil trying just to hold on. "What's wrong with this world?" he asked himself stupidly. Nearby

Lana was whimpering. Baer called out encouragement as the ground kicked and everyone went sprawling. The fires were scattered, and Tael was half thrown into one. In spite of his fright, he cursed angrily as he scrambled up and out of it, only to fall to the ground once more.

The earth heaved again and again. Each time people cried out in fresh terror. A rumble overtook them from the direction of the cliff face. Sounds of rocks falling, rolling, being scattered by an unseen force, swallowed all other sounds. A cloud of dust enveloped them, and they choked on the stifling rock powder, coughing and gasping for breath. Then there was a horrendous sound, a long drawn out screech, ending in a sudden explosive crack as the roots of rocks were torn asunder, and the wall face was split once more. Rocks of all sizes came cascading down. This time, the rock slide almost reached them on the open slope. Makar, sure that he was going to die, ran in open-mouthed terror till a new thrust threw him to the ground. He stood up, but the ground was yanked from under him.

The shaking increased anew, built to a new crescendo, then ceased temporarily. The dust started to settle. Dazed people were looking around. It was hard to see in the darkness, for the fires were scattered embers giving off little light. Sosa whimpered, "Mommy, Mommy," and Tay just gasped with fright. Her mother Yaya clutched her, but the terrified child was beyond comfort. Kor cursed, for when he toppled during one of the heaves, he fell on his face and chipped a tooth on a piece of rock, cutting his lip. He had few teeth to lose. To his surprise, Chaiko was hurt too. He had a good-sized burn on his left forearm, though he could not remember when it happened. His mouth was dry with the taste of blood on his tongue. His body, however, was drenched in sweat from the effort of hanging on. Though he felt a sense of relief that the awaited danger had finally materialized, a feeling of unreality weighed on him. Then the shaking began afresh, lightly at first, but soon building to a violence that tossed them about again. The earth bucked and rolled under them as wave after wave passed through the ground. Like an echo, lighter tremors followed, but still the shaking continued unabated, rattling their teeth, flesh aquiver on a rack of bones.

Then there was abrupt silence. Without any transition the violence turned to an unreal quiet. The world stopped shaking as everything was abruptly frozen into stillness. It left them hanging, listening to their own labored breath, still seized by terror. Why was it so quiet now? In a way it was more frightening than what went before; in the movement of being tossed about helpless, there was at least a sense of time passing, but now...? Now they were left waiting for it to start again. Slowly sound returned, filling the void: a groan, a few hesitant calls, a few tentative stirrings of limbs, a trial of movement. Several staggered to their feet, but the rest remained on the ground wide-eyed in expectation of further violence. But since the sense of helplessness was greater lying flat on the ground, more and more made the attempt to struggle to their feet, legs shaking and eyes dubious.

People stumbled about, not exactly sure how much to trust the ground. It was almost as if they had forgotten how to walk, confidence and self-assurance being a core component of walking. Even being upright required firmness of the ground to support it. Had not the roots of earth just danced? Had the rocks not trembled in fear? Did they not claw into the earth to hold on? But when the earth moved and trembled, where was there a place to stand? Now that the ground was still again and they had miraculously survived, people thought about what they had just escaped. Only the eldest of them had experienced earthquakes before, though all knew about them from oft-told stories. Those stories would have more meaning from now on.

Three more times before daybreak the ground shook, rousing them from sleepless stupor. It tossed them onto the ground, rolled them, tumbled them, playing with them like a raging river with a piece of driftwood. They were helpless against the power unleashed by forces they could not understand. They were sprawled on the ground jabbering in the language of terror. But each time, the shaking, jerking and tossing became less violent and those who could, took courage from that fact.

Chapter 7

With daybreak the devastation of the night's tumult became evident. The cliff-face was split in several places. A fresh pile of rubble spread out at the base of each new fissure. Well-known rocks were gone, and new ones were everywhere. The upright rock that gave the clan its name was leaning precariously to one side. The side of the cave that was first touched by the morning sun was buried under rubble. Part of the slope had also given way and slid halfway down, opening an ugly gash of yellow clay from which protruded grey boulders like bones. Tall-Frog tree was torn in half, a part still standing, the other in pieces on the ground. Further down trees were uprooted everywhere. Massive older trees lay shattered, their yellow cores exposed, while younger trees were plucked intact from ground and cast aside. Birds were stunned, hidden among the branches, afraid of light, afraid of every shadow. There were no animals to be seen and no sounds to be heard other than the rush of wind through the leaves.

It was as if overnight they had been reborn into a new world; a similar world, yet not what it had been. The familiar was everywhere dislocated, made more strange by its very familiarity. But the greatest change was felt on the inside. All remembered the utter helplessness as the ground shook and kicked, and they had felt powerless, tossed about. The stronger the man, the greater was the feeling of helplessness and the more impressive was the power of the forces toying with him. Perhaps children had a more realistic perception of the events; after all, they were more used to being helpless, at the whim of others. The night left many scars, and everyone remembered vividly its sheer terror.

Among all other feelings, Chaiko felt a release from the burden that had so oppressed him. First, because they survived, second, because his warning had been in time. Daylight dispelled some of the terror of the night, like awakening out of a nightmare. Terror fed on darkness; light always diminished it. But Chaiko knew that although the memory would fade in time, the fear would remain and mature into something that was more, something even worse than the original experience. Horror and fright, bad as they had been, were mere blossoms on the root plant that was Fear itself, that lurked just beneath awareness to flash into consciousness and spawn fresh dread. A destroyer of peace and confidence. In time to come, it would be that Fear they would remember.

Befitting a leader, Baer recovered his composure first. He checked his mate and child, made sure they were all right, comforted them briefly, then looked about, did a quick head count and found no one missing. "Is everyone all right?" he asked, going from group to group, noting the shock etched on faces. Miraculously nobody was seriously injured. He waved to his companions to join him. He also beckoned Chaiko. Tusk came reluctantly, his face compressed with worry and confusion. He had met something more powerful than himself last night, Chaiko reasoned. Cosh was more cheerful. He had survived, and the elation buoyed him up; he could not stop grinning. Samar, on the other hand, seemed lost, his eyes looking troubled and cloudy. Of them all, he knew more about earthquakes, yet he had been as shocked by the event as everyone else. "The ground shook to its roots, and new mountains and valleys appeared," so told an old tale, describing the violence they had just survived. But there was little feeling in those words, no helplessness, no terror, no injury. After this, though, there would be a new understanding of those words.

The leaders went aside and sat down out of earshot of the rest of the clan. It was unreal to sit here in sight of their normal conference place in the cave. Tusk cast a baleful look towards it and the surrounding devastation. Baer looked at them in turn, assessing the impact the earthquake had had on each. As for himself, he had already put away his feelings for there were too many things to attend to, but he needed the assistance of the others. Tusk required careful handling, he cautioned himself. The big man's confusion was turning to resentment that was looking for an outlet. Would he have to direct it toward himself? Baer wondered. He was amused by Cosh's elation, recognizing it as the release from the terror of the night before. They all shared in that relief, a reaction much easier to channel. Samar look dazed, his eyes watery and unfocused. Baer frowned; they needed him, especially now. Although Chaiko looked calm, Baer hoped it was not delayed shock setting in. However, his eyes were clear and alert with the customary inquisitiveness flashing from here to there.

Baer turned to Chaiko and said in a muted voice, "Your warning was right. Without it many of us would be dead now. Thank you." He glanced toward the cave, strangely alien at the distance, shrouded by dust. He looked at the rest of the clan huddled dazed and confused in the surrounding chaos. How do you thank someone who has saved your life, your mate's, your child's, and all the rest? Words were entirely inadequate to span the void between deed and gratitude. "Thank you, Chaiko," he repeated the words, his eyes full of things left unsaid, but Chaiko understood. Cosh added his thanks and clapped him on the back in expression of a camaraderie he had rarely before exhibited. Tusk maintained his morose silence, merely frowning, nursing his disaffection. The earthquake had robbed him of a comfortable, fixed view of the world that could not cope with such shocks or too much change. Samar remained untouched.

"What's next?" Baer asked more of himself than of the others. Turning to Chaiko, he questioned "Do you think....?" then paused, unsure of how to phrase what was needed. It occurred to him that the stone Chaiko had talked about had finally found its splash, much too loud a splash. "Do you think the danger has passed? Can we go back to the cave? Can we...?" he trailed off.

Chaiko considered this. His warning had come from a sense of the unusual: the animals, the birds and even insects had called his attention to it. But this morning everything was unusual and strange; the animals and birds were all confused by this new world they found themselves in. There was no help from that source. Yet he had heard something else too, and had felt the weight of the cliff pressing down on him. What does your feeling tell you now? he asked himself. Aloud, he said uncertainly, "I'm not sure. There seems to be danger still, but it seems at a distance, as if waiting. I am sorry, but that's all I feel now."

"Well, good. But if you start feeling ... danger, you let us know. Samar ...?" Baer focused everyone's attention on the old man. Surprisingly he was ready for them; he had been searching his memory for something useful, and a trip through his past seemed to have refreshed him. His eyes shone brightly.

"When I was young, we were on a hunting trip. There was a quake, not as violent as this, a mere trembling in the ground and we did not think much about it. But when we returned to the cave, we found two dead and five hurt from falling rocks. Stow's father's father was one of them. There were two more quakes that day, three or four the next, but each less noticeable than the one before. The last one, about four days later, we noticed only because the water in the pool was quivering... and the floating leaves were trembling on its surface ..."

Finally, some real information, both Baer and Chaiko thought. Tusk broke in. "Do you mean there's going to be more of these?" By the end, his voice became accusing, as if to hold the old man responsible for any such reoccurrence.

"Each weaker than the one before," Samar repeated, his watery eyes reflecting no offence.

"Then we have seen the worst," Baer concluded, extracting the one reassuring bit of information. "We will stay out of the cave till they pass."

The others accepted readily; no one trusted rocks at this point. "But we have so little food with us out here," Cosh said, his sense of life returning, asserting itself, and he felt surprisingly hungry.

"Then you can go into the cave and dig out the food yourself," Tusk said with irritable hostility; he was still not hungry. "We ought to go hunting." Hunting he understood; maybe, by doing routine things, the unexpected could be held back somehow.

"We will do both," Baer decided, heading off any confrontation before it could develop. "Tusk, you take Tael, Stow and Malek and go hunting. We will need meat. But don't go far ... and if the earth shakes again, you come right back." And that will get you out from underfoot, doing something useful, he added silently to himself. "Cosh, you take Makar and Crow, go into the cave and get anything you can. They are young and quick. They can go in, grab something, then get out. Quick, only one person in the cave at a time, you understand? Do not tarry. Weapons and food first, then furs and skins." Cosh nodded as Baer yet added, "I will stay and help you."

Tusk and Cosh left on their separate errands. Baer looked at Chaiko then Samar. "You two stay here and watch for signs. If you see any, hear any ... or feel anything, you yell and I will know." He, too, left.

With the leaders walking about issuing directions, the clan was goaded into action. With movement a sense of purpose returned and hope was resurrected. Things could not be that bad if there was time for hunting.

The assigned hunters collected about Tusk, shared whatever weapons were available, and set off.

"The game will be skittish, still scared from last night, so have patience," Baer called after the departing group. Tusk's face turned to stone. He resented being instructed, but did not want to show it in front of the others. Noting this, Baer held back the rest. "Good hunting."

A group of women left to forage. Their dried food and spices were buried in the cave, so any roots or leftover seeds to be gleaned would be very welcome. The remaining men, women and children went to collect firewood. Only the old people were left, congregating around the fire, wondering among themselves about a world turned suddenly so unpredictable.

Having finished dispatching the work groups, Baer hurried to the group that was concerning him the most. In the meantime Cosh had had a chance to examine the cave from a safe distance. Most of the visible damage affected the west wall. A good sized piece of the cave roof had given way and had buried that side under a mass of rubble. There were some new cracks in the wall as well. Baer joined him, and Cosh quickly pointed out the more obvious damage.

"That side," he pointed to the east side of the cave, "escaped damage. For the rest..." he shrugged his shoulders. "Had we been caught in there sleeping ..." His face turned distant, shutting out the nightmare possibilities. He turned again to the task at hand. "It looks safe on the morning side."

"Are you sure?" Baer peered into the dim interior, appalled by the confusion. Their well-ordered cave was nearly unrecognizable.

"Yes. That's just a layer of stone dust. We can get to most hearths, though Malek's things are buried rather high. The good news is that the food storage pits seem only lightly covered."

Both men paused, thinking. Was it worth the risk? At any moment a new quake could strike and collapse an already weakened edifice. Having a decision to make, Baer looked at Cosh and raised a questioning eyebrow. Cosh shrugged his shoulders in comment. There was just no way of telling. Baer waved Makar and Crow to join them.

"We will take turns going in there, a person at a time." Baer was pointing vaguely into the cave. "Grab something useful, then get out. Weapons, foodstuff and furs. Everything else can wait. Don't stop to dig, it's not worth the ... time." He had nearly said "the risk to your lives." It was best not to conjure up more doom.

The two boys were very earnestly attending to his every word. Crow, the newest hunter, wanted badly to impress Baer. Baer took one quick glance back at Chaiko then made up his mind. "I will go first." A leader must lead by example and share fully in the risks.

Moving quickly, Baer entered the cave, heading for the less damaged side, grabbed a basket of foodstuff, a fur wrap and a skin carryall, and was already on the way back. Quick, but not hasty. Cosh was right; this side was covered with heavy chalk dust that clung to everything, but no other damage. He moved into the open and realized with some surprise that he had been holding his breath the entire time.

Cosh went next. He strolled in with an indolent disregard for the towering stone above and proceeded to pick through the scattered stuff on the ground. The clan had kept the cave tidy and clean, sweeping frequently. It was amazing how even a little rubbish could make a place hardly recognizable. He extracted a fine piece of skin, soft and supple, Yaya's prize possession, from under layers of dust. Yaya will be happy, he thought. Then, from somewhere outside, the rumble of a rock slide reached him; he snapped up his head, startled like any deer, and thought better of lingering any longer. He picked up the items he had collected and left much faster than he arrived.

After a short pause, it was Crow's turn. He went in a hurry, his ears straining for every trickle of rock, every shifting pebble. He was set to jump for safety, if need be. Had he not seen Chaiko become trapped in a rock slide and lose a leg? He found a few items, but his mind was so preoccupied with the threat above that he could not choose between Kor's bag of flint nodules and Ido's collection of colorful rocks. One a vital tool, the other a kid's curiosity. So he took them both. A fresh trickle of rocks against the back wall hurried him on his way. A short dash and he was glad to be out from under the rock, breathing again.

Makar emulated Cosh's unconcern. He knew that they were watching him and enjoyed the attention. He almost forgot the dangers. He went deeper into the cave than had the others. He was rummaging around where he expected Kor's fire to be, but was confused by the rubble.

14 Stones

Everyone knew every bit of the cave, the exact space allotted to each, so that there would be no disputes. Territorial awareness and respect was taught to every child. There were strong taboos about touching other people's possessions, and here he was doing just that. Makar was tickled by doing something normally forbidden. This was turning out to be a real adventure! Very much enjoying the circumstances, he turned and waved to the others outside. How they must be admiring his courage, he preened. Outside, even Cosh was muttering under his breath, "Hurry up!"

Makar began to extricate a length of rope, laboriously woven by Rea, who was the best at it. Makar was just congratulating himself on such a valuable find when he was suddenly surprised by a ground tremor that quickly increased to violent shaking, tossing everything about. Immediately dust filled the air. The ground heaved suddenly and Makar lost his footing, fell down and struggled to get up. He screamed, instinctively crawling toward the safety of the outside, but the ground was swaying beneath him so strongly that he could make little progress. A crack in the back wall opened up and disgorged a flood of rock fragments. The cave filled up with a cloud of stone dust and Makar was lost from sight.

Outside the others were struggling on all fours, trying to hold onto the bucking ground. The terror of the night before came flooding back and the memory of it was added to the terror of the present. Chaiko had felt the same sense of helplessness four years ago, when the rock slide carried him along. The déjà-vu gave him a strange sense of detachment. He noted that this tremor was not as strong as the first, and did not have a back kick to every heave. He also sensed that this would not last long. He tried to yell encouragement to the others, but his voice was lost in the general rumbling as the whole world resisted being moved, yet had to.

Chaiko, his mind emptied of terror, relaxed against the forces playing with him. With a heightened clarity that surprised him, he measured the tremor passing, a heartbeat at a time. His pulse slowed, and he even smiled; Earth do your worst. Then the ground stopped shaking, and an eerie silence embraced them all.

They struggled to their feet, looking confusedly about. Baer quickly scanned everything, saw the old people staggering around but unhurt.

There was no one else in sight. The cave was obscured by a dense cloud of dust spilling out and they all thought of Makar still in there. Running toward the opening Baer and Cosh called loudly to Makar but there was no answer. Baer tried to decide what to do. It was impossible to see, and he held a restraining hand against Cosh, not letting him in. "There's no use in getting lost in there. We will wait." And they waited for an agonizingly long time for the dust to settle a little. Occasionally they heard a pebble roll, a rock fall and a sudden rush as rocks disturbed from their balance point toppled, taking the rest with them. Then, faintly at first, they heard coughing. "Makar is alive!" thought Baer in a rush of relief. The coughing increased as Makar struggled to consciousness, trying to find air in the dust. Instinctively, both Baer and Cosh moved into the cloud toward the sounds. Immediately they found it difficult to breathe and were forced back. Between fits of coughing, Makar was calling, panic-stricken; he could not breathe nor could he see; his eyes were filled with the dust that blotted out the cave. Spasms of coughing continually racked him.

Baer told Crow to stay; he had no wish to worry about the boy's inexperience. Crow was crushed, but there was no time for niceties. Cosh picked up a grass matt and wrapped it about his head leaving only his eyes free. "This will keep some of the dust out." He waited for Baer to do the same, then they waded into the obscurity of the cave.

Although the grass weave did help in filtering some of the dust, it still was impossible to see with the cloud hanging heavily in the air. The eyes started to water, the tears dissolving some of the chalk dust that burned the eyes. Blinded, they kept bumping into each other and stumbling over things. They tried to follow Makar's plaintive whimpering for help.

With his hands extended, groping about, Baer found one of Makar's arms. A quick search by feel indicated that Makar was half covered with rubble, pinned down by the weight of stone across his legs. Luckily, a bundle of skins and furs that he had salvaged had protected him at impact. But he could not feel his legs, grown numb with the weight on top, and he was badly frightened. "We're here," Baer told him reassuringly, his voice calming the boy a little. Working blind, feeling around with their hands, Baer and Cosh started to uncover Makar. One by one they rolled the larger stones aside; the smaller ones they simply swept out of the way. Makar was half buried at the foot of a rock spill that extended from the cave wall. Had the fragments come from the roof, they would have killed him.

"Careful," Baer cautioned as he heard the volume of rocks near the top shift, threatening to come down and bury them all. The air was stifling with dust and the heat of their own efforts. They had freed one leg, but the other was pinned under a larger rock that refused to budge. Both men pushed and strained against it unsuccessfully. They cleared some of the rubble and worked the stone down the small incline they had made. Their muscles quivered with the effort until the stone finally gave and rolled away, but pulled some stones after it which incited the rest to follow. Cosh yelled a warning, "Watch out! The whole thing is set to come down." Baer threw himself between the helpless Makar and the shifting mass of stones. He grabbed the largest and tried to hold it as a shield against the rest. Desperation gave him the strength, and he was able to stop the large stone; the rest, thus deflected, cascaded harmlessly around it. Cosh grabbed Makar under the armpits and pulled hard. Makar cried out in pain but there was no time left for gentleness. Cosh yanked Makar free. One stone, about the size of a fist, came tumbling down, careened off a rock and hit Baer full on the side of his chest. A flash of searing pain coursed through his body, staggering him, but he held off the overspill of the rest. Crow appeared out of the haze and helped Cosh pull Makar to safety. Once in the open, Cosh yelled to Baer to let go and get out. Baer pushed himself off and stumbled toward the open, followed by a rumble behind. He emerged doubled up, clutching his right side in agony.

Then they were all safe outside. They cast off the grass mats, gasping for breath. The fresh air, however, reawakened their coughs, and they were racked by new fits of hacking. To Baer, this caused excruciating pain in his side and he started to break out in a cold sweat, the rivulets tracing strange patterns on his dust-covered face. He was visibly shivering from shock. His knees buckled and he sagged to the ground.

All of them were covered in white dust, looking quite inhuman to Samar and Chaiko, hurrying up to them. Both were out of breath, driven by their concern. "Are you all right?" they gasped in unison. Kneeling beside Baer, Cosh shrugged then sent Crow for water. Makar sat up, his leg was worrying him. The numbness was wearing off and feeling was returning. It hurt, but he was smiling, for he thought that he had lost his leg like Chaiko. "I hurt," he moaned. "Oh how it hurts!"

Actually, he was surprised to find himself alive; he had believed the whole cave had come down on him.

Crow returned with a water skin. Makar drank greedily and Cosh washed out his eyes. Wincing against the pain each movement caused him, Baer washed his face but could not wash away the sickly pallor. Chaiko was shocked by his brother's obvious pain. He had never seen Baer really hurt; Baer was above pain, pain did not happen to him. Baer sensed his brother's concern, smiled at him, but shocked Chaiko even more for his eyes remained so clouded. Samar knelt beside Baer, and his finger gently probed the bruised ribcage. He, too, watched the eyes and thus saw the flash of pain, clenched teeth and stiffened body. "You broke a rib or two," he said in a quiet matter-of-fact voice. Baer, not trusting himself to speak, simply nodded, and closed his eyes to hide his agony from the rest. But that was the wrong thing to do, for suddenly he found himself alone with the pain, the hurt filling him with a throbbing pulse, taking over all of his consciousness.

Throughout the day, as people returned from their various tasks, babbling in relief about surviving a new quake, they were shocked to learn about Baer's injuries. They collected about the fires and commiserated in hushed tones. First the earthquake and now Baer, people lamented. What's next? they wondered. The recent successful hunt and the celebration of First-Fires were forgotten, supplanted by this most recent rush of events.

Baer was lying down, propped up on some furs, favoring his right side. Tanya fussed over him trying to make him more comfortable, struggling not to show her concern. Baer also made every effort to remain casual to dispel the growing gloom that descended upon the entire camp. "Bad luck," people muttered. "What're we to do now?"

No one could imagine life without Baer leading them, no one ... except Tusk. The sight of an incapacitated Baer elated him. The weaker Baer appeared the stronger he felt. Yes! He sensed his time coming, but was unsure of how to take advantage of this opportunity. Though he was not particularly sensitive to the emotions that swayed others, he sensed the overall despondent mood, and knew that he could not meet this head on. Thus Tusk pretended concern for the injured leader, but sat apart from him withholding support of his authority. Like a vulture that spots weakness and opportunity even from a great distance, he knew instinctively that this was his chance to contest the leadership that was his right.

Cosh, the third leader, a practical person who was used to doing things rather than thinking about them, had an intuitive knack for doing the right thing at the right time. However he was not driven by vision, as was Baer, nor by entitlement, as was Tusk. Besides, he was too close to Baer to be aware of the subtle undercurrents that were already eroding their authority. He will always be a good helpmate but not a leader in his own right, Chaiko thought, immediately conscious of the power shift. Observing Tusk, he recognized the hidden elation and suspected the design. He moved protectively closer to Baer, and tried to distract Lana, with Tanya hovering nearby. A little later, Chaiko saw Tael join Tusk, forging a new alliance. Chaiko looked at Samar. He needed allies, too, but could he depend on the old man? The three of them, Chaiko, Cosh and Samar would have to protect Baer's back. But nonsense, Baer was going to be all right; he closed his mind to any other alternative.

Chapter 8

But Baer was not all right. The next morning found him delirious with fever. The ugly bruise on his ribs was turning purple with a greenish edge. Tanya washed his flushed face with a wet skin, trying to cool him. By the fire, Emma was brewing a mixture of plants, something to soothe the fever-tossed Baer, but it had few of the necessary ingredients that were buried someplace in the rubble of the cave. She fussed and complained to herself. Her usually kindly round face was crimped with worry. Like her son Crow, whose disposition she shared, she did not worry well. It ate at her and robbed her of all else. It was therefore not surprising that she reached so quickly for some superstitious convenience. She shuffled about the fire consumed with a desire to help but could do little.

The clan was quiet, waiting dispiritedly for the day's events. Would Baer be all right? everyone worried. Chaiko went to Cosh, and together they joined Samar. They discussed Baer's condition and likelihood of a quick recovery. Cosh was optimistic, Baer had always been strong; no mere rock could strike him down. Samar kept quiet as he did not want to dampen their spirits which Chaiko understood all too well. From his own experience he was well attuned to others' feelings about illness and injury. So like the rest, they waited.

Tusk did not join them. Briefly he visited Baer's hearth, inquired after the leader's condition, uttered a few unfelt condolences, then went aside to consider his actions. He ignored Cosh, Samar and Chaiko; without Baer they had little credibility in his eyes. He then went around the fires, organized the women to gather firewood and collected the hunters about him. For once he did not want to hunt as it would be inopportune to be away from camp at this time. Things were brewing and he wanted to be near to await developments. But he also wanted to be perceived as leading them and was making sure of that. He praised Makar and Crow for their bravery in the salvage attempt, but implied it was unwise for them to have undertaken such a foolish venture with the ground so unstable. "It's not like Baer to make such mistakes, but..." artfully he trailed off; he had made the point he wanted and left the rest to hang in the air. Others of the clan nodded. Yes, it was foolish, come to think of it, thus laying the responsibility for Makar's injuries on Baer as well.

Midmorning was interrupted by an aftershock, and the ground danced again, trees swayed, and rocks spilled. But even the most terrorized now recognized that it was weaker and lasted only half as long as the earlier episodes. Afterwards, there were animated exchanges as each felt that they had somehow bested the quake itself. Tusk fed their elation, going from person to person, praising their courage and fortitude. "This will pass," he promised. He himself continued to feel uneasy, but his present plans overshadowed his fears, as he threw himself wholly into turning the situation to his advantage. He laughed a little too often, and spoke louder than needed. He wanted everyone to admire his fearlessness and to acknowledge his bravery. And people did just that. They were ready to look to him; they did not like the uncertainty of Baer's illness. They were not aware of any conflict among the leadership or if so, chose to overlook it. It was more comforting to think that Tusk was simply shouldering the leadership by himself until Baer recovered.

As another good sign, the birds reappeared. Their flying at first was unsure and exploratory, but as the sun climbed higher in the sky, more and more birds appeared in flight. They seemed to take courage from each other, and their chattering soon filled the air. The earthquake had uncovered new feeding opportunities for them which they were quick to exploit. Broken trees exposed their innards to probing beaks; dislodged rocks no longer gave cover to creeping and crawling things; and gashes in the soil had unearthed colonies of ants, termites and bugs of all sorts— all busy trying to repair the damage.

Four-footed creatures also reappeared, timidly at first, for they were obviously confused with so many changes in the landscape. The birds in the sky were still able to orient themselves by the larger features of the land: the lake was there, unchanged, as were the cliffs and the hills in the distance, providing them with line of sight bearings. But to a fox and to a rabbit whose world was more myopic, everything had changed. A landmark tree or rock was all too often gone and landslides covered up well known trails. In places, the innards of the earth lay exposed, torn tree roots sometimes spanning the gaps. Unaccustomed dank earth smells overlaid the scents they had used to mark territories and to orient themselves. The small creatures went about sniffing, investigating, trying to make sense of all the changes, their appetite suppressed by anxiety.

People were feeling the same. The earthquake had stripped them of their sense of well-being, centered about the security of the cave, now denied to them. In the suddenly hostile world they felt vulnerable under the open skies. But there was no safety anywhere. Certainly not in caves and under rocks. They sat about the fires, waiting gloomily for something to happen that would miraculously resolve the impasse in which they found themselves. Like someone stuck on a steep slope, they could proceed neither up, nor down. Deprived of their leader, they felt trapped. Baer had the instinctive awareness of what was needed and the wisdom to express it in terms that everybody could accept. But Baer was injured, and although his fever had broken several times, he seemed none the better. He fell into an exhausted sleep.

The other most looked to in times of trouble, Tusk was sitting quietly flanked by Tael and Stow. Although he was deeply disturbed by the earthquake, he had the mentality that could rearrange facts to support whatever he needed at the moment. By a simple mental twist he was able to blame Baer for this catastrophe— he must have violated some taboo and thus have invoked the quake. Therefore, Tusk was able to channel all his anger toward where he wanted it anyway, centered on Baer. Baer's betrayal of them justified anything Tusk was now prepared to do to wrest leadership from the stricken man.

On the whole, Tusk was well pleased with how things had been developing so far. As a hunter he knew that the most vulnerable moment was that brief instant when the prey was recognized, marked and focused upon. From then on it was a matter of patience and endurance until the kill. Well, Tusk the Hunter had made his decision and had selected his prey. Now for patience. The patience of a stone, he reminded himself, all things would come to a patient man. He turned toward Tael and Stow, and since under the circumstances it would not be seemly to smile, nodded to each in solemn acknowledgement. Though he was appreciative of their support, it was also his due. Other people came, sat a while, waiting for leadership to emerge. "Wait," Tusk prompted himself, "even a headless snake must first twist and turn before it realizes it needs a new head."

Cosh was sitting by Baer's side, watching his friend's suffering, helpless to assist him in any way. His earlier optimism evaporated as Baer's condition worsened. He was miserable and wished he could have acted more quickly back in the cave so there would have been no need for Baer to hold back the rocks with his body. It was, however, not in his nature to blame himself or others. Cosh was of the happy disposition that did not look for trouble. He did not worry about forestalling problems, yet when faced with difficulties, he did not question or deny them, but did his best to find a pragmatic solution, which he most often did. So, though he noticed the comings and goings about the fires, to him it forebode no trouble.

On the other hand, to Chaiko sitting near him, the situation was highly suspicious. He was aware of the sudden shift of power in Tusk's favor. Tael's and Stow's obvious support did not escape him. He reacted instinctively, roused himself to protect his brother. But how? He had no status, no followers. Nobody looked to him. He needed allies. Cosh was too impervious to the undercurrents, and it would be a waste of time to warn him, but when the time came, he would stand by Baer. Samar still had power within him, though it was often slumbering. He, too, would help. But Chaiko needed more support to stand against Tusk if need be. Covertly he gestured to Crow who was at the next fire, busy passing around pieces of meat. Crow gave Chaiko an encouraging half-smile. Yes, Chaiko nodded back, Crow could also be counted upon. Then there was Tanya, of course, of great personal charm and power. Chaiko suddenly felt reassured.

His immediate concern was to decide how much of his suspicion was actually based on reality rather than on his dislike of the man. His distaste, though, was not on his own account, for like his brother, he tended to think of the clan first; here he perceived an incipient danger to them all, but could not confirm it. After all, Tusk had done nothing thus far, other than to ignore them. Yet Chaiko acutely felt Tusk's disdain. As a cripple, he could expect no consideration from him. He wished he had his leg, which though missing, tended to hurt in times of stress. Chaiko absently rubbed his other leg to alleviate the phantom pain.

Rea and Gill sat by their fire, two unmated men of middle age, provoking each other as was their lifelong habit. Rea was despondent over the absence of leadership and was unreasonably angry with Baer for being injured, like a child often was, reacting to feelings of abandonment.

"He'll be all right," he assured himself, erecting a defensive wall against the unthinkable.

"Baer's strong, but a fever can burn a body up right quick," volunteered Gill dispassionately. He had seen strong men succumb before to illness from an infection arising from a ridiculously small wound. "He could heal up or could just as well die," Gill summed up the two possibilities, weighing one against the other. He shrugged his shoulders ... there was nothing he could do about it.

"He'll not die!" Rea was shocked by Gill's cold-bloodedness.

"Tell you what, I'll wager my throwing stick against the bear claw you took off me for the new bison robe. If he dies, I get my bear claw back. If he lives, you get the throwing stick."

"Gill!" interrupted Rea, scandalized.

"The throwing stick is full of carvings, good luck charms..." Gill bragged, inflating its value.

"How can you bet on the lives of others ... especially Baer's?" sputtered Rea. Sometimes he just could not understand his friend.

"I am only guessing. I am not deciding his fate," Gill shrugged his shoulders again. Why, Gill wondered, was he so upset? Does lightning care where it struck or about the forests it burned? Death was death. They had seen enough of it to know.

At his fire, Tusk was expounding on the theme of luck. "Baer's luck must have surely changed. His younger brother lost his leg, did he not? That is very bad luck. Their father drowned. So bad luck runs in the family. And now, Baer has brought bad luck on himself and on the whole cave. Perhaps it would be better to find a new place..." It would also be easier to exert his leadership in new surroundings, unfettered by reminders of old loyalties.

People came and went, and each took a thought back to his own fire. By evening all discussions were centered on the issue of luck, a very important consideration in their lives. The clan was constantly faced with the arbitrariness of nature. Whether it was a chance accident or an earthquake, luck was seen as protection against the unpredictability they faced daily. A shaman must channel that luck, but a leader must command it. Baer had been considered lucky up until now. He had a fine-looking mate, a healthy, cheerful daughter and the respect of the whole clan. What he undertook usually succeeded. But wait, did not Tanya lose a son? And Chaiko a leg? And then this injury? Was the family indeed dogged by bad luck? And though people came to Baer's fire and were genuinely concerned about his condition, there were also many sideways, surreptitious glances toward them. Could it be true? Chaiko felt their furtive looks and shared their unease.

"We have had some hard years behind us. The winter two years ago was especially hard. Did not Kray's father die, weakened from hunger, as well as little Co-Co, barely two?" Tusk seemed lost in his musing.

Tael, who had stayed by Tusk's side most of the day was beginning to see a certain pattern and knew how to react. "Did not Baer call off the hunt that would have given us more than enough food for the winter?" He, too, like his mentor, allowed the question to hang in the air, letting each person find the answers for himself. Neatly ignoring, of course, that they had had two injured hunters to carry to safety and to care for. But was that calamity not another indication of bad luck? Bad luck attracted attention like a bad smell, and it was hard to wash off.

Tanya was worried. Though the fever abated at times, allowing brief respites from the tossing and turning, it would return even stronger, gradually wearing down Baer's resistance. Emma's bitter herb concoction helped to quiet him, but was unable to stem the course of the raging fever. At its height, Tanya would wash his body with a water-soaked chamois, cooling it. She tried to make him drink, but could not force the liquid down his throat; it all came spluttering back up through parched lips. Each time the fever broke, she would wipe off the sweat, keeping him dry, then pile covers over him, for next he would be racked by chills, trembling and shaking uncontrollably. His eyes, when they opened, were clouded and he did not recognize her. Occasionally he babbled something incomprehensible. She obsessed over him, fighting her anxiety. She had never seen him so helpless before. Emma sought to help, but could do little. She wrung her hands in distress. Cosh sat beside Baer throughout, feeling useless, but he wanted to share his friend's suffering. Samar sat there, rocking back and forth on his heels, reciting under his breath; "Pain eats a man from the inside ... devouring his thoughts ... consuming his intent ... But pain shared is pain divided ... First spear is the pain itself ... Second spear is the fear that follows ... Third spear is the worry it spawns ... Make your claim."

Recognizing that he could do nothing in the situation, Chaiko took Lana aside and sought to distract her. The girl was clearly worried, her sense of security eroded by the earthquake, then by her father's injury. It was inconceivable that her powerful father could be so struck down. To make things worse, nobody was answering her simple questions, "Is he going to be all right?" and her deepest fear, "Is he going to die?" People shook their heads no, but would look away from her beseeching eyes. Her mother was busy tending to her father, and had no time for her. But mother had always had time for her before. Chaiko sought to reassure her without lying to her. "Your father is strong, both in body as well as in mind. He's fighting the fever and your mother is helping him. It's best to stay out of the way." He told her stories to keep her mind occupied and off her worries.

"Man is a puny creature. He's born naked and helpless, crying into the world. Even grown, he has no fangs, no claws, no beaks and neither fur nor shell to protect him. Yet he walks with lions, hyenas and wolves and shares the world with bears." Chaiko shook his head, as if wondering at the audacity of man. "People believe many things, but this much is true: what People needed, People took." Chaiko emphasized this with a large grabbing gesture. "Man was hungry, he hunted and he killed, taking meat from the animals. He was cold, he took furs from the animals. He had no place to stay, so he invited himself into the cave of the bear. He also took knowledge from all around him. From the wolves he learned to hunt. Man had no fangs, no claws, so he made some: spears and clubs, and knives.

"And when the night was dark and the air was cool," Chaiko's gesture swept the whole sky, "he made fire. Around the fire he did not feel afraid. For no other creature had fire."

"But fire was the gift of the skies," Lana gestured, signing the lightning streaking down striking the earth, and then the sign of fire. She was referencing an oft-told tale with a child's triumph at being able to correct an adult. To her, only three years older, Chaiko was an adult.

"And so it was," Chaiko conceded easily, "but what People needed, People took, and what they could not take, they made. Like the water skin. No creature takes its water outside of itself, but the People. At night we bring water into the cave so we do not have to go into the darkness."

"And we make baskets of grass and twigs, so we can carry things more easily," Lana contributed.

"Exactly," Chaiko confirmed. "When we need something we take it or make it." He was turning it into a game. "When we feel cold, we shiver and let our teeth rattle ..."

"No! We make fire," she threw in, delighted to join in. Though it was a childish exchange, she knew from experience that he liked to improvise twists and turns to surprise her, so she remained expectant. She knew most of his tricks.

"And when we are re-e-al cold?"

"We wrap ourselves in furs to keep warm," she jumped in.

He showed her the Singing-Stick, but she reacted with only mild interest at the hum he produced. He was a little deflated, for he had expected more from her because of her musical ability. It was his secret treasure, he struck the string to accent his singsong voice:

> "When we need to dig for roots
> A claw is more than handy.
> When we need to cut up foods
> A chopper axe will have to do.
> When you need just anything
> Take it, or else, make it
> Make it, or else, take it
> Then you will have it, too.
> Claw or fang, just take it.
> Knife and spear, just make it ..."

At each refrain "make it" he invited her to sing along and she did in her pure voice. He soon ran out of things to make, but was not yet ready for the song to end, as it was adapted from a much longer melody. "When we need a ... a nose ..." he improvised. "Make it," she came in on the correct beat, laughing. "When we need a head," she was laughing ahead of him, "We make it." He was astonished at her uninhibited laughter that forgot the terror of the earthquake and her father's injury. The freedom of her laughter dissolved his tension as well, and he knew that whatever else might happen, life would go on, and he was able to look beyond his most pressing worries. He would do whatever he must, he knew, to protect his brother, family and the cave. But for now, he would continue distracting Lana. He substituted body parts freely, and giggles bubbled up in her anew. "When we need a toe ..." was followed by "an arm," and then "a leg;" he was fast running out of body parts. She was laughing uncontrollably, "We m-a-ke it." Then she looked at him in surprise, for he had suddenly stopped, the last note on the string fading away. Chaiko was no longer there, his eyes focused on some distant spot, hiding the pain he felt. "A leg," he had said, she realized, and felt the pain for him.

Later in the day Chaiko spent time with Crow, testing his thoughts on his friend, but Crow at first refused to consider even the possibility of malevolent intent by Tusk. He had always considered Tusk to be an ideal person. Tusk was big and his movements large, without subtlety. He got attention for his size alone. He was always able to let others know what he wanted them to do. This was the secret of his success. Though Crow respected Baer above all others, he could never see beyond the thoughtful eyes; to him, Baer was unreadable. And so was Chaiko, even though he was an age mate and a friend, but he had an intuitive feel for Chaiko that allowed the two to be so close. And though he did not share Chaiko's concerns, experience had taught him to respect Chaiko's worry-spun conjectures. So reluctantly he promised to keep an eye on Tusk.

That night, Chaiko was busy analyzing the situation. While he instinctively felt the threat that Tusk presented to Baer's leadership there was no evidence for it. Still he must not let down his guard. As long as Baer was unable to protect himself, it was up to him to protect his brother. But how could he fight an adversary who did not show himself? He would only make a fool of himself in front of the whole clan. As a cripple, he was enough of a fool already. He was loath to risk the gains he had made the last few days. This prospect unnerved him and softened his resolve to undertake something. But no matter where he started in his thinking, he came to the same conclusion: he was sure of the threat. Tomorrow, he decided, and though he would not fight shadows if Tusk did not emerge, he would try to repair Baer's reputation that was being eroded by things said or left unsaid. He had overheard snatches of conversation around the fires. Everyone needed to be reminded of Baer's many services to the clan.

"In all fairness," he thought, "with Baer down, the clan will need Tusk's strength." Dutifully he examined that thought from all directions. Yes, the clan must have a leader. If not Baer then Tusk. Suppressing his distrust, he forced himself to look impartially at the man, judging his value to the clan. Tusk was strong and people were willing to follow him. In this crisis what else mattered? "Doesn't a little spoiled meat ruin the rest?" Chaiko argued with himself. It would be dangerous to follow a man who had vision only for himself, and in his mind, the clan was there to bestow the rightful respect due to him, status preceding responsibility. Still, the crisis was now. "In this situation, is a little darkness in front of one's feet more important than the great darkness far off?" Once again, Chaiko resolved to do something the next day... but that something would have to be cunning.

Chaiko reached for his Singing-Stick, plucked it, humming quietly to himself the song he and Lana had sung earlier in the day. The simple melody had stayed with him, like a worm quietly nibbling at the edge of his awareness. "Take it or else make it ..." the refrain came back to him. The quarter moon sailed across a cloudless sky, its wan glow barely illuminating the landscape. Small noises filled the void, but the usually watchful Chaiko was lost in thought.

Several times throughout the night Baer called out, unintelligible sounds, rousing Tanya from a fitful sleep. She would soothe him as if he were a child, talking to him softly, patting him reassuringly, stroking him. He would quiet down and both would drift back into sleep.

During the latter part of the night there was a weak aftershock, a gentle tremor that did not awaken the sleeping clan. Chaiko himself barely felt it.

Chapter 9

The next morning found Baer's condition unimproved. The signs were a confused mix of good and bad. Although the fever had broken earlier in the morning, his skin tone was pasty and stiff. He was in a deep sleep and his breathing was much less labored. But he appeared wasted; the flesh had melted from his frame and his cheeks were hollow. Tanya called to him softly, but there was no response. She lifted the furs and examined the ugly bruise on his ribcage. The color had turned to splotchy black and blue, the swelling still quite pronounced; her hopes wilted at the sight. Emma, too, was discouraged. Obviously there was still infection there which could start feeding the fever again. Samar came over and muttered some incantation to boost Baer's spirit to fight off the sickness. He waved and passed the wolf talisman over the affected area to use the power of the relic to heal the injury under the bruise. He could do no more for Baer. His face, weathered by time with a myriad of wrinkles, was unreadable to the anxious Tanya.

The rest of the clan stayed by their fires. It was obvious to all that the illness had not run its course. It was thus better to stay out of the way. The women brought over foodstuff and remedies which Emma accepted with strict interrogation as to ingredients and efficacy. Even several hearths away, people spoke in hushed tones and continued their anxious vigil.

Crow had been busy, sent by his mother hither and thither to find certain plants that grew only in certain places at certain times of the year: plants, roots, seeds, lichen, bark, dried flower tops. She kept adding to the list, and off Crow went on yet another errand.

"Good, good," she would encourage her son. "I'm glad you found that ... No, this is not crowfoot, this is deer-heart, similar but not the same. This is good for keeping swelling down; this is good only for fixing something else in a concoction." Emma leafed through the inventory of what he brought back from one of his forays. When Crow grew discouraged, he reminded himself of Lana's brave smile and was ready again to forage the rest of the countryside.

Tanya, who at first had been thankful for her support, grew weary of Emma's constant fussing and began even to question the potency of her varied medications. But she dared not say anything that might deprive Baer of even the slim chance that her potions might have some positive effect on his condition.

The others watched closely all the goings on and drew their own conclusions. Discussions of the day before, about luck, once again made the rounds of the fires. Luck was a visible component of leadership. Why else would people follow it? An unlucky man was to be avoided, lest the bad luck be transmitted like fleas. Everyone seemed to know what luck was, though there was no consensus about it. Listening quietly, Chaiko mused to himself that luck was what you made of it. Ela considered it luck when a startled bird took flight underfoot, for she had not stepped on it or on its nest. Further, she had stirred up the bird, not some predator stalking her. To her mate Tael, the same would be considered unlucky, because it called unwanted attention to his whereabouts, alerting any prey he was stalking. He would be most critical of his own stealth: unskilled, if not outright unlucky.

Luck, on the whole, was usually judged in terms of outcomes. Any unexpected outcome was attributed to luck, though Chaiko noted that skill and luck often went hand in hand. Chaiko saw luck more as an attitude or expectation that foreshadowed the outcome. It explained why some people were consistently lucky, whereas others habitually unlucky. Up to now, Baer had been lucky, and he, Chaiko, was considered unlucky. Vigilance on the pathways of choices could make the difference. Had he noticed four years ago how the loose rock shifted, he would not have taken the risk and would still have his leg, his luck and a normal life. These were no idle concerns. Oft, the difference between hunger, and even death, was the luck of the hunt, the luck of the season.

In line with his decision the night before, Chaiko went about from fire to fire putting in a hopeful word about Baer's improved condition. The timely warning he had given about the earthquake had boosted his status, and people received him kindly, though the reception was overshadowed by his brother's injury. The mood around the fires continued to be brooding. What else would befall them next? This apprehension was slowly eroding their confidence. Only Tusk was well content. The cave, in such an unsettled state, would offer less resistance to him taking control; till then their lethargy suited him. They would be happy to be led again.

Tusk's more immediate problem was to determine in which direction to move. He lacked vision to illuminate his way. He did not allow himself to confer with others, as this would dissipate his own confidence by opening his counsel to questions. With a shock he realized he was alone with the burden and responsibility of leadership. Whereas before, Baer, Samar, and Cosh had deferred to him, and sought his advice, the final decisions came out of general consensus, and he had not felt the weight of it. He was good in executing a chosen course of action, but poor in planning it. Yet, unfortunately for those who followed him, he was blind to this lack, as were they.

Still, he felt superbly confident that he could do a better job at leading the cave than Baer. He was not yet aware of the fact that he needed a certain resistance that he could push against. It was the counter force itself that often gave him direction: he pushed and it resisted, then he shoved more to follow up an advantage. In reality, Baer was able to lead him quite easily to a desired decision, although Baer always listened and considered Tusk's advice and concerns fairly on their merit.

At present Tusk felt himself up against the cave, and this gave him a sense of opposition, and hence the direction he needed. He would have to move them away from the accustomed track. He must remove them from Baer's influence.

Calla was becoming concerned. Her fine nose could smell the intrigue brewing and she, too, wanted to stir the pot. After all, who else was more qualified? She was not at all pleased by the turn events had taken. She considered her situation carefully, and came to the conclusion that her standing was based on an existing relationship with Tanya and Baer, and that she had better undertake something to protect it. Once she made up her mind, it was to her credit that she acted wholeheartedly, and took no precaution for herself should the tide turn against Baer.

"Tusk is an upstart," she observed to her mate. Kor blinked; he had been in the middle of explaining to her about the hardness of agate, when she came forth with this. But he was used to such interruptions, as if he had never spoken. He shrugged his shoulders, squinting at her, testing the direction of the wind.

"Well, he is!" came bubbling forth from Calla's discontent. "And he is cutting off the perch we are all sitting on."

Kor knew better than to ask what perch, but looked around to see what metaphysical perch she could be talking about.

"Go, give Tanya your sharpest flint blade from that nodule you found by the pits ... near the smoking-waters," she ordered him. He was shocked that she demanded that he give from the shrinking collection of his most prized possession: a flint so flawless and sharp, without the brittleness of lesser flints. Everyone knew how rare and valuable that flint was. Did she know what she was asking of him?

She knew. Of course, she knew. She wanted to send a clear message of Kor's and her support for the beleaguered head of the clan. The special quality of the stone would do that admirably. He sighed, but made ready to comply, and she rewarded him with the warmest of smiles, such as he had not seen for many years.

Nearby, Kray and Yaya were sitting by the fire. The earthquake was still fresh on Yaya's mind, so she kept her children close. Kray was working on a spear to ingratiate himself with Tusk, but not so overtly as to upset Baer's faction. He did not miss Tael's first overtures, then his outright support for Tusk. "The fool, he will soon regret that mistake," Kray muttered to himself. "A male lion oft kills the cubs of other lions..."

Yaya was using a handful of twigs to bring some order to Sosa's unruly hair. He was, of course, resisting her efforts and complained loudly and bitterly that she was killing him. "Be still!" she ordered, and slapped him none too gently on the back of the head. Deciding to change tactics, he cried, "Look, Ork is allowed to run about."

"Malek and Nebu are much too lax with their children," Yaya retorted. "Look at how Ruba is allowed to do anything, yet he is only eight."

Kray only grunted; he respected Malek's power of painting and was not going to undermine the relationship. He had seen the drawings on the cave wall in the farthest recess: the bison, elk, horses; graceful herds of them, in charcoal and ochre. He had looked for the spirit held by the work but could not discern any. But then, he was only a hunter, who worked with wood.

Sosa tried yet again, "Look, there goes Ork with Crow to get some medicine plants for Baer. I should go and help them." He struggled briefly against the firm grip holding him back. Yaya knew better than to believe her son's altruistic motives, but let him go anyway. Sometimes a nice pretext was better than no pretext at all; besides, she wanted to spend time with Ela to repair some skins. Though their men often feuded with each other in a semi-friendly fashion, and the two women were rivals themselves, they spent a great deal of time together, each trying to give as much as she got. As she prepared to go off, she snapped at Tay, "Put your wrap on!" and slapped the young girl's rump.

"What is wrong with her?" Kray muttered, looking after his departing mate, and shaking his head. "Women! What man can understand them?"

The younger children were becoming restless. They were not used to being so constrained to the nearness of the fires. The adults huddled in closed groups waiting to see what would happen. Baer had to get well. They could not imagine a future without him. Even a consideration of such an eventuality was to be fought off, so as not to inadvertently call forth that calamity.

One by one the children wandered off. The bravest even dared the danger of the cave to search for useful and valued items. A group of boys collected further up the creek, and once out of eye and earshot of the adults, reverted to their carefree selves, playing, shouting and chasing each other. The girls collected dried herbs and scented buds in sun-drenched meadows. There was laughter that shook off the terror they had experienced over the last few days. The resiliency of youth could not be suppressed; so easy to be hurt, but quicker to heal. Underneath the scar, the memory remained. Lana and Ido were looking for spring flowers to weave into a garland, but it was too early in the season. They then decided to look for rocks along the creek bottom.

They both shared a passion for pretty rocks, the more colorful the better. Ruba trailed them, hoping for some attention. Ork and Sosa followed close behind him, with identical smirks on their faces, just to get in his way. Makar came around the path, and whatever Ruba's intent, it quickly evaporated at the older boy's approach.

At noon a sparse meal was passed around and eaten gloomily. The realization grew that something had to be done. There was game to be hunted, firewood to be gathered, roots to be dug up, and something had to be decided about the cave. But still everybody waited for someone to take charge, for someone to organize and resume their daily routines. Someone to restore their confidence and security. Chaiko felt the need, but knew instinctively that his suggestions would be resented. After all, even dogs had their order. A cripple could not lead, not because the cripple lacked wisdom, but because people would not follow. So Chaiko went to Tusk.

Tusk looked at him in wide-eyed surprise as Chaiko boldly sat down in front of him. On either side, Stow and Tael were taken aback as well, ceasing their conversation and squirming about not knowing what to expect. From several fires away, Crow hurried over, with a worried expression on his face.

"I come to speak for my family," Chaiko started, using the form that prevented the others from turning away and rejecting him out of hand. "This would Baer say: 'You must now lead the cave. The cave needs your skill in hunting, but even more, the cave needs a head. While Baer lies stricken down with fever, he cannot lead. Tusk, we look to you to lead us. We are in need of your strength."

All within earshot were taken aback. By some unknown mechanism, quite a group had collected about them, somehow aware that something unusual was about to happen, and they were right. Even those most unaware of alliances felt Chaiko's plea to be out of place. Chaiko was expected to plead and protect his brother's status, rather than to give it away. No one was more surprised than Tusk, but so hungry was he for the power he craved that he instinctively snapped at it like a fish at a baited lure. He could not help himself. Chaiko gave a little shove, and all the pent-up ambitions and emotions were loosened, gathering momentum on their own. There was now no turning back. Tusk rose to his feet with a large gesture that embraced the whole cave. "I shall lead," he proclaimed. There was a gratified murmur from the crowd, a genuine sense of relief. Tusk had his audience, as he had dreamed and planned, but to his own surprise he found himself with nothing to say. "We will hunt tomorrow," was all he could think of and he sat down lamely, but it was enough. They were looking forward to some normalcy. With Tusk in the lead, most felt they had it.

In any case, Tusk, having accepted the leadership, now had to lead. He had to prove himself capable, and be measured against Baer's competence. If he should be found wanting, it would soon be obvious. There was also the chance that a real taste of the burdens of leadership would quench Tusk's ambitions. Chaiko had flushed him out into the open, out of Baer's shadow, to be tested on his own merits; all his actions would henceforth be public. And if there was real leadership in him, it would benefit the clan.

Chaiko, accompanied by Crow, returned to his fire. He was reasonably pleased. Events had started rolling: Tusk had made his move, though he had tried to hide his intent. Chaiko had made a counter move, and things were now visible for everyone to see. He, who had no real role to play, had made one for himself. People would remember that it was he who had gone to Tusk and challenged him to be a leader. He had wielded Baer's authority and Tusk, eager to accept, had inadvertently validated him. Yes, people would remember at the very least that he had had a part in making decisions. And though some might feel that he should have better protected his brother, all would remember his stand, gaining for him even more stature: first, through the timely warning that saved their lives, and then by his role as an emerging person of importance.

By now, the sun was high in the sky. To the west a line of clouds was building, threatening rain for the morrow. Chaiko squinted against the glare and examined the clouds. They had a strange coloration about them. He was puzzled, but the nagging worries of the present drew him back and he was asking like the rest, "What's next?"

Needing some rest from the heavy anticipation all around him and needing some space to think, he decided to try fishing. Today with the scarcity of meat, even fish would be welcome. With his peculiar hobble he worked his way down the slope, often detouring around a fresh obstacle created by the quake. By the time he reached the creek he was tired and was forced to rest. He lay flat on a stout tree branch overhanging the water and watched the quiet pool in the shadows for signs of fish. It was immediately obvious to him that the water was murkier than it should have been. The bottom was barely visible, and he could discern only an occasional flash that marked a fish. He surmised that somewhere upstream a landslide of exposed earth was washing into the creek filling the water with sediment. At this spot the water had a chance to spread out and to slow down to a leisurely pace, but still it appeared almost brown from the weight of the mud it carried.

As he lay along the branch, the hardened bark impressed its ridges into his flesh. A faint smell of drying moss tickled his nostrils. He loved this spot, often watching the water roll downstream, mesmerizing and relaxing him. A piece of wood came drifting by within easy reach. Attracted by its smooth look, he plucked it from the water. It was a stout branch, about half his body length, the thickness of his arms and surprisingly heavy. It must have been in the water for some time to acquire its smoothness, but not too long to have lost its hardness and strength. As he looked closely, he noted the straightness of the grain and the absence of knots or twists so often found. The piece of wood was nearly perfect, but for what? Experience had taught him that with a little time the wood would reveal its purpose. He laid it aside and turned his attention to fishing.

The muddied water had probably upset the fish's feeding habits, he reasoned; he would probably have better luck by the lake. Reluctantly he got up and continued along the path that followed the creek downstream.

Near the lake he had to skirt a large marshy delta filled with an impenetrable looking tangle of reeds, weeds and bush. Right at the edge the ground gave way, sucked at his one good foot and swallowed his walking-sticks. Off balance, he pulled himself along by the few bushes, but the going proved difficult and he soon grew tired. There were clouds of insects everywhere getting into his eyes and nostrils. Birds loudly followed his progress, swooping out of the sky to feed on the swarm he stirred up. All around, frogs complained of his presence, grew still as he neared and then jumped from under foot into the water with a fat splash. Green slime wrapped itself around his foot and a miasma of dank fetid smell assaulted him, with each step sinking into the ooze of mud. Finally he emerged onto a sandy beach drenched in sunlight. The sand was coarse and grainy, but its dark shade absorbed the heat of the sun and Chaiko luxuriated in its warmth. This had turned out to be the warmest day so far. He walked west along the shore, his nose sorting the smells, a tangy mixture of sweet decay curiously freshened by onshore winds.

From underneath a dead bush, whose roots gave protection to a small abandoned den, he drew his fishing implements: several fishing spears tipped with barbed bone and a length of painstakingly knotted jute with a carved bone hook. He took the line, then with the support of his walking stick hobbled along the shore. He overturned several rocks and found just the sort of bugs the fish went for.

He was tiring once again, when he reached a group of boulders along the shoreline adjacent to a deeper pool of water. This was his favorite spot to fish on the lake, and rarely did it fail to provide him with a generous catch. He eased himself down on a familiar perch and using the weight of a small stone, he cast his line as far as it would go out into the pool. There was only a slight breeze that made the sunlight dance on the water and rustled the leaves in the trees edging the lake. The balmy air and the warmth of the sunshine soon lulled him to drift off. He was alone, except for the occasional bird that flew over to investigate the likelihood of scavenging. It being past midday, he felt unafraid, since predators following the rhythm of seasons and instinct, also rested.

A tug on his line brought him instantly back into full awareness. Something was nibbling on his bait, cautiously tasting it. At the next tremor he gave the line a firm jerk and felt with satisfaction the instant resistance as the fish, too late, tried to back off the hook. Judging by the strength of the pull Chaiko knew it to be a fair-sized fish, and the way it worked the line from side to side, undoubtedly a catfish. He liked catfish; with a little watercress and strong-root it made a succulent meal. With practiced patience he worked the fish ashore, clubbed it, strung it through the gills, then put it back in the water to keep it cool. He put on fresh bait, cast out the line and settled into comfortable waiting again.

Chaiko loved fishing. It did not require the use of the missing leg, and even a big catfish did not overreach his strength. He was the best fisherman in the clan, knowing more about the subject than anybody else. Too bad that fish was not so highly prized and fishing not invested with as much prestige as hunting. Otherwise he could have had a secure future supporting a family and trading for what else he needed.

On the way back up the slope, a string of eight fish slowed him down. On top he paused to enjoy the view of the peaceful lake, the expanse of calm water in a shimmering haze and the far shore hidden by the distance. He thought of all the fish that swam in it and again that the lake would always assure him some sort of future even if the clan had denied him the status.

To the west the cloud bank had grown and spread across a quarter of the sky. Chaiko felt stirrings of disquiet; he liked neither its shape nor its color. It seemed to be hanging rather than floating in the air, and the sunlight was swallowed by a grey pallor.

Back at the camp the fish were gratefully divided. The hunters had brought back little, but with the fish and the few edible roots and winter-dried berries, it sufficed to provide a meager but adequate meal for everybody. With Tusk distracted, the hunters had lacked confidence and focus.

There were no more aftershocks that day. With every hour that passed, people relaxed more and more, suppressing the terror of the earth shaking. But as fear receded, their dissatisfaction increased at their dislocation, the cave so near yet denied to them.

One of the youngsters, Sosa, after relieving himself, from habit returned by the usual path and to his surprise found himself back in the cave. He yelled in sudden realization of this and ran as if the entire cave was coming down on him. The people around the fires watched him; some smiled, some laughed outright at the lad's discomfiture. Humor released the final bonds of remaining fear, and smiles smoothed out the worry lines. After days of tense expectation, now giddiness swept over them and they laughed at little or even at nothing in a surge of relief that the earth had shaken and that they had somehow survived. The whole earth, shaking, could not kill them. What then did they have to fear?

Darkness fell early as the bank of clouds blotted out the setting sun. It disappeared in a quick brownish hue that faded rapidly. Out of habit most saw the sun set but found it unworthy of note. What weather did it foretell? Chaiko wondered to himself, not remembering the like of it before. The day had seemed to last longer than the previous day, more nearly normal, and people settled down for the night in a more purposeful fashion.

That night while tending the fire, Chaiko worked on the piece of wood he had found. With a flint shard he rounded off the jagged broken end; the other end had broken neatly. The wood had lost its slippery wet feel, and there appeared to be no soft spots in its entire length. He wiped it and rubbed it with a handful of sand. "... And make it, we make it..." he hummed. Let the wood dry thoroughly and we shall see, he told himself, laying it aside.

In the middle of the night the leading edge of the clouds covered the moon, and before dawn rain began to fall, a light drizzle that continued. Soon Chaiko was soaked, but the night air was warm and he did not mind. It was nearly morning when he first became aware of a peculiar taste, ever so slight or faint. He could think of nothing to compare it to, yet there it was, elusive on his tongue. Then slowly he got used to it and, having enough things to worry about, forgot about it.

Chapter 10

The next morning the rising sun cloaked itself in an unusual array of colors. A bright yellow lit up the entire eastern arc of the sky with mauve and greenish striations that soon faded as the sun rose higher, but the pallor remained. The birds wheeled and swooped in normal morning flight and the cacophony of insects denoted nothing unusual. Ever since the earthquake had been presaged by the unusual behavior of birds and animals, Chaiko had been more observant of their behavior.

As usual, after the night's vigil, Chaiko's eyes were dry and the smoke of the fire still burned in his nose. This morning the stump of his leg ached and it made him irritable. Baer was still sleeping, his strength sapped by the infection. At the moment he was quiet. Tanya looked tired from waking throughout the night checking on him. Near morning Baer had awakened. "His eyes were focused and his speech was clear though weak," Tanya reported. "I must have drifted off," Chaiko concluded, "to have missed it."

Cosh and Ile crossed the boundary stones, making this an official visit to inquire after Baer's progress and offer Tanya encouragement. It had become clear even to Cosh that some form of visible show of support was called for to stop the slow erosion of Baer's prestige. He carefully kept his voice light, his countenance bright and his gestures confident for the benefit of all the onlookers. Playing a role was not his forte and he overplayed his casual stance, but he gave as good a performance as could be expected from a person of his disposition, that eschewed any and all posturing. Ile was much more natural, giving Tanya the last of her honey (which she had been saving for a very special occasion), in the hope that the rare treat would reawaken Baer's appetite to eat and gain some strength back. Tanya smiled gratefully at both of them, the lines of tiredness briefly eased by their caring.

The two returned to their fire and sat in comfortable silence. Ile was a quiet person, thoughtful and purposeful. She had a calm easygoing manner that fit well with Cosh's practical approach to life, and the two had a peaceful, harmonious relationship. Both were slow to react to provocation and neither was emotional. What they lacked in excitement they more than made up for with consistency. It was thus interesting that their only daughter Ido, though mostly quiet and shy, was hot of temper and given to an occasional emotional storm which the parents could not understand. Tanya had had to mediate a few such outbursts for them.

Typically, when there was some controversy raging about them, they stayed calm and detached, exchanging knowing looks with one another that were only slightly smug, the feelings that calm people often experienced in the face of full emotions. Yet they were never arrogant and both listened patiently and gave due consideration, though they tended to be a little short on the response. But then most people needed only to be listened to. They were both well liked, partially because there was nothing much that people could find to dislike about them.

Tanya and Ile were good friends, having come to the clan as mates for Baer and Cosh after the same Gathering; both being new, they had naturally found each other. In all that time, nigh unto twelve years, Tanya had seen Ile lose her patience but once, toward Krii, a single male who had eaten at her hearth for a number of years. He had made it his habit to give uninvited comments on her meals, her choice of seasonings, cooking and preparation. For years she endured his picky asides stoically, until one day he denigrated her sautéed sweet carrots once too often and she, to show her appreciation for his remarks over the years, dumped the rest into his lap, grabbed him by the ears and flung him halfway across the cave. After that he was not welcome by her fire. In fact, he had to go join another clan because no one was willing to put up with his disposition. Tanya still smiled at the incident. Their girls were close friends, being age mates, inseparable. At the moment Lana and Ido were out looking for early willow blooms.

The rest of the clan was going about morning tasks. Get the fire started, relieve oneself, eat something and wash up. "Yawn and stretch then scratch," went the saying people used to describe a leisurely awakening. Crow came over to Chaiko, his face troubled. He had had a disturbing dream and wanted Chaiko's views on its spiritual implication. In the dream, Crow was hunting with Tusk and Cosh when they suddenly came upon a big black bear. The bear reared up on its hind legs and roared at them. Tusk and Cosh moved to attack from the front and they wanted him to attack on the exposed side. "Go on, do it," they yelled at him, but though he tried to move his feet they refused to budge. "Do it!" And he tried to lift his spear but his arms would not move. He tried to yell but no sound could escape him. Thankfully he woke up, but could not shake off the dream. This morning he was going on the hunt decreed by Tusk and was afraid that, through the dream, the spirit world was warning him of something dire about to happen. He wanted to know Chaiko's opinion.

Chaiko looked at his friend in sympathy. Listening, he had concluded that Crow was realizing in a roundabout way that being a hunter also had its share of burdens. The ceremony a few days before gave him prestige and status, but today he would have to earn it. And day after day from now on he would have to merit it. Crow was not afraid of danger, Chaiko knew full well, but he was afraid of letting the others down, and the dream showed it. Are we not all afraid of letting down those depending on us? he asked himself.

Chaiko thought about the best way to help Crow; certainly not with reason, as reason was a poor weapon against unreasoning fear. He would have to try something else. Knowing how superstitious Crow was, Chaiko decided to use that against itself. "Set a fox to catch a fox; for only a fox truly knows a fox," as the saying goes. He carried about his neck a tell-mark, given to his mother by the great Bogan, and she had given it to him. She never told anyone why Bogan had given it to her. Chaiko prized it for her sake, not because it had once belonged to the great shaman. But he knew how much Crow revered the stone. For his friend, a piece of Bogan was still in the stone. Well then, let Bogan himself fight fear, Chaiko decided. He took the stone from his neck, gave it to Crow and said in his most solemn voice, "This I lend you to keep you and those with you safe. Many years it hung about Bogan's neck, and it kept him safe and purposeful. May the stone help you also."

Crow's face lit up. Reverently he placed the stone about his neck and felt safer already. With a light heart he arose to prepare for the hunt.

Tusk was anxious to get started. He wanted to hunt and bring home lots of meat to show the value of his leadership. It did not please him to see Baer's improved condition and the obvious lifting of spirits all around him. Today he must make his mark. He sent runners ahead to scout for likely game and then harried the rest to get moving. Soon a group of hunters had gathered around him waiting for the customary send off from Samar. But the old one had hardly started into his gestures when Tusk interrupted him, not unkindly, but obviously in no mood for a protracted ceremony. It was speed and strength that counted, not some muttered words by an old man. "Give me but a good spear," a hunter was wont to say. The more experienced, however, knew the value of the mind-set built by the ceremony and the focus it conferred. The group set out, hopeful eyes following their progress down and then around the slope. A good full meal of fresh meat was wanting again.

Meanwhile, the women gathered around in an awkward huddle. Normally, Baer's leadership included them with specific instructions in preparation for the day's tasks, but not this time. It was not that the women needed special instruction—they knew very well what was needed—but they now felt slighted by being so ignored by the rush of the hunters. It made their contribution seem less valued, and consequently they felt off balance. But in a little while, under Tanya's gentle directions, they too organized and set off in various groups to get firewood, to gather herbs for smoking meat, to weave cords, or to build and repair racks for hanging meat to dry.

With the hunters gone and the women dispersed, Lana and Ido with them, only Samar, Kor, Chaiko and Baer, with Tanya attending to his needs, were left with the children. Ruba, flanked by his two minions, Sosa and Ork, was set to go on some grand adventure, but was hamstrung by the presence of Tay who was left in the care of her brother Sosa.

"Why did you bring her?" Ruba demanded of Sosa in full ill humor.

"I did not bring her," he protested, "I was told to take care of her."

"How are we going to climb the cliffs looking for eagle feathers with her along?" he wanted to know.

"Fetters? Taj love fetters!" Tay clapped her hands rejoicing.

"We could ask Chaiko to take care of her," suggested Ork, trying to be helpful.

"Chaiko?" His older brother frowned, but then shook his head no. Chaiko had too many strange powers that could see into the nothing, and feel an earthquake growing. Ruba was sure that you do not ask a person like that for little things. The others did not question him, and the four of them left the camp to explore the creek bed. There was always something of interest to be found there. The last time, they had stumbled across an abandoned wasp nest. They had stuck pieces of the waxy comb onto sticks, which they lit, and ran about the camp with blazing torches. In so doing, they had inadvertently set fire to Gill's prized wolf pelt, and to make matters worse, while Gill was still in it. Yelling and flailing away with his arms, Gill had tried to extinguish the blazing fur, having a hard time undoing the knot that held it. By the time he managed to free himself, the fur was half burned, quite useless and possessed of an evil smell. Malek and Kray had to offer him compensation for the damage caused by their sons. Thus Ruba and Ork had to collect firewood for a whole moon for Gill's fire, and Sosa had to collect a large pile of moss for Gill's bedding.

Though there were no specific instructions given, the cave remained closed; no one wanted to risk being hurt like Baer. There had been no aftershock for a whole day, but still no one had suggested they could go back into the cave. So co-operative effort was hampered by lack of the implements or utensils, still in the cave. Kor was busy making chopping axes from fist-sized river pebbles, perhaps the simplest of tools, but effective and relatively easy to make. Later there would be time to make the more intricate, sharp flint blades. Though cognizant of their need for these simple tools, Kor grumbled discontented that these were much beneath his skill.

The backwash of all the ongoing activities fed by renewed hope and purpose made Chaiko restless. He looked over all the possessions he had salvaged and the pieces he was working on. The piece of wood he called Straight showed signs of drying out. He rubbed spittle along its length; it would not do to let it dry out too quickly. The wood might split or lose its greatest virtues: its density and hardness might be diminished. Then, he shaved both ends to nicely rounded shapes. He decided against searing the wood in fire, thinking rather to rub it with crushed flax seed to smooth and temper it.

Next he picked up his Singing-Stick, bent and tied it, and strummed it, delighted by its sounds. By varying the tension on the string he changed the tones, some sounding pleasant, some not so, and again he wondered how to control them reliably. The morning quickly went by in that happy pursuit, erasing his earlier irritability. For the moment he was able to forget his worries about Baer and the conflict over leadership. Activities flowed around him but he hardly noticed. A few youngsters came over and watched him for a while. Ork, Sosa and Tay were hoping he would tell them a story as he often did, but today he was busy and when he did not pay attention to them they drifted away. It was Tanya who finally broke into his concentration. Baer was awake, sitting half-upright, supported by a pile of skins and furs, and was asking for him. Chaiko hurried over, warmed by his brother's attempted smile. Baer appeared drawn and exhausted, but his eyes were alight and interested. Chaiko leaned over and squeezed his brother's hand. He was too choked with emotion to speak, but the weak return grasp told him much and his elation subsided.

Throughout the day the women drifted back from their various pursuits. Lana and Ido returned with armfuls of willow switches that they were going to weave into strong carrying baskets. At present, Lana was sitting beside her father weaving grass blades into cup shapes to hold the berries that would be ripening soon. Emma fussed about at the other side of the fire; she too was vastly relieved that Baer was conscious, and she secretly praised herself and her herbs. The poultice seemed to have worked, for the swelling had gone down and Baer appeared relatively comfortable, if very weak. Cosh was absent, having gone on the hunt, accepting Tusk's leadership without question. Someone had to do it, was his attitude. Besides, he was not going to sit by Baer the whole day again, helplessly watching his friend's struggles. He had wrestled with himself all day in a conflict of emotions, but finally made peace with himself. Though Baer was his age mate and closest friend, and though he would do what he could, it was not in his makeup to strain against what he could not affect, and should Baer not recover, Cosh would live on and would not dwell on the past.

Generally, people about the fires looked busy with various tasks but paused often to look for signs of the hunters' returning, or at Baer. These were the most important thoughts for the day. They did not come over yet, knowing what he needed most was rest and quiet. Baer, too, was turned to face the expected return of the hunters, Tanya having filled him in briefly on the events that he had missed.

"Has the quake passed?" The words slowly formed with an effort on his lips.

"Yesterday, midmorning, there was a brief tremor. Nothing since then," Chaiko replied, still at his brother's side.

"Are we safe then?" Baer's voice lilted expecting a hopeful reply. "Or is there still danger?"

Chaiko had to roll the question around in his mind. He felt no imminent danger, but could he trust his feelings? He shrugged his shoulders, both palms turned up, but still said, "No." Baer closed his eyes in exhaustion, but the answer reassured him.

Samar, too, came over and quietly sat down beside Baer. The two exchanged glances of understanding; words sometimes just got in the way.

Tanya offered Chaiko and Samar some smoked mushrooms filled with roasted grubs sprinkled with crushed hazelnuts. Samar held up a hand to decline her offer; his gums were too sensitive to crunch on the hazelnuts. Chaiko munched on the tasty mixture happily till he suddenly realized what he was ingesting: grubs. The taste suddenly turned sour in his mouth and he swallowed quickly. He had been feeling incredibly light, now that his brother was awake and alert, conscious of a great load taken off him. Even in his weakened state Baer offered more reassurance than anybody in full strength could, and this radiated throughout the whole camp like a good fire offering warmth and comfort.

Swarms of flies, frisky in early season rites, buzzed around them. Lana fanned them away from her father. He smiled weakly at her and drifted off to sleep. The rest remained quiet, not wanting to disturb him. Tanya hovered over them, anxiously guarding her mate's rest.

After eating, to shake off the growing lassitude, Chaiko headed into the woods to search and gather. He followed a path he alone used. Most people were reluctant to wander here by themselves in the closeness of the trees, as predators could be lurking in the undergrowth. Chaiko, however, was not afraid and welcomed the loneliness; away from the prying eyes he moved about faster and with less effort. As far as predators were concerned, with his back to a tree and a spear in hand he felt equal to a lynx or even a mountain lion. "Do not turn your back on a lion, thereby inviting its charge, but show it the sharp end of your spear and slowly back away," Chaiko thought, recalling the hunting lore that was taught to every child. The greatest danger here was big brown bears, but the creature made so much noise in moving through brush and trees, it could easily be avoided.

As Chaiko moved under the trees he scanned the ground for small creatures crossing his path. The earth between the girth of two tall trees was worn bare and well marked with sharp imprints of many paws, so he set a noose snare hoping for a raccoon or a rabbit. A little further on he followed many tracks again as the animals tried to skirt a line of rocks. The scent of pine needles drying was strong there. A woodchuck and another rabbit seemed possible. He propped a heavy flat rock with two sticks delicately balanced, baited with young celery shoots. The blow would be fatal.

He came to a clearing and the glare that greeted him suddenly hurt his eyes. Higher up, a haze shimmered and scattered the light. There was no depth of blue in the sky at all. At the foot of a lone walnut tree he dropped his carryall. He hefted his spear in his right hand, taking confidence from the smooth feel of the shaft. He rocked back, then snapped forward at the waist, swung his body around the left staff, and launched his spear into the air. He struggled hard to keep from falling. The spear landed among a clump of ferns, a disappointing throw which missed its mark, short on distance. Again and again he tried, and though his balance improved, the spear continued to fall too short. He could match maybe a throw from a ten year old. Why, he threw better four years ago, before his mishap. Discouraged, he sank to the ground, winded by his efforts. When he won back a calmness of breath, he tried again, then again. He concentrated on smoothness of movement rather than depending on strength alone, and was rewarded with better accuracy and a somewhat longer range. He tried to launch into an even motion early on and maintain the flow, especially through the awkward swing around his left crutch, the final snap of elbow straightening, and the follow through to regain his balance. With practice the movement became more natural but though his accuracy increased, his range did not.

The exertions tired him and he had to sit down. Though he was disappointed by his apparent lack of progress, he knew that all things took their own time to develop. He rubbed his good calf against a cramp. Most times he lived with a pervasive stiffness from the constant effort to compensate for his missing limb. Any new activity tended to incite cramps.

He realized that even if he could increase the throw to twice the present distance, it would still not be enough for a hunt, and he did not have the mobility required for the chase or the final rush to finish off a wounded animal. Could he hunt from a blind hiding spot, ahead of the expected path of an animal? A rare event, when an animal came near enough to a fixed spot. That was more akin to hoping than hunting, Chaiko concluded. Anyway the kill was the consummation of the hunt, a small part, between the long trek to find game, track then chase, the rush to kill followed by butchering and dressing the meat, and a long haul home. Even if he could last through all that, he would slow down any hunting party.

He needed hunting magic that the stories talked about, but no one he knew had actual knowledge or use of it. He had carefully reviewed all the songs that spoke of magic, but the few clues were vague and nondescript, seeming to hide more than to reveal. Still, magic, too, was aimed and then cast like a spear. Maybe at the next Gathering due three years hence, he could learn more about it. It seemed to him that the great practitioners the songs spoke about were all long dead. But then for him there could be no Gathering, so far away, certainly beyond his reach. Everywhere he turned he found only another way closed to him.

The clan had missed the last Gathering because of the harsh winter that preceded it. There had not been enough food and hunger and illness preyed upon the weak. A few had even died that winter. The rest were weakened and some became ill; they had needed all their energy just to hunt and gather to restore themselves. They could not take time out in midsummer, with the storage-pits all but empty, for the long trip there and the long trip back. It was a prudent choice to forego the pleasures of the Gathering, but they had all missed the much looked-forward-to event. The next winter was milder and the food stores were adequate, but the fear of hunger was always in their midst.

Chaiko had been to the Gathering twice; the first when he was only five, which he barely remembered, and then when he was nine. He was most struck by the crowds of countless people, numerous as bison on the plain, all doing something, all belonging somewhere. To a nine-year-old, used to the comfortably small clan, the sudden extent of all the clans was nigh incomprehensible. He had been an impressionable child anyway and all the activities excited him beyond measure. He did not know where to look first or what to do next. Crow, who did not have to know everything, had a great time running with a pack of age-mates, joining in all the mischief, the jokes, the singing and dancing, the feasts and the storytelling. Chaiko was overawed by all the traditions he saw and all the wisdom he was surrounded with. Would he ever see another Gathering? Most likely not - the Gathering was outside the range of a cripple - that sad fact kept repeating in his thoughts.

He lay back on the grass and let the future with all its problems go. He shut his mind to the insistent voices in his head and tried to find shelter in the present. He listened to the buzz of insects and the restless rustle of the wind among the grass and leaves. The noise of a small creature scurrying in the undergrowth reached his ears but did not break into his awareness. Slowly the tension went out of his body, the curve of his spine relaxed and he melted into the soil. He felt the push of the earth supporting him, and was filled with yearning for the Earth Mother, wishing her to be true, wishing he could believe in her. The feeling was gone in an instant, leaving him questioning. Sunlight danced on the leaves of the walnut tree above and he closed his eyes against the disconcerting glare of the open sky.

Suddenly, the loud staccato burst of a woodpecker working on a nearby tree wrenched him fully into the present. The hard and precise series of knocks compelled his attention. A quick burst, followed by a new sequence, came reverberating across the glade. He could not block it out or ignore it, but followed the rhythmic cadence of the hammering. In one of the pauses he tapped on the tree trunk with the butt of his spear in imitation of the cadence. The woodpecker was surprised into silence by this unexpected reply. It flew off to a new perch, its claws digging into wood. Chaiko repeated the sequence, trying as hard as he could to imitate the burst of crisp energy the bird had shown. Even to his ears it did not sound quite right, but the bird, intrigued, flew near, swooping into view to spot the source of the sound that was not a woodpecker. In a short glide into the open, the man and the bird looked at each other, their eyes met... and recognized each other's curiosity. After circling his location a few times, the bird flew off, but even from afar the staccato rhythm reached Chaiko's ears for a while.

Perhaps a part of the magic of drawing an animal in close is to arouse its curiosity, Chaiko thought, yet the in-built caution of most animals unleashes flight at anything unexpected.

The sunlight was slanting steeply through the foliage when he started back. Neither snare had caught anything but he found a cluster of mushrooms and that pleased him. A little further he found a nest in a thorn bush that held three eggs. Lana would be delighted with the speckled eggs, he mused.

Once he left the cover of the trees and was on the open terrain he noted the strange shadow high in the sky. It seemed more marked on the weather side to the west. He had to pause several times on the steep slope leading up to the open crest before the cave where they were temporarily encamped. The smoke curled from the fires, each surrounded by a group of people. They appeared subdued and hardly noticed his arrival.

The hunters had come back—empty handed. Earlier, Kor and Calla had dared to go into the cave, and had opened one of the storage pits in the back so there was plenty of meat from the first hunt. The spits were turning over the fires and the tantalizing aroma floated in the air, but it did not lift the sullen mood of the hunters. All day Tusk had driven them in search of something worthy to bring back. They had ignored a few lesser game since he was so intent on bison or giant elk, but they had seen none, not even in the distance, not even any spoors.

The hard pace and the lack of success had made them irritable, and Rea had snapped at Gill who bit back, snarling. Tusk had not intervened; he had wanted an angry pack of wolves he could point at the game, and so the dark mood of the hunters suited him. Yet when they had found nothing by the end of the day, he too was snarling. People stayed away from him, warned off by the angry cast of his eyes. It did not help his mood to see Baer's improvement and the resurgence of hope this occasioned. He wanted to be their rescuer—and weak as he was, Baer was upstaging him. His brooding countenance darkened even more.

Crow returned Bogan's tell-stone, more than ever convinced of its efficacy. Even though they had not found game, it had kept them all from harm. "Guard it well," he admonished Chaiko as he relinquished the stone. "It doesn't just belong to you, it belongs to the whole clan." This astonished Chaiko, as he was not used to Crow taking such a large view of anything. He resolved to value the stone more, in respect of his friend's admiration of it. After all, he reasoned, the tell-mark had to have power to achieve such an effect on the usually impervious Crow.

From his place Kor looked up from his work and watched the ugly mood painted on the hunters' faces. "Bah, what kind of hunters are these?" he asked in a half tone that only Calla could hear. "These have the patience of water, not the patience of stone," referencing indirectly the most often used quote of hunting lore. Well, if anyone knew then it was Kor, the worker of stone, about how much patience stone really had.

At sunset, the color display of the morning was repeated with a rich magenta hue mixed in. The sun seemed to linger longer than usual before disappearing below the horizon. Cosh and Baer were quietly talking on the other side of the fire, and Chaiko felt his brother's eye on him repeatedly, but he was not called over to take part. Baer was tired still, with a curious flatness to his voice that lacked the usual resonance. He soon settled down, joined by Tanya and Lana, in a close family huddle. All around, the talk petered out as the camp succumbed to the darkness that seemed darker than usual.

The pale moon barely reflected off the smooth waters of the lake. The crickets' strident song filled the stillness. Occasionally feeding wood to the fire, Chaiko replayed the day, trying to determine what was nagging at him. Over the past few days there had been moments of enjoyment that overtook him by surprise. He had felt guilty that these moments distracted him from the self-appointed task of watching over his brother and the clan. Still, they loosened another knot in the tightness with which he had bound himself after the loss of his leg. Was it this thaw in his soul that was bothering him? Or was he sensing danger building up again? What danger? He chewed on the thought for a while, and decided that the quake and all that had happened since had made him oversensitive.

Somewhere an owl hooted, the eerie sound amplified by the cliff wall and the darkness. A bat flitted by; Chaiko felt the wings beat the air rather than heard it. "The bats are feeding," he thought with reassurance, and allowed himself to drift off for a brief sleep.

Chapter 11

At dawn the next day the rising sun seemed to be reflected by a heavy pallor that dominated the western skyline. The birds greeted the new day out of habit but lacked the usual exuberance that heralded the ascendance of light over darkness.

By midmorning, when it should have been fully bright, it was still but half-light as the smudge covered the entire sky and obscured all but the very centre of the sun's glow. A featureless grey mist arched overhead like the roof of a cave, with a steady sense of movement toward the east. It looked like dirty fog, but who had ever seen fog so high?

The people reacted uneasily to this new surprise. What was happening to their world? First, the earth shook and opened up in places, and now the sun hid itself. How did the old story go? Father Sun and Mother Earth. The People called themselves Children of the Earth, and talked vaguely of the Earth Mother when trying to explain their origins. All living things came from the Earth Mother, did they not? But Father Sun was a murky concept, and certainly no one of the Standing-Rock Clan understood it. If it was obvious to most that the light and warmth of the sun was needed to bring fertility to the soil, the deeper comprehension of this was certainly lost to them in the morass of superstition that permeated their lives. Now, facing a new unknown, the more fearful among them clutched their lucky talismans to ward off this new menace. The children were told to remain near and not to wander off.

Chaiko was sitting by the fire, a little off from the rest, assessing the import of the darkened sky. Although he had noticed telltale signs days before, he had attached little significance to them. Now with this upon them ... it bore looking into. He carefully scanned the sky, every bit of it, but the shapeless mass obscuring it gave him no clue to work with. He tried to concentrate, but there was some concern blocking the way of his thoughts. What was it? he asked himself irritably, but found no easy answer. A hunter on a chase must follow one prey at a time, focus on it or risk losing it all. He knew that first he had to clear his mind from this nagging preoccupation, so he could concentrate on the new problem. He forced himself to look at it dispassionately from a distance.

Repeatedly over the last few days he had had moments of enjoyment that he was unable to explain. For the past four years, suffering had so overlaid his emotions that joy had become unfamiliar, nay more, quite foreign to him. True, the earthquakes that shook the earth had also stirred up emotions long suppressed by pain and self-pity. Now the feelings welled up and spilled forth, refusing to be stuffed back out of awareness. The pain was still there but was mixed with glowing moments of joy and pleasure. Though he felt deep anguish over his brother's injury and helplessness, at the same time he also heard laughter of children around him that reached the forgotten child within him.

It was as if, after years of being afraid, and of shallow breathing, he was beginning to take full deep breaths again, the fresh intake of air clearing the gloom that had permeated his mind for so long and had become expected and habitual. He had resolved to change from an attitude of grim determination to one of freely given service; of watching and of guarding the clan without recognition or expectation of gratitude. He would serve like his brother without looking for his own advantage. And like him, he would serve because it was in him to do so and because he was capable of it. "Let him that can, do! And let him that can do well, do better!" he commanded himself in dedication. That was something Bogan had taught. He had freshly buried his severed leg. He had let go of his bitterness. He knew that he was no longer a prisoner of his past, he just had to learn to act according to that knowledge. The joy was an unexpected reward of the changes in him, and with that, too, he would have to learn to live.

Thus, having cleared his mind of this preoccupation with the past, he could look to the present. It had been four days since the quake, and then the aftershocks. They were obviously linked. Could this strange overcast be somehow connected to the quake? "Why should that be?" he asked himself, searching his memory for like events. Sometimes, looking west to the weather side, one could see clouds disgorging rain over the mountains and see the rivers rising the following day, flooding the plains the next. Perhaps this, too, was an event linked but separated in time. Was he looking at two different faces of the same event? He struggled to stay his mind on track; he sensed an understanding, but full insight was just out of reach.

He scanned the skies and tried to follow the flight of a few birds in the dim light against the featureless mist. They seemed to stay well below the cloud level, but one large eagle, looking for its normal cruising height, disappeared into its murky midst. Almost immediately it tumbled out of it, disoriented into an erratic flight. It soon recovered but made no other attempt to climb again while Chaiko tracked it. It quickly faded into the grey as if absorbed.

Still, as the morning passed and no real threat materialized, the people became reconciled to the cover over the sky to the extent that they were not going about craning their necks skyward expecting pieces of it to fall and crush them. It was just darker than normal, they told themselves, almost like a heavy overcast day. All the same they were reluctant to leave the nearness of the fires.

Tusk awoke to the strange skies and was filled with foreboding. It confirmed that this place was somehow cursed, though the concept was ill defined. Malevolent bad luck? Bad spirit effects? He preferred to blame Baer for it. He must have done something to bring on this additional menace. The sky also strengthened his wish to run, but where he could not decide. Here they were exposed in the open, the shelter of the cave denied to them, so they might as well be anywhere else. He was a man of action, but no good course of action suggested itself. Still, to flee grew and took hold of his mind and all the other thoughts turned to it like flowers turning toward the sun. It did not seem incongruous to him that yesterday he wanted to be the new master of the clan, but today all he wanted was to run away from it. Without having decided, he was already embarked on his new course. He cast a quick look about—who would he take? Not the whole clan— that would slow him down too much. To Tusk speed was always the essence of action. Speed in judgment, decision and action.

Near him, Stow and Tael noticed right away from the change in his body posture and his calculating glances that something was afoot. As hunters used to reading intent from small gestures of the prey they hunted, they could also read each other, and they moved in, interested. Having chosen this alliance they did not want to be left out of it. They had already learned that Tusk was wholly devoted to his own concerns and quite oblivious to theirs. He led by leading and his followers had better learn quickly to keep up with him. It was clear that he would lead even if no one followed. Actually, Tael found this disconcerting.

He followed Tusk because he calculated that the nucleus about Baer was closed to him. If he wanted more status than his years entitled him to, he must risk it on the only other source of power that he could find in so small a clan. Now, he was faced with the realization that his support for Tusk might not be reciprocated. Had he then risked all for nothing? No, he concluded after a short reflection, because Baer was not a vindictive type, and overlooked missteps by others. That reassured him for then he was covered at both ends.

Stow was a young man of seventeen who needed an object of focus. He had tried Baer first, but though the leader treated him kindly, he refused to accept the homage the youth needed to bestow. Baer was hard to understand as well. Furthermore, daughter Lana rejected his attentions and thus twice slighted he turned elsewhere—to Tusk. Indeed, the lead hunter was an impressive character, clearly the strongest man in the clan with few to rival him anywhere. He was a renowned hunter, and though he did not crave admiration, because of an ingrained conviction that took it for granted, he did not reject it either. This allowed Stow to make the lead hunter into an object of his admiration.

At the other fire, Baer awoke to find the camp frozen in indecision. Weak as he was, he called for a meeting. Cosh, Samar, and Chaiko came, but Tusk pointedly ignored the summons. Baer's eyes narrowed but he said nothing.

"What is this?" he asked Samar directly, gesturing at the skies, dispensing with all pretense at form.

Samar had been puzzling over this all morning and had an answer ready. "Long, long time ago, so far back I can hardly remember it, there were large forest fires in the distance. The sky was somewhat like this at that time. Smoke high in the sky."

"Then this is forest fires burning far away?" Baer wanted to know.

Samar did not answer him right away, seeming to be lost in some memory when he was still full of life. Reluctantly he tore himself back to the present and said: "The smoke was so, but it smelled different."

Cosh and Chaiko looked at him in surprise; a faint smell was there but hardly obvious. The old man shrugged "My eyes are blurry, but my nose is still keen."

"Can anyone see fires to the west?" Baer wanted to know. Cosh shook his head.

"Can you see the mountains?" he asked again. From where he was lying not much could be seen, but Cosh had been to Lookout, and reported, "There are no fires on the mountains. The smoke must come from beyond." No one had been beyond.

Baer thought a while. "How is the grass in the plain?"

"Still green enough to withstand flames," Cosh replied evenly, having been there the previous day with Tusk's hunting party.

"Good." Baer nodded with evident relief. He sank back into a more relaxed pose and Tanya gave him a wooden bowl (that Chaiko had carved from wild cherry) of fresh water. He drank slowly with so much gusto that Chaiko himself felt thirsty.

Baer considered again, looking in the dim light at the people about the other fires. He knew them and from a look he could read their worries. "If it is not forest fire, what could it be?" He addressed this to Samar directly.

The Old Man shrugged, "It just smells different," was all he would say.

They sat around quietly, each trying to figure out the puzzle. Cosh roused himself and said tentatively, "It smells a little like the bubbling mud in the hills."

Chaiko saw the two look at each other and read agreement into that exchange. He had never been deep into those hills, though he had heard tell of it, where the mud bubbled and steamed and the waters were hot, foul-smelling, brackish and undrinkable. Yellow salt crusted the earth crunching underfoot. Most were impressed by the overpowering smell of the unbreathable vapors, causing stinging eyes and choking spasms.

Chaiko looked up at the sky; the fog vault seemed to have settled closer to the ground. "It will smell stronger before the day is through," he said, not sure how he knew. The others looked at him in surprise. They sniffed the air.

Baer had seemingly accepted Tusk's decision to withhold his counsel. He sensed without anybody telling him the subtle shift that had occurred while he was sick. He knew the People of the Clan and, like all hunters, was good at reading small signs and gestures of the body. Now he looked at the clan and saw them as a small herd of bison, milling about disoriented and confused. Then he saw the impatience of Tusk growing, and likened him to the bull that with a sudden bolt would take half the nervous herd with him.

"Cut him out," he told himself. "Send him away, before he can stampede the rest."

"There is some danger from the west," he summed up their thoughts. "We had better look for safety to the east." He waited for them to react, then continued, turning to Cosh. "Go to Tusk. Tell him to check the route to the east. If we are forced to flee from this ... this new thing, we must know what direction to take. After the earthquake, the known routes may be blocked." He was thinking of the deep gorge they would have to cross. "Let him take Stow and Tael. They would want to go anyway. And Malek." Chaiko approved. Even if the others kept running, Malek was reliable and would come back with vital information they needed. "Do, but ask nicely," Baer called after Cosh, unnecessarily, for Cosh would ask in his direct manner unworried about consequences.

They watched Cosh go up to Tusk, and squat down at a respectful distance, waiting to be invited, a very formal gesture between hunting compatriots. Just enough time was allowed to pass to make Cosh aware that he was asking, but just short of being insulting. Tael and Stow waited for Tusk, studiously not noticing Cosh till he did. Baer and Chaiko watched the flow of conversation among them, reading from body language the progress of the proposal. Cosh leaned into his earnest attempt to convince Tusk of the necessity of the path-finding. His hand motions remained calm and measured, but conveyed urgency and need. They watched Tusk's stiffness melt, then get drawn into the proposal, and finally, when the gestures stopped, turn inward to consider it. From afar, the watchers knew even before Tusk that he would accept. They saw the determination growing in the set of his jaw and the forward lean of his body as he nodded finally in agreement. Cosh came back, pleased with his efforts and they smiled with him.

Tusk was pleased too. He had the reason he had been looking for all morning. Scouting for a safe route to the east in case the whole clan needed to flee this threat was a great pretext to break camp, without looking as if he were running away. A quick pace would burn off the accumulated tension from these damned dark skies weighing so heavily on him. Maybe if they moved fast enough they could outdistance the darkness. He looked appraisingly at his companions. Stow and Tael would be welcome, and Malek would be acceptable. A couple of days on the trail, moving quickly, would trim them into shape. It didn't bother him that it was Baer who had come up with this plan; it fitted so well with his own inclination that in his mind, he assumed ownership. To the clan, he would be looking for a safe passage for them all, Tusk the leader serving the good of many, and would be admired for it.

The four wasted little time. They gathered the necessities, broke camp and disappeared in a fast lope down the slope. The youngsters followed them for a short distance, and their shouts of well-wishes could be heard echoing after them. By now everyone in camp knew that some danger was expected from the west and that safety was sought to the east. No one had trouble agreeing that Tusk was the best choice to find them a safe route in case they had to flee. On the whole, the clan felt reassured and sought things to do in the half light.

Nebu and Ela were commiserating with each other because both their mates had gone on the scouting expedition. Nebu had been near tears as she took leave of Malek and had struggled for something meaningful to say, but all she could come up with was, "Don't bring back any rabbits." Malek had looked at her with a strange expression—this was not a hunting expedition - but promised that he would not.

Ela had clung to her mate as they made a great show of leave-taking. Ela had cried copiously and Tael had reassured her with a considerable display of affection. Friends had to peel her off her mate, and support her, so overcome was she by the drama of the moment. After a while, even Tanya became irritable and snapped at her, "Pull yourself together, girl; he is only going for a short time." Ela then sought to engage Nebu in a show of sorrow and devastation, but Nebu would have none of it. Though she secretly envied the younger woman's abandonment of herself and her freedom of expression, she could not bring herself to emulate it. In fact the more Ela carried on, the more stone-faced Nebu became.

Simm was with the rest of the clan watching from the sideline, smiling somewhat sardonically at the show. Both Tael and Ela had played their roles with as much publicity as they could garner. They did this all the time, Simm groaned inwardly. He was glad that Tael's absence would give him a respite from all this; Ela was so much more real when Tael was not around.

As the day advanced, the layer above them seemed to grow heavier and to settle closer to the ground. All sign of the sun disappeared and the day turned into a long dusk. From time to time an unpleasant odor mixed among them.

Gill and Rea had not been speaking with each other since the ill fated hunt of the previous day. Since they shared a fire with the other unmated men, they could not avoid each other but each pointedly ignored the other.

A pocket of foul air swirled down from above and enveloped Rea in its embrace. It reeked with such concentration that he nearly fainted and was forced onto his knees. He clutched his throat and gasped for air, but every intake of breath increased his pain.

Gill, who only got a light whiff of the stuff, looked askance at him at first, then grew angrier and worked himself into full rage. "Water, water," Rea pleaded, trying to shut down all his senses at once.

"You faker, stop pretending!" Gill exploded. Then the miasma overtook him and he choked too. The foul stench was bad, very bad, and penetrating. Dead fish that had stayed in the sun too long was not as bad as this. Passing gas after ingesting spoiled meat was not as bad as this. The collective outpouring of the sweat glands of the entire clan was not as bad as this. In fact all of these things taken together, were not as bad as this.

Mercifully, a gust drove the stink out of the way, leaving the two helpless men on the ground gasping for air like fish out of water. In spite of their excruciating need, the two sipped shallow breaths of air, afraid to trust a whole lungful. "What was that?" Gill croaked through parched lips.

"That was foul, rotten ... vile," crackled Rea when he finally found his voice, looking for words to describe the experience. His mouth, nose and eyes burned, and he was nauseated. Both were totally unnerved. They were, however, talking to each other once more, and neither brought up their previous disagreement again. To their surprise, in the half-light nobody had noticed their miseries and no one else seemed similarly affected.

Sitting near the broad opening of the cave with a good view of the skies, Chaiko kept a close eye on the slowly descending fog. The formation lacked detail or features, a shapeless, opaque mass that sealed the sky from horizon to horizon. It looked menacing and oppressive. The air was noticeably heavier, and Uma who had weak lungs, found it almost impossible to breathe. A whiff of choking odor set her coughing, and she was racked by spasm after spasm.

As much as the dim light allowed, Chaiko watched the birds. He sensed more than saw them, in short flights that stayed well clear of the layer above. They were quiet and confused. In the absence of the sun and the bright light of day, some of the night birds also were flying, looking for their usual prey hiding in the undergrowth. The day thus met the night, and creatures of both were disoriented by the pallor that was neither dark nor light.

Then without notice, day passed into night, and people, animals and birds were caught by surprise, their settling down routines disturbed by the suddenness of the darkness upon them. It had been a most disagreeable day, the threat all the more ominous because it was so ill defined, arousing all sorts of fears. They had thus lingered aimless all day, suspended by their own apprehensions.

During the night the darkness deepened, no moon, no stars able to penetrate the prevailing gloom. Only the fires of the Standing-Rock Clan struggled weakly against it. The smell grew stronger, stinging the eyes and the inner membrane of the nose.

Later still, the wind picked up, whispering along the grasses and rustling among the leaves. The turbulence stirred up the layer above, driving it toward the east, shredding it, pushing pockets of fetid air down onto the ground. Lightning flickered in the west over the mountains, illuminating for an instant a quarter of the horizon, being absorbed and reflected by this strange vault in the sky. The storm was rapidly coming closer. Lightning flashed over the plains, its brightness alive for seconds, then swallowed by the gloom. The distant rumble of thunder rolled and grew. The clan stirred uneasily watching the storm approach. Children and adults alike were awed by its power. Baer, his voice rising above the tumult of wind and growing thunder, yelled for everyone to take shelter in the cave. "Move! Get into the cave! Deep as you can! Make sure you hold onto your children! Help each other!" The rest was drowned out by a fresh burst of wind that raked over them.

Stumbling about in confusion and disoriented by the darkness laced with flashes that showed a dance of light and shadow, the clan, clutching its few possessions, ran for the cover of the cave. It was preferable to be crushed to death in the cave than have to face the storm in the open. Hard choice. It was a foot race between the clan and the fury of the storm. They were hardly under the overhang when the first stinging drops of rain pelted them. They sought shelter in the very deepest part against the back wall, huddled in a close mass, both for comfort of sharing the peril and for warmth in the sudden chill.

Then the leading edge of the storm was fully upon them. A gust of wind tore through them, throwing a stinging whirl of dust in their faces. A flash lit up the surroundings in sharp relief, held it for a flicker then winked out into total blackness. The clap of thunder was immediate, soul-shatteringly loud, with a back snap at the end. Immediately, there was another flash, then another, and their sounds merged into one continuous crashing rumble that shook the earth beneath them and the sky above. It rattled their bones and their innards resonated to the war of noises. The People cried out in terror, clutching each other, seeking to press themselves into the stone. Then the suffocating smell seared their throats and filled their eyes with tears. They choked and gagged as they fought for air through constricted throats that wanted to close. Even in the very back of the cave the gust drove the rain at them, flailing drops stinging with grit.

Time stopped, as hearts seized in fear of the awesome clash of light and thunder, continually roaring and flickering. The sounds boomed in their ears, the pain of it boring into their bones. The people covered their heads and ears protectively to escape the rumble growing to a continuous rolling of sound high in the sky, coming nearer and nearer, then the splitting of the air with a horrendous crack as a thunderbolt struck the earth boring into the ground, shaking and vibrating with the impact. The brightness burned through clenched-shut eyes and the rumble pressed into their stomachs and chests, lungs rattling in resonance. The smell of discharge, burnt grass and wood mixed in the air with the foul stench that was about. The wind whipped at them, tearing at their hair and furs, as they were pelted by hard rain they were soaked, gasping for air.

Cowering against the cave wall, Chaiko felt puny and helpless in the face of this violence. The wind buffeted his body, alternatively tearing at him then slamming him hard against the rocks. He struggled for the next breath, his lungs burning for air. He had never seen a storm this intense before. Fear ate at him. Though he knew Baer could not help him now— no one could—the thought of his brother gave him strength. Beside him, Uma was trembling in terror, and he put a protective arm over her heaving shoulders.

The sights and sounds of the storm continued unabated. A flickering blue light filled the inside of the cave. Chaiko shut his eyes against the blinding flashes and confusion of dark and light jumping from place to place, reflected off the cave wall. His ears were ringing, and he covered them with a corner of his fur wrap. Still every inch of his body felt the rolling thunder overhead, then the sound slapping his face with stinging blows as the lightning discharged time and time again. His senses were overloaded and he could not think. He fought down the rising panic, a cramp growing in his belly. A lightning bolt struck the ground very near, split wood, split rock, split the earth, and the sound of it was too loud to be heard, but lashed out as a blow that threw Chaiko into the midst of a protesting, struggling mass of limbs. Smoke swirled about and a new smell of singed earth was heavy in the air. Then a peculiar jolt hit them all and they convulsed as one heaving mass of flesh suddenly rigid with the fading power of lightning coursing through them, leaving them jerking and trembling uncontrollably, struggling for breath, struggling for control. Someone near him, unrecognizable in terror, was screaming open-mouthed, but Chaiko could not hear him; he felt but a painful throbbing in his ears. Another lightning strike nearby flooded the cave with light and sound that rebounded from the face of the cliff. The cave trapped the sound which reverberated in its confines, like the inside of some giant drum. The wind beat at them, robbing their lungs of air, and flinging them about. A branch was swept into the cave. And a dead bird. A gust nearly tore Ela's baby from her gasp; only Simm's great hulk kept them anchored.

The very heart of the storm was passing over them in a continuous barrage of lightning and thunder that rent the air and split soul from bone. The storm was so strong it could not grow any stronger, and in that slow realization, Chaiko was the first to find hope. "If the first blows of the storm did not kill us, maybe we can yet survive ... we will survive." And he felt the rush of joy of all survivors, and he wanted to stand up and shake his fist in defiance of the elements railing at them, if they would let him. The panic had passed, the fear receded, but the joy also subsided as reality intruded. There were still lightning, thunder, wind and rain, but he could watch them composed, disinterested in the outcome, as an observer.

This detachment allowed him to appreciate the beauty of the storm. In the confusion of his overburdened senses, he could still find beauty in the intensity of the raging tumult. The display of light and sound was dazzling, but it was the power that was most compelling. That power could sweep him, his clan and all living things in the valley into nothingness. Had this power sought to kill them, and failed? Like a hunter hunting the hunted, had it missed its target? Or were they just in the way, as if surprised by a moving herd of bison? Or had Baer's luck saved them again? Were Tusk, Stow, Tael and Malek caught in the open? He shuddered at that possibility.

In his musing, he almost missed the subtle change. The storm was no longer pushing but was pulling at them. With a triumphant jump of his heart he realized that the back end of the storm was now passing. The lightning was still as intense and the thunder as loud, but the wind was no longer whipping the rain to drench them. The air was lighter and the stench abated somewhat. It was becoming easier to breathe. The centre of sound had shifted as well; it was no longer hammering at them from all around but seemed to be coming more and more from the evening side. When he heard an echo from the east, he knew for sure that the storm centre had passed. All his muscles ached, he had a cramp in his stomach, his head ached, his ears buzzed when they did not ring, his skin stung, and his throat and nose were swollen; even his hair hurt. Otherwise I am quite well, he commented to himself, and still alive.

Tentatively he tried to stand against the painful stiffness of his limbs. He had a few bruises from being tossed about that would hurt as soon as the shock passed. Baer appeared next to him, grimacing against the pain in his ribs. Chaiko hoped that his brother had not reinjured himself. Baer was saying something, his mouth forming words, but Chaiko could not understand the sound because of the ringing in his ears, and was too drained to make an attempt to concentrate. All around people were slowly realizing that the worst was over and were daring to lift their heads. A few, pummeled into insensitivity, babbled and trembled still with shock, eyes wide, mouths slack, salivating.

Chaiko, Baer and Cosh went to the mouth of the cave to have a look around. There was not much light to see details, and each shut his eyes reflexively against lightning strikes further off, but they could sense the storm coursing to the east. The lightning flashed more and more in that direction. A gentle rain washed over them.

As they stood there and looked out at the darkness through the cave opening, each realized that they were in the cave, staring at the abandoned campsite in the open. They exchanged quick looks and the eyes agreed that, quake or no quake, the clan would not go back outside to camp. For better or worse, they would stay in the cave. Chaiko tasted the rain; it had a gritty feel to it and when he wiped his face there was a coarseness he could not explain. Then suddenly the darkness all around them lit up and an explosive crack of sound lifted and threw them back deeper into the cave. A blue light hit a tree beside Tall-Frog tree, in a shower of sparks and flame that raced down the trunk and ribbons of blue light separated like roots and bore into the ground. Instantly there was a glow to the opened core of the tree, and a sudden billow of smoke rose up. The tallest limb swayed and fell, heavily crashing to the ground, breaking into many smoldering pieces. As far as they were from the tree, they still felt the shock that hit them an instant later, leaving them strangely numb.

Chaiko realized that they had been hit by lightning again, luckily not directly, or as bad as last time, but he was a little more aware of it, since there were fewer events competing for his attention. He had felt the power radiate out from the tree through the ground, then he was thrown down by the jolt of it. His limbs trembled; he had no command of them. The whiteness of his vision faded, and sight returned but he could not focus properly. Around him lay people struggling where the lightning had cast them. After several false starts he got up shakily, fighting the spasm still coursing through his muscles.

But that was the final parting shot. After that, the storm pulled away quickly, leaving just a gentle drizzle in its wake with a steady mild flow of air following the storm. People were recovering slowly, though some still moaned convulsively, unable to stop. They milled about dazed.

Chapter 12

After a fitful sleep of exhaustion the clan woke to find the sky lightened of its load, as if wrung out by the storm. The sky was higher than before, though a pale veil still shrouded the sun, already high in its orbit.

There was a light covering of ash on the ground, speckled with black grit beaten down by last night's rain. A light odor lingered in the air, but the rain had rinsed most of it away.

With light, the devastation was apparent everywhere. The landscape that had barely recovered from the convulsion of the earth had once again been assaulted, this time from the skies. The tree near the cave that was hit by lightning was a charred trunk still smoldering. There was debris everywhere, from small twigs to branches, to whole trees, which, shorn of their leaves, lay all about the ground scattered by the force of the wind. Here and there bushes lay uprooted, and there were bald spots where even the grass had been plucked out of the ground. There was no wind shadow to catch and accumulate debris, as the wind had swirled from all directions in its macabre dance of destruction. The people were thankful for the solid rock around them, so recently feared.

People cautiously ventured forth picking a way through the heaps of destruction scattered about everywhere. The women started collecting some of the branches blown into the cave and examining their own hearths with a mixture of gladness and sorrow: gladness, because each thing found was cause for rejoicing. People tried to talk to each other over last night's wind that was still hissing in their ears. Released from the terrors and the tensions, smiles and laughter erupted spontaneously. As if by agreement, no one spoke of the earthquake and of the danger still threatening from possible cave-ins, which now seemed preferable to the dangers of the open.

The world outside the cave was also recovering. Ants, termites and bugs that hid beneath were busily repairing their abodes. Insects buzzed about in swarms, having amazingly survived the night. Birds took flight and swooped among the clouds of insects, or sought grubs in exposed wood, or devoured worms flushed from the ground by the rain. A fox ambled by within sight, dragging two dead birds in its mouth. A squirrel was trying to find its hoard, trying to find its lair. The tree was gone. A bird circled anxiously above, looking for her nest and her three brown eggs.

People returned loaded down with birds and animals caught by the storm. The child Sosa, having dared to go as far as the creek, came back babbling about fish floating belly-up in the water.

Chaiko had slept through what remained of the night, the first time in almost four years that he had not kept vigil by the guard fire, and in spite of his aches awoke refreshed and clear-headed. All the fires were out, first drenched by the rain reaching into the cave and then the ashes scattered by the howling gusts of wind. Leaning heavily on a stick, he hobbled over to the tree struck by lightning, held a tight twist of grass against a smoldering crack in the trunk and blowing gently, fanned the heat back into his face. The grass dried, turned brown and curled in a wisp of smoke. Blowing with steady gentleness, Chaiko nursed the entire wad to catch the smoke and a new fire was born. This was how it must have happened that first time, Chaiko thought, as a man took possession of fire and accepted the gift of the sky. Tanya was there with an armful of grass and leaves to bed the fire. She then covered it for the short trip back to the cave to ignite the big communal fire in the centre. Eager hands brought wood and kindling and the fire soon took hold, giving a new heart to the cave. Things were slowly returning to what they should be and the People of The Standing-Rock Clan took comfort.

Crow came to Chaiko dragging a reluctant Makar with him. Since his father had died of illness during the bad winter two years ago, Makar had been taking meals with Emma and Crow, but slept with the rest of the unattached males at a separate fire at the back of the cave. Makar and Crow were friends of sorts, but Makar did not know how to react to Chaiko, which explained his reservations. Chaiko looked over both of them. They looked worried. As Crow explained it, they felt oppressed by the series of untoward occurrences happening to them; first the earthquake, then the smoky sky, the black rain, and now this storm of all storms. And there was no game anywhere. What was wrong with the world? Crow railed against these forces out to destroy him ... personally.

Makar, who did not like this presentation, broke in. His usually lively face and laughing eyes that looked for jokes everywhere were constricted with worry. "Perhaps **we** broke some major taboo, and thereby called all these misfortunes upon **ourselves**."

Apparently they had been scaring each other, Chaiko decided. Watching Makar's face, remembering his many jokes played on them all, with mock fierceness he asked accusingly, "And what taboos have you broken?"

Makar froze in terror at the accusation, his jaw dropped open, and he nearly wet himself in fright. So he **had been** blaming himself for all this. Makar's face then changed to white and then abruptly red. Unexpectedly, he turned and ran. "What the ...? Where's he going?" Crow asked, then glumly went after him. What could Makar be blaming himself about? wondered Chaiko. For the injuries Baer had received in rescuing him? Most likely. He knew that to Makar all gestures were large and grandiose. It was what made him so entertaining. What he felt he immediately expressed. But as this episode proved, he bore his troubles with equal zeal. Chaiko shrugged, people always surprised you.

He disliked talk of taboos as a facile way of trying to find the cause of an unexplained event. Yet, he could not dismiss it either. In the senses world they, too, were surrounded by taboos with lesser or greater effects. One does not throw fire into dry grass without the risk of burning the whole field and perhaps beyond. One does not jump off a cliff without some expectation of meeting what lies below. There are thus physical taboos one does not ignore without risk of consequences. It was, therefore, reasonable to surmise that spiritual taboos, if broken, would produce resultant spirit effects. Ones they could not see but, as Chaiko had to concede, would have to be inferred from an outcome. Mostly he was frustrated that he could not get his hands on the whole spirit world and could not understand how the rest seemed so willing to accept spiritual explanations and not search beyond.

Tanya with Ile cleared the space on the ledge reserved for the leaders and with Cosh's support, Baer was set on a pile of furs. From here he could see the entire cave and a good piece beyond: the open slope, and in the distance, the occasional flash of sunlight reflected off the lake. The layer above them was slowly lifting and the sun's warmth increased steadily.

Baer and Samar were talking in low tones as Cosh listened. Baer was trying to figure out what to do next. He raised his head, and his eyes swept over the clan as they busily cleaned and tidied their hearths. His eyes caught Chaiko's, and he waved his brother to join them. Even in the tumult of the night he did not miss his younger brother's steadiness and how clearheaded he remained in midst of a crisis, and he was glad. He remembered, on the other hand, Makar's heedless flight into the cave, scattering everything on the way in his rush to safety. Gill had been right behind him.

Baer looked at Chaiko and said but a single word, "Tusk," his gesture both uncertain and hopeful. Chaiko shrugged, indicating the debris all around and indirectly the power of the storm. Samar was content not to speak.

Finally Baer roused himself and told Cosh to go no further than the Willow Pond Cut to look for some sign of Tusk's party, smoke in the sky perhaps. Baer was uneasy with the thought that he had sent them off, and wondered if his luck had indeed changed. Cosh took Rea and they left.

A little later the women brought food prepared from the windfall of the night. Chaiko became pleasantly aware of a new respect, as the food was offered him. Ile's face was quietly solemn as she opened the leaf to present a roasted piece of duck with mushrooms, marsh onion and a sprig of calla. The meat steamed appetizingly, but Chaiko could barely smell it past the memory of the foul odor still burning in his nose. He drank deeply from a bowl that was offered, trying to wash away any residue of the night before.

The rest of the day slipped away in picking up, cleaning and settling into a "new" cave, the excitement fresh in their minds from their most recent brush with death. Both the cave and the people had changed, but it was only Chaiko, the observer, who really noticed how much. Baer felt it; the rest were caught up in it. The shaking of the earth and the pounding from the sky had stripped them of their taken-for-granted security, centered about their cave. The events had exposed their helplessness and the limits of human strength. But these same things also reawakened their joy in living.

Later in the afternoon, as the shadows stretched away from themselves Cosh returned with no sign of Tusk. He and Rea had gone as far as Willow Pond Cut, as instructed, and had seen devastation and wind damage everywhere, but they saw little else. There was no evidence of game, and worse, no tracks at the usual watering places. Even the marsh seemed empty of fowl. The sky continued to clear and the heat rose as the sun shone brighter.

Lana was playing with three-year-old Tay so that her mother Yaya could go to find some soap root with the rest of the women. (Even if the sky fell down people still had to bathe, especially after winter, having been so long prevented by the cold. One of the summer's pleasures everyone was looking forward to was swimming and bathing at every opportunity). Lana cradled the little girl and rocked her gently while singing softly to her. Nearby Chaiko enjoyed the sound of her sweet voice. Tay soon fell peacefully asleep and Lana eased her down onto the coverings. She hummed a while yet as she watched the young face relax. Soon after, Yaya came back, her carry wrap full of soap roots. Her words of thanks to Lana, though softly spoken, reached into the depth of sleep and her young daughter struggled awake. Yaya tousled Tay's hair and gave her a delicate piece of shell she had found in the sand. Tay looked with delight at its smooth pink sheen, then ran off to find Sosa and to brag to him about the new treasure their mother gave her. Yaya smoothed down the covers, frowning at the allotment of space, puzzling over its extent. It appeared too short. Then she noticed that the boundary stones had been moved. She called to Ela, her voice full glad to aim its hostility at her favorite target.

Soon Yaya and Ela were embroiled in an intense dispute over the exact locations of key boundary stones that had separated their sleeping places, somehow dislodged by the rush of people to safety in last night's storm.

"I tell you, these stones belong here," Yaya declared, her voice rising to call attention to the justness of her claim.

"They most certainly do not," retorted Ela, making her counterclaim known, proving once again that she was not shy. "She's trying to steal an arm-length of space from me," she asserted with gestures, inviting all to judge for themselves.

"Look, the fire stones have not been moved, and this fur has lain fully stretched between them and the boundary stones. Kray and I lie on it, night after night, year after year." Yaya marshaled her evidence to the crowd quickly assembling. "Look and see, it is she who would steal an arm from me and next she would take a leg as well."

"No, no. You're wrong," interjected Ela in a shrill voice, defending every bit of her nest. It would not do to have Tael come home to find them cheated. She took a deep breath to blow away the opposing Yaya.

"Wait!" commanded Tanya moving between the combatants, her face calm but determined. She did not want to draw Baer into this dispute. "Show me your claim. You first," she said to Yaya. Yaya placed the stones where she thought they belonged, then Ela where she was convinced they had been all these years. It was clear to all assembled that the same stones could not be in two places at once, as the distance of a good arm separated the competing claims. Tanya bent over the ground and carefully examined the lay of it, but the quake and the storm had obliterated all signs with a fresh layer of dust and sand. She shook her head, undecided how to proceed.

"Let the stones tell you where they belong," said Chaiko moving awkwardly into their midst. People looked at each other puzzled; how are stones going to tell you anything like that? Yaya pursed her mouth, her face reddening; Ela placed her hands on her hips. Both women were set to battle on.

Chaiko bent over the disputed ground and with a wing of an owl carefully swept away the debris. "Stones have roots in the ground," he murmured in that peculiar way of his, as if all wisdom was on his side, but many eyebrows were raised in contradiction; everyone knew that stones were not trees. Chaiko ignored their muttering, and continued his sweeping down to the original hard-packed soil, revealing the shallow depressions into which, one by one, he placed the stones—each a perfect fit. "The ground remembers," he said, pointing at the evidence. "The stones belong here, for here are their roots," he declared looking up at the two women. "You were both right," he continued kindly, indicating the stones that were now halfway between the rival claims. The crowd nodded wisely; they, of course, knew it all along. Tanya smiled to herself, glad of his phrasing; Chaiko could have equally said "You are both wrong," but chose not to.

By nightfall the cave was orderly. The old ground rights of families, confused by the earthquake, had been reasserted and boundaries re-established. A general feeling of relief prevailed that they were back again in the cave. The fires smoked thickly, because too much green wood had been piled on to burn off the sudden harvest plucked by the storm. There was some laughter, but voices were subdued as if still very much aware that nature was listening. Children cast off their caution first, calling to one another and laughing freely, a tribute to the moment that minded not the past nor yet feared the future.

Makar made a nest of his furs, then pretended to be a bird; he squabbled noisily with his nest-mate over space. He played both sides of this dispute, scolding and squawking, accompanied by excited flapping of wings. At this display even the adults laughed out loud so that he redoubled his efforts. Only Yaya and Ela could not see the humor in the performance.

This, of course, inspired Ruba to evict his brother Ork from the nest, but all it got him was a cuff from his father. Which went to prove that strength alone was often not enough; one also had to observe the prevailing pecking order and alliances.

Outside, the sky continued to clear, and the moon and a few stars shone through the veil that remained. The insects had recovered their competing voices. Once again by the guard fire at the opening of the cave, Chaiko watched the smoke sweep up and the sparks leap into the lightening air. He was still too tired to do much more than listen. He wondered where Tusk was. And he kept worrying about what had caused the upheaval in the west.

The following day the sun rose clear and gained quickly in intensity. Soon the air was filled with oppressive moisture trapped in its unmoving mass. Further into the day the heat increased, but still no wind rose to bring any relief. People kept to the shadows and did as little as possible. Even the children soon wilted in the heat. It was strange how this heat wave suddenly overtook them.

Still no sign of Tusk. Cosh went to the rim of the ridge that backed the cave, to scour the countryside for any indication of the expedition. The heat haze had built into a curtain that hid more and more of the distance. Cosh shaded his eyes against the glare of the scattered sunlight, but his eyes could find no relief from its piercing rays. He did not stay long, his skin glowing with the heat.

Throughout the day, Nebu and Ela went to Lookout, looking for signs of their mates. "Can you see anything?" Nebu asked the other hopefully; her eyesight was sharp normally, but ever since the hunt her eyes, irritated by smoke, were clouded by a small inflammation, especially sensitive in this haze.

"No, nothing," replied Ela, dejected.

"Look more to the east, along the Sandy Trail," Nebu suggested. Ela did, but she saw only the countryside suffering the build-up of heat.

"Do you think they could have fallen into the Gorge? Or been pulverized by lightning? ..." the younger woman would begin, painting a dire possibility, limited only by her restricted imagination. But fear was a great artist. Nebu shook off each of her conjectures. The sun was blazing fiercely and they fanned themselves, forcing some air past their faces, but could not stay long, exposed as they were.

The third time they went, Tanya and Ile joined them and sought to reassure the worried women. Although Nebu was deeply concerned, nevertheless she suffered quietly as was her nature while Ela made a show of it. They all searched the view, but the distance failed to yield its secrets.

The day passed slowly in listless misery. Once again no work was done. People tried to keep cool as best they could, drinking water and dousing their overheated bodies. For a while, the boys Ruba, Ork and Sosa made many trips to the creek to replenish their water supply, but after a time they got tired of this unselfish chore. Ela wrapped her baby in moist skins to keep him cool, but the baby cried, complaining, and would not be comforted.

The sun set with a gaudy display of colors. Chaiko regarded it with distrust; there were colors there that did not belong to the sky: the greens, the browns, the mauve among the yellows and reds. Don't react but observe what is there, he cautioned himself. There were still gases in the air, for every once in a while, the stench of rotten eggs would briefly swirl by. His mind searched for parallels. As the sun reflected in the rainbow that painted the water in the sky, so the gases painted the air as the sun shone through them, he thought. But where had those gases come from?

In the stillness of the night he realized with a shock that he had not thought of his mother or father in years. Both had died when he was young, and since his accident he had not spent much time looking back. Having so recently made his peace with the past, now he could look back and begin to reconnect with all his memories. He could recall his mother, father and himself when he could still walk and run. Yet, not having thought of them or of his own boyhood for so long, they and even he himself were strangers to the present. Thus he had but a confused reaction to the surfacing memories. An easy step at a time, he cautioned himself, immediately aware of the irony. To a cripple no step was easy.

The day dawned with another gaudy display, but some of the odd colors were leeched from the air. The sun rose into a cloudless sky, and soon the day promised to be hot again. While it was still bearable, people made a beeline for the creek to fill all the water bags. By midmorning the heat had built into an oppressive haze that pressed down on them, sapping everyone's vitality. Afraid of sunburns and sunstrokes, Baer decreed another day of rest. This promised to deplete their stores of food further, but in the heat, people ate little anyway. Only Simm's appetite was unaffected, though otherwise he suffered acutely all the other discomforts and at times could barely breathe in the heavy air.

In spite of the heat, Cosh once again went to scout the adjoining land but still could find no sign of Tusk. The distant view disappeared in a shimmering haze that the eye sought out, then recoiled from in confusion. Cosh was not prone to dejection, but his expression was downcast and drawn. Soon his report made the rounds at the fires. The people shook their heads apprehensively. What could have happened to them? Tusk was a powerful man; had he met his match in the storm and been bested?

Nebu and Ela went to Lookout and peered into the distance, but the heat haze obscured the view. Nebu held a piece of grass matting over her head to block out the merciless sun. Ela shaded her eyes with both hands. She was much subdued; the night had worn away at her, and frown lines worried themselves into her smooth young face. Seeing her fretting so, Nebu felt more sympathetic toward the younger woman.

By midday the heat was again unbearable. The motionless air, full of moisture, sat like a clammy weight upon them; even in the shadows sweat drenched their bodies, and their matted hair was itchy and uncomfortable. Their skin crawled with irritation from heat rash. It was difficult to breathe, and Uma was suffering acutely.

Some tried to find relief in the back of the cave, squeezing through a narrow passage to the interior gallery where Malek did the paintings on the cave walls. It was cooler there in the darkness, but the place was so airless that they found themselves panting, then gasping. They stayed only a short while, the heat being preferable to suffocation. How could Malek spend endless hours in this airless interior? Few of them could understand the soul of an artist, his overriding need to interpret the world and communicate it to future generations. For their art, artists suffered any discomfort.

Outside, the heat was unrelenting. Even the birds stayed out of sight, out of the scorching heat of the air. The few fires, lit to keep insects away, burned dispiritedly, the smoke unable to rise because of the heavy humidity. In this weather only the insects seemed to thrive. Huge swarms of all sizes buzzed about, getting into eyes, ears, noses and even into mouths. Most were not even bothering to wave them away but suffered the infestation listlessly. The flies came to lick salt from the skin.

Yaya went to get some water, for there was a great need to keep people cool. She was laboring up cave hill, a water skin in either hand. Tay, half naked, came running out to meet her on the open slope, pursued by Sosa trying to catch her. Yaya dropped the skins, spilling the water, then scooped Tay up and railed at her son as they all hurried back to shelter. "It was not my fault," mumbled Sosa, with the resigned tone of one who didn't expect to be believed.

14 Stones

Nightfall brought some relief from the heat, but the humidity remained clammy and heavy in the air. Most could sleep only in short snatches before being awakened by the irritation of their own bodies. The youngest whimpered even in their sleep. People drank from water bags tepid from the heat and were not refreshed, sinking back exhausted into a short slumber only to wake more tired than before.

Chaiko drifted in and out of sleep. He kept the fire burning or smoking with green leaves to discourage the insects, who would not be discouraged. The hum, the buzz, the strident sound of the bugs was unceasing. It seemed to grow in loudness and filled every part of the mind, making thinking nigh to impossible.

The next day and the day following were the same. Sweltering temperatures, suffocating humidity and clouds and clouds of insects. Almost everybody was showing open sores from their frustrated scratching to ease the irritation. There was an edge of desperation in the mood of the cave. Uma was breathing rapid, shallow breaths, followed by a desperate intake of air, then gasping in the rising panic of a person drowning. Emma was soaking her with water to try to keep the frail body cool. Emma herself found it difficult to breathe, so conscious she was of Uma's suffering.

The afternoon of the following day a light breeze sprang up from the west and brought instant improvement. The clouds of insects were driven off and the air started to lighten. People gratefully spread their limbs to allow the airflow to wash over them. The heat persisted but the oppressive weight of the humidity was gone. Slowly Uma was able to breathe more easily, though at times her anxiety returned and gripped her like talons around her throat, choking her. Ela was concerned about the rashes that made her baby miserable. Nothing seemed to help; neither root nor leaf-medicines could ease the discomfort. Oils squeezed from seeds, usually so efficacious, only softened the protective scabs that were forming.

The wind continued to be warm and picked up strength, swirling lightly about the cave. Refreshed, life resumed again. Baer sent a small party to scout for availability of game. He was developing a growing concern that so little had been sighted lately. Where was the large migrating herd of bison that by now should have covered the plains with their thundering mass? Where were the herds of antelope, horses, the wild cattle on the hoof? And where were the hunters, the lions, the tigers, the wolf packs and wild dogs? The few hyenas they saw had shrunken sides, ribs showing, testimony of a meager diet.

The women and children continued to collect the cast-off branches for the fire. A large pile grew by the cave wall. A couple of the men went to see if they could catch some fish in the river and came back loaded down. They confirmed that the fish had been dying, because the creek banks were littered with their carcasses. Judging by the smell ever since the storm, they were still dying in numbers, but the ones they brought back were very fresh, the meat still firm and springy and the sheen on the scales not dulled. The women quickly cleaned the fish, impaled them on sticks and set them over the fire.

With a break in the heat, people had rediscovered their appetites and fish seemed the ideal food for such temperatures, but most were suspicious of the unexplained nature of their deaths and were reluctant to partake. Many suggestions were offered, but finally Chaiko's explanation that the ash rain and the bad smell from the storm had poisoned the fish was generally accepted as the most likely. If it had not killed the people before, it should not kill them now. Regardless, there were still a few who abstained and chewed on dried seed cakes instead, the last of the last till harvest time.

By sunset, though the temperature had not dropped much, the air had dried out and the heat had become easier to bear. With nightfall the wind subsided to a gentle constant breeze that was most welcome to keep the air flowing over hot bodies.

The night was uneventful and to Chaiko, by the guard fire, it seemed that everything had returned to the usual. At least all the sounds that should be there, were reassuringly there. The waxing moon sailed across a cloudless sky in the centre of its bright glow that bathed the landscape in silver. Occasionally the shadow of a hunting bird would fly across its face making good use of the light to drop on its prey. Still, somewhat constrained by all that had happened in a short span of time, Chaiko was uneasy about trusting this seeming normalcy. He felt that if he let his senses be lulled by this ... the whole world might erupt ... again.

To divert his mind from uselessly chasing its tail with such thoughts, he worked on his Singing Stick. In spite of the constant tension of the string pulling against the bend in the wood, when released the wood still showed the tendency to twist markedly to one side. Chaiko had to admit to himself that he might not be able to straighten the wood out. It could not be a spear, he mused, looking at the wood to reveal what it should be—but it could sing. The wood had a rich smooth feel; some of that feel came from rubbing with finer and finer grains of sand, but the smoothness and density were inner qualities that emerged through the rubbing. No amount of rubbing could turn the light skinwood into this smoothness, the wood tending to peel off in long grains.

Perhaps it will stay a Singing-Stick, he mused, and tried to improve the sound to a consistent pleasing tone when struck. He found that by jamming a short stick between the string and the bent wood he was able to change the sound with some predictability. With the stick halved, the sound plucked from either half of the string was about the same. But as he shifted the stick towards one end of the Singing-Stick, the shorter string produced a higher tone, and the longer string a deeper. He spent a good part of the night experimenting with the length of string and the quality of sound and soon found that he could mark the position on the string that gave the best sounds, with a spot of berry dye.

So engrossed was he in this pursuit that he barely noticed the passage of night and was surprised by the first tentative calls of a morning bird in anticipation of the sun already lightening the east. Chaiko put away his Singing-Stick and concentrated on the awakening day. Insects and birds were first to show themselves. Soon, sounds of small creatures in the bushes reached his ear. A rabbit hopped into the open, then froze in an upright posture, intently regarding him, its nose wriggling and sniffing the air. Reassured, it hopped away on its rounds following a path that was worn bare by its many passings.

As the sun climbed higher into the sky, and the shadows shortened, the gentle breeze freshened into a constant wind out of the west. It dried what dew and moisture had accumulated in the grass. Once again there were no clouds and the sun beat down on them ruthlessly. The women went to get extra water and the children chased each other, dousing one another, and playing even in the heat.

Baer appeared to be somewhat better, but was still just a shadow of his old self. He favored one side and kept quiet as much as he could. Though the mark of pain was still etched into his face, his features were less drawn and more relaxed. Tanya thrilled at the flash of his quick smile and the sparkle in his eyes. Although he was still weak, his vitality was returning. Lana came and hugged him with careful tenderness. She then combed his hair and tied it together in back with a leather braid. Chaiko, too, was relieved to see his brother's improvement. He could feel the strong personality reasserting itself and casting off illness and fatigue.

The rest of the clan also noted that Baer was coming out of his illness. If only Tusk and his companions would return, the world would be a safer place again. Expecting to be led, they watched Baer's fire with anticipation for coming signs of the day ahead of them. Cosh came over and sat on his haunches, still chewing on a dried piece of fish. Samar came more slowly and after making a quick examination of Baer, settled down on the ground content to be silent.

When Baer spoke, the purposeful tone was back in his voice. He turned their attention to their most pressing concern. "We have to find Tusk," he declared, referring to all four.

Cosh nodded. "We could look more toward the north, where there is more open ground; through there they could have found an undisturbed passage to the east."

Chaiko, his eyes red from the smoke of the all-night fire, squinted at them. "Tusk might not follow the most direct path in this case. Try by the Salt Licks. When he was young he killed a giant bison there; I oft heard him talk of it. He likes to revisit that site."

Both Baer and Samar agreed, recalling the many times they too had heard Tusk tell the story over the years. Tusk had led many greater hunts since then, but this was from his early youth; the giant bison had left its mark on him. Cosh took Kray and left, promising not to venture too deep into the foothills. Throughout the day the dry wind blew steadily from the west, easing the heat from a fierce sun that blazed down on them out of an empty sky. The brightness was so intense that it dulled everything rather than highlighted. Even the shadows looked pale. The wind carried the heat along in a desiccating breath that sucked the moisture from the ground. Already the grass was wilting in spots where the soil was thin.

The working parties soon returned to escape the heat in the shade of the cave. Rea told of seeing a hyena give up a chase, its tongue hanging, and crawl into shade. It took a lot to deflect the greediness of a hyena following a blood trail.

"I tell you, the hyena crawled under a bush and lay down in the dust, his sides heaving, panting, tongue hanging out. It looked at us but did not move," Rea told Gill, shaking his head. "We too spent half the time hiding under some shade. That is a killing sun."

"I heard tell that a sun like that can drive a bison mad," contributed Gill to the discussion. "A whole herd searches out some water hole and they all crowd in for relief from the heat. Of course there is not room enough for all. The few squeezed out had better find a way to hide from the sun. The more experienced kick some dust over themselves for cover, but the younger ones do not know what to do. They burn in the sun, getting hotter and hotter, their dark coats absorbing the heat. Finally, because they do not know what else to do, they start running and running. The heat of their body increases, but they keep running until they drop. Dead." Gill wanted to best Rea's story.

"That's sunstroke," chimed in Emma, "I have seen old people and the very young drop like flies on days like these."

Early in the evening, Cosh and Kray suddenly appeared on the slope, between them supporting Stow who was having trouble putting weight on his right foot. It was Ruba who noticed them first and gave a mighty shout of discovery. The whole cave rushed down to meet them. Eager hands took Stow and carried him up the slope. Though it was against etiquette and custom, they barraged Cosh and Kray for details. Panting from the exertion of their fast pace, the two could only gesture for the rest to wait until they found their breath.

Back in the cave, they set Stow down, made him as comfortable as possible, while Nebu (whose meals he shared) fussed over him, hoping to hear some word of Malek. The people crowded around eager to read any detail on his face, but Stow was completely drained. His eyes, seeking to fix on something familiar, struggled against the waves of exhaustion, became unfocused and rolled back into his head. His eyelids could only half close. Someone called out to give him room and the crowd reluctantly pulled back, then slowly shifted to Cosh and Kray who were trying to report through ragged breaths to Baer. The crowd dared not intrude until Baer invited them closer.

Cosh did not know any details. They had found Tusk and the rest struggling across the open slopes just south of Salt Licks, all of them injured. Tael had broken a leg, the bone showing through the skin. He was already delirious with fever from his wound. The rest had exhausted themselves carrying him. Malek had a painful sprained shoulder and ankle but dragged himself along helping as much as he could. Tusk had pulled a muscle in his leg and his back. They had made a sorry sight when Cosh and Kray came upon them stumbling across the field under the weight of the injured Tael.

Ela grew pale at this news. Her hands went to her mouth protectively to ward off this pain, and her eyes grew large with the shock of worry. This time reality had outstripped her worst imagining and she did not like it. Calla hurried to her, patting her back comfortingly. "He'll be all right, child. You will see. Tael is strong and your cooking keeps him healthy." But it was not easy to reassure someone who was driven by an inner sense of melodrama.

The men had tried to decide what to do, but the group had been exhausted, barely able to keep moving. Their tiredness had clouded their minds with confusion, and every thought had been a weary battle against their lethargy. After much trouble it was decided that Cosh and Kray would help the more lightly injured Stow back, while Tusk and Malek would stay with Tael and await further assistance from the cave. Other than hearing some vague utterance that they had fallen down some cliffs, Cosh could add no more to this bare report. Of course, everyone wanted to rush off at once, but Baer ordered quiet and time for consideration, and for Cosh and Kray to recover. Obviously Tusk and party had not eaten for a while so food also had to be taken; Baer set the women to prepare that, while he ordered the men to gather skins to transport whoever needed to be carried back.

Having drunk and eaten, Cosh set about organizing the rescue party. Though everybody wanted to go, he chose carefully whom he would take along, over weak protests. They left in fading light, taking along torches to use later. The plan was to get there tonight, feed and cover the injured, make them comfortable, and attempt to return only in the light of day, but before the heat became intolerable. Before he left, Cosh said a few concerned words about Tael's condition to Baer and Chaiko. "In spite of fever, Tael was looking ... ashen," he warned, and regretfully shook his head.

14 Stones

The kids and part of the cave called out encouragement as they accompanied the departing group partway down the slope. When they came back to their places, the cave could not settle down, but there was general relief that Tusk's party had been found. They commiserated about the injuries and wondered about what had taken place to cause them. Tusk was considered to be too good a leader to be surprised easily. They recalled how the fierce storm mauled them even in the shelter of their cave. If the massive stones could not protect them from the full fury of the storm, then how much more violent it must have been out in the open. But they would have to wait to find answers to all their questions. Wait. Always wait. Often they were forced to wait like this, but they did not wait well, full of impatience, mouthing the well worn saying, "Have the patience of stone." Only the stones surrounding them waited patiently, for they waited without feelings, without hope. Chaiko thought, time waited for no man, but advanced at its own good pace; sometimes it crawled, as now, toward some expectation, when it should have hurried, sometimes it leapt over an event, a joy, when it should have crept to allow more leisurely enjoyment of it. Who was the master of time? Surely not man? Does the sky ask man when it may rain, or even where? No, few things waited for man. Stone being one.

Chapter 13

There was no one awake to witness daylight dawn upon the landscape. The twittering of birds seemed more subdued, perhaps because of the scarcity of insects in the present wind of this heat wave. The sun was swollen, already bright and shimmering. A heat haze was building on the horizon and the line of hills dissolved in a dance of confusion.

The rays of the sun reached a good way into the cave before someone stirred, then the whole cave seemed to swarm, aroused by the memory of last night's excitement and the anticipation for the new day. A line of watchers grew at the mouth of the cave, expectant.

"Ah what," someone offered, "They would only be starting back now." All the same, the line remained. People would come stand awhile, watch a spell, then go back to whatever they were doing. Periodically they would return, exchanging a few words with neighbors.

Around midday the line drew everyone, though by now it had moved back into the cave to hide from the direct rays of the sun and was skewed to stay in the full flow of a steady breeze. The anticipation was laced with nervous tension. When would they come? A youngster would stride into the open with every intention to go to the Lookout, but half way would turn around, his resolve wilting in the hot sun.

Chaiko could smell the dryness in the air, and feel the crow's feet around his eyes that grew from squinting into the glare deepened with worry. Everywhere he looked, plants sagged and trees drooped. Little by little, the grass was turning from dull green to brown and finally to sun-bleached yellow. The color of leaves gave a clue as to how far the roots of the plant reached into soil. The parched ground cracked as it shrank, and still the breeze blew to dry the moisture laboriously sucked to the surface by deeper roots. Chaiko scanned the west but found no clouds in the dancing haze. He started to worry about the tinder dryness and resolved to speak to Baer about it. A spark now could set the whole world on fire.

14 Stones

A small starling, beating against the wind, suddenly fell from the sky. Its wings fluttered sadly in the dust, then the last twitching ceased; a victim of heat stroke. The strident chirping of crickets sounded drier than usual, irritatingly so. A large bee hunted half-heartedly among the flowers for some nectar, but found only dried up lumps. Four buzzards high in the air circled something hidden below. "Death is not near yet," explained hunter Gill, who had come to stand beside Chaiko, "They're too high up. But something is hurt there. When they land, then you know death is nigh."

Waiting was tedious; the whole mind-set was focused on some future event and every moment seemed to delay it rather than to bring it closer. Was it not strange that waiting so displaced all other activity? Like a stone cast into water pushed the water aside to make room for itself.

Then abruptly, a figure emerged from the background around the lip of the down slope and behind him were others. The details blurred in the heat, but soon everyone recognized the purposeful gait that was Cosh's, followed by Rea and Kray carrying someone slung into a skin. The rest of the group came straggling into view, Tusk's great frame limping noticeably. Malek was being supported on either side. The cave surged to meet them, surrounding them, even Chaiko, hobbling on his crutches.

Close up, signs of exhaustion and waste on the three were shocking. Tusk's face seemed to have sagged, all power melted from him. Malek looked emaciated, his face drawn and exhausted with patches of skin peeling off from sunburn. Tael was unconscious; his limp body sagged in the skin wetted to keep him cool. Under the intense sun their skin looked red. Baer ordered everyone into the cave.

All hurried to make the returning party as comfortable as circumstances allowed. Tael was taken to his fire. Ela made little mewing noises of anguish as she and others eased his body down carefully, supporting his injured leg to prevent it from being jarred. They stretched him out; the bearers straightened gratefully and stumbled back to let Tanya, Samar and Emma take a good look at his leg.

Malek was escorted to his place, his face screwed up in pain from the cramps that were racking him. They eased him down and he let himself collapse onto his furs. Nebu hovered over him, her face full of worry. He attempted to smile reassuringly at her, but managed only a grimace that split his heat-cracked lips. She clucked her tongue in dismay, hurrying to give him a bowl of water to drink. His hands shook, and the water splashed from the trembling bowl. He drank a little, water spilling down his chin. Exhaustion closed his eyes, the bowl dropped into his lap, and he sagged against Nebu. She eased him back gently, crying silent tears. Ruba and Ork stood by watching wide-eyed, hoping their father was going to be all right.

Tusk refused all help, made his way back to his sleeping place and dropped unceremoniously onto his furs. He looked around at all the faces, then turned his back on them, settled himself down and was instantly asleep. After three breaths a steady snore could be heard. People shrugged their shoulders: Tusk always knew what he wanted to do in any given moment. This time he wanted to sleep.

Their concern and curiosity at a fever pitch, a crowd collected about the relief party, pestering them with questions. Cosh told them how difficult the return had been. They had started early before light, but under the blazing sun had slowed to a crawl. At one point he had considered holing up until the evening, but there was no good place to do so; totally exposed and needing to be near water, they had pushed on. He also spoke of the plains being bone dry with no sign of game.

"No bison?" Baer asked, fear growing in his heart. What would they do for winter? He forced the thought away. They needed to face the problems of the present; the future would have to wait. With painful slowness he ambled over to Tusk, but the big man was already sleeping. Tael's leg had been set and bandaged by Emma and Samar working together. Now the shaman was washing Tael's face to cool the raging wound fever. Ela hovered nearby, comforted by Tanya and Emma. "His leg was broken in three places. In one place, the bone poked through the skin," Samar informed Baer. "But he will survive if he can fight off the fever."

Malek was deeply asleep also; he clutched his covers, exhaustion having brought on the shakes. Even in his sleep he was shivering. Stow, having slept through the night and day, was showing signs of coming around. People found excuses to be near, in hope of catching him awake and being the first ones to hear what had happened. Cosh had made it known that the rescue party had concentrated on getting the injured home and knew little of their experiences.

14 Stones

A little after sundown, Stow awoke. With assistance he went and relieved himself, made his painful way back to the fire, then asked for food and water, which were quickly provided. His place was surrounded by the curious, who watched him eat. When it seemed he was finished, Baer came over to sit by him. Everyone jostled for position to be closer.

"I am glad you are home," Baer said simply, and his words were echoed by a chorus of murmurs from all around. "The others are also back, safely." He gestured toward the sleeping forms and the crowd parted to let Stow see. "We would all like to know what happened out there," he said leaning forward. The crowd pressed nearer to catch the answer.

Stow looked around at all the faces trying to guess the words on his lips, faces dancing in the firelight, and he tried to gather himself for the long-awaited explanation.

"We went ... to the hills... saw the storm coming ... had to find shelter ... but the tree had fallen and the wind pushed me down ... The rain came and filled the hole ... the rain ... the water ... washed us over the cliff. Tael broke his leg ... Tusk carried him ... Malek and I carried each other..."

The words came stumbling out past a swollen tongue, lips cracked from heat. And with the words, the memories flooded back, the fear and the pain and the bone-weary tiredness. Suddenly his eyes were full of tears and he was crying, a soundless cry, his chest heaving with great big gulps of air. Some of the women cried too. They had not understood the jumble of words but understood the emotions that were being released. Samar put an arm around Stow and patted him comfortingly. The men fidgeted about embarrassed, while the kids watched in wonder a grown man cry.

The outpouring of words, having given but a glimpse into what happened, merely whetted the appetite to know more, and their curiosity grew uncomfortable like an unreachable itch. There were murmurs of, "What did he say?" Baer held up a hand for quiet to allow Stow to recover his composure, but the heaving, gasping sobs came on their own. Someone passed a bowl of water which Stow drank in one swallow, easing the constriction in his chest so that the convulsive sobs diminished. Finally, when he looked around at the circle of faces, his eyes were clear once again, the disorientation washed away by the overflow of emotions.

"We headed north along the ridge and at Three-Rocks we turned toward Great Salt Lick. Tusk hurried ahead and by the time we got there we were all tired and strung out but within sight of each other. I don't know why we had to go so fast. After resting, he made us go on again though we were still tired. We reached the Gorge and walked along it for a while. The sky was getting darker all the time, and we could see the hills on the other side, but the Gorge was too dark. Tusk went ahead but soon came back saying that the old route was gone, the ledge had collapsed from the earthquake in several places that he could see. He said we had to wait for daylight to explore it in more detail. Tael asked, 'What daylight?' as it was very dark by then and the Gorge was an impossible darkness itself. We made camp there on the lip of the Gorge with no trees or shelter about. We did not even make a fire. Soon I was asleep from the hard day, lying there on the bare ground." Stow paused to order his recollections, and everybody could sense that things were about to happen in the story. The approaching storm of course. Had they themselves not lived through that, though sheltered in the cave?

"I awoke because Malek was shaking me hard. The wind was blowing strongly and it was difficult to stand against its push. We all had to crouch and crawl on all fours. Tusk was pointing to the west where lightning was showing. He said we had to find cover. Cover, but where? There was nothing on the plain side and we did not dare to go near the Gorge for fear of being blown into it by the winds." He paused again searching for some detail.

"That is when I lost my spear. I must have left it on the ground. It was a good spear. A lucky spear," he added with regret. "On First-Hunt it hit the bison true, sank deep..." He was interrupted by a growl from the restless crowd to get on with the tale. "I lost a good carryall, rope, my fire pouch..." He was fumbling about his neck where the pouch used to hang that contained dry tinder to catch the heat of a drilling stick. It was obvious that this was the first time he had inventoried the items he lost and was saddened.

Noisily he cleared his throat, and drank from a bowl of water someone pressed in his hand. In stronger tones he continued. "The wind was blowing hard. Straight into the Gorge. I was lying down on the ground. We were all flat on the ground, holding onto it. The wind was roaring and I could not hear the others. In the darkness I feared that maybe I was alone and that they were blown down into the Gorge." He paused and shivered at the memory.

"What happened next? Yes, tell us!" came from all around.

"Tusk crawled along the Gorge and found a cut that led into it. We all crawled down and there the wind was less. But as the storm got nearer, the wind got stronger even there. Further down we found a tree halfway uprooted by the quake and we crawled into the hole to hold onto the exposed roots. The lightning was terrible. The whole sky was afire with a blue light. The thunder was rattling and shaking the air. It was shaking my bones, and my insides rattled like dried seeds in a pod. The rain fell in large drops. Then water poured down like a river on us. I could not breathe in the thickness of the rain. The hollow filled with water and rushed down the cut into the Gorge. I was the first to go. The water was pushing and pulling, the roots I was hanging onto got very slippery and my arms became cramped. One hand let go and I could not make it go back to hold onto something else. Malek held onto me ..." He said this with wonder, for the first time giving recognition to Malek whom he had looked down on before, because he did not look like a hunter or act like one. Stow did not know what to think of paintings or painters.

The crowd pressed closer, hanging on every word. "Malek held me, Tusk held Malek, but the water was too strong—and rising—pulling at us, ready to wash us over the edge into the blackness of the Gorge. We could not stay there. We would drown. I tried to climb up on the tree trunk but lost my footing and fell. The water carried me away. I was tumbling with the rush of water. I was tossed and turned around and around. Hit a rock then another. Then I am not sure what happened. I must have fallen into the Gorge ... rushed along by the water. I do not remember. Later I ended up hanging onto a small bush growing out of the wall of the Gorge. The water somehow threw me there, onto a narrow ledge. I crawled higher along it, hanging onto a crevice."

Stow struggled to bring order to his memories. Strangely he could not remember the continuous flashes of lightning and the roll of thunder reverberating in the confines of the Gorge. He remembered only the smell of rotten eggs so strong it took his breath away and left him choking and gasping. Of all the things that happened that was the worst. His eyes stung and his skin burned as if scoured with sand. After that there was no specific memory but a jumble of impressions that refused to stay in order. There was no sense of time, just a floating feeling as if time had refused to go forward. The storm had passed when he finally became aware again. His ears were still ringing. He felt rather than heard the storm pass to the east. The wind ceased to try to push him into the roaring waters below. He fell asleep, so exhausted that he didn't even worry that he might fall off his precariously narrow ledge.

"When I ... awoke, I was deep down the Gorge looking up at the light above, clinging to my narrow perch. Not far below me the raging waters of the night before had shrunk to a slow trickle along the bottom. I could not see anybody. I could not hear anybody. I figured they must all be dead. And I could not understand why I wasn't dead." He paused, remembering the wind, the storm, the power of the water, still wondering how he had survived. His right leg had a big bruise above the knee and did not want to bend. He clambered down to the bottom, wincing with the pain. He worked back along the bottom slope, laboriously crawling over boulders tossed about by the rush of waters, the loose piles of stones that shifted underfoot not having settled yet.

"My leg hurt," he said simply, rubbing his right leg just short of the ugly bruise. "I crawled up the Gorge looking for the others. I thought I should go down the Gorge to look for bodies, but I was too tired. It was very difficult. There were rocks, sticks, branches and whole trees blocking the way." I should have gone to look for them, he now told himself, feeling the guilt of his omission; I would have been wrong, but I should have gone.

He was almost ready to crawl into a hole and give up when he heard Malek from above calling for him. With a burst of renewed energy he clambered over the last rock croaking out a reply. Malek heard him and came to help him over the next stretch to lead him back to Tusk and Tael. Amazingly they had all survived, but Tael had broken his leg when the water smashed him against a rock wall, and he was suffering greatly. A small piece of bone was showing through the skin, surrounded by a dark red wound. The shock had worn off, and with eyes shut tight and teeth clenched, he fought against the pain. He rolled his head from side to side, uttering an occasional groan that made all of them wince.

"Malek found me and took me to Tusk and Tael. Tael had a broken leg and was in great pain." The three had spent the night clinging to each other in the lee of a rock that deflected the full downflow with the backwash of the water pinning them there. Amazingly the four were reunited, each hurt in some way, but all of them alive. How was that possible? The sky had tried to kill them; the air tried to kill them; the water nearly drowned them; the rocks almost smashed their bones. Yet here they were, hurt, but still alive.

Tusk had already scouted ahead and had a plan. He organized their effort, with each one doing as much as his injuries allowed. They spent the day working slowly up the Gorge. Exhausted, they spent the night at the foot of a cliff wall that they eventually needed to scale, with no way up the smooth surface. At first light Tusk explored further along the Gorge looking for another way up, but came back without finding one. They were dejected and not even the clear skies looking into the Gorge helped to lift their mood. Though the humidity was high, the air followed the fault in the ground and there was a resultant good airflow channeled by the Gorge to make it at least bearable. Stow watched Tusk chew on his lip in exasperation looking for a solution out of this death trap. The way down led nowhere, while the way up ended at an unscalable cliff. He alone could doubtless have made it, but with the burden of the others weighing him down he saw no way. He seemed ready to give up. Then Stow heard Tusk ask himself "What would Baer do?" Then he spent a goodly amount of time in deep thought. Without saying anything he backtracked down the Gorge to reappear later with a small tree he had found. Eight times he went and returned, each time bringing back a tree or a large branch. He propped them against the sheer wall so that each overlapped and supported the other. With branches and stubs interlacing, the construction provided enough foot and handholds for him to clamber up as near enough to the ledge as could be negotiated. He came back down and told each what needed to be done. Then he and Malek went up helping each other, till Malek was safely on the ledge. Tusk came back down and Stow was next. It was surprisingly easy, once the way was shown, and with a little help he was also up on the ledge. Tusk went down again, packed Tael into the only hide-wrap they had, and slinging it onto his shoulder, shutting out Tael's frequent cries of pain, worked his way up to join the others on the ledge.

There was still some way to go to reach the top, but there was a narrow crevice cut into the smooth rock face that led upward. Tusk pulled some of the branches up from below, broke them into suitable lengths, then jammed the pieces across the crevice to use for support on the way up. Once worked out, the progress was again surprisingly easy.

Halfway up, Stow's right leg gave out from fatigue and he started to slip down but was grabbed and held by Malek. But the two were teetering dangerously off balance and started to slide down. Malek held onto him and Stow managed to grab a rock handhold, but still they slipped toward a fall. Tusk, with Tael still on his back, reached out, grabbed them both and held them steady, all of their weight supported by the awkward arch of his body. There was a sickening snap of a tendon jumping out of place in Tusk's shoulder, but still he held them, his face screwed up in a grimace of pain and determination. Somehow, they made it up, muscles trembling with effort, fingers cramped and drenched in rivers of sweat. Then they lay panting on the open vista of the lip above.

"Tusk carried us to the top. He found a way and like a spider took us up the wall with Tael on his back, I in his right hand, Malek in his left. Up he took us ... straight up the side of the Gorge." There was an incredulous murmur of disbelief and appreciation from his listeners. "He saved us then. Then saved us again," Stow said with pride and conviction. Chaiko listened carefully, guessing at what had been left out in the narration. There was no mistaking the gratitude in that voice. When he had time, he would think about Tusk again, he promised himself. This Tusk was new to Chaiko.

Once under the open skies, the heat of the sun and the humidity soon weakened them even more. They found a small depression and crawled into it. Then, digging into the soft soil seeking a cool embrace of bare earth, they found the soil too dry to give much comfort. They waited out the heat of the day and emerged once the sun was low on the horizon. Their progress was painfully slow and what had taken them a hard day's march, now turned into an agonizing crawl from one bit of shelter to another. Like a scorpion running from shade to shade to avoid the killing heat of the sun.

"The way back was impossible. It was too hot. No shade. No breath left in the air. The ground was burning with heat. There was no water or what little there was, tasted bad. I do not know how many days it was or how many nights. It seemed to go on forever, then beyond it there was still more to go. When Cosh found us we were nearly done," he concluded, tired of his tale, tired of reliving those memories. In the depth of exhaustion one step, just one more ... and again and again, just one more. An entire lifetime in those steps. Their past became the last step, their whole future lay in the next, if they could take it and make it.

Stow sank back into the skins, exhausted. He closed his eyes, shut out all the people looking at him with curious eyes and he sought refuge in sleep.

Baer nodded, understanding what it took to bear the full burden of the hopelessness of others. He was immensely glad that Tusk had taken that burden on. He looked down on Stow, onto the exhaustion stamped into the slack lines of his face; he waved for silence and dismissed the crowd.

The gathering slowly dispersed to their hearths. They did not want to; they wanted to stay, ask questions and talk. They wanted to share and understand what had happened. But it was late into the night, and Baer wanted them fresh for morning tasks. "No fires tonight," Chaiko said in parting, and Baer just nodded; he had been thinking the very same.

Ruba had listened open-mouthed to Stow's tale, his imagination excited by the adventure he heard in those words. He had already forgotten how scared he had been when the storm had swept over them all in the depth of the cave. Beside him, Ork whispered deprecatingly, "I would have gotten out with no trouble. I would have swum down the Gorge."

Ruba looked at his brother and considered stepping on him, but this was not the moment for that. He had a rare sense of pride in his father's accomplishments. Had Stow not said his father had saved him twice and held on to him at his own peril? Yes, though Malek was a slight man, he had done all right. Ruba had sometimes secretly wished for another father, big and strong like Baer or Cosh, and envied Lana and Ido at those times ... but a boy should not envy any girl. He settled down for the night, Ork beside him. Nebu was sitting by her mate, anxiously watching over his sleep.

Throughout the night the air flowed steadily. It was more than a breeze, but not quite a wind, unwaveringly out of the west, its breath a whisper of dry heat. In the moonlight, the field of grass undulated reluctantly, protesting with arid stiffness. The rustling of bushes and trees had become the rattling of shriveled, curled-up leaves. The heat of the air continued to draw moisture from the soil.

Baer was up before light, rousing some of the hunters. He wanted them to scout for game before the heat of the sun made it impossible to be out in the open. The men rose slowly, yawning and scratching, sorting through their gear, straggling into a group. The women hurried about putting together something for the hunters to eat. "Go to the best watering place you know," Baer told Cosh, "and find some game. We have not seen bison or antelope on the plain, so do not go there, but the deer might come from the hills to the watering holes. The water head is shrinking." Indeed, the creek had all but disappeared, shrunk to a mere trickle. "Stay out of the heat of the day. Come back in the coolness of the evening." Baer looked at Samar and the old man made quick gestures of hunting magic and then dismissed them with the good hunting sign. The hunters moved off, Crow among them, still stiff from the night.

Baer then went to check on Tael whose fever had broken a little earlier and who was now sleeping restlessly. His leg was an awkward looking bulk of bandages. Ela looked up at him dazed, her eyes red with sleeplessness. "He's going to be all right," she mumbled repeatedly. Baer smiled, nodded but said nothing. He went and checked on Malek and then Tusk, but both were deeply asleep. Tusk was snoring heavily; the sound would at times cease disconcertingly then after a long pause would resume. Baer wondered if the others got any sleep around his fire or had gotten used to it after so many years. Luckily, the hearth was a distance from the rest, the noise not bothering others much.

For the rest of the morning, Baer, Samar and Chaiko stayed together, each preoccupied with his own thoughts. Baer was thinking of the hunt and the need to find more food. Where are the bison? In this dryness there is no water for them to drink and no grass for them to eat. But without the bison and the antelope, there was no place for the clan here. In the open there was not enough meat to support them and with the vegetation so sparse and stunted there also would not be enough seeds, roots and fruit. In his mind, hunger loomed, if not for the summer, for the winter surely. They were already far behind, and had been forced to consume almost the entire bounty of the First-Hunt. It would be a long winter without food, but first they must survive the summer, he reminded himself.

Samar was thinking of food as well. When he was young they still went north to hunt the Woolly Rhinoceros and people still talked about the Giant Mammoth by the ice fields. Even back then the beasts were already very rare. But one kill could feed the clan for the whole winter, rich in mouth-watering fat. There is nothing, he recalled wistfully, like a piece of mammoth hump, singed in fire, dripping juices and fat. His mouth watered at the memory. But now the ice fields had shrunk, and the Mammoth and the Woolly Rhinoceros were gone. Where had they disappeared to? Some held they had ranged further north where the ice still grew. There are still bison, large thundering herds of them, but where are they this year? Has the earthquake blocked their way somewhere? Has the storm turned them? Someone has to go west to find the answers.

Chaiko was thinking about Stow's tale. He knew him to be a straightforward person, not given to much elaboration. Though he did not lack imagination, he would not stretch the truth to make it sound better. The facts revealed, according to his tale, that Tusk had acted out of character. He had saved the rest without thinking of himself, but unselfishness was not a quality he was known for. Others were attracted by the single-minded purpose he showed in pursuing his own needs. He led because his needs always gave him purpose, and others followed simply because he had a purpose. His needs had been enough to give him light before. Why would he change now? Had he overestimated Tusk's dislike of Baer, or himself?

Lana came over and passed around some dried fish to each. Samar looked at his with mistrust as he had few teeth to chew the tough dry piece. By his fire, or rather, Kor's and Calla's, his piece would be soaked to soften beforehand. Still he was too polite to say anything and quickly hid his reaction. Observing the quick play on his face, Lana laughed delightedly, her voice ringing with pleasure. She pulled a small bowl from behind her back, a piece of fish softened the way he liked it, and offered it to him. Grinning back sheepishly at her he took the bowl and busied himself. Chaiko chortled in appreciation, reached over and tousled her hair, but she danced away giggling, enjoying her little joke. From across the unlit fire Tanya watched her antics indulgently. Baer too, had a brief smile to soften his worries.

Around the council fire the mood quickly turned somber. "It seems we must go from here," Baer said with quiet finality. The other two looked at him with shocked surprise. What had he said? Go from here? Where? Why? "The bison have not come in numbers. We have seen but a few antelope. Where are the elk, the horses?" He paused painfully. "Without them, we cannot survive here." He let the thought sink in. They all knew it to be true but were not ready to accept the unthinkable, not yet. Where did Baer get the courage to even utter such an eventuality? But it was unavoidable; without the grazing herds, the plains were empty and life for the clan was insupportable. "In past years when meat was scarce the seeds and roots, fruits and berries were good and tided us over the winter. But this year ..." He motioned toward the burnt ground for proof.

"The fish, too, were poisoned," added Chaiko to the list, his stomach tightening with the thought of winter ahead. "But where can we find anything more than we have here?"

"In the hills, maybe," answered Samar, his voice brittle. "In the small valleys, maybe. By the ponds and the swamps, maybe. Among the rocks, maybe. In bird nests, maybe. Under rocks and in trees, maybe." At the mention of the last, both Baer and Chaiko shuddered at the memory they shared from childhood of a feast of raw grubs dug from a decaying tree. It had given them much needed nourishment then and would do so in the future, but left them with revulsion to stifle any appetite.

"On the plain one can see far. The hunter can spot the animal from afar—less need to search. But the animal can see the hunter too, and move off, resulting in a long chase and a long trek home," Chaiko said, thinking aloud. The others watched him, waiting patiently for his direction to reveal itself. "In the open, a lot of hunters are needed to herd the animals into a favorable position for the kill. In the hills and forest it is easier to stalk and trap an animal against a feature of the land," Chaiko tried to explain. "Hunting on the plains requires lots of hunters, and if they do not find food then there is no food. In the hills and forest, one hunter or two alone can stalk and kill a deer, a wild pig, even a brown or sand bear and bring it home. Two hunters here, two hunters there. Hunting in many places. Somebody will bring home food." Chaiko struggled to make himself clear, aware that he was not a hunter and that he was talking about hunter things. But Baer nodded in understanding: small hunting parties in many places ... one large party concentrated in one place. He preferred the latter, when the herds were running, but they were not running now.

"Even if the herds were to come back now, there is no food or water for them here." With that, Baer closed the matter for the present. He would wait to see what Cosh would have to say.

14 Stones

For his part, Samar did not know what to do, but he knew Baer was right; to find food they must move. He cast about in his memories trying to figure out what he as shaman must do. Was there some ceremony or rite required of him in the serious task of moving the clan to a new location? Should he look for signs? How could he prepare the clan for the move, spiritually? How could he help Baer to win agreement and the co-operation of all. What must he do first?

Baer was asking himself the same questions. He had decided to move the clan, but what must he do to get the clan moving? He would not have time to build agreement by patient reasoning. The food stores had dwindled and what was left would be needed for the move. Unless the hunters met with success ... but the signs were against it.

Chaiko rattled off some of the obvious drawbacks. "Water is bad. We cannot risk fires in the open. Must avoid the Gorge as there is no way across it. No shelter. Not enough food. We have old people and babies." The cripple, he did not mention, but kept it to himself.

Chaiko realized suddenly how much was being asked of him. He was facing a very long march. He resolved that whatever it took he would do, not to slow down the rest. He would have to travel light, and started to list what he would take: soft-wrap and a stiff-wrap, a small water skin and his leather carryall; a few pieces of flint and a chopping axe, fish hooks, a line and a length of rope. With regret he relinquished all his prized possessions, even the Singing-Stick, a handful of spears... and the woods he was working on. He must leave his skins and furs as well, but perhaps they would be back; he must store them carefully.

He smiled at his brother in support of the heavy decision he was bearing for all of them. He made two fists in front of his chest, a gesture of strength and resolve. Baer returned the smile and the gesture, then got up to look for his wife and daughter.

The clan looked out on a parched landscape. The green had faded and more brown and yellow showed. The distance danced in the heat. The grass hung limp, unresisting to the wind. The dryness rustled, rattled in its flow. Dust cones twisted across the field plucking fine silt from among the roots, stealing future growth. More buzzards were in the sky, patiently circling. They, at least, were not bothered by the heat.

From their high vantage they counted the living, the dying and the dead.

At midday, Tusk roused himself from his resting place. He stretched and grimaced against the stiffness and the aches. The stretched tendon in his shoulder nearly paralyzed his arm, which was capable of only the slightest of movements, and hung uselessly by his side. The rest of his body ached. The muscles of his leg resisted all motion; he could limp only with conscious effort of will. In a slow shuffle he went to relieve himself, every eye upon him. On his return, he took a long drink, then went to Stow to talk with him briefly. Stow's face glowed with gratitude and admiration. Tusk smiled back, patting the young man's back, glad that he had recovered so quickly, the severe sunburn on the other's face and neck notwithstanding. Tusk wondered if he himself was as badly burned, but it was an idle, unconcerned thought—overshadowed by the fact that they had all survived.

After that, he went to Tael and talked with Ela who was solicitously taking care of him. She was worried, but reported that his fever had broken in the morning, and a little while ago he had even come around briefly. His eyes had been clouded with pain, but he knew where he was, drank, then escaped back into sleep. Tusk nodded and said only, "You deserve some sleep yourself."

Then he went on to Malek. The painter was stirring, cautiously stretching his limbs testing the limits of his movement. He scowled with pain but was pleased by his assessment. He was stiff and sore; there was some localized pain in his leg, but he had survived and was even functional. He knew he could yet paint and for him that was enough. (Already his mind was visualizing how to paint unrelenting heat, thirst and bone weary tiredness.) He smiled up at Tusk. Nebu was behind him massaging his sore back and carefully daubing some grease onto his sunburns, her face a tender concentration of care for him. For the first time Tusk was filled with pangs of longing for a mate who could so ease his discomforts.

Next, Tusk went over to Baer, settled himself down, and said straight off, "There is no way across the Gorge. The old way, the rock ledge leading down, has collapsed, and the one leading up is blocked. I walked the Gorge almost its entire length but found no suitable place to cross. Leastwise, not for the whole clan." His eyes flashed from Baer to Chaiko, including them both. He leaned forward peering into their faces. "What's wrong with the world?" His question was frighteningly naked in its intensity. Baer did not try to answer.

"The oldest tales talk of the earth shaking, bringing forth rivers of fire, smoke in the sky, bad smells and black rain," began Chaiko struggling to recall as exactly as he could the tale he had heard at the one Gathering when he was nine years old. It had not seemed relevant at the time; now he wished he had listened more closely. Both Baer and Tusk nodded; they recalled something vaguely too.

"The trouble with old songs is that they leave too much out," Baer said in exasperation. "They could have easily included that for days, the earth shook again and again."

"Perhaps when you make your next song, you could include all those fine points," Chaiko could not resist interjecting, on the verge of laughter. Baer only looked balefully at him and Chaiko had to swallow his mirth. "Whatever happened, it happened to the west," Chaiko went on. "Could it also have turned the herds? And swept the clouds from the sky? And brought the heat upon us?" He was not sure if it all hung together so neatly, but he knew there were reasons for most things.

They had experienced the shaking of the earth, smoke in the sky, the bad smell and black rain. But rivers of fire, what did that mean? Could there be fire to the west? If so, since the whole plain was tinder dry, one spark could set the whole ablaze. They were thinking of crossing a piece of the plain. Even up here, the cave was edged by an open slope, ready to burn and fill the cave with choking smoke. Was there safety anywhere? In the hills, maybe, behind a ridge-line of rocks giving them a fire beak.

When Samar came over, they were still discussing possible causes for the string of misfortune besetting them. The old man listened, then added his piece. "When I was a boy, on a long trek to the west with the clan, I saw a mountain belch smoke that grew into a black tree high into the sky, then white ash fell from above for many days. It accumulated like deep snow on the ground, covering everything, suffocating it. And this was high summer. We turned away but the ash followed us for days." He paused to clear his throat before continuing. "I think this time must have been the same. The earth split and burped up its hot breath, and spewed ash into the air. If you look closely at the sky, you can still see tiny specks glinting in the sun. I think that layer is storing up the sun's heat to produce this dryness."

"How long do you think this drought will last?" Baer wanted to know.

"Hard to say, but already plants have lost their growth. The soil is parched and everything is thirsty. We'd best think that things will get worse before they get any better."

"But what about the rain that came with the storm? Where did that water go?" Chaiko, who had been silent, suddenly asked.

"That was mostly ash falling, mixed with a little rain. It was more a lightning storm that came with the ash cloud," Samar said. He reached into the cold fire pit and scooped up a handful of ash that he let slip through his finger. The others watched, trying to come to terms with his opinion.

Later, Baer told Tusk of their need to find safety and a new place somewhere in the hills. To his surprise, Tusk accepted the decision without question. He had developed a bad feeling about the cave anyway and had felt the pressure to move on. The two brothers exchanged questioning glances. This was unexpected. Samar, meanwhile, had fallen asleep.

Near evening the hunters returned. Except for a few gaunt birds, they had found nothing worthy to chase. Cosh shook his head, "There are no signs, not even at the watering holes." This was indeed worrisome. In times of drought, water acted like a magnet attracting all creatures to its life-sustaining wetness. At a time like this, animals should be crowding upon such a precious resource; friend and foe forced together by their overriding need. Where had the life gone from the plain so suddenly?

Baer waved Cosh aside and quietly filled him in on the decision made. Cosh, not unexpectedly, merely nodded. If it was good enough for Baer, it would be good enough for him and his family. That was Cosh's heart, a deep trust of Baer.

The birds were quickly plucked and quartered, and because there were no fires they would be dried in the sun the next day. The cave noted with approval that the leadership was solid again. Tusk's exploits in the rescue of his companions had vastly increased his standing, so people were glad to see Baer and Tusk's differences settled and the two leaders in harmony. Only the more perceptive noticed that something more than usual was going on. For one thing, there seemed to be too much talking that would stop when someone came a little too near. These guarded expressions bode no good.

Kor was working on a stone implement. Working was his answer to all life's challenges. There was drought on the plain? Work the stone! There was no game on the plains? Work harder! The chips were flying, Calla sweeping them together time and time again, murmuring under her breath.

Kor worked, his attention focused on the stone. When he would pause to look about, his eyes would settle on the leaders talking. "There's something cooking," he finally said.

"What are you talking about, you old man?" Calla asked in her usual querulous manner that overlay her fondness of him.

"There's too much talking going on," he said, nodding his head toward the council fire.

"Your eyesight is bad and you see shadows where there are none, you old fool," she chided him, but she started sniffing into the air. There did seem to be a faint smell of intrigue someplace!

"I know what I know," he said stubbornly, then the chips were flying again.

In a lull around the fire, Chaiko asked Tusk about the Gorge and how he managed to lead them all out of there. Tusk answered readily without embellishment. In a matter-of-fact tone he described the interlace of tree limbs that allowed them to climb out and the supports he jammed into the crevice. When Chaiko asked how he came up with the idea, he was rocked by the answer, "It's what Baer would have done." Chaiko had heard this before from Stow's recital, but to hear it out of Tusk's own mouth was jarring. (When Chaiko later related this to Baer, Baer was somewhat dubious about the credit Tusk was so willing to bestow upon him. The two brothers marveled at the change of attitude in Tusk. Chaiko was also aware that this called for a reassessment of his own view of Tusk.)

Tusk had discovered out there that he did not really want the leadership role, but had to take it when it was thrust upon him, for there was nobody else. The decisions he had made were vital, choices between life and death for all of them, and he had had to weigh all of their interests. Probably for the first time in his life he was challenged enough to look beyond his narrow view. In so doing, looking inward from the outside, he saw himself and did not like what he saw; he clearly detected his own limitations. He had a brief insight into what it took to be Baer, and though the illumination was brief as a shooting star, the memory of that insight lingered, and he promised never to oppose Baer again. He had also realized that to survive himself he needed the support of others as much as they needed him, so he had given all his strength and effort to bring them home. For the first time since childhood, he felt good! And for the first time as well, he could look a cripple in the eye and still feel good.

In the night there was no guard fire, but Chaiko kept his usual vigil. Without the fire he felt naked and vulnerable, so he kept a spear close at hand. He caught himself looking to the west, expecting a river of fire. He shuddered involuntarily as he remembered his own river of stones.

Chapter 14

The next morning events happened quickly. Soon after first light the leaders gathered, drawn by the pressing need to plan the details of the clan's move to the hills. Baer would have preferred a slower approach, allowing him time to gain agreement of the whole cave instead of confronting them with this urgency as they were forced to do now. This time he would have to use his authority to the full and command them to go.

The whole clan noticed the early goings-on, as well as the intensity revealed by their leaders' body postures. They rightly read agreement into them, but were puzzled as to intent. What was in the air? They noted that Chaiko was also included in the group. A few days ago this would have been a source of astonishment, but with all that had happened and Chaiko's role in saving them, it was tacitly accepted.

The people began to move purposefully about, but the morning routine was hampered because only one fire had been allowed for cooking for the whole cave. Not that people were hungry in this heat. But the fire was part of the morning ritual of waking up as they gathered about in its smoke, scratching and yawning. Tanya, aware of the tinder dryness outside, fed the fire cautiously with a few sticks. It was good to have all of them safely back in the cave, even if some were injured. She glanced about appraisingly at the people, knowing what was being proposed, and making her own assessment.

She looked first at Ela and Tael, the latter sitting propped up by a bundle of furs. His face was tense from the pain that throbbed like a drum hammering away at him from the inside, a pain that Emma's potion could not dull entirely. Ela was busy suckling the baby but continued to cast anxious glances in her mate's direction. Tanya had to wonder how they were going to move Tael, but then Baer always thought out everything beforehand.

Tanya then considered Nebu and her mate Malek. He was standing up, moving about stiffly, talking with Rea, Gill and big Simm. It looked as if he could walk on his own, maybe with his son Ruba's help.

Next, her eyes sought out Stow and found him in a tight cluster talking with Crow, Makar and Kray, the two girls, Lana and Ido, listening shyly at the periphery. They were besieging him with questions and he was answering them animatedly with free movement of his limbs. No problems there. His young body had quickly recovered from the exertions of their ordeal. Yes, it looked as though Stow would be all right. Likewise, Kor and Calla should give her little concern; they were tough old birds and had each other for support and encouragement. On the other hand Chaiko, Samar, Uma and even big Simm were each a cause for worry, as each had an impediment to slow them all down. Then there were the children: Ork, Sosa, Tay and Ela's baby. How could they stand up to the trip? There was always something to worry about, she concluded, and the largest part of leadership was having to brood about all the people. Sometimes Tanya wished that she and Baer could be led instead of leading all the time.

Outside the cave the heat built quickly. The wind blew continually from the west and there were no clouds in the sky with even a hint of rain. Already this early in the morning the horizon danced in the rising heat as the sun lifted itself above the land. Every living creature sought out the shadows. Thankfully, there were few bugs, as there was no dew on the grass to drink and the wind was too strong for most of them.

Around the council fire, talk had ceased as each was considering how best to break the news to the rest of the cave and how to anticipate and head off their protest. Chaiko sat among them, by invitation. He was not a leader, but he was more than just a guest. Most certainly he was part of this decision. So newly elevated from his passive, observer role, he found it difficult to adjust to the more active participation required of him in this council. He had been quiet for so long that silence had become a habit with him. He listened as, one by one, they began to air their concerns and discuss details. Because of his night vigil he felt tired, but clearly the day promised to be very interesting.

With all the decisions having been made, the time had come to convince the rest of the cave. That was Baer's task. He sat there intent, sunk into himself, ordering his ideas, rehearsing the words he would say. The others watched him quietly, seeing the set expression of his face change with the new mood to be conveyed. This was a critical speech, for their whole future hung in the balance. He must convey hope and confidence in what he needed to propose.

Suddenly resolved, Baer stood and the others rose with him and moved to center stage deferentially at Samar's slower pace. Instinctively the clan moved in, surrounding them at a respectful distance, but with growing curiosity and no small apprehension. Clearly, something important was about to happen. Baer motioned for everybody to sit. Hurriedly they complied, forming tight anxious groups. Many questioning looks were exchanged.

Baer took his time, slowly turning about. He looked at each. Finally he spoke in a clear voice, going to the heart of the matter. "Dear friends, it has been decided to move the whole clan to the safety of the hills for this summer."

Shocked silence greeted this announcement. Breath froze in mouths, and hearts skipped a beat. The statement, hanging in the air, left all wondering if they had heard what they thought they had heard. But surely that could not be right? Ela's baby whimpered in the sudden tension; Ela patted him reassuringly, but who was going to reassure her?

After the silence grew into a painful awareness of itself, it broke, and like water denied the downslope, the reaction gushed forth in murmurs of incredulity. "Leave the cave ...?" "Move the clan ...?" "To the hills ..?"

Baer allowed the murmurs to subside before he spoke again. "We, the people of the Standing-Rock Clan, hunt the bison. Our fathers hunted the bison as did their fathers before them. We hunt the bison, cook its meat, use its hide to robe ourselves and cover our sleeping places. It is bison meat that sustains us through the long winters. We made bison our lives, for our lives and the life of the bison are intertwined." He showed them his hands locked with fingers interlaced. "Our destinies are bound." People nodded in confirmation.

"When there are lots of bison," Baer continued, the sound of his voice booming between the cave walls into the waiting silence, "the hunting is good, and the people are full and content. When there are but few bison, the people go hungry, for the storage pits are only half full. This year the plain is empty. There are no bison out there in the plains. Not even one! No bison have been seen since the storm, since the Ashrain." He paused to let them remember the storm and its power.

"There are no lines of bison on the horizon, converging, coming over the crest of a hill to descend into the valley below. There are no thundering herds raising dust from one end of the plain to the other as far as the eye can see. There are no hooves to stamp their passing into the soft ground. There are no shaggy beasts fighting each other head to head, shoulder to shoulder, breath bursting till one will yield or both die on the spot. There are no cows to drop their calves. No lowing or bellowing. Can you hear a calf, lost and confused, call for its mother? Can you hear the challenge of a male? Can you hear the beat of hooves that make the ground tremble? No, for there is only silence. Silence on the plain, silence in the valleys and silence at the watering places. Can you not hear the silence of them, only the wind whistling empty through the grass?" He ceased speaking, and they all strained to hear something from the plain.

"We hunt the bison and the antelope and wild horses that run with them. But where are these creatures we depend on? With what shall we feed our hunger? Shall we run after the wind, now, for there is only wind on the plain? We hunt the elk and wild pigs. But this year there is none to hunt. Will you eat the wind for supper? There is no prey. The lions know it - for where are the lions? The wild dogs know it - for where are the wild dogs? The wolves know it - but where are the wolves? We have seen only a few hyenas."

A pause followed before he went on. "A long time ago the people learned from the bear to live in caves. A long time ago they learned to hunt from the wolves. Today the wolves tell us there are no bison to hunt, nor elk nor antelope. Will you not listen to the wolf? Will you not learn from him as your fathers did?" The people considered the question fairly. Put like that, people were ready, of course, to listen to the wolf and to learn from him; Chaiko could see willingness to learn glowing in the faces about him. The oldest tale told about fire being the gift of the sky; the next about the bear and the cave; the third, learning to hunt from the wolves. Few teachings were so ingrained as these three. Yes, the people were ready to listen to the wolves.

"Or will you listen to the hyena? His ribs are now hollow and his stomach is empty. He's forced to drink mud, for the water hole that used to be full, is now dried up. He is whining ... 'Something will surely turn up.' His nose drags in the dust, sniffing for some promise of something to eat. Count his ribs, for each one is showing. Look into his evil yellow eyes. What has he taught you in the past, but to mistrust him? Will you now listen to him?" Baer paused to let the question grow in their awareness. All around people shook their heads; no they would never listen to the foul-smelling beast. "We are hunters and we will not wait for something to turn up. No, hyena, we will not listen to you, for you smell of death and talk deception. We are brothers to the wolf and follow his teaching." People nodded with enthusiasm. Sensing their mood, Chaiko put his head back and howled the long drawn out call of the wolf. Others joined in; the wailing sounds of wolves rang through the cave again and again. Only reluctantly, the brothers of the wolf quieted down, to hear what their leader had left to say.

"We have had lean years before. Two years ago the game was scarce, and do you not remember the hunger of the following winter? Nebu lost a child because her milk dried up from hunger." In the back row Nebu started to cry; friends reached over and patted her consolingly. "Old Farr died that winter too, for he gave his share to young Makar so that he could grow into the young man we see today." All the heads were nodding in memory of Old Farr. "The game had been scarce then, but there's nothing now. Will you go and face winter with nothing in the food cairns? We have just enough to feed us till we get to the hills.

"We are hunters," Baer struck his chest proudly. "We look for signs. In a good summer you look into the sky and in the distance you will see a flock of carrion birds circling the plenty below. And beyond them you will see another flock wheeling in the air, and beyond them still more, because the bounty below casts off a few so that even the carrion birds can eat and live. Look to the skies now. How many birds can you see circling high in waiting? I will tell you. None." His hands motioned to the empty skies. "The wolf tells you to go, even the vulture tells you to go, for there's no game here. Or will you have the wind for your meal? Will you drink the heat in your thirst? And having eaten and having drunk, will you not ask for more?"

Chaiko could sense that Baer had swayed the crowd for there was a general nodding of heads. But Baer wanted to make sure they all could remember the points. "Maybe tomorrow, or the tomorrow after that, the bison will come, and they will come in numbers. But what will they eat? The grass is burned yellow and dry. Will they, like you, drink sand? The water courses are almost dried up. And where will they find cool shelter from the heat of the burning sun? The trees have lost their leaves and the shadows have lost their coolness.

"The Standing-Rock Clan hunts the bison as it has always done, but what will the clan do when the bison disappears? Will you eat the scorpions? Will you eat ants? The creepy-crawly things under the rocks? Will you stalk the snake? Will you hunt frogs in the soft mud of the lake? Will you fight the badger for the last root?" There were loud no's from the crowd at the suggested menu, perhaps none louder than Simm who was known for his discriminating appetite.

"It is clear that we cannot stay here. Look at the desolation around you. Feel the dryness of the grass. See how the trees droop. See how the soil shifts with the wind. No, we cannot stay here."

"Where shall we go then? Where shall we find food and safety?" They all leaned forward; they already knew the answer, but they needed to hear it, and be reassured again and again. "We shall follow those who have left already. We shall follow the wolves into the hills. We shall follow the deer that went before. Into the hills." Dramatically, he pointed toward the far off hills, and involuntarily people glanced in that direction.

"I tell you, we must go to the hills, where every hill has its valley, and every valley its cool running stream shaded by tall trees. Under the trees are deer grazing on sweet grass and tender shoots. There are wild pigs digging in the cool soil searching for succulent roots. There are black bears and brown bears to show where the best berries are. There are rabbits, giant squirrels and foxes in the undergrowth. There are fowls in the grass, their nests full of eggs. There are grouse in the clearings, ducks and geese in every pond, and turtles. The streams and marshes sparkle with fish. And under the trees the air is pleasantly fresh and cool."

As his brother talked, Chaiko's desire for the hills grew. He smiled to himself remembering an almost forgotten memory of his father saying that Baer could talk the fish out of the water, just as he was now talking the clan into the hills.

"So friends, do not listen to the hyena; follow the wolves into the hills. Why even the wind hurries there, tired of this heat, to find cool shade." Bear looked most dignified. He had given them a vision, and he himself believed every word of it. They would now have to go to the hills to find out for themselves. As he talked, he looked into every eye, and they looked back with growing enthusiasm for the move.

"I am going to the hills." He struck his chest, then pointed at Tanya and Lana with a sweep of the hand that included Chaiko. "My family will go to the hills." He paused, then asked in an intimate voice, "Who else will go with me there? Who else will start a new life under a forest of trees?"

The taciturn Cosh was the first to jump up. "I will," he shouted with eager energy. Then somewhat more slowly Tusk arose, his chest heaving with emotion. "So will I." Then everybody was standing and yelling, "I, me, too..." The clan stood together as one, fully committed to the decision to go. Chaiko also was swept up by the contagious excitement all around him, and for the first time in a long time felt that he truly belonged. Crow was beside him pounding on his back.

Baer finally motioned for silence and waited till he had everyone's focus once again. "We shall take only what we must and leave what we cannot carry. We will pack well what we cannot take, for when the bison returns so will we: as the Standing-Rock testifies, this is our cave and out there is our land. The pictures in the back of the cave, where the spirits of animals are captured, will confirm that this is our cave. Even the bear and wolf will heed our smell and know and respect our claim." Thus, Baer extended their security over all they would leave behind. Then having said all he had intended, he sat down and looked around to see the effect of his speech. Half the crowd was chanting, "To the hills, onto the hills ... hills, hills." The rest were howling like the wolves they were determined to follow. Makar, at the sight of so much demonstration of feelings, was bursting from his skin. He ran like a wolf howling "Hiiiiiiillls, onto the hills," then mixing his metaphors, he flapped his wings to get there faster. Only slowly did the emotions subside, the movement and sound recede, and order return.

With that demonstration, the meeting was over. Some details still needed to be settled, but with the main decision accepted, the task of sorting and packing began. Baer sat recovering from the heat of his own speech while Tusk and Cosh went from group to group, giving specific instructions. It was made known that they would start the next morning as early as the dawn light allowed, then walk only as far as the heat of the day would let them. Their first destination was a camp at Broken-Tree. There, a low ridge would give some shade and shelter, with water trickling from a spring nearby. Then, in early evening, they would continue on and reach perhaps Frog-Pond. There were to be no fires at all.

Packing proceeded quickly, with animated conversations back and forth about the trip ahead and what they could expect once they were in the hills. Learn-from-the-animals seemed to have excited their imagination. "I will learn from a skunk if need be," Makar declared with loud bravado. "A skunk has nothing left to teach you," someone interjected into the general laughter.

The heat outside was stifling. It burned the exposed skin, forcing the clan to stay in the shadows. The sky had a peculiar bare haze that robbed it of color, much as the scorching heat robbed the ground of color. The wind drove dust into the air like a drifting smudge over the landscape. Grains of sand rolled and floated across the ground to pile up in wind shadows and to collect in depressions. It seemed that the land itself, little by little, was leaving for the east, following the life that had already gone.

As the day wore on, the reality of what they were about to do started to sink in. A few dissenting voices were raised. Immediately, the people around accused the protesters of listening to a hyena. Since no one wanted to admit listening to hyenas, and all wanted to run with the wolves, the voices of doubt were soon quieted. Still, a sense of sorrow prevailed as people sorted their possessions, disheartened by the large pile to be left behind and the much smaller pile to be taken. Eyes sought out familiar landmarks and said quiet goodbyes. "Where will I find sloe berries in the forest?" moaned Emma, whose sloe berry cake was considered the very best by all. "Never mind, in the forest you will find foxtails," consoled someone, knowing that they were good against dry skin and itches, both of which Emma suffered with bad humor.

Repeatedly, Baer, Tusk and Cosh went among the people reminding them to take little, as the way was long and even a small weight grew heavier with every step. Simm remained unconcerned; he intended to eat his pack to lighten it, and stuffed it full of smoked meat, some dried mushrooms and a skinful of hazelnuts. "With each step my pack will grow lighter," he promised. "Check your waterskins," the instruction went about.

14 Stones

Tay burst out crying piteously, and with a great deal of energy and determination insisted that she did not want to go because her brother Sosa had told her there were monsters in the hills waiting for them—monsters that ate children. Sosa received the usual cuff to the back of his head, to show him that monsters waited for no one.

Chaiko selected the few items he would take: his light wrap, a small carry-all full of smoked meat, a small water bag, his crutches, in a separate pouch his modest collection of flints, a fishing line and some hooks. Around his neck hung a soft skin pouch of 13 small stones and Bogan's tell mark. He looked with regret at the pile of things to be left; all the things he had been working on. Chaiko picked up the Singing-Stick and caressed the smooth wood affectionately. He wondered if he would ever see it again, but shook off the disheartening thought; of course they would be back, when the bison returned. Collecting all the wood, he tied it together into a firm bundle and stacked it against the back wall of the cave. He would have to be satisfied with that.

The furs were shaken, spread out in the sun, baked on both sides in the light, made into a tight bundle, then packed into the now empty food cairns. When full, they were carefully covered with rocks and soil. They would be there when the clan returned, they reassured each other. The fireplaces were cleaned of all scraps so as not to attract scavengers, and everything that could not be packed or taken was dumped on the trash slope.

By nightfall the work was mostly done. Everyone was stripped down to essentials, the rest packed away or discarded. The lightness of their baggage was sobering, and the clan was dejected, the elation of the morning forgotten.

Chaiko went to Samar, who was drawing patterns in the sand to hide his agitation. Though he saw the necessity of the move, personally he feared that his old body would not survive the trip. Chaiko looked at him in full sympathy. He himself had misgivings that he would not make it on his crutches. But he must try, as must Samar. In a way their very weaknesses fed their determination and they would strain themselves to the utmost not to slow down the rest.

"When the bad-tempered wolverine leaves what it cannot carry, it spoils it with its scent so no other animal can make use of it. We are much like wolverines, are we not?" Chaiko asked the old man, to distract him from his apprehension. Intrigued, Samar looked at him intently, wondering what he really wanted. He grunted in acknowledgement of the question but wasted no time on an answer.

"Tomorrow, we leave this place for the hills," Chaiko said, his voice tinged with regret. "Most go with heavy hearts as bones of parents and children will be left behind in the burying ground. Most feel comfortable in this place and are loath to leave it. Yet it would be better for all if they could leave it not having to look back so often, missing what they left behind." Baer had come up, listening to Chaiko. As he sat down he winced from an unexpected twinge of pain that shot through him from his injured ribs. Chaiko wondered how much reserves Baer had left; hopefully enough for the trip.

"I do not know of any leave-taking ceremony," answered Samar somewhat reluctantly. Looking at the two brothers, he was struck by a similarity he had noticed before: a certain quality they shared, a forward looking, purposeful set to their personalities that had been in neither parent. "There's no ritual that fits the circumstances."

"Then make one up," the brothers chorused in unison.

"You do not make up traditions!" Samar retorted, shocked by their suggestion. Not being a full shaman, he defended the shaman's prerogatives all the more vehemently. Traditions grew from successes that needed to be taught and rehearsed, not made up on whims of the moment.

"Why not? Each tradition must have been started by somebody," Chaiko said almost harshly. He had little patience for blind fixation on ritual and ceremony for its own sake, but was not averse to its serving the very real need of reassuring people so that they could start tomorrow calmly and without regret.

"It would be good to say goodbye somehow to the spirits of the cave; ask them to guard the cave or to come along," Baer suggested, in a conciliatory tone.

"But we invited them in so recently during the First-Fires," Samar said, somewhat confused. He understood what they wanted— a ceremony that would ease the pain of parting from the cave and its surroundings. Yet he was offended that the office of the shaman was so lightly construed, implying that he, Samar, did not really believe in what he was doing. But he saw real concern for him and for the clan in those faces, and his anger evaporated. "I suppose some form of rite could be arranged," he murmured, but promised them nothing specific. After some thought, he went off to tell Stow what to do, leaving the two brothers alone.

Chaiko looked at Baer closely. His brother's face sagged slightly and his eyes appeared to be deeper set. He had lost weight from his injury plus worry over the fate of the clan. Pain had left clear lines on his face and his mouth tended to frown more easily. *How much strength has he left; how much do I?*

"Brother," Chaiko struggled awkwardly to find the proper phrasing for the burdens of his heart, "tomorrow we embark on a new future, uncertain though it may be, especially for the likes of Samar and me. Samar is old and I am a cripple," he said striking the stump of his leg for emphasis. "Samar might not make it, and the way is long for a man on crutches."

Baer interrupted him, "I have seen that a man with a will and spirit to live can outlast a stronger man who is weak in heart and resolve. I tell you that you have heart, and rooted in your heart the same desire as I, to see our people safe. I need your eyes and ears and mind."

Chaiko looked at his brother and struggled with his emotions. "Who knows when we will have time again to talk of private matters? I need to tell you of my gratitude for how you have stood by me all my life, especially since I ... lost my leg. I have been a burden to you and the clan ... but have found myself. There is peace inside." Chaiko patted his chest. "But I could not have made it without you. No, let me finish," he insisted, warding off his brother's painful protestations. "As you can see from my few possessions, my burden is light, and my heart is lighter, free of bitterness, (Make yourself light, the owl said, 'so your spirit can soar') and I start this journey in full expectation of reaching the hills. But should something happen to me or to you, I want you to know that you have been brother to me, a father and the leader of my clan. And because you are the head of this clan, and because Tanya and Lana need your strength ..." he paused to ease the constriction of his throat, "you must promise, that if it comes to a choice between me and them and the clan, you MUST choose them over me."

Baer was rocked back by the intensity of this request. All his life he had looked for clear choices, even more so as a leader, but he hated this choice now presented so brutally clear to him. He shook his head. "Do you not know that everyone of us is the clan? Can you separate me from my arms? From my legs? From my heart?" Only belatedly realizing this was the wrong track to take with a man who had lost a leg, he lapsed into silence.

"Brother, it would ease my heart immeasurably, if this trip were to be my own. I will then live by my own strength or die from the lack of it. But it will be my destiny. And I will promise to do all I can to live and survive."

"Chaiko, I will not lie to you. This trip will be hard on us all, with the old people, the injured and the young to take care of. Our future in the hills is perhaps no more certain than here, notwithstanding my speech earlier. But we shall make it. Focus on that. We shall make it. When choices come we will both do what we must."

"Then you promise?" Chaiko queried.

"To leave you behind if you can't keep up? No, I will never promise that." Baer ended on a note of cold finality that brooked no redress.

In the meantime, the clan focused on Samar who had broken into a shuffle to the beat of a hollow tree trunk pounded by Stow in a simple rhythm. The booming sound had a hypnotizing effect. In slow undulating steps, Samar moved about the cave, muttering incantations, holding a long, smoldering feather which he waved about him. The smell from the feather wafted about in a thin wisp of smoke that was so overpowering, bitingly acrid, that people backed away from the shaman in haste. Samar continued unconcerned by their reactions, the odor not seeming to bother him. He wove his pattern through the cave, his progress marked by a scramble of humanity trying to escape the burning smell which the old man was insisting on waving under their very noses. In spite of himself Chaiko watched bemused as Samar elicited cries of consternation wherever he went. How was this supposed to help the clan become reconciled to leaving their familiar haunts behind?

Voices of irritation were raised against their shaman when he threatened to come toward them again, but Samar produced yet more feathers, and the smell grew even more nauseating. For a good while the old man persecuted them all, driving them hither and thither, the sense-blurring smell bitingly pungent. One whiff and Kray had an instantly dripping nose, probably the last thing that he would have wished for himself. His mate Yaya looked at him in open disgust at all the viscosity that was hanging in a long strand from his nostrils. He mewed pitifully. The cave was like a riled-up beehive, with lots of irritable buzzing and flying about. Finally Samar doused his feathers and seemed quite satisfied with himself as he headed for his sleeping place.

"So?" Chaiko, having approached Samar, let the query hang in the air.

"So, think you they still regret that tomorrow they leave this place?" Samar flung back at him. "No, they are much too angry with me to be burdened with sorrow. They will curse me and not pine away the night. Or do you think that a person who lost his foot, still bemoans the toes he hurt previously?" he asked in viciously biting tones. So he did smell the feathers after all, Chaiko concluded. Certainly the irritation Samar created with the feathers would distract the people from their apprehensions. But did he not have the analogy reversed? If the cave was the foot, what did the toes stand for? Then, Chaiko found himself thinking about his own toes. Tomorrow he would tell Samar that yes, even after four years, he missed his toes, even though the loss of the whole does overshadow the loss of each part. One still grieves.

After being so riled up for no reason they could see, the clan settled down fairly quickly for the night, but sleep came slower after all the excitement of the day and the unknown facing them. Out of habit Chaiko stayed awake, though there was no fire to guard or feed. The moon shone bright and a few thin transparent clouds floated by. The wind blew incessantly, its hot breath sucking moisture from an already desiccated ground. Chaiko could almost hear the stalks of grass breaking from the dryness. He could smell the baked odor of pine needles from a cluster of trees not far off.

His nose felt dry; a whiff of Samar's feathers had not helped him either.

Chapter 15

Before dawn could creep over the horizon, the clan was up with last minute preparations. The cave was a beehive of activity, but not everybody was caught up in the general excitement. Ela's baby cried in weak protest at the unaccustomed hour. He was still bothered by heat sores. Samar too was cranky, though he tried to hide it, fearing the rigors of the day ahead. Calla was exhorting her mate to take yet one more thing. Cosh had to intervene and refuse over half of what she claimed to be bare essentials. With large wicker baskets strapped to their backs, the women vied with each other to pack more comfort into their stacks, with large bundles of dried herbs stuck on top. Again and again, people were cautioned and then told to repack. The men, too, tended to take just one more item, an extra spear or a lucky throwing stick, one more trophy testifying to their skill and status. The people looked with sour regret at the pile of discarded treasures growing higher and for the time being, ownerless.

Crow sought out Chaiko who was trying to cut his pack down to essentials. He was going to be sent ahead, he thought, and he wanted to make sure Chaiko would be all right. Chaiko patted his crutches and said lightly, "These will carry me on their own." Crow looked dubiously at the two stout sticks. "Don't forget you have Bogan's stone to protect you," he said in all sincerity. Chaiko smiled wanly at his friend and wished he had as much confidence in the talisman.

Three groups were organized. Tusk, who due to his great vitality had recovered quickly, was sent with Stow and Crow to the front to scout ahead. The main body was lead by Baer with his family. Tael had to be carried by two hunters, Kray and Rea, in a hide sling, with Gill, Simm and Makar on reserve to change them up. Kor was assigned to assist Samar. Generally the weaker had someone stronger to help. As was his wish, Chaiko was by himself, resolved not to lag. Cosh and Malek were sent to the rear, to keep an eye on stragglers and to guard against predators following their trail. They had not seen any, but it was prudent to be cautious.

14 Stones

The word was again passed up and down the groups to keep moving so that they might reach Broken-Tree before the sun and heat became unbearable. Then without any ceremony the clan was on the move: out of the cave, down the slope to a narrow cleft in the cliffs that led to the north, and a slow descent onto the broad plain. There were but few backward looks, so intent was everybody on the journey ahead.

By the time the sun rose above the rim of the earth, the clan was into the salt marshes of the plain. The white and yellow salt crust lay about like froth crunching underfoot. This salt was inedible, causing severe stomach complaints when ingested, and even the animals learned to avoid it. In places cracks crisscrossed the ground where the constant wind had sucked all moisture from the soil. The place looked more like an uninviting desert than a marsh. The dried out hulks of reeds no longer offered shelter. Here and there they came upon the remains of some small creature that had died and been fought over by carrion birds. Fine dust flew on the air, caught by the least irregularity of the ground, obliterating any tracks, then drifting on.

The first two hours had been easy, with the air still fresh and the excitement of an unknown future beckoning them on, every step taking them northward, farther from their present problems. But now the heat from a blazing sun increased until they were bathed in sweat. Cast off dried-out fragments of stalks blew about on the air, and cleaved to their sweat-plastered bodies, their sharp edges and points working into the skin. The few remaining bugs disturbed by their passing buzzed about their heads and faces, aggressively going after any moisture, especially about the eyes and nose. More and more, people reached for their water skins.

They had made it about half way to their first destination, Broken-Tree, traversing flat open ground covered only with dried-out stubs of vegetation and scrub bushes that had lost all their leaves. There was no shade anywhere, and the wind blew constantly at them with a hot breath that carried fine gritty sand to plaster their bodies. Chaiko was already tired and had to concentrate to keep the rhythm of working his crutches. He had slipped to the back of the main body, but was determined not to be caught by the vanguard. His armpits were sore, the skin between forefingers and thumbs already raw from the constant friction with the wood. His palms ached with the effort of holding on, and his right leg was too tired to cushion the shock of each step. He felt the ache build in his muscles and knew he was not equal to this pace. Slowly he lost ground, but was determined to fight for every step. Happily the ground here was even and firm, a lot easier to traverse than a track of yielding, loose sand. The heat on his skin was unbearable; the whole right side of his body burned, while the cooler left side only reminded him how much hotter the other side was. Sweat poured from his forehead, the salt stinging his eyes, but half blind he stumbled on. He had no hands free to wipe his face. He did not try to fight the build-up of pain, but tried to focus his mind on the next step. He was aware of the rearguard closing on him and tried even harder.

The column was now strung out over a distance. Kids had to be carried and old people supported. Ahead, Baer looked back appraisingly. Tanya and Lana were all right, and so were most of the others, but the sustained effort was beginning to show on the old people. They had about a third of the way still to go until Broken-Tree, but with the sun climbing ever higher in the sky the heat was sapping everybody's strength. Samar, like the tough old bird he was, with Kor's help managed to keep up. The lightness of his body made it easier for his spider legs to carry him. A way in the back, Baer saw his brother struggling and his eyes squinted narrower into the glare. The next stretch was going to be the hardest, he warned himself, yet nowhere could they stop for a rest before Broken-Tree, because of the lack of shade and fresh water. He lengthened his step just a little, forcing the line forward. On they marched across a dried wasteland, in single file, like an army of ants.

The sun beat down relentlessly. Its rays burned into the skin in spite of the grease that people rubbed on to protect themselves, but the grease plugged the pores and hindered the sweat from cooling the body. It also picked up every grain of sand blowing about, the resulting layer storing the heat immediately close to the skin, inescapably intimate.

To the rear, Chaiko struggled not to fall further behind. His perception shrank to inner turmoil as his mind fought against the weariness and effort of each step. "Sit down on that inviting rock," his mind suggested, "Stop and take a sip of cool water," flooding him with promises of relief if only he obeyed. But Chaiko fought off the temptation, forcing himself to keep a rhythm, at times faltering.

He lurched forward, the earlier smooth fluidity gone, planting his crutches on the hard-packed earth in front, feeling the shock under his armpits impacting into his aching shoulders and radiating along the shoulder blades. He pushed off with his right leg, carrying his weight over the balance point, riding the crutches, his right foot swinging ahead, planting it on the soil, to ease the body down against the jarring impact. He would then launch himself into the next sequence, before his mind could have a chance to think and his body to refuse. He knew that if he yielded on one step, his whole resistance would cave in. He kept plodding on, not daring to look ahead to face the stretch of expanse still to go, or to look behind to be reminded of how little progress had been made. Thus, he heard more than saw the rearguard close in. Though he had little energy to spare, he pushed harder to stay ahead.

The situation was turning desperate for the whole clan, not just for Chaiko. Now even the older children, not having the endurance of an adult, were fading and starting to lag. Exhaustion erased all expression from Ruba's face and only a dull dazed look remained. Sosa and Ork were dragging their feet noticeably. The old people, too, had to shorten their steps to keep their stiffened muscles and creaking joints going. The pace had slowed to a crawl, as each struggled to find reasons to keep on moving. Their wake was littered with their hopes, as they sought to lighten their burdens: a favored skin, a fur, a digging stick, a few clubs. Superfluous items of comfort or display—discarded.

The sun was now near zenith, and blazed fiercely down at them. Out in the open, it seemed twice its normal size, malevolently dominating and baking the surrounding countryside. The brightness pierced the eyes like needles, in spite of lids slit against its onslaught. They turned away screwed up faces, the dust collecting in every wrinkle and every fold. Throats were parched, and no amount of lukewarm water could slake their thirst. The nostrils became crusted with sand and flies buzzed about their faces. Their skin grew numb from the combined assault of burning sun and desiccating wind driving grains of sand into every pore.

There were clusters of thorn bushes about, devoid of leaves, a few bird nests still clinging to dried out branches. A few cactus-like plants seemed to retain a vestige of color; the rest were uniformly the grayness of dry death. A passing foot stirred up bits and pieces of their shattered hulks, stabbing into calves and ankles. Here and there they crossed a dried-out river bed, the pebbles and rocks rolling loose underfoot, the mud having dried and shrunk away, releasing its grip on the stones. They came upon a deeper hole full of bones and dried up scales, where fish had died en mass as their last refuge dried out. Now, only dust swirled along the exposed waterbed.

Shading his eyes with his hand, Baer scanned the land ahead, aching to catch a sight of Broken-Tree. They were coming up to a high point in the gently rolling plain from which he hoped their destination would be visible, giving new heart to the exhausted clan. They needed a boost to their spirits. He himself felt immeasurably weary, his side aching with the effort of his breathing forced against his healing ribs. He peered with apprehension about him. Tanya looked tired but still seemed strong in spite of the large backpack she was carrying. Lana was dragging her feet listlessly, her eyes dulled by the mindless shuffling across a burned-out land that danced in the heat. He took her hand and squeezed in encouragement. She looked up at him and her blank look barely recognized him. Her parched lips cracked as she attempted a slight smile, and her face dissolved into a grimace frighteningly devoid of recognizable expression. He gave his spears to Tanya, then swung his daughter onto his shoulders, wincing against the pain in his side. Lana clutched his forehead and sagged against him. Baer was shocked by how much she weighed. Looking about he could see that most of the kids were being carried, something having been cast away to make room for them on sagging shoulders and aching backs. Let the present carry the future. Baer could see desperation growing in the faces. But they stumbled on. To his surprise Uma was doing well; she did not seem to mind the heat at all. Samar was also holding up, his feet shuffling on in unvarying rhythm, the rest hidden by his stone-set grimace. To the rear he could just see Chaiko limping along; his heart ached, but there was nothing he could do about it. His brother had asked to be on his own, refusing help, and as far as he could, he would give Chaiko the chance he wanted, but he would intervene when the situation demanded it. For now, Cosh would take care of him, he told himself. Lana was heavy and he had to shift her to a more comfortable position. He too was struggling to keep command of his aching body. Just one more step, he told himself, just one more.

At the rear Cosh and Malek were following Chaiko at a slight distance. Cosh knew that Chaiko wanted to do this on his own and he gave him enough room to do so, even slowing their pace somewhat and allowing the rest to get ahead. He knew that they were nearing their destination, which was just out of sight, over the rise. Then several times Chaiko stumbled, just barely recovering, and Cosh gestured for them to move in. "Well done, Chaiko. We are almost there," he said, laying a steadying hand on him as did Malek on the other side. So supported, progress was easier. His mind was now completely numb to the pain, to the heat, and too exhausted to resist or to care.

Ahead of them the main group reached the crest, then disappeared beyond it, and the three were alone in the landscape. Chaiko hardly noticed as they, too, made their way to the crest one step at a time. Then they were there and paused to view the ground laid out in a gentle slope to the north. Still ahead was Broken-Tree towering above the surrounding bushes and trees, its crown noticeably broken off to give it its name. The clan was already halfway there, their pace freshened by the sight of their goal.

As they neared, a pack of wild dogs appeared snarling at the newcomers. They looked ready to defend the only watering hole in the vicinity. But as the men approached with spears ready, the lead dog backed away, growling in frustration. The pack hesitated then followed the leader into the scrub bush to the north. It seemed that they too were retreating to the hills.

There was a copse of wood by Broken-Tree, hugging a small pond fed by an underground spring. Leading up to it was a deep washout that provided shade whatever the time of day. The clan rushed the pond, drank deeply of its refreshing coolness and splashed about washing away the dust and grime. Baer had to warn them not to stir up the silt in the bottom; he wanted the water clear and drinkable. He also warned them not to drink too quickly and bloat themselves. Soon, the exhaustion drove them to find a resting place in some shade and, one by one, they gratefully sank down. Most were soon asleep.

Chaiko did not remember how he reached the shadows. He did not remember Tanya bringing him fresh water to drink and that she then washed his face and carefully the raw places on his hands. He did not remember Baer coming over to check on him.

His mind, released from the bondage of determination to push on and on, refused to focus. Instead he was amazed by a small blue flower in the lee of a bush. He had not seen something so delicate and tender since the wind-blown heat wave took hold. His eyes drank in its fresh blue color, in its way as restoring as a cool drink, so devoid of color the last days had been, with sun-bleached tan and pale yellows dominating everywhere.

Chaiko lay where he had collapsed against a rock ledge and the bush. The rock felt cool against his burning skin. His leg cramped occasionally, but his mind hardened by the forced march was inured to the complaints of his body. Chaiko thoroughly enjoyed his motionlessness; it was so good not to have to move, not even to stir. His eyes swept the sky; from his shelter the sun was not visible, and he noted how much friendlier the depth of sky looked. His eyes wandered freely about the blue expanse without squinting. In the middle of such idle observation he, too, fell asleep.

It was decided not to continue the march that evening but to wait for the pre-dawn. This leg of their journey had proved so grueling that time was required for the whole clan to recover. Luckily, on the next stretches, water and shade were more abundant. Baer, Tusk and Cosh went meticulously over every person to assess their reserves of strength. Baer was most concerned about Chaiko, but Cosh was able to reassure him by reporting how well he had done all day. In the end, Baer trusted the fighting spirit of his brother; he had to trust it as there were no alternatives. Everybody was in need of help and he had no one to spare. Tael had been carried but was painfully jarred by stumbling missteps. The bearers, even taking turns, were exhausted.

Three days later the clan was two thirds of their way north-east across the plain. In the distance ahead their destination, the gap in the hills, was clearly visible beckoning them on. The heat was as intense as ever and the wind blew unceasingly from the west. They leapfrogged from one pocket of shelter to another in the burned-out land that offered precious little refuge.

Their progress was slow and difficult, though a routine had developed. The scouts left markers to show the best trail, which the rest followed at a measured pace that allowed even Chaiko to keep up. The rearguard was dispensed with as they had not seen any animals at all to protect against. During the last part of each stretch the younger kids had to be carried and the older people assisted. But all had toughened up and bore their exertions with quiet weariness. They marched on in the silence of grim determination, making the least movement or effort that was required. The common measure was one step, just one step, behind the person ahead. One foot leading the other, in a weary shuffle through the dryness of a coarsened land. The eyes were downcast to hide from the piercing glare and to shade the mind from the confusion of the distance that danced in the heat. They crawled along like insects which having lost the shadows, crawled to survive a merciless sun, pushing on and on until they either reached safety or died.

Though their aiming point lay tantalizing ahead, it did not seem to be getting any closer. The depth of the plain was deceptive and swallowed up any appearance of progress. It had few distinct features to give them a sense of proportion. Though the leaders reassured them that they had indeed covered over two thirds of the distance and exhorted them to push on, still they lacked the rewards of waypoints reached, and found it disheartening. It seemed a useless exercise against a hostile nature, trapped between horizons.

Chaiko was doing quite well, although he was again dropping behind. He was able to maintain a steady rhythm as he pushed his weight along smoothly on his crutches. He had aches and pains but he accepted them, and even his mind got so used to it that he took less and less notice of the many complaints his body generated, but also did not seek to escape them. Chaiko concentrated on his breathing, as his whole rhythm depended on it. Every sequence started with a deep intake, which he held as his weight rode over the crutches, then the shock of impact with the ground driving a prolonged exhalation. The trick was to balance all components to achieve the harmony of breathing and motion. The breathing also had a hypnotic calming effect on his mind, and he found that time seemed to pass swiftly enough even though his body could in no way escape the harshness it was exposed to. His mind was thus insulated by this increased concentration, while his body was cut off from any conscious recognition of its suffering, at the behest of the imperative to keep moving, marching, a step at a time.

He also kept his mind within safe bounds. Do not look back, do not look ahead, one step at a time. He did not try to anticipate difficulties or relief. He tried to stay in the moment just one step at a time. "Keep going, move your feet," he told himself, "foot" he corrected himself. Reduced as he was to a most basic state, he found this to be amusing enough to burst out laughing, in reality sounding more like a fit of a coughing. Just one more step, over a landscape that seemed not to change, just one more step for a prisoner of the horizon.

Chaiko was picking his way through loose shale, careful to plant his crutches to get a firm purchase. Loose bits of dried out moss lost their hold on the rock and were carried away by the ever-present wind... blowing from the west. Chaiko could feel the windburn on the back of his neck and ears, a dull prickly sensation from the driven sand. His eyes burned from the dryness and the dust, with sand crusting in the corners. The well-trodden path he followed blurred in front of him. He took a quick look ahead to orient himself and saw the main group at a standstill, bunched up. In surprise he pulled up short, wondering what had caused them to stop and cluster like that. He was too far back to make out any detail, but still the body postures and group reaction showed the shock of frozen surprise. The tight group indicated a measure of threat somewhere, drawing together protectively for reassurance.

Chaiko squinted across the distance, trying to make sense of what he saw. He noted that the group was facing west; was this the source point of some danger? He quickly scanned the west, but saw only the open plain and the range of mountains in the distance. There was no suggestion of any threat. Yet he felt apprehension rising at the unseen danger and noted that his heart was beating fast. He took a couple of deep breaths to quiet himself, then started off taking a less cautious route through the shale and broom grass.

Ahead there was an obvious meeting, some decisions being made. That must be Baer, Chaiko told himself, identifying the focus of the tight cluster. Then one person separated from the group and headed toward Chaiko at a fast lope. The rest of the group formed a marching line and set off at a forced pace.

Chaiko could not imagine what could have caused all this. A closer scrutiny of the west revealed nothing to account for it. The uncertainty was gnawing at him, and his apprehension grew. By the reaction of the clan there was some imminent menace out there that he could not see from his lower position.

Peering at the approaching figure, he recognized Crow from his mannerisms. The gliding gait was unmistakable. When they were kids he had often raced against him and was familiar with all his motions. Being taller and longer of leg, Crow won most of the short races, but the longer ones belonged to Chaiko; he ran not faster but smarter, pacing himself and taking every advantage of the terrain. He clucked to himself disapprovingly as Crow took a shorter but more difficult line to him. He recalculated his course to intersect with Crow's path.

He noted that the main group was moving faster on a new heading, taking the most direct course to the hills: certainly shorter, but more arduous, as there was a number of ravines to traverse as well as an awkward switch-back trail up a steep slope. The original course would have taken them north to the broad river that flowed to the west and offered a comfortable path into the hills upriver. They had been looking forward to fresh-flowing water and a respite from the burned-out land they had been travelling. But the clan was now trading ease and comfort for time and a shortened distance.

Chaiko increased his pace, aware even at this distance how much faster the main group was moving now. The children were being carried, he suddenly realized, and his heart gave a jump. Were things that desperate? The fear rose within and constricted his throat, but an apprehensive look to the west still revealed nothing. What could it be? Instinctively he hurried his stride more and nearly fell. He steadied himself, set the usual stride, then gradually built up speed letting all the components of his movement catch up to the new demand.

Crow's lope was getting to be ragged, fighting loose sand up a light incline. He was laboring with the effort. "Just like him, to set too quick a pace and use himself up," Chaiko commented to himself, "instead of calculating the whole distance." He slowed somewhat, admonishing himself, "Better take your own advice."

A confusion of feelings swirled within. A need to know fed his critical impatience at Crow's progress, yet was mixed with love and appreciation for his friend who was making such an obvious effort to get to him; to warn him of what? The west remained silent.

Off ahead, the single line formed into two lines moving side by side over open ground. Better to help each other, Chaiko reasoned. In front of them were probably the scouts, led by Cosh and Tusk, to find the quickest line to the hill. Why the quickest? He could read the desperation into what was happening, but still could find no reason for it. The gap between cause and effect increased his disorientation and flooded him with feelings of unreality that were stronger than any spirit effect he had ever experienced. Ahead was his clan, and he could feel their panic, but because he could not find the cause, he could not use his reason to fight the rising fear in himself. What could be driving them?

The person who could tell him was making every effort to get to him, winding his way through scrub bush and buffalo grass. Crow was floundering, his gait uneven and his chest heaving to gasp in more air. His knees buckled, and he stumbled forward, but he forced himself to maintain the punishing pace. Chaiko's heart swelled because of Crow's great concern for him that fuelled this effort. He, too, pushed on, forcing his crutches to reach a little further.

While in the foreground, his mind was beset with the growing unreality of the situation, his reasoning mind was working methodically in the background. It was clear that there was a danger threatening from the west and that safety lay in the east. The margin of safety appeared to be slim, so quick was the new pace and so marked the deviation to the present course. How much time did they have? That seemed beyond their control. Then, how much time would they need to reach safety? This was something the mind could work on. Under the original plan they had about three days left of travelling in easy stages. Today's segment would have taken them northward to the river, then two days along its broad banks into the hills. The new route, directly east to the hills as the birds flew, without pause, without hiding from the sun at midday, would still require the rest of today to complete. Would that be enough?

"How far can I go? How far and at what pace?" he asked himself soberingly. Mentally, he shrugged his shoulders at too many imponderables, but he did a quick assessment. He felt worn down by the trip so far, beset by accumulated aches and pains, but also felt trim and lean as he had lost some weight and gained some toughness. The resultant weariness gave a good mind-set for the unrelenting effort that was required. His mind had hardened, ignoring the protestation of his body, concentrating on smoothness of movement, wandering not far from the reality of the present. His mind now found it relatively easy to say no to the body and insist on its will.

He took a quick look at the group ahead working up a slight incline toward a ridge, made a quick search of the west, still unable to find anything to arouse his concern, and then settled on his friend now within shouting distance. Sweat was pouring down Crow's face and his arms pumped stiffly to force the pace of his movement. His knees buckled much too often, lending a curious bobbing motion to his progress. His face was flushed crimson and was contorted with the effort of keeping his body moving. They met and Crow collapsed, his chest heaving. So greedy was he for fresh air that he had no time to expel the used-up breath, but gasped convulsively after more, with nowhere for it to go.

"What is it?" Chaiko demanded from his friend, exasperated with his inability to answer. He had hurried to get here, but now was unable to say anything. "What is it?" he demanded again, loading all his fear into the "it."

Crow was still unable to speak; he half stood and pointed to the west with a shaking arm. He struggled to get a few words out: "... smoke ... fire ..." was all he could manage, but it was enough. Chaiko's head snapped around to the direction indicated, his eyes searching westward, but still he saw nothing. He rescanned and this time found a smudge line obscuring a bit of the background. "It could be fire," he concluded. In the dried out plain a fire was burning almost smokeless, driven by a steady west wind. Earlier, he had looked too far to the horizon and then too near, and missed the spreading smudge that did not call attention to itself but hid in the general washed-out tan of the dried-out landscape and the dancing heat. It was a narrow line of flames, driven by the wind, greedily consuming the dry grass, burning smokeless. The shimmering heat haze hid the rest.

At this distance the fire did not look dramatic or even dangerous. But he knew it was deadly. With a steady wind behind it, it was racing across the plain toward them faster than they could run, faster than a bird could fly; a wall of intense heat that seared everything in its path and left behind everything smoldering char.

Faced with the fact of fire, he wasted little time resisting the thought of it, but started to calculate, estimates of time, distance, rate of progress and of course, the speed they would need to reach safety in the east. He looked at the main group pushing toward the hills in full flight. "Maybe they would make it," he concluded "but you won't." He recalculated, using more generous margins but came to the same conclusion. He looked at Crow and saw confirmation in his friend's eyes.

Somewhat recovered, Crow pulled him by his arm to get him moving toward safety, and the two started about a quarter of an afternoon behind the rest. Chaiko knew he could not maintain the fast pace the main group was setting and that the gap would widen with each stride. However, he pushed himself and was able to hold a smooth rhythm. All the while, his mind worked feverishly, juggling time and distance. He lacked numbers and mathematics to solve such a problem, but had an uncanny ability to judge distances and travelling time that came from experience, not from abstract reasoning. He settled on a speed that would be needed to reach safety. Crow smiled encouragingly, but Chaiko knew that it was a speed he could not maintain long. His heartbeat increased to match his breathing at this forced pace, trying to stay synchronized. He barely had time to expel the used up air before the next breath was incoming. Pushing his weight forward was relatively easy, but the shock of the ground was already putting strain on the knee of his good leg. His calf muscle was stiffening with each impact. The calluses on his hands were starting to crack under the added friction and would soon be bleeding. Chaiko knew that he could maintain this punishing rate for only a brief time longer, and would totally exhaust himself far short of safety. He kept at it though, realizing that he must, for Crow's sake, but he would have to pry his friend loose somehow.

With an effort, he pulled even with Crow, who looked at him in gratified approval. "What did ... Baer say?" he forced out the question between breaths, but did not slow down.

"'It is as you had wished' ... Baer said," Crow replied, still puzzled by the cryptic message. "Or, 'as you had wished.'" At the time, the exact wording did not seem important, as long as he could get to Chaiko and then to safety. Chaiko smiled to hide the shock of confirmation from his brother. Baer had made his calculation, too. How hard it must have been for him not to turn back himself and help his brother.

He looked up, ahead, to see two lines in full flight, like insects moving across a broad landscape. He looked hard at a point that stood motionless, seemingly looking back towards him. "Brother...," Chaiko half spoke as a parting thought across a distance that denied him safety. Crow looked at him shocked, then saw the direction of his look and understood. He lowered his head, to give Chaiko privacy.

In the west, the smudge grew, gaining on them. It was creeping north as well but was racing toward them on the wings of the wind. In spots, a column of darker smoke now rose into the air, where the fire had found something more substantial to consume. Among a group of trees or bushes, the fire leaped into a sheet of flames, in a delirious dance of destruction. The fire now hid part of the horizon. Time was running out for them.

"Crow," Chaiko called to his friend, "you must go."

"Go and leave you? ... Never!" his friend replied. Not a shock of surprise at the request, but the quickness of the reply told Chaiko that Crow, too, had made his calculations and had made his decisions. He hoped his friend would not get into a stubborn mood, which he knew from experience was difficult to overcome ... yet overcome it he must.

"Raven ... you must go. You will have to live for both of us." Crow's eyes widened. Chaiko had not used that private name for Crow since his accident ... the significance was not lost on Crow ... but it was preferable to die with one's friend than to abandon him. No, he shook his head, he would stay.

"My friend," Chaiko said, all his feelings trembling in his voice, "dying is easy, it is living that is hard. You must do the hard part and live for both of us." A swirl of smoke passed like a shadow over them and the smell of burning was growing stronger. Chaiko was fighting for breath, but he had to talk. "Dying is easy, but knowing that I would cost you your life, makes my dying very hard ..." Tears were coursing down on Crow's face but he shook his head no.

The curtain of smoke reached high in the air and now the fire extended as far north as to the south. A flight of birds passed overhead straight-line to the east. They had not seen any animals all these past days, but were now overtaken by a small herd of antelope. The famine from the drought had sculpted hard ridges into their ribs and lines of bones. Driven by fear they passed quite close taking no notice of them.

"You must help Baer," Chaiko pleaded, with great effort forcing out the words. He knew how much his friend respected Baer, but Crow only shook his head.

"You must help Lana," he tried again, knowing of Crow's fondness for her. Crow stumbled ... that was something he had not thought about. So, his friend was more than just fond of her. "Lana likes you," Chaiko pressed on, trying to imply more than the words said. Crow's eyes grew rounder still—his dilemma played out on his face—but still he shook his head.

They had finally intersected the path of the main group and fell into their tracks. Littered along both sides were favorite possessions, and even essential items lay discarded everywhere. Even parcels of food, Chaiko noted with shock! That bespoke the desperation more than anything else could have. The people ahead had nothing left but their lives.

Behind, the fire had noticeably gained on them. It seemed to be coming faster as the distance shrank. To the south the fire front was more advanced and the horizon was blotted out by driven smoke. To the side, they passed a clutch of rabbits, noses nervously sniffing the air, haphazardly milling about, not yet overwhelmed by the panic that was sure to come.

Ahead, the two lines of the clan were disappearing into a draw, then all were gone except for a lone figure on the hilltop, watching them. "Brother..." Chaiko murmured. His sides were hurting and he ran lopsided to ease the pain. He was running out of time, in more ways than one. He must get Crow to break out on his own; till then he must run with him. But how? If love could not loosen his resolve, what would—duty perhaps?

"We both know that at this rate the fire will overtake us." Chaiko squeezed the words out between breaths. Crow shrugged his shoulders. If he had to die it was fitting to die with one's friend and in his mind the matter was settled. "The wind might change," Crow said, not unreasonably. It hadn't for weeks, Chaiko thought sourly.

Desperately he sought a solution to the cruel dilemma that faced them. He must find a way to free Crow from the feeling of loyalty that tied them both. A stray thought crossed his mind and desperately he grabbed at it. With some difficulty, from around his neck Chaiko took the odd shaped tell-mark, a curious looking stone on a rawhide thong and handed it to Crow. "This belonged to Bogan," he reminded Crow who needed no such reminder. "This must not be lost to the clan," he added simply. Crow looked with reverence at the valued object. Some of Bogan's spirit still must cleave to it and he knew that it must be saved. Chaiko saw the wavering of resolve on his friend's face and pressed on, "You hold a piece of the future of the clan in your hand, and you must save it." Crow could argue about not leaving a friend and dying, but he could not argue about the future of his clan. He clutched the precious item protectively close and a fresh flood of tears blinded him. Perhaps if the decision had required of him a change of action, he still would have balked, but fate required of him only that he do what he was already doing, run and keep on running.

With the last of his strength Chaiko pushed Crow forward speeding him on his way to safety, he hoped. Crow stumbled, but recovered, and loped off with the future of his clan in his hand. He dared not look back and see himself leave his best friend behind. But the knowledge that he had, and the sense of betrayal he felt guilty of, would follow him all his life.

Chapter 16

Panting with exhaustion Chaiko dropped to the ground and watched his friend Crow running away from him. He was flooded with intense relief and gratitude that his friend, by saving himself, had given a life back to Chaiko—all that, to save a valuable relic for the clan. Now, if it had to be, he could die more easily.

Crow, unencumbered by a cripple's pace, was able to put some distance between them. "He'll make it," Chaiko reassured himself, "he must make it." Lifting his eyes to the distant hill top, to the lone figure there, Chaiko's heart was filled with sadness. Baer too must see the distance grow and have his answer, Chaiko thought. "It's as you have wished....," he repeated his brother's last message, knowing that had there been any other choice, Baer would have made it. When he looked again, the hilltop was empty. Crow too had disappeared in a cut in the land, and Chaiko was alone.

"What now?" he asked himself. The sudden aloneness gave him a strange sense of freedom. Whatever he did now, he would do by himself for himself. He turned and observed the fire calmly. With the clan hopefully safe in the hills and Crow gone, the fire lost some of its threat. He estimated that he had some time left, not enough to reach the hills to the east, but maybe enough to head north to reach the river and find refuge in it. Maybe. He owed it to himself to try, and to Baer and to Crow, for he had promised both. He rose against his stiffness and headed north forcing his aching muscles to obey.

As he hobbled along, over his left shoulder he saw the fire approach, the smoke filling the whole sky, obscuring the sun. The fire had now extended fully to both north and south, like some fiery bird unfolding its wings over all distance, flame for its feathers, a trailing plume of smoke its shadow. Chaiko was following a course that ran parallel to the advancing fire front, chancing that he could beat the fire to the river. Once there, then what? Would there be enough water to shield him from this bird of prey? Could he fight the fire for air to breathe? He had to try.

14 Stones

Increasingly animals ran across his path: a marten, a family of coyotes, deer, raccoon and rabbits, but they all ignored him. Only a fox paused and looked at him perplexed; manchild, why are you going that way? A flock of birds flew overhead with heavy wing-beats in the air. On the ground insects and bugs scurried about, perhaps aware of the growing danger, seeking shelter underground, beyond the reach of fire. Chaiko envied them. He had no wings to fly to safety, nor four legs to run with; he had only one ... no three, he corrected himself, laughing mirthlessly, his mind grasping at humor in the face of fear. Life felt sweeter and more precious in its peril. He would do what he could, he resolved, and let the fire do what it could. He would soon know the result. He had a flashback to this same feeling of suspension and calmness when he was younger, caught in a river of stones, unable to help himself, but not yet knowing the consequence. The price he found out only later: pain, loss of a leg, loss of status and loss of a normal life. And what price would he have to pay now?

The smoke was growing thicker, a wide curtain rising high into the sky. Chaiko's sense of unreality increased. This fire was made of the same stuff as the tame, servile fire, hand-fed and confined to a circle of hearth stones. Familiar and docile. Unleashed, the fire became living, breathing on its own; unfettered on wings of the winds, racing toward him, devouring everything in its path. And therein lay its evil nature. It had no regret, driven by its all-consuming greed. "More, more, I want more!"

Determined, Chaiko drove himself north. Ahead, still impossibly far ahead, there was a belt of green that extended across his path marking the river. Could he make it? The ground was hard and he made good progress toward it. He came to a rocky ridge and instinctively chose to follow the side away from the fire. Beyond it he reached the level land of the river basin. Here the vegetation was still green and grew greener still as he neared the river, but it was also denser, and he found it harder to pass through. Under a sundried crust the flood plain was soft muck so that his leg and crutches sank ankle deep, making each step all the more difficult.

To his left the fire grew. He heard a dull roar, its angry crackling and felt its hot breath on the wind. Smoke veiled the sky. There was a thick interlocked mass of bushes that kept him from the safety of the river, if indeed there was safety there. He saw the water glint through the lush vegetation but could find no way to it. He turned east now, parallel to the river, with the fire at his back, looking for an opening. Behind him thick smoke and a storm of ash swirled all around him, burning his skin; he had but minutes. The vegetation seemed endless, and it was beginning to look hopeless, but stubbornness drove him on. He wrestled his foot free of the mud, then his crutches and threw himself forward. Desperately he plodded on, the heat warm on his back. Then in the smoke he almost missed it, a broad open pathway to the river used by herds of bison and other herbivores to reach the drinking places. The ground was churned up by many hooves of past years; the drought had hardened each print into an uneven, difficult obstacle for his crutches. But he could see the river and strengthened by a surge of hope he strove toward it.

The smoke was becoming denser and breathing more difficult. The acrid smell burned his nose, and his throat was soon raw. His eyes blinked at the salt of his sweat and tears welled up to clear them. The heat was rising and perspiration ran freely down his body. He marveled that he still had so much moisture to spare. He pushed on, suddenly falling as his crutch got stuck in a hole and snapped under him on the uneven ground. On all fours he crawled, the palms of his hands and his knees scraped by the hard ridges burned into the soil. The smoke was now too thick for him to see, but the hoof marks pointed the way and he crawled by feel.

The sound of the fire turned into an angry roar and was almost upon him. Mixed in were anguished cries of animals trapped by the flames. A bird refusing to leave its nest with two eggs behind, cried piteously, then the fire enveloped it, consuming it. To his left, a deer struggled exhausted in dense bush, the flames licking at him. A large bird emerging from the smoke, its feathers on fire, plummeted to the ground in a smoking heap of twitching flesh. Blind, Chaiko on all fours struggled on, fighting for air in the heat and for hope in desperation. Then finally, his hands touched moist mud and he clawed his way into the water until he was waist deep and then fully submerged, the water cool and reassuring on his skin. None too soon. With a blast, the fire engulfed the shore he had just left in one solid sheet of flame. With the force of a blow, a wall of heat hit him as he ducked under water. He held his breath as long as he could, then with lungs bursting, he came up to take a gasp of hot, hot air then went under again. The next time he came up for air, his body convulsed as it struggled for air in the dense smoke and stifling heat. He panted in quick shallow breaths but did not find enough air to escape under water. With his hands he splashed water over himself to keep his hair from catching fire and his skin from being seared by the intense heat.

Toward shore he saw a warthog run from the burning underbrush into the water, his short hair on fire, squealing piercingly. He rolled about in the shallows and, dousing the flames but not his pain, his eyes rolled crazily and he charged back into the fire, his death noises embraced by the roar of the flames and the hissing at the water's edge.

Even in the middle of the river the heat was unbearable. Chaiko dipped himself as often as he could to cool his exposed head, but could not stay under because his lungs had not found enough air. Several times he became dizzy and almost passed out, but each time the water revived him enough to struggle on.

A new wave of flames passed over, and Chaiko felt a flash lick his face again; his hair was singed and his eyebrows were burned away. He dipped himself, stayed under as long as he could, then came up to wrestle the fire for air. He gasped, the smoke making him cough, convulsively still trying to take a breath. Along the shore, rocks were bursting from the heat and the water was boiling around them. The flames drove the smoke into the air, beneath which Chaiko could see quite well. Something was burning there, still moving; sickened, Chaiko turned away. Was the same fate awaiting him? Then the heat forced him under again.

When he surfaced, things had calmed somewhat. The flames had shrunk, the sound of the fire was going away from him and the smoke was being pulled along by the retreating fire wall. The fire too was struggling for air. Still, all around the ground, trees and bushes smoked. Everything was blackened and charred. Then as fresh air was pulled in, the flames burst awake and settled down to burn at a more leisurely pace, as if they had all the time in the world.

Chaiko could still not get enough air, and he gasped and gasped lungfuls but seemed not the better for it. His lungs, throat and nose felt scalded. The delicate linings were raw. His eyes burned with a sting that a whole river could not wash out. In a couple of places blisters were rising on his cheeks, he felt them gingerly. He was tired, and though in water up to his neck, very thirsty. But he was alive. Still dizzy, he crawled into the shallows afraid that he would drown if he passed out, not daring to go ashore. Fire was still there, heat was there and smoke was there. The sound of the fire front was receding. Chaiko could almost start planning what to do next. If only he could breathe.

On the near shore an elm tree was burning along its entire height; its crown was already consumed with only the main limbs left. The trunk was alive with glowing embers and a streamer of flame and smoke trailed in the wind's wake. The wood crackled explosively as the fire ate deeper into its core, splitting it. A gust of wind toppled the burning column into the water quite near him. Hissing, the flames were doused; sizzling, the embers winked out and steam and smoke boiled to the surface. Chaiko splashed his way into deeper water.

Then out of a wisp of smoke, a water-buffalo appeared, heading aimlessly upriver. Its hump was smoking and its skin was burned off, flesh and muscle smoldering, hanging in shreds from its sides. Blood-flecked froth dripped from its mouth and rumbling bellows of surprise more than pain followed it. It splashed about in knee deep water, the eyes already glazed, uncomprehending. Some instinct still drove him along the watercourse. He vanished back into the smoke.

The secondary fires took hold and once again the heat built, though it did not have the intense blast of the first. All the same, Chaiko retreated back to the middle of the river again till his foot no longer touched bottom. The current embraced him and carried him gently west away from the heart of the fire. He was not a good swimmer, but he could tread water and float. Still, he was tired from the efforts of the last few days; his movements became more and more feeble. When a fair-sized tree floated by, he grabbed it gratefully and with the last of his strength, pulled himself up among the branches. It too had passed through the fire; the leaves and the smaller branches had been burned off, in places still smoking and smoldering. Chaiko made himself as secure as he could among the remaining branches, and before he knew it he was asleep. He woke again and again, suffocating, his bruised lungs hungry for air, in a restless sleep of exhaustion that did not restore him.

The tree kept drifting past the burned-out landscape at a lazy pace, as the rains had not fed the river and it was sluggish and slow. Every once in a while, it would catch on a shoal, swing about, then continue drifting west. In the early evening Chaiko awoke briefly, looked about, found himself further west than ever. Both shores looked uninviting, fire blackened and dead; smoking branches and trunks reached in stark supplication to the sky. The tree trunk bobbed gently in the lazy flow of the river, slowly turning in the eddies. The shoreline drifted by, in its slow way adding to the distance, taking him further and further away from his clan. He was too tired to care, content to let the river find him a new destiny. He drifted back to sleep.

Later still, he was suddenly roused by the complaining, raucous call of a bird that took a dislike to his presence on the log. It flapped its wings threateningly, and screeched a further complaint. Chaiko waved feebly at the bird, and it flew off in ill humor. Chaiko raised his head and looked about. The water had spread itself and the current was barely noticeable. The sun was low in the skies; hours must have passed while he slept. Near and far, there were clusters of reeds sticking out of the water, most of the stalks burned off by the passing fire, only short stubs just above the water left. The shoreline was fire-blackened, here and there still smoking. The smell of burning was still very strong in his nose. He scooped a handful of water to his lips and drank carefully past a swollen tongue and an aching lump in his throat. The water tasted of fire, though he suspected that his senses were temporarily overwhelmed and he should not trust them. After several handfuls, his mouth still felt unwashed and gritty, and his stomach sloshed and gurgled with all the water he had drunk. He realized how hungry he was, but after days of denying the needs and demands of his body, the nagging sensations were coming from far away. Not urgent at all.

He looked more carefully about, and was surprised to discover a raccoon nibbling on the few surviving leaves on the other end of the log. Between mouthfuls the rodent would pause, look at him with beady eyes, then resume his ritual of washing and chewing on the leaves. How had it survived the fire? Where did it come from? Chaiko shrugged to himself; he had other more important things to think about. But he noted with a detached puzzlement that his mind refused to concentrate, wandering about aimless, almost outside his control. At the height of his peril, his mind had focused in wonderful sharpness and detail, but in the aftermath of the danger his mind was sluggish and rebellious. To reorient himself and to refresh a sense of purpose he looked to the far horizons. He noted that the river was still bearing to the west, and the western hills were much nearer, whereas the eastern hills shrank in significance. He had a flash of anxiety about the clan, but he forced it back down and hoped for their safe escape. He would have to hang onto that hope for them as well as for himself.

Leisurely, the log floated by a rock outcrop blackened by soot, surrounded by burned vegetation. There was a small noise among the ashes and a rodent-like creature poked its head above the debris, the nose twitching inquisitively in his direction. It, too, had survived, Chaiko marveled. Probably deep in some burrow—but how did it breathe against the fire's rapacious need for air? Remembering how the fire had sucked air from his lungs, he wondered, "How did I survive?"

His attention was drawn by a sudden splash just ahead. He was too late to see what caused it, but right after, a fish jumped out of the water, its side sparkling in the slanting rays of the setting sun. The droplets of water blazed with color. There was another splash and another fish. A spit of land deflected the river back onto itself, and the waters trapped in its backwash collected slowly spinning flotsam and debris, full of insects that had succumbed to the heat and smoke. The fish were feeding on the collection. The log was drawn toward this turning pool, but was too large and heavy to be drawn fully in, and slowly it drifted by. Chaiko saw a large white fish, rising close to the surface, make a dart toward the rotating float, make a grab, turn away in a flash, then unexpectedly clear the water and arch into the air, spitting out a mouthful of water and a piece of charcoal which it must have mistaken for a tasty morsel. Again and again it jumped, its mouth agape and spitting ... if a fish can spit. Chaiko smiled to himself briefly as he thought how funny the story of the spitting fish would be around the clan fire. But the smile vanished: where was the clan and where was he? He looked ahead to see the sun already perched on the tops of the hills toward which he drifted. The wan light caressed his face with the gentle warmth of its afterglow, but his body numbed by the waters below felt the building chill of the approaching night. He wedged himself more securely into the crotch of branches and drew himself into a tighter bundle, clear of the water. The raccoon watched him suspiciously and retreated into the far extremity of the tree. Chaiko considered striking out for one of the shores, but concluded he was safer where he was.

The sun disappeared behind the hills, and for a while the western skies glowed in the full color of its setting, tinting the hilltops gold but robbing the rest of the landscape of color. Little by little the hues faded altogether and, soon after, the grayness turned to full black, though the river still reflected a pale starlight. The air was completely still, Chaiko noted in some surprise, remembering the relentless desiccating wind. But that seemed so long ago. The lethargy that had settled on his bones also claimed his mind. Somewhere there was a splash and somewhere a snap of breaking twigs, but he was unaware of them, and he drifted off to sleep.

A sudden smell of fire ripped him awake; he rose in panic, and nearly fell into the water. His heart was pounding, but there was no fire, only darkness everywhere. His blood drummed in his ears. Slowly he reassured himself and settled down again. The smell had been very distinct, very real ... and he even felt the accompanying heat. He shook his head to clear the nightmare from his mind. The sky had darkened and the stars stood out in bold relief; if there was a moon, it hid behind a building bank of clouds. In the darkness only the river was visible, a ribbon of silver-blue between the shadowed banks. The water course was narrower, and the flow faster. The tree was bobbing more energetically among the ripples. A gentle lapping sounded from the shores. Chaiko was cold; he hugged his knees to his chest aware of the thinness of his one remaining skin girding his loins. He heard the raccoon moving about on the other end, probably responding to his movements. "Brother raccoon," he reached out in sympathy, "we both lost our cave (did raccoons live in caves?) our families and clan." Sleep came but slowly.

The next time he woke, the stars were brighter and the moon sailed in and out of the clouds. The air had become comfortably mild, filled with a drifting haze of smoke. The raccoon was gone and he was alone.

Chapter 17

He awoke to the heat of the sun on his back and neck, while the rest of his body was numb yet with cold and the dampness of the water so near. He opened one eye but shut it immediately against the harsh light that flooded in. Carefully he opened his eyes a crack for the light to seep through, letting his eyes get accustomed. His lids were swollen and the tears blurred his vision. He squinted into the glare. The full light of the sun danced on the water, blinding him. He cast his eyes toward the shadows and sought relief there; slowly details emerged. The log was floating by a pebble-strewn shoreline, capped by sand dunes held by clumps of weeds, now charred and burned, their hold loosened on the soil, the sand shifting gently from among the exposed roots in a light breeze.

He had been drifting on the log for three days now at the river's gentle pace. Several times the log had been grounded by its roots and he had clambered ashore to look about. Without crutches he had been forced to crawl on all fours; his hands and knees, softened by the water, were soon raw. He found a few roots and stuffed them into his mouth only to spit them out, unable to eat in spite of his hunger. His stomach had shrunk and was full of water from constant drinking. He had had better luck with some green shoots from underwater, and had chewed the crisp stalks slowly to let his stomach get used to them. Later, he had found the remains of a bird and he picked at it. With each bite, his hunger gradually returned, so that by the end he was hungrier than when he had started, but he found little else to eat. As a consequence, his hunger soon faded and his appetite receded once more.

Each place he landed was more inhospitable than the last in the aftermath of the devastation; he returned to the log and drifted down the River of Destiny. He knew that he was being carried further from the clan, but there was nothing to sustain him— even this far the destruction seemed complete. So he was forced to go on.

The western hills, which three short days ago were only distant projections on the far horizon, were now startlingly near. A harsh cliff face loomed large ahead, and Chaiko suddenly realized that he was now drifting to the south. How many times in the past had he looked in this direction, from the vicinity of the cave, to see just an insignificant line of ant hills, wondering what lay there ...? He looked around with suddenly piqued interest. Yes, the river met the western hills and made a bend, looking for a way to the south. The other side was unendingly flat, the distance hiding the eastern hills beyond the horizon. Both shores showed the violence of the fire that had spared nothing. Charcoal and ash, the fire had burned all other colors from the landscape.

He moved cautiously against the numbness of his limbs so long cramped by the unnatural posture of his perch. His arms and legs did not feel like they belonged to him, and he had to force them to move. Slowly the reawakened circulation warmed him and a feeling of pain returned to his limbs. Even his missing leg ached. The pain should have reassured him that he was still alive and should have spurred him on to make some accommodation with his circumstances, but the feeling of detachment prevailed and he remained disinterested in his own future. Without thought, without resistance he watched the river carry him further west, then south. He felt that his lot was predetermined and that the river was an able arbiter of his fate, certainly, at the moment, better than he.

His mouth still felt gritty and his nose was still full of smoke though no fire was anywhere visible. He drank deeply, the water splashing about in the hollowness of his stomach drowning any hunger pangs. He should be hungrier but was not, he noted disinterestedly. He washed his face, wincing at the sting of water on the open sores of the blisters on his cheeks: the fire had marked him well. His eyes were still very light-sensitive, so he turned away from the sun to ease the discomfort, and suddenly among the further branches where the raccoon had been some days ago, was a small snake coiled tightly about a branch, the sun glinting on its speckled bands. Now where did that come from? Could it be poisonous? He did not know, but since the snake showed no inclination to move, after a while Chaiko relaxed, but kept a vigilant eye on it.

The warmth of the sun melted his stiffness and a degree of well-being returned. He was barely aware of a distant nagging of hunger. His mind was still lazy and reluctant to deal with the problems facing him. He was thus content to let the river carry him where it would and not look ahead. At the moment, Chaiko was free of real pain or of a need to move; the present would do him for now and in the rising warmth, he dozed off.

He awoke suddenly to a feeling of coldness enveloping him. He found himself in the shadow of a cliff, the darkness all the cooler on his sun-warmed skin. He shivered and drew himself together to conserve heat. Lack of hunger notwithstanding, he would need to eat soon. He looked about again.

The landscape had changed from gentle slopes to a rugged terrain of rocks, steep hills and cliffs that forced the river to twist and turn to find a way through the many obstacles. In places where the river narrowed abruptly, the water had to hurry to push through the constriction. At these times, the motion of the log became more insistent and urgent, forcing Chaiko to take a firmer grip on the branches. He considered striking out for shore, but the water looked discouragingly cold and both shores steep and slippery. The way ahead looked no worse than the present stretch and as he listened intently, he could hear no roar of a waterfall above the ambient murmur of the river. His mind was still slow to react, sluggishly grappling with each decision. Finally he resolved to stay with the tree but kept a careful watch ahead.

The river was more active and seemed to have a sense of purpose as it gathered strength and pushed against the rocks confining it. Still, it knew where it was going—it was Chaiko who did not. "How does the river know where to go?" he mused to himself. An idle thought, meandering ... he had been on this flow too long. His mind, too, was becoming waterlogged.

Then the river swept around a curve, and cliffs built even higher on both sides hemming the river once again into a narrower channel still. The current freshened and the water splashed and lapped eagerly against the cliff sides. The log also bobbed with more energy; repeatedly the water washed over the whole length of it and over his foot onto his lap. He was soon uncomfortably wet and cold. Ahead there was white water; the pressure of the flow increased as it divided around a rock outcrop in the middle of the channel. The swift current led the log through the gap and sped it down a chute of white water. The tree bucked and threatened to roll. Hanging on tightly, Chaiko's arms grew tired and his skin was scraped by the rough bark. Mist, like smoke, was quickly shredded by the wind growing strong in the narrow confines, moaning in its hurry back upstream in a counter flow to the rush of the river.

At water level, the light was quite dim, only a ribbon of sky right above was aglow with sunlight. In most places the water was pitch dark, only white froth showing the treacherous turbulence below. The river surged then backed up as water fought water for a place to go. A sudden upwelling, like a river of its own, forced another stream under. The log fought its way through the turbulence, lifted by a wave, pulled by the suction of a downflow. Alternating, the root end and the branch end of the tree went under as it bucked its way down stream. With the splash and spray hitting his face with a cold bite, Chaiko grimly hung on. His grip grew numb. He noted that the snake was gone.

Now and again the log rolled ponderously and he had to scramble from handhold to slippery handhold to stay atop. The stump of his leg braced awkwardly against a limb. The cold water surged up around him, the current eagerly tugging and clutching at him. Time and time again he managed to hang on, to stay aloft as the tree righted itself, his knuckles white with cold and effort. He was shivering and his teeth chattered uncontrollably.

Then the leading root end hit a crest and slid sharply off to the side, the roots catching against the cliff wall. Instantly, driven by the current, the rest of the log swung across the flow and jammed itself into the far wall. The obstructed water welled up, washed over the log and wedged it firmer still. The log shuddered with the strain of the full weight of the river above, the current gushing over Chaiko, tearing against his weakening grip. "This is the end," he thought, his hands slipping, "Bye Baer, bye Crow." The pressure of the water on him increased, but the conjured vision of his brother and his friend gave him extra strength. Still it would be so easy, tired as he was, just to let go, to let the inevitable play itself out and be done with it. "I shall do all I can to stay alive." He recalled the promise he made to his brother and desperately hung on.

The log quivered, slipped with a bone-jarring jerk, then a root broke and the tree leapt free of the wall, again powered by the pent-up energy of the river. The log bounced from wave to wave. The front rose into the air, hung there for a heartbeat, then slammed down nearly pitching Chaiko into the cold deep. Wind and water filled his eyes, the banks spinning by in a blur, as the tree raced from crest to crest down the chute.

Chaiko's senses were overwhelmed; he could not see in the rush, he could not hear in the roar, nor could he feel his body at all. He could only hang on, barely, unconsciously, stubbornly hang on. He was unaware of the rest of the rush, had no memory of it, knew only that time passed as it stood still, paused between heartbeats, his life suspended in between. It was as if it had all been decided already and he was merely waiting to see the outcome—coolly, calmly, detached. To live or to die? Only "brother" echoed in his mind.

Then the surge slackened and the tree quieted as the river suddenly opened up into a wide sun-filled basin. The sound of the water and the wind died away. But Chaiko was unaware of it all; he still hung on, his grip frozen in a cramp, his mind at a distance, his body rigidly locked in last grim determination. After a time the warmth of the sun finally reached his awareness, and he slowly came out of his stupor to insistent pain, proof that he was still alive. Little by little his death-grip relaxed and some clarity returned to his mind.

Ever since the fire, his mind had refused to focus, perhaps afraid to look at realities that he might never again see his clan, never again hear their voices. It was an instinctive reaction to cling to the tree to carry him from danger, but it was inertia that kept him hanging on to it all this way down the river. He had made no plans and no immediate plan suggested itself, but he knew he could not risk another run like he had just been through; he would never survive it.

He examined both shores carefully, realizing that he must make landfall soon. At this point the basin was quite wide, spreading between generous shores. The east showed a gently climbing slope, strewn with large boulders pushed there by raging waters of previous flood crests. Looking at the high-water mark, at least a man's height above the present level, Chaiko realized he would not have survived even a modest year's flow— the drought had saved his life. Here and there piles of driftwood had collected in heaps too moist to burn even by the passing fire. The few bushes were burned to black tracings of themselves. Further still, the scar of fire burn extended into the distance.

On the nearer western shore, the hills had retreated allowing a gentle valley that extended into a split back to the hills. More importantly, here and there healthy vegetation showed, untouched by fire. Without much thinking Chaiko rolled off the log into the breath-catching coldness of the water. He stood about chest deep. For all its placid surface, the current was still quite strong; it pushed him downstream stumbling among naked boulders, where the sand and gravel had washed away. Swimming, bobbing and hopping on one leg he laboriously made his way to shore and collapsed on the warm sand, trembling with cold and exhaustion, his teeth chattering. He had no strength left.

The sun warmed him and slowly restored some energy. He realized he had to feed a hunger he could no longer feel and cast about for a likely food source. His eyes were drawn to a circle of carrion birds in the air not far away, intent on the windfall the fire provided. With a length of driftwood he hobbled toward the direction of the wheeling birds. His progress was slow; he missed his well balanced and measured crutches. Not in the direct path of the fire, but in a slower back burn, in a strand of soft woods he found the carcass of a small deer, trapped by its own panic and confused by a slow-moving fire. A hyena was circling the deer, keeping the carrion birds away. (Why was it that hyenas, of all creatures, always seemed to survive?) Chaiko yelled at the four-footed pest and threw stones at it. The beast, already satiated by other meals, gave up easily—there was no reason to fight when the picking was so plentiful. With a baleful look and a backward growl it slunk away to disappear in a hollow. Chaiko bent over the lump of charred flesh, but underneath the outer char, the meat was well-cooked, still tender and protected from spoiling. He plucked a handful of meat from the carcass, carefully removed the burned portions and stuffed the rest into his mouth. Immediately, juices flooded in and his stomach growled in anticipation. It was young lean fare but tasted more delicious with every bite in his reawakening hunger. Chaiko took his time, chewing slowly, resisting the urge to wolf the meat down. Afterward, in a sheltered hollow, he found a clump of tender grass and clover, and thoughtfully chewed on a handful to balance out the full flavor of the meat.

Restored by the warmth of the sun and the food, he started thinking beyond the present. He realized that he had lost everything, except for the soft wrap about his middle and the bag of year-stones around his neck. He was alone and a long way from familiar ground. He had no weapons, no tools, no shelter and no fire. The weapons and tools would have to wait, but shelter and fire were urgent.

After a brief rest he made a slow exploration of the area. Not far he found a ledge with an overhang that hid a narrow fissure extending back into the rock. An ideal hideout for one person, he concluded. Wary of possible wild animals, he crawled in, his stick ready to repel any attack. But the hollow was empty, though there were aged signs of occupancy. Relieved, Chaiko enjoyed the security of being surrounded by rock again, and enjoyed the good view his new shelter provided of the river. He allowed himself a small nap.

Chaiko rose rejuvenated. The sun was leaning toward mid-afternoon. He went back for what remained of the deer and dragged it back to the "cave." On the shadow side of the ledge, he dug a pit with his hands, then buried the meat and covered it with stones to keep animals from getting at it. He then struck out again and collected a pile of driftwood that was dried enough to burn. After several trips he had accumulated a neat pile and found two sticks that fit him better for crutches.

The remainder of daylight he spent spinning a stick between his palms, drilling it into a hard piece of wood to make fire. The process proved very slow, tedious and exhausting. He was struck by the irony: here he was trying to bring fire to life, to serve him, when a few short days ago it had nearly killed him. He knew he would never look at fire with the same complacent eyes again.

By nightfall Chaiko had a modest fire burning at the entrance to his hollow. In the flickering firelight, he worked a straight shaft into a crude spear. With a stone shard, he smoothed the wood and hardened the point in the fire. He would have to get the balance right in the coming days, but now he had a weapon to defend himself. He banked the fire, then crawled into a pile of dry grass, moss and leaves he had collected earlier. He had hardly lowered his head and settled himself comfortably on this nest, piling some of the grass and leaves over himself, before he was asleep.

His sleep was restless. He had nightmares of blazing fires and of being burned, alternating with being pulled under into cold dark waters. Still, he awoke only once, out of a dream of being around the clan fire and shared merriment; the joy turned to tears.

Chaiko spent the next days making himself more comfortable in his new place. He searched out more carcasses preserved by the fire and stored them. He collected more firewood and built a proper hearth of a solid ring of stones. "You will not escape the circle that binds you to serve me," he addressed the fire, uttering the incantation taught in Fire Rituals. "You will burn and I shall feed you and from my hand you shall eat. Fire to show light, fire to shed heat." In the aftermath of the recent conflagration the well rehearsed words had acquired a new and deeper meaning. Chaiko shaped the words and focused his mind to exert his will on the fire. "You shall not escape! I have planted you in the ground, bound you with stones and rooted you in your ash, so that you will stay."

Nearby he found a small valley that cut into the rock face, untouched by the fire. He collected some moss and gathered aromatic grasses and herbs to sweeten his bedding. He harvested mushrooms in the lee of a decaying wind-ripped tree. In a low squirrel's nest in a hollow of a tree he found some of last year's nuts and pine cones. For the present he counted himself well provided.

In the evening he worked wood, wove a basket, and twisted a strong string out of grass that, next morning, he fashioned into a snare to catch small animals. He would need furs and hides to cover himself. He worked long reed grasses into a covering, which he used for clothing till the sun warmed up the air—but he was leery of sitting close by the fire in something so obviously flammable.

Each day found him better adjusted to this new place. He further improved on his crutches and could get around more easily. He quickly learned the lay of the land, the paths and watering places that the animals used, and the places where they bedded down for the night or waited out the heat of the day. He found the best grassland or clearing for fruits, such grains or herbs as the season would provide, a salt lick, a likely place to find flint, and even prized ochre-colored earth.

Day by day he established a routine. In the mornings he would fish, trap or explore, but would stay closer to the "cave" in the latter part of the day. In the evening he worked around the fire, to better equip himself. From the river bed, he brought up smooth fist-sized pebbles rounded by the ageless rush of waters, broke them into two, then chipped the broken end into a serviceable sharp edge to fit into one's hand, a chopper axe.

But with each new habit, his loneliness grew, for each habit freed his mind of a preoccupation and gave it time to consider more fully his situation. He was totally alone in a strange land. Even the rocks could not speak to him of a shared history. There was no prior event that tied him to this place; the trees knew him not, and to the animals around, his smell was foreign. Even the spirits must be strangers to him here, he thought with some dread. Looking about he realized that there was nothing here to remind him of his past; he was isolated even from his memories. His heart grew heavy with sadness and he grieved all he had lost. To fill the emptiness, he found himself talking to himself just to hear a human voice, to seek comfort in his own company. By the fire he would sing softly to the rhythm of the work at hand. He would often think aloud and sometimes carry on an argument in two distinct voices to hear the flow of ideas. Also he would prompt or give orders to himself; "Pick it up," "Put it down," "Move along," or such. Worse, he would talk to trees and rocks—as if they could respond— and to the wood he worked, "You will like the smooth feel this rub will give you."

The nights were worse. Falling asleep alone to the song of the wind or to the music of insects. Dreaming of being around the clan fire, hearing and seeing in sharp detail and clarity all that his days now missed, all that his soul ached for and required ... only to awaken to the hoot of an owl or the distant bark of a coyote, alone ... the brief happiness turning into bitter reality.

All his life he had been within shouting distance of company—now the others would likely think him dead. And dead he would soon be unless he could get his mind to focus and his body to obey. There was a winter to prepare for, and there was nothing and nobody to depend on except his own strength and skill. It would be up to him alone to survive or not to survive.

Trying to walk back to find the clan was out of the question. He was on the far side of the plain, nearly out of food, poorly equipped and still tired from his exertions to get here. A trip back would require planning, stores and stamina and at the present, he was short of all three. Still, he would manage it in easy stages. There was not only the distance of the ground to be covered, but the obstacles in his mind to overcome; the river had carried him here but could not carry him back against the rush of currents. The perils he had survived on the swift waters had certainly increased the distances in his memory and increased the feeling of isolation he now felt. And then there was the fear that perhaps the clan had not survived, but had been trapped by the advancing fire and perished. Crossing the plain would confront him with that possibility. Yes, the distance loomed larger than it really was, and sapped his motivation to even start planning his return to the clan. The immediate problems of the present were daunting enough, certainly all he could cope with right now.

Yet, in his loneliness there was an odd mixture of relief—it seemed that all his life he had felt in some way responsible for other people, a trait he shared with his brother. It had compelled him to serve the clan, oft at the expense of his own needs and desires. Now there was no one else to care for but himself. He was free to make all and any choice he cared to without regard to others and their needs. "But not Baer," he thought of his brother still shouldering the load. He hoped fervently that the clan was safe in the hills somewhere far to the east, below the horizon.

He had collected and stored all the carcasses in the vicinity, and knew that somehow he must hunt soon. Fishing alone and trapping small creatures would not suffice. Uninitiated or not, Hunter or no Hunter, he must hunt soon, he repeated to himself. Under the circumstances, being a cripple was not enough of a reason not to try. He had spears but lacked the necessary mobility to get near the deer or other prey. Still, he reasoned, in the confines of a narrow valley his chances were better than on the open plain. One morning he had come upon a small herd of deer grazing by a water run, but his approach had been too clumsy and noisy. They had taken flight before he could get near.

He dared not go after wild hogs, although signs of them were all around. The creature was too irritable and ill tempered, would likely turn and charge any stalker, and he had not the balance to fend off such an attack. So, paradoxically, he needed a prey that would run from him, but not too quickly for him to get near and perhaps allow him to cast a spear.

Each morning he made marks on a stick for a day here. One-two-three-four-five, he could not count farther than this, and still more nicks showed, one-two and three. His right hand held the counting finger on his left.

This morning he decided to climb to high ground to have a look around. A nearby hill appeared gentle enough for his capabilities and he set out to find a way to the top. At first the going was easy, firm solid ground with only a moderate slope. Higher up, bare stone and water-scoured crevices and depressions made upward progress more difficult. Covering moss hid a slippery clay layer that made his crutches lose their purchase and suddenly slip out from under him. He had to move carefully. A sprain would be a disaster, a broken bone his death. The sun warmed his back, so that he was sweating profusely when he reached the top. From there he had a good view of the surrounding land.

Close by, to the west, lay the line of hills extending north and south. Behind them were more hills with lots of hidden valleys possible. Here and there a touch of green among the rocks indicated pockets untouched by the fire.

To the east, on the other side of the river, the great plain spread out in gentle undulation and low slung hills. It was crisscrossed by tree-edged water runs and secret folds. The land was still burned, and though there had been little rain since the fire and only the heavy dew in the mornings, a green hue was creeping back into view. From this vantage high above the valley floor, the line of eastern hills was again visible on the curve of the horizon on the far side. Chaiko spent a long time looking there, hoping to catch a wisp of smoke or any sign of the clan. Wishful thinking, he finally dismissed the thought.

Nearer, there was nothing to be seen. No smoke. No sign of roving herds. Here and there, the wind would catch a scattering of ash and would further disperse it. Chaiko sat down, and taking his time, scrutinized each part of the foreground. For the present, he had to make a living on this narrow strip. At this distance, the river looked insignificant, but the memory of its power was still very fresh. How comforting the fire was in a hearth, he thought, there confined by man to do his bidding, but how terrifying it was when burning on its own, setting the whole of the earth ablaze. Along the river edge he saw an occasional dark spot, at this distance seemingly motionless, and then some more along a pathway across a crest. Grazing animals, deer most likely, maybe elk. He marked these places well. He ate a midday meal then reluctantly started back. Up here, he was above all his troubles and his daily concerns seemed far away. A fresh breeze tugged at his hair and a wide open blue sky glowed above him.

By evening cast of the sky he was back in camp, reawakening the banked fire into a cheerful dance of flames. He stared long into that dance, seeming less friendly now that he knew that the spirit of the fire ached to grow, yet was fed by man a starvation diet. "I can burn worlds," it seemed to crackle—but it had already burned Chaiko's world.

14 Stones

The light faded quickly as the sun settled behind the hills that projected a long shadow across the landscape. Near the fire Chaiko sorted feathers he had collected and carefully packed, according to size. He had some broad wing feathers of stork, gull, crow, and blackbird that he tied with a twist of twine into an overlapping mantle of feathers, tying knot after knot. The covering was light but strong and the feathers waterproof, the tiny quills leading the water down and away from the inner surface. Chaiko tried it on and was reasonably satisfied with the result. It would have to do till he found some real fur. The rest of the smaller feathers he gathered into a reed basket for some future use.

"Will need fresh meat," he told himself in a clear voice as if there were others around to share in the conversation, "and some furs." Hunting was his greatest concern but at least here no one could tell him he could not be a hunter, cripple or not. In contrast, everything demanded that he hunt. The problem was how? To hunt successfully, he needed to get closer to the prey or be able to throw his weapon farther. Nearer to the prey and throw farther. Nearer and farther. The idea chased itself around in his mind. His crippleness made "nearer" difficult as he could not move on his crutches with either speed or stealth and his clumsiness easily gave away his position. The awkwardness of throwing while balanced on his crutches made "farther" as problematic. Still, if he reduced the weight of his spear, maybe... but that would rob the spear of its bite. Again and again, one thought chased the other, but no matter, so "farther" never got "nearer."

With all his limitations considered, the most realistic course seemed to be to wait in ambush for game to pass on some well-used path. There were several such paths that he had noted already, where some constriction in the land forced an animal within an easy spear-cast of a hiding place. The waiting would require much patience, which he had in abundance; but he was of an active nature and reluctant to wait passively for an animal to come near him by chance. If only he had some spell, to call to the animal's spirit and snare it, but he had none. He must find a better way than simply waiting. "Winter will not wait," he reminded himself; provisions must be found and stored. Farther, nearer. Farther, nearer; he rolled the problem around his mind, but found no clear answers. Finally, he gave up and tried from a different direction. He needed to free his hands for the throw, but could see no way of achieving it; his crutches were in the way. Could he stand on one leg unsupported and throw his spear? Should he throw from a sitting position, or braced by a tree? His thoughts boiled in his head but he could not escape the fact that he needed his missing leg. A hunting cripple had to depend too much on conditions outside his control. The animals would have to come to him.

If he could only grow a leg, his problems would be solved. When he had his leg, he was quick, fleet of foot and long-winded, the pride of the family, a hunter to be, his place in the clan assured. The girls had smiled at him. His heart beat painfully in his chest. Where were those dreams now? He was facing an uncertain future, alone, every movement reminding him that he was a cripple. But even a cripple needs to eat and to breathe. He would need to prove that even a cripple can survive. What his body lacked, his mind would have to make up. His brother believed in him; could he do less for himself? No, whatever the future held, he would face it, his eyes and heart open, not shriveled up in fear and bitterness. Still if he could grow it ... He looked at the offending stump, a useless lump of flesh hanging just beneath the knee. He bent the knee, testing its flexibility, feeling the awkwardness of the movement. A sigh rose to his lips from deep within. He threw more wood on the fire and followed the rising sparks into the pitch-dark of the sky.

He closed his mind to the thoughts that led nowhere, but was still too agitated to settle down for the night. With a stick he stirred the fire, chanting an incantation. "Fire, fire, firelight, guard the cave day and night, light the face of darkness deep, chase spirits to their sleep..." It was an old song, sung mostly to children to quiet their nervousness in the face of darkness. To Chaiko, alone as he was, it seemed most appropriate. "Fire burn and fire glow, eat the wood steady slow, keep out the night, guard our sleep, cast no shadows on our dreams..." How many times had he sung this softly to Lana to ease her into the night? Certainly, long past the age she really needed to be so reassured; it was a ritual they both enjoyed. And oft, she sang it to him in her pure voice.

Thinking of her reminded him of the song he had lately composed for her and he broke into the refrain,

> "When we know what we need
> We take it or we make it
> We take it or we make it...."

He wished he had Singing-Stick with him, to accompany his voice, though its absence allowed him the freedom to improvise on the melody, beyond the few tones the Stick could produce. He tried to remember the exact words of the song, and tried to imagine Lana being just across the fire listening. He closed his eyes to foster the illusion. Already he felt less alone, warmed by the vision of Lana. His voice grew bolder, the tone reinforced by the echo from the rocks around him. Again and again he sang, the song holding back his loneliness.

> "When we need to dig for roots
> A claw is more than handy.
> When we need to cut up foods
> A chopper axe will have to do.
> When you need just anything
> Take it, or else, make it
> Make it, or else, take it
> Then you will have it, too.
> Knife and spear, just make it..."

With repetition the song lost some of its naive charm and freshness and he began to listen to it more critically. "Take it or else make it?" What had he been thinking of? Was there any sense to this? Just a child's rhyme ...

The refrain froze on his lips. A sudden recognition flooded his mind. Of course! Why had he not thought of it before? *He would make what he needed!* He would make a leg. He would fashion and shape it out of wood. Just like a real leg it would be. But how to fit it? The wood to the flesh. The one with feeling to the one without.

His mind raced feverishly. He threw a generous armful of wood into the fire, moved to the pile of wood he had collected, and examined each piece in the light of the freshened blaze. One seemed suitable enough, a stout limb; straight, strong, dense and thick enough for what he thought he needed. He saw clearly in his mind a leg made of wood and wondered why he had not thought of it before. It seemed so obvious.

He worked with excited energy through the night, driven by the vision of a new leg. First, he whittled away the wood, one end tapered, the other end hollowed out to accommodate the stump of his leg. When the shape was about right, with a flint shard he scored a deep groove just below the cup end, for a fastening rope to fit. He held the wood to the fire, warming it, hardening it. Then he rubbed it with handfuls of sand, his hands soon tender from its coarseness. The wood became dryer, harder and smoother to the touch. With two twigs he picked up a glowing ember from the fire and placed it into the hollow to burn the wood and slowly deepen it. He moved the ember about to burn away the wood evenly, enjoying the distinctive smell of the rising wisp of smoke. Again he scoured with sand, smoothing and polishing. Now and then he placed his stump into the hollow and marked where adjustments had to be made.

As his hands were busy working, seemingly on their own, his mind looked ahead and celebrated the coming freedom from crutches, freedom to walk, freedom even to run again! It answered all his needs of movement: to walk straight and upright, to follow and stalk the game, and, dared he hope, to chase, his hands free to hold a spear, to cast it far? He was amazed that he had been blind to this possibility when it was so clear and obvious now. Why had no one seen it before? he asked himself over and over again.

Morning light found him still at work putting on finishing touches. The length was good and the fit excellent. Finally he was ready. He put a handful of moss into the hollow and a layer of downy feathers to soften the joint. He placed the stump of his leg securely in the hollow then with a winding of grass rope he secured this wooden contraption. He stood up, tottering at first, and took an unsteady step. His knee buckled under the unaccustomed weight, pitching him forward. He found it difficult to get up, the new wooden leg clumsy and unyielding. He tried again but with no better result. He picked himself up, bruised from the fall, his mood dampened but not discouraged. It was not going to be an instant freedom, he told himself ruefully. His short leg was too weak and his walk geared to movement with crutches; he found it strange to stand on two "feet." Yet, when he tried to add crutches, the new "leg" interfered with the flow of movement and he quickly discarded them. The sooner he got adjusted to the new reality of two legs, the better it would be.

He practiced some more, taking short stiff steps, falling less often but tiring very quickly. His knee did not want to bend fully, and his leg muscles cramped as the rest of his body tried to compensate. He had to stop, take off the strange attachment and rub his stump for relief. There were red bruises on it and he knew that more padding would be needed to soften the contact area. Also, he concluded that he would have to deepen the hollow to get more support from the wooden leg and a better connection. Though this first attempt was not as successful as he had hoped, he was pleased enough with the progress he had made, for his balance had improved and his hands were free. It would take much work to become proficient, but Chaiko was used to work; for a cripple, most things were work. Only to the child he had left behind had things come easily.

Driven by a need to finish and the promise of unfettered mobility, he set about deepening the hollow with the burning technique—being careful not to burn away too much. His eyes watered from the curling smoke rising into his face but he kept a close watch on the glowing ember. When it lost its heat, he replaced it with a new one from the fire. It was nearly midday by the time he was satisfied with his work. This time he stuffed the hollow with extra moss and down feathers, then tied the leg on. He wished he had a soft and supple chamois for this and leather strips for the tie-ons, but he had to be satisfied with what he had. Later he would improve on this lack. Now when he stood up and straightened, he found the leg somewhat short, but curiously the shortness seemed to help with his stride. He had to take shorter steps anyway when leading with the wooden leg, so as not to have the wood slip under him. This unevenness gave a curious hobble to his movement. Soon tiring, he had to take the leg off because his stump was sore and swollen from the pressure placed on it. He would have to grow into his new "leg."

He ate a sparse meal, the last of his provisions. Tomorrow he would fish first, then he would hunt. His excitement succumbed to growing tiredness, and he fell asleep by the fire, the leg still in his hand.

Chapter 18

Chaiko woke late that night and found that the fire had died, not having been properly banked the day before. Afraid that he might have to use the tedious fire sticks again, he carefully uncovered the ashes and found a hot spot. By blowing and gentle feeding it with dry grass he coaxed the fire back to life.

Eager to exercise his new mobility, Chaiko put on his leg after packing some extra padding and practiced walking around the fire. His stump was sore, but he was able to move about quite well, to stop and turn smoothly enough to please him. Once again he noticed that the shortness of the wooden leg worked in his favor though it made his gait somewhat lopsided. Any adjustments would have to wait until he developed more expertise in its use. The most critical part, the hollow, seemed to give him a firm connection though he expected to have to enlarge it as his stump strengthened and grew into it.

His greatest difficulty was getting up and down from the ground, the wooden leg awkward in its stiffness. Upright he felt steady and more secure, and most importantly his hands were free. Much too quickly, however, he had to stop walking because of the tenderness of his stump and the twinge of pain in long unused muscles suddenly called upon.

Notwithstanding the fever pitch of activity this contraption occasioned, once he sat down and gathered his leg under him by the fire, Chaiko felt the emptiness surround him. A good part of his last years had been spent in quiet observations of the clan, their deeds, habits and interactions. Now, alone as he was, the observer had nothing to observe. The self-appointed guardian of the clan, the eyes and ears he promised himself to be, had nothing to protect. Cut loose by circumstance, he felt bereft and without purpose. So accustomed had he become to attuning himself to the needs of others that merely taking care of himself seemed of insufficient worth or value. He hoped they were all right. Although his body and his hands were busy with daily tasks, and even with all the planning that was required, his mind was unchallenged by some context outside of himself. He sought to achieve a new balance between his inner life and the nature he faced so alone and yet so intimately.

He thought briefly of the ill-defined spirit world but did not know how to approach it. He needed a shaman to initiate him and guide him through its complexities. On his own he knew neither how to proceed nor how to tap into the power that was there.

He had never felt great affinity for the Spirit of Grey Wolf, and already as a child had lost reverence for the relics that Samar displayed on special occasions. Even less did he understand the relation to Earth Mother; to him she seemed supremely indifferent toward all her children. Though he never outright denied the spirit world, he could not comprehend it and was left with only what he could see. He refused to explain away everything he did not understand with some spirit effect argument, as many of the clan were inclined to do. He had long decided to let the spirits fend for themselves; he would watch nature to find out its secrets. Still, it would be nice now if he could access its power.

Repeatedly throughout the night the fire shrank and had to be replenished. It was a small island of light in the vast surrounding darkness. The rising smoke embraced him, filling his nose with the pleasant odor of seasoned wood burning. A soft breeze gathered up the smoke and swept it out of the circle of light. A light drizzle fell and he pulled the grass mantle closer to ward off the wetness. A frog called into the night, answered by a chorus. His eyes lost in the glow of embers, he roamed wherever his restless mind led him.

The morning sun broke upon his musings. The birds took to the air and greeted one another. The hum of insects grew and filled the background with a rising and falling intensity. A bird landed in the bushes bordering his camp and launched into a series of off-pitch calls that sent shivers down Chaiko's spine. The bird, obviously expressing its enthusiasm for the new day, was inspired for a long concert. Chaiko, with teeth clenching as the sound grated on his nerves, threw a stick in its direction, but the bird, like a true artist, was not easily discouraged. Chaiko followed with a deer's thigh bone, several rocks of growing sizes and even one of the fireplace stones. The bird squawked its protest at this ill treatment and flew off to continue its concert somewhat further away. "Don't come back, Crier-Bird," Chaiko called after it, exorcising it.

At peace at last, Chaiko considered the coming day. It would take some time for him to get accustomed to his new leg, to gain facility as well as endurance with it. His hunger, however, could not wait that long; he resolved to hunt, to wait in ambush for chance game, then go fishing if the hunt failed. He was grateful that fishing always gave him an option to exploit.

He picked up his crutches and looked at them with new eyes. Already they were less a part of him. Still, with their aid he was able to move about with accomplished ease and with less effort than his new leg required. With some practice, he expected this situation to change soon. For now, the crutches would serve as they had so well over the past years. He set out taking two spears with him, his hands already awkwardly full with the crutches.

He followed a trail that converged with more tracks into a narrow defile as it wound through steep stone on either side, penned in with dense pine and brush. On the rocky path he saw stones turned, and in a softer spot read the many imprints of deer and goat and the claw marks of smaller creatures passing through. Then he found the ideal spot on the shoulder of the hill overlooking the path. A little further along he clambered up a switch back access to a ledge above, hedged by evergreens. The ascent was steep and difficult but the blind gave him height and a good view in either direction, with a screen of sparse grass to hide behind and look through and hide behind. Here his crutches were useless; he laid them aside. He lay down in a thick layer of pine needles, hoping that the heavy pine-pitch odor about him would mask his scent. He readied his spears by his side, judging the distance to the far wall to be within an easy throw even from a semi-prone position. Now he would wait for an opportunity to present itself, and wait he did. It seemed to Chaiko that the rest of the world was waiting too, as there was no motion or movement near about.

He sent out a Call, a directed thought. "Come, deer, come. The grass is tender green. The water is fresh and cool. Come with your brothers and sisters; bring your kin. Find the succulent shoots and young bark that await you here. There is much soft moss to lie on, and clean sand to roll in. Come, deer, and find me..." he thought-talked. He visualized as clearly as he could a herd of deer coming up on the path, heads high, eyes sparkling, unwary. Tawny sides with light beige spots, the prance of dancing feet. Vapor of breath lightly smoking from the nostrils in the stiff morning air. More would follow, he wished, and held onto the vision.

Time passed slowly as it tended to do when it waited on itself, especially more so in expectation of some earnest event. Someplace above, water babbled in a brook, tumbled over rocks and splashed into a hidden pool. A small rock rolled clicking downhill. Again and again, the snap of a twig somewhere beneath the pines testified that life went on, smaller creatures living on a smaller scale often overlooked by the larger world. Below, a ferret-like creature explored the pass with familiarity that showed that it knew the way. Chaiko became aware how in this narrow cleft of rocks, robbed of the wide vista of the open plain, even small events grew in significance. A squirrel followed halfway up the path, then dashed back down when a shadow passed overhead. A little later, a solitary rabbit hopped by, nose twitching nervously. A blackbird landed on a nearby bush but sensed Chaiko's presence and flew off complaining, broadcasting its warning of an intruder's presence. Chaiko tensed, but stayed still, practicing being a stone.

The sun stood overhead, flooding the pass with sunshine and filtering through the needles to him. Chaiko was becoming tired of waiting, and restless, as his body protested being still so long. "Stone ... the patience of a stone. The stone that waits," he reminded himself, all the while thinking that surely he would have had more success fishing. An ant crawled up his leg and shattered whatever concentration the stone still had. Pine needles were sticking into his skin and he itched all over. His stomach growled and he was thirsty. All the same he did not move from his prone position.

Then he heard it. The unmistakable clicking sound of hooves on stone coming closer. "Let it be deer," he concentrated. Judging by the sound it was a group, the rhythm bold, not cautiously pausing or hesitant. They too, knew the way. Chaiko felt confident of his hiding place, knew he was above their eye level, but he kept absolutely still, all discomforts suddenly forgotten. Finally a female appeared, an upland deer somewhat smaller than its cousins on the plain. She was soon followed by others, one with a rack of new antlers, half grown and covered with velvet, then more young ones and some does. They looked well fed on high meadow grass untouched by the fire and appeared fresh and rested. The herd was high-stepping its way uphill, heads proud and steady. A juvenile pranced by the side with graceful nervous energy.

With careful slowness Chaiko readied himself, rose to his knees, took a spear in either hand and made ready. His heart was thundering in his chest; even his hair rose in excitement. The group neared, and he let the lead deer pass, choosing a fair sized female in good meat and with shining hide. The bunch in the back were less alert. Slowly he raised himself above his cover, coiled, then as she reached an adjacent spot in front of him, he cast his spear. The deer sensed the movement and shied to the side, but the spear bit into the soft tissue just in front of the hind quarter. She fell down grunting in pained surprise. The rest scattered in an instant, half uphill, the others back down. Chaiko quickly switched hands, and cast the other spear at the stricken female. This hit too, a grazing blow, tearing a ragged wound across the throat, then glanced off to the side. The wounded animal struggled to her feet again, then staggered downhill, a spray of crimson blood from the neck and a gurgle of pain marking her agony.

Chaiko grabbed his crutches, scrambled and slid down hill scraping his legs on the rough texture of stone and bush. He hobbled after the blood trail pausing only to retrieve his spear. Arriving on the open slope he could see no sign of the wounded deer, and his heart sank in disappointment. Could it have somehow escaped? Can't lose it now.

He followed the trail of bright blood clear on the bare slope. It was amazing how much of this precious fluid the animal had in her. Still there was no sign of the deer. His nostrils quivering with blood lust, Chaiko followed the trail, "If need be, across the mountain, across the river ..." Then, at the foot of a rock ridge, he found her crumpled body, the spear still poking from her side, quite dead, the eyes glazed over, blood still seeping from the wounds.

Relieved, Chaiko knelt beside the slain animal and cradled her head. "Thank you, sister. I meant you no disrespect. Your meat will feed my family, your skin will cover our bodies. Spirit of deer, take with you our gratitude." He blew into her nostrils "I make my claim." They were words of an aged ritual, recited without much thinking, but this day he meant them—as her death bought a piece of his life, for a time. He pulled the spear out and wiped it on the long grass.

After resting awhile until the heat of excitement and the trembling subsided, Chaiko packed the carcass over his shoulder and tied it securely. Then, bent under the weight, awkwardly balancing on his crutches, he made his way back to camp, pausing often to rest. He gratefully dropped his burden by the hearth, much relieved to be back. In his tiredness the triumph faded, though the confidence of success remained to buoy him. He refreshed the fire, then, with the only flint shard he had, set about skinning the deer. He spread the hide flat on the ground and scattered some cold ash over it to soak up the blood and to keep insects away.

He gutted the animal, the entrails slippery in his hands. With his chopper axe, he butchered the meat. He spiked half a rump on a stick and had it roasting over the fire, the delicious odors soon teasing his nose. The rest he cut into strips which he strung on a rope in the smoke trail of the fire.

It was evening by the time he was done and could enjoy the succulent roast. He could not remember when he last tasted anything as good. Pride was a great seasoning that he had almost forgotten about, while a defeat had such a bitter flavor he remembered all too well. He was sated; the deer skin was drying by the fire; he was well satisfied with the day. If he could only have some company.

In spite of being full, he attached his wooden leg and practiced walking about the camp. He noted some improvement and hoped that his stump would callous soon so he could use it for longer periods of time.

He kept the fire going in full smoke banked with leaves and earth. As the strips cured, he worked the hide, scraping it with a small cast-off antler he had found and rubbed more ash in it. He knew that a skilled worker would use urine, but did not know why or to what effect. Also he recalled that for extra softness the skin was chewed. His hands moved over the hide solicitously.

"It is too small to make a full wrap," he was talking to himself yet again, "but will do to cover the upper body." The skin had the advantage, over the grass blanket and feather mantle, of being quiet, especially on the move; the rustling of dried grass and feathers would not give away his presence. He lifted the skin and examined it in the firelight. The animal had been healthy; consequently, the hide was of good quality. He would need more skins, many more, for footwear, covering, carryall, waterskins, thongs and straps. This was the first of many, he hoped.

Throughout the night he kept the fire smoking about the meat, the faint aroma of drying pleasing to his nose. He was satiated, full beyond hunger but not uncomfortably so. In his mind he reviewed the hunt and was proud. He had picked the right animal. The larger male would have provided more meat, but would have been much too heavy for him to lug back to camp, and would have forced him to butcher the animal there on the spot. The smell of death would have hung about and ruined a good place for hunting for some time. He hoped to use the ambush spot again, as it was an ideal location along such a narrow, well travelled pathway.

The moon stood high in the sky, casting the landscape in silver light, deepening the shadows. The rocks glowed with this illumination and the midsummer waxy leaves of a nearby copse of poplar flashed and winked, trembling in the light breeze. The air felt chilly with a touch of dew settling to the ground. Chaiko hugged the grass mantle closer around him and threw a few branches on the fire, then covered it with a handful of green grass. The smoke billowed into the air, spreading a bitter smell.

Tomorrow he would make the customary mark on the cave wall to commemorate the kill. Mark of a hunter, he thought with satisfaction, to claim a kill and to claim this cave! He wished that his brother were here to share this victory. And Crow, of course. The kill had made him a Hunter; cripple or not, a hunter he now was. He wished his new status could be recognized in a ceremony with the whole clan there to share his joy and witness his election to the rank of a Hunter. To sit among the men, cripple or not, the blood he shed testifying of his right to be there in the elect company of Hunters. A Hunter! His mind lingered reverently on the status, and dreams that had been suppressed for four long years, the dreams of childhood, had become a reality. The irony was that it was his very loneliness that had forced him to become a hunter, yet the same loneliness robbed him of the reward of prestige and recognition of his new stature. Still, cripple or not, a Hunter he was. Nobody could henceforth deny him that self-awareness. Alone, the prestige felt somewhat hollow, but he was not disappointed, for he knew that this victory was largely in his heart and spirit. He had gained much in feelings of self-worth and mastery, all paid for by the blood of a deer. He was grateful to the slain animal and wished its spirit well.

Sitting in the smoke trail of the fire protecting him from the swarm of insects, Chaiko's thoughts returned to the clan and he wondered how they were all doing. Was anybody watching over them as he had, the self-appointed guardian of the night? Had they found shelter and safety in the hills? Were there animals enough to feed them? In his musings he found many questions but no answers. Finally, he shrugged the sadness off; he was here and they were somewhere there and a broad plain lay in between, the distance made longer by the perils of the waters that carried him and by the dangers of the firestorm that swept over him. In his mind the past divided itself into a period before and after the fire. His life had changed, the rules of survival had changed, and he had better change with them. Yesterday was yesterday, in the care of the clan, but today had been a victory.

He thought about the logistics of crossing the plain, finding the clan in the far, far hills, and rejoining them. A surge of joy at this vision was dampened by the reality of all the obstacles facing him. Maybe when he grew into his leg, it would carry him all the way back. For now he must look at the coming day. He would fish and he would trap, collect more long-stemmed river grass for rope, and look for eggs and feathers among the reeds. He would have to find some flint; his only piece was disappearing from overuse. He would have to find new wood to fashion a new leg once experience of its use taught him all he needed to know for the final measure.

Between thoughts, sleep overtook him and his head sank forward on his chest. But still, thoughts chased each other, some practical, some nonsense, as his mind cast off the fetters of reality and was free to roam where it pleased. And then he saw her, as he had many times before in his dreams, embellishing on a brief glimpse of reality. She was the daughter of a stranger visiting the Standing-Rock Clan about a year ago. Her father had new skills in curing hides and he trekked from clan to clan teaching the new technique. But Chaiko had learned nothing; he had had eyes only for the girl and had heard only her laughter everywhere. Dove was a season older than he, and aware of herself, driven to search for a mate. His gaze and thoughts had followed her, but she had no eyes for him, seeing only a cripple. He was envious of the smiles she had bestowed so freely, even on Crow ... and resentful of the laughter she had so lightly given away. He had been possessive of her every gesture and could not bear to see her share her time with anyone, leastwise his age-mates. He had tried to hide from her his crippleness.

One day, he had been fishing, hidden from the sun in the shadows bordering the creek. He had been at it all morning but had only a perch and an undersized trout to show for it. However, fishing like hunting was in large part patience, and so he had waited for the fish to bite, dreaming of Dove. The intensity of his yearning for her confused him. Just then, Dove herself strolled from under the trees onto the small beach by the pool just below him. She paused, stretched languidly, then in one smooth motion opened and stepped out of her wrap. She stood there fully naked, fully revealed, with the whiteness of her skin aglow against the dark ferns. She turned into the embrace of the warm sunshine, her hands outstretched, her fawn-colored hair twirling with her, afire from the light caught by its strands.

A White Dove, Chaiko mumbled to himself, his heart hammering in his throat as his eyes swept the proud arch of her neck, along the graceful curve of her back and down the long lines of her legs. Her body was lithe, glowing with the blush of youth, with the vitality of health. Her breasts were pert with faint pink nipples and the secret place of her body covered in light down. She was heart-stopping beautiful and the urgency of his need welled up within him. But Chaiko dared not move and risk frightening this lovely vision away. Was it truly real, or some woodland spirit taunting him?

The vision walked into the pool up to her knees, then cupped the water in her hands and poured it over herself. She shivered in delight at its cool freshness and her laughter twittered infectiously. Again and again the water rained down on her, a shower of jewels to tumble sparkling down her skin. She bent down, scooped a handful of clean clay from the bottom and rubbed it onto her body. The smooth sensual feel of the clay on her flesh seemed to mesmerize her, and the flowing rhythm of her hands playing over her body became more languid, pausing here and there, caressing. Chaiko wanted to caress her, too, and share her intimacy. The clay dried to chalky whiteness and she turned into the wood nymph he suspected her to be, but then she dipped herself, rinsed her hair and with a flick of her head sent a fan-like burst of water spray, spinning, sparkling through the air. With her hands she swept the remaining wetness from her body, pausing to enjoy the pleasures of a tender touch on her sensitized skin in the cold afterglow.

Then she stood still, face lifted to the sun, on full display. She presented herself. Womanhood, yearning for her destiny, straining for the future awaiting her.

She must have felt the burn of his gaze upon her, for she turned on him full, then froze like a startled doe when she saw him there under the shadows. Her eyes opened wide and mouth flew agape prettily in surprise. Then instinctively she covered her breasts in a flush of confusion and stood transfixed; for that instant time froze too, in mutual embarrassment.

Then she laughed and broke the spell, a joyous tickling laugh he could share too. Like a deer, she pranced, splashing through the water onto shore. She scooped up her wrap and disappeared - leaving him alone with his heaviness of breathing.

Throughout the day and the next, he could not take his eyes off her, but when she looked at him, he turned away, afraid his eyes would betray his begging need of her.

Then one day she was gone with her kin, on to the next camp. Tanya saw his sorrow and gently consoled him. "Your time will come," she murmured, however, in her wisdom she did not seek to take away the pain that he must taste and learn from. She did not deny him the feelings of abandonment he felt. Had he not been a cripple, he would have followed Dove, counting her his destiny. But she disappeared from his life, leaving him only a dream vision of her.

Since then he had dreamed of her again and again and the dream had become a well rehearsed play—his passion straining after her, and she, playful, teasing, remaining unreachable. Yet each rehearsal robbed him of a little of her, the yearning having turned more into need, the blush of innocence fading as he had lost more of his vulnerability. The White Dove he pined for became less a feeling of her, and more a feeling of himself, and his needs. Drop by drop White Dove the person was lost, having turned into this ritualized vision that said more and more about his desires. A look of enticement had replaced the smile, a peal of seduction overcast the ring of her laughter. Time had blurred those edges of memory.

Once again as she laughed he awoke to frustration, the spell broken yet again; he tried to shut his eyes and crawl back into the dream looking for her. After a while his breath calmed but the feeling of loss left him more slowly this time.

Free of the clouds the moon shone brighter over the sleeping land. A thin wisp of smoke curled from the fire. Rousing himself, Chaiko piled on a new handful of twigs letting them light before smothering the flame with grass. The smoke billowed up and the acrid smell of burning green filled the air. He checked the meat hanging on the strings in the rise of the smoke. The strips had hardened but when he twisted one, it bent easily enough; it still had a soft core. By tomorrow, perhaps they would be ready, stiff and hard for storing.

To the north he saw distant lightning reflected in the sky, but could hear no thunder. The storm came no nearer, though several times during the night it drizzled lightly.

Stick in hand he stirred the fire occasionally, piling on more wood and grass as needed. In between, he slumbered, hoping to find his dream. But each time he awoke, he remembered only a confused mix of images and fragments of memory. "Tomorrow we fish," he said aloud to no one. The sound of his voice was swallowed up by the night, sounding strange even to him, one lone human being in an empty land.

Chapter 19

In the morning Chaiko awoke with a start and found the sun already high above the horizon with its rays warm on his cheeks. He shrugged off the grass mantle, rose, put on his wooden leg and went aside to relieve himself. He wandered off to gather some wood and paused by the brook for a drink. His stomach was still full from the feast of venison the night before. Crier, from a dense bush, insisted on greeting him. His strident calls grated on Chaiko and sent unpleasant shivers along his spine. He threw a rock in its direction, but the bird was not easily deterred. What bird would find those calls attractive, he wondered to himself shaking his head. The calls continued for a while and followed Chaiko about.

On his return, the camp greeted him with a welcoming sense of familiarity that was reassuringly comforting. He checked the curing meat, but found it still somewhat pliable, though he judged the sun would probably do the rest. He woke the fire, then covered it with the last of the grass he had at hand. The smoke rose up, swirling about the camp indecisively until a gust scattered it.

On his day-counter stick he made a new mark and matched two hands, each of five, against the incisions, but had no name for the count. He would say "five and five, or two hands of five." He picked up the new deer skin, the hide stiff and unyielding in his hands. He rolled it, twisted and pulled at it working some flexibility back into the hide.

He had planned to go fishing this morning. "Hurry," he prompted himself, "the fish will soon stop feeding in the rising heat of the day." He collected his spear, a length of tightly wound twine and the hooks he had made of fire-hardened jagged pieces of bone.

He walked down to the river and on the way, turned over some rocks until he found some fat worms which he packed into a moist clump of moss tightly wrapped in a broad leaf. A bit upstream, he settled down under a gnarled old willow that had seen many floods and was sending out new green shoots from fire-scorched branches. The air was alive with the hum of insects that annoyingly swarmed around his head, getting into his eyes, nose and ears. He slapped at them ineffectually. He baited the hook, unwound the string and cast it into the current of the river. He played out the line, loosely held in his hand, and waited.

Above him a host of gulls wheeled about crying noisily. A sandpiper worked a nearby pool of water, its beak combing the shallows. A large dragonfly droned by. This was much like old times, when as boys he and Crow went fishing. He had tried to teach his friend his passion for fishing, but Crow endured it only for his sake. "Too much waiting," Crow had said disparagingly, "I am going to be a great hunter, not a fisherman." "No greater than me," the young Chaiko had retorted then. Under the willow, Crow's presence was so strong that Chaiko turned toward where his friend should have been, only to be confronted with disappointment.

The line jerked once in his hand. He tightened his grip and felt the snap of the line as a fish bit down, hooked itself and then tried to escape. Chaiko pulled it in, a good-sized trout. He clubbed the fish with the butt of his spear, strung it through the gills on a piece of twine and put it back into the water, tying the other end to a low-hanging willow branch. Soon, he had two more trout, and a catfish. After that the fish stopped biting. Leaving the fish in the cool water, he went along the river to explore. He was looking for some flint in the jumble of rocks piled up in profusion on the flood plain, by sand banks—here one day gone the next—and along the pools of trapped, shallow water full of slimy algae. The going was difficult among the rocks, his wooden leg slipping on smooth stones, catching in crevices or sinking in soft mud and sand. Mounds of debris were piled up, wood, matted grass, and even bones of some animals caught in an unyielding current and here cast ashore. "Could have been me," he said, remembering the boiling rapids.

In the grass basket he carried he collected half shells, fist-sized pebbles, dried water reeds, feathers, and quite a few eggs from nests in thorn bushes edging the river. He broke off a few thorns to use as needles to work skin and hide.

He noted that on the other side of the river, green was fully asserting itself again. Only the trees looked forlorn, shorn by the fire of their mantle of leaves. Some bushes were sending new shoots from the roots. Life was not going to be denied.

14 Stones

By the middle of the day, Chaiko was back in camp pleased with his efforts of the morning. He unstrung the cured meat, wrapped it tightly in dried fronds, then buried it deep in a pit against the inner wall of the cave. It wasn't much, but it was a start toward a winter larder.

He then cleaned and filleted the fish, stringing it out to dry. The catfish he cooked and ate, relishing the taste as the tender flesh melted in his mouth. Some spice-root added a tangy flavor to the meal. He took off his leg and rested. The stump was somewhat sore, but there were no tender spots and on the whole it had stood up quite well to the full morning use of the leg. He was pleased ... at least on the surface. And why not, he had the comfort of a camp, fire, and food. On a full stomach the future seemed not so bleak. But underneath he felt dissatisfaction growing, of not knowing the fate of the clan, of being alone, and of the silence surrounding him where an answering human voice should be. He could not see himself mirrored in a human eye, in a friend's reaction. Alone, without the clan, he was but a shadow, living the life of a shadow, seeking an object to attach itself to.

Man was not meant to live alone, he concluded. He would have to work his way back across the plain and find the clan, maybe when his leg was strong enough. He decided to go up to Lookout Mountain to check the lay of land again from the high vantage, to search for a way back and for signs of nearby animals. In any case, he needed to hunt. He strapped on his leg and set out.

At first the slope was gentle and he had no trouble climbing it. But when the pitch of the hill increased, he experienced growing difficulty as his knee was weak and not used to bending. It buckled without warning, and he had to use his spear again and again to stop himself from falling. About half way up, a light drizzle fell from a passing bank of clouds. The wetness felt cool and refreshing on his body, but the track became treacherously slippery and he had to be extra careful where he planted his wooden leg. Still, he was able to make good progress up the slope. By the time he reached the top, his body was sore and he was quite out of breath. Dizziness overtook him; the hill swayed under him. He leaned heavily on his spear, looking up into the full haze of the sun blinding him. The familiar figure of his brother, back-lit against the glowing sky, appeared. "You promised to keep yourself safe and to save yourself. And now you are dead. Dead!" the figure said accusingly. "No!" Chaiko shouted back, "I'm alive. I am alive," as the figure dissolved. "I'm alive," he repeated and heard the echo return from below "live."

Finally his breath calmed and the grayness of his vision faded. Though the apparition had only been an outline, the recognition had been instant and achingly vivid. He was badly upset by this confrontation and was wondering if he was losing his mind. At the Gathering, there was Ulak, a weak-minded sort, who went about muttering and talking to nobody there; was Chaiko turning into someone like him? He had to get back to his people to find sanity and normalcy again.

From the peak, the plain showed an even darker hue of green. That at least was encouraging. The drought had passed, and though there had been little rain, each night a heavy dew wet the topsoil generously, speeding the recovery. Then, in the far distance he saw dust in the air, catching his attention; dust meant movement and movement meant life stirring. His heart skipped a beat. The clan? No, a line of dots seemed motionless at this distance. Bison? No. Bison moved as a herd bunched up on a broad front. This was a single line cutting across the land. More like elk, he guessed, but so far south so late in the season? All the same, finally, some larger game, even if not bison.

A careful sweep of the near ground just on the other side of the river did show more movement; family groups of deer, dispersed on the yet sparse grass. Before the fire, they had been invisible in the height and color of vegetation, but now they drifted like shadows. He studied the nearest group of four females with only one young tailing behind them. There should have been three maybe even four. Must have been the drought and the fire, he told himself. The group was spread out, leisurely feeding, meandering along a water course. They appeared unconcerned, not bunched up and vigilant, he concluded, so it was likely that no human or animal had hunted them in the last little while. The soil on the plain was thickly dark and fat grasses of many varieties grew there, the reason why the plain grazers were so much bigger than their highland cousins growing up on leaner fare. Now that he knew what he was looking for, the plain appeared more populated than he dared to believe, as he spied group after group. Still not the herds that blackened entire valleys with their numbers, the ground shaking under their thundering hooves. Far off, he spotted a wheel of birds circling, cruising the air—already harvesting.

He checked the narrower strip of land along this side of the river, his present hunting ground. Scattered were copses of trees, in full green untouched by the fire, and between them stretched lush green grass and dense bush. Here and there were fire burns that had crept under the backwash of the driving winds and backtracked valleys into the hills, consuming everything. The old tangle had burned away and already the new grass was growing to the enjoyment of the deer. On this side the pattern of destruction appeared so haphazard; untouched wood adjacent to a burn scar.

Turning fully west, he saw the hills, lined up behind each other all the way back till the distance turned back his gaze. There were hidden valleys there, he surmised, but he could not find a clear way to them. On a rocky slope not far away he saw a mountain goat or sheep bounding sure-footed uphill. He wished he could have their expertise since he still had to get down. High in the sky he saw an eagle glide on still wings, and in the fashion of all who were earthbound, envied the freedom and the view the bird enjoyed. Nearby a short-winged harrier hawk was mobbed by an angry pair of smaller birds, distracting and driving the larger bird from the vicinity of the nest of young they had to protect. Their shrill cries reached him faintly. He sympathized; yes, life, at most times, was an earnest struggle.

He then looked to the east, where the land disappeared in the distance. Of course, aside from the faint blue outline of hills there, he could see nothing. The sun stood at his back and its light was reflected by a receding line of rain clouds now over the plain. Their shadow moved beneath on the ground. His eyes followed the river back north and concluded that a shorter way could be found overland heading more east. A broad level track opposite looked promising but he could not follow it very far in the many folds of land. At least the fire had cleared out the dense undergrowth, which would make cutting across the plain easier. His eyes grew tired and watery peering into the distant glow of haze. He had seen what he came to see: the game he needed to survive, and a way back so he could hope again.

He scanned the river itself, a ribbon of silver cutting a twisting path across the land. Did the river carve the land or had the land hemmed the river in its present course? He would have to cross it before the autumn rains swelled its waters to an uncrossable rage, trapping him here on this shore. Did he choose the wrong shore? No, at the time, this side had the only intact green to feed and shelter the game he needed.

He looked east again, and saw the scattering of clouds shedding their rain. Long streamers were hanging from the overcast and the sun sparkled on the face of it. Then slowly an order of colors emerged, a striation of reds, yellows and greens with a faint blue on the inner edge. The colors stood on the ground to either side, and little by little the arch filled out to join in a perfect semi-circle ... so uniquely strange and singular in its perfection in a nature that thrived on irregularity. "The Rainbow Gate," Chaiko marveled, his heart beating faster in his chest as a surge of longing, as always, welled up in him.

As a young boy of nine at the Gathering of the Clans, he had stopped by a blind shaman telling his stories to whoever cared to listen. Chaiko had listened, then listened to the retelling of it, and committed the tale to memory.

"Tomee had entered the world we live in through the spirit-gate and brought with him all the knowledge that was known and practiced on the other side. He knew all questions and had answers ready. There was no question that eluded him for he brought with him ancient wisdom. The people of the clans listened to him and marveled that one man could know all things.

"Tomee had come through the spirit-gate, an opening in the sky, the feet of which were rooted in the ground and the head of which reached the clouds. The color of it was red, yellow and green and the shape of it round all around. And it glowed when it appeared, so that no one who had eyes to see and a heart to hope, could miss it.

"It was said that whosoever passed through the spirit-gate would find answers to questions that had not yet been asked. He would know all things, understand all things and there would not be any secrets hid from such a one. Tomee knew and he never went back. He sired Kilik, who was the father of Soma, who was father to Tomee the Younger.

"Yes, Tomee knew all knowledge and he taught it to his son, Kilik, who likewise told it to Soma, who passed it on to Tomee the Younger. But each generation took no care to listen carefully so that the memory of that knowledge was lost a word at a time. A word here, a word there, as each generation lost a little of what Tomee had brought into this world. Today we barely remember him, he who knew all things..." The old shaman blinked back tears from sightless eyes. Young Chaiko was shocked that such precious knowledge had been lost. Then and there he resolved that if he ever had the opportunity he would go through the spirit-gate to retrieve all knowledge for his people again.

Samar had cautioned him that it was an old story and as stories were wont to do, it grew with each telling. "Hope is a better story-teller than truth," the old man had said, but to young Chaiko, the age of the story spoke for it rather than against it. He felt convinced that there had to be a place for all knowledge, and he would gladly claim that prize for the clans and bring wisdom back to the world. Samar had to caution him again that wisdom was the right and proper application of knowledge ... and that knowledge alone, without integrity, in the wrong hands, was a dangerous thing.

Still Chaiko felt convinced that the story was true. For one, the legend was not popular; he had heard it only three times in his life, but each time it grew in significance for him. If the story was so rarely told, it was unlikely to have been embellished much, so its truth could have survived.

Chaiko had looked at this puzzle from the other end as well, at all the things that would tend to disprove it. For instance, if Tomee had indeed known all knowledge, why had he survived only in this one tale, and how were his generations so soon forgotten except for Kilik, Soma and Tomee the Younger? Should not Tomee be deserving of more honor? But Chaiko had seen the answer all around him, how his people welcomed a comfortable answer at the cost of truth. Indeed his world walked in the shadow of truth rather than in the light of it. Surely such worlds, in the past or in the present, would not have recognized the value it had in Tomee.

Like a fever, a quest for knowledge consumed his mind and he resolved that as much as he could, he would find it. He reasoned that knowledge did not change. One had merely to uncover it, and make it known. And then remember it, he hurried to add, recalling the lesson of the story itself.

Thus Chaiko believed the story, believed in the spirit-gate. From the brief description of it, he concluded that the rainbow was the sign of such a portal, and he would have to pass under it to prove or disprove the rest. Samar pointed out to him that, to his knowledge, no one had passed through a rainbow, except maybe Tomee. "Exactly," the young Chaiko had exclaimed.

Standing on top of the hill, confronting the vast panorama of the plain in front of him, he watched the clouds drift away and the rainbow dissolve slowly from the top, the colors receding back into the grayness of the distance. Almost against his own nature, he believed in rainbows, for he felt that they held the promise of answers to all the questions, and he had a large store of them already. The question he needed an answer to now was when to start back to look for the clan, and then, which way?

Satisfied that he had seen what he came to see, he turned and started down again. The way down the mountain-hill proved harder than going uphill. He had to brace himself against the pull of his own weight, and often felt as if he were falling over the stiff wooden leg. He rested frequently, not wanting to be short of breath so as to call forth another vision of his brother. Once on even ground, walking was easier in spite of his fatigue. Back in camp he took off his leg, rubbed the red chafe marks and rested, chewing on a piece of sun-dried fish.

After eating, he checked his traps. He found the first two empty, then two rabbits in the next snares, choked by their own panic to escape, and a small badger, its head crushed under the weight of stones in the cunningly balanced trap. He could use the furs but found the rabbit hairs to be sparse and mottled. Back in camp he skinned them and roasted the meat. He ate and felt full again.

Afterward, he worked the deer hide, scraping and rolling it to break up the stiffness of the hide. With a few cuts for his neck and a few rope stitches he fashioned it into an upper-body covering. Crude but serviceable, he thought, as he slipped it on. He flicked his hair out of his face. The hair ends were still brittle from being singed, but his eyebrows had grown back. He had assured himself, checking his image in the reflection of standing water. The scars of blisters on his cheeks had also faded to faint traces.

Sorting through the sticks he had collected he found a smooth piece of wood that reminded him of his Singing-Stick, so he set about shaping it. The wood was denser, stiffer and it took more strength to bend it and to tie it into shape. The sound was harsher, less pleasing to the ear, not as pure of tone. Tomorrow he would bend the stick and train it some more. He hummed to himself as he worked, hands busy, his mind wandering. He would have to cross the river soon, the thought kept repeating, and be one step closer to home. Home? Home was a place one has been to, but where was the clan? The clan, not some cave, was his home. He thought of Tanya, her smooth skin and warm smile, but it was her gentleness he missed the most, a gentleness that had included even him. His brother was lucky. Would he ever have a mate as nice as her? Who would want a cripple? His humming turned harsher.

The night came with a sudden chill; he banked the fire with dirt and ash, and crawled into the cave. Tired as he was, sleep overtook him quickly. His last thoughts were regret at having to leave the comfort of camp he had made for himself, and then of Baer, Tanya, Lana and Crow. In a few days, in a few days, he promised himself, he would be on his way back to them.

Chapter 20

Chaiko hurried through his morning chores, eating, cleaning up and gathering and stacking firewood. Yesterday he had noted that blueberries were finally ripe and he wanted to gather some before the animals got them all. He knew just the spot—there was an open place on a hillside not far away with lots of bushes.

He put on his leg. In spite of all his walking and climbing the day before, he hardly noted any sensitivity in his stump beyond a slight stiffness in the knee. He stuffed in extra down and moss to soften the contact. With use, the muscles had strengthened and the stump had already grown into the cap of the wooden leg. He took but one spear for protection and a tightly woven grass basket he had made days before that had a long loop to sling over his shoulder. He set out, following a path that led through the woods. The light was soft under the trees; the canopy of branches and leaves shielded the forest floor. Drops of dew adorned the serrated pattern of ferns everywhere. A rich, varied smell from the damp soil rose into the air as he passed. The ground was soft and yielding, and in places slippery. He had to be careful as his wooden leg tended to slide out from under him. In a hollow, a large pool of water had collected to flood some bushes and trees. Water reeds abounded in profusion, and at the edge willows were taking hold. Mist swirled above the surface of the pool and hung about like smoke. Ahead a flutter of birds took flight noisily, wings flapping, shrill cries echoing alarm at his approach. Wild doves, he thought, reminded of White Dove. He wondered where she was now. A bittersweet feeling washed over him. "I am a Hunter," he reminded himself, "a craftsman. A survivor." He had come a long way since then. His mood lifted, freed from the momentary passing of a shadow.

It felt good to walk in the fresh morning air and he stretched his stride. The movement felt smooth and natural, with none of the jarring impact that he experienced with his crutches. His head was up and alert and his hands were free. The full realization that he was walking hit him suddenly. He was walking just like any other human being ... on two legs! He could stand erect ... on two feet. Years of self-conscious awareness, years of hiding his deformity, suddenly awoke to the pain it had been hiding from, but an upsurge of victory faced down the pain and soon receded. Chaiko was filled with joy: the joy of being alive, the joy of walking through the woods pierced by the sunlight, the joy of a growing mastery of being on his own, and prevailing. In a way, he was a cripple no longer; this emotional realization fed his growing exuberance. He felt taller than he was, full of strength and energy, and certainly, more than what he had been before.

Abruptly the path opened into a sun-filled glade and the burst of light blinded him. He pulled up short; ahead there was a small herd of deer frozen in surprise, too, eyes and ears on him. The hunted looked at the hunter, and the hunter looked back at them, each recognizing the other. The hunter was instantly ready to pounce, the prey ready to flee. Chaiko's fingers tightened on his spear, but the big buck sprang into the air and disappeared into the woods. The remainder exploded into motion and in an instant they were gone, the sound of their escape fading. Chaiko bit his lips in exasperation at having missed such a chance. But he was still too happy about his new leg to be dissatisfied with himself for long.

Shortly after, he reached his goal, an open meadow sweeping up onto a hillside, blueberry bushes crowding each other. The slope faced south into the bright flood of sunlight. Countless butterflies fluttered in the air, the white wings opening and closing, flashing in the sun, performing to some intricate choreography that only they understood. His eyes were captured by broad slashes on a nearby tree trunk and he went closer to investigate. There were deep vertical grooves in the bark, with bright yellow weeping sap. "A bear marking his territory," Chaiko observed to himself. He stood next to the marks but could not reach the top. "A big bear." He looked about apprehensively, but the marks were days old. He relaxed and looked closer at the signs. Here the bear scratched his back against the tree, a crack in the bark still holding a tuft of hair. "An old bear." He noted the white hairs among the rest and felt their coarseness. He wrinkled his nose at the light pungent odor that still lingered about the hair and the site. This bear was no longer looking for a mate but was marking his claim as he had for many years. Other bears would know it, too.

"Brother Bear, I just want a few of your berries," he said aloud out of respect for the animal who had marked this claim. The bear was old and all signs bore it out. There was, however, still plenty of strength left in him, for the grooves in the tree were deep. "Probably ill-tempered too," Chaiko surmised, knowing the solitary nature of the bear.

He walked to the nearest bush and stuffed a handful of berries into his mouth, enjoying the tangy woodland flavor. They had a subtle taste, not as sweet as field berries, but pulpier. The bushes were full of them, but they were smaller than those of other years because the summer had been so dry. It took him quite a while to pick the basket nearly full. All the while he ate to satisfy a pent-up craving for fruit, spitting out with distaste the occasional berry ruined by a stink bug. Repeatedly, a bird would land nearby, peck at the berries till it was satiated, then fly off. With the heat of the day the insects became more bothersome and he swiped at them half-heartedly. Finally when his stomach complained of the growing sour taste, he stopped picking and started back to camp.

After the sunshine of the open slope, it was cooler and dimmer under the trees. The leaves filtered out the sun and the occasional shaft of sunlight that penetrated had a magic quality as the colors glowed in its luminescence. Occasionally, a twig would snap nearby and he would freeze to listen. "Readiness to act is a hunter's weapon," he thought, reciting hunting lore well worn into the consciousness of all boys and men. "Inattention of a wandering mind" was the weakness the hunter must abjure, the backside of the same instruction. Thus he approached carefully the spot where he had been surprised by the deer, not really expecting them to be there, but he did not want to miss a second chance. The glade, however, was empty. He took time to examine their track. One deer had a chipped hoof, the stride showing it was favoring it. There was a multitude of droppings, indicating that the herd had had plenty to eat; the darkish color, regularity and firmness of the drops suggested that the animals were healthy. Flies buzzed about on the piles.

There were bite marks where the deer had chewed the tender ends of shrubbery. In places the entire branch was stripped of skin. The bark held some ingredient that the deer needed to keep them healthy.

Farther along, the path opened up into a clearing between dense bushes. There were flowers among the grasses and insects flew in pilgrimage from petal to petal. A lady bug investigated him close up, landing on his nose; he gently flicked it off. When a bee caught Chaiko's eyes, he paused, thinking how delicious honey would taste just now. He kept his eyes on the bee and followed at a distance, resolved to let it lead him back to its hive. The waist deep grass closed about him as he pushed his way through; grasshoppers jumped into him with hard little knocks. He rigidly kept his eye on the bee knowing how easy it would be to lose sight of it. His ears helped him out, tracking the buzzing.

A sense of danger warned him. Abruptly the bush in front erupted and a large warthog stood quivering with hostility before him. It was a large boar, the short hair on its back erect, the snout pulled back into a sneer, showing a wicked looking set of sharp tusks. The eyes glinted yellow in the scowling folds of flesh. It was momentarily confused by the smell of fire that hung about the human, then predictably set its head and launched into a full charge in a drumbeat of hooves. Transfixed by the shrill squeal of rage, Chaiko was barely able to step aside at the very last moment, flinging the basket of berries from him.

The yellow tusks came within a finger-width of his legs as he felt the brush of coarse hair on his skin. The hog's momentum carried it by; it pulled up, slipping in its eagerness to turn and get at him, stood and lunged at him again. This time Chaiko had time to plant the butt of his spear on the ground and vault over the charging form of the hog, out of its way. It squealed its outrage at being thwarted, whipped about again and came charging toward Chaiko now lying helpless on the ground because the wooden leg had folded under him on landing. Desperately he rolled to the side and brought the spear tip protectively to the front. At full tilt the hog impaled himself. The rush tore the spear from Chaiko's grasp and the animal, though already dead, crashed into him.

Panting with the suddenness of all this, Chaiko stood up on trembling legs, grabbed his spear and jerked it free of the hog. The blood gushed forth from the wound and splashed on his leg. Breathing heavily he backed away, when a second hog charged at him from under the same bush. Instinctively he stepped aside and smote the hog with the length of his spear as it raced by. It wheeled about, paused and studied him with malevolent eyes. It was smaller and had undersized tusks, but it was as ill-tempered as the other. It charged again, its hurtling speed easily able to break a leg. With hooves to trample, tusks to slash with and those teeth to bite into flesh, it was a formidable opponent. As he leaped free, Chaiko was able to stab it with a glancing blow that drew blood and a shrill squeal of pain and rage. The hog turned and grunted menacingly at him, but watched him with a sudden wariness. This hog was smart enough to be cautious, and it studied the human intently. It made a charge but pulled up well short; Chaiko slowly backed away. It feinted another charge but stopped short again. Slowly but steadily, Chaiko retreated further. The hog backed up as if to charge again, but then wheeled about and, crashing through the bush, made his getaway. Chaiko stayed still, spear at the ready, staring after it, straining for the fading noises of the hog's retreat. At last, except for the hammering in his ears, the thumping in his chest, all was still again.

Chaiko sat down on a moss-covered rock. His leg was drenched in the pig's blood and flies were already buzzing at the mess. His stomach was still heaving at the speed and violence, his mind trying to catch up and reassure himself. He was still shaking. With distaste he wiped the hog's blood from his leg and to his surprise found a wound hiding underneath, slowly seeping from a gash that he could not remember receiving. He shook his head in confusion. The wound, however, was not serious and soon stopped bleeding.

Once his chest eased its convulsive gasping and he was able to catch his breath, a measure of self-control returned and his hands ceased trembling. He examined the boar's carcass. It was a heavy beast, compact and dense; he would not be able to carry it whole back to camp by himself. His brows furrowed in concentration. He walked over and swept the scattered berries back into the basket. Then, taking the chopper axe from the carryall, he knelt by the boar and hacked off the two hindquarters. Without the two ham portions the rest was considerably lighter. With his spear he loosened the topsoil, scooped a shallow depression which he lined with grass, and dragged the carcass into it. He covered it with grass again and then dirt. On top of this, he piled rocks, hoping to prevent scavengers from digging at this temporary cache. He then picked up the basket of berries and the hams and headed back to camp. Under the weight of all he carried, he soon broke into a sweat and a swarm of flies pestered him. He had to watch his step as his legs still felt wobbly from the sudden encounter with the warthogs.

Back in camp, he woke the fire with fresh wood and banked it with earth, allowing only enough air for a steady glow of heat and smoke to gently bathe the ham portions stuck on spits above it. He then returned to the battle site to retrieve the rest of the kill.

He spent the remainder of the evening butchering and smoking the meat. The liver and kidney he cooked and ate, and sucked the marrow from the bones. From the creek bed he collected tender fern heads for salad to cut the richness of the meat. He was stuffed. Because he was alone, it was not the festive meal it should have been. There was food in abundance, but without laughter and shared merriment, it was just a heavy meal.

With a piece of bone, Chaiko pried the tusks loose from the jaw for a trophy of this victory. Certainly, his new wooden leg had saved him, because had he been on his crutches, he would have been unable to avoid the mad rush of the beasts and surely would have perished. The wooden leg had also freed his hand to hold a spear in his defense. The memory of the boar's shrill squeal set his back shivering anew. In those evil eyes he had looked at death.

Finally he was able to rest. "A hunter went to pick berries and came back with pork. Dare the hunter hunt for pigs? What will he encounter then ... if a spear is needed to pick berries?" he said aloud conversationally. He found this hugely amusing and started to laugh. The laughter grew as the release of tension set his belly shaking. An echo came rolling back from the rocks, and Chaiko had a strong sense of Crow beside him, sharing in the laughter, just like in old times. Sobered, he asked, "What's wrong with me?" Sighing heavily, "Loneliness," he answered himself.

Still he enjoyed the glow of pride that he had bested such a formidable foe, such a cunning and aggressive beast. This triumph, however, was tinged with the unsettling realization of how close he had come to death in this encounter. How casual it had all been; one moment he was thinking of honey, the next he was fighting for his life. He shook his head at the unreality. Death had touched him. But how could his whole life come to an end in one mad rush? What would happen to all his thoughts and memories? What was beyond death? A spirit world? His head started to ache and he rubbed it frustrated, finding all the ways blocked.

Maybe we live only in the memories of friends and family left behind. That thought caused a sudden upsurge of guilt, as Chaiko immediately realized that he had not thought of his parents for a long time. Would his father be proud of him now? Would his mother still care for him, even though he had lost a leg? Of course. Mothers always cared. He shut his eyes to calm his thoughts. He did not know how to look at death. He was used to looking ahead to the needs of the living. As long as he was alive, he would look ahead and let go of all the burdens of the past, he resolved. He would have to find a way back to the living; he would have to find the clan.

As the last chore that night, he threw all bones and offal on the fire, the scraps sizzling in the flames, so that the garbage would not tempt scavengers into the camp.

The next day he woke to overcast skies and by midmorning, a steady rain was falling. He had quickly built a small fire in the cave just out of reach of the rain. The smoke soon filled the interior as it had no way to escape, although an occasional gust would reach into the cave and clear it out. He had also brought in the strings of pork that were curing on the line. He did not want them to get wet and slow the curing process.

Chaiko was sore from the exertion of the day before. He had unusual aches and found bruises on his ribcage as well as a tender spot on his back; neither could he associate with a specific memory. He was driven by instinct to stay alive, had reacted without thinking. He recalled once rolling on the ground but in the rush of events not much else, especially not how his leg got gashed. The wound was already covered with a dark scab; there were no soft spots oozing or other signs of infection, for which he was grateful, since he possessed no medicinal herbs.

He worked on the Singing-Stick. It was just a little shorter than he, the wood stiff and strong, so that it took all his strength to bend and tie a curve into it. The sound he plucked was false, not pleasing at all. His brows furrowed as he wondered what he was doing wrong. He twisted a piece of wood into the tensed string and by winding it, could easily change the tension and thereby the pitch of the sound. He experimented but could not eliminate the unattractive harmonics. Crier, on the other hand, found the sound more than pleasing and expressed its appreciation with strident calls. Chaiko's exasperation quickly turned to irritation at the bird who was expressing its joy at finding a soul mate. He laid the Stick-That-Refused-To-Sing aside, but Crier kept at its hopeful courtship calls. Finally, Chaiko picked up a stick and cast it into the bush where the sound was coming from, and heard the bird fly off protesting.

Chaiko ate, then as the rain eased, he walked down to the river. There had not been much rain since the Black-Rain storm; the following drought had dried out the land, so this rain was being absorbed greedily by the ground. Still, as he looked out over the rolling waters, he noted immediately that the water was higher and faster already. The bare

14 Stones

cliffs had cast off the rain and already the river was swollen. He picked up a piece of wood and threw it into the flow checking the pace of the current. The wood was swept along at considerable speed, bobbing then spinning in an eddy. Chaiko pursed his lips in concern. Not wanting to get trapped on this side of the river, he resolved to cross as soon as he could.

The next day Chaiko crossed the river. He packed all his food, stores and belongings and hauled them down to the river's edge. He tied armfuls of branches into a raft and piled his stuff onto it. Without hesitation, he waded into the river at its widest point. The water was cold and his apprehension increased as the water got deeper. The current tugged at him, pushing him steadily downstream, but did not sweep him off his feet. The wooden leg found good anchoring between the rocks; before he realized it he was emerging on the other side. It was a whole lot easier than he had feared.

In several trips, he lugged his possessions to high ground. He also saved the wood of the raft for firewood. Relieved that the crossing was now behind him, he was able to rest. He looked back onto the far shore he had gotten to know so intimately, yet from this perspective, it appeared to have grown strange already. He knew he would never see the place again. "Good bye, Crier-Bird," he said charitably even to such a pest in an upsurge of sentimentality, honoring the companionship the bird seemed insistent upon. For a brief time, this had been an important waypoint. Here, he had come face to face with himself, had measured himself against the task of survival, and had found the necessary confidence to continue. Thus, though the memory of this place was already fading, it would never lose its significance for him.

Chaiko set up camp on a low hill top, built a fireplace circle and from the clay-lined bundle of packed grass and moss, fanned the ember alive onto the new fire. "Fire, fire, friend to man, find a home in a new place..." he intoned. He tried to relax, but the new place felt strange and it fed his unease; it had all been too easy.

The next days he explored the lay of land, fishing and trapping as needed. He followed the way east for a day with half his possessions and established a camp. The following day he trekked back and moved the rest of his possessions to the new camp. In like manner he planned to leapfrog east across the plain till he found his clan or until winter overtook him.

As Chaiko walked toward his future, someplace in the east, he paused and looked back to where he had been. For a long time he could still see Lookout-Hill, but felt that the distance growing was more than just the steps leading him away. He realized how rooted he and his kind were in the present and how quickly the past faded from focus. The boar had lost some of its stature too, yet it would remain a symbol of dread, of vicious surprise, for some time to come. Looking back over the years, the cave of his youth was a symbol of comfort and protection. But when he thought about it more, he realized again that home was not in a place but wherever the clan was. Chaiko hungered to hear a voice, but he worried when occasionally he heard a voice so clearly in his mind that he turned about expectantly, only to find himself alone. He worried that his mind was conjuring up images to feed this hunger. Could he still trust his feelings, because he was too willing to believe what he was longing for? Yet there was a growing sense of confidence to counterbalance these questions about his sanity. In spite of being cast naked upon this land and in spite of his handicap, he had overcome daunting obstacles and survived—nay, prevailed. He had learned to walk again and learned to be a hunter. He sensed a future for himself again, as with each accomplishment his hopes were being given back to him. How much would he then dare to dream?

Physically Chaiko felt good. He looked after himself, highly aware that there was nobody else to take care of him should he fall sick. He made sure he ate well, greens as well as meat, and that he slept and rested enough. His stride using his wooden leg improved. The knee and thigh of his left leg strengthened with further use so that he was able even to run, though not with the graceful glide of a hunter on a chase with that minimum of motion that called no attention to itself. He had to pump his arms to help his balance and his gait was interrupted, half fluid, half stiff, as he rode over the wooden leg.

After the rain the grass grew quickly and gave him cover to stalk game, but he could not get near enough for a spear throw. He saw that he needed to double the range of his throw, an improvement he did not know how to achieve. If there were more people, some could drive the prey to a waiting ambush, but on his own .... he did not know how to accomplish that.

14 Stones

At times he waited in ambush by a watering place or by a well-worn path but had to watch frustrated as game passed by just out of his range. Still, he kept his senses sharp looking for opportunities. One day he came across a deer trapped in a mud hole of a creek bed. The animal was young and obviously inexperienced. There were already foxes awaiting their turn, as well as a few birds cruising the sky above. Chaiko piled brushwork over the mud and crawled out on it. With a swift stroke he dispatched the deer, then wrested the carcass from the mud. At a cautious distance, the foxes followed him back to camp. They watched him skin, butcher and smoke the meat, and clean the hide, whining and yipping their desires. Then, with nightfall, their eyes yet blinking in luminous reflections of the fire, they finally melted into the darkness. In the firelight Chaiko fashioned a head covering from the head of the deer and the skin of its neck, still sporting its small horns.

Two days later, Chaiko came to a fair-sized pond. The water was murky, the bottom obviously stirred up by some larger animal wading through it. A moose perhaps? He scanned the surroundings but found no trace of the animal. On the other end of the pond, there was a flock of water fowls drifting on the water and diving under the surface in search of food. After some consideration, he collected reeds, leaves, a carpet of moss and some slimy algae, formed a loose bundle which he wrapped about his head, then slowly, so as not to create even a ripple, slipped into the murky water; only his head was above, hidden by its covering. Slowly he "drifted" across to the other side. The birds took no notice of him as he came within easy reach of them. Underwater, he stretched out an arm, grabbed a bird's legs and jerked the bird under water, holding it down until it stopped struggling. The other birds seemed unconcerned and took no alarm. He got three ducks this way. Quietly he left and slipped ashore, pleased with his catch.

On the way back to camp, he came across a level open spot covered with many prints of animals passing to and fro. He knelt and with interest examined each, trying to read in the print details of the animal that made it. There was an elk, then crosswise a handful of deer, a horse at a gallop, and an antelope most recently, but no bison tracks anywhere, he concluded regretfully. Then skirting the edge of this soft area, he found some strange prints which he could not identify. There were three of them, smaller than his palm, close together - about half his stride, with no distinct features beyond a light depression in the soil. He circled the area looking for more such prints, circled wider again, but could find no more signs of it. It was as if the creature took pains to avoid detection. What animal did that? Disquieted, Chaiko gazed about and on the way home more than once looked over his shoulders wondering. He liked things in order, and did not like surprises, especially not after the boar charged him. Unconsciously, he touched the boar's tusks hanging about his neck.

The next day was the day that changed his life. It was completely unexpected, and he remembered every detail of it, and enjoyed telling it to whoever cared to listen—every little bit of it. It is therefore only fair to let the principal relate his own story.

Chapter 21

"It was years ago, in my Year-of-Becoming, but I remember it as well as if it happened just the other day.

"That was the year the great fire ate up the whole plain. The west wind raced with the fire and drove it into our faces. Smoke covered the sky from one horizon to the other and flames consumed the earth. Every tree was blackened and every bush was burned. Birds lost their nests, the wolves lost their lair, the deer lost the grass they fed on, the clan lost its cave, and I lost the clan. ... But that is another story.

"That day, every animal fled before the Great Fire, but many were overtaken and died. The river saved me. The water sheltered me from the flames and the current took me downstream, out of danger. I drifted for days on a log, far to the west, where the river meets the western hills and turns south. That was a long way from here. From there I could not even see yonder hills, far away from all I knew and recognized, far from my clan. I was saved, but I was alone. I was left almost naked with no weapons, no food and no supplies. I was marooned, not to see a face, not to share a smile, not to hear a word but my own, nothing but my thoughts and worries to keep me company. Every day I woke to find no one there. And the same the next day.

"A moon passed, and yet again a half. I was walking back across the plain looking for the clan, hunting as I went, making camp at day's end. The grass was just growing back after the fire, all fresh green, but the herds were not back yet in the valleys, and the game on the meadows was scarce. I had to make do with what I found. Some days I feasted; most days I went hungry to sleep.

"On the day I am telling you about, the sun was in the sky although it had lightly rained as I set out from camp. I had spear in hand and a carryall on my back. Throughout the morning I searched, but found nothing. In the distance I saw movement, and part of a herd, but too far away. A little later, I saw a pack of wolves heading north, so I went south. But still I saw nothing within my reach but birds in the sky, insects in the grass and a snake coiled on a rock.

"Finally, with the sun getting lower in the sky, I gave up the search and was heading back to camp; nothing found but hunger in my belly. I came to a crossing through a shallow stream and saw in the mud many prints, some old and overlaid, some fresh that had not hardened yet. But there was one that puzzled me, the track of a three legged elk. It is true ... the right forefoot print was missing. I felt sorry for the injured beast. But then hunger in my belly reminded me that I was hunting, and my thoughts said better me than a hyena. The prints were very fresh and I had no difficulty following them.

"It was not long after that I saw, just ahead, a big elk hobbling along on three legs. The one injured he held aloft, the lower half flopping about. The elk grunted with pain at each jarring step. I was truly sorry for him, he was as I, a cripple. It was a wonder that no other four-footed hunters had found him yet, so it must have happened recently. Again I reminded myself, better me than hyenas as I would give the elk proper respect and would stop its suffering from a grievous injury that could not heal. I moved in, my spear ready.

"He saw me coming. Had he been healthy, he would have charged me and it was I who would have been in trouble, avoiding those antlers leveled against me. But as it was, he was injured and tried to get away. He crashed through some blackened bush, I after him. He lumbered across a meadow, I right behind him. I raised my spear and that's when I stopped ... I halted in my tracks. I froze because my senses told me there was something wrong. I did not realize right away what it was ... it was smoke.

"Yes, smoke. In the middle of the plain I smelled smoke where it did not belong. For smoke belongs to fire, and that meant danger. I whipped about and looked to the west, but there was no fire there. I looked to the south, and found no fire there. I looked to the east, the same. The north sky, too, was clear, no smoke anywhere, but I smelled it still, and my nose was full of it, yet my eyes told me that the earth was not burning. The smoke must mean man; ... the clan, I thought, was searching for me. Ah, what, I told myself; I was imagining things again. You see, my loneliness protested and to appease it, my mind conjured up a sign to awaken hope that I was not alone... or so I thought. I set after the elk again, trying to close my mind to the smell still in my nose.

14 Stones

"The elk ahead was tiring and I was once again just a few steps behind it as we came around a small hill to an open space. I raised my spear for a cast, when I was frozen yet again by a definite smell of smoke much stronger than before. The elk burst through the bushes on the far side, its breath rattling in its chest. In spite of the heat of the air, vapor puffed from its mouth and his tongue hung out in exhaustion. I still heard it crashing through bushes further away. Then the noise of his retreat faded."

Chaiko never once failed to stop here and wait for some reaction from his audience. He usually got one, even if the audience had heard the story many times before, which was more than likely.

"What happened next, you ask? I've been trying to figure it out all these years and still I am not sure. The elk? Oh, the elk got away. Me? Oh, I was thunderstruck.

"Turning to the side, I found the fire I had been smelling, burning almost smokeless, in a small clearing. And beside the fire was this small, slight figure, hands held to the mouth, eyes wide, wide open looking up at me. I could not believe it. I shook my head to clear it. Rubbed my eyes. But the apparition was still there and had not moved. Was this more wishful thinking? Then I noticed that it was shivering. No, not shivering ... trembling. The poor thing was full of fright of me.

"I dropped on my knees beside it and put an arm out to reassure it. But it shied and pulled back. Out of its mouth poured words like water ... I shook my head to clear my ears for I could not understand them.

"It said something that sounded like gibberish with only a few words in between that sounded familiar. I could not understand what it was telling me. I shook my head again and again. It was still frightened, I noticed, and cringed at the sight of me. I quickly dropped my spear and showed my empty hands. 'I will not harm you,' I must have said. It just looked at me out of wide blue eyes. I had not seen eyes like those ever before. Bluer than the morning sky. Bluer than the soft blue flowers we call bluebells growing in every sun-drenched meadow.

"I reached out again and it pulled back, but not as far, and I paused my hand there not moving it forward or back. I did not know what to do. I made baby sounds as if to soothe a frightened child. 'Coo-coo-coo,' I said over and over again and saw something flash in those eyes and the fear went out of them. Then it looked at me.

"Slowly and carefully it looked at me, into my eyes, and into my face. It reached out a tentative hand and touched me ever so gently, yet that touch burned me and I started to cry inside. I had been alone so long, you see, the touch reminded me what I had been missing. My skin tingled from the contact, shivers coursed through my body, and my chest grew tight with a backlog of emotions long suppressed.

"Gently it turned my hand over and traced along the lines of my palm onto my forearm, and still I cried. Then the hand slowly rose to my face, brushed back the folds of my deerskin cap, touched my cheek so gently ... and all the tears that filled me up inside started to overflow from my eyes. It then made cooing sounds of its own and still I cried. All the loneliness that was in me flowed through my eyes.

"And as if it understood, it put an arm about me and gently cradled my head and, reassuring, patted my back. And my hands went around it. And then we both cried.

"It did not seem real at the time. In the middle of a wide open, empty land, two lost creatures met and seeing each other's loneliness, hugged and cried in recognition of need. The tears washed away the pain and the distance between strangers. It was soul talking to soul. Consoling. Reassuring.

"Then I squeezed this creature in my arms and pulled back, for my hands had touched something soft and warm. I suddenly realized I was holding onto a girl.

"I pulled back further to take a good look at her. She had wide blue eyes, a small mouth with a tender set, a smooth, glowing complexion. Her neck was graceful, her shoulders, though slender showed strength and bearing. Her hands were held in quiet repose, waiting. She had on a soft deerskin wrap, well fitted to her body. Around her neck was a string of beads and charms. There were traces of color patterned into the wrap. She sat straight, with legs tucked daintily beneath her, waiting patiently for me to finish my examination.

"The questions piled up in my head. Who was she? Where did she come from? What was she doing here, of all places, in the middle of an empty land? Well, not so empty, apparently. Who were her people? Where was her family? Her clan?

"I looked about her campfire and found but a basket and a digging stick. No sign of anyone else. But how could that be? A girl here, alone? It made no sense to me.

"We sat and watched each other for a while, each of us wondering. She would speak words that I could not understand, and she would frown in concentration at my speech, shaking her head.

"Finally she straightened up on her knees, looked into my eyes, crossed her hands across her chest and said something that sounded like 'Doon' and patted her chest. I realized she was telling me her name, so I pointed to her and said 'Doon.' She smiled briefly, shook her head prettily and said 'Doan.' I repeated 'Doam' and she corrected again, so I said 'Doan.' She smiled fully; 'Doan' she confirmed.

"But Doan had no meaning for me and I scowled in concentration as she watched me, so earnest and serious. 'Doan?' I asked, and her smile lit up her face like sun unfolding over the land in the morning, and I knew that I would call her 'Dawn.' I so called her, pointing. Puzzled, 'Doan' she said, but I shook my head and pointed at her, saying with great weight and determination, 'Dawn.' She sighed and then said 'Dawn' pronouncing it a lot better than I had her Doan.

"I then told her my name. She was good at imitating and 'Kaeko' was soon corrected. But we needed more words. I hugged myself and drew a circle about me and pointed to the east to tell her that I and my people came from the east. She nodded that she understood, pointing in her turn to the west. It was my turn to nod.

"Then we both, at the same time, pointed at the fire and our hands swept to include the whole land. We each nodded making regretful clicking sounds. I was telling her I was alone. I assumed she was telling me the same.

"Then I smoothed the dirt by the fire and drew the hills to the east, the hills to the west, and the river that cut the plain first to the west, then south. I took a handful of pebbles, placing them in the east hills for my clan; then took one, pointed to myself, and placed it in the middle; took another and placed it beside mine and pointed at her. Her face was quiet and watchful of all I had drawn and gestured. She looked over my design, took the stone that represented herself and hugged it to her bosom, then placed it back. She took a piece of charcoal from the fire place and put that between 'us,' representing our camp. Then took 'me' and touched my chest with it, and when I nodded she placed 'me' back by the fire. She frowned, then took some pebbles of her own and placed them farther to the west for her people. We then both understood where we had come from, and that we were both alone. It was a sobering thought. Still I looked at her and smiled. And she smiled back at me. A sweet smile like an early morning dawn.

"And that is how she and I met," Chaiko would say in a grand flourish of hands, and a broad smile.

Dawn tells the story somewhat differently, but always with a kind, indulgent smile of fondness. She, too, likes remembering that day on which they first met.

"If he tells you it was raining, believe him for I do not remember it. If he tells you it was an elk, believe him not, for it was a moose. A large moose with an antler molting and a broken left foreleg. He will tell you differently, but that's how it was.

"He calls me Dawn, but in my language it is Doan, meaning soft-water. But try telling him that. I have been telling him these many years now and still he calls me Dawn, and now I too barely remember who Doan once was.

"If he tells you he smelled fire but could see no smoke, it's probably true. I was in a strange land. With a small fire of dry sticks there was no smoke to tell everyone where I was.

"It was some demon-spirit that chased the moose. It had the head and face of a deer and the body of a giant eagle." ("It was my deer cap and my feather mantle," he could not resist interjecting into her narration.) It had giant talons and there the demon hulked over me against a bright sky and it uttered strange noises at me, none of which I could understand.

"It scared me nearly to death it did. The breath stuck in me and my heart stopped beating. I was frozen with fright. But then the demon did not attack but sat there open-mouthed watching me. I did not believe it and it did not believe me. I touched it and it was warm. That's when I knew it was human. No demon ever cries ... it would devour first. But it cried. And that is when I cried too.

"He told me his name was Chaiko and called me Dawn. He said he was from the east but he came to me from the north-west and later took me back that way. He was separated from his people, as was I. Two lost souls stumbling across each other in a wide broad land. What is the luck of that, now I ask you?"

Chaiko was right about the elk, Dawn was right about the molting antler. He, the hunter, would remember things a hunter attends to, and she other things more important to a woman. The molting velvet reminded her to look for cast-off horns, to make useful implements.

Neither memory was entirely correct as it was overlaid by many years of living and in those many years they had negotiated and refined many of the details. At the time he was thunderstruck ... as she was overwhelmed. And though they could not speak with each other they instinctively understood that their destinies were henceforth intertwined.

Chaiko awoke slowly from deep sleep but as the events of the day before seeped into his awareness, he sat bolt upright to ascertain that he had not dreamt it all like he had time and time again of White Dove. But across the fire there she was, curled in her bed of moss, breathing lightly. Relief flooded through him. No, it had not been a dream. He wasn't going crazy.

He quickly looked about the land but nothing seemed amiss. He piled more wood on the fire then sat back and watched her.

Dawn was turned toward him, her reddish-brown hair cascading over half her face, hiding the line of her throat. Her eyes were closed but he shivered at the memory of those clear blue eyes on him. He looked at her high cheekbones, at the delicate lines of her nose and mouth that showed a well proportioned, balanced face. She was very pretty, he concluded. Yesterday his emotions had blinded him and he had really not noted her charms. Under her wrap her body was lithe and had the flow of grace about it. Her breasts were small, but he remembered how soft and at the same time firm they had felt. He got warm just thinking about it. He would have to watch himself around her, seeing how tender and fragile she looked.

Chaiko was himself neither large-boned nor tall, but felt he towered over her, and around her all his instincts welled up to protect her. From whom? Mostly from yourself, he answered himself mockingly. But beyond the silent laughter, he felt something build up within him, something very familiar, some call to action he did not understand yet. He was only aware that he must do something—an imperative—but did not know what. Ever since he got separated from the clan he had been responsible only for himself without having to worry about the rest of the world. But yesterday he had found something new and exciting, and the weight of responsibility grew about him again. So be it, he resolved, and dedicated himself to protect her.

Yesterday she had looked him over thoroughly. First, with a critical eye she had examined the deerskin covering his upper body, then gently but firmly had peeled it off him. After a few cuts and deft adjustments she had returned the garment to him. He had put it on and had been amazed at how much better it fit, freeing up the movement of his arms.

Next, she had looked at his leg, the missing one, that he had tried to hide from her. But with the gentleness of dealing with a child, she had made him show it and even to take his wooden leg off. With soft hands she had traced the ridges hardening on his stump and he blushed with pleasure and embarrassment. Looking at the wooden implement, she had shaken her head and he had drawn back defensively till he noted her expression of wonder and admiration.

When night came he had stayed at her fire, careful not to crowd her. She was nervous, but finally fell asleep. Chaiko stared up at the stars; it took him longer for sleep to come.

The sun peeked over the horizon and the patches of mist glowed white. Chaiko was awake, impatient for the day to begin, but it could not until she awoke. The day was waiting for his Dawn. The morning dew lay heavy on the grass, but the insects were already buzzing about. A fly landed on her face and her hand twitched to shoo it away. Slowly her eyes opened and Chaiko watched as realization met memory. Her eyes widened to see him there and a smile lit up her face. Well named she was, Dawn. A gift of fire, he told himself. The fire that took so much also gave back, as it gave the new grass a chance by burning the old.

Chapter 22

Realizing that the fire was burning and she was not alone—he was there on guard—Dawn gratefully closed her eyes again. She snuggled herself into the moss nest and her face relaxed, her expression fading as she slipped back into sleep. Vaguely disappointed at being so deprived of her company, Chaiko could hardly wait to find out more about her. He put more wood on the fire, and for the fourth time he reattached his leg and hid it under him. He kept a close look about.

The sky grew brighter and the mist was swallowed up by the rising light. The usual morning excitement of the birds gradually subsided. The hum of insects settled into a steady drone. A muskrat emerged from the grass, stood for a moment on hind legs, nose twitching suspiciously at him, then dropped to all fours to scurry off into the thick grass. A line of ants marched nearby and, watching them, Chaiko wondered if rain was coming, since he knew that ants and other insects had the ability to sense the weather. There were some clouds in the sky, but none of the heavy feel in the air that sometimes presaged rain or a storm. He looked around again but, finding nothing to hold his interest, looked at her, so cozy, curled up in her nest by the fire. He fidgeted about restlessly, and was hungry but did not want to leave her to look for food.

Finally, she stirred, her eyes opened, and she looked at him. The smile warmed her face and set his heart racing. Why should he feel this way? he asked himself, quickly looking away.

Dawn got up, shook herself and pulled her wrap aright. She riffled through a basket but could offer him only a handful of berries and nuts, and a couple of eggs. She could survive on that meager fare, but he could not. All the same, he made a show of taking some of the berries and nuts, chewing on the mere handful. She ate her portion, watching him with eyes that sparkled with humor. She said something in her tongue, the words flowing expressively, but of course he could understand none of it. Still, it was so nice to listen to a human voice, and hers was more melodious than most.

She then dropped to her knees in front of him, and sat back on her haunches, her back graceful and proud. Her eyes seemed to penetrate his head and an uncomfortable feeling grew within him that she could read his mind. Those blue eyes of hers; he had to look away. When he looked back her eyes were downcast, and she threw only quick glances at him.

She pointed to the fire and said something like "aoel." She waited, then pointed and said again, "aoil." He too pointed and said "fire." "Aoil" she said and he replied "fire." "Aoil," said she and he echoed "fire." Then very slowly he said "f-i-r-e." "Aoil?" "FIRE," he said with more emphasis. Looking at him with big eyes she said tentatively "fijr." He nodded encouragingly. "Fire," he repeated and "fire" came back. He smiled with a big grin. "Fire," he said pleased. That simple exchange established which language was to be learned.

"Spear," he showed her his spear. She said "labba." "Spear," he said again and waited. She hesitated than said "spir." He laughed, and corrected, and this time she said "spear."

He pointed to all the objects nearby and told her their names. Stone, skin, earth, basket, head, finger, nose, ear, and she dutifully repeated them, getting better as she gained some practice contorting her tongue around the strange combination of sounds. Hair, arm, tongue, he stuck it out to show her, and they both laughed. Elbow, face, eyes ... and he had to stop. She waited for a bit, reached out and touched his wooden leg, the eyebrows raised in a question. He grimaced, took her hand and placed it on his good leg, saying "leg." And "leg" she answered, but her eyes were soft and tender.

Then, standing up, he put on his deer cap with the horns and his feather mantle; with his spear in hand, he became a hunter, not the demon-spirit she had first met. He took his foraging basket and gestured for her to follow— trying to make it a hopeful invitation, not a peremptory command. She thought for an instant about what she should do. Should she follow this stranger who beckoned? What other choice was there for her? Those clear blue eyes looked at him, read him, and perhaps in the hope he displayed, she saw their future. She nodded her head once, so be it, then bustled about the camp. She scattered some sandy soil on the fire with him helping, then got her basket and digging stick. She was ready. He turned and strode off to the north and she followed him, forced to take two steps to his one to keep up. This gave him a new perspective on himself; he was outpacing a whole person. Who's a cripple? he exulted, energized through and through by his sudden turn of fortunes.

By the afternoon they reached his last camp. The fire was out, his bedding of sand and leaves scattered, and an animal had made an attempt to dig up his meat larder. He looked sourly at the fire which he had banked, but he had been gone too long. All the same he carefully uncovered it, searching for a hot spot to awaken but found none. He groaned, remonstrating with himself, when she handed him a compact nest of moss that held a smoldering ember. Good girl, he thrilled; quick as she had been in following him, she had had the foresight to pack an ember for later use. The two of them quickly built a fire. He uncovered the cache and took a piece of dried venison for each, and they sat by the fire munching on the meat. Even though the flavor was slow to emerge from the tough strips, Dawn's eyes sparkled with pleasure at eating meat again. Noting her eagerness, Chaiko gave her another piece which she soon stuffed into her mouth. Hunger eats such a big hole in one's stomach as well as in one's eating manners, he observed to himself, but remembered his own pleasure at eating meat after a longish abstinence. He smiled at her reassuringly, and gratefully, she smiled back. Afterward, they both drank from a nearby water run.

He dug up his skins, offering them to her, and with delighted surprise she took possession of them. He made motions as if pouring from a drinking-skin, and she watched him, nodding that she understood. They did need a waterbag.

They went looking for dried grass, moss or leaves that had survived the fire, to collect enough to make bedding for her. The fire had spared little, but under the brittle remains of a dense mat, they found some grass seeds still useable though it smelled strongly of the fire. They returned to camp, and she made a nest on the opposite side from his.

Then they spent more time on words, practicing old ones and trying new ones: water, walk, run, skin, throw, sleep, up and down. She was fast, surprising him at how quickly she learned and how well she remembered the words. "Fire hot," she made her first sentence. He beamed but seemed not to hear her translation, "Conna a aoil."

Chaiko showed her all of his possessions, beginning with the chopper axes that fit into a hand with their carefully worked cutting edge. She clucked in joy at the sight of his prized flint blade. She was puzzled by his collection of bone hooks till he pantomimed the fish fighting against the line. "Toi," she said in triumph of understanding; "fish" he told her. He loved the way the uncertain frown was suddenly erased, and how her face lit up in understanding, and how her eyes blazed in joy at each victory as they exchanged a word. He gave her new things just to see her reactions. She marveled at the smooth feel of Singing-Stick; she could not see its use but was intrigued by it. He took it in his hand and with some effort, bent the wood and strung it. Then he struck the tense string, and it responded with a tone that started out pure but quickly turned dissonant. He struck it again and again, but the note hung about sourly in the air. Dawn looked at him wonderingly. She could not understand his preoccupation with such an unpleasant sound. He saw a trace of a perplexed frown on her face and laid the Singing-Stick down.

They looked at each other: two people cut off from their families and clans. They were hungry for companionship and understanding, but could not communicate. He wanted so much to tell her about his clan, his brother and his friend Crow. He wanted to tell her how much he missed them and ... he could read the same need in her face; those steady eyes of hers just watching him, in a quiet way. If he looked up, she would look down, having seen how uncomfortable he seemed under her gentle stare. It was frustrating for both not to be able to communicate fully. He strained against this limitation, while she bore it with the patience of women. He spoke slowly and a bit too loudly, as if talking to a child, to force understanding. It was obvious that she was treating him as one too. The lack of a common language robbed both of the wisdom that shone in the eyes of each.

The realization of how much his knowledge was locked into words surprised him and fed his feeling of discontent and inadequacy in the situation. How was he going to communicate with her? There was nothing he could assume about her, he realized, and was struck at the same time by the thought that she must feel the same about him. He smiled. Immediately she smiled back. Each could sense the many questions in the air, but lacked the words to frame an answer. The questions were probably the same, he surmised.

Not surprisingly, before long they were back at learning words and practicing words they had already defined. He would hold up an object, and she would give its name; he would do an action and she would give the word defining it. On a new word that she did not understand, she would shake her head emphatically, screw up her face in puzzlement, overacting her lack of comprehension. He would try again. When she understood, she would speak the word in her own tongue to commit it to memory, alternating the languages as a way of prompting herself.

By evening they had practiced many words, her head buzzing with all that had been crammed into it. She shook her head 'no' when he tried just one more. She was afraid that everything would come gushing out and they would have to start all over again. His head was full too, with thoughts of how to present a word so that she could understand. Objects were easy, if one could lay hold of them and show them. Actions were also simply acted out. All movements were exaggerated to emphasize meaning, and she often burst out delightedly at his antics. Her laughter filled him with joy, sounding so free, so uninhibited. She found and took pleasure where he did not, yet her laughter reflected it for him so he, too, could recognize and take pleasure in it. Her carefree manner melted his grimness, and he became the child his misfortune had robbed him of, to live in the moment and to enjoy it fully. Let the future take care of itself.

They ate more dried meat, chewing deliberately and long, the flavor filling their mouths slowly. She closed her eyes enjoying the emerging taste. She had had no meat for quite a while, but had subsisted on berries and roots. Afterwards, she came and sat beside him, untied his hair, then combed it with a four-pronged twig. The feel of her hand on his shoulder, neck and head set him shuddering with pleasure, though he tried to hide it. Her hands were firm; the fingers radiated spine-tingling shivers through his body. Each touch left an afterglow of pleasure and at the same time a longing for more. Chaiko was acutely aware of her body so close beside him, could feel her warmth and softness. However, he dared not think of it, fearing to frighten her away. So he sat there motionless, enjoying the pleasure of her touch, but not allowing himself to think of any promise it might hold for him. Finished, she drew the hair tightly back and tied it, like he had, in a tail.

The light was fading from the sky as the moon grew in brightness. "Moon," he said pointing, and obediently she repeated "moon." "Stars," he said, pointing again. She followed his hand, then in turn pointed to some clouds. "Stars?" she asked, wanting to be sure he had not meant the clouds up there. He shook his head and pointed again. "Stars." "Stars," she said and quietly to herself, "Takomas."

Chaiko put more wood on the fire. He watched her settling into her bedding, trying to cover herself with some of the grass and moss for protection against the chill of dew to come. Already there was a light wetness on the grass. Chaiko walked over and covered her with his feather mantle and she flashed a grateful smile up at him. He said unexpectedly, "Sleep, night, fire," in her language. She sat bolt upright, mouth open in astonishment; he had been listening after all! Thoughtfully she settled down again.

He stayed awake watching the sparks leap from the fire, rising into the night air. He heard the hoot of an owl nearby, a bark and yip of a fox out late. He slept and woke, put more wood on the fire, listened to the night and slipped back into sleep. He dreamed of White Dove, but she had the face of Dawn, with tender blue eyes and he wanted only to protect her. Still, the dream stirred up a confusion of feelings: Dove still carried all his urges, Dawn all his hopes.

He woke early the next day. He did not want to miss the dawn of her smile and the sunshine it filled him with. Then he had to wait, for she was deeply asleep. A hunter waits like a stone, he reminded his impatience. The dawn crawled by. The birds rose in the sky, all a-twitter. The insects launched into their irritating serenade. Chaiko thought of his Singing-Stick. Then he thought of the coming day. Time to hunt, he told himself, but realized that there were now two of them. Women did not hunt; but neither did a cripple. Would she follow his lead? He could see an immediate advantage; she could drive the prey toward him.

He was so full of plans by the time she woke that he forgot the pleasure he had been looking forward to since sunrise. He made motions with his body and hands, shaking his spear at the picture of a deer he drew on the ground. "Hunt," he said to her, and she dutifully repeated it, nodding her head in agreement. When his motions included her also, she nodded again and her face brightened. They ate quickly, covered the fire to slow its burn, hung all items high on a bush and set off.

They followed the water course, scanning the land ahead, looking at the ground for signs. There were tracks, the split hooves of deer most common, and an occasional broad print of an elk. There were also wolf tracks and those of a solitary fox. Near a shallow pond, tracks of many birds were imprinted in the soft mud. The reeds that had grown in nicely since the fire gave them good cover. On the water he saw a few ducks and geese, but today he was after bigger game: they needed skins to cover themselves. On a nearby island Dawn spotted a nest. Wading through the shallow water and stirring up a cloud of mud, she took two and left two of the eggs. She came back and gave one to Chaiko. They broke the tops and sucked out the contents.

Suddenly Chaiko bent down and pointed to four leeches clinging to her ankle slowly growing fat. He made to pluck them off but she stopped him. She knew that the leeches would cling, and plucking them by force would only tear them and leave a part of the parasite in the wound to fester and infect. He knew this himself, from clan lore, but the sight of them on her legs made him precipitous. They waited till the leeches had their fill and dropped off her leg.

The wind changed and Chaiko turned to face it, letting it lead them. He did not want their smell to spook any game. They came to a slight ridge. He dropped to all fours, she behind him likewise. They crawled until they could see over the crest onto a broad expanse of a valley within the plain. Some of the bushes were showing green, new shoots from seared branches. Here and there groups of deer grazed, drifting along a line of march that crossed the humans' path. There was always one animal with head up, watching, on guard. The ears rotated and twitched, ready to catch any sound. Chaiko considered their choices. A group, not the nearest, offered the best chance, as there was good cover on the downwind side to screen their approach, and there was a depression in the land to help them get even nearer. He backed up out of sight, motioning Dawn to follow. On a bare spot he drew a quick sketch of the ground ahead and the grazing deer. He showed her what he intended to do, tracing a way for himself and one for her. She nodded that she understood, but he made her point his and her way through the sketch before he was satisfied. To be successful, they had to work together.

They crept back to the lookout, checked that nothing had changed, then backed up again to walk to their left out of sight below the ridge line. He found a water run, defined by a line of bush and taller grass that cut a way across the ridge and down the far slope. They moved cautiously, careful not to step on a twig and give away their presence. Deer had very acute hearing, Chaiko reminded himself, as well as sensitive noses, and their eyes were quick to spot any movement. He winced as he felt something snap underfoot; angry at himself, he waved to Dawn to be quiet.

After a slow and tedious approach they were in the hollow and could clearly hear the noise of deer feeding, the teeth clicking and grinding, and the occasional grunt. He motioned for her to sweep around behind the deer and he pointed to where he would be ... best positioned to intercept the deer once she got the herd moving toward him. She nodded back at him and disappeared in the tall grass crawling on all fours to the location indicated. She was to stay there and wait for him to get into position, then deliberately give herself away with gentle sounds, not enough to alarm the deer into flight, but just enough to hold their attention, giving Chaiko his chance to move in while the deer were so distracted.

Chaiko waited, listening. He sensed the herd's shift of focus toward the right and ever so slowly moved to head off their drift, his spears ready. He rose just a head above the grass and saw a young buck in front of him peering towards the spot where Dawn was making light noises. He rose to full height, gathered himself, and cast his spear with all his strength. The spear flew true and buried itself into the chest from behind, piercing lungs and tearing flesh, to come out on the other side. The deer jumped once in pain and fell, crashing heavily to the ground. Chaiko readied his other spear, but all the deer had already fled, leaping and bounding across the landscape.

"Dawn!" he called loudly and she rose above the grass wondering; was that it? Did she do well? He waved her over. She came, face flushed, breathing heavily from the pent-up excitement and looked with wide open eyes at the dead deer at their feet. Her expression changed from surprise to sorrow and she knelt down beside it. As Chaiko pulled out his spear and the blood started to seep from the wounds, she dipped her finger in it and drew a sign onto the forehead of the deer, muttering in her language. Then she marked herself on the forehead. Chaiko guessed it was a hunting ritual her people adhered to. Not to be outdone, he paid his respects to the deer, thanking it for feeding and sustaining his family. Then he blew into its nostrils to set its spirit free.

He found a stout, blackened branch and they tied the deer's feet to it, then lifted and lugged the carcass apace. Dawn carried her end without protest, though his taller size had shifted the load onto her end. He was surprised by her strength and endurance. They lugged and rested, again and again, wrestling with the awkward load, until they were back in camp. Chaiko was tired and his stump ached from the sustained effort. Dawn, on the other hand, still looked fresh, eager to set about taking care of things that needed her attention. He had to marvel at her resilience. She held out her hands to him, and he gave what he guessed she wanted, his prized blade of flint. Expertly she set about skinning the deer. He watched her awhile, admiring her skill and the ease with which she worked. Obviously, she must have come from a hunting tribe, he told himself, rather than one that ate nothing but seeds, roots and fruits. At Gatherings he heard tell of such people, living far away, reportedly small of stature. It was good to know that Dawn was not one of them. He watched as she finished butchering the meat.

Shortly after, a portion of liver and kidney was cooking on the fire, and an orderly line of meat strips was hanging in the smoke. He was breaking bones and shared the marrow with her. Both sucked greedily at the exposed core to extract the pulpy softness from the hollow. "Marrow is good, a great restorative," Chaiko observed, reciting for her the wisdom of his people.

They worked quietly side by side, with an occasional sound of satisfaction to reassure the other. Each knew what needed to be done and did it, smoothly dividing the tasks between them. Life was going to be much easier, Chaiko exulted quietly.

After eating, Chaiko worked on the antlers. Three of the tips could be used for spear heads, a lower part to carve into a comb and the remaining broad juncture of horn could be made into a ladle to catch dripping fat from the meat roasting over the fire. Dawn, in her turn, set about cleaning the hide. What would she make of it, he wondered?

That night he taught her the words kill, dead, sad and hungry. He took his time, making sure she understood. He was pleased how much she recalled of the words already. Later he took his leg off and rubbed his stump gratefully. He was pleased that his wooden leg had worked so well. His mind was beginning to accept the wooden appendage as a part of himself, and to interpret subtle pressure clues on his stump as if originating from the wooden part of him. A very odd sensation indeed, the mind telling him of feelings in his wooden leg. Throughout the day he had become more aware of it, the mind smoothly integrating from the living, as well as the wooden tissue.

By now he felt weary, tired and sore. She came beside him and those gentle hands soothed his soreness, his stump beginning to feel very good at her ministrations. He wished to point to other body parts that were begging for her attention, but refrained, biting his lips.

The next day they spent about the fire, bathing the hanging meat in the smoke. The day was pleasantly warm and a bright light filled the sky. Everywhere they looked, waves of grass undulated in the breeze. There had not been much rain, but every night a heavy dew had seeped into the soil making this growth possible.

After the excitement of the hunt the drowsiness of the day was welcome. Chaiko worked leisurely on the spear tips, shaping and sharpening them on a piece of rough-grained stone. Later, he worked on the Singing-Stick, shaping the wood, hoping to find the elusive clarity of sound his first stick had. His mind was busy analyzing the hunt. He was pleased with the result, but if they were to provision themselves for the winter, they must do better.

Next time, he thought, he must make sure to cast his second spear at a second target. He was pleased how he and Dawn had worked together. In spite of not understanding each other's speech, they had communicated the plan of action well with gestures. Her timing had been good, and she had done just enough to hold the deer's attention without frightening them off. They needed to be a pack of wolves. Wolves, by taking turns, drove the prey round and round in a great circle, exhausting them before fresh wolves in waiting pounced on them for the kill. They would have to use the hunting strategies of the wolves, somehow, although a he-wolf and a she-wolf hardly made a pack. He chuckled to himself, drawing a look of appraisal from Dawn.

She worked on the new deer skin; having scraped it clean, she now spat and rubbed ash on it till it became pliable and soft. While she worked, she hummed a simple melody, as he remembered his mother used to do. His mother could weave the tightest grass baskets, and spent a lot of time doing so, her fingers hardened from bending tough river grass and smelling of its juices. Chaiko well remembered that smell.

The morning passed quietly. Many looks were exchanged and the looks burst into smiles for no reason at all. His good humor just could not contain itself but jumped into his eyes and face. "I am grinning like some idiot," he told himself but did not wipe the expression from his face or close his soul to it. Dawn did not worry about why she was smiling, she just did, and her happiness radiated from her, even Chaiko could see that. He felt very comfortable by his fire surrounded by his possessions, the work of his hands. This was his hearth. But it was she who made him feel this way. He looked at her and she looked back. "Not sad?" she asked, to which he shook his head vigorously. "Happy," he tapped his chest. And she too said "happy" with a big smile and laughter in her blue eyes.

The sun stood high in the sky. She looked up and pointed, "Noon. Time to feet." He burst out laughing, "Feet?" "No, no. Time to leet," she was looking for the correct word. "Eat," he said, still shaking with amusement, and she joined in.

After lunch of some venison and young sorrel leaves, his mood turned serious. They had plans to make. He cleared the ground in front of him and started to draw in the dirt. The hills in the east, the hills in the west, the river to the north. Dawn watched this intently, her face set in concentration. About a quarter way into the plain he placed a small circle of stones, with some charcoal bits in it. This was their campfire. He then took a fat round stone and placed it beside the fire, then a smooth white stone with curves beside it. "Kaiko?" she asked mischievously, picking up the smooth white stone. "No," he said smiling, but he stayed serious.

He placed a collection of pebbles for her people in the west and a handful for his in the east. From their fire he drew one path to the east and one path to the west. She watched the ground and held her breath, the idea of the drawing slowly becoming clear to her. Chaiko took and placed the smooth stone on the path to her people and placed the rough stone on the path to his, and he waited for her reaction, his heart beating furiously. Dawn looked at the ground, then at him, then at the ground again. When she looked up again her eyes were full of tears and Chaiko's blood drummed in his ears. He reached out and placed his stone further along the track to his, and hers closer to her people. "Tay, tay, tay ..." she repeated and brought both stones back to their fire.

"Yo, Doan, Yo. We must. Winter will be coming," and he placed the stones onto their respective paths. But she shook her head, again putting the stones back by the fire. "Kaiko, Dawn here," she stated determined. Their eyes locked briefly, then the defiance went out of her eyes and she looked down.

14 Stones

Sadly he shook his head. He placed the stones further along the diverging paths. She was crying silently, tears running down her cheeks. Chaiko felt bad, but they had plans to make. Dawn reached out with trembling hands, picked up the smooth white stone, and placed it beside his on the way to the hills to the east, toward his people. A tidal wave of relief washed over Chaiko and filled him with tenderness. She would give up her people to follow him and tie her future to his destiny! He took her in his arms gently as if afraid to break her fragility. "Kaiko, Dawn, one. One path. Go same," she said through the tears, and nestled into his arms.

Chapter 23

The next morning Chaiko awoke to intense feelings of relief. In his grogginess, he could not account for this at first, then recalled the momentous decision Dawn had made for both of them. Joy welled up in him till he thought he would burst. There was just too much feeling for his chest to contain. He wanted to shout, and even to sing. He did neither, but a deep contentment filled him. He felt a similar eagerness and appetite for the coming day. It was as if he were a child again, as if the future had been given back to him.

He didn't quite understand this emotional upswing, however it felt right: as it ought to be. Maybe, because this was a solution to his loneliness that had been eroding his sense of being part of something and belonging somewhere. His isolation had diminished his sense of identity. "We need others to tell us who we really are," he reasoned. Well, even if they had difficulty communicating, Dawn gave him focus again.

She lay on the other side of the fire, peacefully sleeping, trusting him to guard them both. He wanted to lie with her last night (for had she not said they were one? "Kaiko, Dawn, one," were her exact words), but kept back, afraid of his strong urges that were somehow both tender and violent at the same time. There will be other times, he told himself; after all she had made a promise to him, had she not?

Why did she choose to go with him? Why did she accept his destiny? Had she no family to go back to? Who were her people? He sensed that she was as relieved as he was at stumbling into each other. It was dangerous to be alone in this hostile world.

Chaiko stirred up the fire and watched the lightening sky in the east. That was the direction they would take today, he told himself, to be one day closer to the People of The Standing-Rock Clan.

For the first time in a long time, he was at peace with the world he was born into. She had given up her people, her customs and even her language. She had given away years of her childhood to stay with him.

It filled him with wonder. Was he worth all that? In her eyes he must be, so he would have to live up to the measure she set for him.

The light brightened even more and rich hues emerged. Yellow melted into orange, a burst of crimson piercing the pale clouds that stood against the deep blue of beyond. Even the birds held their stirrings in a hush of breath that waited for the glory of the morning to unfold. Chaiko went to Dawn and gently shook her awake. She opened her eyes, and he pointed to the east where the colors were blending and glowing. She sat up and together they watched the spectacle.

The crimson slowly consumed the line of clouds and in turn succumbed to the rising orange, followed by a yellow radiance. Darkness retreated before the change of colors. Just as water must flow downhill, Chaiko thought, dark must yield to light. Then a slice of the sun appeared over the line of hills, retouching the hilltops with gold. The sunlight raced across the landscape. With each heartbeat, the splendor of dawn unfolded as the blazing orb broke free of the horizon, liberating each soul of its fear that hid in darkness.

"Dawn," Chaiko said to her.

"Dawn,'" she replied, wondering how had he equated her with all of that? Yet the comparison warmed her through and through. This big strong man was hers. Or was he?

He pointed to the east. "Today we go. Find my people."

"Yes, we go." She simply accepted it. Henceforth she would go wherever he led.

The rest of the day was full of activity. They packed, broke camp and set out following a well-trod animal path that led east, northeast. He was loaded down and so was she, with over half their possessions. The rest would have to wait for a second trip.

He set an easy pace at first and looked back at her often to make sure she was keeping up and not tiring. But if she was, she did not show it, and he admired her quiet endurance. The day was warm, a beautiful high summer day, but he, the worrier, could sense the autumn behind it and even the winter coming nearer with each passing day. Now that he had to think for both of them, the nicer the day was, the greater the threat of bad weather that was sure to follow. He lengthened his stride for they had ground to cover. Uncomplaining she kept three steps behind.

By late afternoon they were far from their last camp, and as he looked back he could see no landmark that pointed to it. The distance that hid the way ahead closed behind them as well. He took careful bearings since he would have to find the way back there again. He pushed doggedly on, stopping only briefly to drink from a clear pool of water they came upon. He was growing weary and his leg started to ache. Behind, Dawn kept pace with him.

They came to a creek bed that cut a clear path along a vale, so he turned to follow its course. He found deer prints and with the instincts of a hunter he tracked the animal from print to print. He tried to think as the animal would, taking his cues from what he saw. Certainly that tender bark with chew marks invited his attention as it had the deer's. He chewed on a piece, swallowing the slightly bitter taste. Then as the deer had, he, too, pressed on toward a tender patch of water reeds.

So intent was he upon being the deer that he almost missed it, a chalky lump a little smaller than his head that lay half buried in the gravel bed. By chance the hoof of a deer had nicked it, revealing the greasy smooth sheen of its interior. With a greedy shout of joy he pounced upon this valuable find. He cradled it carefully in his arm and showed it to Dawn who frowned at it, seeing nothing remarkable about the stone.

"Flint," he said joyfully. In this nodule he was holding more flint than he had ever possessed. Still Dawn looked at him, not comprehending the strange word. "Flint," he said again, showing her his one blade that had grown smaller with each use. He had enough flint now to make many blades. Her enthusiasm soon matched his. Every woman knew well how valuable and useful flint was.

"This is a good sign," Chaiko said half aloud to himself. "Where there's one there are bound to be more." He looked about quickly, scanning the ground, but saw no other. Still, maybe there was more upstream.

He looked about for a campsite and found an attractive level spot a little way off. It was a clear, sandy place: soft, suitable for bedding, giving a good view to all approaches, and lying snug in the lee of sheltering rocks. It was elevated enough to be away from dampness or the reach of high water, near enough for fresh drink, far enough so that creek noises would not mask the noise of any intruder. There was a pile of driftwood in the bend of the creek that had somehow escaped the firestorm. The fire had licked at the stack, but had not had sufficient air to consume it, nor the time, it seemed, for the fire was impatient to get at the rest of the world.

He set down his spears and the rest of his burdens and straightened gratefully. He felt as if he could fly, so light had he suddenly become. Dawn laid down her digging stick, easing the grass basket from her back and the leather carryall filled with their provisions.

"Fire here?" she asked for confirmation. When he nodded, she quickly set off, built a circle of stones, gathered firewood and kindling, and blew life into the ember she had carried from the last fire in a lump of carefully folded clay. She had the fire burning before he finished rubbing some feeling back into his stump. She was quick, he noted appreciatively. And tireless as well, he added. Indeed, her eyes were bright with the joy of making a nest, her nest ... their nest.

From somewhere she found some dry grass, leaves and moss and made their beds, not on opposite sides as before, but closer together, though not side by side.

She handed him a piece of dried meat, some shriveled up dried mushrooms, and some leaves that tasted bland, vaguely sour. They chewed in silence, listening to a gentle breeze play among the grasses and the rise and fall of the hum of insects. Both were thinking of a busy campfire with lots of talking, laughter and storytelling that would follow a day of travelling. It was very quiet, with just the two of them. But still, so much, much better than being alone. A bird flew over, then swooped to the side, avoiding the smoke of the fire. It was good to rest after a day of walking, carrying heavy packs.

After the meal he lay down thinking to rest, but she came over and made him sit up. She undid his hair, and with a wet deer skin wiped his face and hair. Then with the bone comb he had made for her, she combed his hair smooth, free of insects and bits of grass. Her hands were so gentle, the play of her fingers on his scalp raised delicious bumps on his skin. He closed his eyes and gave himself over to the pleasure of her touch. All too soon, she had finished with him and tied his hair at the back. She then sat down by the fire and groomed herself. She crushed some berries and rubbed them into her hair, after which she combed the long strands, making them shine with a dark sheen. Her body swayed with the grace and rhythm of her hands, combing in a sensual down stroke, and her body arched and flexed, revealing its soft contours and suggesting secret folds. His eyes drank in the sight of her; he could look nowhere else. When he could stand it no longer, he walked down to the creek and splashed water on his face. Even for a summer evening he was much too hot.

Back at the fire, she was working on the deer skin, having cut it into a number of pieces and somehow attached them together. She huddled over her work, her face set in concentration, her hands moving expertly over the pieces of skin.

He took out the flint nodule and carefully examined it. He had never worked this much flint before. He thought of the old master, Kor, of his gnarled fingers caressing the stone, and the knowing eyes scrutinizing the texture of it. Chaiko tried to see what Kor would see, then as he had seen Kor perform many times, he cradled the stone in his lap and with an antler tip he carefully chipped one side to get to the layer beneath. Even with a light pressure the chips seemed to splinter from the stone. Underneath, the stone changed to a shiny grey. Even color, he noted with satisfaction, with no pockets of porous rock, or unwelcome veins of chalk in the core. Pleased, he could find no blemish whatever. Now he had to decide what to make and then how to make it. They needed cutting blades most urgently, he decided, but not the double-edged ones that required a handle; rather single-edged, blunt-backed ones to be held safely in the hand without causing injury to the user. Refinements could come later when he had more time and practice.

Should he make flint spearheads? He quickly dismissed the idea. Flint spearheads were too vulnerable to shattering. One spear that missed its aim destroyed hours of work in a single throw. Unlike Cosh, he preferred an antler or even just fire-hardened wood.

He worked the flint nodule with the antler tip until it was uniformly round, then he placed the whole in his lap on one of the rabbit skins. He took the antler tip, pointed it close to one edge, then gave the antler a light blow with a fist-sized rock. A long flake split from the rock and fell onto the rabbit skin. He picked up the piece and examined it carefully. Not bad, he concluded; a little chip here, a little there, and they would have a serviceable blade. He rounded the other edge to remove any sharpness so that it could be held comfortably in the hand. Then he made another blade and soon, another.

14 Stones

While his hands worked, his mind sought to evoke Kor, and he tried to remember all he had heard and seen the old master do. Kor had always maintained that working stone required both respect and confidence. First, respect for the qualities of the stone, then confidence to work it. "Let the stone tell you what to do! Do not force yourself upon the stone!" How often had he heard Kor say that? He learned that stone had great patience and endurance. It also had great memory; for every chip remembered the other, every shard recalled where it had come from. The stone knew, as well, what held it together, was aware of its own strength and conscious of every weakness. Why not then let the stone crack according to its nature? Along lines it chose, along the planes of its preference, going with the grain. Then, a light blow was all that was required. A great force could not compel it, would only shatter the stone into fragments. Planning and foresight was what was needed, sensing the lines of fractures, working with them. "Let the stone be stone! Respect its nature!" Chaiko heard Kor instruct Tael, who had his own ideas about stone. Finally, the hapless apprentice was persuaded that perhaps stone work was not for him.

One who would work stone must do so with confidence. "A man may work stone with his hands, but a patient man works stone with his ears. He listens to the stone speak. A gentle tap will tell you a lot about the stone." Throughout the years Chaiko had attended to the words Kor had said, and locked them in his memory. "Each piece of stone has a distinct sound, find it and you control the stone, miss it and the stone is the master of your work. Work long enough and even a raccoon will make a perfect cutting blade. But to make each cutting edge perfect ... that takes a stone worker." Kor tended to talk in obtuse references but he would mix in some good practical advice. "A stone about to break gives back a shortened sound. No echoes, no resonance, no reverberation ... just a bone-dry sound. Hit lightly at that point and the flint will break clean and smooth into a sharp line. Hit the stone harder and the force will radiate out in all directions and the smoothness and sharpness will be gone." Over time, Chaiko realized that one had to look beyond the mysticism to find the workman practicing his craft. But how does one speak a language that has no words to articulate the skill of years and the dexterity of practiced hands?

"You can hear the confidence of the worker in the steady clicking of the stones he works, the blades peeling off and falling away, steady as rain from a midsummer sky bright with a rainbow." There was always a pleasing rhythmic quality to Kor's work.

Soon, a third of the flint nodule was gone. Chaiko sorted through all the blades he had made, inspecting each critically. On the whole he was quite pleased with his efforts and thought that Kor would have approved of his fledgling workmanship. Of course, much more improvement was required, both in listening to the stone, and making the stones sing. His rhythm was still too hesitant and interrupted to testify of confidence. Still, a hunter he was, and now, a worker of stone as well. He smiled. After years of darkness, the skies were brightening and sunshine was filling his world.

Dawn came over and squatted by him, hugging her knees. With eyes filled with wonder she watched his magic as blade after blade separated cleanly from the stone. She tested the edges and laughed delightedly as it cut cleanly through grass and even twigs.

A little later she brought over the skins she had been working on. Coverings, he guessed: a very soft piece of something, then a water bag—now that was what they really needed for travelling and for night time use. He smiled as she ran to the creek and brought it back full for him to try. He drank deeply, ignoring a slight taste that was not water, smiling broadly to show how pleased he was. Her eyes laughed back at him. He drank more till he was near bursting just to see the light of joy in her eyes. He smacked his lips appreciatively, overdoing it perhaps, but he had not the words to tell her what she already meant to him.

Dusk surprised them enjoying each other's company in a quiet, comfortable way. As he worked, he would pause and look up at her; she, sensing his eyes, would pose herself, show herself to best advantage. She firmly believed that a quarter view of her right side was the most harmonious, mysterious and even tantalizing. Her girlfriends must have told her so. So it was not surprising that Chaiko got to see much of that side of her without being aware of its significance.

With darkness deepening, Dawn put away her things and settled down on her bedding. Sleep, however, did not come easily in spite of the hard travelling she had done all that day. She tossed and turned; she was too aware of him. The leaves and grass rustled under her, drawing his gaze to her. The firelight reflected the hunger in his eyes, but she was unafraid of it, day by day having grown more secure in his care of her.

Chaiko put away the flint; he needed good light to continue. Besides, they had more than enough blades for now. So he worked on the Singing-Stick. The sound was still all wrong, but it fit his mood, also slightly out of tune. He was off balance, the nearness of her at hand, yet the gulf of language and different customs separating them. "Careful," he reminded himself, "she is not like girls you have known. You cannot tell her what you need and she cannot tell you what she wants of you. Don't assume she agrees with you just because she cannot tell you different." He sighed deeply, so much of being wise depended on language. He must look like a fool to her, sometimes, and he sighed again.

He bent the stick more and was intrigued by the elastic strength stored in the curve of the wood. The snap of the string rubbed his finger raw plucking it. He took a piece of twig and used it to strum the string as he applied more tension. The twig hooked the string and he pulled back against a growing resistance. In her sleeping place Dawn turned, the bareness of her legs flashing in the firelight, attracting his eyes. He peered at her, seeing more than the dim light actually provided, seeing more with his imagination. So distracted, his grip relaxed and the twig slipped out of his hand as the string snapped, and the wood disappeared into the darkness.

"Eh, what," he muttered casting the Singing-Stick aside. The sudden howl of a coyote quite near startled him. How did it get so close without his noticing? "Watch out," he reproached himself, as he remembered witnessing a stag so intent on mating that a rush of wolves overwhelmed it in its heat. He did not want to be a stag in rut, similarly diverted, and to grow so unaware that he endangered them both. Hunger, he shrugged? A wolf was hungry all of the time. Besides, hunger was good, it fed the appetite.

Next morning, he made a great circle about camp to see how close the coyote had actually come. It was a fair way before he found the tracks and followed them. The coyote had come across their tracks and zigzagged along them, checking them out, then had veered off to cut through the bush. Most likely the animal distrusted their smell, and detoured around them rather than risk the chance of a confrontation. As Chaiko was coming back he found, caught in the branches of an evergreen, the twig which he had used the night before to pluck the Singing-Stick. The sun bleached wood stood out in sharp contrast to the cradling dark green needles. He froze in surprise. But that could not be right; it was too far from the campfire, much farther than he could throw a stone! Shaking his head in puzzlement he cast the twig aside, but there was no question that it was the same piece of wood. Some animal must have moved it there; but why would any animal do such a strange, unexpected thing?

A little later, they started back the way they had come to pick up the rest of their belongings. The dew soon made their feet wet as they cut across the grassy slope. Without a load they made good time and could avoid some of the difficult sections that had given them trouble before. Dawn spotted a useful herb beneath a group of trees, so they stopped to collect a large bundle for later drying. Chaiko did not recognized the herb, which had a strong aroma clinging to it and stained his hands light yellow. By early afternoon they were in their previous camp which they found undisturbed.

Dawn took her digging stick, and they went looking for roots. They soon discovered some, but they were mostly small and stringy because of the drought and the fire. Dawn broke a piece off and buried it back into the hole, tamping the soil firmly around it. What a strange ceremony, Chaiko thought. It must be honoring the plant that bore the fruit.

They made a small fire and sat in its smoke to keep the insects off. They ate dried meat and roots, and drank water from the new waterbag, settling into what was fast becoming a comfortable routine. Quiet companionship, eyes and gestures talking, with smiles providing needed emphasis. His eyes followed her about, though he made sure to look around for any danger that could lurk in the surrounding landscape. She refreshed their bedding, moved around, stretched languidly, posing for him, daring him to look. She threw a sideways glance at him from lowered eyes, caught him looking, and her laughter of delight filled his head with responding joy, but his face flushed red at being caught.

He was working on a piece of wood, a digging stick for her, smoother, straighter and longer to give her more leverage to pry into the soil. The wood was resisting him and he was muttering to himself, drawing her eyes to him. "Stubborn wood," he declared somewhat defensively.

"Stubborn?" her eyebrows raised.

"Stubborn," he reaffirmed, "doesn't want to help .... does not want to change."

"Ah, the WOOD is stubborn?" she asked sweetly, archly, and he reddened again.

"I am not really ... I said the wood was stubborn!" he muttered at the point of petulance.

"Yes. That is what I said," she hastened to agree with him. "But why would the wood be any less stubborn than the one who shapes it?" Those were not the exact words she used, mixed as they were with strange words, but her tone certainly implied it, and his mind interpreted the rest. Anyway, there was no good rejoinder to that.

The heat of the sun woke them the next morning. Chaiko had not slept all that well, but was surprised to have missed the dawn. The fire was still smoldering, a thin wisp of smoke curling toward the sky. Dawn fanned the flames alive and stood in the column of rising smoke to deter insects buzzing around her. Smoke made every living creature, except man, uneasy. Chaiko watched the smoke flow over her body, embrace her, envelope her. Then she shifted to the morning side of the fire and stood silhouetted against the bright sky, the contours of every curve and every angle accentuated. Chaiko quickly had to find something to do.

In the freshness of the morning Dawn was full of energy. Like a deer she pranced into the dew covered grass, picking an armful of flowers. She returned wet and shining, her face aglow, her eyes sparkling. Chaiko did not know where to look. So much happiness was hurting him.

She cast the flowers down, knelt beside them and with a quick twist, a tie and twist again she made a garland of flowers that she placed on her head. The white and yellow petals stood out against the dark sheen of her hair. She was humming a melody, every once in a while breaking into words of her tongue.

"We have to go now," he said more gruffly than he intended, resisting all his yearnings.

She flashed a smile and was ready before he had time to pick up half his load. He led; she followed. He remembered next to nothing of the way back to the advanced camp since he was so consumed with awareness of her. She laughed and softly sang, it seemed like the whole way. What was with her? Did she eat some laughing-weed? But her laughter tickled him and the harshness of the years softened without his being aware of it. He was confused by his own reactions. He found himself grinning for no reason at all. What was wrong with him? What was happening to his manly grimness?

They arrived back at their advanced camp and found it much as they had left it, the animals by and large having avoided their smell. They unpacked and stored things away in their proper place, Dawn alone knowing where these places were as she took possession of the site.

With the load they carried, they should have been tired, but were not, buoyed with feelings that they did not fully understand, but felt instinctively as natural. She laughed and he made a grim face to hide his smile. Quick as a flash she was on him and tickled him till he collapsed on the ground helplessly roaring with laughter. She leapt on him, then they rolled on the grass as one. Face to face, body to body, thigh to thigh. The laughter suddenly left them. Breathless, she pulled away, overwhelmed by her feelings; momentarily confused, she backed away. He rose after her, but stopped half way. He sensed a line that he could cross only once, and he, too, backed away. He did not quite know why, but trusted his intuition. They were quiet the rest of the evening. The playful heat and the carefree mood of the day evaporated, replaced by a solemn pledge; they now belonged to each other. Unspoken, as words just got in the way. It was enough that he had read that promise in her eyes. Suddenly the urgency and longing that he had stored up all his life was dissipated and there was no hurry at all, for he now had all the time in the world. He could look at her unabashed and enjoy her every move and every mood and nuance of expression. He no longer needed to steal a look or capture a smile, for she was his as he was now hers.

In her turn, she felt the bond fully as much. She trusted him. Had he not found her lost in the wilderness where she had sought refuge from the fire? Had he not rescued her from the loneliness eating her? Had he not given his life to her to share? But most telling, he became the focus of her caring, the object of all her generosity which needed to be shared so that it could renew itself. Also, she trusted him because she needed to trust. She gave to him because she needed to give. It was her nature to provide and to be helpful. When she was on her own on the plain she could not help herself; she needed an object on which to lavish all these needs and, for better or worse, Chaiko was now it.

They looked at each other, she in her favorite pose, right quarter side to him, chin resting on her knees that were drawn up and hugged tightly to her chest. He sat quiet on the other side of the fire breathing in the promise she exuded. For that moment, the whole world shared in that contentment; there was no anger, no hurt, no pain ... just a promise.

The next day both were subdued. The intense emotional peak of the day before burned away the passion, for the time being at least, and left them reflective. It burned away doubt in self and in the other, making them feel closer and more secure in the evolving relationship. They had not explored its extent or discovered its boundaries. For the moment each enjoyed the sense of its limitlessness. There would be time enough later to come face to face with personal barriers, old wounds and memories, but for now the promise of a wide open tomorrow sufficed. In a way it helped that they could not speak with each other, and had to let their bodies talk, their emotions respond, without getting side-tracked by many words. There could be little preconception for they were equally exotic to the other. And each reached out, tentative at first, not wanting to startle the other.

"Kaiko, what is between man and a woman? What call that feeling?"

"Love?" he tried, "caring?"

"What is love?" she seized upon the word, sensing the tenderness behind his tone.

"Love is caring, a bond, a promise," he struggled. "Love is like fire, it gives light to see by, warmth to share ... Without love is a world without fire, cold, no heart ... Love is like the sun, it brings light to the world, makes sense of the darkness ... In the same manner, love gives sense to life ..."

She did not understand all the words but she read the feelings in his expressions and those she understood. "Shalandar" she said softly and Chaiko thought shalandar expressed love somehow much better, and he marked the word so he would remember it.

Chapter 24

Chaiko followed the well used trail that meandered along the creek, the water splashing cheerfully among the rocks on its way downstream. At times he had to duck under branches and push through a tangle of interlaced twigs that barred his way. Sharp points raked at him and caught on the soft leather covering he wore as he passed through some pines, heavy still with the smell of burned needles. He was checking the snares he had set the day before, keeping an eye out for anything useful like a stick, some herbs, fruit or eggs in a nest.

As he walked he was preoccupied with thoughts of Dawn back at the campfire, surely busy with something; perhaps bending gracefully as a willow to pick something up, or sitting with work in her lap, her back proud and straight, filling the water bag in this same creek, water drops running like pearls through her slender fingers. She, dancing through the grass, lifting her wrap to keep it out of the dew. And the way she laughed ... Even at this distance, her vision reached out to him and he found her so alluring, he nearly missed turning with the path. Regretfully he banished the vision from his mind and forced himself to concentrate on the present.

Between a blackened trunk and a fire-licked rock, he found a rabbit in the snare. In its panic, it had choked itself by its struggle to get away, flailing legs scoring the dirt. He undid the snare and felt its fur, which had recovered from the molt, evenly soft, about a finger's width deep. Lacking only about another finger's thickness of growth, this too reminded Chaiko that winter would be coming. He dropped the rabbit into the carryall slung over his shoulder. Some steps further he restrung the snare knowing that animals who did not hunt avoided the smell of death, and animals who did were attracted by it.

The creek opened up into a series of pools crowded with rice-grass and water reeds. In one corner a profusion of lily pads choked out other vegetation. Chaiko found it simpler to wade upstream in mid-channel than to fight through the tangle of greenery and the sucking mud of the shoreline. He was following a ridge of gravel washed free of debris by

14 Stones

the flowing current. Still, occasionally his wooden leg would sink deep in a hole of soft muck where cross currents met in a swirl of eddies. Just ahead of him frogs jumped from lily pads into the water and bird noises quieted in the reeds as he passed by.

He came upon a small beach of clean sand, and upon it a pile of bones. He went closer to investigate. The bones were old, from before the fire, he noted, as he observed a trace of burn on the edges. By the size of it, a full grown moose, he guessed. The legs and the head were missing, doubtless dragged into the bush by some scavenger. On the bones he saw some peck marks and chew marks of smaller carnivores. Was there something left he could use? A broad pelvic bone perhaps, for digging? He pulled upon the ribcage and it fell apart. His hand raked through the soft sand and came unexpectedly upon smooth wood. He pulled, and as the sand yielded, he held a broken spear shaft with a flint head in his hand. The spear had found its aim, but the moose had outlived the pursuit and had gotten away to die of the pain buried in its side, here on this spot.

He knew at a glance that the spear was not made by his people. The shape of the flint tip was alien, more curve in the edge than was common with all the clans. The stone itself was of a yellowish color not to be found hereabouts. Might have been made by her people, he guessed. But nothing she had said indicated to him that they had penetrated this far into the plain itself—their hunting ground lay to the north-west, on the other side of the western line of hills. As he mulled over the puzzle, he brushed the sand and mud from the spear, appreciating the expertise and sharpness of the edge, and the secure binding that tied the flint to wood. He carefully looked around, searching for some clue to tell him how old the scene in front of him might be, but the only evidence was the bones themselves. He examined them carefully for signs of ageing. The graying of the bone, fading of chew marks and the dry bits of tendons still adhering indicated to him that the death must have occurred not this spring, but maybe late last year.

One bone had been half-buried. The buried half, protected by the soil, showed scrapes and incisions much more clearly than the exposed part. He also looked at the inner core of the bone broken by powerful jaws. The porous matrix of the inner bone crumbled when he nicked it with his nails. Last year, definitely. He decided to return to camp and find out from Dawn what she thought of it.

She looked up surprised to see him back so soon, but right away noted the shadow of worry in his expression. "What is?"

"This." He offered the broken spear to her. She took it in her hand, turned it this way and that, looked at it with interest and asked, "Why Kaiko give Dawn broken spear?"

"That is not from my people," he said as simply as he could. With renewed interest she looked and tested the edge of the flint.

"Dawn knows not about spears. This flint is not from my people. This strange color." In spite of his focus on the spear, he was again surprised by how well she spoke. In a very short time she had picked up his words and remembered them. He found her alert and always listening. She had to be smart to learn so quickly.

Returning to his problem, Chaiko chewed his lower lip in consternation. If it was not Clan-people, and was not her-people then who was it? Were there other People about? Quickly he scanned the sky all around, looking for telltale smoke. Dawn's face, too, turned serious, the blue eyes wary, looking around.

Suddenly his heart skipped a beat; he had left her alone. All that time and the time before she had been alone, unprotected! He could not risk that, if strangers were about. Strangers were rare, not usually hostile, but not above taking a few things from an unguarded camp. Especially a lone girl. Fear of losing her gnawed on him.

"Eh, what." He tried suppressing his worries. "I have found a stranger already and it was Dawn." But whoever wielded that spear was a hunter, not so easily dismissed.

Chaiko squatted by the fire, and motioned for her to sit where he could see her. "Tell me about your people."

"My people?" she asked, frowning, surprised by the abrupt shift of focus. She took a deep breath, thought for a moment, searching for words, then stumbling and hesitating at first, she spoke, stringing words together that often made no sense at all so that she had to start over again. Bit by bit, the story emerged about her people and their lives, with Dawn sometimes lapsing into her own language to relieve the pressure of wanting to tell him everything. Her face was screwed up in concentration; her brows knit with the effort as she struggled with phrases to say what she wanted, instead of the words leading off on their own somewhere unintended. At times she sounded fluent, then she would stumble over a turn of a phrase and required time to recover the thread of her formulation. As she talked, Chaiko listened to her speech: the pauses, the tenseness of the tone, the pace, interspersed with sounds of frustration at being unable to find the right sayings.

Her people, The Clan of the Elk, or Those-Who-Follow-the-Elk, lived during the winter on the northern plain on the other side of the hills. In late spring they moved north with the large herds where there were many lakes but few trees that could stand in the cutting wind. There were numerous bands that followed the elk, three or four families to each. In the High-Time they all came together to celebrate the great hunt of the year, by the shore of a swollen river that all the herds had to cross. Then each band would follow its own herd to the summer pasture grounds that lay still further north.

In Dawn's band, there was her father, something-Eagle (or Who-Sees-Far-on-Wings, Chaiko could not be sure); her brothers Boar and Bear, for short; a sister, Fire-Dancer, who was mated to Hollow-Tree. There was Little-Fart, and Big-Fart. That is what she called them. And Hair-on-Fire, Otter, and White-something, besides other names that made even less sense. She had difficulty with the names, limited as her vocabulary was, and often spoke them in her own tongue rather than translating them. This often left him confused, but he did not interrupt her, letting her tell the story. After all, this was the first time they were actually communicating with each other beyond everyday objects and events. She needed to tell him these things; the words would stumble over each other, stop for an instant, but then pile up and tumble forth at the insistence of her desire for him to understand.

This year there was a great trembling of the earth and water that flowed uphill. Then there were no herds of elk to follow. Some said that the trembling scared the animals and they stampeded to the south and in the great darkness that followed they could not find their way back. The Wisemen sat in counsel, but could not agree. The People of the Elk argued among themselves and groups went on separate ways to live as best they could, on what little they could find, in a world disrupted by such cataclysmic events. Doan's family went into the hills to fish and trap, and hunt along a river. She talked of the dryness that followed. Then the great fire (Tuha maku aoil, she called it) that swept up from the plain and drove them east further into the hills. In the swirl of smoke she fell and when she stood again she could not find her family. More smoke, more heat. She crossed a creek, and when the fire came she hid behind a waterfall that protected her from the flames, but she almost died from lack of air. Later, she looked for her family but could not find any trace of them. At this part, tears filled her eyes, fearing they might have perished.

A pack of dogs had picked up her scent and started to stalk her. She escaped into the river, and the current took her far downstream. Nearly drowning, she landed on the far shore, further from her people. She built a fire, dug for grubs in the soil, and ate whatever she could find. Birds, fish, nuts, moss and things, she shuddered. She saw nobody, till a demon-spirit came upon her while chasing a moose.

"An elk," he corrected softly.

She smiled, but telling the story brought back all the fear and anguish of separation from her kin and the smile trembled. Her eyes were moist, as she blinked back the tears. He put an arm comfortingly around her. He had many questions, but there would be time later, when her language had improved and the pain faded. Now he had to distract her.

"Did the People of the Elk live in caves?"

"In winter, cave yes. In summer, they in ..." she paused searching her mind "... in flar. Skins."

"Skins?"

"Yes. Skins on sticks?"

It took her a while to explain: elkhide stretched over poles. The Clan did not have a word for tent, so 'flar' became part of Chaiko's vocabulary.

"We will make flar, too," he decided, pleased with the added comfort her description had painted for him, "before winter comes."

Dawn snuggled comfortably in his arms, and he held her against the warmth of his body, stroking her hair and the nape of her neck reassuringly. Safe, she soon fell asleep, and he dared not move to disturb her.

14 Stones

So she was not a gift of the fire, as he had thought earlier, but a gift of the river, the river that had saved them both and had found them a new shared destiny. He had not understood all she had said, and had to wonder how much of what he guessed was in fact what she had meant. But it had been good to challenge his mind, to unravel the puzzle of her origins.

Then his thoughts returned to the hunter whose spear tip he now had. Who was he? Where did he come from? Where was he, this hunter? Was he alone? Or with many? It was strange that they saw no signs of any others. The possibility of their presence somewhere nearby bothered him and robbed him of his peace of mind. It grew into a very uncomfortable feeling, always there just behind his present thoughts like some mouse, nibbling at the edges of his awareness but disappearing when he looked for it. He resolved that henceforth he would not leave Dawn alone for any length of time. Now that he had something of such value, he dared not risk losing it. He had been alone before, but without her, the loneliness would be even more empty, because he had sampled her companionship and sensed something yet to come. For now, they were alone together and this aloneness he enjoyed, for it allowed them to focus on each other without any distractions. Cramped, he gently set her down onto his bedding and covered her against the dampness of the settling dew.

In the darkness of the night, in the dream state of his mind, the mouse that nibbled turned into a lion ready to pounce. The worry turned into fear, and the fear grew into a nightmare vision of being alone again. In the night, in the firelight, all dark thoughts seemed possible, likely and even unavoidable. All night he fretted and got very little sleep, but by morning he was able to wade through some of the confusion. With the obvious threat of strangers in the vicinity, he had to focus upon the clear need to protect both Dawn and the camp from any intrusion.

He was calmer now. After all the moose had been killed the year before, and whoever had done it was probably long gone to where he had come from. Alone or in a group, there was no sign of them. His thoughts moved on, to himself. Chaiko the observer, so wise in the ways of others, felt so foolish in this man-woman thing in which he had found himself. At every turn he seemed to be fumbling with incompetence, like some child. And like a child he so wanted to be stroked and pampered by her. He could not recognize himself. He, Chaiko, the Hunter, of One Leg, he added quickly not to be presumptuous in a title he gave himself. But to so fawn upon this girl, so eager to please her, and so afraid of disappointing her ... made him feel a stranger to himself. Where had all these feelings come from? Then he recalled White Dove, but understood no better.

The scare of a stranger's presence nearby burst his bubble of security and he suddenly found himself questioning everything, including himself. This conflict between the hunter and the child awoke the cripple in him again, the cripple that had fed on hurt and rejection for so many years. The cripple that had belittled him, and was not at all pleased with this new cocoon of contentment. The cripple who suspected all smiles, who distrusted all laughter. It was the all too-familiar pain that the cripple welcomed; it was suffering that he could deal with. Joy turned sour in the cripple's embrace, for joy was the greater threat: joy could elevate him only to dash him into darker and deeper despair. Familiar pain was preferable to the fickle joy of hope. No, the cripple would not let him enjoy himself. "Surely," a voice whispered, "she could not be that nice. For if she is, then you are not worthy of her."

The voice continued its mocking, "Love is but a feeling; any wind of change will blow it away. Like a fire, once the wood is burned and the passion is gone, it will die out." He shook his head in denial but the voice persisted. "You were sure of the future once before, and it was taken from you by a River of Rocks. Be careful that the future you hope to have will not also be taken likewise, by a river of soft words and sultry looks," the voice in his head insinuated.

Then there was Dawn, a combination of joy and innocence, yet with the quiet wisdom of her sex better able to keep in perspective what was real and important. Family was, and the here and now was. She was not distracted by what could be or what might happen yet. Fear had not taken root in her thoughts as it had in his.

But there were other compelling reasons for his concerns. Chaiko knew how babies were conceived, and the approximate number of moons that pregnancy lasted. He had often heard the pain of childbirth ring in the cave and a few times shared in the attending sorrow of death. He did not want to risk that for her. He had to get her back to his people so that the clan could assist and protect her. And there was no certainty that he could find the clan by winter, for they could have moved on further still. What if something were to happen to him now, and she would be left alone with her pregnancy? No, he could not risk that. He would wait and not press himself on her.

"Do not think with your desires, for desires are blind and headstrong, taking you wherever they will, for they live on dreams and hopes, and ignore realities." The real might not have feeling or color, or substance other than itself, but it was the one sure path he, the Hunter, must follow, for both of them.

It was strange, he thought, having once buried his leg and come to terms with his bitterness, how much harder it was to face even the fear of losing the sweetness she represented. Why, then, was love so bittersweet? Let not sweet taste bitter or bitter hide in sweet, for how then shall one be able to tell them apart?

And thus had the cripple awakened; bitter at the sweetness it found, a sweetness denied to him these past years, a sweetness that it would not let Chaiko enjoy. And reason had hurried to its assistance, to find even more reasons to deny Chaiko what he most craved; a caring acceptance of him. Then like a snail that felt the first drop of rain, Chaiko withdrew into himself. Retreated and wrapped himself in self-denial.

Next morning Dawn quickly noted his detachment, but could find no cause for it. "What have I done wrong?" her eyes queried him. But the snail felt comfortable only in its shell. The snail and the cripple, a strange combination, emotionally slow and both defensive.

By the afternoon the gulf between them had grown into real distance. They sat on opposite sides of the fire, silent in their isolation. He moped about, hands working lackadaisically over reluctant wood, his expression guarded. Her looks of concern, in his mind, turned to looks of reproach, and he wished to escape them, to go off by himself, fishing or trapping, but he could not leave her alone. Surreptitiously he scanned the skyline for smoke of campfires, but found none. He settled deeper into his gloom.

Dawn was hurt and confused by his sudden withdrawal. She could find nothing to account for it. Certainly her actions did not merit such a reaction and she could think of nothing that could have provoked it. Thus, not knowing the cause, she could not fix it. That more than anything else bothered her. She was so set on fixing things. She chewed her lips in exasperation.

Getting up, she made sure to flash a glimpse of her thigh. He noticed but then pointedly looked away. Had he lost interest in her? Already? "No man ever loses interest in that," her mother had told her, "Not till they die, they don't. Just make sure they are interested in you and not someone else."

"Then why is he ignoring me?" she asked herself, wishing she could ask her mother for advice. Her heart ached for her family. How were they all? Alive she hoped. Where were they all? Did Fire-Dancer have her baby yet? She was big the last time she saw her and must certainly be due by now. Dawn so longed to hold the baby in her arms.

"He is strange, this Kaiko of mine. What means Kaiko anyway? I am called Doan, meaning soft-water, but he calls me Dawn, of the morning." And she remembered with a warm glow the sunrise he shared with her. "Why is there such storm on his face now?"

"He thinks too much. Even when he is resting he is thinking—thinking all the time. How can there be so much to think about? Was not the day already long enough with things to do and take care of? Must it be made longer with such heavy thinking? One gets up, eats, drinks, hunts and gathers food, sleeps and makes love. What is there left to think about? Is the tree not enough, that it has leaves, fruit, and casts its seeds? Must it also hold up the sky with its branches as its roots hold onto the soil? Is it not enough that there is a nest in the tree, a bird in the nest and eggs under the bird? The nest reminds of the past it was built in; the bird is its present, and the eggs are the promise of the future. Is there room or time for more? Why must there be so much significance?

"It is good for a man to work with his hands and keep them busy, but it is also good for him to use his mind to ask questions and think. There is nothing more boring than a man who takes things only for what they appear, take things for granted and cannot see the tears hidden behind a smile, cannot sense the feelings behind the gestures. Such a one sees sunrise coming and turns away, sees dawn but takes no joy. How tiresome is a man who has a ready answer for all things and whose tongue gets ahead of his thoughts. Chaiko is not such a one. His eyes dart from things to things, as his mind darts from thought to thought. But so much thought cannot be good for anyone."

She liked it the best when his eyes were on her, alight with fire, his nostrils flared, and his breathing heavy. Do men not realize how funny they look so full of wanting? Like children wanting honey-soaked seed cakes. But his gaze on her felt nice, like a hot caress of excitement on her skin. Certainly it could shorten her breath.

She looked at him appraisingly, so quiet on the other side. Should she cross the distance between them? Should she cry? Should she wait for him to rescue her? Should she pout?

There were times, she noticed, that men wanted to be by themselves in the company of other men, to share jokes and laughter that no woman was meant to hear. And there were times when they sought out solitude—to be all alone. Perhaps this was one of those times. A man who thinks all those deep thoughts needs to be much alone.

"You can contemplate all you want. I shall certainly not bother you. Just do not shut me out. Do not hide your feelings from me. I will not steal them. Just tell me you care for me ... still.

"If Chaiko means the turtle, then he is well named, so ponderously full of thoughts. He thinks he can hide in his shell forever. But I can be patient—a woman can always be patient—it is men who must always be rushing off to action, the poor things. Not a moment's peace they give themselves. Everything they make so important, and then they must respect it, and revere it. But life itself is important; everything else is but a pulse of life. Yes, I can wait. When he peeks out of his shell, I shall still be here.

"Oh, but sometimes I just want to shake him. Shake him so hard that all those fine and important thoughts fall out of his head onto the ground. Then I will say to him, 'Surely all those together cannot have been worth all that silence.'"

She pouted to herself, now only half angry, only half hurt. But she concluded that it could not have been her fault, so she was not going to waste her time chewing on her worries. It seemed to be his problem, so let him then fix it. She sensed that any attempt on her part to reach him now would only drive him deeper, and then he would hold her responsible for being so deep in solitude in the first place. After that he would hold her responsible for getting him out of it. "No, no, no. You dug the hole, you climb out of it. I shall smile and say sweetly it is such a very nice deep hole, but I shall not climb down into it to join you."

Chaiko the turtle, her thoughts softened with sympathy. "But he's my turtle," she reminded herself and was again almost content.

She sat quietly as if she, too, were by herself and worked with long willow twigs weaving a strong basket out of the flexible switch. She looked at him several times but let him alone.

Her quiet composure and her acceptance of his mood piqued him somewhat. What was the use of striking a posture and having it overlooked? Was no one going to react to it? Thinking like a child again, he remonstrated with himself.

They ate in silence the food she served. Between mouthfuls they reached for the waterbag at the same time and pointedly yielded to the other. Finally it was Dawn who drank first, her head tilted back, her throat a-throb and her breasts straining in her wrap. His eyes flickered and his expression softened for an instant, then he cloaked himself again in his moodiness. Already he missed hearing her sparkling laughter and watching her litheness of motion and the sway of her hips ... but he could not be moody and gay at the same time, and was trapped in the role he had set for himself. Why was she not even trying to get him out of this—for this self-imposed emotional exile was quickly draining him.

Casting about for something to distract himself, he picked up the Singing-Stick.

Chapter 25

The next day the strain of silence continued. The pressure to maintain his detachment, however, was wearing on Chaiko and he found it increasingly difficult to remain distant in her proximity. His eyes sparked involuntarily in her direction and his thoughts followed. He reminded himself that he was doing this for her.

Dawn was content to wait patiently for the turtle to show himself. Intuitively sensing that his taciturn moodiness was, in part at least, artificial, she indulged him by not challenging it. Had she thought otherwise, that this was indeed a real crisis, she would have waded into the fray to salvage him. In the present situation, her instincts told her that such was not yet warranted, and her practical turn of mind allowed her simply to bear it with more comfort and patience than he was experiencing.

The day was beautiful. The sky was clear and full of sunshine. Birds in droves were performing their aerobatic flights, swooping into swarms of insects invisible in the distance. The fields of grass undulated in the gentle wind that whispered across the countryside. As the two sat by the fire, Dawn turned into the breeze, enjoying its gentle caress on her cheeks and throat, her hair sweeping back in graceful swirls. She was full of longing for the days of her childhood, remembering many such sweet days of sunshine, laughter and companionship. This time of the year usually found the People-of-the-Elk on the move across treeless grasslands in search of dispersed herds. There would be constant travelling, merriment and jokes. They moved lightly on the trail, taking only necessities, hunting and preparing the meat as they went, storing it into underground caches dug deep into the cool soil. On their return they would retrieve these stores, consuming what they needed as they worked their way back to their winter cave. It was a time of plenty, a time of excitement and easy congeniality, especially for the children who enjoyed a greater sense of freedom because they were constantly on the move, away from the claustrophobic confines of the cave, where everybody's conduct was public property. The adults would be busy themselves socializing or planning the next event. She sighed deeply.

Where was her family, her people? Here she was, in the dour company of a man who was determined to waste such a beautiful day with some dreary preoccupation.

But in this she was wrong. Chaiko also found the day much too nice to squander on moody posturing. He was, however, caught in the trap of his own making. It suited him to maintain this posture, especially since he had already invested so much effort in it, yet he did not want to forego the day because of it. The dilemma was how to enjoy himself without appearing to do so. He needed to keep her at a distance, but he could not leave her alone as there were strangers about, of that he was certain. Chaiko reached half-heartedly for the Singing-Stick (it seemed of late that he was reaching for it much too often to distract himself). He ran his hand along the length of wood, enjoying its sensual, smooth feel. He had rubbed and polished it with animal fat, giving the wood its rich burnished sheen. He leveraged his weight against the strength of the wood, bent it and looped the loose end of the sinew over the other tip of the stick. The string vibrated with the tension that held the curvature in the wood.

Chaiko plucked the string. He wished to evoke the rich, pure tones of the original Singing-Stick left back at the Standing Rock cave. If he could not fix this, he would have to rename it the Crying-Stick; he thought sourly of the irritating sounds of Crier-Bird. He plucked the string again and winced as the tender spot on his finger complained. He selected a straight branch to strum with, and remembering the last time, fitted the branch to the string; holding the string and the branch together, he pulled back against the resistance of the bending wood. He let the string go. With a twang, the string snapped, the bent wood straightened, and the branch disappeared in a blur of motion. He felt a burning pain as the string slapped the inside of his left arm, scraping it.

He looked, but the branch was nowhere in sight. Now where did it go? he wondered. The sequence of unexpected events was too quick for him to sort through and left him confused. He got to his feet stiffly, and hobbled along the flight path of the branch scanning the ground for it. He was about to give up when he found it at an incredible distance from the fire. He picked it up to make sure that it was, indeed, the same piece of wood, for he could hardly believe the evidence of his own eyes; the distance it had covered was over four spear throws away! Then he recalled the day he found a previous stick caught in the branches of an evergreen as far away. Perhaps it had not been carried there by some animal, as he had surmised.

Excited, he went back to the fire and repeated the exact sequence. The string snapped and scraped over the fresh welts, but he ignored the pain and kept his eye on the piece of wood. He noted the gentle curve of flight and how the branch hit the ground even farther away and skipped along the grass. He was possessed of an odd feeling of unreality, as if he were dreaming, but the sharpness of his vision lacked the fuzzy, undefined quality of a dream state. He shook his head but could not dispel the dislocation he felt.

Again he retrieved the branch and again launched the shaft, careful to use the same set of motions so not to risk losing the magic of it. He fit the wood to the string, drew back and released, keeping his eyes rigidly on the flight of the wood. He saw how it wobbled and turned slightly in flight from a true straight path. The eyes observed, and his mind automatically analyzed and concluded that he would have to make the shaft heavier in front to steady its flight and make it thicker overall to stiffen and thus stabilize it. Since Chaiko was an accomplished spearmaker, these observations came on their own, but then the full import of this all hit him. Here was a means to the distance he had been searching for! With this, any prey within four spearthrows was now within his range! His heart thumped wildly as he looked at the branch. Could this slender stick really kill a deer? Maybe he should use something stronger, like his spear. He picked up the lightest of his spears, fitted the butt end to the string, pulled back and released. The spear flew a disappointing short flight, landing within half a spearthrow. The spear was too long, too thick and too heavy. What he needed was something about half its length. He sat down and started working with a spear he had intended to turn into two shafts for his Singing-Stick.

In his feverish preoccupation, he had not noted Dawn's growing interest in his activity. Dawn had immediately noticed the change of mood in him, his mounting excitement. Then, she, too, saw how the branch flew over this incredible distance, and she noted how he winced with pain each time the released string slapped at his extended arm. She saw how welts appeared and were turning an angry red. When he sat down to make shafts, she set about working with her skins.

When he was finished with a reasonably well balanced shaft with a hard point, so was she, and she stopped him as he was about to draw back the string. He looked at her questioningly as she pointed to the red welts on his arm. Where had they come from? He had been so engrossed in his concentration that he had not really noticed them. She wrapped his left forearm in a soft piece of deer skin and tied it securely. He could still move his arm unencumbered, and appreciated her thoughtfulness.

He fitted shaft to string, pulled back and released. The shaft flew in a smooth, steady curve, to bury itself in the ground even further than the best before. Euphoria filled him. They both raced for it, she graceful like a gazelle, he with the lopsided rhythm of his wooden leg. They arrived, she slightly ahead of him. The shaft was embedded a third of its length into the soft ground. Looking at the depth of penetration, he concluded that the shot could have seriously wounded or even killed a deer. Chaiko beamed with satisfaction. Dawn, her face flushed from her run and eyes alive with the excitement of the moment, glowed with energy and pleasure. The turtle peeked out and was on the run. He had to tear his eyes from her and reroute his thoughts to the task at hand.

He fitted the shaft and shot it back toward the fire. This time it struck a rock and shattered along its length. Chaiko was irritated with himself for not foreseeing this eventuality, but at the same time was pleased with this new evidence of the striking power of the shaft. Yes, it would bite deep into whatever it struck. With the repetitions, things were falling into place, and he was noticing them one by one. He was also pleased at the protection of the wrap about his left arm; he had hardly felt the slap of the string. "This is very good," he patted the wrap, "Thank you." It did not occur to him that this was the first time he had thanked her for anything, but she realized right away, and smiled in a flush of pleasure at the gratitude his eyes radiated.

Chaiko made himself comfortable by the fire and sat about making more shafts. He no longer cared that the Singing-Stick sang false; in his mind it was already transformed into a hunting weapon of great power. He was still disbelieving the strength stored up in the wood and felt that it must be somehow magical. He could not throw the shaft even a fraction of the distance. But if he was not the source of power, then it must be the wood. He looked with new awe at Singing-Stick. Did all wood possess this quality? It took nearly all his strength to draw it back into a full curve. He had better find a new name for it; Singing-Stick was no name for a hunting weapon. Chaiko knew that a name imbued an object with characteristics of the name. Certainly Mighty-Bull conferred more power to the bearer by that name, the honor of it a source of added strength. Naming, therefore, was an important ritual. Fretting over many names, he finally settled on Falcon. Yes, both struck from the sky, and he hoped with practice that his aim would be as sure and as lethal as a falcon's.

"Falcon," he announced, waving the Singing-Stick in her direction. "Falcon's talons," he said of the shafts. Dawn did not understand the words, but understood the glow of satisfaction and mastery in his voice and gestures. The turtle was turning into a lion, at least it could roar like one. She smiled to herself with pride of ownership.

By day's end he had made four talons of respectable workmanship; straight, well balanced, and with sharp points. He practiced shooting into the fading light, making sure to choose soft spots for targets. He took great satisfaction at how quickly his aim improved. With a little more practice he would be able to hit anything about a deer size within three spearthrows. His fingers were turning raw from drawing the string. Dawn stopped him long enough to tie a small pad over the irritated area. He smiled at her and thanked her for the second time.

Chaiko had intended to hunt the next day, but he was now so obsessed with this new toy that he kept on practicing, determined to improve his skill. He was elated with every hit, frustrated by every miss. By the afternoon he had the satisfaction of being sure of his mark within three spearthrows. His motions of shooting had become smoother, more confident, much more economical. He no longer jerked the string back but pulled in one fluid motion, held only for an instant to confirm his aim and release. There was less strength required and no waste of effort. He had reasons to be pleased with his progress.

During a meal break he tried to explain to her what it all meant: that he as a cripple, even with his wooden leg, would be unable to keep up with other hunters, and how in the past he had been unable to get close enough to the game for an effective spear throw. But now with Falcon, he would be deadly at a distance, the talons making up for what he lacked in speed and mobility. She listened intently, not understanding everything he said, but hearing the promise in his voice that told her they would not be hungry anymore. She smiled back at him, rewarding him with her radiance and rapt looks that warmed him through and through.

His excitement claimed Dawn also, but while keeping an eye on him, she was busy, drying herbs and making grass mats for their bedding. They still did not have enough skins for a proper covering, so she made do with the grass and frond mats to lay over them as well as under. She recalled the excitement before a major hunt, but this was somehow different. Here she was seeing something for the first time; by some magic the wood was made to fly. How clever Chaiko was in commanding the wood where to go.

Chaiko shot again, the talon spanning the distance, striking into a clump of grass. "Yihha!" he celebrated, running to it and shouting back to Dawn, "Deer." He mimicked pulling the shaft from the carcass of a deer. "Deer!" he shouted again, and she waved back, her face aglow with his triumph.

Remembering her brothers practicing with their weapons, she set about bundling together long-stemmed grass. Then with a rope and a few sticks for support, she deftly joined the tight bundles into an amazing likeness of a deer, with wood antlers and a long neck. "Deer," she called to him and set it up for him to practice on.

The next talon hit the deer in the neck and went right through the tightly packed bundles. The next burrowed into the chest area just behind the front legs. Both shots would have been lethal. The third missed the throat by a breath. He was delighted; if only Crow and Baer could be here now to share his triumph. Dawn ran to retrieve the talons for him, his excitement heating her with enthusiasm.

Chaiko encouraged her to try shooting but her strength proved unequal to the task, and the talon flew in listless flight for only a short distance. She dissolved into laughter. "Me big hunter," she boasted of her prowess, performing a sham victory dance. Tickled by her antics, he erupted into laughter that made him weak-kneed; he had to drop to the ground short of breath, belly quivering. When they next looked at each other the distance between them was gone, the strain melted by the excitement of discovery.

That night as Dawn slept and Chaiko worked on more talons, he was buoyed by the afterglow of success. He regarded the Falcon and the talons with reverence as having touched something magical—although he was also developing a more practical view of it. He had a new tool to make their lives easier. He was satisfied with his progress in using this weapon, for his skill level had increased markedly after only two days of practice. Also he thought he had found a good explanation for the power of Falcon. It seemed that the wood turned the strength he used to bend it into speed to launch the talons on their flight. Strength was turned into speed. The mystery lay in the combination of power, weight and speed that somehow converted into distance and hitting power.

He noted also that whereas in the beginning it took all his strength to draw Falcon, with practice he found it a lot easier, and he was already considering increasing the weapon's length and thickness, the two qualities which he suspected affected the strength of the wood. He now had a handful of talons, smooth shafts with fire-hardened points. He also notched the butt end of the talons to provide a secure fit for the string. He was itching to try the new weapon for real, and decided to hunt with it the next day.

The sky was golden in the morning light and the distance disappeared in a light haze. They ate some nuts and smoked meat, packed quickly, and set out. Chaiko carried Falcon and five talons, Dawn a basket on her back and one of his spears.

Chaiko led them north-east as he wanted to look over the path they would soon be taking to find a way to the eastern hills. The grass was wet from the dew; Chaiko was amazed that it alone could feed the growth of vegetation all around, as there had been little rain since before the drought. They followed a small brook, passed through some bushland recovering nicely from the fire, and skirted some pools of water seeping from the ground. Frogs jumped into the water at their approach, a few birds erupted noisily into the air, filled by the heavy hum of insects. A large dragonfly buzzed them, then an orange-black butterfly led them on for a while.

They passed by an evergreen that had miraculously survived the fire and a nest with it. A twitter of activity among the branches drew their attention. A pair of finches. They stood still and silent as they watched the parents encouraging their offspring to fly. The young chick had been hatched late, the fire disturbing the timing. "Gather the air under your wings," Chaiko whispered, remembering the Owl's advice to the Eagle who walked. Wings flapping, the bird fluttered to the ground. Cries of fright and distress were mixed with sounds of determination and encouragement before the trio moved off in a series of short bursts of flight, their sounds fading. One more sign of the passing of seasons and the approach of winter, Chaiko reminded himself.

As they came over a crest, a long slope of the plain unfolded to their view. Open grassland surrounded a few islands of trees and bushes. Far to the east, a blue line of hills showed their destination. Someplace in those hills was the clan, but where exactly? One thing at a time, one step followed by another, he thought, just like on the great march during the draught. It was too discouraging to look too far ahead and get lost in the hopelessness of the task. A river of greener vegetation cut across the landscape, a path the herds had stamped into the ground, seeded and nourished with their scat. That would be the best way to follow; the lush greenness would lead them across the plain. Where were the herds now?

The distance ahead looked far, but strangely he wasn't intimidated by it and that confused him. Then he realized that having gotten used to his wooden leg that so eased his travelling, distance alone no longer caused him anxiety. He walked upright, not hunched over his crutches, and felt equal to any man with two legs. The wonder hit him again of how he had improvised these improvements.

They looked for game, expecting to see small groups moving about in abundance, but found only a few, much too far away. Disappointed, they paused in the sparse shade of a tree, most of its branches barren, only a few showing signs of recovering life. A woodpecker was busy hammering away at it, digging for grubs. They shared some water and some seed cakes.

"Kaiko," Dawn asked, "your people, the clan, dress in skins or feathers?"

"In skins and furs," Chaiko replied wondering why she was asking. He considered concocting that in summer the clan wore no clothing at all, to enjoy the freedom of the season, but quickly banished the thought—but he chuckled, enjoying the vision of how she would look.

"Good. Doan does not make dress from birds." Her mind was set at ease. She remembered the feather cape he had worn the day she first saw him. She watched his eyes drink in the sight of the eastern hills. What if his people would not like her? What if she were judged too ugly? What if she were not fat enough? The People-of-the-Elk preferred girls of more substance, reciting to herself the popular saying

"Woman as soft as feather down. Soft are her eyes. Soft are her lips. Softer still her embrace. Softly she cradles you in the warm billows of her passion. May you sink deep in her charms."

"Kaiko, are my eyes soft?" she wanted to know, feeling much too sharp and angular to be desirable.

Chaiko could read the plea for reassurance in her eyes, but was wary, for he could feel the wind though he could not yet sense its direction. "Very soft," he said carefully and noted with some relief her brightening.

"And are my lips soft too?"

"Yes," he ventured. "I would love to find out," he added to himself.

"And my eh, race ... brace too?"

What brace? What is she talking about? "Yes" he hazarded, "that too."

His answers seemed to have stopped the flood of questions, but left him edgy. What was she getting at?

Time passed and the sun was right above them, but still no game showed nearby. Vexed, he chewed his lip, frustration building in him. He so badly wanted to try out Falcon. Until the first kill, this was all just a thought, an untested concept. He needed concrete proof of its effectiveness. His eyes searched for a worthy target, but anything suitable stayed tantalizingly out of range.

To pass time he carefully scouted the land ahead, planning their route to the next camp. A bare rock promontory about half a day's march ahead looked promising. If they couldn't find a cave or some shelter they could always build a ... (what did she call it?) flar.

He pointed. "We could make a flar there?"

"A what?" Her question surprised him.

"A flar," he repeated.

"What is a flar?" she asked wondering.

"Skin on sticks," he said, using the words she had used describing flar to him.

"On stick. Something to eat?" she tried to help him out.

"No. To sleep in. Flar." This time exasperation showed in his undertone.

"Oh, flarr!" she exclaimed in enlightenment, putting the emphasis properly on the r where it belonged. "Yes, we can build a flar."

They waited in the shadows and watched over a quiet landscape dozing in the midday heat. Nothing moved but swarms of irritating insects. Dawn drifted off while Chaiko chased his thoughts about in his head. There seemed to be so many places for an idle thought to hide, and it seemed to him that he had to be forever searching for something useful.

When the shadows started lengthening the other way, he shook her awake, and they headed back to camp empty-handed, except for the few roots and leaves that Dawn had collected on the way.

The next day they got up at sunrise, packed, and were on their way, carrying half their possessions. Soon they passed their waiting spot of the day before, and shortly thereafter they were on the broad venue stamped into the ground by the passage of herds over the years. By early evening they reached the rocks he had seen and made camp in their proximity. The sky was clear, so he decided no flar was needed to protect them. They made fire. After the exertions of the day, they quickly settled down and fell asleep.

The next day they trekked back to the old camp, stayed the night, then made the trip again to the new camp with the rest of their belongings.

Chapter 26

The new camp was well situated on the broad crown of a hill, sheltered enough to be out of sight, yet within steps of a panoramic view of the countryside. The only drawback was that fresh water was a fair distance away in the valley below, but at least their remote location would not invite inquisitive animals following along a water course.

Chaiko found two tall boulders suitably close to each other, and by placing some branches across the gap, he made a snug weather shelter between them. Dawn covered the branches with overlapping grass bundles, reeds and pine branches blackened and still smelling of the fire. Soon the shelter promised to keep out even the rain that was approaching from the west. Grey clouds were poised overhead and the air was heavy with hushed expectation; even insects paused for the rain to start.

They made a circle of stones close to the shelter, the fire guarding the southern approach. The opening to the north was secured by a steep drop off. They packed their provision of smoked meats in a dry fissure and covered the tightly wrapped bundles with dry sand and a layer of rocks. They collected a large pile of wood, some already half burned by the great fire. Chaiko took some of the wood under cover to keep it dry. Dawn discovered an abundant supply of fresh moss, which she stripped and spread out in the back of the shelter for their bedding.

Midmorning, a gentle rain started to lighten the burden of the overcast skies. It was a steady drizzle and as the dampness increased they retreated into the shelter, making a small fire within, just to keep the flame alive, to return to the main fireplace once the rain had stopped. Dawn fed it some aromatic grasses and the pleasant odor lingered in the air.

Chaiko had found a straight piece of yew with a long yellow grain and started to work it, thinking of making another Falcon with more strength. He stripped off the fire-licked bark, but underneath the wood was fresh and pliable. Its thickness resisted bending; however, by shaving it with a flint shard, he expected to get it as flexible as needed. He wanted it longer and stronger than the first, to be able to reach even farther with the talons. He had lost some of the earlier awe he felt for its magical properties, but he still marveled at its simplicity once he understood how it worked. Why had no one ever made one before? It was so simple, so obvious once one saw it. How many other secrets were hiding before his very eyes just waiting to be discovered?

Dawn was weaving more grass rope by braiding three threads to make a light but strong strand. Under her nimble fingers the coil around her grew visibly longer. She paused, looked up at him, then looked at the land surrounding them, and suddenly felt the isolation of the two of them alone in an open empty plain. She looked to the hills in the distant east and wondered about the future that awaited her there among his people.

The rain gently spattered the covering above them, a reassuring, soothing sound. All around, the grass in view glowed with the wet greenness of spring rather than with the mature high summer hue. Only a few flowers showed, where, in a normal year, there should have been an abundant carpet of colors. A bird landed nearby, and shook the wetness from its feathers, squawking its displeasure at the heaviness of the air. Chaiko was engrossed in his work; the wood shavings in tight curls spilled from his lap all around him. Dawn reminded herself to save some for kindling.

The wind freshened out of the west and the clouds moved at a faster pace across the sky. The rain increased, and driven by a downburst, pelted the shelter in earnest. The cover above them started leaking in places, and they huddled to find warmth in each other's nearness. She looked shyly up at him and though he smiled back at her, his eyes did not soften. She longed to cuddle closer, but sensing his refusal in the frozen posture of his back, refrained. He pretended not to notice as she pouted silently.

The weather moved over and past them and a quiet followed. A blanket of low clouds drifted across in moody hues of grey, like smoke among the shadows. The air was lethargic and heavy with its burden of moisture; the rain had washed the warmth from the air and left behind a damp chill. No creature wanted yet to wade into the wetness. A moist smell choked the air and a pervasive gloom settled over the land. Shivering from the clammy closeness of the sky, Dawn clutched her skins tightly about her.

14 Stones

Suddenly the sun peeked out from behind the retreating clouds and flooded the world with light. The sunrays captured by the raindrops clinging to the grass exploded into colorful sparkling jewels. Near them on a bare bush, a spider had spun its web, the strands dewed with drops like strings of pearls, decorating its delicate design, highlighting each strand against the dark green of the grass. To the east a rainbow rose from the ground and arched its span across the whole of the sky as the sun stretched after the withdrawing rain. "The Rainbow-Gate," Chaiko thought, his heart fluttering. As always he wanted to run and pass through it to claim the knowledge hidden on the other side. This time he had the legs to do it, he thought with a flash of pride. The colors shimmered for a little while, then faded back into the hazy hue of the sky. Dawn saw the longing on his face and wondered what thoughts had inspired such craving in him. Chaiko wondered too. Of all the spirit arguments, why had he chosen to believe in this one? But a rainbow was such an unlikely thing, so perfect, so eye-catching, so out of context with the rest of nature that surely it had to have a greater significance than its mere existence, here one moment, gone the next. The only purpose he could see was that the rainbow called attention to itself, to mark something in time and give it a location. This fit with the story of Tomee well, so if there was a place that held all knowledge, then why not behind the rainbow-gate?

The line of clouds passed over, and behind it the sky opened up bright blue. The rising light woke up the world. Birds rose into the air en masse in a short flight of recognition, then landed onto their nesting sites squabbling over space and proprietary rights. A little slower, insects took to flight and soon their hum aggressively filled the air. Chaiko held a smoldering branch close to his head to drive off these pests.

A little later, he put the new Falcon aside, reattached his wooden leg and ventured into the damp grass. He walked slowly around the perimeter of the hill top, scanning the land spread out before him. He saw no smoke but some movement of animals, much too far away. Then to the north he spotted a group of deer moving in single file into a copse of wood. Actually, he first saw the path they drew in the fresh green grassland, which led his eye to the small herd. He waited for them to emerge from the bush on the other side, but they did not, so he surmised that they must have settled down in the shelter of the thicket. He waited patiently to confirm their intent.

Decided, he called to Dawn, "Deer," and made the hunting sign. He grabbed Falcon and four talons while she picked up her new willow basket and a leather carryall. They paused only a moment to ensure that the herd had not left the bush, then using a zigzag goat path they descended onto the plain. Driven by impatience to try out his new weapon, Chaiko took generous strides and occasionally his wooden leg slipped under him on the wet soil, but he pressed on, Dawn close behind him.

Soon they were on a slight rise just above the bushland sheltering the deer. Chaiko paused, made sure that they were downwind of them, motioned for Dawn to stay low, then slowly rose to peer through a thick thorn bush. He saw nothing at first but waited patiently and caught a slight movement at the very edge of the bush. Must be an inexperienced young buck, he concluded. He sank down behind the cover of the bush, then the two of them slowly backed away, out of sight to the other side of the rise.

The wind swirled slightly and Chaiko worried lest their smell be carried to the herd. He wondered what he could do about that. He found a patch of broad-leaved rhubarb-type plants. He broke the stalk and cupped the slowly seeping green sap into his hand, which he then rubbed all over himself, his hair, face, torso, arms and legs. He motioned for her to do the same, but she shook her head vehemently in refusal, her nose crinkling in distaste at the pungent odor that emanated from him. Her eyes on him were wide, wondering where he had disappeared under the dark green color. Again he gestured, but this time he was no longer her Kaiko, but some peremptory woodland spirit whom she could not gainsay. She broke off a few leaves and shuddering with distaste, worked the evil smelling slippery sap into her face and skin. She dabbed it here and there, but he growled and she rubbed in earnest. Soon she was as changed as he; only her blue eyes shone, frowning disconcerted from under the dark green. Like chameleons they were both well hidden in their surroundings and their odor masked by the fetid smell of the plant.

He made a quick sketch of their location on the ground and drew up his plan. He would circle around on the downwind side to a point overlooking the most likely escape route the deer would choose, while she was to approach from the uphill slope slowly and cautiously. Then gently she was to excite the herd just enough to flush them out of cover but not to frighten them into full flight. He gestured over the drawing

14 Stones

and spoke in hushed tones. She nodded understanding, eyes aglow with the excitement of the coming event. He went through it again much to her rising impatience. Then they separated.

Chaiko slowly worked his way to his position. He found a rotten tree trunk overgrown with thick moss and climbing vines that hid him well but gave him an excellent view of the far side of the thicket. He fitted a talon onto the string and readied Falcon for a shot. His heart pumped with the exhilaration of anticipation. To steady himself he took slow, even, deep breaths till his pulse slowed to a more comfortable pace and his hands stopped trembling. He stood frozen beside the tree, his greenness blending into the vegetation, invisible as long as he did not move. He kept his eyes unwaveringly on the edge of the brush. Nothing stirred yet. Their timing had to be right; Dawn had to play her role with finesse; give away her presence just enough to compel them to withdraw, but not enough to push them into a mad rush to escape. Beads of perspiration ran down his face, washing salt and "rhubarb" juice stinging into his eyes. He blinked but dared not look away. It was time. Where was she?

Then the bush trembled and from behind it a deer's head emerged, ears nervously rotating about to catch the slightest sound. The eyes were wide open, suspiciously drinking in the view as it looked about, then turning its head on its long neck to look back beyond the brush. Another deer emerged, and quickly two more, then the whole herd came drifting out of cover, moving with intent, nervous but not overly alarmed.

Chaiko tensed, slowly raised the Falcon and pulled the string back but did not apply real strength yet. He waited for the best shot to present itself. But the lead animal already began to angle away, the rest of the herd after him. Chaiko compressed his lower lip in frustration as with every step the herd was getting further away and the chance of a good hit decreased. He thought about making a charge and shooting at a run, but quickly choked down that impulse. He steeled himself to wait, when every fiber of his being wanted to take action to prevent the herd from slipping out of range. Then a trailing pair emerged from cover and ambled after the rest; a large dam and an accompanying fawn. She was having difficulty making the fawn follow; they too started to drift away.

These were the only targets left, and Chaiko was determined not to let them get away but risk a long shot. Already, the large dam was over four spearthrows away, the fawn close behind her. Chaiko could wait no longer, stepped clear of the tree, and in one smooth motion pulled the string back, sighting along the shaft, aiming high and to the left to allow for a light cross wind, then he let the string go. The talon leapt into the air in the exhilaration of its freedom, climbed gracefully, then like the falcon it swooped out of the sky to strike into the left-hand side of the chest cavity, slipping through bundles of muscles, burying itself deep into the soft inner tissue. The deer leapt into the air, came crashing down, thrashed about on the ground, then raised itself to stagger along an uncertain path.

Already a second talon was on its way toward the smaller deer. It would probably have missed, but the animal was startled by the dam's sudden collapse and jumped right into the flight of the talon. The shaft bit into its neck, pierced the bronchial tube, and lodged itself into the neck bone, severing the spinal cord. The animal was dead before it hit the ground.

Then a third talon was loosed, boring through the air and hitting the dam's barrel chest just behind the foreleg. Still the animal staggered on, instinctively following the rest of the herd that had already disappeared over the far slope of the draw. Chaiko jumped over some thistle weeds and fitted the last talon into the string, but held up shooting it, judging the animal's fading strength. From behind, Dawn emerged into view, saw him and came running. They found the dying deer lying on the grass sprinkled with her blood. The head lowered slowly to the ground; her eyes blinked and the light went out of them. It twitched once then was still. The side deflated as the last breath escaped the lifeless body.

Chaiko's bloodlust receded slowly, the thumping of his heart eased, and the roar in his ears faded, but the feeling of elation at how effective the weapon was, remained. He was jubilant; he couldn't have hoped for better results. All three talons hit and each was deadly. He looked gratefully at the carcass at his feet, at the same time feeling pity for the animal he had just killed. "Rest, sister, for you the journey is over. For you the sun won't shine, the wind won't blow. Your eyes will not look upon this world again. You have no need of water, no need of food..." Because he was uninitiated into the secret rites of the hunting society, he did not know the proper words to unlock the soul from the dead body of a kill. He knew some words from old tales, but they were considered too old-fashioned to be effective. So he adopted the words said over people, to mark and honor Falcon's first kill. The blood had made the wood into a weapon, just like his first kill had turned him into a Hunter. Falcon was now a part of him, to use to good effect. With pride that did not overwhelm his sadness for the slain deer, he caressed the smooth curve of the wood. Dawn knelt by the animal and with its blood drew the designs of her people to mark and honor the kill.

Chaiko then showed her the fawn, the talon deep in the neck. At the sight Dawn's joy turned sad, remembering all the children she grew up and played with, like the fawn must have, but she repeated the ritual to claim the kill. Behind her sorrow for the death was the glow of pride for her hunter, who had spied the deer, tracked and followed them, cunningly ambushed them, and unleashed death with his strange sticks. There was magic in that wood of his, the one he called Falcon.

When Chaiko showed her where he had stood behind the dead tree, she could hardly believe the distance. "The herd was going away. Farther and farther away and still I had no good shot. I thought I was going to lose all chance at them. Then these two came into view, still too far off, but it was they or nothing. So I shot and sent the talon on its way. Then two more. And they all found their mark." He shook his head, disbelieving his own feat. The distance was impressive. There must be magic somewhere after all, between intent and the deed accomplished. He could not remember actually aiming; it was as if the weapon did it all on its own, and he was just its bearer. In a way he was right. The many hours of practice had made the motions automatic and taken them out of his conscious control. The talons, once loosened, became messengers of death.

"The young one died right away. The dam staggered on. The rest ran over the slope there." He pointed the way. Had the deer taken a more advantageous route, as he had expected them to, he could have made another shot, so there might have been four kills altogether, one for each of the four talons. As it was, he had made the best of a less than ideal situation. He could not have gotten further ahead of them without alarming them, either by movement or by the smell of his presence.

He looked at her painted green, and at himself, and started to laugh, all the accumulated tension of the hunt erupting through the laughter into release. She was swept along with his mirth though she did not know why they were laughing. "Good," he exclaimed, slapping her lightly on her back. "Dawn did good. Dawn is a mighty hunter." She drank in the pleasure of the praise along with the gentle teasing. They worked well together, with exact, intuitive timing. Twice now, she had given him a chance he would not have had without her collaboration. He pulled out the talons from the wounds and wiped them on the grass.

Chaiko looked around appraisingly. It was already late afternoon and they had a lot to do, to butcher and to prepare the meat. It was too far to return to camp loaded down as they were with both carcasses. Besides, it would never be good to lead a fresh blood trail back to their camp, an open invitation no hunting animal could refuse. He looked about for a place to make a fire. A little distance off, there was an open gravel spot, free of grass and bush, just right for their purpose. They each grabbed a hind leg and dragged first one then the other to this bare spot. There was also a convenient pile of wood from an uprooted tree that had been protected from the great fire by a dense covering of vine that overgrew it, as well as a pool of fresh water at hand, fed from an underground spring. Chaiko went to investigate, thinking what an ideal spot it would be for a campsite, then froze, for just ahead of him was a circle of stones, ringing hardened ash and bits and pieces of charcoal. STRANGERS!! He spun about and made a quick scan all around. It was an instinctive reaction, for he already knew that the site was old.

Dawn came running up to stand beside him. "People?" she asked, but knew from his reaction that it was not his clan. Could it be her people? She looked closely. A fire is a fire. All people used fire; it was what made them different from all other creatures. People had learned to live with fire, to live in smoke. Chaiko found a pile of bones, and dug among them trying to estimate when and for how long the campsite had been occupied. He recognized some bird bones, partial deer and rabbit skeletons, and more odds and ends. He uncovered some quills of a porcupine. His people did not eat porcupine, considering them too sympathetically after the many stories the creature was featured in, to teach children the value of perseverance and honesty. Did hers? She shook her head no, but then shrugged her shoulders. Who knows? She was remembering with distaste the beetles and worms she had had to eat when she was alone after the great fire.

There was little left to read into; the weather had erased all other signs. Chaiko picked up a stick, sharpened to a point on one end and obviously used as a skewer to hold the meat to the heat of fire, but he could not read anything more into the crude workmanship of a throwaway implement. He estimated, from the pile of bones and the pack of ash in the fireplace that the fire had been used by one person, male, about a year ago, maybe for a handful of days. Probably a hunting camp, by the same person who had hunted the moose and lost the spear tip. Not the clan or her people. This fresh evidence of strangers, even if old, was unsettling. The mastery he had felt a short while ago suddenly dissipated because of an unknown presence with whom they shared this part of the plain. But then he shrugged his shoulders; stranger or no stranger, they still had things to do. Dawn already had the fire going in the circle of stones. She was skinning the animals in turn, with deft, practiced movements that he had to admire. Chaiko took his chopper axe, and hacked away at the carcasses.

They worked late into the night, cutting and portioning the meat into strips to hang in the smoke, the task made easier by the many flint blades they had at hand. All that they needed was coming from her basket, he realized admiringly. All he had grabbed was Falcon and four talons, but she had come prepared, saving them a trip back to camp to fetch the needed tools. He was grateful for such a long-sighted helpmate.

It was approaching morning by the time they finished cutting and hanging all the meat over the smoke. They had built three other fires around to discourage predators who might be prowling nearby, attracted by the smell of the kill. A coyote barked in the near darkness and somewhat later a sudden squabble erupted among the waiting hyenas. Chaiko thought he heard the deep-chested cough of a legendary saber-tooth, but that was impossible, since no one had seen a tiger alive; it now lived only in the many stories people still told. Throughout the night they heard other noises of prowling scavengers, but none ventured into the guarding circle of fires.

Both were tired. Too tired even to eat in spite of the tantalizing smell around them. Above all, they wished to wash off all the blood, gore and green plant stain, but dared not go into the darkness. At least the green seemed to keep the insects away; Chaiko stored that bit of useful information.

At first light, as a narrow ribbon of gold peeked under a ceiling of low clouds, Dawn, with a spear in her hand, ventured to the pond. Not wishing to dirty the clear water, she filled the waterbag and brought it back to the fire. They washed themselves gratefully, scrubbing with handfuls of sand at the tenacious green color on their skin. It was easier to put on than to take off, Chaiko grumbled to himself. She had to make several trips before they both were clean enough for her satisfaction.

They spent the next two days in the stranger's camp, curing meat. Dawn worked on the two new skins while Chaiko worked on more talons. With the effectiveness of the new weapon so well proven, both felt more assured of the future. They exchanged smiles across the fire, smiles that were proud and confident. They still had a long way to go, he reminded himself.

When the meat was cured, they wrapped it into hides and buried it in gravelly sand. In a couple of days they would pass this way again and would add the cache to their load. After that, they cleaned up the campsite, doused the fire and said farewell to the stranger's camp.

By late afternoon they were on the hilltop again. Their shelter was still weather tight and no animal had been too inquisitive among their possessions. Chaiko enjoyed the commanding view of the countryside, aware that few things could surprise them there, a good quality to have in any campsite. The air was always fresh as the wind flowed over the brow of the hill at any time of day. Dawn secured their packs and draped their footwear over a bush to dry. Then she made fire while he took off his wooden leg and scratched his stump. His calluses had hardened but at times he was plagued by itches that seemed to hide beneath the toughened fold of skin, unreachable. They ate, drank and rested, quickly growing sleepy after a day of movement.

The fire collapsed onto itself and its radiance retreated to hide among the ashes. A thin wisp of smoke climbed into the cooling evening air. As the light faded, he looked about the comfort of the camp with regret, knowing they would be leaving it soon, this time for good.

Chapter 27

After a few more days Chaiko was growing restless. He found himself wanting to be on the move again, to find his clan. But they needed to rest up before they could undertake the next stretch. He estimated that in six days of steady travelling they could reach the hills, but where to go from there? The clan could be anywhere in the maze of valleys and hills. And if the clan, for whatever reasons, had to move beyond those hills, how was he going to find them?

Should they surge ahead or should they continue leapfrogging across the plain, from camp to camp, hunting and preparing for the winter as they went? He chewed on this dilemma, or maybe the dilemma chewed on him; it was often hard to tell which. His emotions spurred him to take a chance and to push for a quick search, but his reason advised caution: winter waits for no one, and they had only themselves to depend on. The long winter's hunger of the past was deeply etched in his memories and he could not turn his back on them. Unlike animals, fear of the future was the curse as well as the salvation of his kind, driving man to anticipate and prepare for whatever waited ahead. The future was a large part of the present, and the present lived in its shadow. No, they would not rush into the unknown but make their steady but slow way across the land, preparing as they went.

The success of the hunt had reassured him; he felt more confident about the future. He, Chaiko, was now a Hunter as he was becoming fond of reminding himself. The blood of the kills had made him one, he had claimed all the slain animals, and he needed no other ceremony to confirm it. This recognition was now a core part of him. Although Falcon gave him a huge advantage, it was still only a tool; it was his confidence that was the true Hunter. The cripple who had overcome his handicap now walked the path of a Hunter with confidence. Falcon was thus more a proof of his tool making: the finding and taking advantage of what he had discovered and how he had turned the flexibility, strength and resistance of the wood into the weapon it now was. And he had called it a Singing-Stick! He smiled to himself, but immediately became serious for he realized what a narrow path had led him to uncover this weapon of great value that had been hiding in the Singing-Stick. At the time he had not been working on a weapon at all; he had been trying to improve on a musical oddity that struck his fancy, which itself was uncovered by accident from trying to straighten a crooked piece of wood. Was life itself just a series of accidents, a string of luck or misfortune? That cannot be, he reasoned; the dire urgency of his need, as alone as he had been, had set his mind to search for anything useable that would help him survive. And he had had full expectation of finding something, which he did, in recognizing the potential in Falcon. But if discovery was a mind-set, a recognition, then the opposite must also be true; he must be constantly overlooking things of equal or even greater value. What had he overlooked? Not recognized? Must he then look for things not there as well as for things that were? He rubbed his forehead as his head started to ache from such an unending circle of reasoning.

Chaiko looked at Dawn. She was on her knees beyond the fire, scraping the deer hides yet again to make them even more pliable. She worked in a steady rhythm that ignored the boredom and weariness of the task. He was amazed at how tenacious she was at everything she undertook and how strong she was for her size. Step for step, carrying a heavy load, she had kept pace with him. He had not heard her complain once. She did not allow even a sign that she was tired, or that the task was beyond her. In a level-headed way she knew what had to be done and did it: she did not seem to worry about it. She did not ask him for direction, or if she did, it was out of courtesy, of recognition that he was a man of stature. His respect for her grew; her size was entirely misleading, she was not small at all. If size was measured by quality, she was probably taller than he.

As they worked companionably side by side, he was having difficulty keeping his eyes off her. She noticed it, too, and did her best to encourage his interest by keeping herself in front of him. Gone was his rejection of her. He had laughed and smiled with her. The head of the turtle was looking about once again, but she knew that the nature of the turtle was to be slow and cautious. She, too, smiled. It was a woman's destiny to find her mate, to find the father for her children. She had not been given many choices in life, but she had been fortunate to find the only man to be found in this forsaken emptiness. Looking at him, her turtle, her heart grew warm with thoughts of him; she was content with the choice fate gave her. But why was it so difficult for a man to see the obvious? What could he be waiting for?

14 Stones

"Kaiko," she asked "what means Kaiko?"

"Chaiko is from the old language of the clan, it is not used much anymore. It means the snail." He did not tell her that, for the clan, the snail was a symbol of contentment, for wherever a snail went, it carried its cave on its back; therefore, it was always at home. He was unsure if it actually meant snail or the contentment that a snail was reputed to enjoy in abundance. He had, in any case, come to despise his name as a cruel misnomer, not finding much contentment in his life up until now. But perhaps, now ...?

Her understanding of his language had improved greatly, but this word she did not know. "Snail?"

"Snail," he replied evenly, gesturing with his hand to show the shell on back, the slow crawl on the ground, the hornlike extension of the eyes, but this did not enlighten her. Finally, with a talon he was working on, he drew a spiral in the sand.

"Snail," she said aloud. "I knew it," she said to herself, "but to me you will always be a turtle; hard of shell, not soft at all."

After the rains, the vegetation had freshened and flower buds appeared retouching the green with tender bits of color. It seemed that nature knew that summer was well advanced and it now sought to catch up. Insects buzzed the flowers checking for nectar flow. Some of the trees and bushes that had survived the fire now sent tentative new shoots from blackened trunks. Though a bush was burned, the roots still had enough energy left to send forth new growth. There were seedlings of pine poking through everywhere. The fire had burned off the old but given the land a chance to renew itself.

It is strange how tragic it had all seemed when the fire came and visited death and destruction upon the land; how the clan had run in front of it, and how near he had come to being burned himself, Chaiko thought. But the fire had also given him Dawn, for without it they would never have met. He had lost the clan but gained her. These events were linked and he could not choose just one and reject the other. The good came with the bad, hand in hand.

While he was lost in thinking he was looking at her and did not notice her looking back at him. With his mind so distracted, his eyes spoke their own language, a language she understood better than he. He suddenly awoke to her eyes reading the hunger in his. He reddened and quickly turned away to hide further thoughts from betraying him. For a while after, they played the game of eyes, looking at each other and then quickly looking away.

For midday they had the last of the roast she had cooked the day before. Chaiko preferred venison above all meats. It had a subtle mild flavor that worked well with most herbs to accentuate the taste, and it was usually tender, certainly not as tough as bison or elk could be. Dawn had uncovered some seeds cracked by the heat of the fire but protected by the thick mat of grass the fire could not penetrate. She had ground the seed, crushed some nuts found in an abandoned squirrel's lair and added water, mixing it into a paste. She formed flat little cakes and let them dry in the air. They munched on the crispiness, grateful for a different taste. It would be almost fall by the time they could count on real variety in their diet with the ripening of fruits and roots.

It was a pleasant sunny afternoon and after eating he felt drowsy, lay back on the skins and gazed up at the sky. Soon his gaze lost itself in the sparkling blue, reminding him of her eyes. A man could get lost in them too. He felt content and let his mind wander, to dream the dreams the cripple had not dared. What was it he wanted? Recognition of worth certainly, to be effective in some vital undertaking; and then he wanted Dawn, his companion and partaker in his future. A sweet ache of longing filled him, but with the upswelling of emotions the dream quickly turned to want. I want, want, want ... Dawn sensed his eyes on her, looked up, saw the greed therein and quickly looked away confused, color rushing into her cheeks. Had she not wanted this? But Chaiko's eyes were so full of demands, exacting what she was willing to give ... but not let just be taken. Her face turned away, carefully blank, so as not to betray her vulnerability to him.

Chaiko felt her retreat, but did not know how to reach after her. He remonstrated with himself, "I want, always want, but what does *she* want? Day after day she serves my needs, but what would *she* like?" Had she in some oblique way already asked and he had somehow had not recognized it? How could she be so opaque when he felt so transparent? He searched her face, the gesture that her body spoke, hands folded in her lap, quiet and far away. Where did she go? asked the turtle, on the verge of alarm. His eyes tried to pierce her solitude. But this was worse than before: Dawn felt naked before the quest of his eyes looking into her soul. Both were full of emotions, much too powerful to be comfortable. They averted their eyes and carefully studied the distance. Somehow, each had come too close. Where did one person end and the other begin? Boundaries colliding, feelings intruding. This was too much for a turtle; Chaiko got up and stretched. The cripple was right about feelings, he observed to himself; they were too unpredictable and went their own ways.

Chaiko walked about somewhat stiffly, stretched again, then resolving to escape his emotions, grabbed Falcon and a handful of talons. He motioned for her to follow. She jumped up eagerly, quickly banked the fire, collected the waterbag and her carryall, hefted proudly the finely worked digging stick he had made for her and they were on their way. He had no specific plan, just wanted to walk off his restlessness and take a look at the countryside they would shortly be travelling on the next leg of their journey.

They passed by the thicket of the deer hunt and visited the stranger's camp. While she filled the waterbag from the clear water of the pool, he made a circle of the camp reading the signs. There were tracks of dogs, foxes, coyotes and hyenas, all attracted to the site of the recent butchering. The pile of bones they had left were scattered and gnawed by the scavengers, but their meat cache was undisturbed.

He looked at the camp closely with the eyes of the stranger who chose it. The spot gave the best view of the main route led by the lay of the land. From this side of the fire, the stranger could see everything without having to turn to look. In spring the bedding would be over there in the flow of smoke drifting in the prevailing wind to keep away the swarm of insects. In summer, the bedding would be on the opposite side to catch the cooling flow of the breezes. In autumn, it would be there by the rock to conserve and reflect the heat of the fire onto the sleeping place. But only a fool would risk winter here in such an open place. He shook his head, convinced that here, on this spot, the stranger would sit to best keep watch.

With a talon he raked through the small pebbles and coarse sand looking for some small sign of the stranger's presence. He turned up a few shell fragments. He looked at them with interest. They were a type of shell with a sharp cutting edge that people used to cut hair instead of singeing it off and then putting up with the unpleasant clinging smell.

Was the stranger from the south? For the shells did not belong here but came from the lake further south.

Then he found a shard of yellow flint that linked the stranger with the hunter who had lost the moose as well as a spearhead. That had been yellow too. This flint piece was too small to be of use, perhaps a flake off a larger tool that the stranger repaired. He slipped it in the fold of his carryall thinking to check the shard against the spearhead he had left back in camp.

Digging further into the sand, he found a puzzle, a long piece of bone on a thong. The bone was long like the leg bone of a crane, the ends cut off and hollow all through its length. There were curious holes along the bone. What could it be? What was its use? He turned the thing over and over in his hand but nothing suggested itself. He noticed that the thong was frayed and must have been torn, allowing the bone to fall, to hide here in the sand. The thong was just long enough to place this strange thing around one's neck. He retied it and placed it on his own neck. Odd, he mused, but then a stranger would do strange things to make him a stranger.

He narrowed his eyes and took one more look about. The stranger was a hunter from the south, with confidence to dare the unknown by himself. He cut his hair, so did appearance matter to him? What was he doing here, so far in the wilderness away from his people? What was the bone for? And where was he now? Chaiko scanned the surrounding emptiness. The signs were made last year, the few weeds growing in the ash pit told him so.

Dawn waited patiently while he mused. She had never known someone who took up so much time with just thinking. Not even the Old One of her people thought for so long. "Where does he find things to think about? It is strange that people who seem to think the longest appear to be the least sure of answers. You ask them a question, but instead of answers they ask more questions until one forgets what the first question was. And that was wisdom? That you think yourself into losing an answer? That kind of wisdom I do not want. A body knows what a body needs to do and that should be enough. How can he sit there and think and think and not notice that I am here waiting, waiting for his good pleasure? Indeed, the turtle is as slow as any snail."

Finally Chaiko rose and they continued beyond. They soon came to a rise that hid further sight of land. They approached cautiously. Bent over with talon nocked, prepared, Chaiko slowly rose to peer over the covering grass. Nothing was in sight. They walked along the ridge of the crest scanning the land that unfolded before them: a slope down to a narrow basin then a gentle slope up again, until the land disappeared behind a further crest. Chaiko sat on a rock and leisurely examined the view.

There were many tracks, but there was a main track along the principal axis of the basin with other feeder tracks intercepting. It was a busy valley, so it seemed. From this vantage point, every track showed clearly in the grass, even the occasional foraging and grazing off to the side by a herd. He should learn something from this rare view. The patterns should tell him something, but what? He had the growing feeling that there was something obvious that he was overlooking. He frowned.

He was thinking again, Dawn observed with some dismay. What could she do to fill her time while he thought all those important thoughts? Does he have to think about taking but a step, or even relieving himself? What was he looking for? Looking at? Her eyes roved over the area he seemed to be searching.

"Ah," she uttered in recognition.

"What?" he queried, half annoyed at the faint smugness of her tone.

"There." She pointed to where a broad side track intersected the main path. As soon as his attention focused on the detail, he recognized it too. The main path carried most of the to and fro movement of the valley, that was clear, but why should such a wide track come in from the side that seemingly led nowhere? As well, there seemed to be other narrower tracks converging onto a bushland off the far side.

"Waterhole?" Dawn asked, but he shook his head, pointing to the three or four pools along the main route which were more convenient.

"What then?"

He shrugged his shoulders. "Let's find out." They descended into the level basin and soon joined the main path. To the side and ahead the grass was trampled down and revealed an unbroken bare trail. There were many prints, most of them shallow, made before the recent rain. The droppings and scat were mostly dried out and hard. When they reached the side trail, they were surprised by the many prints, and even Dawn who was not trained could see them leading in and coming back out. Chaiko shook his head to forestall her questions and turned onto the side track. Soon the bush closed in and he was wary of its narrowness, a bad place to come upon scavengers. Then the view opened abruptly again to show a yellowish pool with a gravel bank bare of any vegetation. There was a yellowish crust scattered about.

"Con!" she exulted.

"Con?" He did not recognize con.

"Yes, con." She stepped into the open, bent down, broke off a piece of crust, touched it to her lips and offered it to him. Cautiously he licked it and instantly a sharp flavor filled his mouth, even to the very back. "Salt!" he exclaimed. All around them was the precious commodity, there for the taking. They set about collecting the crumbling crust. No wonder the animals detoured to this place.

The clan got its salt from the salt lake to the south, where they journeyed every four or five years. They would fill rock fissures with brine, let it dry in the sun, and collect the salt residue. It took a long time to collect all the salt they would need for several years. If this was not done right, the salt would cause them all to have severe stomach complaints, and he remembered on one occasion the whole clan running to find privacy.

Soon they had all they could carry and left quickly, for he was nervous to be in such a popular and frequented spot: where there were animals, there were also hunters who preyed on them. The thought occurred to him that if he ever needed meat, this was a sure place to find some. He took careful bearings to find this spot again.

Back on the open slope he felt safer. Yet just then, a pack of hyenas appeared. The creatures were on a different tack, but as soon as they spotted the two humans they headed over to investigate. Their hunched-shouldered lope began to close in on them. Chaiko turned to face them. Her heart racing, Dawn clutched her digging stick, the sharp end toward the advancing troop. Chaiko waited; he allowed them within two spearthrows, then shot. The talon ripped into the lead hyena, instantly killing him, the lifeless body still tumbling from the speed of his charge. The rest pulled up in surprise. They were experienced hunters and could immediately recognize death, but could not connect the death of their leader with the two humans. Wary, all the same, they closed in much more cautiously, fanning out on a broad front. Chaiko shot again, and one hyena went down into the grass and then another. Their hackles raised, and snarling their frustration, the rest backed away from the death facing them. Foaming at the mouth, a big male growled, spun about, retreated a few strides then turned again, considering his chances. Chaiko pulled the sinew back and aimed. The big male retreated, turned aside, grabbed the dead leader and dragged him back into the bush, where the rest of the pack fell on it and tore it to pieces.

Chaiko spat with disgust after them and eased the tension on the string. No respect for the dead. Then a thought struck him: "Were you going to kill it just because you could?" he asked himself. Most held that hyenas were to be killed on sight, but Chaiko felt uneasy at such narrow thinking. Surely even a hyena must find a place in this world, just like a cripple must. And once again, it was the cripple who made the decision. Chaiko lowered Falcon to let the beasts retreat. Did this weapon gave him such a mastery that he could so arrogantly and callously dispense death? At a distance it was all too easy. He would not see their pain and suffering, just a distant object, a target for his weapon. "Let it not become too easy," he warned himself. Beside him, Dawn was shaking with reaction at this sudden, violent confrontation. Chaiko put an arm around her to steady her, and she melted in his arms, burying her face on his chest, feeling safe. "The turtle has teeth," she thought with pride even through her fright. She hated hyenas.

Chaiko walked up to the nearest carcass, nudged it with his foot to make sure it was dead, then pulled the talon from its body. Keeping his eyes on the bush behind which the rest of the pack still squabbled over the grisly remains of the leader, he retrieved the other. They left the carcasses for the hyenas to dispose of.

Back in camp, both were subdued by their brush with death. Had they not seen the beasts coming at a distance, and had they not had time to prepare for their attack, the rush of the hyenas could have easily overwhelmed them. These were merciless killers with powerful jaws and an implacable hatred for the rest of creation. At close range, their attack would have overtaken the two humans before Falcon's bite could strike fear of death in their hearts and stop their charge. Chaiko might have killed one but the rest would have reached them. It was the confusion that turned the killers back; they could not figure out from where death was falling on them. Chaiko resolved to be on the lookout. These were cunning and vicious beasts of opportunity; he would have to make sure not to give them an opening.

"Kaiko," Dawn said uncertainly, "you use magic of Singing-Stick to send your sticks to kill the evil beasts. They do not forget. They will remember you, me. Follow us even." She shuddered at her own words.

"Shush, shush," he calmed her, and said with a nonchalance he did not fully feel, "Hyenas are no worse than the rest. They hunt to feed themselves and their young." But he did not say all he thought: like humans, even when full they are still hungry, for it is not a hunger of the belly that drives them but the hunger in their minds. They do not have respect for the living, much less for the dead. Look how they went after their leader, how they tore his carcass to pieces. Aloud he continued, "Do not fear, they will not follow us. For death is their business, and death for them is so commonplace as to rob it of significance. Thus they do not know vengeance. Ask yourself this: does a fish in water know what thirst is? Does the fish know it is wet? Hyenas will follow any blood trail, and to them one death is like any other. It is need that drives them, not memory. And if we meet them again, Falcon is hungry too."

Dawn smiled at his boast, though the worry lines about her eyes remained.

That night Chaiko stayed awake with Falcon beside him and talons stuck in the ground to be ready at hand. He let the fire burn brighter than was his habit. The moon, too, gave good light and he felt safer because he could see. Later, he heard movement in the grass and smelled a carnivore. He gripped Falcon tightly and had a talon ready for flight, but the noise moved off and he relaxed.

Still, he thought-walked into the darkness, sensing into the periphery hidden in shadows. He concentrated, trusting what he felt. He encountered no sense of malice, nonetheless remained fully vigilant. In a mesmerized state, he was patrolling beyond the circle of fire light. His trance led him to thought-touching Dawn. He felt the rise and fall of her breathing, the warmth of her body, the shiver of her muscles as she struggled with something she was dreaming. What could be bothering her? He sent calming thoughts toward her, and in a short time she settled into a relaxed pose. His concentration was gone and he allowed himself to slip off.

As he drifted in and out of sleep, he recalled Dawn seeking the protection of his arms, the warmth of her breath on his chest and the way her body molded into his, wooden leg and all. A delicious shiver tingled up and down his spine, but he held onto the feeling of being strong for her. Eventually, it was not the feeling of his holding her that stayed with him; it was her need of him and the fact that she trusted him that warmed him the most.

The next morning he was tired and irritable, but her eyes alighting on him filled him up and his energy returned. Suddenly he was looking forward to the day.

Chapter 28

In the midmorning brightness a pair of geese flew by overhead, the wings beating the air with smooth, powerful strokes. The male was in front and the female in close synchrony behind. They made several wide circles then settled down on a pond. A little later Chaiko saw an adult male with four juveniles likewise flying patterns in the sky. This group was less attuned to one another and the geese kept drifting out of position until the insistent honking of the lead goose got them back in proper alignment, for a while anyway. They were starting to practice for the long flight south. Winter is coming, Chaiko thought with dread, for they still had so much to do to prepare. His first impulse was to rush out hunting to increase their provisions, but on brief reflection he thought better of it. It would be better to move camp again and then hunt, saving themselves the burden of lugging additional meat to the new camp. He told Dawn his thoughts and she listened to him intently, calmly accepting his decision. She approved: it would be good for him to find his people.

They spent the rest of the day dividing and packing the load. Their possessions kept increasing, so that they were just short of having to make three trips in order to transfer everything to a new camp.

Next morning they secured the camp, hiding and burying the possessions to be left behind to await the second trip. When they moved off the hilltop onto the open plain, the sky was lightly overcast, the air mild, perfect for travelling. The early distance was strenuous until the loads settled and they found their stride. They arrived at the stranger's camp, opened up the cache and added half its contents to their load. The heavier burden slowed them somewhat, but they pressed on. Soon they were at the salt licks, and then moved beyond onto sandy ground that supported only sparse vegetation and few trees. It became harder to walk on the loose soil. Chaiko found his stride breaking because his wooden leg sank into soft spots. His stump, which he hardly noticed anymore, now started to ache under his heavy burden. He said nothing, because Dawn behind him did not complain and kept up with him, step for step.

14 Stones

Occasionally they paused, threw off their load and rested. They drank from their waterbag, feeling incredibly light, almost floating, without their baggage to hold them down. Chaiko allowed little time on these rests, fearing that lethargy would set into their cooling muscles. Much too soon they were on their way again, ants loaded down, marching in a wide open plain.

The land became more arid, since the sandy soil could not retain water and only the hardiest of plants could survive. Here and there was a solitary thorn bush; in its shelter, a small animal like a lizard or a mouse scurried about. And there were nests amongst the thorns. It seemed that life in however modest a form found a place to survive and even thrive. But humans needed more, much more.

It was late afternoon when they paused for a longer time. Gratefully they laid down their load and sat down on the ground. They chewed on dried meat and drank water in slow careful sips, too weary to talk or even to think, just enjoying that they did not have to move. Fighting his drowsiness, Chaiko roused himself to speak. "This place is called Drifting-Sands, for the moving sands that build new ridges then move on. The clan doesn't come here, since nothing grows here but the heat, and the place is empty of useful things. There are scorpions and sand beetles, spiky plants and thorn bushes. Look there," Chaiko pointed to a nearby mound of compacted sand with wave upon frozen wave of ridge lines contoured into its surface. "That is the breath of wind, drawing in the face of sand where it flows and how it flows, leaving behind its footprint. See how it crisscrosses there." Dawn eyed the sequence of many lines, neat and concise, yet hopelessly confusing in its strict order.

"Look at that soft sandstone, how the wind ate at the base of it a grain at a time. It looks ready to topple." Dawn looked at the rock he pointed to, the mass of it balanced on a narrow foot, imperceptibly eroding away. "You see the intent of the wind, patiently moving the world, a grain at a time. He is in no hurry, for time waits for him. So why should the wind even bother to remember? But it does. Look at the lines in the sand. It flows hither and not back thither." Chaiko's thoughts were roaming as freely as the wind.

Dawn nodded. "Far to the north, there's a great flat plain of grass and rocks. No tree can stand in the cutting wind. My people call the place Wind-Wide because it is the birthplace of the wind. There it always blows, sometimes gently, sometimes angry and strong, but mostly steady. There you can stand with your back to the wind and lie back in its embrace. Tiku, my father's brother's son, once lay back in the wind and it held him standing and he fell asleep. A little later, when the wind took a breath, he fell to the ground and was wrenched awake. He was shocked, but we all laughed." That was not quite how she told it, for she mixed languages readily, and it took all his knowledge of her tongue and a few guesses to understand her longest discourse to him. He smiled at her proudly, then looked to the north, acutely aware of how small his world was, and how little he knew of what lay beyond. If he could only pass through the Rainbow-Gate, he would then know everything.

After eating they stretched out on the sandy ground and fell into a short, refreshing nap. Then it was time to go. Chaiko helped to set the load on Dawn's back, straightened it, picked up his own, and they moved on. Their muscles had stiffened during the brief rest; it took a while to find their stride again. The land was level and continued sandy and arid. The green in the distance beckoned them on. The ants marched in the footprint of their shadows.

Sunset found them still on inhospitable terrain, but in the fading light they could see a river and green not too far ahead. They found a couple of bushes, made a small fire and carefully rationed the sticks to last through the night. They dutifully ate, but were too tired to be hungry. Still, Dawn did not complain and even had a weary smile for him. Chaiko took off his leg and felt his stump. It was amazing how used to the wooden leg he had become, as if it was now truly a part of him. Indeed, he could no longer feel where the flesh ended and the wood began. His brain was happy not to have to worry about it either. She came over and rubbed some greasy salve into the tender areas. He laid back enjoying her ministrations, his fatigue pressing him into the sand. Unaware, he drifted off to sleep.

He awoke to darkness until the moon cleared the clouds and painted the blackness with its wan glow. Dawn was nearby; he could hear her gentle breathing, and the crickets' song, even in the emptiness out here. He threw a few sticks onto the fire, settled himself down and was soon asleep again.

By morning light he was awake, watching the sunrise bring color to the land. Not far to the northwest, where he intended to go, was a river and beyond it, green grasslands again and groups of trees. It was strange, he mused, how trees had clans of their own; it was rare to see a solitary

14 Stones

tree. He tracked a route for them to follow, a river to cross, and he thought a gentle hill in the distance promised to offer them a good view and shelter. Beside him Dawn stirred, then slowly came awake. As he had watched the sunrise, he now watched her eyes open and consciousness and recognition dawn in them. She smiled brightly when she saw him looking at her, then indulged herself the luxury of a long, languid stretch. He beamed at her one of his rare smiles, which she found so heart-wrenchingly attractive, in part to reward her for yesterday's hard march and his admiration for her quiet fortitude. She cast an appraising sideways glance at him and returned his smile. She then rose and was all business. They chewed on meat, the flavor only slowly filling their mouths. She covered the remains of the fire with sand and they picked up their burdens. The ropes pressed into tender flesh. The first steps were awkward, resisted by the stiffness in their muscles, but it soon melted away; they made good time and before long they were on grassland again. The green was a welcome relief from the piercing glare off the sand.

Soon they were at the river and forded it easily, the water barely reaching their knees. They threw their packs down on the other side, then climbed back into a deeper pool for a swim. In a quick motion, Dawn pulled off her covering, threw it ashore and in a flash of skin dove into the water leaving him wondering just what he had seen. She surfaced, splashed and frolicked in the other end. He stripped as well, took off his leg and went diving after her. But she was quick as a river otter and just as playful; he could not get near her. She laughed and laughed, splashing water in his face. By the time he looked she was in another place. Finally he gave up, and just watched her. Behind the reflection of the water and in the froth she stirred up, he caught a glimpse of her breasts, a flash of whiter skin, and outlines and shadows that excited his imagination. Even the fresh water could not cool the heat rising in him.

She stopped playing, watched him calculatingly, then waded to shore to rip a handful of ferns from the banks. She then scooped river mud from the bottom and worked it into the ferns, till it became a smooth green mass. This she worked into her skin and even her hair. She took her time, rubbing herself all over, standing up in the water exposing her naked back to him. Then she dove under and rinsed the mud off her body.

339

After, she came over to him, up to her chin in water, made him turn around and started working the slippery mixture into his hair, head, neck and shoulders. The velvet feel of the mud made her strong fingers slide easily on his skin. The pleasant odor of the fern masked any hint of dankness of the mud. She massaged his back, her fingers leaving a tingle of sensations that begged for more.

As she worked she said softly, "Sometimes you see a duck moving across a pond, gently pushing through the water without any apparent effort. Then from beneath her wings come forth ducklings, first one, then many more. Some climb onto her back, the rest follow in a straight line behind her, little legs moving to keep up. Then a cross wind comes up, and the surface of the water shivers and the little fluffs of tender yellow are pushed about by the blowing. The duck stops, unfolds her wings and her brood hurries to hide safely under them." Her voice was soothing, the words of two languages mixing in a soft flow, but the sense of the story eluded him. "There is confusion in the world, but there is also harmony."

"Confusion?" he asked, looking back at her through big eyes that tried not to look too far down.

"The wind brought confusion into this little world," she tried to explain earnestly. "The mother duck acted in harmony, protecting her ducklings, countering the confusion." That seemed clear to her, but the point so understated was still lost to him. She tried yet again, "The mother duck did not fight with the wind. She gathered her brood safely under her wing, and turned into the flow. Or do you think she turned her back to it, letting the wind under her feathers? No, no. We can learn much from a duck, such a gentle nature ..." she went on in considerable detail praising its many virtues. He listened to her pleasant voice droning on, barely aware, but at some distant level came to him the thought, "My wolf would make short work of your brave duck." He would have fallen asleep, but he was much too aware of her naked body so near his, and every once in a while they would touch underwater and that would send shockwaves of feeling coursing through him. He would reach toward her, but she would slap his hand noisily and tell him to behave, in a tone used on a child who would not hold still for an infrequent washing. Her hands moved to his back and chest, and his breathing changed as if he could not find enough air. She kept on talking in gentle tones, but all he understood from her speech was that she prized harmony. "Who doesn't?" he asked but was much too busy with her fingers rubbing and massaging the muscles, first his back and then his chest. He dared not move. "Harmony," she said: "Yes, yes, more harmony," he replied. Her hands moved to his waist and paused, lingering a while. Finally, he turned around; then as she dove away he lunged after her, but his arms found only an empty spray of water. He saw her clamber onto shore, water dripping from her body, then she disappeared behind some bushes. Chaiko muttered and grumbled as he washed away the mud. He could not believe the difference her touch had made, and the excitement it traced across his body. He had never felt it so strongly before ... and he wanted more, yes, much more.

He climbed onto shore, waited for the water to dry, then put on his skins. At the packs he found her, combing her long hair, eyes on him, vigilant and so clear a blue. He wanted to rush her and bury her in his arms and do what it was that people do when they felt this way. He knew in part but was not quite sure. What little he had seen in the cave, or much rather heard in the dark, of intimacy, struck him in the past as some comic interlude that he could not take seriously. It seemed that informal instructions came in jokes and with much too loud laughter. Looking at her, he pressed his feelings into a tight little place where he had learned to hide overwhelming things like emotions. She smiled tentatively at him. Had she gone too far? she asked herself. She was ready, but the timing was wrong and this was out of place.

Without speaking they loaded up and set out again. He did not feel the weight of his pack. He kept chewing in careful little bites on what had happened and the way he had felt. His eyes were looking inward with this preoccupation, and he nearly missed the turnoff he intended to follow in order to look over the slight elevation of the ground, and the promise of shelter. They went up the gentle incline through waist-deep grass that thinned as they got nearer the top, and came to chalky limestone protruding from the ground.

When they reached the top his heart beat quickly, for in front of them in a looming rock facade he recognized the hollow of a cave. A cave! Home! Shelter! Instinctively the thoughts flashed in his mind. They both dropped their packs. "Careful!" he called out to warn her as well as himself. This might already be home to some creature. He nocked a talon into Falcon and made ready. Behind him, Dawn clutched one of his spears. Carefully they advanced toward the cave, pausing to listen, pausing to sniff the air. There could be a bear or even a mountain lion;

less likely a pack of wolves or dogs, since they changed lairs frequently. But no movement, no sound and no animal smell returned to them. Cautiously they approached. The cave looked good; a large open space sheltered below an overhang, narrowing and disappearing into dimness at the back. Chaiko scanned the ground looking for tracks, but found only a few small prints. Between the rock boulders strewn about, the grass was thick but not tall. As they moved under the overhang there was still no sign of any habitation. Beyond a smooth rock ledge, the floor was even, sandy amidst interspersed clusters of rocks, showing no tracks or prints, and there was still no smell of scat or kill in the air. They went far back into the dimness and found the cave completely empty. Relieved, Chaiko turned around and relaxed the tension in Falcon. The grassland, trees, bushes and a distant view of the valley were framed by the generous opening of the cave to the outside world. Yes, this was a good place, big enough so that the whole clan could easily fit into it.

They went outside and collected the packs. Chaiko squinted into the sun, calculating. The cave had an ideal orientation, looking to the south, south-east facing the morning sun. Still cautious, though more confident, he explored the outside of the cave. He heard a trickle of water and found a tidy clear pool in a circle of bush and small trees. This is a good cave, he thought, generous space for shelter, water so near, and a great view of the valley below.

Why had not the clan discovered this cave before on one of their hunting forays? he asked himself. But he then remembered a description of the sandy wasteland that kept the clan out of these parts. Bare and useless; nothing grows there, it was told.

If Chaiko was happy with their find, Dawn was ecstatic. This was a real cave that could easily house her whole family and more. And it was empty, just waiting for them.

"Kaiko," she called to him, "t'is a good cave, no?"

"Yes, Dawn, this is a very good cave," he answered. "There's a lot of room inside, a good view outside and there's water." He said this as if pronouncing a momentous decision just like his brother used to do. "There's no harm in making an occasion special, so that it can later be remembered and relived," Baer had said a little over three moons ago. Had it only been three moons? he asked himself astonished. No, it was two moons and a half, but in that time he had grown and his life had changed so much that he barely recognized the person he had been. Then he had been a cripple, now he was no longer, he told himself with pride; he could now stand on two feet like any man. Then he had been useless; now he was a Hunter with Falcon to hold in his hand. And he had Dawn, gift of the River of Destiny, the gift of fire that drove him across the land so that he could find her ... and she him. His heart melted and his pride in her shone so brightly in his eyes that she nearly missed a step because of their intensity. Wide blue eyes looked back at him. Was she ever going to understand her turtle? she wondered.

Dawn, too, felt blessed. Here was her cave; she knew it the instant she saw it. This was her nest, her flar, her home. This cave was here because of her, of that she was convinced. She, no they, must claim it. A cave and a mate. She knew it. Yet this was not how she had imagined it as a child, talking with her friends—dreaming of the future. This was better. She looked sideways at him; would he also claim it? Why was he grinning so? Why was he not thinking? Here was something real to think about, so think yourself a home. Here was water. There was a fertile plain to hunt. There was wood all over. You could carve another Singing-Stick or another Falcon if you must, but make this our home.

"Kaiko," she called to him, wanting to ask him if they could make this their home, but then when he turned toward her, she remembered his clan in the hills and quickly swallowed her question. "T'is a good place, no?" She hoped that he would recognize it himself.

"This is good," he affirmed, but sensing that something else was required.

Dawn smiled at him, but to herself she thought, I will prove to you how nice a home I can make here, so that you yourself will not want to leave it. She brightened instantly and set about organizing their possessions.

A little later she walked about inside the cave, thinking, planning. She decided on the best place for the fire and set about selecting the fire stones, clearing a place around it. She called Chaiko to prepare a place for bedding adjacent to the fire. He rolled heavy rocks out of the way and brushed loose pebbles clear. "After a hard day's walk the body is tired," he grumbled under his breath, though not unkindly. When he was finished and inclined to rest, she gave him a piece of skin and sent him to find sand to soften the place they would lie on. Grumbling, he went out, found some sand, loaded it into the skin, and staggered back into the cave to call attention to the fact he had earned a rest; but he was ashamed that, day after day, she had followed him without complaining, and here he was not doing his share. He scattered the sand and got some more. They found some moss near the pool, brought armfuls back into the cave, and soon had an inviting nest ready. He noted how she had organized their places so close to each other.

Next, they collected fire wood and made a neat pile against the cave wall. She arranged dry grass kindling, small twigs, branches and thicker branches. She then carefully unrolled her clay clump and from its bed of moss she blew the hardwood embers to glow and was about to place them in the midst of the kindling when he stopped her. Without explanation, he took the embers from her and cast them outside.

"First Fire," he said seriously, "we must make a ceremony of First Fire."

"To make claim of cave?" she wanted to know, her heart racing, her throat pulsing with excitement.

"Claim? First Fires is to renew. To welcome the new." He struggled to define it with words. There was something else about spirits, but that had never made any sense to him.

Rummaging through their pile of wood he selected a flat piece of dry wood and a hardwood shaft. He settled himself, spat onto his hands, and started to spin the shaft between his palms, drilling the hardwood into the flat. Dawn watched him, her brows furrowed. You threw away good fire to do this? But who can understand a ceremony? Only the Old Ones can. She knew, however, that any ritual must be performed in strictest observation of all of its parts.

Chaiko hummed a primitive melody, on the downbeat forcing the sound and putting extra pressure on the stick. Her ears picked up the rhythm and soon both were humming in unison. Beads of perspiration ran down his face but he kept the stick spinning. Dawn put her feet on the flat wood, took the stick from him and continued spinning. Chaiko gratefully relaxed his complaining muscles. Fire was the gift of the skies, but was hard to awaken once it fell asleep. Wood rubbed against wood, the spot deepened from the relentless pressure and slowly it darkened as the heat of friction built up. Now she was sweating as well and he took over. Soon a thin wisp of smoke rose from the point of contact. Dawn pressed a wad of dry grass near it and with her face close, gently blew on it till thicker smoke arose and flame appeared.

Holding the flaming wad in her hand, she looked at him questioningly. "Is so?" she asked, thinking of the ceremony, and when he nodded she put the wad into the kindling. They watched mesmerized as the flames spread. Soon a cheerful fire crackled and the shadows danced for the first time on the cave wall.

In this solemn moment Chaiko felt compelled to add a touch more to the ceremony: "To the fire that drove us here, to the river that bore us to safety, to our feet that carried us here, let it be known that this cave is shelter, let this cave be safety. Let the fire be content in its circle, let it eat the wood we feed it, let it give us warmth and light, and cook our food. Let it stand guard at night against the hunters of the darkness and the spirits that look for a place to hide. Let this cave hear our voices, let this cave know our presence, let it be filled with our smell. So we claim," he added to please her.

"So we claim," she added triumphantly. The ceremony was good, very good, she concluded.

Darkness fell upon the land outside. The two huddled by the fire, eating dry meat. It would be nice to have something fresh again; he thought of hunting on his hunting ground. Not yet; tomorrow they must make the return journey to the old camp to get the rest of their possessions. But after that, he promised himself.

Later, in a festive mood, he hummed her a melody and sang all the songs he could remember, his voice deeply resonant. In her turn she sang the songs of her people. In a clear voice that flowed like pure water cascading from rock to rock, she sang. He could not understand the words but could feel the emotion beyond the meaning. There was one song he really liked and she tried to teach him, laughing when he got the words almost right, laughing harder when he didn't.

The moon was at mid-sky when finally he crawled into the bedding facing the outside. She had yet to bank the fire to allow a little flame and light but not to let it burn too fast. Then she, too, crawled into bed and cuddled up to his back. Chaiko tried to turn around to face her but she put out a restraining hand. "Not yet," she whispered. There was still a long way to go, and Chaiko knew it too. A day and a half there, and a day and a half back.

"Sometimes one has to live on a promise," his mother used to say. Well Chaiko could live on a promise, but sleep did not come easily to him that night.

The new morning greeted them with a cheerful sunrise that flooded into the cave. Dawn was up, yawning and stretching. It took Chaiko somewhat longer to rub the sleep from his eyes. Then both were up, enjoying the secure feel of the cave about them. There was much to do to get ready. They gathered empty baskets and carryalls, with a little food to get them there, and their weapons. They walked into the open, and away from the cliff. Dawn already found it hard to leave her cave, and she paused and looked back as if to take the view with her on the trip. Chaiko, too, looked at everything around him with new eyes, for now it all belonged to them somehow. It was their trees that they were passing and they were laying a new path that they would follow back and forth in time to come. My grass, my rocks, my birds, he claimed with each step.

They crossed the river. Chaiko wanted to take a bath again, but Dawn wanted to get the trip over with in a hurry, so they continued on. "A body needs to have a bath," Chaiko grumbled just loud enough so that she would hear. "You're clean enough," she let him know.

As they passed through the wasteland again, they felt the sand hot under their feet in the full sun. Reaching the grassland beyond, they rested and ate then pressed on. Without the heavy burdens it was much easier; the distances melted before them. They camped for the night by some rocks and fed a small fire. This time after a full day's march, Chaiko fell asleep much aware of Dawn pressing into his back. "A body needs to have ..." he muttered to himself, but fell asleep, dreaming of promises. He had his old dream of White Dove, but she was becoming transformed more into Dawn, with those disturbingly clear blue eyes.

The new day was sunny again and after the dew dried, the grass rustled crisply. Dawn showed him where the seeds were almost ripe and would soon need to be gathered. Finally, greeted by the familiar sight of the stranger's camp, Dawn rested while Chaiko looked around once more, hoping to discover something else about the stranger, but came across nothing new.

They found the hilltop camp much as they had left it. Out of the way as it was, few animals came across it. They had made good time and it was but mid afternoon. Dawn quickly made a fire while Chaiko took Falcon and set off to look around. On a southern exposure he found a groundhog colony with many creatures eating and sunning themselves. A few stood on guard on top of their earth works, each looking in a different direction to give them an all-around watch. Chaiko, hidden by a bush, notched a talon, aimed and shot. The talon found its mark, a fat woodchuck that by instinct still dove for its hole, but the crosswise shaft prevented it from vanishing down the narrow tunnel. With loud piercing whistles the rest disappeared into their burrows in a flash.

Chaiko retrieved his talon and dropped the groundhog into his carryall. He figured it would take the rest a long time to recover from his intrusion. He would look in on them on the way back. On the south side of the next hill, he found another colony, but no groundhogs visible anywhere. Then he saw a badger digging furiously at a burrow, the yellow soil flying high and wide. Chaiko went closer to investigate. The badger was half buried in the hole, widening it. The front feet dug up the earth, passed it back, and the hind feet ejected it into the air, spraying down slope a long streak of yellow soil. The badger sensed his presence, backed out of the hole, fur raised in irritation at being interrupted in his hunt, and charged him in fury. It did not matter that Chaiko was ten times his size. Chaiko backed away, for badgers had a ferocious reputation. Those teeth were sharp, the claws long, and for its size it could inflict a surprising amount of damage in a hurry. Anyway badger was tough meat, very muscular, and its fur coarse, certainly not worth a talon. He avoided the badger that snarled and growled menacingly after him before returning to his furious digging.

Chaiko continued on but saw nothing else of interest. On returning, there was no sign of the badger. At the hole where it had been digging, there were blood marks, so the badger must have been successful. The colony on the next hill was empty too; perhaps the badger had been there also.

Back in camp the fire was just right, a bed of embers. Dawn took the groundhog from him, skinned it, skewered it and within moments it was roasting over the fire. Finally they were going to have some fresh meat. With full stomachs they went to bed. Groundhog, grown fat on fresh vegetation, was amazingly tasty.

Early light found them already on their way, heavily loaded down with the rest of their possessions. They made good time, however, driven on by thoughts of the cave waiting for them. Both were anxious to get back to it, Chaiko to explore the vicinity, and Dawn to feather her nest. They overnighted in the wasteland again. The night passed uneventfully except for an infestation of sand fleas that left them scratching and hunting among their skins.

By midday they crossed the river, both wanting to reach the cave; they hurried on, up the slope, the brow and then the crown of the hill, and finally they were back. They divested themselves of their burdens and gratefully collapsed by the fireplace. Chaiko was tired, but Dawn seemed energized. "A cave is not a cave without a fire; a cave without a fire is but a hole in the rocks." She repeated the saying of her people and set about quickly to make this hole into a cave again. A short time later, smoke welled up and reached for the roof of the cave. Chaiko, lying on his back, watched the smoke being drawn further into the cave and up. He guessed there was an opening up there; otherwise, the smoke would be filling the top of the cavern and then spilling out of its mouth.

That night she moved close to him, pressed her body into his back and blew gently on the nape of his neck, sending delicious shivers up and down his spine. But they were both truly exhausted and were soon asleep.

Chapter 29

The next day the air seemed fresher, the sun felt warmer and the colors appeared brighter than usual. His senses gloried in the day and his mood thrilled in its promise: a very unaccustomed feeling and he had trouble accounting for it. To be sure, they had a new cave and already she had made it comfortable. A glowing feeling dispelled his habitual seriousness and he found himself unable to go about his customary worrying. This worried him all the more but he could not hold onto the worry. It was just too nice a day, even for thinking. He was again restless to do something vital and significant, if he could only figure out what that could be. Then he found himself smiling for no reason at all.

Dawn noted his mood, and adapted herself instantly to match his. Humming a song, she began to dance, her lithe body swaying to the rhythm. She dipped and twirled and his eyes were immediately captured by her motion. Her hair loosened and fanned out around her head as she spun around, and he thought he had never seen anyone as fetching as she, not even White Dove. She kept looking over at him, gaining little sips of encouragement from the desire shining in his eyes; her own eyes twinkling with mischief and merriment.

It was amazing how a little attention can sparkle a girl up, she thought to herself, but at the same time a more critical part of her warned that it was not good to become too dependent on his moods or approval. A turtle always had a place to withdraw to and the natural inclination to do so. But she pushed the thoughts away; today she would be happy, she promised herself.

She basked in his attention and glowed with the pleasure of it. Her feet stamped the rhythm into the sand and she lilted, dipped and turned, her body gracefully flowing from one position into the next, drawing attention to a curve here and a gesture there. He could look nowhere else.

She danced, she floated on this feathery feeling inside her, soft and tender, as if her feet hardly touched the ground. That irrepressible side of her, which she could not control and most certainly was not wanted here and now, mocked her gently. You are putting yourself on display, girl, she heard the voice inside her head. Why not make him dance and present himself? With most birds, it was the males who had the plumage and the feathers; let him strut on display. It was the drab female who made the choice among all the suitors vying for her favors. Dawn pushed the thought away, and danced on. She did not have the voluptuousness of a mature woman and her young girl's body felt inadequate to the task, but she had a mystery and glow about her that awakened Chaiko to think less with his eyes and more with his desires. And his desires were fully awake.

Dawn danced, her face flushed and aglow, her eyes brilliant. She felt that this time she had the color, the plumage and the choice, and found confidence in the reflection of his eyes drinking in eagerly, hungrily the sight of her dancing for him. She felt intoxicated by the power of his attraction, saw him totally captive to her allure, and because she believed it, she radiated it and he was helpless to escape her enchantment.

The rhythm of her dance of seduction compelled Chaiko to stand and join in her song and he danced with her, his movements slower and more deliberate, but no less graceful. She was quick and light on her feet. She caressed him but was away before his hands could catch her. Then she was on the other side, nestling into him again briefly, then slipping away from his arms. The heat was rising and the passions mounting. The playful game suddenly turned very serious. She backed and enticed him after her, and as he lunged, she artfully fell, surprise oh surprise, onto the softness of the bedding of moss and furs.

He fumbled with eagerness, and in fever-haste the skins came off. They joined and melted into each other, their bodies pressing skin to skin, their hearts beating in a rhythm neither had yet experienced. With the greedy impatience of youth, they sought one another wildly, in a close press of contact, eager to discover and take pleasure in each other. Then the pleasure took over, melted all the barriers of self: skin and flesh ceased to be, rising to a storm of feelings, spiraling higher and higher till there was no higher left to crash upon itself. Breathless in each other's arms, each wondered what had just happened, for this, this was not what either had expected.

14 Stones

Chaiko, who was the doubter in most things, was hopelessly romantic when it came to thoughts of love. Perhaps all males were, in the beginning of any courtship. He was awed to discover that the pleasure of reality far exceeded his dreams. The intensity of the tension that had built and the total release and the pleasure of the afterglow took him by surprise. In the end he turned to water, flowing with feelings of peace and contentment ... his mind suspended ... silent for once.

Dawn, whose practical side usually browbeat the wistful, fun-loving part of her, was silenced too, so overwhelming was the experience. First, she was shaken by the hunger his touch awakened in her. As he explored, it robbed her of breath, and she nearly fainted with the intensity it stirred up in her. Then she melted, yielding, yielding as he pressed into her. She had been ready to give him pleasure, but to receive it? Sigh after sigh escaped her lips, then calls like doves.

Utterly spent, Chaiko quickly drifted off to sleep. Beside him Dawn lay snuggled in his arms, her body still hot and palpitating in the stillness that followed the receding rush of feelings. She stroked the arms that held her, and she felt fulfilled. She had been prepared for pain, as her mother had warned, but not for the all-consuming pleasure. The intensity had been frightening. Was this not violence of sorts? A steady rhythm building to a new pulse of awareness, absorbing the passion, the insistence, inescapable, demanding, gathering strength until the pleasure itself became unbearable, to finally burst, to release in a flood of all feelings so stored, to rush forth and wash away all emotions, leaving only a spent contentment. She inhaled their fragrance, a mist, joy-filled and intimate. She sighed in reflex, wonder-filled. Finally, now she understood the sounds she had heard in the nights, a straining impatience ... striving for ... this release. Did he do what he did, and did she? Had they been one as the songs talked about?

When he awoke, she was not beside him and he found her standing naked at the lip of the cave, the warm sun bathing her bare skin. Shocked, he almost told her to put the skins on, but bit the words back. They were mated now, that was for sure, and he enjoyed looking at her. She turned about and made a present to his roving eyes. She was small, just a slip of a girl, so fragile and vulnerable framed in the light spilling through the mouth of the cave —she did not seem to be the woman who had ridden with him the rite of passion. *She is my girl!* His heart swelled with pride and love, and roused to protect her. She reflected his smile, and he burst out laughing with contentment he could not contain.

She ran to him, threw herself beside him, melted in his arms and the two tumbled backward into the moss bed where they spent a very pleasant afternoon exploring one another.

They could not get enough it seemed, with years of hunger to catch up on; and when they could do nothing but lie in each other's arms, still they caressed and stroked each other. And in those most gentle moments the cripple inside was healing.

It was nigh evening before Chaiko became aware of his hunger. His stomach growled and Dawn hurried about, finding things to eat. He ate ravenously, but not really tasting because he was full with the feel of her. Through and through content, she felt she could not take much more of this happiness or she would surely burst. Yet her body still glowed with the awareness he had awakened. She could not understand where all those feeling had been hiding all these years. They looked at each other and broke into silly wide grins of happiness. The turtle and the dawn. Mated and One.

The following days were filled with pleasure so long denied them. Time and time again he reached for her and she was there to yield to his need of her. It felt so good to give in to him and ride out the waves of pleasure, and though his hunger was great, her thirst was greater, and she would come to him and crawl into his lap and hug and kiss, nibbling on his ears, till he was ready in spite of himself, groaning with his soreness. *Mother never told me about this*; she wondered about that repeatedly. And in this the two parts of her mind agreed, there was always going to be time for pleasure.

"Kaiko," she asked one time, "have you been with other girls? Like now?" She nested in his arms.

"No," he could reply truthfully. After all, White Dove was but a dream based on a brief glimpse. "And have you known a man before?"

"No," she replied but held back the many kissing games and secret groping she had taken part in with her age-mates and friends. Most boys wanted girls with big breasts and wide hips, and flat as she was, she had not been the preferred target of their attentions. Still she had got enough, for it seemed to her that boys were more demanding but less discriminating; anything with the proper body parts would do in a pinch. Still those budding pleasurable feelings were nothing compared to this. She smiled at him and never tired of looking into his brown eyes. "Chu, chu," she cooed gently, stroking his face, and he closed his eyes with delight.

Next morning they woke to honking in the skies as big circles of geese were practicing flying formations. A large flock of black birds collected in the nearby bush and trees, their varied and shrill calls breaking upon their pleasant reveries. The sight and sounds woke up the responsible Chaiko; it was time to get back to work, he concluded regretfully. When Dawn came sidling up to him to entice him into some pleasurable pursuit, he slapped her on the rump and unceremoniously sent her for wood as he got ready to hunt.

"Mated but few days and already he is ordering me around ..." her playful grumbling for his benefit trailed off. But she liked his taking charge. It was time to awaken from the dream, a very pleasant dream, but it was time. Still she stood on tiptoes and insisted on a kiss; he dutifully pecked her on her cheeks, but when a shadow of a frown crossed her face, he laughed at his teasing of her and gave her a real bear hug that lifted her off her feet and pressed her close to him. Looking after her, he recalled and understood the depth of fondness between Baer and Tanya, and wanted badly to present Dawn to them.

Chaiko descended from cave hill and followed the river till a swamp blocked his way and forced him more inland. There were signs of deer, antelope and the split hoof of bison - the first sign of bison - and his pulse quickened. His clan depended on these beasts; it was good to see some signs of them.

All around there were prints as he read the ground. In the middle of this preoccupation came a vision of Dawn, beckoning him, and an impulse to hurry back to her took possession of him. A feeling both urgent and demanding stopped him in mid-stride. He shook his head vigorously to awaken himself. He was disgusted that he, Chaiko, the Hunter, the Master of Falcon, was so easily diverted from his concentration by however lovely a vision of her, and in the middle of hunting ... tracking. He closed his mind to the vision.

He came across fresh deer tracks, ground water still seeping into the prints, and he followed them, expecting to see them just ahead. The tracks led into a narrow draw with steep sides that finally opened to a large, open round place that had no other exit. And there on the other side were two deer, a male and a female. They had no way of escaping him and were driven by their alarm hither and thither. Chaiko lifted Falcon and drew back on the string, sighting down the length of the talon squarely onto the male. The female ran trembling to hide behind her mate and he shielded her from Chaiko's view. She uttered little noises of distress and her feet danced in fright and nervousness, but there was nowhere for them to go. Chaiko eased the tension off the string and lowered the weapon. On this day, he could not let the string go to speed the talon on its way. On this day, he would not hunt, and moved aside to let the two terrified creatures escape.

He walked back through the blind draw, looking, thinking and calculating. Perhaps ... perhaps, he nodded to himself. The cave hill was near at hand. He carefully studied the lay of the land, the flow of valleys, dips and hills and tried to see how animals would cross and find their way.

Suddenly he realized with a shock that the fire had not scorched the land here, had not devastated trees and bushes, and that the grass was tall and full of flowers. How? he asked himself, not comprehending. He looked to the west, and there in the stretch of wasteland he saw the answer. The sandy emptiness had provided a fire break that protected this piece of land from the destruction of the firestorm. He and Dawn had been so preoccupied with their growing desires for each other that they had overlooked the obvious. Perhaps Dawn was right after all; this place was waiting here for them. He shook his head, incredulous that he had not noticed this before.

He looked to the hills visible to the east and wondered where the clan could be now. He was reminded of the dilemma that he had pushed from his mind. He needed to find his clan, but he knew that Dawn would not lightly leave their cave and he would not want to ask her to. Still, the needs must somehow be reconciled; but he put the problem away yet again, and returned to his exploration.

This island of green that remained untouched by the fire had attracted a large number of animals that found food and shelter here. This would explain the many tracks and frequent sightings of game. He came across a pile of bones, picked bare and scattered, and it warned him to be cautious; the hunters and scavengers had also found this place.

All in all, he was pleased with what he saw. Here they had everything they would need. Foremost, they had each other, and he smiled. He returned to the cave to find Dawn waiting for him with a bright smile on her face. She ran into his arms and he lifted her, and carried her into the back of the cave.

Much later he lolled indolently beside the fire while she worked with her skins. She then made him stand, stripped off his skins and enjoyed looking at his nakedness and his reaction. She patted him affectionately then slipped new skins over his head with holes for his arms, reaching to just above his knees. The shirt was incredibly soft and fitted him like a second skin without hampering his motion. She made him walk, stop, turn and walk the other way while she mustered him with critical eyes. Finally, she pronounced herself satisfied. He rewarded her with a big hug, body next to body, and with a lingering kiss. This time it was she who drew him into the back of the cave.

Later again, Chaiko was very tired, barely able to keep his eyes open. Dawn hummed, content, and fussed over some woven thing. She was hugely pleased with herself. Although she missed her family and kin, she was glad that they were here alone, to get to know each other without the distraction of other people around. She knew her brothers and friends would have dragged him away with many ribald jests and dirty laughter. No, this was much better.

She hummed happily and watched over her mate drifting in and out of sleep. The poor dear, she said to herself with the kindest of ironies. She was the small one ... but it was he that was worn out. She thought about their play, blushed, then started getting hot again. But this time she knew it was no use; nothing much could rouse Chaiko anymore today.

She wondered about herself. Perhaps after so many years of believing herself to be unattractive, her hunger for attention and affection was hard to satisfy. To a person on the verge of starving, eating alone was not enough; being stuffed to overflowing was still not enough. It was not till the memory of that hunger faded that they could again be satiated. Maybe someday, she too would be full, but not yet, she smiled secretly to herself.

Chapter 30

They awoke to the soft light of dawn flooding the cave, but did not move from the comfortable warmth of their nest. However, when she reached for him, Chaiko growled and she quickly withdrew her hand, pouting in mock offence at being so summarily rebuffed. She recalled that when she was but a girl, a newly mated cousin had been so bored by the attentions of her new mate that he had to grovel and beg for her favors, to the huge amusement of family and kin. Dawn had then resolved never to humiliate her mate so, should she be so lucky as to find one ... and she had not; it was he who now said Enough! But then she herself had not expected to like their play so much.

Chaiko rose refreshed, eager to meet the coming day. Last night, after she had finally left him some time to think, he turned things over in his mind and came to a few resolutions. If this was going to be their cave, as she so desperately desired, then they must provision it for the winter. They would need a successful big hunt to do that; he had a glimmer of an idea how to accomplish it. If they were successful, and stuffed a larder full, the two of them could mount a quick expedition to find the clan in the hills, not having to worry about the coming winter and about lugging all their possessions with them wherever they needed to go, for this was their home now, and neither would be willing to give it up.

He chewed on the meat she gave him, lost in thought. The turtle was thinking again, Dawn noticed fondly. Well, let the thinker think, she would not want to change that. For her part, she was content to let her hands do the thinking; the day would always find the right thing for her to do. Later, he went off into the woods and returned with hardwood branches to make the many more talons they would need for his plan. Then he practiced with the new Falcon. It was considerably stiffer and harder to bend, but the talons flew faster and farther, and hit much harder, boring an extra hand's breadth into the ground. He was pleased as he practiced to accustom his aim to the added strength.

Chaiko planned to explore and study the lay of the land. He was still reluctant to leave Dawn alone, but the cave gave both a new feeling of

14 Stones

security. Dawn felt protected by the massive walls of rock around her, and likewise, Chaiko felt reassured by the aura of comfort and familiarity they had acquired in such a short time. The cave contained them not only physically, but mentally and emotionally as well. It seemed inconceivable that someone or something would dare intrude into the privacy and domain that they had claimed as their own.

During the night, he had remonstrated with himself for having given in to his urges and for having broken his resolve not to touch her until he could count on the assistance of his clan, should Dawn become pregnant. But she was so eager for their play, and Chaiko could not withstand her seductions for any length of time. The heat of his own appetite had an easy time overwhelming the reasoning part of his mind. In fact, once aroused, the mind was quite willing to find reasonable grounds for giving in to these urges. It was doing so now, he noted with some amusement. In brief: she had converted the cave into their home, but home was meant to hold a family. A childless couple was not yet a family. Should she be with child, then so be it, he concluded, smiling that his pleasure was safeguarded. "A mind that wants, bears watching," he warned himself. But the mind was indeed devious and conjured up for him visions of his son helping him to hunt and to provide, visions of just the two of them in the grassland, tracking a herd of deer, Falcons in hand, finger-talking in the silent communication of hunters. Father and son. Chaiko had so much to teach him. He was filled with intense longing for the bond that even so short a foresight presumed. "But what if the child would be a girl?" He smiled, "Then she would be beautiful, strong and brave like her mother." His heart was melting with the fantasies his mind fed it.

By midmorning Chaiko left to scout the valley further, reading the signs left in the soft soil. He found a small herd of bison foraging along the river where the grass was the most tender and sweet. Yes, they would do, he told himself.

"Bison?" she asked, after his excited report; it was not a word she knew. He hooked his fingers by his ears to indicate horns, hunched his shoulders to show the characteristic hump of the beast, stroked a beard beneath his chin and emitted deep-chested grunts. "Oh, bison." She understood and smiled widely at his imitation then mimicked it back to him. Both were laughing hard pretending to be bison, pushing each other head to head, till he tried to mount her, and like the good bison she was, the grunts soon turned into sounds of pleasure that no bison ever uttered.

Somewhat later, he returned to the topic of bison. He showed her three full hands and then three fingers, to indicate how many. She made him do it again, and with deliberate slowness counted with words his clan did not have. "Eighteen," she said pleased with herself. He made her repeat all the numbers, till he could say them too, remembering her words for the count. Again he was lost in thought. Yes, eighteen or a part of eighteen would do nicely, he told himself.

Then he started talking and Dawn listened. He talked with a quiet intensity, often reflective and self-absorbed, for he was thinking out loud. She loved hearing the cadence of his voice, the sound of reasoning, often heavy and ponderous. Though she did not catch every word, she understood the whole well enough, and she was excited by his showing her how he linked ideas and thoughts together into something meaningful. She found herself thinking along with him. So that is what he does all day! Weaving a mat of thoughts, connecting one strand to another. She also realized that it was not all that different from her thinking. It was just that she did not take the careful steps he did, building upon the previous thought toward some narrow focus. She kept wanting to interrupt, to bring in so much more for his consideration. He read into her fidgetiness her wish, but held up a hand, "A hunter who wishes to hit the mark with Falcon had better take time to aim and not point the talon every which way." He felt surprised by the flush of pleasure at having woven wisdom around his new weapon. Such self-indulgence surfaced more often of late, now that the cripple was not in control to deny him pleasure.

Dawn marveled at how different their worlds were. He needed so much thinking to do something, the choices so hard to contemplate. For her it came so easy; when there were choices to be made, she made them with everything that she had, with an intuitive leap, and she was right ... most of the time. She did not break things down as he did, into parts and segments; she did not pit one reason against the next and let them fight it out. It was enough that if the whole was smooth then the parts must be also. It was strange how they looked at the same world, but saw it so differently.

So Chaiko talked and Dawn listened. And his talk gave her insight into this man-woman thing. The male logic seemed to be like their weapons. Made to aim and throw. Fight and force the issue. Take apart to put together. Always about some underlying mastery. The female logic was softer, wider, like an embrace; accepting, not fighting with realities. Man said, "I want;" the woman replied, "Here I am." Both sexes were strong in the things they knew and did, but stronger still together.

Chaiko was dazzled by the brightness in her eyes, as if that clear blue needed any more brilliance! In the midst of showing her his thoughts, he wondered what she was thinking. He told her a little about his clan's beliefs and habits: that they had learned to live in caves from the bear, and that fire was a gift of the skies; about the shaggy beast, the bison, on whose herds they depended; and how the wolves had taught people to hunt.

"Wolves are most silent creatures, 'ghosts of shadows,' we call them sometimes. If you hear them howl, watch out, because they want you to hear them. There is a message there in your hearing, to recognize and to respect their territory. There's always some purpose, you can count on it. Otherwise you can rarely hear or see them. The shadow of shadows, they are.

"When they hunt— and you can go a lifetime without being lucky enough to see them, I've only heard it told myself—they use wonderful cunning. It is not known how they decide, but it is known that, unlike other animals, it is not the strongest that leads, but the smartest, the one who knows when to bend to the will of the pack and when to bend them to his will.

"The whole pack hunts; the lone wolf is against type. They pick a herd, and the whole pack creeps and slinks, each into a position; then the scouts go out to start the herd moving. With a few charges, the herd starts moving, running to escape the wolves that do not really follow. Each wolf guards an area, to keep the herd from escaping, but they sit and watch the herd milling about. The herd runs and runs, in a giant circle, around and around in front of the wolves. They run until tongues hang from the mouths, until breaths smoke from the heat of the chase. Then the lead scout selects a target, someone small, weak or slow, and the whole pack marks that one, and for that poor beast there's no escape. The wolves move in and drive that creature, each taking a turn, till the animal is exhausted, and a rush of wolves overtakes it and brings it to the ground. According to protocol, the animals take their turn at the carcass." Chaiko paused, the scene clear in his mind's eye.

"It would be so wonderful to see it," Chaiko concluded with much longing.

"Wonderful?" Dawn recoiled at the horror of the story. "What can be so wonderful about that? The poor, poor creature, to be so hounded to death." She was on the verge of crying.

"But don't you see? It's amazing how they all work together, each knowing just what to do, and when to do it. They use the strength of the animal against itself ... the speed of the animal against itself. Seeking to escape, the prey wants to run? Let it. The sooner and faster it runs the better. By mock charges the animals are set up to run; their way of escape is to run, but there is no escape for the one that is chosen. Let the runner run and run and exhaust itself. It will think it is escaping, but the wolves know better. The wolves will await the right moment with proper patience, and only when the time is right will they charge in."

"But that is so bloody—how you say?—bloodthirsty," Dawn cried out to protest her distress at the vividness of his description. "It's the small one they kill, and the old."

"Yes, but the wolf will take a portion back to its den to feed its young and to ensure the pack's continuance. It is the wolf who keeps the herds healthy, by taking the weak and infirm. The wolves take the worst not the best. The strong survive to be the parents of the next generation. It is the nature of things that all creatures must suffer those that prey upon them. So no creature gets too proud or haughty."

"But no creature bothers wolves, does it?" Dawn countered.

"No. Not many. But the number of wolves is set by the number of those it hunts. Otherwise, having eaten all, it must eat itself." More deadly arithmetic. "Like all creatures, wolves have a right to live and to exist. Are we so different from wolves ourselves? Do we not buy our lives with other creatures' flesh? Man is more bloodthirsty than wolves. For wolves kill only what they can eat, and no more."

She shook off her mood and asked matter-of-factly. "Kaiko, what mean this ... this story?"

"We, the Clan of Standing-Rock, like all other clans, learned to hunt from the wolves. The point is we hunt with our heads first and last.

Only a small part of hunting is strength or speed or luck, but each one of these is an important part." He paused, his eyes looking inward, searching for some key to the puzzle, their place in the great design. She hugged her knees and pulled herself into a tight defensive ball. "We do not hunt as one, as the lone wolf, who is bound to die for he has no pack, as a person without a clan is bound to die..."

"Kaiko alone. Dawn alone. Kaiko not die. Dawn not die." Her arithmetic was so simple, but hard to argue against.

"Because Kaiko found Dawn ... we are our clan," he added with some exasperation at her interruptions. "The hyenas would come and take Chaiko alone, Dawn alone. But Chaiko is not alone anymore." He paused and then continued evenly, "Chaiko has Dawn and Chaiko has Falcon," as a central statement of fact.

"The point is," he said with emphasis to forestall further interruptions, "when the clan hunts, we hunt as the wolves do, together, each one playing out a rehearsed and practiced role. None has to do it all by himself; we all share the load and we all share the risk," he concluded with a self-satisfied flourish. "And we all share the rewards," he hurried to add, "according to need, not merit." Dawn would have mentioned rewards first.

"So?" she asked, not because she was contentious, but that she had gotten so caught up by his words that her exclamation was involuntary. She wanted to know the point of all this, if there was one. This man-woman thing could get confusing.

"So? So, if Chaiko and Dawn must hunt, then we shall hunt like the clan, like the wolves we learned from."

"Kaiko and Dawn hunt together, yes. Clan is far away," she puzzled, trying to tease the answer apart like some elusive strand in a tight and narrow weave.

"He who wants water to drink must carry a water-skin, else walk to the river. But he who carries water in his hands, shall see it slip through his fingers and shall be thirsty. We go prepared to want; we go ready to hunt." He had this infuriating habit of offering clan homilies, usually in a discrepant context, when he wanted her to think beyond the obvious. Dawn knitted her brows in concentration; what could he be wanting now? But no matter how she looked at it, the two of them added up to only two.

"Kaiko and Dawn hunt," she tried to sound assertive, but knew it was not the answer he was waiting for.

"Yes, Kaiko and Dawn hunt ... with own clan." He watched the frowns of bewilderment deepen in her face.

"Where own clan?" she asked stammering.

"We make 'em!" he almost trumpeted in triumph. He moved closer to her and elaborated, his manner intense and intent. Now and again she nodded her head. No wonder he needed to think all the time, she concluded, about his audacious plans. But if they were going to do it, they had a lot to accomplish and they had better get started on it. She took a length of rope and together they went and brought back bundle after bundle of water reeds, which she bound and shaped as he had asked, one after the other. Once she got going it was quite fun and the day passed swiftly. In the meantime, he had made talons and torches of tightly wound grass strings on a stick soaked with melted pitch.

The next day they were all over the countryside, planting stakes in the places he had chosen, and collecting and dragging large piles of fire wood to where they would need them. By nightfall their preparations were complete.

That night there was no love play; both were too preoccupied with the coming hunt, too tired with a full day of preparations behind them. Weary and worn out as they were, they could not sleep, the anticipation of the coming day much too high and exciting.

"Kaiko will t's work?" she wanted to know.

"We have to try to make it work," smiled the lead wolf into the darkness, and set up a loud howl that raised even the smallest hair on her back. "Kaiko!" she protested, and jumped on him, flailing at him with a soft rabbit skin for having so startled her with his noises. They rolled about on the bedding in playful wrestling and much laughter. She won because she tickled him mercilessly into submission. But still sleep was slow to come.

The next day both were silent and earnest. He asked her for some sweet grass, which he burned to cleanse them of spirits and whatever else the good-hunting ceremony was supposed to do, hurriedly mumbling through the words. Then they set off, he carrying Falcon and many talons in a long pouch she had improvised for him, she a spear and her carryall. Each also had an unlit torch and a pouch full of river pebbles.

They found the herd where he thought they might be, grazing peacefully along a water run, munching on grass and chewing their cuds. Insects buzzed about them in swarms and a few animals rubbed up against each other to rid themselves of these pests burrowing into their coats of fur. A few rolled on the ground, turning and twisting in the dirt. Others irritably tossed their heads to shoo away flies from the mucus of eyes and noses. Though they saw the two coming, they did not react to their appearance, not having met people before. Since this herd was much too far away from the cave, the first part of the plan was to get the herd moving closer in that direction. Chaiko motioned Dawn into position and they advanced on the herd, making much noise and beating sticks together. The massive heads rose and looked in their direction. A nervous tremor ran through the herd and they started bunching up, the biggest facing them, shielding the others. This was a critical point in the plan; the herd must not charge past them. They made more noise, at the top of their lungs, and waved their arms and pieces of skins to make themselves appear larger and more hostile than they were.

The lead bull was full of wisdom and courage, but had no experience of hunters like these and was undecided as to what to do. He knew wolves, lions and bears and would have gladly fought them, but did not know what to make of humans. His indecision affected the whole herd, and they started shifting about nervously. Chaiko took a rock and hit a younger bull at the edge of the group, counting on his reaction to turn aside, which he did, bellowing his irritation. Chaiko threw and hit the animal again; then they were both throwing rocks, yelling and waving in between. A rock hit a younger animal on its nose. The animal, confused, backed away and when a second stone hit its side, started running from something it could not understand. A few turned with the young bull, and in a ripple effect, the rest of the herd followed, leaving the lead bull still facing the humans. Then it must have occurred to the bull that as leader he should be in front and not behind the herd, so he charged off to find something to lead. Elated, Chaiko and Dawn followed at a run along the twist of a small vale, through sparse bush, then over a slight rise into the next depression. There they caught up with the herd just where Chaiko had predicted. They paused, short of breath. Dawn was beginning to see the value of all his thinking.

This time the herd was much easier to move and reacted to their noisy approach by drifting in front of them following the contour of the land. Just ahead was a rise; beyond it, a choice point between diverging paths. The herd had to be deflected to the left, toward the cave. They came over the rise, and the herd pulled up short, for on the right-hand path was a line of grass dummies holding smoking torches blocking that route of escape. The herd milled about as the lead bull tried to make sense of all this. Chaiko threw a stone, aiming carefully at the young bull, hitting him on the side to get him moving in the desired direction away from the line of grass dummies. The rest was again inclined to follow. This time, the lead bull was not going to let the herd get ahead of him and thundered off, taking the rest of the herd just the way Chaiko wanted them to go. He thanked his silent clan holding the smoldering torches.

Twice more they repeated this maneuver; a line of silent clan denied the herd the choice to go somewhere else. They were now close to the cave, the herd bunched up opposite the blind draw where Chaiko had cornered the two deer. Now he was ready to spring the trap in earnest. He yelled, waved and threw stones. But the lead bull was suspicious and refused to go into the constricted passage. The animals milled about again and looked ready to make a run for it. However, this too had Chaiko foreseen. He and Dawn ran to light fires they had built in advance and soon a line of flames and smoke blocked the way. The bison knew about smoke and fire, and backed away but still refused to go into the draw behind them.

Chaiko took a fair-sized burning branch and chucked it into the press of shaggy bodies. The bison snorted in alarm and drew away from the burning piece of wood. Chaiko threw yet again, creating (like the wolves) movement amidst the hunted. The motion soon turned to flight, as alarm fed fear and fear grew to panic. Against their will, the animals charged into the trap. Chaiko and Dawn hurried after, lighting fires as they went to plug the neck of the trap. Soon, a wide curtain of smoke hid and denied exit. Keeping cautiously to one side, Chaiko led Dawn up the draw. They found the herd milling about in the basin, facing them, bellowing in confusion, dust stirred up by the uneasy shuffling of hooves. Chaiko found a high spot on a man-sized boulder and they clambered up on top to safety above the herd. His wooden leg slipped on the smooth rock face, but Dawn steadied him with surprising strength hidden in her small frame. She was amazed. Everything had gone just as he had planned, down to this detail of the two of them on the rock facing the herd.

Chaiko braced himself on the rock and looked over the bison. He held up two hands and arched his eyebrows questioningly at her. She shook her head, showing five fingers then one, settling on six. Chaiko made Falcon ready. Which six? his expression asked. Dawn looked at the herd, the young and the old, just as she had said, and did not want to make the choice now. She bit her lip in distress—but they must each do what they had to do— and pointed a shaking hand. Chaiko raised Falcon and a talon was on its way, true to the mark, buried itself deep into a shaggy side, slicing between ribs, piercing the heart. The animal collapsed, then in quick succession five more. Truly, the weapon was well named the Falcon. Its talons falling out of the sky were swift, deadly and mercilessly efficient. Six times they flew; six times they struck and six lives were taken in quick succession. Then the killing stopped. Dawn was crying with the realization that it was hard to be a Hunter. Chaiko was glad that his aim was good and the animals had died without suffering. Just a slight moan of surprise then a shaggy body dropped crashing to the ground, and before the animal could regret its passing, its sight darkened to see no more. Chaiko's hands trembled, his breathing was ragged and there was a drumbeat in his ears. There was always a price to be paid for shed blood, he reminded himself.

Then they waited and rested on top of the rock. They would need to save their strength for six animals had to be prepared. But they were within sight of the cave, and Dawn was filled with pride for her "thinking" mate. They could not have gotten any closer to the cave than this.

No need for noise now. Little by little, the herd settled down though still nervous, seeming to recognize by some ancient wisdom that a price had been paid. They accepted the deaths, just as they accepted a wolf pack culling the herd, year after year a traditional give-and-take struggle. Hide in numbers, was the defensive strategy of the beasts. The unlucky few had paid a blood price for the safety of the rest. The smoke blocking the way out abated, and the herd gathered itself to escape. When they could clearly see their way onto the other side, they sprinted through the last of the smoke and retraced their route, thundering by the silent clan and the still-smoldering torches.

Back at the killing ground, Chaiko howled, half in triumph and half out of respect for the kill, and to help the spirits of the slain find their way, for it was known that the destinies of the wolf and of the bison were intertwined. These were ancient adversaries who well understood each other. Humans were late comers to this conflict.

Then it was work, work, and work: animals to skin and butcher, meat to cut, fires to feed and meat to hang for smoking. Sometimes it seemed to Dawn that half their lives were spent in doing just this. There had to be a better way. If Chaiko could think himself into having the meat deliver itself almost into their cave, she too would find a better way someday. Her hands worked at cutting the meat while her mind explored this novel idea.

It would be nice, likewise, to have plants come to the cave to be harvested. Bah, plants cannot move. She was about to dismiss the idea, but stopped herself. She had not seen straw hunt before, either. So maybe there was a way for plants to bring their fruit to the cave! Dawn was excited by the strangeness of her thoughts. She was so used to thinking about practical things ... but these thoughts did not have a head or tail to get hold of. It was hard to ignore all the other thoughts that intruded to block her thinking. She realized that she must give up preconceived notions and look beyond barriers of the conventional. Let thoughts have the freedom to find themselves, as his did, she instructed herself. This was hard work, she was beginning to realize. How can doing nothing be so tiring? She put these thoughts away, but resolved to return to them when time allowed.

They were both soon covered in blood and gore from head to foot. Even their hair soon became matted with the unwelcome stickiness of their work, but they continued on. They worked through the night, until Chaiko finally stopped her, afraid that in her exhaustion Dawn would cut herself with a sharp flint. He took her aside and made her lie down and almost instantly she was asleep. Two short hours later she was back again somewhat refreshed and started cutting again. After a while she chased him off to take a nap. His sleep lasted twice as long as hers. When he awoke there was still work to be done but it had shrunk encouragingly.

14 Stones

In the morning light a large flock of vultures collected above the kill. They wheeled in a great circle high up above, letting the whole plain know of the slaughter. Soon there were more than twenty birds cruising high in the air. Some of the vultures landed and waited in ungainly lines, squabbling among themselves. As graceful as they looked in mid-air with wings extended, masters of the air currents, they appeared awkward on the ground with their side-to-side lurching and stiffly holding their folded wings out of the way. The carrion birds' presence brought the hyenas into the open, but none dared to cross the line of fires. Dawn shuddered, looking at the scavengers gathering about them, just awaiting their opportunity. What was the difference between humans and them? The price of life had to be someone else's life. Those were the harsh rules of living, Chaiko had said. It was enough to make one stop thinking, she thought tiredly.

Then they were done with the cutting and butchering, but there were still days of smoking the meat ahead of them, as well as skins to be scraped clean. They washed themselves as best as they could with water from their water bag. Chaiko kept giving Dawn broken bones so that she could suck out the marrow, still steaming, hot from the fire. Both their people prized marrow as a restorer and strengthener. However, with six kills, even a good thing was turning unappetizing.

Sometime in the afternoon Chaiko buried the offal and the bones, for it was not good to let scavengers profit from the effort of humans and to develop unwanted expectations and a following. Chaiko crossed the gallery of scavengers and retraced the hunt to collect all the grass dummies to be stored in the back of the cave. They had served their purpose well, and he thought there might be use for them sometime in the future. He made sure that all the fires they had set were extinguished. It would not do to burn down the valley after it had survived the great conflagration.

Chapter 31

It took them five days of hard work to preserve the six bison; cutting the meat into strips, stringing it over six smudge fires, checking and turning as the meat dried and shrank into hard, tough strips, and finally storing the meat in cairns Chaiko dug in the back of the cave. Chaiko walked the rounds, from fire to fire, feeding them a careful diet of aromatic grasses and wood like hickory or smoke-bush. Time and time again, he restrung the lines to ensure that the meat was drying evenly in the rising smoke. Dawn rendered bison fat and poured it into skin bags to congeal for storage in a special pit, sealed with an extra layer of clay. Then she cleaned and worked the stiffness out of the hides, scraping and rubbing the insides smooth. By the time they were done, they were both exhausted. Their eyes were rimmed red; they smelled of smoke themselves; their hands were callused from the hard work, laced with many cuts from the sharp edges of their flint blades. But such was the price of the bounty of six bison. Smelly and grimy as they were, they collapsed and moved little for two days. They rose only to wash and feed themselves and tend the fires that kept the scavengers away. They were heavy and lethargic with a glut of fresh meat.

The success of the hunt was a great relief, for even if they hunted no more, they had enough meat to last through the winter. This gave Chaiko some peace of mind. Dawn was less apt to worry, as she was generally more confident about the future, but she was glad to have her mate reassured, and assumed that this would improve his mood in general. In years to come, she would learn better; a worrier can always find something to worry about. She was as yet naive about this facet of his character.

Chaiko was working with some sinew for Falcon, hoping to improve it so that it would not be affected by the weather: shrinking when it got dry, going slack when it got wet, and turning brittle when cold. Thongs performed no better, and twisted grass strands tended to unravel under the constant tension. He was trying to combine sinew with braided flax strands, certainly the most promising combination that he could think of, and the initial trials looked good.

14 Stones

He strung Falcon anew with this mix, plucked the string and listened to the pleasant hum that came from the vibration. The sound was almost as good as that which the original Singing-Stick had produced, but this was no longer a Singing-Stick, rather a marvelous hunting weapon. He regarded the implement with an odd sense of dislocation. On the one hand, the initial mystery of its power still remained; on the other, he had become familiar with the instrument and could draw and aim it with practiced ease, as the six bison had proved. One bison, one talon, each finding a vital spot, severing a life line. In spite of this evidence, it remained an enigma, its strength and capabilities hidden in its shape. If anything, it looked fragile, like a child's toy in comparison with a hunter's stout spear. Yet it gave him a tremendous sense of power and competence, something that he had not developed before a River of Rocks made him a cripple ... but this wooden thing in his hand made even a cripple a master of his world. Would this likewise rob winter of its fear of hunger and threat of starvation? He plucked the string, and Falcon hummed with power: yes!

His wooden leg had stood up well to the demands of all the work they had to do. His short leg became more tired than the whole one, and he tended to limp more as he grew weary. Still, his range of motion was incomparably better than relying on crutches. He got so used to it that he hardly thought about it anymore. All the same, the deep wounds suffered by the cripple still remained behind his conscious thoughts.

Dawn resumed working on the bison skins. She planned to make some winter wraps for them and covering for their bedding. The bison fur had recovered from the summer shed, and was still very soft and smooth, none of the coarseness of a winter coat having grown in yet, perfect for what she wanted. With smooth pebbles about the size of her fist in each hand, she was rubbing the inside of the skin, spitting on it, smoothing and softening it. It took patience to do work like this, but Dawn liked to work at things and she sang softly to herself songs of her childhood. She felt happy. They still had fresh meat, a full larder, and the luxury of six bison furs. The sky was full of sunshine, the air was warm and the breeze a gentle caress. The crickets were chirping loudly as they were wont to do at this time of the year joined by the strident whirr of cicadas. She looked up at Chaiko who seemed preoccupied with the thing he called Falcon. Dawn was grateful for that magic piece of wood that had brought them such abundance. He looked up and their eyes met; she smiled but he really did not see her as he was lost in his thoughts. He was thinking again, she noted to herself, but having seen such dramatic proof of his thinking, this time she felt no resentment except a curiosity as to what he could be thinking about.

Dawn was immensely impressed by the result of the hunt and was very proud of her mate, how he had foreseen every detail and so smoothly executed his plan. She was aware of how much she had been a part of all this, from the beginning to the end. He had made a special effort to explain everything so that each segment had been clear in her mind. As the result of all the planning, the bison had delivered themselves practically into the cave. Had they been forced to hunt and prepare the meat where they had first found the herd, they could have handled only two at most, instead of the six.

Inspired by the results of the hunt, she resolved to think her way through the plant puzzle she had set for herself. How could the plants deliver themselves and save the extensive seeking and gathering that was now required? The reasons why it could not be done all rushed to the fore, while the other side remained quiet. She had to suppress the flood of thoughts that argued against the concept, to look beyond their limits for what could be done. So she allowed thoughts to surface, looked at each in turn, stored it, and dismissed none—not yet. However, she found it difficult to keep herself focused on such a narrow path. She was used to looking at things from a broad perspective, in the context of everything else around her, and now she struggled against the intrusion of the rest of her world into this problem. How to keep oneself open, but focused, seemed to be the challenge.

She got a little further along in her thinking. If plants were going to move, they would have to move as seeds. She had naturally observed how birds and other animals scattered seeds wherever they went and therein she thought to have her answer. A rooted plant could not move, or could it? What stopped her from bringing a small plant to the cave, planting it into the soil and letting it grow and mature? Or just to plant as seeds? Near the cave? That seemed possible. She saw, dimly as yet, a field of plants conveniently near at hand, no need to wander in search of what she needed. The idea warmed her and she resolved to try replanting a young plant nearby. And a few seeds too. But she knew it was not the time for growing, so late in the summer. Her experiment would need to wait until next year.

On the other side of the fire, Chaiko roused himself and took a long drink from the water skin that was always filled with water so that it

14 Stones

would not dry out, shrink and crack. He sat down beside Dawn and watched her rhythmic motion. He wrapped himself in one of the skins she had worked on and luxuriated in its soft embrace. "Hhummm." He uttered this sign of contentment and she flashed him a smile of pure pleasure. Men were so sparse with their praises, and a woman always had to be satisfied with what little they called approval. A stingy "good work" or a mild pat on the back passed for enthusiasm with the man folk. Admiration for the worker, not just for the product, was required. Why do men awaken an itch and then do not scratch it? But she was pleased that he had noticed. Her song changed to a lighter and higher tone reflecting her happier mood. The smooth round stones slid easily over the inside of the skin, adding a rhythmic measure as the stones clicked against each other.

Chaiko listened to her singing, and the clicking of the stones reminded him of his years. From around his neck he took the small bag and the stranger's bone full of holes. He had almost forgotten about that. He held it in his hand, looked at it and wondered what possible secret lay hidden there. He concentrated on it, but saw only a long hollow bone with holes in it. What good was it? He frowned at it, but nothing in the bone suggested any use for it. There were no barbs so it was not used to catch fish, like the bone hooks he had for that purpose.

He next turned his attention to the bag and spilled its contents onto the bison pelt. The clicking of small stones caught Dawn's attention and she asked what they were.

"These are my years," he said simply, spreading the stones out on the pelt, explaining the custom of the clan to commemorate each year with a small stone, to count one's age. Clan wisdom held that he who forgets the past is blind to the future. He counted them, one by one, using her words for the count. He picked one up, one of the smaller stones. "This was for the year I was born, a hard year full of hunger, my mother said. That is why there are so many edges on the stone, to remind me that it was a painful year. If you put it in your mouth it feels rough and uncomfortable." The stone was unattractive with sharp bumps on it, and as a child he had put it in his mouth.

"This was for my fourth year," he continued, "the first year that I have a memory of. It's all pale and white. My mother chose it for me to remind me that my younger brother died. I remembered running in a field of grass and flowers with my friend Crow. He was faster then."

"This was the first stone I chose for myself for the sixth year, a year of flooding. The water was very high; I saw fish swimming among the branches of trees. Crow and I wanted to see if they would lay eggs in the abandoned nests of birds. Look how it has this sparkling vein in the grey stone." Dawn looked at it closely but could not see flooding in the stone. "I just thought it looked very pretty the way it sparkled, especially when wet. I was only six."

One by one Chaiko told her the memory preserved by each stone. She listened raptly. She liked this clan custom of remembering. There was one stone she noted, misshapen, which he had not talked about. And when he stopped recounting, she naturally asked, "And this one?"

After a long silence he said painfully, "That stone chose me." His voice was very low and shaky. "And it cost me a leg." She looked at him, shocked by the tension of his words and the pain in his face, and did not know what to say for a moment. She suspected she was about to meet the cripple whom he had been so careful to hide from her. She waited expectantly, her face reflecting quiet sympathy. He began slowly at first, with words struggling to find the long way to the surface, from some deep hidden recess where he had tried to bury all his pain. He told her about the child he had been, carefree like any other, full of future promise, then about his friend Crow, and about the race across the loose stones and then the River of Rocks and the time thereafter. He told her how, with the leg he lost, he also lost his future and had no standing in his clan. He was to remain a child forever, overlooked or worse still, pitied. The awakened cripple struggled anew with the hurt. Words after anguished words were forced out of him by the pain, and without his wanting it to, the past came rushing out. Shudder after shudder racked him, tears stained his cheeks and sobs, long repressed, burst forth. Dawn said nothing but held onto him, and when he struggled for control, she gently stroked his hair and shushed him like a child. In her arms he slowly quieted and the pressure went out of his voice. He told her about his brother Baer, Tanya and Lana, then Crow and Samar and one by one the rest of the clan. Dawn listened and she heard the pain gradually change to pride.

The telling eased the tumult within and when the words stopped and the sighs ceased, she said softly, "All you have been and all that has happened has led you here to be with me. I am grateful that you found me. We are each other's future, you and I. You are a hunter, a thinker, master of Falcon and my mate. And your children will call you father."

In her quiet words he saw himself as she saw him, and the words were healing as her strokes were calming and reassuring. She made it all sound so simple, simple enough even for a cripple to believe.

Outwardly calm and consoling, Dawn was nonetheless also shaken by his revelation of the depth of pain he was harboring. After all, she saw him as a complete person, strong, competent and self-assured. To her, the missing leg was irrelevant; his genius had found a way around it and she marveled at the solution he so devised. In all aspects of their lives she saw only strength in him. The sudden revelation of hurt, so closely juxtaposed with this strength she came to rely on, was highly confusing to her. All the same, her protective instincts welled up, and she sought to ease his pain. "Heal," her hands caressed his tense body, "heal," she smoothed his brow. She hugged him, lay her face next to his, feeling the wetness of his cheeks, feeling their hair intertwine. Gentle cooing sounds issued from the back of her throat. She wanted to share his pain, take more of it onto herself. In her embrace and care, the tenseness slowly yielded and went out of his body. His breathing eased, his eyes opened and his mind returned to the present. As control returned, he shrugged off her embrace, imperceptibly so, perhaps ashamed of the weakness he had exhibited. She then brought him water and gave him food, a woman's remedy to feed the body and to solace a hurt soul.

A short-winged harrier hawk flew over them, wheeling and turning to get away from a pair of starlings mobbing it to drive it from the nearness to their nest, even though the young were grown and ready to fend for themselves. It was late in the season. The six bison in the cairns were reassuring.

Dawn, sensing that Chaiko needed space to recover his balance, went back to working on the skins. His gaze found rest in the hills to the east and his emotions slowly subsided. He put the stones away but was reminded that the 14th stone still needed to be found. This had been a strange year. The 14th year, the Year of Becoming, the time to change from a boy into a man, had been full of changes and full of challenges. There was the earthquake, black rain, drought, fire, the river and now Dawn. How was he going to express all that in one stone?

Chaiko looked at Falcon. That had to be commemorated too. He, alone ... well Dawn too... knew of it, of its power as a hunter and its power to affect their lives. To them only was it known; to the rest of the world it was still a secret. But if he had discovered it, surely others would? Or did it discover him? Did he not wait for the wood to tell him what it wanted to be? He had been working on Singing-Sticks and look where it had led him. If he had found this wonderful quality of wood then maybe so would others. But when?

If he thought closely about it, before Falcon there were spears. Who made the first spear? What was before spears? Clubs. And before clubs? Stones. Someone discovered the use of each, so that in his time, Chaiko too could use them. All those things now belonged to whoever made them and used them. Falcon was therefore not his alone; it belonged to the clan. Falcon could improve their hunt as well, and assure them a better future. He must find the clan because they too needed this implement.

He felt the sudden weight of responsibility again. Lately he had been responsible only for the two of them, but the recognition of what he had discovered and needed to share with the rest of his world, reawakened his sense of duty with all its burdens. It was true that he had found it, but if he could not teach it, the knowledge could be lost for how long? It was now up to him.

"Dawn," he called and she came over. He gave her Falcon to hold. "This is a great thing. It shot six times and six bison died honorably to feed you and me. I have never seen one man kill six of anything so effortlessly at one try." Indeed the ease of the kills still bothered him. No creature should lose its life so lightly; the ease of killing left him unworthy to claim the kills, because it had cost him so little to earn it. "Six talons, six kills." He restated the deadly arithmetic. A hunter can claim one, even two, but six? Was there not some danger in so arousing six angry spirits against oneself at one time? How could he defend against them? He wished he could get away from spirits once and for all. "Enough meat for the winter." She nodded in agreement.

"But Falcon belongs not just to the two of us, but to my clan ... and to your people," he added, ashamed that he only now stumbled upon this afterthought, "and to all people beyond, so that all people can hunt like us and feed their families. We must take this to show and then teach the people how to make use of this."

"Leave the cave?" she asked, her voice tremulous, apprehensive of the direction he was taking.

Yet, she could not argue with him, for she wanted his people and her people to have this marvelous new weapon so full of magic certainty, but she was torn by the threat this presented to their new home which she did not want to leave. Sensing her thoughts, he hastened to reassure her, "It will be for only a short while, to show the clan and teach them its use. We will come back, for this is our home." She smiled at him gratefully for this commitment. But still she was regretful of the necessity of leaving her cave, when they had so newly found it and had just made it so comfortable. They had found happiness here.

They discussed details of an expedition to find the clan and all the things they still needed to do to prepare. They agreed that they must leave the cave fully provisioned to see them through the coming winter. Dawn pointed out that they needed to collect a full store of firewood, moss and down for winter bedding; seeds, cones, grains and roots; bark, mushrooms and herbs for medicine; wood for him to work; and willow, cane, broadleaf and long-stemmed grass for her. There were leaves and fruit to dry and on and on it went until he grew discouraged. But each item gave her a little extra time to bind them more securely to their home.

"How long will all this take?" Chaiko asked in growing dismay at her expanding list of things left yet to do. It was obvious that her list of winter necessities was much longer than his. To a hunter a larder full of meat seemed enough.

"Not long, half a moon." Dawn smiled sweetly at him, but half a moon was twice as long as he was willing to wait. He sighed deeply. Yet if it was his decision that they must go and find the clan, then he must allow her to set the time. As she worked, the realization grew within her of shortly meeting his family and kind, and she warmed up more to the idea. It had been good for the two of them to be alone to learn about each other, but their children would need a community to embrace them so they could count the generations and learn their customs and heritage.

Dawn immediately set about organizing what they would need to prepare for the journey. She wanted to make them new hides to dress in, to make a good impression on his people. She also wanted to take some offerings, as was the custom among her people when visiting: some herbs and spices, pitch to burn, salt, sweetgrass and such ... something that could always be used. A bearer of gifts was welcome, more so than one who came only with wants and needs, proclaimed a saying of her people that Chaiko got to hear quite often as they prepared for their journey.

Having become more familiar with his clan's way of doing things, Dawn found herself with two sets of values to uphold, two sets of conduct to maintain. Certainly, she usually yielded to his, giving his needs full precedence over her own. Beyond his, however, she felt obligated to adhere to hers. It had been his decision to look for the clan, and while this protocol of his did not conflict with hers, she layered two additional requirements onto it. Thus she wanted them to look good and to make a fine first impression, as well as to be bearers of gifts to assure their welcome. Chaiko was aware of Dawn's self-imposed double burden, but she bore it with such patience and self-assurance that it did not appear cumbersome for her at all.

"But why go to such an extra effort? Do we not have enough to do already?" he asked her, hoping to shorten their preparations.

"The effort is not of consequence (ramara, she had actually said in her tongue), but good form is. Your people say he who forgets the past is blind to the future. My people say that the shape of things are as important as the things themselves. Though we do not mistake one for the other, each is important and has its place. Strength, therefore, should look strong, just as conduct should be framed with good manners. Therein is harmony. One seeks to balance the outside with the inside ... and the balance shows in peace of mind, and in the orderliness (kuolam) of one's life." As she struggled with the words, she looked hopefully at him to see if her words found understanding. It was hard to explain (in any language, even hers) such core concepts that never needed explanation before. It had been part of her culture, had been taken for granted.

He tried very hard to make sense of her mixing the languages, so hard that he felt a build-up of an ache behind his surface thoughts, but he could not find her perspective. Though she had become more accomplished in his tongue, complex reasonings like these overtaxed her new vocabulary. He knew he was questioning the constants that she accepted without reservation and needed not to be justified. Still he fought against the underlying implication that his manner was not as refined as hers; in fact, if he understood her unspoken reactions at times, it was not only inferior but downright rude, though she never reproached him for it.

"Soma teo la fabeloras," he surprised her with a key turn of phrase, that he thought meant, "We shall speak of this again when time allows," without the prejudice of anger, rejection or quality other than a recognition that the topic had not been resolved but remained of import. She inclined her head in acceptance, with that quiet dignity of her culture, and he beheld that quality again, so attractive, so suited to her, that he resolved to protect it in her. He returned her bow with like composure. Again she bowed to him, a little deeper this time. Chaiko felt they gained something in this transaction but was at loss to identify it. Carefully, however, so as not to disturb the feeling of value (a piece of her harmony, perhaps?), he rose and returned to his pursuit and she to hers.

So, while she worked with renewed vigor on her skins, he set about making yet a new Falcon. They would have need of many more when they found the clan. He had several sticks that seemed suitable. He shaved the pieces of wood, giving them shape. As he worked his thoughts ranged far and wide but always returned to the bag of stones around his neck.

All the things that happened this past year were important to him, to Dawn, and to the clan, but none as important as Falcon, for he saw now that it belonged to all men. So for this one time, perhaps, the 14th stone needed not to be a stone at all. It could be a small piece of wood from the tip of the first Falcon, to remind him that all men were born and lived and died, but the things they learned and passed to the next generation lived beyond.

That night both dreamed of the coming journey and of the reception they would likely receive. Chaiko was certain of rejoicing, but Dawn felt apprehensive and wondered if his clan would be as accepting as he was of a skinny half-sized girl.

Chapter 32

The morning light stole upon them softly. The sun warmed the bison pelt and like a flower greeting the rising light, the pelt opened a little at a time, to reveal the two within. First the arms and shoulders, the faces hidden by a tangle of hair, then slowly the torsos and the legs emerged, close together, the limbs hopelessly intertwined. The warmth increased and bathed their skins and they stirred, unfolding from each other, limb by limb. Finally Dawn rose to begin their morning routines. Chaiko yawned, stretched, and through slit eyes peered into the blue sky. Another night was behind them and another day in front.

Then as he blinked again, memory slowly caught up with the present and the mood of the previous day filled him anew. He felt emotionally exhausted and subdued. After the outpouring of the day before, he felt flat and wooden. He was shocked at how easily the past had come gushing out, even after years of burying his feelings. An innocent description of a year-stone had unlocked his memories and the past became dislodged; the River of Rocks flowed again. Still, there was a lightening behind the sense of emptiness. A burden released, perhaps? Could he so renounce the past?

Dawn looked him over guardedly, trying to gauge how badly the opening of such deep wounds had pained him anew. It was not reassuring to find him so lethargic. My poor turtle. Men allowed themselves so few feelings that when they encountered some they did not know how to cope with them. She sighed. From past experience with her menfolk, she knew that there was little she could do if they insisted on denying past events, always looking for some convenient hole in which to hide them again. Her brother Boar was one such, who denied his feelings all the time. For seasons he had yearned after a pretty girl named Summer. As was custom, he left his token in a private place only she used. She would recognize it and if she returned it twined with a token of hers, it would mean his suit was welcome. Though it was the parents who arranged pairings, the girl had the right of refusal; Boar's hopes were thus in her hand. And though Summer had looked at him significantly, there had been no token returned. And though the asking and the response were very discreet to avoid public humiliation, the silence of no response was nonetheless very painful. Only three people knew of this petition, Summer, Boar and Doan, for he had confided it to her. And though he claimed he was not hurt, his eyes followed Summer about and he never left a token for another. When Doan tried to console him, he evaded it, and sank deeper into silence. And each time the hole got deeper and the silence grew louder. Looking at Chaiko now, she resolved to be gentle with him, though she wanted to shake him awake. You must accept the past for what it was and then face the future.

Dawn threw herself into the activities that needed to be done. This flurry of tasks distracted her from the unease she felt at the impending introduction to his clan. At the mere thought a storm of butterflies awakened in her stomach. The more nervous she became the harder she worked. She sorted through her skins and found that she had enough to make herself a new shirt, but just. She had recently made Chaiko something new, so he was covered. She also wanted to make them new footwear and would need some more skins, but decided that it was not the right time to ask him for some. She set about cutting the pieces and tacking them together. She also needed some porcupine quills for fine stitches, but that would have to wait too.

She went out and gathered moss which she spread out in the sun to dry and later stored in the back of the cave. Not far away, on an adjoining cliff, she had found a large colony of birds with precarious nests pasted with birdlime to the stone facade. Below, there were many discarded feathers. She remembered how striking he looked in his feather cape when he first stumbled across her and decided to make one for each of them.

"Kaiko, do your people make many feather things?" She did not want to compete against experts.

"No. But a feather is sometimes used for decoration."

"Oh. Well then ..." she brightened. His cape by now looked worn, with feathers missing or broken. If the truth be told, it was not all that well made to begin with, little sorting or selecting, barely held together by a loose matrix of knots, but it was nonetheless ingenious how the feathers had led moisture down and away from the inside leaving the wearer quite dry. Immediately she set upon improving the design. For the shoulders she wanted short broad feathers with good overlap, on the straight piece down the back matched, long feathers laid out in tight, covering lines. She went off to the cliff and soon came back with a huge pile of feathers which she started to sort.

Dawn's activity induced some stirrings in Chaiko. He got up and went to collect some firewood, which required the least amount of thinking or planning. Soon there was a large pile growing in front of the cave. She suggested that he sort and then store them in the back of the cave according to thickness. He made trip after trip, for he was collecting for the winter. With exertion his stiffness melted and his mood lifted. He was able to smile at her, and by the evening he was starting to have more intimate thoughts. Then that night, under the soft moonlight, the two embraced in their cozy nest by the fire, stroking and caressing one another as such intimate times called for. This time, however, their play was more comforting and reassuring, less the driven heat of passion.

The next days were beautiful soft late summer days, not too hot, pleasant to work in, full of activity for both of them. Chaiko found a porcupine for her needles and she completed her shift. She used some berries to stain some patterns around the neck, alternating good luck signs with good weather and happiness signs.

Chaiko also shot two more deer, from which she prepared some footwear for them. She would have preferred moose skin for these, or elk at least, for they were hardier and more water-tight, but she made do with what was at hand. She also made them new carryalls, and for him a new container that could hold eight talons and hang from his belt at the back, out of the way, yet within easy reach.

They spent a good part of each day strolling across open fields collecting sheaves of grass, spikes of grain, seed pods, roots and herbs. They collected late ripening berries, blueberries, sloe berries and sour red berries. Back at the cave they would sort according to kind. Chaiko least liked the sharp brittle feel of grass and the tediousness of getting the seeds out of their husks. The roots were easy: wash, clean, dry and store. Of the berries, what they did not eat they dried in the sun. Dawn hung bunches of herbs to dry, their pleasant though sometimes sharp odors filling a corner of the cave, making him sneeze anytime he went near.

Chaiko and Dawn were grateful that this part of their world had survived the great fire and now brought forth all this abundance for them to harvest. Chaiko hoped that his clan had found as bountiful a place to fill their needs. Dawn also quietly wondered how her people were doing. In a normal year they would be organizing the last big elk hunt before withdrawing to the winter caves. But this year?

It was still too early for nuts and cones, but there were plenty of mushrooms to pick. They conferred carefully and picked only the ones they were sure were edible. Dawn strung them on long loops hanging in the cave. Both were pleased with their progress and each handful and armful of foodstuff was an assurance against the winter.

These were good days for both of them. The weather smiled with balmy mildness, and the sun filled their world with golden light. The days passed in happy pursuit of harvesting the bounty of nature all around them. They had already collected and gathered enough for their needs, but because it was there, they collected to overflow. Chaiko dug more cairns in the back, lined them with mud, and hardened them with slow-burning fires. Soon cairn after cairn was full and carefully sealed against spoiling.

Because they were happy, the work got done as if by itself, amidst good humor, banter and lots of laughter. He would chase her as they gleaned seeds in the fields; she was quick but sometimes allowed him to catch her. And then with the sun warm on their skin, there would be sounds of pleasure.

Around the fire, as they each worked on their respective tasks, he on a new Falcon and talons, she on the feather capes, they talked cheerfully. He told her of his clan and introduced her to all the people one by one; she told him about her people and their customs. Her understanding of clan language was very good, though in her speech she insisted on using some peculiar twists of phrases that she could not or would not correct. Such as, "It would be nice, useful or valuable ..." to hide some imperative.

In fact, as her familiarity and fluency with his language improved, he began to note a few more peculiarities in her use of it. For instance, something like, "It would be nice to have fresh water with the meal," would generally earn his agreement. To the follow-up, "It would be nicer with fresh water," he would again agree. When this was in turn succeeded by, "It would be even nicer to have it with fresh water," he would begin to understand that some response other than just agreement was required of him. "It would be most nice ..." was rarely reached, because he would get the fresh water she had been obliquely requesting, or she would get it herself. Interestingly, as things got "nicer," her tone grew more exasperated.

Similarly, she had the odd habit of referring to herself as "this girl," or "this woman." Often an adjective got involved in this expression as well. "This girl is happy to do this or that." Chaiko understood this to be an agreement of sorts. But when she said "This worthless woman would dare not refuse ..." he found it more difficult to interpret. After a few experiences with like phrases, however, he concluded that the woman was indeed daring to refuse. In fact, when she applied words like useless, lowly or insignificant to the woman, it made him aware that often the opposite was intended and that he should be wary. The more insignificant she got, the more attention he had better pay to it!

In like manner, he found disconcerting to be referenced in the third person. She would say, "He can do this without difficulty." He would have to ask "Who?" And she would have to elaborate, "He who sits across the fire from this worthless woman." There was this word "worthless" again, he noted, pricking his ears up.

In later years, he was able to track these idiosyncratic usages to the moral and ethical constraints built into the language of the People-of-the-Elk. Her culture stressed harmony and non-confrontation to such an extent that all expressions were subjugated to it. Imperatives were cloaked in neutral-sounding, almost incidental, "It would be so nice to's." Self-effacement was used to eliminate gaining stature at someone else's expense. So worthless and useless were commonly used to describe oneself, less from a sense of modesty than from lowering one's own status in order not to appear threatening. Questions were phrased to avoid triggering refusal, and the third person was often used to avoid direct personal address. Competition was likewise discouraged, so comparisons were rarely made. Even an innocent-sounding declaration, "He is a good hunter," was considered bad form, for it obliquely also implied the opposite. When such statements were unavoidable, the form, "He has the reputation of being a good hunter," was preferred, for this was seen as a statement of consensual fact, which was better, calling on the authority of the whole group.

At first, her learning presented no problems as she was trying to survive in his language and the words were simple and basic. Her biggest problem was dealing with the directness of his language. He looked at her directly, addressed her directly, and asked her directly for things that left her no way out to avoid or refuse. To her ears, these sounded like ill-mannered demands and triggered within her a full linguistic prejudice against him. Her upbringing compelled her to accept and agree. This Chaiko saw as well-behaved and obedient. However, the more she developed appreciation and use of his language, the more her thinking in her language intruded into his. Once she explained and he understood her background, this was no longer such a big problem for Chaiko. He just saw these oddities simply as holdovers from her culture. It was harder for her to overcome her feelings of constantly being offended by his directness.

When she started thinking in both languages, things got even more confused and Chaiko had to learn a different set of rules for interpreting her use of his language. Was it the old Doan or the new Dawn talking? He soon learned that "it would be nice ..." or "highly desirable" still carried a disproportionate weight, and he had better heed them. Also "useless" and "worthless" remained key words to alert his attention.

Yet, on the whole, in spite of all the things that needed to be done, this was a quiet time for both of them and they continued to learn about each other. She was delighted when he talked about himself and his people; he readily accommodated her, telling all the long stories he could remember. Listening to these stories, little by little she lost her fear of his clan as she grew to understand them more, though her apprehension as to how they would perceive her remained. But if the days were good, the nights were better, warm in their bedding, clinging to each other, giggling and teasing. They had learned each other's responses, knew what pleased the other, and their play grew more assured, and then more varied. Though the newness had worn off and the painful intensity was gone, their love-making had matured, and become more deeply satisfying. They were so much more in synchrony, the heights they reached were mutual, and the peace that followed was more secure as they lay in each other's arms. In this sunny afterglow, both were healing. Chaiko forgot about the cripple inside, and saw himself with her eyes, growing with her esteem. And with each day and each night, Dawn felt herself becoming more beautiful, forgetting the skinny little girl she had been so afraid of. It was enough for both of them that they were together, mated for life.

They both looked forward to the nights, when all the work they set themselves for the day was done, and they could loll about the soft glow of the campfire, just talking or listening to the sounds of the night around them. At times he would feel expansive, and before he knew it he was telling her yet another story.

"In the old, old days before there was memory, a great bison roamed the plain. But there was only himself. Alone he grazed on the sweetest of grass, alone he drank of the clearest of waters, and alone he lay at night in the softest of places. He should have been a most happy beast, but was not, and knew not why. He saw the fox run in pairs, male and female. He could not count the number, so many rabbits were about. 'Why am I alone?' the bison bellowed, but received no answer.

"After many years the Spirit of the Sky grew weary of his bellows of frustration and asked the bison what he wanted. The bison said, 'I do not want to be alone.' The Spirit then said, 'You are not alone. Look about you, you are surrounded with life on all sides.' But still the bison shook his head objecting, 'But there is none like me.' And so the story ended." Chaiko smiled, pleased as if he had shared with her some great secret. But this left Dawn mystified and she asked, "Kaiko, what means this story?"

"It means what it says. It's a story we tell children." He shrugged his shoulders as if that explained it. Dawn struggled with herself. She wanted to ask him again what the story meant, but did not want to imply he had somehow misled her although she had noted the mischievous sparkle in his eyes. The conflict played out on her face, and Chaiko had to laugh, then said, "The bison must have gotten his wish, as their numbers darken the valleys nowadays." He sobered quickly and thought that the story sounded better in other years, when the valleys were full, not nearly empty like now. He tried another tale.

"There lived a squirrel in a cozy hollow between gnarled limbs of an ancient hickory tree. Year after year the tree withstood the winds of storms and changing of the seasons, but it was growing tired and very old. Its roots loosened and the soil slipped from its grasp. The squirrel worried about it, for it was his home. Then one day he searched through his lair, found the largest, the most perfect hickory nut he had and buried it at the foot of the old tree. He watched the shoot break through the soil, turn into a seedling, grow into a sapling and then into a young tree.

"One day in a storm the old tree fell and shattered into pieces on the ground. The squirrel went to the young hickory tree and sought entrance, but it barred its branches and denied him the way. 'Ingrate,' the squirrel muttered, but went away. The next day the squirrel came back and dug many, many holes right beside the young tree and into each he planted a hickory nut. Next it went to the river, soaked its tail in the water then shook the water over the seeds, day after day. And the seeds, too, grew into seedlings, then into saplings and into trees forming a dense press about the young tree, stealing its sunlight, blocking the flow of its air, drinking the water from its roots. Where there had been the old tree there now stood a forest of dense trees, the branches fighting each other, all interlaced so that the young tree did not know where it ended or began. And so ends this story."

Dawn was troubled. Was it she? Or was it he? Where was the meaning in this story? There was one, then there were many, in both stories. But what did that mean? "Kaiko," she began, but he waved her off, "It's just a story." She puzzled over it but looked suspiciously at the merriment in his eyes. As far as she could see, she was faced with two puzzles: one, the riddle posed by the stories themselves and two, why Chaiko was pestering her with them?

"He who looks for seeds should not be surprised if he finds some," he said cryptically, shaking with suppressed laughter. *He is going to drive me crazy with his stories*, she thought wrapping herself tight into the blanket, presenting her back to him. Still, the story stayed with her as she tried to make sense of it.

She would have been even more puzzled if she had known Chaiko's feelings on the matter. He would watch her intently, looking for signs of recognition that she understood, and rejoicing at every sign of it. In fact, he was envious, for questions were the mother of all answers, and there was no one to ask **him** profound questions now. He not only had to find the answers to what faced them, but first had to find the questions that gave birth to them. When he was young and first heard the story of the lone bison, and how the Spirit of the Sky filled the valleys with his kind, he had been glad, for all the clans were grateful for this bounty of nature that sustained them; and the numbers of them were vitally important. Years later, he began to feel a little regret for the uniqueness that the first bison had to give up, to trade in for its loneliness. He had gained a lot to be sure, but in the numbers had lost his individuality. Chaiko had felt the pull of the conflict very personally; his crippleness had made him unique and, like the first bison, he was fighting the loneliness. At the same time he was also aware of how much he had gained by being the way he was, crippled and alone, yet full of inner existence: life of thought, time of observation, light of understanding, qualities of experience he would not trade even for his missing leg. The loss of his leg had bought him a depth that a whole and intact Chaiko would not have found. A life crippled, such as it was, had become precious. Lately, he had been thinking of the bison looking for a mate, perhaps to raise a family. His focus shifted: first, to being alone, then to countless many, then to just two, mated and expecting new life. The thoughts filled him with peace.

As he said, the story was told to children, but Chaiko told it differently, without the inescapable, overstated value to be impressed upon the listener. He presented it in the form of a riddle; let the question awaken thirst for meaning, let the mental journey be the experience. So, somewhat envious he watched her, enjoying even the frustration she showed, for he knew it for a sign that such a keen mind as hers felt challenged to reach some resolution. He then wondered what answers she would find. He was proud, as well, of her growing awareness of the nuances of his language.

We learned from the wolves, he thought. For a time an adult wolf would chew the meat for the cub and regurgitate it on demand, but when the cub had grown, it was ready to hunt on its own and to have its own thoughts. Dawn was not a child, yet the new language she had had to learn had made her a child again. Now it was time for her to be on her own, let her chew on a few bones. In whichever language, he knew, she would do well.

Most nights they spent by the fire, lost in quiet contemplation, filled with much smaller thoughts, watching the ever fascinating ride of sparks into the sky. She would sometimes sing the songs she grew up with, and he would tell stories about his people. Often there was no need to talk at all. They would slip under the covers and the world would become very small and intimate. Afterwards they would sit by a small fire in front of the cave, searching the depth of the night sky, and finding figures in the stars.

"Look, there is a bull," he would say, pointing to some far off constellation in the myriad points of light.

"There is the Elk my people follow," she would point out in her turn. "There is his head with many branches of horns, proudly pointing to the migrating route the herds will follow. We believe they can read the stars, they hold their head so high, even when they run."

Though these days were beautiful, there were increasing signs that the season was advancing. The ripening all around, the flight of birds in the sky, even the behavior of insects, showed that autumn was coming and winter was not far behind. But in those bright sunny days, it was so easy to forget that summer did not last forever. Even a worrier like Chaiko was lulled into a peaceful complacency.

Chapter 33

The half-moon was coming to an end and all things on the to-do list were accomplished. They had stockpiled plenty of all they would need of meats, seeds, roots, firewood, grass and materials to work on throughout the winter. Indeed, they were well provisioned with more than enough to take care of just the two of them.

They were ready to go in search of the clan but were loath to interrupt the pleasant rhythm of these late summer days. They were content—let the rest of the world take care of itself. The weather continued soft and mild as if to make up for the earlier harshness of the drought. All around them was abundance, but they knew that just beyond in the burnt zone, circumstances were not so pleasant - there nature was struggling to catch up with a meager and shortened harvest.

Reluctant to break this idyll, they nonetheless decided on a short scouting trip to check the way ahead and do one more sweep of harvesting of whatever they came upon. They both took wicker baskets strapped to their backs and leather carryalls slung over a shoulder. Chaiko took Falcon and talons, while Dawn took her spear-digging stick. They set out north, north-east.

Soon they were in the plain walking through waist-high grass, with drying flowers and rattling seed pods everywhere. Often enough they had to go around clusters of thistles; their spikes had ripened to piercing points equipped with barbs that hung onto anything passing by. They saw patches of carrots, celery and onions. They marked the spot well for the return trip, since it made no sense to lug the things on the way out. However when Dawn discovered a rare wolf's foot, prized for its medicinal restorative properties, she stopped and collected half the plant leaving the other half to thrive for the next season. A little farther on, she spotted a patch of whiteroot, also a rare find, which she collected as well.

The day had started fresh, but quickly the air warmed up under a summer sun set in a cloudless sky. The heat glazed their skin and built

14 Stones

up in their bodies. Soon Chaiko was sweating, having to pause frequently to wipe the sting out of his eyes. Dawn, who loved hot weather, seemed not at all bothered by it. She hummed happily, but the happier she became the more miserable he appeared. Crossing the trickle of a watercourse, she dipped a soft skin into the slow moving water and wiped the back of his head and upper torso. The coolness felt nice on his skin. Then she drenched his hair and wrapped the wet skin about his neck. Refreshed he pushed on, but soon a cloud of insects enveloped his head, getting into his eyes and nose. One large bug somehow got into his mouth and he inadvertently swallowed it, causing him to go into a convulsion of spitting and hacking, but the bug was already ingested. When his wooden leg sank into the softness of a mole burrow, almost pitching him onto his face, he muttered dark musings of disrespect. When they next paused by water, he waved his hand, declining a similar ministration.

As they were passing a thicket, they flushed a rabbit out of hiding, the creature running a zigzag course toward the safety of some taller grasses. Chaiko raised Falcon, set a talon, drew and released in one smooth motion, but missed the moving rabbit by only a palm's breadth. He did it in play, satisfied at having come so close to a small moving target at such a distance. He retrieved the talon, checked it to make sure it was not fractured, cleaned off the tip, then slid it back into the deer skin holder.

In their wake a long line in the waving field of grass pointed back to where they had come from; ahead, the grass seemed an endless expanse, undulating with every breath of wind. Near the ground the grass was still wet from the dew and their legs were damp and uncomfortable with bits of grass fragments cleaving to them. Swarms of insects rose from beneath their feet and buzzed about their heads and bodies, seeking moisture and the salt of sweat. Occasionally, a bird erupted into the air with a noisy beating of wings amidst shrill cries of alarm. Grouse and pheasants with their speckled feathers blended into the profusion of grass stalks and ripening plants. The birds tried to hide as long as they could, even ran along tunnels burrowed in the dense grass, and only taking to the air reluctantly when every other choice was denied them. It was startling when a whole flock exploded into the air, communicating to each other their panic. A hawk high up in the sky banked sharply and swooped down toward the frightened birds, that in turn dropped into the grass to freeze motionless. It was not as uneven a struggle as it seemed; the ground birds were masters of camouflage and the hawk was reluctant to drop into the tall grass entangling its broad wings in the long stalks. The hunter knew it could not risk any harm to its wings.

The countryside was flat and open here with little to catch the eye. There were no hills and no trees, just grassland extending into the distance. They did come across a few depressions washed out by water draining the plain, in which more variety could be found. Dense bushes and a few trees hid in these hollows. From above they could look into these isolated little worlds, but skirted them seeing nothing to attract their interest.

Then, abruptly, they came to burnout again along a line that extended roughly north south. This had been a slow fire, a back burn creeping under the wind going the other way, reaching this far and no further. The line was sharply distinct. One side showed mature green, the burned side a sparse carpet of paler hue. Both Chaiko and Dawn were once again thankful that their island of green had survived. Here the grass on the far side had grown back in, fresh green still, but the seeds were small and as yet unripe. The few bushes that could be seen were mostly bare branches.

Chaiko strode into the burnt zone heading for a slight rise from which he hoped to see the way ahead, planning to turn back toward home again to collect all the things they had spotted.

From the shallow height there was not much to see. The plain was flat and featureless, and although the hills to the east looked closer, the distance still hid the details. Carefully tracing water-runs and dips in the land, Chaiko picked the path that they would take. They ate dried seed cakes and drank from their waterskins. Then, in the midday heat, they lay down and had a short nap, listening to the soothing whisper of the wind in the grass, and to the distant calls of some birds. The ground smelled of the sun, a rich clean scent of growth and ripening. The shadows stopped hiding behind the shapes they hugged and started lengthening again when the two of them roused themselves, picked up their load and headed back.

They collected a half basket each of red carrots from a fertile patch and Chaiko too, like Dawn, broke and left a piece of the root to grow back in. Then on to a patch of onions. Their hands soon reeked. They washed themselves in one of the many watercourses they crossed, the splash of cool water refreshing on their heated bodies.

They were halfway home again when Dawn paused to gather some dried flower tops, to keep bedding, skins and furs fresh and smelling good. He grumbled good naturedly that no man would waste time on that, but he appreciated her attention to these small details that made their lives more pleasant.

They came across a wet spot, full of reeds. On the sides there were tough broom grasses; they collected several bundles of the stiff stalks that were useful for sweeping the cave floor. Dawn was feeling satisfied to find all these things. She was better than he at spotting opportunities they came across, since Chaiko, often blinded by his sense of purpose, tended to overlook chance discoveries. As they progressed they got more and more loaded down.

They crossed a dry patch of grass and stirred up a confusion of crickets that went bounding off in all directions, colliding into them with hard little hits. Dawn told him how bad they tasted and how she had to eat them when she was on her own. Chaiko told her about grubs and how he disliked them. She countered that grubs with the proper seasoning were good, but Chaiko was not inclined to argue about it. Suddenly she stopped and pointed to a bee buzzing about, and the two of them kept a careful eye on it. The bee flew from flower to flower, but the nectar flow had ceased already, and it took the insect some time to collect anything worthwhile and fly back toward its hive. It flew a meandering zigzag course over the field of grass. The eyes of both grew tired at having to keep such a small moving insect in sight, and occasionally one would lose sight of it and call to the other to point out where it was. With painful slowness they worked back to a rock outcrop where they found the hive in a deep protected fissure. It was of a sturdy construction, a shiny beige mixture of beeswax and resin, impervious to the weather. There was a constant traffic of bees coming and going, a few bees on guard and a few fanning fresh air into the hive. When Chaiko's shadow fell upon the hive, a handful of bees buzzed angrily at him and one stung his cheek. Dawn pulled him gently back.

"How are we going to get the honey?" he asked.

"With patience." She gathered some dried grass, twisted it into a tight wad and held it against the smoldering ember she uncovered from the protective lump of clay. She blew until the wad of grass absorbed some of the heat and started to smoke. She approached the hive and blew the smoke directly into it. The sound of buzzing intensified and there seemed to be increased activity, but none attacked her as they had him. Then with deliberate care she opened the hive, reached in slowly to withdraw a handful of honeycomb, covered with bees. She gently brushed the bees away and put the comb into the pouch. She blew more smoke into the exposed hive then reached in again. When she had half emptied the hive she stopped. "It's best to leave them some to live on; then we can come back next year," she said in a quiet voice as they backed away. Amazing to him, she had not been bitten once. Confidence had to be part of it, he noted to himself.

She licked her fingers and allowed him to lick some, but slapped at his hand when he reached toward the pouch. No, honey was always a welcome gift wherever one went, and she wanted to make a good impression when she met his family. He was more inclined to consider his stomach first, but she was adamant. "It would be very nice not to go empty-handed." He could hear the limits in the "nice" again and noted that she had learned to stress the word more, so he would not overlook it.

When they returned to the cave she set about sorting and arranging all the things they had brought back. She loved organizing, and she had a whole cave to organize and reorganize, just for the two of them. And why not? These were her things and his things and she enjoyed counting their abundance.

Conversing by the fire, they decided to leave the next morning on the great expedition to find the clan, so they set about packing all the items that they would need. Dawn had all the gifts packed already, so she just added provisions and odds and ends. Chaiko had three Falcons and bundles of talons to take. He intended to travel light, but then she loaded him down with one of the bison pelts for their bedding. "Might as well be comfortable," she told him and her smile suggested sweetly the kind of comfort she was thinking about. "Comfort is good, very good," he said, warming to the idea.

All day Dawn kept busy with packing, but as night approached she grew more and more quiet as the realization sank in that they would soon have to leave her beloved cave. He held onto her, consoling, while she quietly cried against his chest. "Strange how emotional women can get," he thought to himself, conveniently forgetting that not so long ago he had cried, while she compassionately held onto him.

14 Stones

Every once in a while she would jump up to rearrange or secure something she had just thought of, then would return into his arms and resume crying. This on-off behavior amazed Chaiko, but he knew how attached she had become to the cave, her home. He felt vaguely uneasy that he did not have stronger reactions himself—after all, this was his home too. He had been fond of telling himself that his home was where the clan was. He now had to amend that; home was where Dawn was, and Dawn had chosen the cave as home for them. She, like a bird, was feathering her nest ... for her eggs? Could she be pregnant? He looked at her significantly but found no signs. "It will be nice to find the clan ..." and his pulse quickened till he realized it did so because he had used her sentence construction. He had to smile at that.

The next morning they shouldered their packs and started on the journey. To Chaiko's surprise, Dawn did not cry, though her face was set. She had spent a good part of the previous night crying, till he had to distract her with many kisses on her wet cheeks.

As at the start of any journey, the anticipation of the goal, of finding and meeting the clan, was high. Chaiko began to feel a budding excitement as he looked forward to seeing his family and friends. Dawn, too, was thinking of the clan: this great older brother Baer, so imposing, and his mate, Tanya, a little too perfect. It was going to be hard to live up to her measure, thought Dawn, somewhat intimidated by the idea of facing two such formidable people. On the other hand, it would be good to have the mother of the clan to turn to for support when needed.

The effort and hardship of travelling quickly pushed any expectations into the background. This was unfamiliar land, and Chaiko was fully challenged to find a clear path for them through the increasingly rugged terrain. The gently rolling view hid some unwelcome surprises. They came to a muddy track where the sludge sucked at their feet; they backed away in alarm before they could become trapped in the soft morass. Since there was no place to cross, they had to make a wide detour around its dangers. A little farther on, they came across a deep fissure in the ground; nothing seemed to grow on its sides and water was slowly collecting in the bottom. To Chaiko it looked as if the earthquake had ripped the land asunder here. Once again they were forced to go the long way around.

Then came a level piece of land mostly of gravel, sparse grasses and weeds, hard packed and unyielding. It seemed to go on forever and reminded Chaiko of the endlessness of the clan's forced flight from the drought. How bone-weary hard it had been then, and in comparison how easy now, for he had two legs to use, even if one was made of wood. It seemed so long ago; so much had happened since. In fact, though he still understood the Chaiko of then and remembered his pain, he was growing increasingly distant from him. To wallow in all that pain for some twisted confirmation of self-worth and sacrifice was unacceptable now, since he had tasted real pleasure and happiness. By his own efforts he was now a Hunter. With or without a leg he had learned to enjoy being alive. The missing leg had become insignificant. "The real person is on the inside," he told himself; still he remembered how low of spirit he had been in times past.

Now they were following a gentle water run and Chaiko was content to let it show the way. "Water cannot lie, it must go downhill," he prompted himself with the rote saying. There was little water gurgling in the main flow, but Chaiko could well imagine its power and surge after a good rain. The clear path of gravel and coarse sand was scoured by the high water rush, with mud and driftwood piled high in places. Occasionally, when the water disappeared under dense bushes, they had to work their way around the green obstruction. They came across few signs of grazing animals, but there was plenty of birdlife about, calling out noisily to each other, and flocks of them in the air. They passed through clouds of insects swarming about the wet spots; once they passed through a storm of butterflies, orange and black wings fluttering and flashing in the sun-filled air. There were countless numbers of them, and they amazingly kept together in that mass, moving slowly but in a purposeful direction. How, Chaiko asked, by sight? Has anybody heard the voice of a butterfly, calling out to another?

On the whole, the journey thus far was uneventful, just a motion of one foot moving ahead of the other. There were no great vistas, no dramatic rock formations to capture the eye; only gently rolling land sparsely covered by grass, slowly recovering from the passage of the fire storm, with the occasional watercourses draining the fields, forming their own little worlds.

Chaiko's mood was reflective, Dawn's was subdued. She quietly followed where he led. She must be missing her cave, her home, he thought. But she was thinking more about the coming meeting with his clan and the likely reception that would be afforded her. She was mostly concerned about how best to deport herself; she resolved to act out the quiet protocol of her people, a non-assertive, gentle repose.

By letting the water course lead them, they were stuck in the bottom of a shallow valley with little overview of the path ahead. Coming to a hill, he detoured up the steep slope, pushing the pace for both of them. His left knee ached with the uphill effort, but he kept stubbornly on. They were still too far from the hills to spot the smoke of a clan campfire, but the notion still drove him. By the time he reached the top and paused, he was quite out of breath. Dawn, carrying her heavy pack of gifts, was less than appreciative of the view. She said in her most oblique manner, "He who hurries must pause often to catch his breath. The Elk who runs the fastest tires the quickest. He who walks a straight path knows where he is going, but he who runs in circles chases himself."

He cast a baleful eye at her. He who? Chaiko wanted to know, he he or some other he? He knew of her people's custom of offering gentle reminders such as these, instead of criticisms which were not allowed in her culture. There was some kernel of truth in each, but he suspected that they lost some wisdom in the translation. By now he knew quite a slew of these. Today he was in no mood to be on the receiving end, and before she could add to his store, he retorted to deflect her, "He who would scratch, must first find an itch." She looked at him in surprise, but then rattled back, "He who itches but scratches not, saves for himself the scratching and the itching, for an itch that is scratched stays not still, but moves and hides, spreading the itch." Did that have to do with self-control, he wondered, or self-indulgence leading to more of the same? Eh what, he dismissed it; he did not want to get bogged down in her linguistic morass.

The view ahead showed little of interest. The hills were still far off. In the near distance, the valley and the spring continued on. They descended into the valley again.

The water run opened up to a sandy spot. On the far side, driftwood piled high to form a bulwark with sand and gravel collecting on its lee side. Noting the clear high ground, Chaiko thought it a good place for a camp, near water but well out of it with plenty of firewood all around. He pointed it out to Dawn who nodded. They passed the barrier then walked up on the gently sloping backside. Immediately they discovered a campfire. The stranger! was Chaiko's first thought. How old? was his next. The fire stones were bare, no moss, no lichen marks on the stone;

therefore, not long. The ash bed, crusted and packed by time and weather, showed no sign of vegetation taking hold, and the usual circle of twigs and branch ends that marked fires was not there. This told Chaiko that the fire had been occupied fairly recently, but before the firestorm had passed over, burning even the charcoal bits and pieces that were part of all fires that simply died out. Through narrowed eyes he looked about. Even after careful searching he found no bone pile of meals consumed and no convenient yellow flint pieces to confirm that indeed this had been the stranger's camp. Nothing but a smudge of tracks. Well, if they met up, he could ask the stranger what the long hollow piece of bone with the holes was for. He combed through the ashes but found nothing.

Dawn had built a fire in the circle of stones, and they rested in the smoke that kept the swarms of insects off them, but soon their noses were full of smoke and the meat they chewed had no taste. The sky darkened slowly overhead and stars emerged as a mysterious glowing cloud in the depth of heaven.

The next day Chaiko led the way along the water course, still thinking that water must flow downhill and that it would have to work itself down to the lower plains to the river, his and her River of Destiny. Both sides of this verdant green strip were eroded by the elements to an uneven and tortuous obstacle course. It seemed reasonable to Chaiko that the stranger must have followed the same route as well, and he kept a close look about for any signs of him. But if there were any, they had been obliterated by the passage of the fire. All trees were burned, charred hulks, but stubs of bushes were everywhere overgrown by new green. The fire must have been especially vicious here, he thought, driven by a wind that was channeled through the narrowness of the valley within a valley. Air also flows like water, he reasoned, often sharing adjacent pathways.

Ahead, he could see a larger expanse of green just before the green funneled between two converging ridges of rocks. With the water level so low, there was plenty of room for them to pass through the gap, and, as the signs indicated, so had many animals. This was a natural conduit in both directions. A recent traverse had been made by a family of warthogs of all sizes, leaving clear tracks in the soft mud. He could see where they had dug holes with their snouts looking for tasty roots and tidbits, and where they spent some pleasant hours wallowing in the mud. From the scat, he could tell they had moved through earlier in the day. They were somewhere up ahead and he cautioned himself to keep a sharp eye about, but a family of this size was bound to be noisy and give its presence away.

He also saw clear prints of deer, fox, rabbits and maybe a badger. On a sandy spot, he saw the smudged esses of a snake, tracing repeating patterns in the soft soil. Chaiko did not know if snakes migrated too. Were they not territorial? Most tracks seemed to be going the same way as theirs, and they could run into some. He followed the track of a coyote or a dog, noting that the right front paw left but a faint imprint and that the stride on that side was short, as if the animal were favoring an injured right leg. Then he came across what he least expected. Sticking out of the coarse sand was the half buried remnant of a spear, the wooden shaft burned to a short stub still attached to the yellow flint head, similar to the one he found by the moose. The stranger had passed through here, just before the fire. But why leave behind a spear of such workmanship?

Dawn did not understand his preoccupation and head-shaking, but waited for him patiently to lead them on. Hunters have such peculiar habits, she noted to herself. He came over and pointed out for her a straight track to follow while he ranged back and forth to the sides scanning the ground, most carefully. Like a dog, he sniffed excitedly at every sign and picked up every charcoal bit of wood. He zigzagged across their advance, his eyes darting over the ground. Then he uttered a sudden cry of recognition, echoing with triumph.

"What is it?" she asked running over to him. At their feet was another peculiar object of yellow flint attached to a bit of charred wood.

"An axe," he replied pointing. "This is the head with the cutting edge and the handle here burned away."

"An axe?" Her people had no tools like this. "What means this? This woman knows not an axe of this shape," she added hurriedly, lest her abrupt question be misinterpreted as questioning his knowledge.

He did not hurry with an explanation; he first looked about as if measuring distances with his eyes. "The Stranger was fleeing the fire through here. It was bad timing, as he would have been safer farther up the bare slopes. But here he was, and the fire must have been close behind him. There he threw away his spear, here his axe and probably all else that he had ... to escape." He looked ahead.

"Did he make it?" Dawn wanted to know.

"Not likely." Chaiko sadly shook his head. "Otherwise he would have been back to retrieve these valuable flints. But if he did ... his best chance lay over those rocks." He pointed ahead to a low ridge.

He quickstepped a straight path to the ridge of rocks, his eyes scanning the ground. On the other side were more rocks and a bare spot with grassland further on, but no sign of any stranger. Chaiko searched both sides but found no evidence of the fate of the fleeing man. Dawn was hoping that he had made it to safety. Chaiko shook his head, shrugged his shoulders, argued with himself. He had been so sure, but then where was the Stranger?

He waded into the sparse grass, tall primitive stalks rooted in the sandy soil. And that is where he found the man. Or, what was left of him. He knelt beside the remains, his hand hooked over his chin, mouth turned down sharply, his peoples' classic gesture of grief. Heart constricted, Dawn small-stepped over to him, hoping in spite of the mounting evidence. Then she, too, saw scattered bones, where scavengers had fought over the remains, a bone here, a bone there.

Shaken, Chaiko circled the spot taking in the sad tableau. The man must have sought shelter among the rocks, too late realizing that he could not outrun the fire, and risking the fire sweeping over him. Chaiko remembering his own experience, recalled the sudden intense heat that must have singed away hair and blistered skin and worse, scorched the lungs. From that second on, the man had slowly suffocated, gasping for air. The returning scavengers must have found his remains, dragged them to this spot and fought over each piece. Dawn was crying quietly for the man and his family, wherever he had come from. Soon she was crying for her family, to whom she was lost as well, like this man.

He must have been tall, Chaiko concluded, noting the long leg bones, and the long arms. A large man of broad girth, he further surmised, if those were his shoulder blades. He could not find the head though he made several increasingly large circles around the location. Solemnly he went back and embraced Dawn consolingly. It could have been them. Both had been saved by water, he by the River of Destiny and she by the curtain of a waterfall. There had not been enough water in the meager flow of the nearby stream to protect the Stranger.

14 Stones

Chaiko shoved his grief into an appropriate recess of his soul and set about with his bare hands to scoop aside the loose sand to make a shallow hole at the foot of the rocks. They gathered the bones and placed them in the makeshift grave, covered them with sand, and placed a few rocks on top. Chaiko uttered the words of sorrow the clan used on these occasions.

"... You need no food, nor shelter nor light for your eyes that see no more. Find a new way in the spirit world. Remember us to our families who have gone before, and tell them that the ... Standing-Rock Clan is still in this land."

Chaiko did not know how else to refer to the man's lineage or ancestry, so he adopted him into the clan to afford him the courtesy of a burial. Dawn stuck a few branches into the ground to mark the grave as was the custom of her people. She uttered a few words in her tongue, sadly spoken and deeply felt, for the Stranger they had never met but whose presence they had felt.

Chaiko realized, yet in detachment, that he would not have to worry about the stranger ever again. But he would have preferred not to have it end like this. Again, they each thought, it could have been me.

Ahead the hills, now much nearer, beckoned them on. Chaiko wondered where he should start looking for the clan in the myriad of valleys ahead of them. He longed to see them: Crow, Baer, Tanya and Lana. And Samar, the dried up old man, half-shaman, his mentor.

Chapter 34

The clan had made a temporary camp on a sandbar in the middle of a dried-up, gravelly river bed. Trees lined the near bank; the high water in the past had washed free some of the roots, creating small nooks to give them extra protection. They huddled about a modest fire, the few that were left: Baer, Tanya, Lana; Cosh and mate Ile and child Ido; Crow and his mother Emma, and Makar. The water bubbled joyously in its narrow course, but the mood about the fire was anything but cheerful. They all waited for Baer to speak but like most days now he had but few words to spare from his silence.

The past summer had not been kind to them. Once they lost Chaiko, they had pressed on to the east into the hills with the fire at their heels and the heat of it on their backs. Barely in time they found a zigzag goat path that led them to safety over the rocks into the next valley. Once on the other side, they had collapsed into heaps of exhaustion. The fire stormed behind them but could not leap the rocky mid-range ridge. The cliff still bore the smudge of smoke burned into its face, but it had stopped the advancing fire wall which burned itself out in a last fierce tantrum of frustration. The smoke driven by a west wind continued for two days more before it, too, succumbed, but the lingering smell of burning remained long afterwards.

At first everything looked just as Baer had promised them. There was cool shelter amongst the trees and bubbling brooks of refreshing clear water and streams full of fish. Pools and lakes filled the bottom of valleys, full of waterfowl. Trapped in the close confines of the many hills, swamps provided home to many more creatures: muskrat, raccoon, marten, weasel, fox and quite a few lynxes. On the meadows there was an abundance of game that had fled the drought and then the firestorm. The fire had followed several of the broader valleys that reached into the hills and burned everything in its path, but most of the interior valleys had been spared. The slopes were full of game and hunting was plentiful. The hunting parties returned loaded down with fresh kill, and one feast followed another, the fires roasting meat to feed the pent-up hunger of the clan.

14 Stones

However, the grasslands of the hills, nourished by a thin layer of soil over rock, were not meant to support such a heavy burden of grazing and with the sudden influx of so many animals, all of them foraging, the grassland quickly disappeared. Cropped to the roots, the plants dried up and the few pastures turned a sickly yellow. As the grass dwindled, so did the game. Hungry mouths then stripped leaves from bushes so that the bushes also died. Even the prickly spines of thistle could not protect its leaves, nor the sharp spikes of thorn bush defend it from the hunger about. Herds drifted in the dim light under the trees, gnawing at the sparse young growth, chewing at bark and devouring even the bitter ferns. Within weeks the bounty of the hills succumbed under the onslaught of so many mouths to feed. Soon, the flesh melted from the flanks of the game, and the hunters returned with shrunken fare. Concerned, Tanya shook her head in discouragement, how was she to flavor meat that was so lean?

The drinking places became muddy from many hooves sinking into the soft soil of eroded banks, churning up the muck of the stream bottoms. When the clear waters turned murky with the sediment drifting in the currents, the fish soon disappeared, too. Vainly did the bear stand in the streams, claws poised to swipe silver fish from the water. The shaggy beast grumbled in irritation as an empty stomach complained within. Vainly did the kingfisher cruise high above, and vainly did the otter dive into the deep. The fish were gone.

Because of the overcrowding and growing hunger, a strange malady took a toll on the deer, and they died en masse, but people were afraid to touch the carcasses they found on account of the disease. But other carnivores were not so choosy and gorged themselves without any apparent ill effects.

The antelope and elk did not like the closeness of the valleys—too many places for a predator to hide—and soon moved out to disperse on the highland pastures to the east. The grazing was sparse there, but it was a wide, open land, full of light and wind. Hunting forays there returned empty-handed.

Then there were the four-footed hunters, the coyote, fox, bobcat, wolf, hyena, lynx, cougar, and the occasional black and brown bears; they, too, had followed the game into the hills. Some of these proved faster and smarter than the humans, stealing meat right in front of them. The wolf howled in triumph, taunting, "Manchild, manchild, will you not learn?" The cougar spat out its warning and challenge. Baer told his men to watch the animals and learn from them. The hunting methods in the hills were different from those used in the plains. Greater stealth was needed, as there was no soft carpet of grass to absorb the noise of approach, and every hillside gave back the tiniest of echoes. The feet needed eyes of their own to pick a silent path through rocks, twigs and undergrowth.

It seemed to Baer that more of the hunters survived than the hunted could support. Samar tried to explain that the hunted reacted by instinct and were quick to seek safety in flight, whereas the hunters first studied their prey, learning to adjust to them. The hunters grew cunning in their need; they planned their attack.

Driven by the fire, each reacted according to its nature. The hunted flew in the heedless panic of the moment as was their nature, even to their doom. The hunter looked ahead, recognized and avoided the death trap closing in. Nonetheless, plenty of hunters had perished in the flames that had consumed the plains, but still, in proportion, more of them survived than the grazers. It was also the hunters that recognized their present predicament of shrinking food supplies and drifted away to the east in search of better hunting.

Baer remembered Chaiko telling him that deer were passive, governed less by a sense of purpose, merely reacting to the dangers around them. It was the wolf that looked about, measured what it saw and made plans accordingly. "We must be like them," Chaiko had said, "and learn from them. Do not be discouraged by failure; it is a better teacher than success. Watch the wolves." The wolves were leaving, Baer realized, should they leave too? "Chaiko, Chaiko, why were you not faster?" Soon, all the grass was gone, and the grazers became weak with hunger and died or moved east. The clan did not follow them into the wide open space of the highlands, since the animals were much too dispersed and could see from afar the humans approaching. The clan tried for a while to survive on smaller game, rabbits, rodents, birds and fowl, but after a time these, too, disappeared. The clan could now appreciate more fully the fertility of the plain and the yearly renewal brought by the migrating herds.

The People of the Standing-Rock Clan were disheartened. Baer himself was not the same; he had never regained his energy, and suffered a relapse after some infection further robbed him of strength. Moreover, he never seemed to have recovered from Chaiko's death. Tanya and Lana were desperately trying to restore him to health, strength and vitality, but such was beyond their prowess. Only a sense of duty kept him leading, but there were grim lines on his face, frozen lines of pain and a growing hopelessness. Late in the summer Samar died, quietly slipping away in his sleep, the thin body even more wasted by the clan's poor diet. As feared, there was nobody to take his place. Baer missed the old man, for with him gone, there was nobody left who truly understood that the clan needed more than just food and shelter. They needed hope, of which there seemed to be less every day. Soon after, Uma and then Ela's baby boy died, and with them another piece of the past and a piece of their future was buried.

Something had to be done. Baer, Tusk and Cosh conferred long. Their food supply was disappearing before their very eyes and soon there would be nothing left. It was presumed that the plain was still bare in the aftermath of the fire and it was argued that it would take at least a year to recover. The general hope expressed was that the herds would be back next spring. After all, it was stamped into the nature of the beasts to return. So the clan needed a safe haven for the winter. It was clear that the hills could not provide for the whole of the clan. "The clan must follow the lead of the wolf and look to the east," Baer proclaimed, his heart contracted in pain, hearing himself echo Chaiko's thoughts. Even dead, Chaiko could help him, he realized, if he could withstand the anguish of remembering. He also recognized that in his present condition he could not go east with the rest as he would slow them down too much.

After much discussion it was decided that the clan would split up and a group led by Tusk would try to find new hunting grounds farther to the east beyond the highlands. The highlands themselves were deemed too inhospitable to sustain them. They would try for the land of the Lesser-Bear-Claw Clan. Baer and his family and Cosh, who refused to leave his friend, would stay behind with Crow, Makar and Emma to help. It was hoped that the nearby valleys could support the reduced numbers. After all, it was argued, they had to survive the winter only; the spring would bring a new abundance to the plain and the whole clan could return. Or so it was hoped.

Amidst great sorrow and a tearful parting the clan split. Tusk came to say farewell, promising to send news back as soon as would be practicable. He was most reluctant to leave Baer and until the last offered to carry Baer himself all the way if need be. He had learned the meaning of clan, togetherness, and having once learned it, he was loath to violate its precepts. Still, there was no other way.

Baer roused himself and tried to formulate a new vision for them all, but mostly to remind them of who they were. "There to the west are the plains, the home of the bison, the horses, the asses and the antelope. The gazelle and the gemsbok drink at the same waterhole. Friend and foe share the air and water of the plains. That was the hunting range of the People of the Standing-Rock Clan. That is the heritage our fathers left to us, so that we can claim it for our children as our fathers have before us.

"The fire burned up the land, dried up the water courses, and drove the animals away, but it could not burn our memories of the land, neither could it destroy the history of our people. No fire can steal our rights to the land. Next spring, of the year to come, the plain will recover. Once again the waters will flow, fed by spring rains; the grass will grow fat again; the birds and animals will come back, and bison ... will cover the valleys, as numerous as grass; and once again the people will return to claim their land ... and hunt where their fathers hunted and where their children will hunt.

"Go now, find safety in the east; find food to feed yourselves; strengthen yourselves for the return journey. But take in your heart these memories to guide you back. Forget not the pathways that will lead you back. Know always that the home of the Standing-Rock Clan is there in those plains ..." Feelings choked off his voice. In a flash of memory, he remembered the first claim of bison he presented to the circle of hunters for their approval. He remembered not long after showing with pride the secret of this land to his new mate. He remembered the joy of his young daughter struggling on his shoulders in excitement at the sight of bison in huge numbers coming over the hill, down to the river, pushing through the water to the other side. Hour after hour, a constant procession of shaggy beasts had passed in review. Was there ever a better land anywhere?

"Those of us who stay will guard the claim of the clan that no man dare say that we left this land empty and unoccupied, free for the taking." Baer tried to give them a bit of reassurance that in their absence, their claim would be safeguarded. No, the land would be still here, but would they also?

Tusk and a sorrowful group departed, disappearing into the line of hills. Subdued, the remainder sat in silence around the fire, afraid to ask the question they were all thinking: "Will we ever see them again?" Baer was inconsolable, his mouth twisted into a bitter grimace. Why lead into darkness and desolation? Why lead at all when he could not see the way? Doubt gnawed at his remaining sense of purpose. He closed his eyes against the searching glances of the rest.

With fewer mouths to feed, providing for the remnant of the clan became easier. Cosh, Crow and Makar did the hunting, and they returned with enough food to eat, but not enough food to put away for winter. So for three moons they subsisted.

At one point Baer sent Cosh to scout out the plain, but he dared not leave for long, going no farther than the burned-out valleys; and though he saw the plain shimmering green in the distance, he did not see any movements of herds or game. He brought the discouraging news back to camp.

Even though most of the grazers had disappeared from the valleys, the scavengers and the killers of the night as well, the land could not simply renew itself in their absence. It had already been robbed of its next season's fertility, because the seeds and fruits were already eaten and grasses cropped close to their roots. The open wounds tramped into the soil gaped, weeping mud into the streams, and drying in the air. It would take seasons for the damage to heal, Cosh concluded, but kept such disheartening thoughts from Baer. He, too, must heal.

Tanya, Lana, Ile, Ido and Emma went searching for roots but found empty holes dug up by bear, warthogs, badger and groundhogs hiding deep in their dens. The women looked for seeds but found few that had not already been collected by birds, the remaining deer and even insects. Nuts and cones were jealously guarded by squirrels and chipmunks and rodents of all kinds that still survived in hiding. Everything was edgy and shy of its own shadow. These were the survivors, the most prudent of their kind. There was little left over for the hunters and the gatherers. A handful of mushrooms was rejoiced over; a tough guinea hen celebrated.

There were few smiles about camp. The two young people, Crow and Lana, were suffering the hardest under this tyranny of constant worry and apprehension. The optimism of youth chafed against the restraint of the prudent, so that they escaped whenever they could into the privacy of the forest to steal a little time for themselves, even daring to laugh, away from the gloom of the grownups. More and more they sought out each other's company and the bond between them deepened. Once in a while they talked of Chaiko, sharing their grief in hushed tones lest Baer should hear. There were many tears in remembrance. Though Lana was too young yet for Crow, he was resolved to wait for her to grow up; they already had a secret understanding between them. In their eyes they were already mated; they had so promised each other. They each swore a heavy oath, Lana on the lives and love of her parents and Crow on the spirit of his dead friend. "May Chaiko come back to claim me if ever I look on another." Then they both cried.

Baer never talked about Chaiko, but Tanya so wished that he would. He kept it all inside. It was part of his helplessness now, that he had been powerless to save his brother. What was the use of leading when one had to drive people from their cave, across an open and desolate land, into the hills to starvation? What was the use of leading if he could not even save his brother, his only kin? Why lead when every step brought more misfortune and suffering? He had lost vision for himself and his clan. He now led out of habit and out of habit they followed him. But everybody's confidence in him and in themselves was sadly diminished.

When he looked at each decision he had made, it appeared correct and reasonable, yet the results were a mockery of all his careful thinking, weighing alternatives and choosing priorities. The truths he lived by— reason, unselfishness, balance—were suddenly turned into lies. The doubt festered and grew, robbing him of all confidence. It seemed no matter where he turned and the clan with him, they could not avoid all these misfortunes befalling them. Samar was not there to tell him different and redirect his efforts or shake him out of his self-absorption. Baer felt that his body had betrayed him ... and that Tusk would make a better leader than he. He was tired of the burden of leadership, still it did not occur to him to step down and allow himself to be led by someone else. Who else was there anyway?

Night after night around the fire there was somber talk of food and winter, then more about food, without ceasing. Crow was tired of it— he wanted to shake them all—this was his life and he wanted a little cheer mixed in with all this misery. It was not fair that it should happen now when he was on the threshold of happiness. In a man's life this was called the Looking-Year, dedicated to the pursuit of finding one's mate. Most men looked back on this time as the most memorable of their lives, and here he was stuck in the mire of the craving of empty bellies. He wanted to do something, strike out at something, but found no other target than himself, and he blamed himself for leaving his friend to face the fire alone to die. Only Lana remained the one constant source of delight, and he hung on to her possessively.

Tanya tried to keep everything in balance. She tried to build and strengthen Baer's spirit, knowing that if she could rouse him to fight off his lethargy, he would be so much better off, and with him, all of them. She tried to present a cheerful face to Lana, and to show interest in all her activities and dreams. She tried hard to listen to Cosh and help him reason, as Baer would have in former days. Trapped in her loneliness, she remained quietly available to every member of the clan. In her concern for others, she forgot her own needs, and this self-denial had become such a habit that she now had a hard time even recognizing her needs. But this she knew; above all else, she needed the mate of her youth healthy and strong, once again the leader. Even a remnant needed to be led.

As for Lana, the misfortune around her had made her thoughtful, and she appeared more mature than her years. She had become quiet, though once in a while her former sparkle and exuberance showed through to her mother's delight. She had her father's determination and keen mind, and her mother's dignity and quiet endurance. The years would give her the wisdom to use these abilities to the full, but right now she, like Crow, was looking for some carefree happiness in the midst of a drab existence. Thrown together as they were, they become dependent on each other's company. She was immensely fond of him, but did not yet understood the hunger that lit his eyes and that he kept under restraint. Still in her mind, too, they were mated, mutually and most solemnly promised to each other. This was much deeper than a young girl's fancy and had the possessive quality of a mature woman laying claim of ownership upon her mate. Tanya found this to be both endearing and disconcerting. She was but eleven, still a child!

Cosh was the only one not caught up in the general gloom. He never worried about the future. He held that the present was enough in itself to worry about, and in his experience, worry never helped anyway. Yet he knew that worry was a large part of Baer's life and above all else he respected Baer. He did not find it incongruous that Baer was under-functioning. To him, Baer simply needed a rest and was entitled to it.

But Baer needed more than rest. He needed to be awakened to how much the others needed him. Their hopes rested in his strength and leadership. But pain often silenced him and he sank further into himself. He had hardened to the pain but likewise had become callused to their needs and feelings, inured to their reproachful looks and uneasy exchange of glances near him. Then, in the early morning discomfort of pain and irritation, he would lash out around him and make Tanya cry in despair and cause Lana to run off hurt and discouraged. Probably into Crow's arms, he would think with disdain, but he would soon repent of his harshness and resolve not to do so again. His melancholy, however, would soon mire him once more.

Then one day, toward the end of the summer, as the few geese that were left took to the air for practice flights, Baer was sitting alone by the fire, brooding. The rest were scouring the countryside for something to eat, and anything to put away for the winter. The air was growing heavy and the sky was darkening with black clouds sealing in the valley. The wind freshened and soon rain was pelting the ground. Thunder approached and lightning flickered high above. Baer was lashed by the sting of rain. He covered his head with a fur but made no attempt to escape the wetness soaking him. In his present mood, it was no less than he deserved.

A clap of thunder rumbled directly overhead and his chest reverberated in uneasy resonance. Lightning flickered in the rolling turbulence of the clouds and the world was obliterated momentarily by a white burst. The glow penetrated through his closed eyelids. The sky flickered and rumbled, the air shook and danced with the unleashed violence of the storm, building up the rage in him. Baer shook his fists at the sky and screamed into the wind defiantly, angry at the world, but most of all angry at himself. "Why did you lead your people here to suffer? Why did you bring your family here to starve? Why did you let the clan split?"

The wind howled in his face and he howled back at the fury of the elements. The sky lit up white again, and blue light arced above, then stabbed down hitting the closest tree only a scant stone's throw away. An electric glow surrounded the tree and a ribbon of blue snaked along its massive trunk, at the base separating into strands that followed the roots into the soil. With a loud crack and burst of smoke, the tree exploded from within, revealing the heat of fire burning at the core. Limbs came crashing down. The power of the lightning bolt radiated out from the tree into the surrounding ground. In the denseness of the soil the strength of the sky dissipated rapidly, but still, when the unseen force reached Baer, it jolted him and threw him flat on the ground. His breath seized, his heart stopped. A rigid tremor shook his limbs and his face contorted into an ugly grimace. All his muscles tensed up, and his body arched off the ground. The power receded, then faded away altogether. His heart started up sluggishly, skipped a beat, then fluttered uncertainly in his ribcage. As he struggled for breath, he lay helpless, his eyes wide open, staring at the ominous clouds passing overhead, backlit by the flicker of lightning higher still. The rumbling quieted slowly as the storm moved off leaving him frozen, stretched out on the ground. At first his limbs were quite useless; a numbness sat on his bones and his muscles refused to obey him. Only slowly did control and movement return to him, and a growing ache, as every muscle complained at being over spanned. The trembling persisted a while yet. But when the others returned he was calm and could explain to them in matter-of-fact tones the shredded tree smoldering on the ground. Next morning there were dead worms all around and beetles still crawled about in confusion.

Much as the storm was gone, Baer's anger had gone, and he felt free of his resentment and bitterness. Though he never told anyone about it, he felt reborn in that lightning strike. Strange, he thought, the lightning could easily have taken his life; instead it gave it back to him. He also felt a certain pride that it took the whole sky falling on him to awaken him, but he remonstrated with himself for this misplaced sentiment; after all, he did not want to turn into another Tael. But if it took the storm to jolt him out of the bondage of his self-doubt, it was his love of Tanya and Lana that gave him new direction afterward. He saw that to help them he must first help himself. He grew even more quiet, but kept a close look about him, gradually realizing how much they all had been transformed. Perhaps he had changed the most, giving in to pain and attending more to the complaints of his body than to what had been happening to his people. Well, there was always time to change. Had Chaiko or his father said that? Baer was not sure, but now was the time to put that wisdom to the test. He moved about a little that day and more the next, each movement testing the limits of pain he could endure, loosening some of the cramp of his muscles. Cautiously he shuffled about, favoring his hurt side. To his great relief, with each day he found the pain receding. He also realized how much his pain had called attention to itself and had taken over his life. But with something else to occupy his mind, the pain was pushed aside. With the exercise his muscle tone improved, and the stiffness of his joints loosened; he slept better and recovered some appetite and interest in life. Then one evening he surprised everyone including himself by laughing out loud at an inane joke Crow was trying to tell. After that everyone noticed and was heartened by his improvement.

Baer still found that everything took so much conscious effort to accomplish. The things that had come to him so easily before, now required real effort of will, but still, day by day, he could feel himself making gains, though so slowly that he had to look back days to notice any progress. To keep himself struggling onward, he borrowed from all around him: from Cosh his loyalty; from Tanya her tender consistency, so that he never snapped angrily again; and from Lana her sense of joy and daring to dream even in their strained circumstances. He recalled Samar's quiet patience; but most of all, he borrowed from his dead brother. He remembered clearly how hard it was for a cripple to move about, always refusing to be a burden to anyone. Even the leader has to learn from those around him, sooner or later. Why, he probably could learn something from Makar, though he would be hard pressed to name it. Irrepressible humor most likely.

His love for his family and sense of duty broke through his depression and lifted his mood. With a new attitude, his responsibilities, which had recently been such a burden, now nourished and strengthened him, as they had before. Tanya fed him the most tender pieces of food to reawaken his hunger and his taste for life. He made gains every day, not as much as he hoped, but enough to encourage him and those around him. His vitality returned before his strength did, but Tanya felt the most reassured when in spite of his pain, he took her in his arms and in the quiet and darkness of the night, made love to her.

After that, he improved steadily, though the tenderness in his side remained and his strength was still limited. He made more of an effort to participate with the others, and even made short forays into the forest to look for anything edible. Most of their time was consumed with foraging in the depleted valleys. Lana found a rock face full of nests, and she and Crow clambered onto the precarious ledges to raid them. Most nests were already empty; the few eggs they found were very late.

14 Stones

They had moved camp again, as they had to quite often, to find new grounds to glean. The sandbar was a clean place to set up camp and the adjacent gravel bed yielded a plentiful harvest of crawling things under the stones. All of them were reluctant to eat this sort of menu, except Cosh—to him, food was food regardless of the form it came in. Of course, he had his preferences, but if bison was not available, he would not turn down anything edible. He could eat ants, even fire-ants with equanimity. So they all learned to eat these lowly creatures, all, that is, except Makar.

Lana was the most relieved of all, and her happy glow in response warmed all of them, but especially Crow. The two young people acted out an idyll that forgot all their troubles and seized the moment for some time for themselves. Off they went into the woods or to the river bank. Emma looked proudly after her son, saw in him the hunter he promised to be, and approved of the relationship between the two young people wholeheartedly. Ido was less sure and felt deprived of her friend's closeness, having to stay by the fire with only Makar for company.

The season was advancing. The mornings were turning chilly and the water smoked in the dawn's light. Emma stayed close to the fire, her joints feeling the approach of cooler weather. The young people led by Lana returned with an armful of cattails which they cleaned and cooked into a rather indifferent soup that was praised by Tanya, who needed to stretch their meager provisions by whatever means possible. There followed various adaptations differently received: moss soup, bird-nest soup, onion soup and plenty of rhubarb. But even Tanya balked at the green slime Lana collected off the surface of a nearby pond.

When the geese started their flight south, and flight after flight of them passed overhead in their orderly formations, the change of season was imminent. Baer and Cosh talked, long and earnestly, debating their situation and Tanya listened in. They had not enough provisions, not enough meat, not enough grain and not enough of everything they would need for winter. Without food, they could not stay here. It was decided, therefore, to leave on the morrow and follow Tusk to the east in easy stages, now that Baer had recovered so much of his strength. Cosh felt that even on the open plateau of the highlands the hunting could not be worse than the picked-over ground here. With the decision made, their future became less uncertain and they all looked forward to the next day's events.

Chapter 35

After living for moons on a wide open plain, the sudden closeness of the hills and the narrow valleys was constricting for Chaiko and Dawn. The horizons they were used to were now hidden from view behind steep slopes. At every turn there was a built-up expectation of danger that might be lurking at close range. Both Chaiko and Dawn, taking her cue from him, were edgy and nervous. The advantage he held with Falcon was most effective at long range, but here a short surprise lunge from close cover could overwhelm him before he could bring the weapon to bear on any threat. Thus he held Falcon at the ready with a talon nocked in the string, his eyes darting about the confines of their path.

They had been moving up a valley that had not been touched by the fire, the first since they had left the green belt about their cave. Looking around here at the unmarked trees in full foliage made Dawn wish she were home again. Under the trees, lush ferns and broadleaf plants were growing through a soft carpet of decay. Here the trees did not crowd each other because the shallow soil could not sustain the denseness found in the plains. Shafts of sunlight easily penetrated through the cover and reflected off boulders and cliff walls. Moss and lichen clung to the shadow side of rocks and embraced with enthusiasm any fallen branch or tree.

Chaiko was concerned. They had seen few signs of animals, and even the usually ever-present birds were wary of them, acting like a quarry that recognized its hunter. They came to a bush with a few berries on it, much too few, and Chaiko went closer to investigate. He saw the bare stems where the berries had been and his heart skipped a beat. This bush had been harvested. There were faint smudges of tracks on the ground. It had been an unusually thorough harvest with only a few dried up berries remaining. All the branches, however, were not broken, unlike the case with bears whose habit was to rip off a branch and feed at their leisure.

They came to a brook trapped between giant boulders, splashing from pool to pool. They followed it, Chaiko hoping to discover a campsite near, or at least to cross some tracks to give him a direction to follow. It was tough going because of rocks littered haphazardly about, dense bush growing unexpectedly across their path, or a tangle of driftwood repeatedly blocking their ways. Branches, spiky weeds and thorn bush, hard to avoid in the constricted path, scratched their skin and caught on their coverings. Often they had to squeeze through a whole mess of them. Then on a level section of the track, as they passed through a dense stand of pines, Dawn paused with a thoughtful frown on her face. "What?" he finally asked when he could not read her intent.

"Do you not see it?" she asked.

"See what?"

"That's just it, there's nothing ... when there should be something there."

Puzzled and intrigued, Chaiko scanned the shadows on the thick carpet of pine needles for something that was not there. Not surprisingly he saw nothing; still he had grown to respect Dawn's powers of observation and kept looking. Then he, too, saw the nothing. Where there should have been a litter of pine cones, there were but few old ones, soggy with decay. He sucked noisily through his teeth, a habit he indulged in when he was concerned, and his face was etched with a deep frown. Dawn tried to read into the worry lines, but he just shook his head and continued on.

A little further, a huge tree had fallen across their path. It must have overturned many years ago, and now was deeply covered with moss. Giant half-circles of poisonous fungi also took the opportunity to feed on the decay beneath. They ducked under the massive trunk and turned to look at its other side. Here the moss had been stripped off and the soft pulp torn away, exposing the orange core. "Someone or something was looking for grubs," he said with a shudder of distaste. "Grubs are good with the proper seasoning," Dawn chimed in automatically.

From then on Chaiko paused often to examine stripped bark on a tree, an overturned stone or holes dug in the ground. He was wearing a perpetual frown.

By midday they stopped for something to eat beside a large pool. He chewed absently on his meal without tasting it, his face furrowed in concentration. Then he picked up a piece of rock and threw it into the water. She followed his gestures, recognizing that he was fighting some discouraging conclusion, and worry flooded her. "Kaiko ..." she started, but he held up a hand to ward off her question.

******

Baer was up and about feeling more energetic than he had for many days. Having exercised with a little effort every day, he could feel his strength slowly returning. His side still hurt at times, but he set his mind to accept the pain instead of fighting and fearing it. It had shrunk to a dull throb with only an occasional burst of sharp pain that coursed through his entire body like lightning. He thus found himself no longer a prisoner of pain and was able to move about with more ease. The others noted this improvement with the delight of resurgent hope, but they also saw his face shut down suddenly as he abruptly froze in mid-movement. They froze with him, too. At these times Tanya hurried to his side, pretending not to hurry, pretending unconcern.

The night before it had been decided that they could no longer delay but must start their way east to join Tusk and the clan that had gone before. The weather signs were changing to indicate the passing of the season. Baer considered himself fit enough for travel and promised to take it in easy stages, not to overexert himself.

Around him, in a bustle of activity, the rest were packing what belongings they had. There was little to pack, for they had thrown everything away in their flight to save themselves from the fire and had accumulated precious little since.

Tanya rolled up and tied a bundle of grass mats. They would be useful wherever they ended up. Lana, Crow and his mother were wrapping each piece of their remaining precious meat into individual wraps of leaves and packing them into wicker baskets for the journey. Makar, Cosh and his family were sorting through some sticks, choosing the best for spears and digging sticks. These were crude implements and Cosh wished they still had Chaiko's expertise with wood. Chaiko,

14 Stones

Chaiko ... he thought sadly, the pain stabbing at his heart. A little later, he, Crow and Makar left to scour one last time the valley they were about to leave, hoping for something more substantial than lean rabbit. Even Cosh was getting sick of stringy rabbit meat. When was the last time they had had a delicious roast of bison, steaming hot, dripping with juices? It was not his nature to strain against the realities of the here and now, but he dreamed about fresh fat meat.

Preparing for anything was preferable to waiting out the luck of the day. Packing gave Tanya purpose that she had lost in the last little while. She had a certain light, heady feel from too little to feed a shrunken stomach, which she mistook for cheerfulness, and as was her habit she unconsciously started to hum. She would have been mortified had she realized that everyone around her knew of this trait to broadcast her contentment. Across the fire Baer smiled quietly to himself reminiscing about how much she had hummed when they were first mated.

Lana came rushing up. "Mommy, can we take this?" she pleaded, showing a highly colorful rock sparkling with small embedded crystals. Tanya regretfully shook her head and explained gently that they must travel light and every bit of weight grew heavier with every step taken, but promised that the very first thing they would do when they got to where they were going would be to go hunt for rocks ... much prettier than the one she held, for it was told that rocks were especially pretty where they were going. "Really, Mommy?" Lana laughed then ran off on some new happy pursuit. It was so good to see and hear her daughter laugh. They had been glum for much too long. And Baer was recovering; the thought coursed through her, warming her. Still, she noted with a tinge of sadness that her daughter was growing up and that with each passing day, she had fewer glimpses of the little girl she had held in her arms, rocking and singing to her, the child who was still interested in pretty rocks.

She had noted with some concern Crow's growing interest, possessiveness and protectiveness toward her daughter, protesting to herself that Lana was much too young, not yet twelve, but had then decided to let the young people have some joy in each other's company. There was little else to look forward to, aside from the trip they were about to undertake. She wished Chaiko were here. She missed him for her mate's sake, then for her daughter's sake, and then on her own account. Chaiko could always find something encouraging to say—to a cripple, anything outside of himself looked brighter. But she dared not talk about him, for Baer grew instantly quiet and retreated inside himself, and Lana's eyes flooded immediately with tears. Chaiko was dead, but not having buried his body they could not let go of him in their minds.

By midday the packing was done and they sat down to a meager meal of stringy gull meat, supplemented by pulpy rhubarb and handfuls of spinach. People ate glumly, making sour faces at the bitter taste. Their stomachs were filled but their appetites were not sated. A swarm of minuscule flies drifted through the group like a cloud. Their days were numbered, as the days got colder.

******

In the late afternoon, Chaiko and Dawn were laboring up a steep slope to cut across to the next valley, as this one had given them but few signs of either animal or human life. The path they followed was an obvious animal track that showed no recent sign of them. The wilderness was closing in on the faint trail, barely discernible now.

Dawn followed patiently, just a step or two behind. It was up to him to lead them, and she observed him as he constantly thought his way across the land picking the best way. Who would have thought that one could walk on thoughts? Her language had an expression for soaring thoughts, but not one that gave feet to thoughts, she mused, momentarily distracted from their anxieties. She had nothing to do but to follow and watch her mate. The deepening worry lines of his face, however, increased her apprehension. What was he so concerned about? If the clan was not here, they would be someplace else, and eventually they would find them. Still, when she looked at him, her chest constricted at the worry he did not share with her. She was too well mannered to ask without an opening.

They reached a crest of the sharp ridge that separated the valleys and looked over the view spread out in front of them. It was a longish valley with a fair-sized pond at the bottom, hemmed in by trees and the surrounding slopes. The eager anticipation on Chaiko's face quickly turned to set determination as his eyes failed to find what he was searching for; it was not a pleasant expression. They climbed down the trail used by animals more sure-footed than they, and finally arrived at the valley floor tired, their leg muscles aching. They reached the pond and collapsed gratefully on a narrow pebble beach. On the opposite side Dawn watched a waterfall tumble from among high jutting rocks, cascade down the steep valley wall, hit the rocks below in a cloud of drifting mist, then finally foam the surface of the pool. Its rumble reached them from across the pond. Chaiko paid it scant attention, doing some rumbling of his own. Why do men take so long to come out and say what is bothering them? Dawn asked herself exasperated, but she was a good mate and finally inquired in a concerned voice what the matter was.

"We have been walking through these hills for days and nary a sign have we come across." He waved his arms in emphasis. "They should be here, but there are no signs on the ground to read and lead us, no smoke in the sky to beckon us and give us hope." Dawn could not understand his dissatisfaction; there were still lots of hills left to search, unless ... there was something else.

There was something else. "The valleys we crossed are stripped of everything edible. We have seen no game to hunt, except for a few birds, and the streams are empty of fish. Every root is dug up, every ear of grass harvested. Mushrooms, snails, frogs, everything." He paused glumly, letting the import of his words sink in.

"Are they starving?" she asked, surprising herself in coming so quickly to the point.

"It would seem so," Chaiko muttered, his face still set. What else? Dawn wanted to know, but resisted the urge to ask. He chewed furiously on a stalk of grass, his mind working. "There's not enough food here to feed the clan." He hesitated then launched into the worst of his fears. "They might have left these hills. Moved on to the north, or even to the east. Hoping to find more food, for there is little here."

The clan on the move? Going possibly away from them? Would they need to chase them to someplace else? Their goal had always been the hills, but now, somewhere else? To go still farther from their cave? This was disturbing news indeed.

"Kaiko..." In spite of herself, Dawn's voice trembled. She wanted to be strong for her mate.

"We came here not to see the hills but to find the clan." He left the words hanging in the air.

She took a deep breath and held it, to push the emotions back down. "And find them we shall," she said with more determination than she really felt. He searched her face and nodded but once, definitively, to finish any further discussion. He had spoken and so had she. They had said all the important things. When he next looked at her, his face was relaxed and the worry lines were gone. You poor dear, she said to herself, if we must follow them to the ends of the earth then we shall, for that is what you need and what you want. The cave will not run away.

They skirted the small lake to the waterfall, listening to its rumble and watching the shimmering cascade descend from high to disappear into the mist. A deer with a well developed rack of antlers came to the pond's edge to drink, but because of the noise of the falling water, did not hear the two humans, and certainly did not see them. Chaiko raised Falcon and aimed an easy shot. The deer would be dead before it could find out what had killed him. At this distance he could not miss. But he relaxed Falcon, lowered the weapon and uttered a loud sound. Startled, the deer jumped and galloped off, bounding into the cover of the nearest trees. Dawn looked at him questioningly but then understood. He did not want to take the time from searching to skin, butcher and prepare the meat. Too bad; a little fresh venison would be mouth-wateringly tasty. Oh well, pass the dry meat, please, she thought resignedly.

******

It was early evening and Cosh, Crow and Makar had met with little success. They had found only a small squirrel-like thing and a handful of hard-shelled beetles. It was said of them that they tasted very good roasted. They had come upon a termite mound, and "gone fishing" for termites by sticking a moistened twig into the termite mound, then, with the lips, brushing the clinging termites into the mouth. Crow felt queasy about putting something that was still moving and alive into his mouth; he could not get past this feeling to remember the taste. But he ate because his body demanded that he eat. He, too, dreamed of real meat, real food, a feast full of abundance. Hunger was such a peculiar sensation. It was born of emptiness in the stomach, but filled the mind to overflowing with craving for food.

They emerged from under the woods onto the lake shore and wondered at the cascading waterfall, as the rushing water filled the air with a pleasant murmur. Makar started along the lake hunting frogs. Crow was about to join him when a deer with sizeable antlers headed toward the water for a drink. Cosh went into a crouch, and raising his spear to shoulder level, made ready to cast. He preferred to run with the animal and thrust his spear, but some instinct told him that he was not going to get nearer to this animal. Beside him Crow imitated his motions and the two silently approached the deer. Makar saw too late what was happening, but did the only thing he could. He slowly raised his hand, otherwise remaining almost motionless, but it was enough to catch and hold the attention of the animal. This brief ruse gave the two approaching hunters their chance to break into a full run. The deer finally sensed them and in a sudden four-footed jump was two lengths away, the spears whistling through the empty spot where he had been an instant before. Crow uttered a desperate cry, and threw his second spear after the fleeing shadow that was already crashing through the bush.

"Too bad," Cosh said evenly, swallowing his disappointment. Makar ran up, feeling that it was his fault for spooking the deer, but Cosh was quick to reassure him that he had held the deer spellbound long enough to give them their only chance. They did not miss, he said; their spears were simply not as fast as the deer.

******

The sun was lowering in the sky, about ready to slip behind the next line of hills, when Chaiko decided to look for a campsite to spend the night. The most likely spot was a raised ridge of clay sand amid a pile of rocks. When they got there, once again they discovered a fire ring. It appeared that someone else had also found this to be the right place to make camp. Excited, Chaiko looked about, reading the many prints left in the fairly hard-packed clay.

"This must be the clan," he called to her, exuberant. "Look, look here! This is my friend Crow. Only he has that crooked bend to his big toe." He ran to other prints. "This is Tanya," he said pointing, "and this is Lana. Look at that small foot, even smaller than yours; of course she is only eleven soon to be twelve. Look, this is her hair, he exclaimed, picking up a long strand caught in a cluster of weeds. He ran closer to the fire. "This must be Cosh. And this..." he paused frowning, "is Baer."

"What is wrong?" Dawn asked, immediately sensing the sudden shift in his mood.

"This is his foot all right, but the prints are so close together. Almost no stride at all. Flatfooted. An old man ... walks like that ... or a sick one." Then a painful silence swallowed the rest of his thoughts.

He strode up and down the full extent of the campsite, visibly growing more agitated. "There is only one fire. There should be about five. There are too few prints here. Where is the rest of the clan? What has happened?" There was pain in the barrage of questions.

"Maybe the rest went hunting," she suggested to calm him.

He sniffed around some more, recognizing Makar's prints. He sought to get control of his emotions, but his feelings refused to go back down in their proper places. And above all he worried.

To the side he found a pitiful pile of bones all small and so well chewed or cleaned off that not even a fox would tarry to sniff through them. He measured the pile with a sinking heart. Measuring the modest ash mound of the fire, he estimated three days. So little, for ... three days? There in that small shrunken pile was the evidence that the clan was starving. Food for nine, ten people? Not nearly enough for one meal let alone for three days.

He looked at the camp as a whole, puzzling the patterns left in clay-sand. He frowned deeply again. There were too few prints here—even for just ten of them for three days. What did these people do, sit around the fire all day? These people were very still, still and tired ... too hungry ... too little energy ... too dejected even to care?

How old was the camp? It was crucial to try to establish it. He raked through the fire. The ashes were cold but still not as cold as the clay ground, certainly not as clammy, so he reasoned that it had been not many days if the ash still retained some residual dryness. He examined all prints again to note any erosion or what had filled them, but came to the same conclusion, the campsite had been used a handful of days ago. This reassured him immensely, for if so, even if they had moved on they would not be out of reach yet.

They made a modest fire and watched the smoke rise into the dusk of the sky. Dawn wanted to ask him all kinds of questions now that they were so near, but did not want to break into his worried solitude. With the sun down behind the hills a chill quickly settled on them. She spread their bison cover on the ground and snuggled in. When he did not come to her side right away she got up, went to him and placed the feather mantle about him to ward off the worst of the chill. He thanked her with a preoccupied look, but did not speak. She rested her hand reassuringly on his shoulder. He merely nodded his head. She settled down again in the warm bison fur and was soon asleep.

The darkness deepened and the sparks traced a glowing ride into the sky until the warmth of their rise cooled and a little bit of remaining soot drifted away. Chaiko's head was still full of worries. He heard the quiet lapping water against the stones. He heard the hoot of an owl, then felt its silent glide to settle in the branch of a tree outlined against the starry sky and the rising moon. It did not move half the night. Not even a mouse stirred in the whole surrounding area. The owl would have noticed if there had been even one.

Unconsciously in his worry, Chaiko was playing with the string of the bag holding his year stones, when his fingers found the odd object of the stranger still hanging about his neck, nearly forgotten. Badly in need of a diversion, he again examined it carefully but was none the wiser for it. He told himself to trust his instincts; over time, most things revealed themselves. His fingers caressed the bone playing lightly over the holes. He noted how the measure of the holes fitted the spread of his fingers. What did that mean? he asked himself, pulled deeper into the riddle of the bone. The stranger could no longer tell him its purpose; Chaiko remembered sadly the lonely grave on the plain. The bone felt like a thing of use, not some trivial decoration or good luck piece. His fingers sensed along the length of bone. If bones could only talk, he mused, but then to his great surprise, this one did! Somehow, the piece of bone fit in his mouth, and most naturally he blew into the hollow tube. The loud pure sound that it gave shocked him. He could not believe what he heard! He blew into it again, and somehow the bone transformed his breath into the shrill sound of an eagle's fierce battle cry. Startled out of sleep, Dawn rose to her knees, looking about fearfully for the source of this shriek. Chaiko blew this time gently and the eagle turned into a baby bird. He watched amused as Dawn rose to look for the poor abandoned thing. He blew again a tender puff of air, and a soft sound was emitted by the bone. Disbelieving, she still looked for the sound, not realizing it was he. Gently and more gently he blew, observing, near laughter, as Dawn tried to find the little bird that must have fallen out of its nest, crying piteously.

Slowly it dawned on her that the season was much too advanced, well past the time of fledglings, and she started to suspect that somehow he must be producing these strange noises. But though she watched him closely, she could not catch him doing it. Still it was odd that every time she turned from him, the bird would call out in simpering tones.

"It is the Crier-Bird," he told her as if that would explain it, but it did not. Finally, she crawled into the bison wrap and covered her head, ignoring the piteous calls of one lost bird that continued into the night even after she fell asleep.

Chapter 36

The next morning Chaiko woke early, filled with restlessness. Night was still in the sky but dawn light was rising in the east. Here in camp he was surrounded by the footprints of his clan, and he was exceedingly anxious to renew the search for them. But where to look first, he queried himself. To the east? Farther to the north? Or perhaps south? He had no indication, no clue to lead him. After thinking about this a while, he decided to climb a high place and from there scan the countryside for any sign of smoke. He reasoned, following clan customs, that after relieving themselves on rising, their very next chore would be to take care of the fire and get it burning. Perhaps from a high vantage point he would be able to spot a column of smoke rising into the morning air.

He wrapped himself into the new feather cape that Dawn had made for him. It was light and would not get in his way while he climbed. He put more wood on the fire and as the smoke rose into the air, left the fire to guard the still sleeping Dawn wrapped tightly and securely within the bison robe. He selected a likely hill to the east that would give him the vantage he wanted. With some branches he made pointers to indicate the direction he planned to take, then in the clay scratched a hill with him on top. That should explain his absence to her, if she woke up before he got back. Satisfied, he headed for the hill he had chosen.

******

With early morning light growing stronger in the east, the clan was about, packing and breaking camp. Crow and Makar had built a fire to warm their chilled bones. Tanya was looking through all the packs and checking what they might have forgotten. She had a thought and called to Lana to get some slippery soap root from the swamp, just beyond the trees not too far away. It would be unlikely that they would find some on the arid high plateau. The young girl grabbed her digging stick and was off in a flash with the unconfined exuberance of youth. She ran splashing through the water like a deer and disappeared on the far bank. Tanya thought that perhaps she should send Crow after her, but Crow was needed here to lift and order the load.

Baer and Cosh were discussing their route. In this Baer depended on Cosh's memory, as he alone had been that way on his hunts and explorations. They decided to take a longer but easier way, and while the main group plodded on, Cosh and Crow would hunt on a parallel course. But that would mean that the rest would have to lug more baggage each. "Food is more important," Baer decided. "Besides, as it is, there appears to be little to carry." Cosh, out of habit, accepted the decision without questions, exceedingly glad that Baer was once again taking on the burden of leadership.

Ile brought them some food, more rhubarb, spinach and overripe heart of fern, which they picked at without much enthusiasm. We have turned into cows, Baer thought ruefully, moose-cows, munching and regurgitating the vegetarian diet. It greatly reinforced his desire to leave this situation.

Not far away Tanya was tying a bundle of rhubarb stalks. She was grateful for so much of this vegetable. Though no one liked the stuff, she at least had something to feed them. It was available in abundance since the rest of creation avoided it because of its bitterness. Crow's mother Emma, a kindly but quiet woman, came to help her distribute the bundles evenly among the packs. When Baer told them that Cosh and Crow would be hunting, they had to reorganize the packs once again, redistributing the loads.

Just then, there was a cry from across the water. Alarmed, Tanya looked up to see Lana come flying through the grass as if something were after her. She hit the water splashing and dashed through it. She ran into their midst and threw herself into her mother's arms: she was trembling! The rest came protectively around them, not a little frightened by the obvious panic they read into her flight. She hid her ashen face in her mother's embrace and shook uncontrollably.

"What is it, child?" asked Tanya.

"I saw ... saw something," Lana stammered out the words, still hiding her face.

"Saw what?" her mother wanted to know, anxiously peering at her daughter's face pressed against her bosom.

"Something ... and it saw me."

"Who or what saw you?" Tanya gently shook her to make sense of her words.

"It was a spirit. A bird spirit. It had a long beak and was talking bird talk. It was a big bird. And ..." here she trailed off, unsure how to continue.

"And?" her mother prompted. What was this child babbling about? Strange. She was not given to imagining. But then what had she seen? She looked questioningly at her mate, but Baer merely shrugged his shoulders; he could not make any sense of the words either. A spirit? Bah! He had never seen any spirits at all.

"It had the face of .... the face of Chaiko. Yes, it was the spirit of Chaiko who came back as a bird ..." she faltered, as she could not find the words to adequately describe what she saw.

But her words were like a thunderclap. Chaiko! The spirit of Chaiko! The blood froze in their hearts. Baer staggered a step back. Chaiko, a bird spirit?

"Where did you see this ... this spirit?" Tanya asked the most reasonable question under the circumstances.

"Near the swamp, by the mud hole where the soap weed grows. You know, where you sent me." The girl stammered out a fairly coherent reply then started shaking again. Dumbfounded, Tanya looked at Baer, her eyes big with questions. Baer, however, was slow to recover from the shock of hearing his dead brother's name in this context. His daughter's words had hit him with a force of a blow and he had difficulty finding his breath. When Tanya's questioning looks finally penetrated the sense of unreality engulfing him, he roused himself with effort, and threw a sideways glance at Cosh, who melted away.

"Tell me again. Leave out nothing," Tanya commanded the girl.

With some pauses, sighs and involuntary shudders Lana recounted her story. Crow hovered near her, concern for her diffused over his face. She had gone where her mother had sent her, to where the soap weed grew. Everybody knew the spot. She was near there when she heard this strange bird call, the likes of which she had never heard before. Intrigued, she had crawled carefully to a bush and peeked over and that was when she saw it. A large bird standing on two legs, as tall as a man, with the face of Chaiko, although it had a ... a very strange looking long beak. It had cried out in bird talk. She had been frozen in shock for an instant, and then she had run screaming, but no sound had came from her throat. She was halfway back to camp before she found her voice again and raised alarm.

Her words stirred up confusion in the listeners, then evoked their dread of spirits. Makar, who considered himself to be knowledgeable about birds, took issue with her description and could not resist contesting her.

"It was standing on two legs?" asked Makar skeptically. "Chaiko had but one leg." With this everyone could agree. Chaiko's spirit would likewise have only one leg.

"I tell you, I saw it. It was the face of Chaiko. I saw it very clearly. Do you think I would not recognize him?" She turned on Makar, who backed away from her vehemence. Everyone had to agree with that; she would surely recognize Chaiko.

"How was he making bird talk?" asked Crow, to ease her back into her story.

"I don't know," she said straight out. "Just that bird sounds were coming from him."

Cosh returned, having made the run there and back in a hurry. He was panting, out of breath. At Baer's questioning look, he merely shook his head. No, he saw no one and nothing, but then he sidled up to Baer and gave him something secretly. Baer looked; it was a large grey feather.

"Uhhh." The wind escaped Baer in surprise. He did not know what to make of it. There was his daughter's story and there was this feather. They did not prove each other, but both were undeniably there. Baer stared at the broad feather in his hand. It looked like the tail feather of cliff birds that liked to nest in large colonies, but there were no such nest sites nearby.

Well, with that flurry of excitement, leaving camp was for the time being impossible, and they sat about the fire discussing this strange turn of events. Crow freshened the fire, the smoke rising tall in the sky.

Tanya held onto her daughter who was still shaking, though it was hard to know if it was still from fright or from indignation at not being instantly believed, or maybe from a little of both.

After the emotions calmed somewhat and the hair on the nape of their necks settled down, the general consensus discounted her story. Such an impressionable young girl, Emma thought kindly. Ile frowned, eyebrows raised at Cosh but he merely shrugged his shoulders. Makar was still skeptical and did not mind expressing it.

"Why would Chaiko come back as a bird? Would it not make more sense to come back as a wolf, or even a fox, or a noble elk? Why would he turn himself into a bird? Thundering Hooves! What good are birds anyway, but to lay eggs. I would not think of Chaiko as an egg-laying type. Does not chaiko mean slug, or some such thing? Definitely not a bird. Why then should he come back as one? It makes no sense ..." Makar was becoming heated by the fire of his own passions. He liked to listen to his own voice. Besides, he had made a reputation for himself through imitating birds and other creatures and felt he needed to protect his prerogative, especially from a spirit creature. Then, as he spoke, his audience that had listened with half-interested indulgence suddenly turned ashen and mouths dropped open in astonishment as they looked right past him. Even Makar had to recognize that such an effect could not be attributed to his abilities alone. The words died in his throat and he spun about to be confronted by the bird spirit standing there in front of him, wearing Chaiko's face.

Time stopped, hearts stopped and the silence deepened to a still version of itself. There could be no doubt about it, in front of them all, covered by feathers, stood the bird-spirit just described. Baer shut his eyes, shook his head, opened his eyes again, but the vision did not clear: the spirit was still there. Tanya's eyes were big as fists and could not close. Lana clung to her desperately. Makar dropped heavily onto the ground, his legs simply giving out under him. Crow rose half way up then froze in utter disbelief.

The bird-sprit moved aside and behind it was another smaller bird-spirit.

Then in Chaiko's voice the spirit said, "This is my mate, Dawn." That was when Makar jumped to his feet and started running in the opposite direction right through a bush and beyond, yelling all the way; they could all hear the sounds of his flight and his cries fading in the distance. The rest were too stunned, frozen in the unreal silence that followed.

Crow stumbled one more step forward but stopped again. This could not be real! His eyes lied, his ears lied, but shaking his head still did not clear the vision.

"Come on, Raven, my old friend," the spirit said, its voice on the verge of pleading. Crow took two more steps toward him, and that was when a small figure flashed by him and threw herself at the bird spirit, yelling "Chaiko!"

That word again flashed through the crowd like lightning, loosening the knots of incredulity and everyone talked at once. "How ... Chaiko?" Lana clung to the bird, ruffling its feathers, great sobs racking her. True or not, they surged in close and crowded about him, touching him, calling out his name over and over again. "Chaiko... Chaiko... how? Chaiko!" Tanya's vision was clouded by tears freely flowing, and her hands trembled as she reached out to touch him. Unemotional Ile was crying unabashedly. Ido, too extended a timorous hand, still much afraid, touched him, then jerked her hand back as if burned. But she had touched warm, living flesh. Cosh's mouth hung open stupidly and he could not close it on account of his great disbelief. It seemed the women were more ready to believe their eyes; the men were still struggling with their mindset, unable to believe the unbelievable.

But it was Baer, who wanted to believe the most that all this was true, who was the last to be convinced. He stayed back undecided. The conflict between his hopes and disbelief was mirrored on his face. He took two steps forward then staggered back—but life would not be so cruel. When he saw his brother's tears flow freely in the press that surrounded him, Baer finally rushed in and hugged Chaiko, wincing with pain. But his face glowed with absolute joy, even though his vision was flooded out by the tears running down his cheeks. The two brothers embraced, their tears mixing. Crow was hugging them both; beside himself, he was pounding them both on the backs. By then everyone was sobbing, and even the unemotional Cosh was crying, a stream of tears pouring down his face. Overflowing with emotions, Emma peed herself, first in fright, then in incredulity, and finally in joy.

Still, people could scarcely believe the evidence of their eyes and hands. Repeatedly Crow slapped himself to see if he was awake or dreaming, then he slapped Chaiko to make sure. Time and time again he stepped back to see if Chaiko was still there, and each time he was flooded with joy. The human heart was not meant to hold so much happiness and there were few moments in any life when the heart so overflowed as when the remnant of the clan welcomed Chaiko back into their midst.

It was Baer who recovered first. "Somebody go get that fool Makar before he crosses the highlands. By Thundering Hooves, nobody talk to him about bird-spirits." Cosh went off.

After that a semblance of order returned. Lana's face was radiant with joy. Crow still looked stunned and was sure he must be dreaming. Emma could not help herself; she cried convulsively, fat tears rolling down her cheeks. Ido did not know how to deport herself, great sighs of nervous explosions racking her. Ile was the most calm; she dabbed her eyes, her face flushed from the excitement. The clan slowly settled down and across from them all sat Chaiko and Dawn. A strange silence grew out of the expectations, no one knowing how to start to ask about or explain this astounding turn of events. The questions mounted and their curiosity turned to an itching need to know.

Once again it was Baer who took charge. With his eyes he motioned Tanya toward Dawn, "to ease her into this," his eyes said to his mate. He took a deep breath to dam up the emotions still coursing through him, then he started to speak in the formal language of the clan. "This is but a part of the Standing-Rock Clan; the rest went east to find better hunting." Having realized that his brother would not know, he flashed this information to Chaiko noting the surge of relief that crossed his brother's face. "I, as leader of the clan, on behalf of all, would like to welcome a son of the clan back with his mate ..." he searched his memory for a name he barely heard in the overwhelming commotion that went before: "Dawn. You are most welcome." They all smiled and their heads bobbed in joyous affirmation.

At another look from Baer to his mate, Tanya rose and went to kneel beside Dawn and formally extended an arm. The two women looked at each other, and in some mystic recognition denied to most men, they naturally and spontaneously embraced each other. A few shy words were exchanged, and everybody strained to catch their voices. The clan's curiosity was heightened to the verge of pain. They saw before them a small girl with big expressive eyes of sparkling blue. Looking in those eyes one lost track of everything else.

"But where are my manners?" Tanya asked herself, shocked at her oversight in protocol. She and the women hurried aside to prepare something to offer the newcomers to eat. They unwrapped some precious meat, and there was no way of avoiding it, the most crisp of the rhubarb stalks. The crowd groaned inwardly at the sight of those, but the presentation was made with grace and dignity and was accepted with the same sentiments, proving that even while serving rhubarb one can still have good form.

Then it was Chaiko's turn to speak for the two of them. He had often dreamed of this moment, but the rehearsed words left him and his heart spoke for him.

"It is good to be home, for where the clan is, there is my home. This is my mate Dawn. She was separated from her people like I was by the fire. I found her on the plains and there she found me. She is my heart, and she has my heart. She is my mate and the mother of my children to be. Treat her as you would me for she is me. We are pledged to each other and we are now one." His last words were uttered as the formula that formally joined a man to a woman, customarily pronounced by a shaman. But since none was present, and since they had already lived together for so long, he took it upon himself to make public vows that henceforth nobody could contest. They were now truly mated. And the clan was happy to be witness of their union.

At this point Cosh returned with a sheepish Makar. But everybody knew that the boy had such an overactive imagination that he could have reacted no other way. When he was afraid, no one feared more than he. Right now he was truly glad to welcome Chaiko back. As he appraised the girl next to him, he was captured by her wide set, incredible blue eyes, and immediately became tongue-tied in her presence.

After that there were many questions and long, long answers as Chaiko did his best to tell his and Dawn's tale to the avid listeners. He told them about his escape from the fire, the long river ride, going over the rapids and the narrows, then the series of camps and how he and Dawn had found each other. He made sure to give her a proper and suitable role to increase her esteem in their eyes. But he did not tell them everything.

In turn he learned with sorrow of the death of Samar and Uma, and of Baer's continued injuries; of the disappearing game; of Tusk leading the rest east in hope of better hunting. And the starvation facing them here. The faces grew glum and despondent, but today they had a great joy to celebrate, and the mood soon lightened again.

Chaiko told them about the animals slowly returning to the plains though not the big herds. And he told them about the green island in the lee of the wasteland bypassed by the fire, where they had made their home. There was food there, meat, grain and fruit and a spacious cave. He invited them to come share it. Everyone brightened and their mouths started watering at the list of all the foods cited. After Chaiko and Dawn exchanged glances of silent understanding, Dawn went back into the bush to the place where they had left their packs, Tanya as hostess following her. When the two returned, at Chaiko's suggestion, Dawn handed out presents all around: a braided leather cord of great strength for Baer, a soft sable pelt for Tanya (though of summer fur), salt and fat for Ile, lumps of sweet-smelling sap to burn for Cosh, herbs for Emma, a delicate pink shell for Lana, a pouch of aromatic dried flowers for Ido, a fold of spider-lace to a blushing Crow (good to enhance potency, or so it was claimed), and a small pouch of soft leather for Makar. Not surprisingly the honey was greeted with the most pleasure, and everybody got some. They licked their fingers and wished they could have more. It was agreed that Dawn's clan had a very nice custom in giving presents when meeting other people. There was an immediate discussion to implement something similar, but Baer did not allow them to be so diverted. It was, after all, Chaiko's homecoming and Baer was determined, more than anybody else, that his brother would enjoy it to the uttermost.

At one point, Lana reminded everyone that Chaiko had grown a new leg out of wood; they gathered about him examining his leg and shaking their heads in amazement at this ingenuity. Who would have thought of that? Some even knocked on the wood. Embarrassed by all this attention, he nonetheless bore it good naturedly.

Later the attention switched over to Dawn and some of the more inquisitive even wanted to look at her teeth (a good indicator of general health and age), but Chaiko discouraged that. They wanted to know if she was a vegetarian. They were amazed at the tone of her voice and the use of their language, understandable enough, with an intriguing accent that put the stress on the wrong places. Still everyone was quick to assure her that it was very charming.

Cosh's mate Ile asked her to say something in her own tongue.

"Abular coha id tall om, shom okole fla shessi omalika," Dawn said in her most melodious voice, amazing them with the flow of her language. They asked her to repeat it, which she gladly did. They were astounded. Why, if you did not quite listen to the exact words, it almost sounded like a real language. They asked her to repeat it again and again.

"And your people can understand all that?" She told them yes, that every child can understand it. They found it incomprehensible that people could speak a language that they alone understood. Then it occurred to someone to ask what it meant.

"You can tell the strength of a fly by the size of the animal it is carrying," she translated smoothly. Chaiko, used to her people's humor by now, chortled aloud, but the rest looked mystified. Even translated it made little sense. He laughed aloud. "Have you ever seen a fly carry a moose?" They remained even more befuddled. "Would you not say that it takes a very strong fly to carry off a whole moose?" He was met with blank stares. He tried to explain but the harder he explained the more the humor escaped them. He gave in and admitted it was a subtle joke at the best of times, but that it had sounded funnier in an empty plain with no other diversions.

This set loose an involved discussion of whether it could be called a joke at all. The conversation then turned linguistic in nature. The consensus seemed to be that it was not worth knowing a different tongue since only strangers could understand it. Chaiko let the discussion lie there.

Crow was sitting near him, his face a picture of bewilderment. In spite of his eyes he could still not quite believe that Chaiko was there in front of him. If true, he was set free from many nightmares. If true, his soul was set free of its most awful burden of guilt. Too often had he dreamed of Chaiko... He reached over, softly and shyly, to touch Chaiko, assuring himself yet again. Chaiko smiled and patted him reassuringly.

During this time Lana came over to Chaiko and asked him to make bird talk. He smiled at her, took the long bone from around his neck and blew into it. The sound rose and fell as his fingers played over the holes. Dawn recognized the Crier-Bird of the night before and flashed him a "just-you-wait" look that every mated man gets to learn quickly. Chaiko merely laughed and laughed. Lana flashed Makar an "I-told-you-so" smile, too. It was as she had said, Chaiko made bird talk.

After that everybody wanted to try Crier-Bird and it went from hand to hand. Makar tried to blow so much air through the bone that it flew out of his hand and hit a less than appreciative Cosh. Yes, the Crier-Bird was a huge success and Chaiko gave thanks to the Stranger.

Cosh came over and expressed an interest in the strange curved sticks that were in Chaiko's pack. Chaiko smiled broadly. "I will tell you tomorrow, my friend. Tonight is a time for celebration." The talk ebbed and flowed and laughter echoed around the fire. There was plenty to tell, plenty to listen to. Baer sat a little to the side. All this joy had taxed his strength somewhat, but he was loath to leave. He had almost forgotten how good it was to laugh and enjoy himself. Tanya watched him with glowing eyes and hoped the change in her mate was permanent. There could have been no better gift (or medicine) to them than the return of Chaiko, she thought gratefully.

But every celebration must find an end and people slowly drifted off to their sleeping places. Dawn, too, crawled into her bison skin. Finally, only the two brothers were left. Both were too excited and churned up by emotions to sleep. For a long time, they sat across from one another in the growing quiet and flickering firelight, content just to sit there within view of one another and exchange an occasional smile. When life was good, it could be very good.

Chapter 37

The next morning people woke not quite believing the astounding events of the day before. One by one they came over to peer down at Chaiko and Dawn wrapped tightly in their bison robe, smiling up shyly at their well wishers. Cosh nodded pleasantly at them, then fingered the soft bison hairs, his eyes aglow. Bison were Cosh's one big passion. After their long isolation, Dawn and Chaiko found this sudden close-up attention very disconcerting.

After they had gotten up, Tanya came over and claimed Dawn for "women talk." They went aside and talked intently for quite a while. Tanya asked her about herself, her family and people, the way they did things and how they thought about things. At the same time she told Dawn about clan ways. Tanya alone realized the full implication of Dawn's presence among them. She was a storehouse of the accumulated knowledge of her people, suddenly made available to the clan. Tanya was excited about new learning, though the information had to be unraveled with patience and with an understanding of the ways of both their peoples. She showed Dawn respect and great courtesy, and Dawn responded with instant liking and easy confidence. The bond of kinship through their mates was thus quickly strengthened by their mutual appreciation of each other. They both realized that they shared the same practical mind-set, though Dawn's focus was still only Chaiko, whereas Tanya attended to the needs of the whole clan. Let men do the things that men must do, but let women attend to the practical things of value in their unobtrusive way. Leave it to the men to do the posturing, they agreed in gentle good humor.

It was not that their attitude stood against men, far from it; women more than men truly realized that it took both sexes for them to survive, each sex contributing its specialized training and knowledge. If men were more set on controlling their surroundings, it was because they faced the more uncertain prospect of the hunt. They had to search, stalk and kill, each step requiring all their skill, the outcome to a large extent still a matter of luck. Not surprisingly, men brought their need to control back to the cave. Women, on the other hand, gathered the plants they had watched growing all season. Plants did not run away from them. Women were rooted as the plants were rooted. If men needed to control, it was because in their lives they felt the lack of it.

The two women talked and smiled freely at each other. They had achieved mutual understanding and liking in spite of the age difference and their separate origins. Both were highly pleased, left with a feeling of budding alliance, something that Dawn, in particular, was acutely appreciative of—being the newest member of the clan. After Dawn came back, Chaiko asked what they had talked about for so long, but she only shrugged, "Women talk." More she would not say, except that she liked Tanya.

Crow, too, came over, somewhat hesitant, not knowing how Dawn's presence would affect his relationship with Chaiko. During the night it had finally penetrated his awareness that Chaiko was back, alive and well, and his present joy had no shadow of disbelief to mar it. It had not been just wishful thinking after all. He sat down across from Chaiko with a wide grin across his face. Chaiko beamed broadly back at him. The two looked at each other, all the memories of their youth came flooding back, and in the exchange of grins, they both felt connected again. For both, the world which had been somewhat out of joint, fell back into place. This was where they belonged, they both thought, reassured.

The second look they gave each other was more appraising, each attending to the nuances that had not been there before. Chaiko saw a depth to Crow that was new and a quietness that overlay the familiar burst of enthusiasm. It seemed that Crow too, had learned not to take things for granted. Perhaps he had left his naiveté back in the hills. From his view Crow beheld a degree of self assurance in his friend that had not been there previously. In fact the change was so marked, Crow could not see beyond it. The familiar was there, but this new quality distorted it. But then Chaiko had always been a puzzle for Crow.

The smiles remained. The bond between them was strengthened by their separation as each had recognized the full value of their friendship. But there were changes, too, and other interests. Chaiko had looked unconsciously for Dawn and Crow for Lana. They both took note of this, smiled again, but each wondered how it would affect the other and how to accommodate the new relationships. Time would tell.

Sensing that this reaffirmation needed no words, they remained silent, content just to look at one another. Thus, when shortly thereafter Crow rose to go, Chaiko did not seek to hold him back.

A little later, after a breakfast of carrots and rhubarb, Baer came over with Cosh to talk with Chaiko. Yesterday he had been entirely a brother, swept away by the overflow of joy at Chaiko's return, but today he was once again the leader of his clan. They wanted to know more about the green valley that had survived the fire and about the cave, hunting, fishing and the ripening seeds and fruits. Chaiko gave the two a detailed account, and as he talked the listeners exchanged looks of longing for this promised land. Dawn appeared and with proper modesty offered the men the harvest of the valley, seed cakes and dried fruits. Baer nibbled on his piece, enjoying its tart-sweet flavor, then slipped it in his folds to save for Lana later. They had not had this kind of delicacy for some time. Cosh gobbled up his piece in a gulp, his mouth flooding with juices at its delicious aftertaste, but he was too well mannered to ask for more.

When Chaiko finished his recital they started all over again asking him many probing questions. He explained about the stretch of wasteland where nothing much grew. Cosh chimed in that he knew the place to be full of thorn bushes, scorpions and sand snakes. And sand fleas, Chaiko added to his list. He then went on to explain how the valley had survived the passage of fire in the lee of the wasteland, blocking access to it. He described the cave and its vicinity and listed all the animals he had seen. Then they wanted some indication of numbers, most anxiously they wanted numbers. But this was problematic for beyond five the clan had no words for numbers; there was but "many." Chaiko tried "five hands of five," but this too was awkward. Finally, Dawn who had been discreetly listening to their conversation from the side, gave Chaiko a heaping handful of straws. And using these as counters and her counting words for each animal, he made a pile indicating their numbers. The piles were comfortably high, the largest being deer. The two leaders exchanged looks again.

"This many bison?" Cosh wanted to know, pointing at a smaller pile of grass stalks. When Chaiko confirmed it, he gave a satisfied nod.

Chaiko caught Dawn's eyes, looked questioningly at her and she, reading the thoughts from his face, nodded her agreement. Chaiko again invited the remnant of the clan to share their good fortune and their cave. Baer and Cosh once again exchanged glances and nods, and Baer accepted in the name of the clan. Everyone was relieved and satisfied. Baer and Cosh saw a new future for the clan in Chaiko's description. Chaiko was pleased that the devalued cripple could offer this service to his people, finally proving his true worth. And Dawn, though feeling a bit displaced by this intrusion of the whole clan into their lives, quickly reminded herself that their children would need people to belong to. Besides, it was easier to bring the clan to the cave rather than the other way around, she thought, laughing silently to herself. It mattered only that she would have her cave back; she was thus also content.

Then out of courtesy and not a little curiosity, Baer asked about her people. Chaiko answered for them both as the form required. He got most things right, but she was not going to correct him in front of his people and kin.

Cosh quickly returned to the point that concerned him the most, hunting. He wanted to know how shy the game was and how difficult it was to stalk them. Chaiko was able to reassure him that the game was placid and did not yet seem to know human hunters; therefore they were quite easy to track and approach. The grass was waist to chest high, giving good cover for the hunters to use. Cosh closed his eyes to better visualize the pictures presented, the anticipation glowing on his face.

"He killed six bison in one hunt," Dawn could not resist interjecting, with pride in his prowess. Noting their incomprehension, she held up five fingers then one more and repeated "Six bison on one hunt."

"Sisk?" Cosh was incredulous. "How?" he demanded to know, always thirsty for more hunting lore.

She was about to tell him, but Chaiko called her name to stop her and she sank back down, head lowered in contrition at having allowed her pride in him to carry her away to break the proper form. Chaiko had thought long and hard how to present the new weapon to the clan and was not going to let Dawn inadvertently spoil his plans. An awkward silence followed. Baer cleared his throat and tried the new word on his tongue "Siss?"

"Six," corrected Chaiko holding up five fingers plus one. He looked at the two expectant faces turned toward him, waiting for an explanation. "Well, good then!" he said in a tone of finality; they seemed ready enough and so was he. He looked directly at Dawn. "Make Mahuar," Chaiko ordered in a clipped voice. She bristled at his tone, but then realized this was not her mate talking but a leader of his people to whom she also owed obedience. It was a dual relationship that she would have to get used to. Yet the incongruity of the situation also struck her: how can a 14-year-old, a boy just turned into a man, be a leader of his people? Just by thinking? These were new people with strange customs. But she was a part of them now, and she had better learn their rules and expectations. She already knew that she had a right and a claim on their attention, but had to observe protocol.

"Mahujar?" How had he remembered her word for deer?

"Mahujar tiku." Did he say deer forms? Then she remembered the straw clan she had made for the great bison hunt. She nodded her head in understanding, got up and hurried away to collect Lana, and the two disappeared into the grass.

"Sikk?" The strange word ill fitting his lips, Cosh wanted to have his explanation. Chaiko held up a hand and Cosh chewed on his lips, full of rare impatience. The three sat in quiet, waiting. It was up to Chaiko to lead the show. Baer marveled at the changes in his brother, so grown up and self-assured. Was this the cripple who used to slink unnoticed about the fires? Most definitely not! This was a new man, who now stood straight on a leg he had made of wood. Truly, this was a wonder and were it not for the love they shared, he was looking at a stranger. Perhaps that little slip of a girl had had a hand in helping him become renewed. He must ask Tanya; she would know, as she seemed to know everything about the clan. He had noticed the two women talking earlier, taking each other's measure. He had asked Tanya what they had talked about, but she had replied simply, "Women's talk." With that he had to be satisfied.

Dawn and Lana came back with huge armfuls of dry yellow grass which they dropped on the far side of the fire away from the men. Dawn sorted, selected, bunched and tied bundles of grass together. Lana watched and helped as best as she could, looking with big eyes at this exotic girl who was mated to Chaiko. The grass bent in Dawn's practiced hands, and soon one bundle was joined to another and a form was slowly emerging. The unusual activity attracted everyone's attention, but they maintained a careful distance, as privacy required, especially toward the new girl. But they all watched surreptitiously, whispering and asking each other what could be going on. Only Chaiko and Dawn knew; of course, Makar professed to know.

Then with a quick twist and tie Dawn joined each of the bundles and assembled before their eyes a deer made of grass, drawing a chorus of involuntary ohs. As a finishing touch, two forked branches served for antlers.

"Mopu abarok." Chaiko, a leader of his clan, commanded, in a tone that also said, "Do just what I ask and no more." Chagrined at her earlier misstep, Dawn did as he asked; she and Lana picked up the deer and carried it further away.

"Abarok." Chaiko waved them further on till the deer was three then four spear throws away. Then he indicated, enough. The girls came running back, giggling at some subtle joke. "That deer won't run away. Even Chaiko could catch it," Dawn had said. Both then visualized Chaiko running with the peculiar gait his wooden leg forced on him, and irrepressible giggles burst to the surface, especially because he was acting so stern and leader-like and because the expectant atmosphere made their hilarity unseemly. But under such circumstances, giggles were especially hard to control. Dawn tried. Lana tried. Their eyes flashed at each other, and there was an instant understanding between them. They both loved Chaiko and in this brief exchange they recognized each other's claim on him. They both shared a right of familiarity.

The clan looked on, puzzled. They saw the straw deer which at this distance looked eerily real, except for its yellow color. What was this, they all wondered. What did Chaiko intend to do? Chaiko waved his arm and a clear path opened between him and the deer. Was Chaiko going to hunt the deer that far away? Impossible ... but so it looked.

They watched as Chaiko took his curved stick and a smaller straight stick and, pointing at the deer, said in clear loud voice, "The hunter sees the deer, but because the hunter is so far away the deer is not alarmed. The hunter is quiet, and moves slowly from rock to tree, from tree to bush, behind cover." And Chaiko stalked the deer, moving in mimicry of his words. "The deer feels no danger, the hunter is still so far away... and it is good that way." He took a few more steps to draw their eyes, then paused. "But a hunter knows that danger often comes unexpected ... and inattention is often its own worst enemy." He raised his curved stick so that the straight stick was now pointing at the deer. His purpose was clear: from where he was, he intended to hunt the deer. But to kill over such a distance? Impossible! How was he going to throw that far with the child's toy of a stick?

Now, Chaiko did a strange thing: he pulled back on the string and the stick bent until it looked to break, the straight piece still pointing at the deer. Then he let go of the string and the straight stick disappeared. It was no longer there. For an instant everybody froze, then a murmur of bewilderment swept through the group. What did Chaiko do with that stick? The watchers stirred uneasily about looking dumbfounded at each other, some with mouths agape. It was Makar who first gave notice with a frightened squawk that the deer had fallen over onto its side. Now what? How did that happen? People shifted nervously; too many unexplained things were happening.

"Shishik," Chaiko commanded his mate: "Get it." The imperative sounded so strange in her tongue, stripped of all polite pretences. Still, she obediently went and extracted from the side of the deer the straight piece. With a flourish she held it high for all to see. Makar rubbed his eyes in disbelief. Others simply shook their heads. That could not be right! But then how? There was some kind of trickery, or worse, some magic here.

"Quiet!" Baer commanded, and was obeyed. "Do it again," he told Chaiko, his tone also stripped of form. Twice now of late, his eyes were telling him things his mind found hard to believe. First there was a bird spirit, now wood that flew. Chaiko nodded; he understood Baer's dislocation. It was rare when an event did not fit into their mindset. The rest were feeling similarly confounded. Cosh pressed to the forefront of the group and never took his eyes off Chaiko.

Chaiko nocked a talon into the string, raised Falcon, pulled back on the string and released. The talon again disappeared. This time the deer did not fall over but remained upright.

"Shishik," Chaiko commanded Dawn, but Cosh put up a hand and said peremptorily, "No shissik!" This he wanted to see for himself; he did not want anyone to disturb the evidence. He went up to the deer, looked it over carefully, then retrieved the talon from still further off; it had gone right through the deer. There was a fresh hubbub of voices

440

again at this result. "Magic! Magic!" the voices called out in superstitious fear.

Chaiko shot and shot again and talon after talon hit the deer-form. Cosh found that the best way to watch the flight of the straight stick was from directly behind to look along its flight path. He saw how the flight curved down gently, like a thrown stone or a spear. That he could understand. But then who threw the stick, for Chaiko did not, of that he was sure. All he did was to let go of the string that held the stick back.

"This is Falcon." Chaiko raised the curved stick and showed it around. "And this is its talon. The Falcon has the strength, the talon has the bite." He shook each in turn, for everyone to see. "Together they are deadly."

Impulsively Makar came up to Chaiko and held out his hands; he wanted to make the talon fly too. Chaiko shook his head denying his request, then looked around on the expectant faces and gave the weapon to Cosh to try. Cosh caressed the instrument, the smooth feel of the wood, the humming tenseness of the string. He held it like Chaiko did, then experimentally pulled back on the string, surprised by its stiff resistance. He pulled harder; Falcon bent but not obediently. He relaxed it again.

"One smooth pull, then release," Chaiko advised him.

Cosh pulled back the string then released and was jolted by the pain of the slap of the string on the inner arm. "Ohhw!" he complained, tenderly feeling the fresh scrape. That was when he noticed the skin wrap about Chaiko's left arm.

Dawn came up and wrapped his arm to protect it. This time Chaiko gave him a talon and showed him how to nock it. Cosh nocked the talon, pulled back on the string and released, but he did not hold the joining of fingers, string and talon firmly seated, and the shaft went off to the side nearly nailing Makar's foot to the ground. Makar sprang aside, squawking in alarm like the bird he liked to imitate. When Cosh tried again, everybody pulled back to a more respectful distance and gave him plenty of clear view to the target. This time it went better, the talon finding its way almost to the target and only slightly off line. The next time when Cosh came within a spitting distance of the straw deer, a cheer went up, and everybody clamored to try it, magic or no magic.

"Falcon took six bison with six talons," Chaiko declared loudly.

"Six? What is this six? Some magic incantation?"

Chaiko counted out six talons and stuck them into the ground, then one after the other he counted as he sent each one on its way; until one, two, three, four, five, six talons were buried in the straw deer in a close cluster. With their eyes they could see the flight of six talons in the air, then striking at the target. This evidence notwithstanding, Chaiko succeeded only in proving and confirming the magic of the wood.

Dawn came into the circle of people and held up the bison robe. "This was number four of the beasts killed," she said guessing, "and here is the hole the talon made on the way to the beast's heart." Everyone came near poking their fingers through the hole and admiring the silky feel of the pelt. Such a small hole for a whole life to escape through.

Chaiko held up his hand for silence again. He wanted to make sure people would remember this demonstration. "Farther," he told Dawn, and she ran to set up the straw deer at six spearthrows' distance. She came running back out of breath, her cheeks glowing warm red. See this, her manner proudly exuded. But Chaiko was suddenly less sure of himself. The trouble with demonstrating distance and accuracy was that one had to hit the target selected. "When one brags, one also has to live up to it," Chaiko thought to himself.

This time Chaiko took his time, carefully measured the distance with his eyes and waited till the tops of grass stopped swaying in the light cross breeze. He took a short breath, held it, then in one smooth motion he raised Falcon, pulled back to full extension, sighted along the shaft, then released. Confidence was also a large part of shooting, perhaps even the largest part. People held their breath as the falcon flew, reached its high point, then angled downward and pierced the throat of the deer instantly killing it. Of that there could be no doubt. Chaiko sighed in relief. But the distance ... the incredible distance. Short-sighted Cosh's wife could not even see that far. This was indeed a magic weapon, everybody agreed. They did not exactly know where the magic lay, but they knew there had to be some. Chaiko told them in one word, "Practice." And then, "Practice some more."

The voices rose to a hubbub again and all came pressing in wanting to touch the magic weapon, even the women, to claim some of its luck and magic properties. Magic was an ill-defined concept that covered everything that people could not find a ready explanation for. They feared it, but at the same time wanted badly to claim it, so they could control it. Chaiko was truly a master of magic it was conceded; had he not grown a leg of wood? Who could do that without magic?

Chaiko went to his pack, took the two other Falcons and gave one to Baer and one to Cosh. Baer tested the pull of his, regretfully shook his head—he had not the strength— and passed it into Crow's hands. The only other male, Makar, looked about for his. Chaiko promised to make him one soon.

After the demonstration, people could not settle down but milled about talking at each other. So much excitement in so short a time. First Chaiko comes back from the dead as a bird-spirit; he brings with him a mate; and then gives them a magic weapon. There were also whispers of going back to the plains instead of going east. And rumors about bison; had not Chaiko killed five and one himself?

It was not until the afternoon, after an unexpectedly generous meal that included more meat than rhubarb, and when the people were settled down enough to listen, that Baer told them what Chaiko had told him of a green valley that was spared the fire, of game, of food and of bison freely roaming. He told them of a cave waiting for them, already prepared. He promised them a new life, with food enough to fill their bellies again. The eyes of his listeners lit up with hope. It was decided to start the journey the very next day, after they had repacked to lighten their loads. Everyone was asked to take only the useful and necessary items. "Ditch the rhubarb!" yelled the irrepressible Makar, and everybody laughed in agreement. Tanya alone blushed; it was not her fault ... they had to eat something.

With that the meeting broke up into various activities to prepare for the next day's journey. After so many days of travelling, Chaiko and Dawn were ready to go, as a matter of habit. Dawn was eagerly looking forward to returning to her cave and to the green valley that sustained it.

Chaiko showed the men how to use Falcon and they all practiced with great enthusiasm. Baer looked on, listening. When he got better, he too wanted to use this new weapon. After the joys of the last two days he felt stronger already. It was always so much easier to lead toward a bright future than toward an uncertain one. He wondered what to do about Tusk and the messenger he was going to send back to report on their trip and condition. In retrospect he did not regret the split-up, for even Chaiko's green valley could not support the full numbers of the clan for long, but would be enough for the remnant until next year. He watched as the hunters got better with this new weapon, cheering each other on. Chaiko had made it look so easy, but each in turn found it difficult, and they had a new respect for Chaiko's skill.

Later in the evening around the fire, people talked eagerly about the events of the day. The men were puzzling at the marvelous new weapon and the promise of game on the plains. The women collected around Dawn and asked her many questions about the green valley. Dawn did her best to answer them all and tried hard to speak correctly, though she intercepted occasional bemused glances among her listeners at an odd turn of her phrases. Tanya praised her and her work on the cave, thus recognizing and strengthening her status. Crow sitting near Lana, hands touching, also listened intently. Maybe he and she had a chance at happiness after all in this new excitement.

Aside, Baer, Cosh and Chaiko conferred. They were trying to devise some method of letting Tusk and the rest of the clan know where they were going. Chaiko suggested putting stone markers pointing to the west at likely spots. Baer thought of piling flat rocks on top of each other to attract attention. "Let the People of the Standing-Rock Clan find the rocks standing to show them the way we went." He was pleased with this solution to their problems and the other two nodded in ready affirmation. Cosh enumerated all the places where they should do this. They resolved to begin the first thing next morning and to erect markers all along the way.

By the time the stars came out, everybody was eager to start a new destiny, but sleep came only slowly as the last two days had been full to overflowing.

After being alone, just the two them, for this many moons, both Chaiko and Dawn found being the centre of attention of the whole clan hard to adjust to. The drama of the reunion the day before, though gratifying, proved utterly exhausting. The demonstration today, in its way, was no less demanding. Though Chaiko had carefully orchestrated the show to best effect and full impact, by sundown he was edgy, although still very excited. He had taken a risk to make the demonstration especially memorable, and thankfully he had been rewarded. Dawn likewise found herself overexposed, an object of curiosity, and could barely keep up with the many probing questions directed at her. Lana and Ido

14 Stones

could not resist touching her, as many also wanted to, to see if she was indeed real, a girl that spoke another tongue that nobody understood, except Chaiko. But that was understandable: Chaiko knew magic and was capable of everything in their eyes.

Throughout the day Chaiko kept an eye on Dawn, to see how she was faring with all this attention. He guessed that having to speak so much in the clan tongue must be wearing her down. But she had quietly answered all their questions and suffered herself to be touched and poked. Seeing her poise and dignity, Chaiko relaxed. Still, when his ear caught the key phrase, "It would be very nice ..." he rushed over to her side, hiding his concern behind a frozen expression. She was talking with Emma and Ile, but looking up at his approach and noting his stone-set face, she laughed and hurried to reassure him, "It would be really very nice to pick late ripening berries by the new cave." This time, nice was just nice, he noted with some relief. Later, he jumped once more when he overheard Cosh ask Dawn, "He who?" but decided to let her handle that.

Lying by the fire, wrapped in the bison robe, warm, with the stars twinkling brightly above, the excitement of the day still would not let go of them. She, and then he, turned restlessly. A snore from the other side sounded loud in their ears. Finally it was Dawn who reached over and caressed and stroked him into excitement. They pressed together in an urgent embrace and joined into the compelling rhythm that took command. He groaned, but she covered his mouth with her small hands, she herself having to bite the robe to keep from crying out in her own ecstasy. They collapsed into a spent heap of arms and legs and their breath slowly settled and slowed. After that he was soon asleep, but she remained awake for a while, floating on the afterglow. Nearby, Tanya still awake with a mental list of things to do, sensed more than heard their play. She smiled to herself as desire rose in her. She reached over to her mate, but he merely grunted in his sleep at her touch; regretfully she returned to her list.

The moon was bright with silvery light peeking in and out of the clouds. A night chill like dew settled down to the ground. People pulled their covers higher and snuggled closer to each other for warmth. Summer was over and the bite of the changing season was in the air.

Chapter 38

Buoyed by the expectation of returning to the plains and to a new cave that waited for them, they were eager to start on the journey. But first, near their campsite, they made a large marker to show the way they went. Two converging lines of stones were placed pointing to the west. Beside it, they erected a carefully balanced structure of rocks about chest height to attract attention. It looked eerily evocative, like the silhouette of a man, mute and motionless.

"Let the stones speak and let the People of Standing-Rock understand their speech," Baer offered in dedication of the stone marker. In the next valley, by an old campsite they would do the same again.

They moved slowly, held to Baer's steps. Although he had improved considerably, he was still weak and had difficulty going up and then down the steep slopes. Cosh, who was leading the group, set an easy pace for Tanya had cautioned him not to burn up Baer's strength too quickly. They had a long way to go but hoped that, on the level ground of the plains, progress would be easier for him. Therefore by mid-afternoon, they stopped at the old campsite they had used in the early days of their stay in the hills. Baer wanted to protest, but knew he had to ration his strength. They made fire and enjoyed a meal with no rhubarb and a generous portion of meat, knowing that six bison were waiting for them at the new cave.

The men went up the valley, hunting, eager to try the new weapon, except for a glum Makar, who had only a spear to carry. The women scoured the other end of the valley for something fresh. They found some small apples and some berries that when soaked made a fresh tasting drink. Dawn picked a patch of sorrel; the women did not know about the plant but were interested in its tangy flavor, a little like spinach in texture. They also found some ripe grass seeds. A little later the men returned with two rabbits. Chaiko got them both after Cosh and Crow had missed one each. Still, their shots had been close so they were filled with excitement at this proof of the new weapon. Since their talons shattered on some rocks, Chaiko was going to be busy making

14 Stones

more. It was a cheerful camp that night. Fresh meat, tasty greenery and the feeling of being a day closer to their new home and a glowing new future. All futures should be this bright, Tanya thought to herself, as she watched the clan. She saw the tender looks that passed between Lana and Crow, a more mature look of companionship between Dawn and Chaiko. Even Cosh and his mate seemed infected with the mood. She glanced at Baer, but he looked tired from the day. She sighed deeply.

Before dark, Lana came, and taking Chaiko by the hand, led him into the bush and beyond, to two mounds of stones piled on the ground. Solemnly and sorrowfully Lana pointed out Samar's and Uma's graves. Then she left him. Saddened, Chaiko sat by the site remembering his old mentor, not a full shaman but a good friend, if there can be a friendship that spanned such an age difference. Chaiko was fond of the old man and missed his presence in the clan. He shook his head sadly at the flood of memories. He also tried hard to think something kind about Uma, but remembered her only as a grey little person worn down by life. But Samar ... He felt a hand on his shoulder. It was Bear. The two brothers missed most the companionship and the wisdom of the old man. With tears misting his eyes, Chaiko piled more rocks on the mound. He wished he could perform a last service for the man Samar had been. "As long as I live, my friend, you will be remembered."

"And as long as I and my family," echoed Baer.

The two brothers stared at the grave, conscious that one day it would be their turn, but not yet; there was too much to do. Baer held out his hand to his brother and opened his fingers. On his palm was Bogan's tell-mark. An unremarkable piece of stone, it had bought Crow's life and, indirectly, even Chaiko's, for if Crow had not left him to face the fire alone, the two would have continued east in a vain attempt to escape the approaching flames. Both would surely have perished. Alone, he had felt free to take his only chance, a desperate drive for the river. Following the chain of consequences, Chaiko realized that without him, Dawn would have perished also, falling prey to a roving band of hyenas or wolves. And lastly, they would not be here to provide the present service to the clan. They all owed much to this grey stone.

Chaiko looked at his brother who was viewing the stone from a different perspective. Why had Bogan, the greatest shaman of all the clans that had ever lived, given this tell-mark to their mother? Baer asked himself. And why had she passed it to Chaiko? Bogan to Chaiko,

Bogan to Chaiko; the thought revolved in his head. He wanted to know if the great shaman Bogan could have foreseen Chaiko, the master of Falcon? Was this some kind of transfer? Of power? Or authority? The questions led to more questions. It would have to suffice that the stone had now returned to Chaiko, both to fulfill their own destiny.

The next day was fresh and they could see their breath, but walking soon warmed them up. The air above was full of wingbeats as line after line of birds passed over them heading south. Ahead, there was but one more hill to cross before reaching the plain, by way of a narrow defile carved out by a stream through the chalky rocks. Chaiko kept his eyes open for flint, but there were but small glints, nothing substantial.

It was an emotional moment when they emerged from the rocks, and saw spread out before them the wide expanse of the plain. They threw their burdens off and greedily drank in the view. From their vantage point the plain looked normal, an even fresh green covering the scar of the fire. On second look, however, the blackened trunks of trees and bare branches bore witness to the destruction they had so narrowly escaped; nor were there signs of the herds that should have dotted the plain ready for the great hunt of the season. Cosh spied a herd of antelope in the distance and then a family grouping of deer peacefully foraging. The sight cheered him, but he knew that they would be too hard to chase over the whole breadth of the plain, too hard to stalk. Then he remembered the new weapon and took heart. He slapped Makar good naturedly on the back, who was overcome by this sign of camaraderie from the usually undemonstrative Cosh.

Dawn, standing beside Chaiko, peered into the distance through squinting eyes, wanting to find her cave. Chaiko told her that the cave was not yet visible, but pointed out to her the slight rise behind which it lay, on another part of the plain, about three days away at their present speed. Baer came up to them, eyes aglow. All this was the land of the Standing-Rock Clan and the wounds in his soul were healing at the sight of it. He sucked in a deep lungful of air, and wondered at how it could smell and taste so much sunnier than the air they had just left behind. They continued on, pausing at a likely spot chosen by Cosh, and arranged a new marker to show the way they took.

"Look, even the rocks want to follow us," Chaiko called out jokingly, pointing to the shoulder-high structure above the height of the grass,

14 Stones

that looked very much like a man. But the rest, so in awe of his magical powers, misunderstood his joke, afraid that the rocks would indeed follow. Makar, unable to get rid of the uneasy feeling between his shoulder blades, kept glancing back.

They marched further into the plain, their fears shedding like old fur as they realized how much they had missed the wide open place and the freedom of the horizons. Each step fed their elation, and there was laughter and joking back and forth. In their light-headedness, they pointed out to each other mundane things as if they were of great import. A towering termite mound, usually not worth mentioning, thus assumed great significance. Makar, pretending to be a passing fox infested by termites, scratched and bit at the itch of them. People laughed. Chaiko wanted to tell him that termites did not leave their nests, but the laughter was what they needed, not correctness.

Even Cosh was affected. Typically he was so even-tempered that he couldn't feel much emotion on his own, and so made it a habit to read the feelings of the people around him to cue him, often puzzled by what all the fuss was about. But not this day; he was elated too. He could smell bison in the air; even if he could not see any, he knew they were out there.

In the open flatness, Chaiko and Dawn took over the lead. It was only right for them to lead the clan to the home they were so willing to share with them. Crow and Lana followed, as they were the most intent on finding a brighter future for themselves. The rest followed at a measured pace. Baer had slowly grown stronger, finding the level ground much easier to traverse. In his smiles Tanya grew noticeably younger and almost carefree; but she was still the mother of the clan and it was she who called a halt and ordered camp at a likely spot near a stream.

The clan, in a mood to celebrate after a meal, broke into singing. Chaiko tried experimenting with the holes of Crier-Bird to follow the melody, adding to the richness of sound. Makar joined in by clapping sticks to reinforce the rhythm. Lana jumped into a dance and flitted uncontained about the fire. Crow joined her but was unable to keep up with her and panting, had to drop out. As the darkness fell, some of the excitement had burned off. Tanya asked Dawn to sing her people's songs, and she did in her beautiful light pure voice. They could not understand her words, but she showed her feelings in her expression and movement, and the listeners were transported by the sheer emotions of her songs. Then she danced. Unlike Lana's exuberance, it was a graceful, polished performance, the movement entirely in time with the rhythm of the music and the clapping. Enchanted, they watched her lithe body turn and spin, the hands flowing with the melody, the feet moving to the rhythm. Crow grabbed his friend and affectionately congratulated him on finding such a talented mate. Chaiko nodded his thanks, his heart too full of pride to speak.

The moon was high but they still kept on, reluctant to let go of the feeling of being one and happy. It had been a long time since they had had such a carefree occasion or opportunity to celebrate. Chaiko had given them back their future and also their sense of fun. Baer was telling Cosh that it was too bad that the rest of the clan could not share in this moment, but Cosh had his distant face on and was again wondering what the fuss was about.

The next day's progress was noticeably slower because of the length of the preceding night, but still, the heat of the celebration had burned off some of the privation of the hills. One could breathe so much easier in the open. And what was more, one could see in the distance ahead where one wanted to go and measure one's progress. This was a journey of jubilation— reclaiming their land, their home.

Again and again they came across piles of bones where some creature, overtaken by the fire, had died. The white bones remained as the only markers of their last agony. Bleached skulls pointed to the east, the direction of a desperate flight for safety in the hills that was never reached. All the other skeletal remains likewise pointed east, recording and freezing in time the mass flight as the whole plain sought to outrun the flames. This was the fate they had escaped so narrowly themselves. Then they looked at Chaiko with amazement, wondering how the fire could have passed over him, that he was here leading them, walking on two legs, with such a skilful and exotic young mate at his side. Surely he must know the ways of magic, Baer thought; surely he was born a shaman as he himself was born to lead! When he looked back upon his life he could see clearly each step that had led him to leadership. Perhaps Chaiko was led likewise. A quiet peace filled him. With the two of them watching out for the clan, their future was assured. Feeling some intensity upon him, Chaiko looked back and the two brothers, as always, understood each other. Tacitly they divided the responsibility for the clan between them. Strangely, however, half the load felt no lighter than the whole.

14 Stones

They made camp on the edge of a burned-out strand of oaks, making fires from the branches they broke off the dead trees. Dawn noticed how the black wood burned with an intense heat and hardly any smoke. She pointed this out to Chaiko and the two puzzled over it.

After the meal, people quickly settled down to rest, wanting to make up for the lost sleep of the night before. Lana came over with Crow in tow, and though she acknowledged Dawn, she shyly asked Chaiko to tell her stories as he used to do before their world was turned upside down. Chaiko agreed, and the others hurriedly gathered about him, straining forward in anticipation. It had been a long time since a story had been told.

"A green frog lived in a small pond surrounded by cattails and reeds. All his life he had lived there, and as the frog grew the pond seemed to shrink especially in the midsummer heat. Finally, either the frog became too large or the pond too small, and so a burning desire grew within the frog to see the rest of the world beyond. However, every time he tried to leave, the tangle of grass skirting the pond stopped him. Jump he would, but the profusion of grass stalks would catch him and throw him back, the roots would trip him, and he could not press through the dense weave of stalks and leaves. Exhausted by each try, he had to give up and admit himself trapped in this bit of swamp.

"'Help,' he would cry despairingly to the dragonfly and the haughty butterfly, but they just ignored him. He could not resist eating other flies before he could find out their opinions on things. In fact, there was only one creature, a sympathetic fox, who deigned to listen to him. 'Why yes, the world is large and much more beautiful and interesting than this mud hole here,' confirmed the fox for the frog. The fox smiled craftily, always so quick to size up any situation and turn any opportunity to his advantage. 'There is a sparkling lake just the other side of those trees, full of fish and colonies of frogs,' the fox spun his tale. 'Why don't you go there?' the fox tempted.

"'I would gladly but my legs are made for swimming and not for walking and I get lost in the grass,' the frog complained. 'Perhaps you would be kind enough to take me there. For you a field of grass is no obstacle as it is for me,' the frog requested of the kind fox.

"The fox looked at the plump frog safe on the lily pad and replied, 'It would be a small service to be sure, seeing how light you are, and it would not be much out of the way for me. And it would be kind of me, and kindness will be with kindness returned,' the fox reasoned aloud through the frog's plea. 'Then you will take me?' the frog wanted to know, jumping to conclusions as frogs are wont to do. Jump at things, I mean.

"The fox answered, smiling sadly, 'I would gladly, but alas it can't be so. For look at your hands, they are made for swimming, for holding water, digging in mud perhaps, but not made for clinging to the fur on my back. I would like to help you, truly I would, but as you can see, it is quite impossible.' The tone was tinged with deep, deep regret.

"The frog was desolate. 'Sir, you have the reputation of being a most cunning animal, surely you can think of a way. It seems such a simple thing.'

"The fox thought a while, then said 'There is but one way I can think of, but since it is quite unpleasant, I hesitate to offer it...' the voice of the fox tailed off, though a fox without a tail is no fox at all.

"'Please tell me, Sir,' the frog pleaded, for so great was his desire to escape the smallness of his world.

"Most reluctantly the fox proceeded, 'I can take you but one way, if you sit quiet and peaceful on my tongue.' This was a novel thought even to a frog and cause for reconsideration. But the fox continued, 'Just the other day I carried a young chick back to its mother on my tongue, safe and sound. But perhaps I should not so offer a ride to a frog.' The fox was turning regretful again.

"'And why not?' the frog asked, unsure if he wanted to be in anybody's mouth, but not wishing to close the one venue of escape the fox represented.

"'I hear tell that the skin of a frog is quite bitter, and I would not like to expose my tongue to its disflavor and spoil the sensitivity of my palate.' The frog licked himself and wondered what the fox was babbling about. 'Not bitter to another frog, but to the rest of us. Be assured, you taste terribly bitter.'

"It seemed there was no solution to the frog's problem, but the fox was a wise animal indeed and soon came up with the required solution. He directed the frog enthusiastically, 'Go roll in good smelling things, like pollen and nectars of flowers, and make yourself sweet for the journey. That way you will not harm my delicate taste buds.' The frog thought it was a most practical suggestion and hastened to do just that. 'Make sure to cover yourself thoroughly to last the whole journey,' the fox called after, so concerned was he for the welfare of the frog. In a little while the frog presented himself, smelling sweet as honey, and the fox opened its mouth to let the frog sit on his tongue, just like on a lily pad. Then the fox closed its mouth." And Chaiko clapped together his palms to show them all. And there the story ended.

"What happened next?" everybody wanted to know. But Chaiko shrugged his shoulders, "I do not know; no one told me."

"Kaiko, what means t's story?" Dawn too wanted to know, but Chaiko said, "It is just a story, and does not have to have a point attached to it."

In her turn, Lana was adamant, "Stories always have a point. So tell us the rest." Dawn was enlightened by Lana's approach, but found its directness jarring to her ears.

"Well good," Chaiko resigned himself. "The reason I can't tell you how the story ended is because I don't know. But each of you know how it ended, so you tell me." But they would not let him avoid the telling and he had to continue.

"What happens next depends not on me, but what you believe. I am sure Lana and Ido here think that the frog discovered the world beyond, courtesy of a kind fox." Lana, who looked reality in the eye only when it suited her, nodded her head yes, but Ido, muttering about stupid frog, shook her head in negation.

"Now I am sure that Makar, here, would think the sly fox had a tasty morsel for his afternoon stroll."

Makar nodded and rubbed his stomach: "So prepared, sweet with nectar, I could eat a frog or two myself." People laughed at this exchange. Most were reminded of Samar, who often told similar tales.

Dawn smiled too—sly fox to talk a meal into its mouth—then sobered as she recalled how the bison delivered themselves to the cave and how her plants would do the same someday. She had to agree with Lana; stories always had a point. Perhaps one point was that if one's hopes could not be contained in one's world, then that world was indeed too small. Or perhaps, and she looked suspiciously at her mate, the listeners had been hanging on Chaiko's tongue too long and are about to be swallowed like the frog.

Crow thought the story was about whom you trusted in life, but he would never argue against Lana's interpretation, at least not aloud.

Cosh could make neither head nor tail of the story and wondered why people were smiling and so animated by it. He had little enthusiasm left over for frogs. Emma thought it was a good story, but did not think beyond it. Tanya, above all, was glad to have a storyteller among them again, to make the night fire alive with the magic of imagination. Sometimes, just the rare times, she wished that Baer had less strength and a little more fantasy like his younger brother, but she quickly hid the thought even from herself.

The light of the next day showed cavehill in the distance so that people had their first glimpse of the green valley. Its mature green stood out from the lighter green of the surrounding plain still recovering. Dawn was excited to be so near, but was impatient to be nearer. Unconsciously they all hurried more to be closer to this promised land. Filled with the hope that was being slowly realized in front of him, Baer had no trouble keeping up; indeed he was exceedingly impatient to get there.

Then unexpectedly, Chaiko called a halt, to everybody's puzzlement. What could this mean, they asked themselves? They crowded near him, but he merely pointed to the ground just ahead of them. There in the grass was a clearly visible line that separated the grassland that was burned from the grassland that was spared. Makar impulsively hurried on to cross, but Chaiko called him sternly back. Dawn looked at him in astonishment, as did everybody else, daring not to move against the authority in his voice.

"This place escaped the flames, the heat and the smoke of the fire so that you, the People of the Standing-Rock Clan, would have a place to return to. Therefore be thankful that this was spared, but forget not your time in the hills, as the bones of our people left there should remind you. Take what you need of the plenty that is still here, but do so with respect. For this place was not spared so you could spoil it. And when you are full and sated, remember that you have been hungry and short of hope. Remember that however bad or lean the time, it passed, and there is a new future ahead of you."

He paused and Makar wanted to rush over again, but was commanded back. Chaiko was not finished yet. He alone sensed the moment of change that lay before them in crossing that line, and he wanted them to fix it in their memory.

"When a stranger comes to you, take the stranger in." He smiled at Dawn but was also thinking of the nameless stranger lying in a shallow grave out there. "That you might remember this day, we shall erect a pile of stones, balanced on one another, just like the next generation on the present. And are we not the Standing-Rock Clan? So make the rocks stand." He dismissed them with a wave of his hands, then went to find a flat rock which he placed on the ground. The others had not understood, but no one was going to argue with the person who knew magic and could make wood fly. They hurried about looking for rocks to pile. Unfortunately, this was not the best place to find them, as the rocks here were rounded field stones and resisted being piled. Thus, it took them longer than anticipated to balance one rock on top of another to the height of a man. But by the end they felt some of the significance of the moment Chaiko wanted them to feel and to relate to their children: how the clan stepped across the burn.

After that there was no holding Dawn back any longer. She not only crossed the line but ranged further and further ahead. Concerned, Cosh wanted to go after her to protect her, but Chaiko held him back. She wanted to be there to prepare the cave for their arrival, and he wanted to give her the opportunity she deeply desired to properly receive them. So they followed at a measured pace.

Just before they crossed the final crest, he held them back again briefly to allow their expectations to rise, then he led them into the clearing in front of the cave.

This time they all paused on their own, taking in the whole of the cave, with its comforting and protective walls of stone, its inviting openness to light and air and the fire burning in the hearth, with bison meat on the spit, smelling delicious. Dawn left the fire, came to meet them, then like a good mate should, pointedly offered Chaiko the first drink from the water bag, in a gesture of welcome. Then one by one she took the bag to each. Dawn too, it would seem, had a flair for ceremony.

After drinking, everyone took possession of the cave and flooded in, exploring. Dawn was struggling with a mixture of feelings, but Chaiko came over to her, gently put his arm around her, and drew her close. "This is our clan, and our children will know them to be our people," he gently reminded her and even more gently patted her stomach, having noticed the slightest little bulge in the flat lines of her body.

A little later, Tanya came over. "This is an excellent cave and has everything a cave should have: deep shelter, open to light and air, water nearby, soft ground to sleep on." Then she added with great simplicity, "Thank you."

That night when Tanya reached over to her mate, he did not push her aside, and they celebrated the new cave in a very intimate way.

In the darkness Lana smiled to herself sweetly. Perhaps the future she had been dreaming about for so long was finally here.

Chapter 39

The next morning the light filtered through a cloudy sky and slowly filled the cave. Gradually people awoke to the realization of the protection of the cave about them. It had been a long time since they had last felt such security.

Dawn stirred to get up but Chaiko held her back. "You are not a servant," he whispered to her. "Let them find their own way about the cave." Obediently, albeit with reluctance, she lay back down but listened tensely to every small sound of people stirring and getting up. These are the people of your children, she said to herself, and placed a protective hand over her abdomen. His hand covered hers. Perhaps it was good so ... and with a deep shuddering sigh, she let go of her cave, and henceforth became just one who shared it.

The Standing-Rock Clan were delighted by their new surroundings. Tanya carefully measured with her eyes the open spaces to apportion each of the clan a just and rightful share. She recalled who was most comfortable with whom to share proximity and she rehearsed several combinations in her mind. Familiarity was most desirable and in as much as Tanya sought to recreate it, the new cave began to look like the old one in the layout of the hearths and sleeping places. There were a few holes in the pattern: Samar, the old shaman, was gone, and so was Uma, sharing a cold hearth underground back in the hills. But life went on. Chaiko and Dawn will need a hearth of their own, of course. Then, her heart constricting with her concern, Tanya thought of her daughter and Crow who would soon need a fire away from their parents, to give them a chance to unfold independently. "She is but a child," she protested to herself. "Only yesterday I held her in my arms as she was nuzzling my breast." A sweet sadness overcame her, sweet for she remembered leaving her parents to embark on an exciting future with a new mate. "Dear parents," she murmured, sending a kind thought of them on the way across time and distance, "it has been a long time, yet it was only yesterday."

Still under the covers, Chaiko nuzzled the back of Dawn's neck sending delicious shivers down her spine. She playfully batted his hand away. What could he be thinking of anyway, in broad daylight? Besides, was he not pleased that they already had one child on the way? She would soon have to tell him for sure, though he obviously suspected it already. Her cave or not, there were things waiting to be done. This time she got up.

Chaiko, too, got up and after refreshing himself and eating, started on a new Falcon for Makar. He had just the right piece of wood for him, a stout ash sapling. It had a heavier pull, and he hoped thereby to slow down Makar's impetuousness to give him a chance for a second look at the quarry. He shaved the wood with a flint piece, the long shavings coiling neatly about just the way they should, the evenness of the strips telling him that the pressure on the flint was right. Surrounded by the clan, with his mate Dawn safely in their midst, sitting by the fire doing what he liked best—working wood— he felt content and at peace.

Dawn and Tanya were talking quietly with each other about some intricacy of sewing leather with the fine thread Dawn had made. Dawn was also sharing with her the many quills for needles and sharp flints Chaiko had made for her. Tanya was struck by what beautiful eyes the girl had, and how full of intelligence they were. Chaiko, you were lucky there, she said to herself. Of all the girls you could have found, you came upon such a treasure, a rare find even if one had a choice, let alone when there was only one. Suddenly she noticed Dawn looking at her, as if she knew what she was thinking, and she blushed deeply red. They both burst out giggling and it was hard to tell from the sound of it who was the younger. The two women settled down, the bond between them deeply felt. In that shared moment Dawn lost her fears of being intimidated by this friendly person and felt at home. In her own cave, she felt at home, she chuckled sardonically to herself. Then the sudden realization of her loss burst fully upon her: the quiet togetherness of just herself and Chaiko, the shared privacy and intimacy of this same cave, suddenly gone, given away, now just a haunting memory. Gone were the shared days of quietly working together, gone were the pleasure-filled nights of uninhibited intimacy. Gone were the times when the cave heard only their voices. Now the whole cave would be listening. Cave and stones have unending patience, people have not. Gone, gone, gone... That was too much to give up, all in one day. Tears rushed to her eyes and she lowered her head to hide them from the others.

Baer, who had been quiet all this time on the other side of the fire, listening to the seemingly inconsequential prattle of the two women, chose this moment to say, "Should ask Chaiko for some more of those feather mantles; they looked very impressive as bird spirits."

Dawn felt the cave close in on her, jumped to her feet, and stammered something like, "This worthless woman ..." Then, not trusting herself to speak more, grabbed the waterskin and ran off toward the creek.

Baer looked after her incredulous. "What is the matter? Was it something I said?" He turned puzzled toward Tanya. "Should I have asked that of her ... ? About the feather mantles?"

Distracted from her concern for Dawn, Tanya looked at him puzzled herself, but for different reasons. She thought, "Why must there be one reason? For all his wisdom and thinking, he often overlooks the obvious. Men have such a narrow focus. Our lives are a tapestry, each of us connected to the others by many strands in a tight weave. You pull one strand and the entire tapestry reacts, draws closer, compensates for the shortened length. It is impossible to change just one strand without affecting the others. Surely that is obvious. Yet even Baer, who is more thoughtful than most, still looks for a single reason to explain things. Chaiko thinks and thinks but he, too, is looking for a single thread. Why are men so fixated on a single filament idea, when the richness of our lives comes from being interwoven and intertwined? We belong to one another, all of us, the whole cave. We did not choose each other, merely learned to accept what we have been given. You, my dear mate, too, are an intersection of many strands tying all of us together, tying our present to our past... and most certainly the future is destined by today's strands that we still hold in our hands. How can a woman explain it if men are so blind to it?" She looked at him and shrugged. "But the blindness of men, is it not also their strength? They are insensitive so they can hunt and kill. Women are spared the burden of shedding blood. Truly there is a price to be paid for all things." The complexity was mind-boggling. She shook her head free of these thoughts, to look at nearer concerns.

Aloud, Tanya said to Baer, "Dawn and Chaiko found this cave; the lost daughter of the Other People found safety here and made this her home. They were happy here, just the two of them, alone. Their togetherness was not shared. Then they went to search for us in the hills, found us, and invited and brought us here to share their cave and the Green Valley. Maybe she was ready to share all this, but was she ready to share Chaiko and her own privacy? Her cave and her quiet peacefulness were invaded." Tanya was looking at the edges of the tapestry searching for her answer, thinking, "What is the heart of the matter? Which strands are how connected? Dawn gave up a lot to get what? Peace of mind for her mate? That alone?" Tanya replayed the last few days looking for small signs, but nothing obvious suggested itself. "A nest, a nest." The thought kept repeating in her mind. In a sudden flash she had the answer, which she should have had before. In a quiet voice that hid her excitement she told Baer, "She is with child!"

"Pregnant?" Baer looked at her in surprise, "Well, that explains that."

Tanya had to smile. Still the single line reasoning. It took her the whole tapestry to see it herself, the one strand that fit into the pattern. "The poor girl paid a high price for the future of her children. But would any mother do less?" She was pleased with herself and smiled brightly at Baer, which left him wondering what she was up to. "Straight line that," she thought, but words of caution immediately rose to her mind. "Let men rule the narrow, and let women take the broad view of things. Together they will be stronger, for there are plenty of narrow things to deal with as there are broad things to keep one occupied." She concluded with the usual flourish when considering men-women issues: "Let men do the things they do best, and let women do likewise."

When Dawn returned bearing a full waterbag, she was composed. Tanya took her by the arm and led her gently back to the fire. They sat and Tanya combed the young woman's hair, talking of inconsequential but pleasant things. "Let her choose the time of telling," Tanya cautioned herself. Their conversation was a little forced and both took the opportunity to laugh over-loudly at some mildly amusing turn of the conversation that surely did not merit it.

Lana and Ile had been weaving grass mats to lie on, but at the sound of her mother's laughter she came over to investigate. "Mommy," the young girl pleaded, "can we go to hunt for rocks like you promised?" Tanya was going to shoo the girl away but then remembered how quickly her daughter was growing up and how rare such moments had become. She got up and the two of them went hunting for pretty rocks, as she had promised.

Cosh took Crow and Makar to hunt. Chaiko did not go with them. After all, Cosh was second only to Baer and the number one hunter present, since Tusk was away. Chaiko wanted to avoid the awkwardness of Cosh somehow deferring to him out of a growing respect, in front of the others. Makar still had only a spear and envied Crow, though Crow had let him shoot with his in practice at a straw deer Dawn and Lana had been kind enough to make for them. The hunting party disappeared into the Green Valley below.

Baer was on the other side of the fire, cautiously testing his limbs. He felt well, even strong, and he noted with satisfaction that he could move both his arms without restriction. There was only a bit of tenderness in his side, hardly worth attention. Good food, the exercise of travelling, and the fresh air cleaned out his lungs, but the best medicine was Chaiko's miraculous return and the bright new future facing them. He felt cured of the black depression that had cast him so low. It is strange how it worked, he mused to himself, how had Chaiko explained it? The spirit ruled the soul, the soul the mind, and the mind the body. For a while, his spirit had given up the fight and had let circumstances prevail. But no longer, he promised himself. He flexed his muscles and his body told him he was all right. It would still be days before he could join the others and keep up with them, but he had promised Tanya he would not overexert himself.

Late afternoon the hunters returned bending under the weight of an elk slung from a carrying pole. They had to pause and rest often, as even the three of them had difficulty handling the heavy carcass. Chaiko hurried over to help. He examined the inert body and the two talons sticking out of its side. He praised the shots, and Cosh beamed with pleasure. Chaiko knew that in his single-mindedness, Cosh would soon surpass him in the use of Falcon. It had always been clear that Cosh was born to be a hunter, whereas Chaiko had had to find out the hard way what he was going to be, and even now he was not so sure. Sometimes he thought he was born to ask questions, for certainly he had accumulated a great many of them. If only he could find half as many answers ... he sighed. Where was the Rainbow Gate?

While the women skinned the elk, butchered the meat and set a generous piece of tenderloin roasting, the men sat by the fire reporting all they had seen. Cosh confirmed that the valley was full of game; herds of deer, swift moving antelope, and lumbering elk returning from their northern reaches. And they had seen fresh bison tracks. Cosh also pointed out that the northern flocks of geese would soon be passing through on the way to the south. There would be lots to hunt and lots to eat; he smacked his mouth for emphasis. Then he talked about the hunt, how they tracked and stalked the animal and at what distance they had shot the first talon. His shot buried itself into the side of the elk. Crow overestimated and his talon went harmlessly overhead, but not by much. Cosh's second talon also found its mark, but Crow then overcompensated and his talon went into the grass just short. The elk collapsed and lay still. It had been so easy, he exulted to Baer. No running to catch up with the fleeing prey, no danger of facing those horns or flailing hooves, no slashing and thrusting with the spear against the toughness of sinew and bone. But even as he said it, a sense of nostalgia for those very things shone through his elation. Cosh was a hunter, through and through.

Chaiko consoled Crow and told him it had taken him a full moon to learn to use Falcon with accuracy. His friend was slow to cheer up but once he did, his eyes went searching for Lana who was working with the women, throwing looks his way. Crow got up and drifted in her direction. As Chaiko showed Makar the progress he had made on the Falcon for him, the young man's enthusiasm glowed on his face, so he sent him off to cut some straight branches for more talons.

The three, Baer, Cosh and Chaiko sat together, each remembering former times when they had so gathered, each thinking of the two who were missing, Tusk and Samar. Then Baer stirred, "We will remember this time of new beginning. In years to come we will forget the hunger in the hills, but we will remember this Green Valley."

"People need a sense of where they have been," agreed Chaiko, his eyes resting on the green surrounding them.

Cosh, looking at the two brothers, was struck by how similar they were, not in looks, for Baer, even emaciated as he presently was, towered over Chaiko. No, they were similar in intent: they thought alike and shouldered the burden of the clan without questioning why.

It also struck Dawn, looking at her man, how Chaiko, her turtle, showed to such good advantage in the midst of his clan and family. Sitting as he was with the other two, she clearly saw in him a leader of his clan. When they were alone on the plain, sometimes he was almost boyish, moody and even petulant. Here, there was a sense of great peace about him, a clarity and largess she had not seen before.

She was suddenly even more aware of how greatly their lives had changed once they met up with the clan. Now, their lives were less their own, as people laid claims on bits and pieces of them. Briefly she felt a longing for the times of solitude, with just the two of them. But then, when she remembered the life she was sure was growing within her, she thought it good so. Still, all this was fast, sometimes too fast for her, the daughter of Other People.

Chaiko too was feeling swept away by all the activity that constantly made demands upon him. Though he felt at peace in a larger sense, he needed solitude to work through all the events engulfing him, but had no opportunity to withdraw. It unbalanced him and he was becoming irritable without knowing why. But Dawn knew. She noticed the small signs, like his eyes that wanted to disappear in the distance only to be called back to focus. Finally she took him aside, made him sit comfortably, then told him simply, "Think."

"Think? About what?" he wanted to know, in surprise.

"Just think!" she stressed, her clear blue eyes compelling him. She then left him alone but stayed nearby to intercept any likely interruption.

He grumbled a little. "Think about what?" But before he realized it, his mind went off into familiar channels and he was happily thinking away, searching for some new balance. Suddenly, in the present adulation of the clan, he was finding as much status as he had lacked before when he was but a cripple wholly dependent on others. He felt dizzy from this abrupt change that catapulted him from the depths to this height. Even his brother Baer treated him with much respect and Cosh showed him a regard he reserved only for Baer. The rest also showed him great deference, Makar and Ido mixing in a little fear as well. They were convinced that he knew and practiced magic. Could he not walk through fire? Did he not grow a wooden leg? And had he not found such a mate in an empty land? He probably turned a bird into Dawn, Makar guessed; Ido thought a deer, for Dawn danced so gracefully. Only Lana and Crow treated him the same as before. But then they had loved him without reservation when he was but a cripple. Should they love him less because he healed himself both in body and spirit?

Chaiko knew he was a man, that only the patterns of his thinking made him different. The respect and the adulation he found embarrassing but he could find no kind way to deflect it. He hoped that they would all soon get used to him again. All the same it was disconcerting that even Dawn was looking at him with new eyes. He needed her to see him for who he really was, not some kind of puffed up straw-man of a sage that she could make with her own hands out of river reeds. No, Chaiko was still that same boy who had chased her down in the meadow and pulled her into the grass to play the game of joy. Chaiko was still that oft moody, sometimes even irritable, mate that she knew and could twist around her finger as she wished. He was still her Kaiko—nothing could change that, he promised silently.

But he knew that he was not the same. The onrush of experiences had changed him. He knew that he would no longer allow his handicap to dictate his life in any way. He was now a man who had lost only part of one leg. He did not fear the reactions of others. Let them look and wonder at his wooden one.

He was a man, better than most, certainly not less. Better than most? He examined this novel idea. Was he not the Guardian of the Clan, the Master of Falcon, the Mate to Dawn? Did not the proficiency in magic ascribed to him (he had to laugh at that) add to his stature? All his life he had respected Baer above all others, but now he saw Baer clearly as a whole person, also his brother. He saw the weaknesses that made his strengths all the more special. Yet Chaiko felt an equal to him, the leader of the clan. Baer had also recognized that. Had he not asked him indirectly to be shaman to the clan?

Be careful, he warned himself, do not forget the journey that has brought you here. Do not inflate yourself like a fish bladder set afloat to be carried away by a river of pride. No, no! Dawn was there to hold onto. And there was Crow, who thought not overmuch on things, but was always steady, and beside him was Lana. And he had his brother's and Tanya's love. He was reassured.

Soon everybody respected his need to withdraw, to contemplate, and he found himself, it hardly seemed possible, even more at peace. Guarding him, Dawn too got into the habit of thinking along with him. Again and again she returned to the puzzle of her plants that would deliver themselves to the cave as his bison had. She recognized that only seeds of plants could move, scattered by birds and animals. She thought she could plant seeds conveniently in the grass slopes by the cave. But there was so much yet to learn. How did plants decide where they grew?

Used to thinking about everything at once, she still found it difficult to stay her mind on one topic. Chaiko listened to her sympathetically, but wisely kept quiet; he knew she could solve the plant puzzle on her own. He commented only that in creative thinking one had to achieve a balance between an open mind and a closed mind. Open enough to be creative, but closed to distractions.

Through these sessions Dawn got comfortable being alone in her mind. She enjoyed the clarity the thinking brought to her ideas, and began to base her actions on careful reasoning rather than on some intuitive response. Chaiko had reached this point because of suffering, while she did so because of her love and respect for him.

The next morning there was a light frost on the ground and hair and furs were stiff with cold, but with daybreak the cold retreated and it turned quickly into a warm and sunny day. The women freshened the fire, checking the elk meat slowly drying in the smoke. Flocks of birds flew overhead, but avoided the rising smoke. The air was full of the sounds of wingbeats and loud calls of birds.

Cosh took Crow and Makar hunting again. Hardly had they left, when they were back again with a large buck between them. It had been fairly struck with both talons deadly in their aim. This time Crow claimed the kill and was granted the hide, which he promptly gave to Lana. She looked at him with shining eyes of pride. "Oh you, my great hunter." Makar grumbled that all he was good for was to carry heavy loads; others shot, and others got all the credit. Tanya shushed him, and quietly suggested he go to the ponds and see if he could get a few of the birds passing overhead. Cheered, Makar hurried off.

Once again Cosh reported on the hunt. They had come upon some grazing deer, and though the deer had seen them coming they did not run away, such was the distance. They both had strung their Falcons, but he had told Crow to shoot first; if he missed, then Cosh would shoot. This time Crow did not miss. Even at a considerable distance he struck the buck fairly in the side, piercing and collapsing both lungs. The second talon was unnecessary, but that had found its aim too. Cosh bragged about the power of the weapon.

Chaiko frowned, then said quietly, "My friend, Falcon is a great boon to us. Because the talons have great range, the hunter can kill at a safe distance. He no longer needs to run after the game and give chase. From an unseen hiding place he can shoot. And the game may not even see death coming. Yes, Falcon is a fearsome weapon that can serve men well..." He paused leaving the thought hanging in the air.

"But ... there is a cost to us and to the land. When we, the hunters, kill at such distances, the killing becomes easy, and we no longer see the animal suffering, no longer see it bleed, and we do not hear the rattle of its last breath. Because of Falcon, we do not see its death up close, we do not see the blood pouring out, the last tremors; we cannot feel its suffering, its parting from life, and thus we lose respect for death. And we lose our sense of thankfulness for the animal that died so we can feed our families. When we see animals only as meat, in our arrogance we lose that which makes us more than animals ourselves—our compassion.

"We must treat this weapon with respect for its power, and use it with fear, for it is death on wings. We must teach the young people, who crave to use it, that same respect that both the weapon and its target deserve. And if we forget the ease with which this weapon kills, and kill all living things on the plain as it surely can, then at what shall the clan aim its talons? What shall the clan hunt then? What shall the clan eat?"

Baer looked at his brother. He had worried for years about who the next shaman was going to be. Perhaps, as he himself was born to lead, his brother had been born to be a shaman. This thought kept resurfacing, confirming his brother's status. Or his missing leg made him one, he thought with sudden insight.

Cosh took the speech to heart, but he put his own interpretation on it, and from then on he become obsessed about building Standing Stones, at the perimeter of the clan's hunting range, that all who passed would know this was the territory of the Standing-Rock Clan and that they might be reminded to be thankful for the animals and the bounty of nature.

Comfortable by the fire, Chaiko surveyed the peaceful scene. The women were smoking meat yet again, the continuing reward of the hunt. Crow's mother and Cosh's wife were talking animatedly over proper seasonings to use. Lana was teasing Crow with a feather ... "I am going to turn you into a bird-spirit ... Just like Dawn did Chaiko ..." then she ran laughing with Crow close behind her, into the woods. Their laughter could be heard faintly for a while. Tanya only looked up when the laughter suddenly ceased.

Chaiko had a further vision; for good or bad, Falcon belonged to all the people. And talking with Baer, it was decided that as soon as Tusk came back with the rest of the clan, they would send runners to other clans calling for a Gathering, so that Chaiko could teach them all the making and using of Falcon ... so that all the clans would have Falcon to assure the future for them.

Only later he thought of the People-of-the Elk. They too deserved such a weapon of power.

For himself there was still much to do, more Falcons to make in expectation of every male wanting one. But when he had completed a few, maybe then there would be time enough for him to work on a new Singing-Stick.

Later that night, watching Dawn working about in the fire light, his heart was so filled with love for her that painfully sweet tears misted his eyes. Just then she looked up and read a meaning which even a thinker like him could not find the words to express. Flooded with a rush of emotions of her own in response, she threw herself at him and the two disappeared beneath the bison robe.

The End

Epilogue

In early spring of the next year, Dawn gave birth to a boy. He had light blond hair and his mother's blue eyes. The birth was more painful than she ever expected, but to those who were more experienced, it had not been a particularly difficult birth, as in later years she herself was going to find out.

Chaiko, the proud father, named him Yael, an old clan word for yellow. Though both Dawn and Tanya hastened to let him know that the blond, almost white, baby hair would not last, he did not change his mind. Secretly, he was thinking of Yellow Flint as he had come to call the Stranger whom he and Dawn had buried on the plain. It seemed so unjust that a person in the prime of life had just disappeared. To Chaiko a birth balanced out a death and somehow the name would honor the Stranger, whoever he was.

It was time for him to pick another year-stone to add to the thirteen he already had and the one smooth bit of wood.

A Parting Word from the Author

Did you like visiting the Stone Age?

I admire Chaiko greatly. Obviously he becomes who he is because of his injury. His loss limits him physically, but makes him grow in the spiritual realm. He observes, looks for opportunities to help, to be of use, to overcome his restrictions using his mind and resourcefulness. Time and time again he is thoroughly tested, yet each time finds a way around a challenge. So you can see why he becomes a prototype of all the characters who come after him.

When I started I only had Chaiko in mind while the other cast members grew out of the story arc. Dawn, however, was implied from the very beginning. She and Chaiko are a good fit, complementing each other well.

Crow is a great foil, useful to measure Chaiko against.

Anyway, I shouldn't over explain, I'm sure you have your own opinions. If you have comments on the book, I'd love to hear them.

If you want to find out more about me, please visit my website at www.seeWordFactory.com .

I thank you for your visit and hope to meet up with you in another one of my books.

I wish you well,

Paul Telegdi

Paul Telegdi

14 Stones

Made in the USA
Lexington, KY
08 March 2018